Never Before Had a woman Captured Him Body and Soul! Never Would She Surrender To a Man Who Bought Her Love!

Under the dark, languorous eyes of the the Duke of Claymore, Whitney Stone grew from a saucy hoyden into a ravishingly sensual woman. Fresh from her triumphs in Paris society, she returned to England to win the heart of Paul, her childhood love . . . only to be bargained away by her bankrupt father to the handsome, arrogant Duke. Outraged, she defies her new lord . . . but even as his smoldering passion seduces her into a gathering storm of desire, Whitney cannot, will not, relinquish her dream of perfect love.

———————⟨∾⟩———————

"THE ULTIMATE LOVE STORY; ONE YOU CAN DREAM ABOUT FOREVER."

—*Romantic Times*

Books by Judith McNaught

Double Standards
A Kingdom of Dreams
Once and Always
Something Wonderful
Tender Triumph
Whitney, My Love

Published by POCKET BOOKS

Judith McNaught

Whitney, my love

POCKET BOOKS

New York   London   Toronto   Sydney   Tokyo

This book is a work of fiction. Names, characters, places and incidents are either the product of the author's imagination or are used fictitiously. Any resemblance to actual events or locales or persons, living or dead, is entirely coincidental.

An *Original* Publication of POCKET BOOKS

POCKET BOOKS, a division of Simon & Schuster Inc.
1230 Avenue of the Americas, New York, NY 10020

ISBN: 0-671-67138-3

First Pocket Books printing January 1985

10 9 8 7

POCKET and colophon are trademarks of
Simon & Schuster Inc.

Printed in the U.S.A.

Chapter One

As their elegant travelling chaise rocked and swayed along the rutted country road, Lady Anne Gilbert leaned her cheek against her husband's shoulder and heaved a long, impatient sigh. "Another whole hour until we arrive, and already the suspense is positively gnawing at me. I keep wondering what Whitney will be like now that she's grown up."

She lapsed into silence and gazed absently out the coach window at the lush, rolling English countryside covered with wild pink Foxglove and yellow Buttercups, trying to envision the niece she hadn't seen in almost eleven years.

"She'll be pretty, just as her mother was. And she'll have her mother's smile, her gentleness, her sweet disposition . . ."

Lord Edward Gilbert cast a skeptical glance at his wife. "Sweet disposition?" he echoed in amused disbelief. "That isn't what her father said in his letter."

As a diplomat attached to the British Consulate in Paris, Lord Gilbert was a master of hints, evasions, innuendoes, and intrigues. But in his personal life, he preferred the refreshing alternative of blunt truth. "Allow me to refresh your memory," he said, groping in his pockets and retrieving the letter from Whitney's father. He perched his spectacles

3

upon his nose, and ignoring his wife's grimace, he began to read:

"'Whitney's manners are an outrage, her conduct is reprehensible. She is a willful hoyden who is the despair of everyone she knows and an embarrassment to me. I implore you to take her back to Paris with you, in the hope that you may have more success with the stubborn chit than I have had.'"

Edward chuckled. "Show me where it says she's 'sweet-tempered.'"

His wife shot him a peevish glance. "Martin Stone is a cold, unfeeling man who wouldn't recognize gentleness and goodness if Whitney were made of nothing else! Only think of the way he shouted at her and sent her to her room right after my sister's funeral."

Edward recognized the mutinous set of his wife's chin and put his arm around her shoulders in a gesture of conciliation. "I'm no fonder of the man than you are, but you must admit that, just having lost his young wife to an early grave, to have his daughter accuse him, in front of fifty people, of locking her mama in a box so she couldn't escape had to be rather disconcerting."

"But Whitney was scarcely five years old!" Anne protested heatedly.

"Agreed. But Martin was grieving. Besides, as I recall, it was not for that offense she was banished to her room. It was later, when everyone had gathered in the drawing room—when she stamped her foot and threatened to report us all to God if we didn't release her mama at once."

Anne smiled. "What spirit she had, Edward. I thought for a moment her little freckles were going to pop right off her nose. Admit it—she was marvelous, and you thought so too!"

"Well, yes," Edward agreed sheepishly. "I rather thought she was."

As the Gilbert chaise bore inexorably down on the Stone estate, a small knot of young people were waiting on the south lawn, impatiently looking toward the stable one hundred yards away. A petite blonde smoothed her pink ruffled skirts and sighed in a way that displayed a very fetching dimple. "Whatever do you suppose Whitney is planning to do?" she inquired of the handsome light-haired man beside her.

Glancing down into Elizabeth Ashton's wide blue eyes, Paul Sevarin smiled a smile that Whitney would have forfeited both her feet to see focused on herself. "Try to be patient, Elizabeth," he said.

"I'm sure none of us have the faintest idea *what* she is up to, Elizabeth," Margaret Merryton said tartly. "But you can be perfectly certain it will be something foolish and outrageous."

"Margaret, we're all Whitney's guests today," Paul chided.

"I don't know why you should defend her, Paul," Margaret argued spitefully. "Whitney is creating a horrid scandal chasing after you, and you know it!"

"Margaret!" Paul snapped. "I said that was enough." Drawing a long, irritated breath, Paul Sevarin frowned darkly at his gleaming boots. Whitney *had* been making a spectacle of herself chasing after him, and damned near everyone for fifteen miles was talking about it.

At first he had been mildly amused to find himself the object of a fifteen-year-old's languishing looks and adoring smiles, but lately Whitney had begun pursuing him with the determination and tactical brilliance of a female Napoleon Bonaparte.

If he rode off the grounds of his estate, he could almost depend on meeting her en route to his destination. It was as if she had some lookout point from which she watched his every move, and Paul no longer found her childish infatuation with him either harmless or amusing.

Three weeks ago, she had followed him to a local inn. While he was pleasantly contemplating accepting the innkeeper's daughter's whispered invitation to meet her later in the hayloft, he'd glanced up and seen a familiar pair of bright green eyes peeping at him through the window. Slamming his tankard of ale on the table, he'd marched outside, grabbed

Whitney by the elbow, and unceremoniously deposited her on her horse, tersely reminding her that her father would be searching for her if she wasn't home by nightfall.

He'd stalked back inside and ordered another tankard, but when the innkeeper's daughter brushed her breasts suggestively against his arm while refilling his ale and Paul had a sudden vision of himself lying entangled with her voluptuous naked body, a pair of green eyes peered in through yet *another* window. He'd tossed enough coins on the planked wooden table to mollify the startled girl's wounded sensibilities and left—only to encounter Miss Stone again on his way home.

He was beginning to feel like a hunted man whose every move was under surveillance, and his temper was strained to the breaking point. And yet, Paul thought irritably, here he was standing in the April sun, trying for some obscure reason to protect Whitney from the criticism she richly deserved.

A pretty girl, several years younger than the others in the group, glanced at Paul. "I think I'll go and see what's keeping Whitney," said Emily Williams. She hurried across the lawn and along the whitewashed fence adjoining the stable. Shoving open the big double doors, Emily looked down the wide gloomy corridor lined with stalls on both sides. "Where is Miss Whitney?" she asked the stableboy who was currying a sorrel gelding.

"In there, Miss." Even in the muted light, Emily saw his face suffuse with color as he nodded toward a door adjacent to the tack room.

With a puzzled glance at the flushing stableboy, Emily tapped lightly on the designated door and stepped inside, then froze at the sight that greeted her: Whitney Allison Stone's long legs were encased in coarse brown britches that clung startlingly to her slender hips and were held in place at her narrow waist with a length of rope. Above the riding britches she wore a thin chemise.

"You surely aren't going out there dressed like that?" Emily gasped.

Whitney fired an amused glance over her shoulder at her

scandalized friend. "Of course not. I'm going to wear a shirt, too."

"B-but why?" Emily persisted desperately.

"Because I don't think it would be very proper to appear in my chemise, silly," Whitney cheerfully replied, snatching the stableboy's clean shirt off a peg and plunging her arms into the sleeves.

"P-proper? Proper?" Emily sputtered. "It's completely *improper* for you to be wearing men's britches, and you know it!"

"True. But I can't very well ride that horse without a saddle and risk having my skirts blow up around my neck, now can I?" Whitney breezily argued while she twisted her long unruly hair into a knot and pinned it at her nape.

"Ride without a saddle? You *can't* mean you're going to ride astride—your father will *disown* you if you do that again."

"I am not going to ride astride. Although," Whitney giggled, "I can't understand why men are allowed to straddle a horse, while we—who are supposed to be the weaker sex—must hang off the side, praying for our lives."

Emily refused to be diverted. "Then what *are* you going to do?"

"I never realized what an inquisitive young lady you are, Miss Williams," Whitney teased. "But to answer your question, I am going to ride standing on the horse's back. I saw it done at the fair, and I've been practicing ever since. Then, when Paul sees how well I do, he'll—"

"He'll think you have lost your mind, Whitney Stone! He'll think that you haven't a grain of sense or propriety, and that you're only trying something else to gain his attention." Seeing the stubborn set of her friend's chin, Emily switched her tactics. "Whitney, please—think of your father. What will he say if he finds out?"

Whitney hesitated, feeling the force of her father's unwaveringly cold stare as if it were this minute focused upon her. She drew a long breath, then expelled it slowly as she glanced out the small window at the group waiting on the lawn.

Wearily, she said, "Father will say that, as usual, I have disappointed him, that I am a disgrace to him and to my mother's memory, that he is happy she didn't live to see what I have become. Then he will spend half an hour telling me what a perfect lady Elizabeth Ashton is, and that I ought to be like her."

"Well, if you really wanted to impress Paul, you could try . . ."

Whitney clenched her hands in frustration. "I *have* tried to be like Elizabeth. I wear those disgusting ruffled dresses that make me feel like a pastel mountain, I've practiced going for hours without saying a word, and I've fluttered my eyelashes until my eyelids go limp."

Emily bit her lip to hide her smile at Whitney's unflattering description of Elizabeth Ashton's demure mannerisms, then she sighed. "I'll go and tell the others that you'll be right out."

Gasps of outrage and derisive sniggers greeted Whitney's appearance on the lawn when she led the horse toward the spectators. "She'll fall off," one of the girls predicted, "if God doesn't strike her dead first for wearing those britches."

Ignoring the impulse to snap out a biting retort, Whitney raised her head in a gesture of haughty disdain, then stole a look at Paul. His handsome face was taut with disapproval as his gaze moved from her bare feet, up her trousered legs, to her face. Inwardly, Whitney faltered at his obvious displeasure, but she swung resolutely onto the back of the waiting horse.

The gelding moved into its practiced canter, and Whitney worked herself upward, first crouching with arms outstretched for balance, then slowly easing herself into a standing position. Around and around they went and, although Whitney was in constant terror of falling off and looking like a fool, she managed to appear competent and graceful.

As she completed the fourth circle, she let her eyes slant to the faces passing on her left, registering their looks of shock and derision, while she searched for the only face that mattered. Paul was partially in the tree's shadow, and Elizabeth Ashton was clinging to his arm, but as Whitney passed, she saw the slow, reluctant smile tugging at the corner of his mouth, and triumph unfurled like a banner in her heart. By the time she came around again, Paul was grinning broadly at her. Whitney's spirits soared, and suddenly all the weeks of practice, the sore muscles and bruises, seemed worthwhile.

At the window of the second floor drawing room overlooking the south lawn, Martin Stone stared down at his performing daughter. Behind him, the butler announced that Lord and Lady Gilbert had arrived. Too enraged at his daughter to speak, Martin greeted his sister-in-law and her husband with a clenched jaw and curt nod.

"How—how nice to see you again after so many years, Martin," Lady Anne lied graciously. When he remained icily silent, she said, "Where is Whitney? We're so anxious to see her."

Martin finally recovered his voice. "See her?" he snapped savagely. "Madam, you have only to look out this window."

Bewildered, Anne did as he said. Below on the lawn there stood a group of young people watching a slender boy balancing beautifully on a cantering horse. "What a clever young man," she said, smiling.

Her simple remark seemed to drive Martin Stone from frozen rage to frenzied action as he swung on his heel and marched toward the door, "If you wish to meet your niece, come with me. Or, I can spare you the humiliation, and bring her here to you."

With an exasperated look at Martin's back, Anne tucked her hand in her husband's arm and together they followed Martin downstairs and outside.

As they approached the group of young people, Anne heard murmurings and laughter, and she was vaguely aware that there was something malicious in the tone, but she was too busy scanning the young ladies' faces, looking for Whitney, to pay much heed to the fleeting impression. She mentally discarded two blondes and a redhead, quizzically studied a petite, blue-eyed brunette, then glanced helplessly at the young man beside her. "Pardon me, I am Lady Gilbert, Whitney's aunt. Could you tell me where she is?"

Paul Sevarin grinned at her, half in sympathy and half in amusement. "Your niece is on the horse, Lady Gilbert," he said.

"On the—" Lord Gilbert choked.

From her delicate perch atop the horse, Whitney's eyes followed her father's progress as he bore down on her with long, rapid strides. "Please don't make a scene, Father," she implored when he was within earshot.

"*I* make a scene?" he roared furiously. Snatching the halter, he brought the cantering horse around so sharply that he jerked it from beneath her. Whitney hit the ground on her feet, lost her balance, and ended up half-sprawling. As she scampered up, her father caught her arm in a ruthless grip and hauled her over toward the spectators. "This—this *thing,*" he said, thrusting her forward toward her aunt and uncle, "I am mortified to tell you is your niece."

Whitney heard the smattering of giggles as the group quickly disbanded, and she felt her face grow hot with shame. "How do you do, Aunt Gilbert? Uncle Gilbert?" With one eye on Paul's broad-shouldered, retreating form, Whitney reached mechanically for her nonexistent skirt, realized it was missing, and executed a comical curtsy without it. She saw the frown on her aunt's face and put her chin up defensively. "You may be sure that for the week you are here, I shall endeavor not to make a freak of myself again, Aunt."

"For the week that we are here?" her aunt gasped, but Whitney was preoccupied watching Paul help Elizabeth into his curricle and didn't notice the surprise in her aunt's voice.

"Goodbye, Paul," she called, waving madly. He turned and raised his arm in silent farewell.

Laughter drifted back as the curricles bowled down the drive, carrying their occupants off to a picnic or some other gay and wonderful activity, to which Whitney was never invited because she was too young.

Following Whitney toward the house, Anne was a mass of conflicting emotions. She was embarrassed for Whitney, furious with Martin Stone for humiliating the girl in front of the other young people, somewhat dazed by the sight of her own niece cavorting on the back of a horse, wearing men's britches . . . and utterly astonished to discover that Whitney, whose mother had been only passably pretty, showed promise of becoming a genuine beauty.

She was too thin right now, but even in disgrace Whitney's shoulders were straight, her walk naturally graceful and faintly provocative. Anne smiled to herself at the gently rounded hips displayed to almost immoral advantage by the coarse brown trousers, the slender waist that would require no subterfuge to make it appear smaller, eyes that seemed to change from sea-green to deep jade beneath their fringe of long, sooty lashes. And that hair—piles and piles of rich mahogany brown! All it needed was a good trimming and brushing until it shone; Anne's fingers positively itched to go to work on it. Mentally she was already styling it in ways to highlight Whitney's striking eyes and high cheekbones. Off her face, Anne decided, piled at the crown with tendrils at the ears, or pulled straight back off the forehead to fall in gentle waves down her back.

As soon as they entered the house, Whitney mumbled an excuse and fled to her room where she flopped dejectedly into a chair and morosely contemplated the humiliating scene Paul had just witnessed, with her father jerking her ignominiously off her horse and then shouting at her. No doubt her aunt and uncle were as horrified and revolted by her behavior as her father had been, and her cheeks burned with shame just thinking of how they must despise her already.

"Whitney?" Emily whispered, creeping into the bedroom and cautiously closing the door behind her. "I came up the back way. Is your father angry?"

"Cross as crabs," Whitney confirmed, staring down at her trousered legs. "I suppose I ruined everything today, didn't I? Everyone was laughing at me, and Paul heard them. Now that Elizabeth is seventeen, he's bound to offer for her before he ever has a chance to realize that he loves *me.*"

"You?" Emily repeated dazedly. "Whitney Stone, Paul avoids you like the plague, and well you know it! And who could blame him, after the mishaps you've treated him to in the last year?"

"There haven't been so many as all that," Whitney protested, but she squirmed in her chair.

"No? What about that trick you played on him on All Soul's—darting out in front of his carriage, shrieking like a banshee, and pretending to be a ghost, terrifying his horses."

Whitney flushed. "He wasn't so *very* angry. And it isn't as if the carriage was destroyed. It only broke a shaft when it overturned."

"And Paul's leg," Emily pointed out.

"But that mended perfectly," Whitney persisted, her mind already leaping from past debacles to future possibilities. She surged to her feet and began to pace slowly back and forth. "There has to be a way—but short of abducting him, I—" A mischievous smile lit up her dust-streaked face as she swung around so quickly that Emily pressed back into her chair. "Emily, one thing is infinitely clear: Paul does not yet know that he cares for me. Correct?"

"He doesn't care a *snap* for you is more like it," Emily replied warily.

"Therefore, it would be safe to say that he is unlikely to offer for me without some sort of added incentive. Correct?"

"You couldn't make him offer for you at the point of a gun, and you know it. Besides, you aren't old enough to be betrothed, even if—"

"Under what circumstances," Whitney interrupted triumphantly, "is a gentleman obliged to offer for a lady?"

"I can't think of any. Except of course, if he has compromised her—*absolutely not!* Whitney, whatever you're planning now, I won't help."

Sighing, Whitney flopped back into her chair, stretching her legs out in front of her. An irreverent giggle escaped her as she considered the sheer audacity of her last idea. "If only I could have pulled it off . . . you know, loosened the wheel on Paul's carriage so that it would fall off later, and then asked him to drive me somewhere. Then, by the time we walked back, or help arrived, it would be late at night, and he would have to offer for me." Oblivious to Emily's scandalized expression, Whitney continued, "Just think what a wonderful turnabout that would have been on a tired old theme: *Young Lady* abducts *Gentleman* and ruins *his* reputation so that *she* is forced to marry him to set things aright! What a novel that could have made," she added, rather impressed with her own ingenuity.

"I'm leaving," Emily said. She marched to the door, then she hesitated and turned back to Whitney. "Your aunt and uncle saw everything. What are you going to say to them about those trousers and the horse?"

Whitney's face clouded. "I'm not going to say anything, it wouldn't help—but for the rest of the time they are here, I'm going to be the most demure, refined, delicate female you've ever seen." She saw Emily's dubious look and added, "Also I intend to stay out of sight except at mealtimes. I think I'll be able to act like Elizabeth for three hours a day."

Whitney kept her promise. At dinner that night, after her uncle's hair-raising tale of their life in Beirut where he was attached to the British Consulate, she murmured only, "How very informative, Uncle," even though she was positively burning to ply him with questions. At the end of her aunt's description of Paris and the thrill of its gay social life, Whitney murmured, "How very informative, Aunt." The moment the meal was finished, she excused herself and vanished.

After three days, Whitney's efforts to be either demure or absent had, in fact, been so successful that Anne was beginning to wonder whether she had only imagined the spark of fire she'd glimpsed the day of their arrival, or if the girl had some aversion to Edward and herself.

On the fourth day, when Whitney breakfasted before the rest of the household was up, and then vanished, Anne set out to discover the truth. She searched the house, but Whitney was not indoors. She was not in the garden, nor had she taken a horse from the stable, Anne was informed by a groom. Squinting into the sunlight, Anne looked around her, trying to imagine where a fifteen-year-old would go to spend all day.

Off on the crest of a hill overlooking the estate, she spied a patch of bright yellow. "There you are!" she breathed, opening her parasol and striking out across the lawn.

Whitney didn't see her aunt coming until it was too late to escape. Wishing she had found a better place to hide, she tried to think of some innocuous subject on which she could converse without appearing ignorant. Clothes? Personally, she knew nothing of fashions and cared even less; she looked hopeless no matter what she wore. After all, what could clothes do to improve the looks of a female who had cat's eyes, mud-colored hair, and freckles on the bridge of her nose? Besides that, she was too tall, too thin, and if the good Lord intended for her ever to have a bosom, it was very late in making its appearance.

Weak-kneed, her chest heaving with each labored breath, Anne topped the steep rise and collapsed unceremoniously onto the blanket beside Whitney. "I-I thought I'd take . . . a nice stroll," Anne lied. When she caught her breath, she noticed the leather-bound book lying face down on the blanket and, seizing on books as a topic of conversation, she said, "Is that a romantic novel?"

"No, Aunt," Whitney demurely uttered, carefully placing her hand over the title of the book to conceal it from her aunt's eyes.

"I'm told most young ladies adore romantic novels," Anne tried again.

"Yes, Aunt," Whitney agreed politely.

"I read one once but I didn't like it," Anne remarked, her mind groping for some other topic that might draw Whitney into conversation. "I cannot abide a heroine who is too perfect, nor one who is forever swooning."

Whitney was so astonished to discover that she wasn't the only female in all of England who didn't devour the insipid things, that she instantly forgot her resolution to speak only in monosyllables. "And when the heroines aren't swooning," she added, her entire face lighting up with laughter, "they are lying about with hartshorn bottles up their nostrils, moping and pining away for some faint-hearted gentleman who hasn't the gumption to offer for them, or else has already offered for some other, unworthy female. *I* could never just lie there doing nothing, knowing the man I loved was falling in love with a horrid person." Whitney darted a glance at her aunt to see if she was shocked, but her aunt was regarding her with an unexplainable smile lurking at the corners of her eyes. "Aunt Anne, could you actually care for a man who dropped to his knees and said, 'Oh Clarabel, your lips are the petals of a red rose and your eyes are two stars from the heavens'?" With a derisive snort, Whitney finished, *"That* is where I would have *leapt* for the hartshorn!"

"And so would I," Anne said, laughing. "What do you read then, if not atrocious romantic novels?" She pried the book from beneath Whitney's flattened hand and stared at the gold-embossed title. "The *Iliad?*" she asked in astonished disbelief. The breeze ruffled the pages, and Anne's amazed gaze ricocheted from the print to Whitney's tense face. "But this is in Greek! Surely you don't read Greek?"

Whitney nodded, her face flushed with mortification. Now her aunt would think her a bluestocking—another black mark against her. "Also Latin, Italian, French, and even some German," she confessed.

"Good God," Anne breathed. "How did you ever learn all that?"

"Despite what Father thinks, Aunt Anne, I am only foolish, not stupid, and I plagued him to death until he allowed me tutors in languages and history." Whitney fell silent, remembering how she'd once believed that if she applied herself to her studies, if she could become more like a son, her father might love her.

"You sound ashamed of your accomplishments, when you should be proud."

Whitney gazed out at her home, nestled in the valley below. "I'm sure you know everyone thinks it's a waste of time to educate a female in these things. And anyway, I haven't a *feminine* accomplishment to my name. I can't sew a stitch that doesn't look as if it were done blindfolded, and when I sing, the dogs down at the stable begin to howl. Mr. Twittsworthy, our local music instructor, told my father that my playing of the pianoforte gives him hives. I can't do a thing that girls *ought* to do, and what's worse, I particularly detest doing them."

Whitney knew her aunt would now take her in complete dislike, just as everyone else always did, but it was better this way because at least she could stop dreading the inevitable. She looked at Lady Anne, her green eyes wide and vulnerable. "I'm certain Papa has told you all about me. I'm a terrible disappointment to him. He wants me to be dainty and demure and quiet, like Elizabeth Ashton. I try to be, but I can't seem to do it."

Anne's heart melted for the lovely, spirited, bewildered child her sister had borne. Laying her hand against Whitney's cheek, she said tenderly, "Your father wants a daughter who is like a cameo—delicate, pale, and easily shaped. Instead, he has a daughter who is a diamond, full of sparkle and life, and he doesn't know what to do with her. Instead of appreciating the value and rarity of his jewel—instead of polishing her a bit and then letting her shine—he persists in trying to shape her into a common cameo."

Whitney was more inclined to think of herself as a chunk of coal, but rather than disillusion her aunt, she kept silent. After her aunt left, Whitney picked up her book, but soon her mind wandered from the printed page to dreamy thoughts of Paul.

That night when she came down to the dining room, the atmosphere in the room was strangely charged, and no one noticed her sauntering toward the table. "When do you plan to tell her she's coming back to France with us, Martin?" her uncle demanded angrily. "Or is it your intention to wait until the day we leave and then just toss the child into the coach with us?"

The world tilted crazily, and for one horrible moment, Whitney thought she was going to be sick. She stopped, trying to steady her shaking limbs, and swallowed back the aching lump in her throat. "Am I going somewhere, Father?" she asked, trying to sound calm and indifferent.

They all turned and stared, and her father's face tightened into lines of impatience and annoyance. "To France," he replied abruptly. "To live with your aunt and uncle, who are going to try to make a lady out of you."

Carefully avoiding meeting anyone's eyes, lest she break down then and there, Whitney slid into her chair at the table. "Have you informed my aunt and uncle of the risk they are taking?" she asked, concentrating all her strength on preventing her father from seeing what he had just done to her heart. She looked coldly at her aunt and uncle's guilty, embarrassed faces. "Father may have neglected to mention you're risking disgrace by welcoming me into your home. As he will tell you, I've a hideous disposition, I'm rag-mannered, and I haven't a trace of polite conversation."

Her aunt was watching her with naked pity, but her father's expression was stony. "Oh Papa," she whispered brokenly, "do you really despise me this much? Do you hate me so much that you have to send me out of your sight?" Her eyes swimming with unshed tears, Whitney stood up. "If you . . . will excuse me . . . I'm not very hungry this evening."

"How could you!" Anne cried when she left, rising from her own chair and glaring furiously at Martin Stone. "You are the most heartless, unfeeling—it will be a pleasure to remove that child from your clutches. How she has survived this long is a testimony to her strength. I'm sure I could never have done so well."

"You refine too much upon her words, Madam," Martin said icily. "I assure you that what has her looking so distraught is not the prospect of being parted from me. I have merely put a premature end to her plans to continue making a fool of herself over Paul Sevarin."

Chapter Two

THE NEWS THAT MARTIN STONE'S DAUGHTER WAS BEING PACKED off to France poste haste spread through the countryside like a fire through dry brush. In a sleepy rural area where the gentry were usually aloof and reserved, Whitney Stone had again provided everyone with a delicious morsel of excitement.

On the cobbled streets of the village and in households wealthy and poor, females of all ages gathered to savor this latest piece of gossip. With great relish and at greater length, they discussed every scandalous escapade of Whitney's scandal-ridden life, beginning with the toad she let loose in church one Sunday when she was eight years old, to the time this past summer when she fell out of a tree while spying on Paul Sevarin, seated beneath it with a young lady.

Only when those events had been recalled in detail, did they allow themselves to conjecture over Martin Stone's reason for finally sending her off to France.

In general, they felt that the outrageous child had probably pushed her poor, beleaguered father too far when she appeared in men's trousers. Because she had so many other shortcomings, there was some disagreement over *exactly* what had driven her father to take such sudden action, but if there was anything they all agreed upon, it was that Paul

Sevarin would be vastly relieved to have the girl out from under his feet.

During the next three days, Martin Stone's neighbors arrived at his house in droves, ostensibly to visit with Lady Gilbert and to bid Whitney goodbye. On the evening before their departure for France, Anne Gilbert was seated in the salon, enduring one of these social calls by three ladies and their daughters. Her smile was more formal than friendly as she listened with ill-concealed annoyance to these women who professed to be well-wishers and yet took a morbid delight in recounting to her Whitney's many youthful transgressions. Under the pretense of friendly concern, they made it clear that, in their collective opinion, Whitney was going to disgrace herself in Paris, destroy Anne's sanity, and very likely ruin Edward's diplomatic career.

She stood when they were finally ready to leave, and bade them a curt goodbye; then she sank into a chair, her eyes bright with angry determination. By constantly criticizing his daughter in front of other people, Martin Stone had made his own child a target for village ridicule. All Anne really needed to do was whisk Whitney away from these narrow-minded, spiteful neighbors of hers and let her bloom in Paris, where the social atmosphere wasn't so stifling.

In the doorway of the salon, the butler cleared his throat. "Mr. Sevarin is here, my lady."

"Show him in, please," Anne said, carefully hiding her surprised pleasure that the object of Whitney's childish adoration had come to say goodbye to her. Anne's pleasure faded, however, when Mr. Sevarin walked into the salon accompanied by a stunningly lovely little blonde. Since everyone for fifteen miles seemed to know that Whitney worshiped him, Anne had no doubt that Paul Sevarin knew it too, and she thought it very callous of him to bring a young woman with him when he had come to say goodbye to a girl who adored him.

She watched him cross the room toward her, longing to find something about him to criticize, but there was nothing. Paul Sevarin was tall and handsome, with the easy charm of a wealthy, well-bred country gentleman. "Good evening, Mr.

Sevarin," she said with cool formality. "Whitney is in the garden."

As if he guessed the reason for her reserve, Paul's blue eyes lit with a smile as he returned her greeting. "I know that," he said, "but I was hoping you might visit with Elizabeth while I say goodbye to Whitney."

In spite of herself, Anne was mollified. "I would be delighted."

Whitney stared morosely at the shadowy rosebushes. Her aunt was in the salon, undoubtedly being regaled with more stories of her niece's past, and dire predictions for her future. Emily had left for London with her parents, and Paul . . . Paul hadn't even come to say goodbye. Not that she'd really expected him to; he was probably with his friends, toasting her departure.

As if she'd conjured him up, his deep, masculine voice sounded from the darkness behind her. "Hello, pretty girl."

Whitney lurched around. He was standing only inches away with one shoulder casually propped against a tree. In the moonlight his snowy shirt and neckcloth gleamed against the almost invisible darkness of his jacket. "I understand you're leaving us," he said quietly.

Mutely, Whitney nodded. She was trying to commit to memory the exact shade of his blond hair and every contour of his handsome, moonlit face. "Will you miss me?" she blurted.

"Of course I will," he chuckled. "Things are going to be very dull without you, young lady."

"Yes, I imagine so," Whitney whispered, dropping her eyes. "With me gone, who else will fall out of trees to ruin your picnic, or break your leg, or . . ."

Paul interrupted her string of self-recriminations. "No one."

Whitney lifted her candid gaze to his. "Will you wait for me?"

"I will be here when you return, if that's what you mean," he replied evasively.

"But you know it isn't!" Whitney persisted in desperation. "What I mean is, could you possibly not marry anyone else until I—" Whitney trailed off in embarrassment. Why, she wondered, did she always go on this way with him? Why couldn't she be cool and flirtatious as the older girls were?

"Whitney," Paul was saying firmly, "you will go away and forget my name. Some day, you'll wonder why you ever asked me to wait for you."

"I'm *already* wondering that," she admitted miserably.

Sighing with irritation and compassion, Paul gently touched her chin, forcing her to look at him. "I'll be here," he said with a reluctant grin, "waiting impatiently to see how you've grown up."

Mesmerized, Whitney gazed up into his recklessly handsome, smiling face—and then she committed the final, the ultimate, mistake: Impulsively, she leaned up on her toes, flung her arms around him, and planted an urgent kiss just to the side of Paul's mouth. Swearing under his breath, he pulled her arms down and forcibly moved her away. Tears of self-loathing filled Whitney's eyes. "I'm so sorry, Paul. I—I never should have done that."

"No," he agreed, "you shouldn't have." He reached into his pocket, angrily pulled out a small box, and slapped it unceremoniously into her hand. "I brought you a farewell gift."

Whitney's spirits soared dizzyingly. "You did?" Her fingers shook as she snapped the lid up and gazed in rapturous wonder at the small cameo pendant dangling from a slender gold chain. "Oh, Paul," she whispered, her eyes shining, "it's the most beautiful, most splendid—I shall treasure it forever."

"It's a memento," he said carefully. "Nothing more."

Whitney scarcely heard him as she reverently touched the pendant. "Did you choose it for me yourself?"

Paul frowned in indecision. He'd gone to the village this morning to choose a tastefully expensive little trinket for Elizabeth. While he was there, the proprietor had laughingly remarked that with Miss Stone leaving for France, Paul must be in a mood to celebrate his freedom. As a matter of fact, Paul was. So, on an impulse, he asked the proprietor to choose something suitable for a fifteen-year-old. Until Whitney opened the box a moment ago, Paul had no idea what was in it. But what was the point of telling Whitney that? With luck, her aunt and uncle would be able to find some unsuspecting Frenchman who would marry her—preferably a docile man who wouldn't complain when Whitney ran roughshod over him. Out of reflex, Paul started to reach for her, to urge her to make the most of her opportunities in France. Instead he kept his hands at his sides. "I chose it myself—as a gift from one *friend* to another," he said finally.

"But I don't want to be just your friend," Whitney burst out, then she caught herself. "Being your friend will be fine . . . for now," she sighed.

"In that case," he said, his expression turning humorous, "I suppose it would be perfectly proper for two friends to exchange a farewell kiss."

With a dazzling smile of joyous amazement, Whitney squeezed her eyes closed and puckered her lips, but his mouth only brushed her cheek. When she opened her eyes, he was striding from the garden.

"Paul Sevarin," she whispered with great determination. "I shall change completely in France, and when I come home, you are going to marry me."

As the packet they had boarded at Portsmouth pitched and rocked across the choppy Channel, Whitney stood at the rail, her gaze fastened on the receding English coastline. The wind caught at the wide rim of her bonnet, tugging it free to dangle from its ribbons, whipping her hair against her cheek. She stared at her homeland, conjuring a vision of how it would be when she again crossed this Channel. Of course, news of her return would be announced in the papers: "Miss Whitney Stone," they would proclaim, "lately the belle of Paris, returns this week to her native England." A faint smile touched Whitney's lips . . . The belle of Paris . . .

She pushed her unruly hair off her face, stuffing it into the crown of her childish bonnet, and resolutely turned her back on England.

The Channel seemed to smooth out as she marched across the deck to stare in the direction of France. And her future.

FRANCE

1816–1820

Chapter Three

Situated behind wrought-iron gates, Lord and Lady Gilbert's Parisian home was imposing without being austere. Huge bow windows admitted light to the spacious rooms; pastels lent an air of sunny elegance to everything from parlors to second-floor bedrooms. "And these are your rooms, darling," Anne said as she opened the door to a suite carpeted in pale blue.

Whitney stood mesmerized on the threshold, her gaze roving longingly over the magnificent white satin coverlet on the bed splashed with flowers of orchid, pink, and blue. A dainty settee was covered in matching fabric. Delicate porcelain vases were filled with flowers in the same hues of orchid and pink. Ruefully, Whitney turned to her aunt. "I'd feel ever so much better, Aunt Anne, if you could find another room for me, something not quite so, well, fragile. Anyone at home," Whitney explained to Anne's amazed expression, "could tell you that I've only to walk by something delicate to send it crashing to the floor."

Anne turned to the servant beside her who was shouldering Whitney's heavy trunk. "In here," Anne said with a firm nod of her head toward the wonderful blue room.

"Don't say you weren't forewarned," sighed Whitney,

removing her bonnet and settling herself gingerly on the flowered settee. Paris, she decided, was going to be heavenly.

The parade of visitors began promptly at half past eleven, three days later, with the arrival of Anne's personal dressmaker, accompanied by three smiling seamstresses who talked endlessly about styles and fabrics and measured and remeasured Whitney.

Thirty minutes after they departed, Whitney found herself marching back and forth with a book on her head before the critical stare of the plump woman whom Aunt Anne was entrusting with the formidable task of teaching Whitney something called "social graces."

"I am atrociously clumsy, Madame Froussard," Whitney explained with an embarrassed flush as the book plummeted to the floor for the third time.

"But no!" Madame Froussard contradicted, shaking her elaborately coiffed silver hair. "Mademoiselle Stone has a natural grace and excellent posture. But Mademoiselle must learn not to walk as if she were in a race."

By the dancing instructor who arrived on the heels of Madame Froussard's departure, Whitney was whirled around the room in time to an imaginary waltz and judged, "Not at all hopeless—with practice."

By the French tutor who appeared at tea time, she was pronounced, "Fit to instruct *me*, Lady Gilbert."

For some months, Madame Froussard visited for two hours, five times each week, instructing Whitney in the social graces. Under her relentless, exacting tutelage, Whitney worked diligently to learn anything which might eventually help her win favor in Paul's eyes.

"Exactly what are you learning from Madame Froussard?" inquired Uncle Edward as they dined one evening.

A sheepish look crept across Whitney's face. "She is teaching me to *stroll* not *gallop*." She waited, half expecting her uncle to say that was a nonsensical waste of time, but instead he smiled approvingly. Whitney smiled back, feeling unaccountably happy. "Do you know," she teased, "I once believed that all one needed to walk properly were two sound limbs!"

From that night on, Whitney's laughing anecdotes about her day's endeavors became a delightful ritual at each evening meal. "Did you ever observe, Uncle," she asked him gaily one night, "that there is an art to turning around in a court dress with a train?"

"*Mine* never gave me any trouble," he joked.

"Done incorrectly," Whitney informed him with mock solemnity, "one is likely to find oneself wrapped in a train that has just become a tourniquet."

A month later she slid into her chair and fluttered a silken fan, eyeing her uncle with a speculative sparkle over the slats. "Are you over-warm, my dear?" Edward asked her, already into the spirit of the inevitable fun.

"A fan is not really for cooling oneself," Whitney advised him, batting her long eyelashes with an exaggerated coquetry that made Anne burst out laughing. "A fan is for flirting. It is also for keeping one's hands gracefully occupied. And for slapping the arm of a gentleman who is too forward."

The laughter vanished from Edward's face. "What gentleman has become too forward?" he demanded tersely.

"Why, no one has. I don't know any gentlemen yet," Whitney replied.

Anne watched the two of them, her smile filled with joy, for Whitney now occupied the place in Edward's heart, and hers, that would have been their own daughter's.

One evening the following May, the month before Whitney's official debut into society, Edward produced three opera tickets. Tossing them with artificial casualness in front of Whitney, he suggested that—if her schedule permitted—she might enjoy accompanying her aunt and himself to the Embassy's private box.

A year ago, Whitney would have whirled around in a rapturous circle, but she had changed now, so instead she beamed at her uncle and said, "I would like that above anything, Uncle Edward."

In silence she sat while Clarissa, who had been Susan

Stone's maid before she became companion and maid to Susan's daughter, brushed her hair and swept it upward, smoothing it into curls at the crown. Her new white frock with ice-blue velvet ribbons at the high waistline and frilled hemline was gently lowered over her head. A matching ice-blue satin cloak completed her ensemble. Whitney stood before her mirror, staring at herself with shining eyes. Tentatively, she dropped into a deep throne room curtsy, her head bowed to the perfect angle. "May I present Miss Whitney Stone," she murmured gravely. "The belle of Paris."

A fine, chilly mist descended, making the Paris streets gleam in the moonlight. Whitney snuggled deeper into the folds of her satin cloak, loving the feel of it against her chin, while she looked out the window at the teaming mass of humanity scurrying along the wide, rain-swept boulevards.

Outside the theatre crowds milled about in gay defiance of the dampness. Handsome gentlemen in satin coats and tight-fitting breeches bowed and nodded to ladies who glittered with jewels. Stepping from the coach, Whitney gazed in wonderment at the unbelievably gorgeous ladies who stood, poised and confident, talking to their escorts. They were, she decided then and there, the most beautiful women in the world, and she instantly dismissed any future hope of ever really being "the belle of Paris." But she did so with very little regret, for there was a wonderful exhilaration in simply being here among them.

As the trio made their way into the theatre, only Anne observed the younger gentlemen whose idle glances flickered past Whitney, then returned for another, longer look. Whitney's beauty was a blossoming thing, a vividness of features and coloring that promised much more to come. There was a radiance about her that sprang from her lively spirit and zest for life, a regalness and poise in her bearing that came from clashing head-on for so many years with adversity.

In the Consulate's private box, Whitney settled her beautiful new gown about her and picked up her ivory fan, using it, as Madame Froussard had instructed, to occupy her hands. She could have laughed at how silly she'd been, wasting so much time on lessons in languages and mathematics, when what she'd really needed to learn in order to please Paul and her father was so incredibly simple. Why, the fan in her hand was far more useful than Greek!

All about her a sea of heads bobbed and dipped, feathers fluttering from elaborate headdresses. Whitney could have hugged herself with the joy of it all. She saw a gentleman receive a playful slap with his lady's fan, and she felt a kinship with all women, as she wondered what impropriety he'd whispered to his lovely lady, who looked more flattered than distressed.

The opera began and Whitney promptly forgot everything else, lost as she was in the haunting music. It was all beyond her wildest dreams. By the time the heavy curtains swept closed to permit a change of scenery on the stage, Whitney had to shake herself back into reality. Behind her, friends of her aunt and uncle had come to the box, lending their voices to the incredible din of talk and laughter in the theatre.

"Whitney," Aunt Anne said, touching her shoulder. "Do turn around so that I may present you to our dear friends."

Obediently, Whitney stood and turned and was introduced to Monsieur and Madame DuVille. Their greeting was warm and open, but their daughter, Thérèse, a winsome blonde of about Whitney's years, only eyed her in watchful curiosity. Under the girl's penetrating gaze, some of Whitney's confidence slid away. She had never known how to converse with people her own age, and for the first time since leaving England, she felt gauche and ill at ease. "Are—are you enjoying the opera?" she managed at last.

"No," Thérèse said, dimpling, "for I cannot understand a word of it."

"Whitney can," Lord Edward proudly announced. "She understands Italian, Greek, Latin, and even some German!"

Whitney felt like sinking through the floor, for her uncle's boast had probably branded her as a bluestocking in the DuVilles' eyes. She had to force herself to meet Thérèse's startled gaze.

"I hope you don't play the pianoforte and sing too?" The little blonde pouted prettily.

"Oh no," Whitney hastily assured her. "I can't do either one."

"Wonderful!" declared Therèse with a wide smile as she settled herself into a chair beside Whitney's, "for those are the only two things I do well. Are you looking forward to your debut?" she bubbled, passing a swift look of admiration over Whitney.

"Not," Whitney admitted truthfully, "very much."

"I am. Although for me, it is merely a formality. My marriage was arranged three years ago. Which is just perfect, for now I can devote all my attention to helping *you* find a husband. I shall tell you which gentlemen are eligible and which are only handsome—without money or prospects—then when you make a brilliant match, I shall come to your wedding and tell everyone that I was entirely responsible!" she finished with an irrepressible smile.

Whitney smiled back, a little dazed by Therèse's unreserved offer of friendship. The smile was all the encouragement Therèse DuVille needed to continue: "My sisters have all made splendid marriages. Which only leaves me. And my brother, Nicolas, of course."

Whitney suppressed the urge to inquire laughingly whether Nicolas DuVille fell into the category of "eligible" or "only handsome," but Therèse promptly provided the answer without being asked. "Nicki isn't at all eligible. Well, he *is*— because he's very wealthy and terribly handsome. The thing is, Nicolas isn't *available*. Which is a great pity and the despair of my family, for Nicki is the only male heir, and the eldest of the five of us."

Avidly curious, Whitney nevertheless managed to respond politely that she hoped it wasn't because Monsieur DuVille was suffering from any affliction.

"Not," Therèse said with a musical giggle, "unless one considers excessive boredom and shocking arrogance an affliction. Of course, Nicolas has every right to be so, with females constantly dangling after him. Mama says that if it were up to the females to do the asking, Nicolas would have had more offers of marriage than us four girls combined!"

Whitney's demure facade of polite interest disintegrated.

"I can't imagine why," she laughed. "He sounds perfectly odious to me."

"Charm," Thérèse explained gravely. "Nicolas has charm." After a thoughtful pause, she added, "It is such a pity Nicki is so difficult, because if he were to attend our debut and single you out for special attention, you would be an instant success!" She sighed. "Of course, nothing in the world will persuade him to attend a debutante ball. He says they are excruciatingly boring. Nevertheless, I shall tell him about you—perhaps he will help."

Only courtesy prevented Whitney from saying that she hoped she *never* met Thérèse's arrogant older brother.

Chapter Four

On the day before Whitney's official debut into society, a letter arrived from Emily Williams that left Whitney lightheaded with relief: Paul had purchased some property in the Bahama Islands and was planning to remain there for a year. Since Whitney could not imagine Paul tumbling into love with a sun-burned Colonial, that meant she had a full year in which to prepare herself to go home. An entire year without having to worry about Paul marrying someone else.

To help quiet her nerves over the ball tomorrow evening, she curled up on a rose satin settee in the salon and was happily rereading all of Emily's letters which were hidden inside a book of etiquette. So absorbed was she with them, that Whitney was unaware that someone was watching her.

Nicolas DuVille stood in the doorway with the note his sister, Thérèse, had insisted he deliver *personally* to Miss Stone. Since Thérèse had tried a dozen other ploys in the last month to put Miss Stone in his way, Nicki had no doubt that delivering this note was a fool's errand devised between the two girls. It was not the first time his sister had tried to interest him in one of her giddy young friends, and from experience, Nicki knew the best way to nip Miss Stone's romantic plans for him in the proverbial bud was simply to fluster and intimidate the chit until she was relieved to see him leave.

His cool gaze took in the fetching scene which Miss Stone had obviously planned in advance so that she would appear to best advantage. Sunlight streamed in the window beside her, highlighting her gleaming cascade of dark hair, a long strand of which she was idly curling around her forefinger as she feigned absorption in her book; her yellow morning dress was arranged in graceful folds, and her feet were coyly tucked beneath her. Her profile was serene, with long lashes slightly lowered, and a faint suggestion of a smile played about her generous lips. Impatient with her little charade, Nicolas stepped into the room. "A very charming picture, Mademoiselle. My compliments," he drawled insolently.

Snapping her head up, Whitney closed the book of etiquette containing Emily's letters and laid it aside as she arose. Uncertainly, she gazed at a man in his late twenties who was coldly regarding her down the length of his aristocratic nose. He was undeniably handsome, with black hair and piercing, gold-flecked brown eyes.

"Have you had an edifying look, Mademoiselle?" he asked bluntly.

Realizing that she *had* been staring at him, Whitney caught herself abruptly and nodded toward the note in his hand. "Have you come to see my aunt?"

To Whitney's stunned amazement, the man strolled into the room and thrust the note at her. "I am Nicolas DuVille, and your butler has already informed me that you have been expecting me. Therefore, I believe we can dispense with your pretense of coy surprise, can we not?"

Whitney stood in shock as the man subjected her to a leisurely appraisal that began at her face and wandered boldly down the full length of her rigid body. Did his gaze actually linger on her breasts, or was it only her confused imagination that made it seem that way? When he was finished inspecting her from the front, he strolled around her, considering her from all angles as if she were a horse he was thinking of purchasing. "Don't bother," he said, when Whitney nervously opened the note. "It says that Thérèse left her bracelet here, but you and I know that is only an excuse for us to meet."

Whitney was bewildered, embarrassed, amused, and insulted, all at the same time. Thérèse had said her brother was arrogant, but somehow Whitney had never imagined he'd be *this* horrid.

"Actually," he said, as he came around to stand in front of her, "you are not at all what I expected." His voice held a note of reluctant approbation.

"Nicolas!" Aunt Anne's gracious greeting relieved Whitney of the necessity of replying. "How lovely to see you. I've been expecting you—one of the maids discovered Thérèse's bracelet beneath a cushion of a sofa. The clasp was broken. I'll get it for you," she said, hurrying from the room.

Nicki's startled gaze shot to Miss Stone. A smile trembled on her lips as she lifted her delicate brows at him, visibly enjoying his chagrin. In view of his earlier rudeness, Nicki felt that some form of polite conversation was now required of him. He leaned down and picked up the etiquette book containing Emily's letters, glanced at the title, and then at Whitney. "Are you learning good manners, Mademoiselle?" he inquired.

"Yes," Miss Stone replied, her eyes glowing with suppressed laughter. "Would you care to borrow my book?"

Her quip earned her a lazy, devastating smile of admiration. "I see that some form of atonement for my earlier behavior is in order. Mademoiselle," he said with laughing gravity, "would you favor me with a dance tomorrow night?"

Whitney hesitated, taken aback by his engaging smile and open admiration.

Mistaking her silence for coquettishness, Nicolas shrugged, and all the warmth left his smile as he said with mocking amusement, "From your hesitation, I will assume that all your dances are already bespoken. Another time, perhaps."

Whitney realized he was withdrawing his invitation, and she instantly decided the man was as arrogant and perverse as she'd first thought. "None of my dances are bespoken," she floored him by candidly admitting. "You see, you are the first *gentleman* I've met in Paris."

Her deliberate emphasis on the word "gentleman" did not escape Nicki, who suddenly threw back his head and laughed.

"Here is the bracelet," Lady Gilbert said, hurrying into the room. "And Nicolas, please remind Thérèse that the clasp is broken."

Nicki took the bracelet and left. He climbed into his carriage, instructed his groom to drive him round to his mother's, then relaxed back against the leather cushions. They drove past a park whose winding paths bloomed extravagantly with spring flowers. Two pretty females of his acquaintance lifted pastel-gloved hands at him in greeting, but Nicki scarcely glanced at the Gainsborough-like scene. His thoughts were occupied with the young English girl he had just met.

Try as he might, he couldn't understand how Whitney Stone and his addlepated chatterbox of a sister had become such boon companions, for they were as dissimilar as lemonade and heady French wine. Thérèse was a pretty thing, sweet as lemonade, but she had no hidden depths to interest a man.

Whitney Stone, on the other hand, was a veritable treasure of contrasts, sparkling like rich, red burgundy with the promise of hidden and tantalizing things to come. For a seventeen-year-old, she had borne his mocking disdain with remarkable composure. Given a few years, Nicolas decided, she would be fascinating. A chuckle welled up in his chest as he recalled how adroitly she'd retaliated for his remark about the etiquette book, by offering to lend it to him.

It would be a pity, he decided, for such a rare jewel as she to be relegated to obscurity at the crowded debutante ball tomorrow night, merely because she was a stranger to France.

Gorgeous tapestries adorned one side of the gigantic ballroom, and the opposite wall was mirrored to reflect the light from the thousands of candles in the glittering chandeliers overhead. Catching sight of her reflection in one of the mirrors, Whitney nervously studied her appearance. Her white silken ball gown was trimmed with broad scallops caught up and held in place with pink silk roses which matched the ones entwined in the heavy curls at her crown. She looked, she decided, a great deal calmer than she felt.

"Everything is going to be wonderful, you'll see," whispered Aunt Anne.

Whitney did *not* think everything was going to be wonderful at all. She knew she couldn't possibly hope to compete with the dazzling blondes and redheads, the demure little brunettes, who were laughing and talking easily with smiling young men garbed in black, but with brightly colored waistcoats of silks and satin. Whitney told herself she didn't care a pin about anything as foolish as a silly ball, but she knew it wasn't true. She cared very much.

Thérèse and her mama arrived only seconds before the musicians raised their instruments for the first dance. "I have the most splendid news," Thérèse whispered breathlessly, looking like a confection in her white lace gown with her cheeks pink and her shining blond hair elegantly curled atop her head. "My maid is cousin to Nicki's valet and he told her that Nicki is coming tonight. *And* he is bringing three of his friends as well—he bet them five-hundred francs against two hours of their time tonight on a roll of the dice, and they lost, so they have to come and dance with you . . ." She broke off with an apologetic shrug to Whitney and bestowed a charming curtsy upon the young man who had come to ask her for a dance.

Whitney's mind was still reeling with embarrassment over this news when the musicians struck the first note of music, and the debutantes were escorted onto the dance floor by their respective partners. Not all the debutantes—Whitney felt her color deepen as she looked helplessly at Aunt Anne. She had known when she came tonight that she might not be asked to dance at first, but she hadn't expected to feel so wretchedly conspicuous at being left standing there with her aunt and Madame DuVille. The feeling was painfully familiar —it was as if she were back home in England where invitations to neighborhood functions were infrequent and, if she went, she was either treated with derision or ignored.

Thérèse danced the second and third dances, but Whitney was not asked for either. When it was time for the fourth one, the humiliation of being passed over again was more than she could bear. Leaning toward Aunt Anne, Whitney started to ask if she could go somewhere to freshen up, but there was a commotion at the entrance and she curiously followed the gazes of the other guests.

Nicolas DuVille and three other gentlemen were standing beneath the arched portico at the entrance to the ballroom. Carelessly at ease in their elegant dark formal wear, and serenely indifferent to the wild attention they were receiving, they surveyed the crowd. In frozen apprehension, Whitney watched as Nicolas DuVille's gaze swept the staring masses of giggling debutantes and young dandies. When at last he saw Whitney, he inclined his head slightly in greeting, and the foursome started forward.

Whitney pressed back against the wall, childishly tempted to try to squeeze herself between it and Aunt Anne. She didn't want to risk another confrontation with Nicolas Du-Ville. Yesterday she'd been too surprised to feel intimidated by him; tonight what pride and self-confidence she possessed were already in tatters, and to add to her discomfort, she was acutely aware of how elegantly urbane and handsome Nicolas looked in his black evening attire.

She watched the men threading their way through the watchful crowd, coming right toward her, and even in her state of paralyzed horror, Whitney recognized the sharp contrast between Nicolas DuVille's group and the other gentlemen in the room. He and his party were not only several years older than most of the young men paying lavish court to even younger girls, there was also an aura of smooth sophistication about them that further set them apart.

Madame DuVille laughed with delighted surprise as her son greeted her. "Nicki, I could not be more astonished if the devil himself strolled in!"

"Why thank you, Mama," he murmured drily, making her a brief bow. Abruptly, he turned to Whitney and grinned as he took her cold hand in his. Raising it to his lips for a formal kiss, he said with an infuriating chuckle, "Stop looking so astounded to find yourself the object of my attention, Mademoiselle. You should act as if this is nothing more than you expect."

Whitney stared at him wide-eyed, not certain whether she was insulted or grateful for his unsolicited advice.

He raised an ironic eyebrow, as if he knew what she was thinking, then he turned and introduced his three companions to her.

The music began and without asking, Nicki simply took her hand, placed it on his arm, and escorted her onto the dance floor. He guided her effortlessly through the swirling waltz, while Whitney concentrated on following the steps she had learned from her dancing instructor.

"Mademoiselle." Nicki's deep voice vibrated with humor. "If you will look up at me, you will find that I am gazing down at you in what our bewildered audience sees as a warm and admiring manner. However, if you continue to memorize the folds in my neckcloth, I am going to stop looking besotted and begin looking quite weary and bored. If I do, instead of being launched into society tonight, you will remain a wallflower. Now, look up at me and smile."

"A wallflower!" Whitney burst out, her gaze flying to his. She saw the humor in his eyes, and her indignation dissolved. "I feel so conspicuous," she admitted. "Everyone in this room seems to be watching us and . . ."

"They are not watching *us,*" he contradicted with a tolerant chuckle. "They are watching *me,* and trying to decide if *you* are what has lured me to this dull assembly of virtuous innocents—"

"—And away from your usual pursuit of vice and depravity?" Whitney teased, while a slow, unconsciously provocative smile dawned across her vivid features.

"Exactly," Nicki agreed with a grin.

"In that case," she mused in a laughter-tinged voice, "won't this waltz ruin my reputation before I even have one?"

"No, but it may ruin mine." Nicki saw her shocked look and said lightly, "It is not at all in my style to appear at debutante balls, Mademoiselle. And for me to be seen like this, actually enjoying myself dancing with an impertinent chit of your tender years, is unheard of."

Whitney pulled her gaze from Nicolas DuVille's ruggedly

chiselled face and glanced around at the young dandies in their bright satin waistcoats. They were staring at Nicki in open irritation, and no wonder! Nicki's impeccably tailored midnight black attire, his air of smooth urbanity, made them all seem somewhat overdressed and rather callow.

"Are they still staring?" Nicki teased.

Whitney bit her lip, trying to hold back the laughter that was already sparkling in her eyes as she looked up into his handsome face. "Yes, but I can't really blame them—you *are* rather like a hawk in a room full of canaries."

A slow, admiring smile swept across his features. "I am indeed," he breathed softly. And then he said, "You have an enchanting smile, chérie."

Whitney was thinking that *he* was the one possessed of a wonderful smile, when it vanished behind a dark frown. "Is—is something wrong?" she asked.

"Yes," he replied bluntly. "Do not let a man you aren't betrothed to call you 'chérie.'"

"I will stare them out of countenance if they dare!" Whitney promptly promised.

"Much better," he applauded, and then boldly, " . . . chérie."

At the conclusion of the waltz, he guided her back to her aunt, keeping his head bent toward her as if he were positively hanging on her every word. He waited there, rarely taking his eyes off of her as she danced in turn with each of his three friends.

Whitney felt a little giddy and reckless and wonderful. Already there were a gratifying number of gentlemen asking for introductions to her. She knew it was because of the extravagant and unprecedented attention she was receiving from Nicolas DuVille and his friends, but she was too relieved and grateful to care.

Claude Delacroix, a handsome, fair-haired man who had come with Nicolas, instantly discovered that Whitney loved horses, and the two of them had a thoroughly enjoyable disagreement about the merits of one breed over another. He even asked if she would care to go for a drive with him one day soon, which was certainly not at Nicki's prompting.

Whitney felt very pleased and flattered, and she was smiling as he returned her to her aunt.

Nicki, however, was *not* pleased, nor was he smiling, when he immediately claimed her for the next dance. "Claude Delacroix," he informed her curtly as his arm encircled her, "is from a fine old family. He is an outstanding whip, an excellent gambler, and a good friend. He is not, however, a suitable companion for you, nor should you think of him as a possible suitor. In matters of the heart, Claude is an expert, but he loses interest very quickly, and then . . ."

"He breaks the lady's heart?" Whitney guessed with mock solemnity.

"Exactly," Nick said severely.

Whitney knew her heart already belonged to Paul, and so it was not in any danger. With a soft smile, she said, "I shall guard my heart with great care."

Nicki's gaze lingered on her soft, inviting lips, then lifted to her glowing jade eyes. "Perhaps," he breathed with a tinge of self-mockery that Whitney couldn't understand, "I ought to warn Claude to guard *his* heart. If you were older, Mademoiselle, I think I would."

When Nicki returned her to her aunt, there were more than a dozen gentlemen, all eager for a dance with her and waiting to claim it. Nicki detained her with a hand on her arm, and nodded toward the young man at the end of the line. "André Rousseau," he said, "would make an excellent husband for you."

Whitney gave him a look of laughing exasperation. "You really shouldn't say things like that."

"I know." He grinned. "Now, am I forgiven for my rudeness yesterday?"

Whitney nodded happily. "I would say that I have just been 'launched' as beautifully as one of England's ships."

Nicki's smile was filled with warmth as he raised her fingers to his lips. "Bon voyage, chérie," he said.

And then he was gone.

Whitney was still thinking about the night before and smiling softly to herself as she descended the stairs the following morning, intending to ride her uncle's spirited mare. Masculine voices drifted into the hallway from the drawing room, and as Whitney started to walk past, Aunt Anne appeared in the doorway, her face wreathed in a smile. "I was just coming up to get you," she whispered. "You have callers."

"Callers?" Whitney repeated, panicking. It was one thing to mouth the usual prescribed platitudes during the dancing last night, another thing entirely to charm and interest these gentlemen who had now exerted themselves to pay a morning call on her. "Whatever shall I say to them?" Whitney begged. "What shall I do?"

"Do?" Anne smiled, stepping aside and firmly placing her hand against the small of Whitney's back. "Why, be yourself, darling."

Hesitantly, Whitney entered the room. "I was about to ride—in the park," she explained to her callers—three of the gentlemen she had danced with last night. The three young men leapt to their feet, each one thrusting a bouquet of flowers toward her. Whitney's gaze slid to the bouquets they were holding, and a smile lifted the corners of her mouth. "It appears that the three of you have just come from there."

They blinked at her as it registered on each of them that she was teasing them about having purloined the flowers from the park beds. And then—surprise of surprises—they were smiling at her and arguing good-naturedly over who was to have the honor of accompanying her to the park.

In the true spirit of fairness, Whitney happily permitted *all* of them to accompany her.

That year Miss Stone was proclaimed "an Original." At a time when young ladies were models of dainty fragility and blushing coquetry, Whitney was impulsive and gay. While other young ladies her age were demure, Whitney was clever and direct.

During the following year, Anne watched as nature collaborated with time, and Whitney's youthful face fulfilled all its former promise of vivid beauty. Sooty black lashes fringed incredibly expressive eyes which changed from sea-green to deep jade beneath the graceful arch of her dark brows. Burnished mahogany tresses framed an exquisitely sculpted face with a softly generous mouth and skin as smooth as cream satin. Her figure was still slim, but ripened now, with tantalizing curves and graceful hollows. That was the year she was proclaimed "an Incomparable."

Gentlemen told her that she was "ravishingly beautiful" and "enchantingly lovely" and that she haunted their dreams. Whitney listened to their lavish compliments and passionate pledges of undying devotion with a smile that was part amused disbelief and part genuine gratitude for their kindness.

She reminded Anne of an elusive tropical bird, surprised and delighted by her own appeal, who landed tentatively and then, when one of her suitors reached out to capture her, flew away.

She was beautiful, but gentlemen left the sides of equally beautiful young women to cluster around her, beckoned by the gaiety that seemed to surround her and the easy playfulness of her manners.

By the beginning of her third year "out" in society, Whitney had become a challenge to more worldly, sophisticated men who sought to win her merely to prove that they could succeed where others had failed—only to find themselves rather unexpectedly in love with a young woman who hadn't the slightest inclination to reciprocate their feelings. Everyone knew she would soon have to marry; after all, she was already nineteen years old. Even Lord Gilbert was becoming concerned, but when he observed to his wife that Whitney was being excessively fussy, Anne only smiled.

Because it seemed to her that Whitney had lately developed a decided partiality for Nicolas DuVille.

Chapter Five

For the third time in ten minutes, Whitney realized that she had again lost track of the conversation, and she glanced guiltily at the girls who were paying a morning call on her. Fortunately, they were all enraptured with Therèse's enthusiastic description of her new life as a married woman and seemed not to notice Whitney's wandering attention.

Nervously, Whitney fingered the letter from Emily which had just been handed to her, wondering as she always did, if *this* was going to be the letter that brought the dreaded news that Paul had chosen a wife. Unable to bear the suspense any longer, she opened it, and her heart doubled its already rapid pace as she began to read:

"Dearest Whitney," Emily wrote in her neat, precise hand. "henceforth, I shall expect you to address me as 'Lady Emily, Baroness Archibald, the Happiest Woman Alive.' I shall expect you to bow and scrape and mince about when next we meet, so that I will truly believe this has happened." The next two pages were filled with wondrous praise of Emily's new husband and details of the marriage which had been performed by special license. "What you said about France is also true of England," Emily said. "No matter how grotesque he is, if a gentleman has a title, he is considered a great matrimonial prize, but I promise when you meet him, you will agree that my husband would be wonderful without any title."

Whitney smiled, knowing that Emily would never have married her baron unless she loved him. "Enough about me," she continued, "I have something else to tell you which I forgot to mention in my last letter. Six of us from home were all at a rout party in London, where our hostess introduced a gentleman who at once took the ladies' fancy. And no wonder, for he was very handsome and tall, and from a distinguished French family. Whitney, it was M. Nicolas DuVille! I was quite certain he was the same gentleman you mention in your letters, and I asked M. DuVille if he was acquainted with you. When he said that he was, Margaret Merryton and the other girls flocked around him to try to offer their 'sympathy.'

"How you would have laughed, for after giving them a look that should have turned them to stone, M. DuVille quite flayed them alive with tales of all your suitors and conquests in Paris. He even implied that he was rather taken with you himself, which made the girls absolutely livid with jealousy. Is what he said true? And why haven't you told me that 'Paris is in the palm of your hand'?"

Whitney smiled. Although Nicki had mentioned meeting Emily in London, he had never mentioned meeting Whitney's childhood arch foe, Margaret Merryton, or the other girls. The pleasure she felt at his defense of her vanished, however, when she considered the possibility that Nicki might truly want to be something more than just her friend. For nearly three years, he had merely been a handsome vision who appeared without warning at her side to claim her for a dance or tease her about one of her many suitors. Then he would vanish with some dazzling female clinging possessively to his arm.

But a few months ago that had suddenly changed. They had met each other at the theatre and Nicki had unexpectedly invited her to an opera. Now he escorted her everywhere, to balls and routs, musicales and plays. Of all the men she knew,

Nicolas DuVille was the one Whitney most enjoyed being with, but she couldn't bear the thought that he might actually have serious intentions toward her.

Whitney stared blindly at the letter, her eyes cloudy and sad. If Nicki were to offer for her, and she were to decline (which she would), she would be jeopardizing her friendship with Thérèse, her aunt and uncle's friendship with the senior DuVilles, and her own friendship with Nicki, which meant a great deal to her.

She forced her attention back to Emily's letter. At the end of it was news of Paul. "Elizabeth is in London for the season, and when she returns home, everyone is expecting Paul to offer for her, since her parents now feel it is past time for her to marry."

Whitney, who had been bursting with joy for Emily's wonderful news, now felt like crying her heart out. After all her practicing, all of her planning, she was at last ready to win Paul's love, but her father was keeping her in France, ignoring her pleas to come home.

As soon as she had ushered her friends from the house, Whitney went to her room to write to him. This time, she would send her father a letter he couldn't just ignore as he had her others. She wanted to go home—had to go home—and she had to do it at once. After considerable thought, she composed a letter to him, this time appealing to his wounded pride and dignity, by telling him how she longed to come home and prove to him that he could be proud of her now. She finished by telling him how dreadfully she missed him. Then she wrote to Emily.

When she brought the letters downstairs to have them sent off, she was informed by a footman that Monsieur DuVille had just arrived and wished to see her *immediately*. Puzzled by this imperative command from Nicki, Whitney went down the hall to her uncle's study. "Hello, Nicki. It's a lovely day, isn't it?"

He turned. "Is it?" he replied tersely, and there was no mistaking the rigid set of his shoulders or the taut line of his jaw.

"Well, yes. Sunny and warm, I mean."

"Just exactly what possessed you to engage in a public horse race?" he snapped, ignoring the polite amenities.

"It was not a public horse race," Whitney said, amazed by his vehemence.

"No? Then perhaps you will explain how it appeared in the paper today."

"I don't know," Whitney sighed. "I imagine that someone told someone who told someone else. That's the way it usually happens. Anyway," she finished with a pretty toss of her head, "I won, you know. I actually beat Baron Von Ault."

Nicki's voice rang with authority. "I will not permit you to do a thing like that again!" He saw her stiffen in angry confusion and drew a long breath. "I apologize for my tone, chérie. I will see you at the Armands' masquerade this evening, unless you will change your mind and permit me to escort you?"

Whitney smiled her acceptance of his apology, but shook her head at the suggestion of his escorting her to the Armands'. "I think it's best if I go with my aunt and uncle and meet you there. The other ladies already resent me for monopolizing so much of your attention lately, Nicki."

Momentarily, Nicki cursed himself for allowing her to get under his skin, when for nearly three years his own good judgment had warned him away. And then, four months ago, after an exceedingly disagreeable evening with a lady who had once amused him and now bored him with her clinging ways, Nicki had encountered Whitney at the theatre and impulsively asked her to accompany him to an opera.

By the end of the evening, he was utterly captivated by her. She was an intoxicating combination of beauty and humor, of exhilarating intelligence and disarming common sense. And she was as elusive as hell!

He looked at her now. Her sensuous mouth was curved into an affectionate smile of the sort one bestows on a loved brother, *not* one's future husband, and it irritated Nicki into action.

Before Whitney could guess his intent, his hands caught her upper arms, pulling her against the length of his hard frame as his mouth began a purposeful descent. "Nicki, don't! I—" Instantly his mouth silenced her startled protest, his lips moving sensuously, tasting and courting hers. In the past, only clumsy, overzealous suitors had tried to kiss her, and Whitney had easily put them off, but Nicki's arousing kiss was awakening a response in her that amazed and alarmed her. She managed to remain perfectly still and unresponsive, but the moment his arms loosened, she stepped back quickly. "I suppose," she said with false calm, "that I ought to slap your face for that."

She looked so coolly unaffected that Nicki, who had been unexpectedly shaken by the feel of her soft mouth beneath his, and the pressure of her breasts against his chest, was furious. "Slap my face?" he repeated sarcastically. "Why should you? I can't believe that I'm the first, or even the hundredth, man to steal a kiss from you."

"Really?" Whitney flung back, stung to the quick by his intimation that she would play fast and loose. "Well, I've obviously just had the honor of being *your* first!" The words weren't past her lips before Whitney saw the rigid anger in his expression and realized that she'd made a serious tactical error in insulting his masculinity. "Nicki—" she whispered in warning, cautiously stepping backward and out of his reach. Nicki advanced on her. She scooted behind her uncle's desk, facing him across it, her hands braced on the top. Each time Whitney moved one way, Nicki countered. They stood, two combatants separated by Uncle Edward's desk, each waiting for the other to make a move. Suddenly, the childish absurdity of the situation struck Whitney, and she began to laugh. "Nicki, have you the faintest idea what you're going to do if you catch me?"

Nicki had an excellent idea what he would *like* to do if he caught her, but he also appreciated the foolishness of the scene. He straightened, and the mask of anger fell away.

"Come out from behind the desk," he chuckled. "I give you my word I shall behave as a gentleman."

Scanning his face, Whitney assured herself that he meant it, then obediently did as he bade her. Linking her hand through his arm, she escorted him to the door. "I'll see you tonight at the masquerade," she promised.

Chapter Six

LORD EDWARD GILBERT STOOD BEFORE THE DRAWING ROOM
mirror, his eyes wide with shock and repugnance as he stared
at himself in the scaly green crocodile costume his wife had
chosen for him to wear to the Armands' masquerade.

His revolted gaze slid from the top of his grotesque head
with its fierce jaws open wide, ready to snap, down to his
claw-like reptilian feet, then along the thick tail dragging the
floor behind him. Precisely at the center of what should have
been the crocodile's sleek green body, Edward's stomach
swelled majestically. Turning his back to the mirror, he
looked over his shoulder and experimentally rotated his hips,
watching in morbid fascination as his tail undulated behind
him. "Obscene!" he snorted in disgust.

Lady Anne and Whitney came into the room at that
moment, and Edward turned on his wife. "God's armpits!"
he exploded, jerking off his headpiece and waving it angrily at
her as he waddled across the room, his tail dragging behind
him. "How am I ever going to have a cigar wearing this, may I
ask?"

Lady Anne smiled imperturbably as she surveyed him in
the costume she had chosen without consulting him. "I
couldn't get your favorite Henry the Eighth costume, and I
was perfectly sure you wouldn't care for the elephant
costume—"

"Elephant!" Edward repeated bitterly, glowering at her. "I'm surprised you *didn't* purchase that getup for me. You could have had me crawling about on all fours, waving my trunk and stabbing people in the rump with my tusks! Madam, I have a reputation to maintain, a dignity—"

"Hush, dear," she remonstrated affectionately. "What will Whitney think—"

"I'll tell you what she'll think—she'll think I look like an ass. *Everyone* will think I look like an ass!" He turned his head toward Whitney. "Go ahead, my dear, tell your aunt I look like an ass!"

Whitney regarded him with laughing fondness. "Your costume is very clever and original, Uncle Edward," she said diplomatically, then she sidetracked him completely by mentioning the name of a lifelong rival. "I did hear, though, that Herbert Granville is coming as a horse."

"No, really?" Lord Gilbert said, instantly amused. "Which end?"

Her eyes twinkled at him. "I forgot to ask."

He chuckled, then said, "Let me guess who you are supposed to be." Whitney twirled around for his inspection. Her Grecian gown of filmy white silk was fastened at the left shoulder with an amethyst broach, leaving the other creamy shoulder tantalizingly bare. Its gossamer folds clung provocatively to her full breasts and narrow waist, then fell gracefully to the floor. The thick clusters of her shining hair were bound with vibrant buttercups and violets. "Venus," he decided.

Whitney shook her head. "Here—this clue will help." She swirled a purple satin mantle over her shoulders and waited expectantly.

"Venus," he declared again, more emphatically.

"No," she said, kissing him on the cheek. "Actually, the dressmaker tried to improve on mythology. I'm supposed to be Prosperina, but she is always depicted in a simpler, girlish gown."

"Who?" Edward echoed.

"Prosperina, the goddess of spring," Whitney said. "Remember, Uncle Edward? She is always shown with violets and buttercups in her hair, and wearing a purple mantle like this one?" When her uncle still looked confused, Whitney added, "Pluto carried her off to live in the underworld as his wife."

"Rotten thing for him to have done," Edward replied absently, "but I like your costume, my dear. Everyone will be so busy trying to figure out who you're supposed to be, they won't have time to wonder who the obese crocodile is." With that he offered his arm to Whitney, and the other to Anne, who was gowned as a medieval queen, complete with tall conical headdress and veil.

Waves of laughter surged across the Armands' over-crowded ballroom, drowning out the efforts of the musicians, then receding, leaving behind the persistent undertow of conversation. On the congested dance floor, extravagantly costumed guests struggled for space to dance to music they could scarcely hear.

Standing on the sidelines, surrounded by her personal entourage of admirers, Whitney smiled serenely. She watched Nicki arrive, nod briefly to his mother, then begin making his way unerringly toward her, recognizing her despite her white demi-mask. He was coming from another party and was not wearing a costume. Whitney studied him with an inward smile; she admired everything about him, from the easy way he wore his elegant clothes to his sophisticated charm. For a fleeting moment, the memory of the way his mouth had felt as it moved over hers tingled through her.

When he was near, he flicked a level, impassive glance over the men standing around her, and they parted to make a place for him as if he had ordered them aside. Grinning wolfishly, he surveyed her Grecian gown, purple mantle, and the violets and buttercups twined in her glossy hair. He lifted her finge s to his lips and raised his voice in order to be heard over the din of conversation. "You are ravishing tonight, Venus."

"Amen!" agreed an enormous banana who was struggling to fight his way past Whitney's group.

"Ravissante!" declared a knight in armor, raising his visor and fixing Whitney with an appreciative leer.

Nicki passed a cold look over the two, and Whitney demurely raised her fan. But behind the silken slats, she was smiling widely. This was her world now, and she warmed with a feeling of security. In France, when she said something unusual, there were no snorts of disapproval or gasps of outrage. Instead, people said she was "witty" and "lively" and even quoted her. Surely when she went home to England it would be the same. She had made dreadful mistakes there as a girl. She knew better now, and she would not disgrace herself again.

Beside her, she felt Nicki's admiring gaze moving over her silk dress, but she did not bother to tell him that she wasn't costumed as Venus. No one at the entire ball seemed to have heard of any female from Greek mythology other than Venus, and the clue of her purple mantle and the violets and buttercups in her hair meant nothing to them. Long ago, she'd given up explaining.

She was in the process of deciding on whom to bestow the honor of fetching her more punch when André Rousseau, one of her most enduring admirers, noticed that her glass was empty. "But this cannot be permitted, Mademoiselle," he said dramatically. "I did not realize that your glass required attention. May I?" he said, extending his hand toward the offending glass.

Whitney surrendered it to him, and he bowed. "An honor, Mademoiselle." With a triumphant look at the other gentlemen, he departed in the direction of the gigantic crystal fountain which gurgled forth a ceaseless supply of punch.

Would Paul think it was an honor to fetch punch for her now? Whitney wondered dreamily. The idea of Paul Sevarin flushing with gratitude over being allowed to do an errand for her was so ludicrous that Whitney smiled. If only he could see her here, surrounded by suitors, courted and sought after.

Abruptly, Whitney jerked her thoughts from Paul back to reality as she realized that she had been inadvertently staring at a man across the room who was costumed entirely in black. Below his black half mask, the man's mouth lifted in a slow, amused smile, and he inclined his head to her in the merest mockery of a bow.

Hot with embarrassment over being caught staring, Whitney turned away so quickly that she nearly knocked the glass from André's outstretched hand. "Your punch, Mademoiselle," he said, offering the glass to her as if he were presenting her with a handful of diamonds. As Whitney thanked him and took the glass, he glanced ruefully at his plum-colored satin waistcoat which was now stained with wet spots.

In answer to Whitney's sympathetic inquiry as to how he had gotten wet, André gravely recounted the dangers he'd faced in the quest for her punch. "It is most treacherous to make one's way through the crowd, Mademoiselle. In the short time I was away from your side, I was trod upon by an inebriated lion, shoved by the same banana who addressed you earlier, and tripped by the tail of a crocodile who cursed at me when I stumbled."

"I—I'm so sorry, André," Whitney commiserated, choking on a horrified giggle at the mention of the crocodile. "It must have been dreadful for you."

"It was nothing!" André contradicted dramatically, making it sound as if it had been something very great indeed. "For you, I would do anything. For you, no task could be too difficult. For you, I would cross the Channel on a raft, tear the heart from my chest . . ."

"Perhaps even attempt another trip to the punch fountain?" Whitney teased.

Solemnly, André declared that he would even do that.

Nicki regarded the younger man with a mixture of pity, amusement, and disgust. "Chérie," he said to Whitney, tucking her hand in the crook of his arm and leading her toward the French doors that opened out onto the patio. "Either marry André, or else cut the poor devil's line. If you do not, he is bound to try something truly dangerous for you, like crossing the street."

"I suppose I *ought* to marry him," Whitney said with an audacious sidewise smile. "After all, you said yourself that he would make me a fine husband, that very first night when you came to the debutante ball and danced with me."

Nicki was silent until they were standing outside on the patio. "It would be a mistake for you to marry him, for André Rousseau's family and mine are old friends, and it would sorely strain that friendship if I were to kill their only son, merely to make you a widow."

Startled by the threatening words, Whitney snapped her head up, only to find that Nicki was grinning at her. "That really is too bad of you, Nicki. I like André, and I like you. We are all friends."

"Friends?" he repeated. "You and I are better than that, I would say."

"Well, good friends then," Whitney relented uncomfortably.

They remained outdoors, speaking to acquaintances who strolled past them on the patio, while Whitney tried to think of some way to restore her relationship with Nicki to the casually impersonal one they'd enjoyed until a few months ago. Suddenly he spoke and Whitney lurched with surprise at the topic. "At what age is an Englishwoman expected to marry?"

"No later than five-and-thirty," Whitney lied promptly.

"Stop, I am serious."

"Very well," Whitney smiled, desperately trying to keep hings light. "No later than five-and-twenty, then."

"It is time *you* think of marriage."

"I would much rather think of dancing."

Nicki looked on the verge of argument, then he reconsidered and offered her his arm. "We'll dance then," he said curtly.

But even in that, he was to be thwarted. A deep voice that seemed to leap out of the shadows behind them said, "Unfortunately, Monsieur, Miss Stone has promised this waltz to me."

Whitney turned in astonishment as a black-cloaked form materialized from the darkness. Even without the almost Satanic costume, Whitney would have recognized that mocking smile—it was identical to the one this man had given her across the ballroom, when he'd caught her inadvertently staring at him. "You promised me this dance," Satan said when she hesitated.

Whitney had no idea who this unidentified acquaintance could be, but she was very anxious to avoid further conversation about marriage with Nicki. "I don't remember promising anyone a dance tonight," she said hesitantly.

"You promised me months ago," Satan informed her, putting his hand beneath her elbow and exerting just enough pressure to begin drawing her with him toward the ballroom.

Smothering a smile at the man's outrageous audacity, Whitney looked over her shoulder and politely excused herself to Nicki, but she could feel his cool gaze on her back with every step she took.

Nicki was forgotten, however, as she stepped into Satan's arms and found herself being whirled around in time to the sweeping music by a man who danced with the easy grace of someone who has waltzed a thousand times and more. Around and around they floated until Whitney couldn't stand the suspense any longer. "*Did* I really promise you a dance tonight?" she asked.

"No," he said.

His blunt answer made her laugh. "Who are you?" she asked conspiratorially.

A lazy grin swept across his tanned face. "A friend?" he offered in a voice rich and deep.

Whitney didn't recognize his voice at all. "No. You are an acquaintance, but not a friend."

"I will have to remedy that," he replied with absolute confidence that he could.

Whitney felt a perverse desire to shatter a little of his arrogant self-assurance. "I'm afraid that's impossible. I already have more friends than I know what to do with now, and they all vow their loyalty to me until death."

"In that case," he said, a smile lighting his gray eyes, "perhaps one of them will meet with an accident—with a little assistance from me."

Whitney was unable to stop her answering smile. His last words held no menace, she knew; he was merely playing verbal chess with her, and it was exhilarating to try to counter his moves. "It would be most unkind in you to hasten any of my friends to their demise. My friends are a disreputable lot, and their final destination may not have a pleasant climate."

"A warm one?" he teased.

With a sigh of mock regret, Whitney solemnly nodded. "I'm afraid so."

He laughed at her, a throaty, contagious laugh, and his eyes suddenly seemed to regard her with a bold, speculative gleam that Whitney found unsettling. She looked away, trying to decide who he was. Outside on the patio, he'd spoken in flawless French, yet here on the dance floor, his English was equally flawless and without a trace of an accent. His face, that part of it which wasn't covered by his black mask, had a healthy golden tan which he certainly couldn't have acquired in Paris this early in the spring. And not in England, either.

The task of trying to place him among the hundreds of men to whom she'd been introduced during the last two years was formidable, but Whitney tried anyway. Mentally, she reviewed the men of her acquaintance, discarding one after another as being either not tall enough or with eyes of a color other than his unusual gray. His height, easily two inches over six feet, was his most outstanding feature. She reviewed the clues but still could not identify him. Yet, *he* knew *her* well enough to recognize her even though she was wearing a demi-mask. When the strains of the waltz died, she was no closer to identifying him than she had been when the dance began.

Whitney stepped away from him, half turning toward Nicki who was standing near the edge of the dance floor, but her partner firmly claimed her hand, tucked it under his arm, and drew her in the opposite direction toward the doors opening off the south side of the house into the gardens.

Several steps from the doors, Whitney began to doubt the wisdom of letting herself be led into the night by a man whom she couldn't yet identify. She was on the verge of refusing to take another step when she saw that there were at least two dozen guests scattered about the brick paths that wound through the lantern-lit gardens, any one of whom would come to her aid if her escort failed to conduct himself as a gentleman. Not that Whitney actually doubted he *was* a gentleman, for the Armands were notoriously meticulous in choosing their guests.

Outside, she reached behind her and untied the ribbons of

her demi-mask, letting it dangle from her fingers as she breathed in the fragrance of the spring night scented with blossoms. They came to a white ornamental iron table and chairs, well within sight of the house and other guests, and her escort pulled out a chair for her. "No, I'd rather stand," Whitney said, reveling in the relative quiet and the beauty of the dappled moonlight.

"Well, Prosperina, how are we to manage our friendship if none of your present friends are likely to do me the favor of dying in the foreseeable future?"

Whitney smiled, pleased that at least one person at the ball didn't confuse her with Venus. "How did you know who I am?"

She was referring to her identity of Prosperina, but evidently, Satan misunderstood her, for he shrugged and said, "DuVille isn't wearing a mask and, since rumor has it that the two of you are inseparable, when I saw him, I realized who you were."

A frown marred Whitney's smooth forehead at the unwelcome news that she and Nicki were being linked together by the gossips.

"Since that answer seems to disturb you," he said drily, "perhaps I should have been more honest and told you that there are certain . . . attributes . . . of yours that made it easy for me to identify you even with your mask on and before DuVille arrived."

My God! Did his gaze actually wander over her body, or was it only her imagination? When he leaned back and casually perched his hip on the wrought iron table, Whitney felt suddenly uneasy. "Who are you?" she demanded firmly.

"A friend."

"Absolutely not! I can't recall anyone of my acquaintance with your height or eyes, or with such outrageously bold manners, especially for an Englishman." She paused and studied him uncertainly. "*Are* you English?"

He gazed down into her searching green eyes and chuckled. "How remiss of me," he mocked lightly. "I should have said 'what ho' and 'egad' and 'quite so'—so that you would know I am."

His humor was infectious, and Whitney could not stop her answering smile. "Very well, now that you've admitted you're English, tell me who you are."

"Who would you like for me to be, little one?" he asked. "Women always admire noble titles—would you like it if I told you I am a duke?"

Whitney burst out laughing. "You may be a highwayman, or even a pirate." She twinkled at him. "But you are no more a *duke* than I am."

The amusement vanished from his smile, replaced by a quizzical puzzlement. "May I ask why you are so certain that I am not?"

Thinking back to the only duke she'd ever seen, Whitney impudently surveyed him from head to foot, deliberately repaying him for the lingering glance he'd subjected her to. "Beginning with the most obvious, if you *were* a duke, you would have a quizzing glass."

"But how would I use a quizzing glass with a mask?" he countered curiously.

"A duke does not use a quizzing glass to see—it is merely an affectation. He raises it to his eye and peers at all the ladies in the room. But there are other reasons you cannot possibly be a duke," she continued irrepressibly. "You don't walk with a cane, you don't wheeze and snort, and in all honesty, I doubt you could claim even a mild case of gout to your credit."

"Gout!" he choked, laughing.

Whitney nodded. "Without the cane, the gout, and the wheezing and snorting, you cannot possibly hope to convince anyone that you are a duke. Couldn't you choose some other title to which to aspire? You might be able to pass yourself off as an Earl if you had a bit of a squint and a clubfoot."

He threw back his head and gave a shout of laughter, then he shook his head and regarded her with a thoughtful, almost tender expression. "Miss Stone," he asked with amused gravity, "hasn't anyone taught you that noble titles are to be revered, not laughed at?"

"They did try," Whitney admitted, with a laughing look.

"And?"

"And, as you can see, they failed."

For a long moment, his gaze lingered on the elegant perfection of her glowing face, then settled on her entrancing green eyes. "But the initial clue that I am not a duke is the absence of a quizzing glass?" he said rather absently.

Whitney toyed with the ribbons of her mask and smiled as she nodded. "You would have it with you at all times."

"Even riding to a hunt?" he persisted.

She shrugged lightly. "If you were a duke, you'd be too stout to ride."

In a deceptively casual move, he captured her wrists, drawing her forward so that her hip pressed against his hard thigh. "Even in bed?" he asked softly.

Whitney, who had been paralyzed into inaction by his unexpected move, flung off both his hands and fixed him with an icy stare while a dozen scathing remarks tumbled to be first from her lips.

Just as she opened her mouth, he stood up, looming over her. "May I get you a glass of champagne?" he offered soothingly.

"You may go straight to—" Swallowing her outrage in deference to his daunting height and powerful shoulders, Whitney nodded. "Please," she choked.

He stood there for a moment, his imperturbable gray gaze studying Whitney's stormy green eyes, then he turned, striding off toward the house for her champagne.

The moment he walked through the archway, Whitney's breath came out in a long rush of relief. Whirling around, she hurried across the lawn, entering the ballroom on the opposite side.

From that point on, her evening declined. She was tense and jumpy, half expecting the black-cloaked figure she would always think of as "Satan" to accost her in the ballroom, even though he remained well away from her, surrounded by a small group of people who were talking and laughing with him.

As she waited with her aunt and uncle to take leave of their host and hostess, Whitney surreptitiously watched Satan's tall figure moving along the line of departing guests in front of them. His head was bent low as he listened attentively to the blond woman who was smiling up at him. He laughed at something she said, and Whitney flushed as she recalled the way he had laughed with her in the garden. Irritably, she wondered who the blond woman with him was. His mistress, she decided uncharitably, for he'd never waste a moment's time with any female unless she was willing to play that role, at least for one night!

Without warning he turned, and for the second time that evening, Whitney was caught in the act of staring at him. His gaze captured hers, and Whitney raised her chin, trying to stare him out of countenance. A strange, unfathomable smile tugged at the corner of his mouth, and he slowly inclined his head toward her. Angrily, Whitney jerked her gaze away. Arrogant, conceited—she couldn't think of enough terrible things to call him in her mind.

"What in the world is the matter, darling?" Aunt Anne whispered beside her.

Whitney started nervously, then cautiously tipped her head in the direction of the front door where Satan was now placing an elegant cape around the blonde's shoulders. "Do you know who he is, Aunt Anne?"

Her aunt studied the couple for a moment, started to shake her head in the negative, then stopped abruptly as the blonde reached up and swept off her demi-mask. "That's Marie St. Allermain—the famous singer," Anne whispered. "I'm certain of it." Whitney saw an odd, awed expression cross her aunt's face as she scrutinized the dark-haired man in the black cape. "And if *she* is St. Allermain, then *he* would have to be . . . my God! It is!"

Anne's gaze swung sharply to her niece, but Whitney was watching Satan move his hand in a light caress over the blonde's back as he guided her out the front door. She remembered how those same hands had drawn her to him and flushed with outraged shame.

"Why do you ask?" Anne said tightly.

The last thing Whitney wanted to do was admit to *anyone* that she'd been foolish enough to go into the garden with a man whom she was now certain she'd never met before.

"I—I thought he was someone I know, but I realize now he isn't," Whitney answered and was greatly relieved when her aunt seemed willing to drop the subject.

As a matter of fact, Anne was *delighted* to drop the subject. She had planned and dreamed too long to see Whitney become just another conquest of the Duke of Claymore. Marie St. Allermain had been his mistress for nearly a year, and rumor had it that he had even accompanied her to Spain when she sang in a command performance before the king and queen two months ago.

For years, gossip had linked the man with every beautiful female of suitable lineage in Europe, but marriage was *not* among the things he offered. Behind that handsome nobleman there was a trail of young women's broken hearts and shattered marital aspirations that would make *any* sensible woman with an unmarried female relation shudder! He was the last man on the continent in whom Anne wanted Whitney to show any interest.

The last man in the entire world!

Chapter Seven

EXACTLY FOUR WEEKS AFTER THE ARMANDS' MASQUERADE, Matthew Bennett left his office and stepped into a splendid burgundy-lacquered coach with the Westmoreland ducal crest emblazoned in gold on the door panel. He placed his deerskin case containing the reports on Miss Whitney Allison Stone on the seat beside him, then stretched his long legs out in the duke's luxurious coach.

For nearly a century, Matthew's forebears had been entrusted with the private legal affairs of the Westmoreland family, but since Clayton Westmoreland's principal residences were in England, it was Matthew's father in the London office of the firm who was personally acquainted with the duke. Until now, Matthew's only contact with the current Duke of Claymore had been in writing, and Matthew was especially anxious to make a good impression today.

The coach had been climbing steadily, winding gently around green sloping hills splashed with wildflowers, when the French country house of the duke finally came into view. Matthew gazed at it in wonder. Situated atop the verdant hills, the sweeping two-story stone-and-glass structure was surrounded by terraces overlooking the panorama that stretched below in every direction.

At the front of the house, the coach drew to a stop, and Matthew picked up his case and walked slowly up the terraced stone steps. He presented his card to the liveried butler and was shown into a spacious library lined with books which were recessed into shallow alcoves in the walls.

Alone for the moment, Matthew looked with awe at the priceless artifacts reposing on gleaming rosewood tables. A magnificent Rembrandt hung above the marble fireplace, and part of one wall was covered with a glorious collection of Rembrandt's etchings. One long wall was entirely constructed of huge panes of glass with French doors opening out onto a broad stone terrace that afforded a breathtaking view of the surrounding countryside.

At the opposite end of the room, angled toward the windows, was a massive oak desk, intricately carved around the edges with leaves and vines. Mentally, Matthew placed the desk as late sixteenth century and, judging from the splendid craftsmanship, it had probably graced a royal palace. Walking across the thick Persian carpet, Matthew sat down in one of the high-backed leather chairs facing the desk, and placed the deerskin case on the floor beside him.

The library doors opened, and Matthew came swiftly to his feet, stealing a quick, appraising look at the dark-haired man upon whom his future depended. Clayton Westmoreland was in his early thirties, uncommonly tall, and decidedly handsome. There was a vigorous purposefulness in his long, quick strides that bespoke an active, athletic life, rather than the indolence and overindulgence that Matthew normally ascribed to wealthy gentlemen of the peerage. An aura of carefully restrained power, of forcefulness, emanated from him.

A pair of penetrating gray eyes levelled on him, and Matthew swallowed a little nervously as the duke came around behind the desk and took his seat. The duke nodded at the chair across the desk, inviting Matthew to be seated, and said with calm authority, "Shall we begin, Mr. Bennett?"

"Certainly," Matthew said. He cleared his throat. "As you instructed, your grace, we have made inquiries into the young woman's family and background. Miss Stone is the daughter of Susan Stone—who died when Miss Stone was five years old—and Martin Albert Stone, who is still living. She was born on June thirtieth, eighteen hundred, at the family home near the village of Morsham, approximately seven hours from London.

"The Stone estate is small but productive, and Martin Stone has lived in the usual style of the landed gentry. However, about four years ago, his financial situation altered drastically. If you recall, that was when part of England was deluged with weeks of rainfall. Estates such as Stone's which did not have adequate drainage facilities suffered badly, and Stone apparently suffered more than most because there was no alternate means of supporting the estate, such as livestock.

"Our reports indicate that Stone then made some extremely large and unwise investments in a variety of risky ventures and, when those failed, he doubled and tripled his investments in more ventures of a similar nature—apparently in the hope of recouping his losses. These ventures were all disastrous, and two years ago, he mortgaged his estate to gain enough capital to make the last—and largest—of the ventures. He invested all the funds in a colonial shipping company. Unfortunately, that failed as well.

"At this time, he is heavily mortgaged and deeply in debt, not only to the cent-per-centers in London, but to the local shopkeepers as well. The estate is quickly falling into disrepair, and there is only a skeleton staff of servants left on the place."

Reaching into the deerskin case, Matthew extracted a sheaf of papers. "This is an itemized list of his creditors, although there are bound to be more that we didn't discover in the brief period of time we had to make our investigation." He slid the papers across the surface of the ornate desk, then waited for some reaction from the duke.

Leaning back in his chair, Clayton Westmoreland scanned the lists, his face impassive. "How bad?" he asked when he finished reading the last page.

"Altogether, I'd say he's about £100,000 in debt."

The staggering sum made no apparent impression on the duke, who handed the papers back to Matthew and abruptly switched the subject. "What were you able to learn about the girl?"

Who, Matthew wondered as he extracted the file marked "W. Stone," should know more about the girl than the man whose mistress she was about to become? Although the duke had not actually said it, Matthew had already guessed that Claymore intended to take the young woman under discussion as his mistress, providing her with a comfortable establishment and an income of her own. He interpreted the duke's interest in the girl's family as curiosity over what kind of opposition, if any, he might expect from them.

To Matthew's legal mind, Stone's appalling financial situation already made the outcome of the matter a foregone conclusion: Martin Stone would have to accept this chance to turn over the responsibility for his daughter's support to Clayton Westmoreland. What choice had he? He could hardly continue to clothe her and keep her amid the Quality for much longer. If Stone's concern was for the girl's reputation, his own was in far more jeopardy than hers. Once his creditors discovered his dire circumstances, as they would at any time now, he would be facing not only disgrace, but an unpleasant stay in debtor's prison.

Matthew flushed as he realized that he'd been silently staring at the girl's open file, and he began at once. "While it was difficult to learn much of a personal nature, without awakening unwanted suspicion, we did discover that Miss Stone was considered rather a difficult child, of an . . . er . . . unpredictable disposition. She is apparently well-read and uncommonly well-educated by a long string of tutors. She speaks fluent French, of course, as well as being proficient in Greek—enough so that she occasionally assists her uncle as translator during social functions where Greek diplomats are present. She reads Italian, Latin, and German; she may also speak them, but we aren't certain."

Matthew hesitated, feeling utterly absurd for telling Lord Westmoreland what he must already know. "Go on," the duke said with a faint smile at Matthew's obvious discomfiture.

Nodding uncomfortably, Matthew continued. "Many of the individuals we contacted mentioned that there was considerable dissension between the young lady and her father.

A few of them put the blame at his door, but most sympathized with Martin Stone as an unfortunate man who had fathered a rebellious, unbiddable child. At the age of fourteen, Miss Stone evidently developed an . . . er . . . rather violent infatuation for a gentleman named Paul Sevarin. Sevarin was ten years her senior and apparently he was no more pleased with Miss Stone's girlish attachment to him than her father was. Because of that, and because Stone apparently couldn't deal with her any other way, her father eventually sent her to France with her aunt and uncle when she was nearly sixteen. They then presented her to French Society at the customary age of seventeen. Since that time, our sources indicate that she had enjoyed an extraordinary popularity here. Of course, if her father's financial circumstances and her lack of a dowry were known, that situation would change drastically," Matthew conjectured aloud, then he glanced apologetically at the duke, and returned to the facts at hand—

"Miss Stone has been on the verge of receiving numerous offers of marriage, but has discouraged those suitors as soon as their intentions became apparent to her. Those gentlemen who persisted to the point of actually speaking to her uncle, Lord Edward Gilbert, were turned down by him, apparently on behalf of Martin Stone. Her manners are reported to be perfectly acceptable to society, although somewhat out of the ordinary. Is there some mistake in this?" Matthew inquired when the duke burst out laughing.

"No. No mistake," Clayton chuckled. "I'd say your information is entirely accurate." In his memory, he could still see her green eyes glowing with laughter as she scoffed at noble titles—*his* in particular. "Is there anything else?" he asked finally.

"Only a few remarks, your grace. Her uncle, Lord Edward Gilbert, as you already know, is attached to the British Consulate here and enjoys an unblemished reputation. Miss Stone is reportedly on excellent terms with him, and with his wife, Lady Anne Gilbert. At present, it is the consensus of opinion that Nicolas DuVille is on the verge of offering for her hand—an offer which Lord Gilbert will undoubtedly find most acceptable. The DuVilles, as I'm sure you know, are one of France's leading families, and Nicolas is their son and heir."

Matthew closed the file. "That's all we were able to learn in the time you allotted us, your grace."

Leaving the solicitor to his own thoughts, Clayton got up and walked over to the wide sweep of windows overlooking the rolling green hills. Crossing his arms over his chest, he leaned a shoulder against the window frame and gazed at the magnificent view, while he considered for the last time the plan which, if put into words now, would become a reality.

Time after time, whenever he was in France and had seen Whitney, he had been drawn to her, laughing silently at some of the setdowns she gave her too persistent suitors. Twice they had been introduced; the first time she was too young for him to consider, and the second time she had been surrounded by a group of beaux all vying for her attention. She had flicked a distracted glance in his direction without really looking at him or listening to his name.

After that, he had avoided further contact with her, sensing that Whitney would require considerable time and courtship to lure into his arms. Of time, Clayton had little. When it came to courtship, he could not recall ever having had to actively court a woman in his adult life, at least not a reluctant woman. They were all too ready and eager to court *him*.

And then, four weeks ago, he had stood in the Armands' garden, drinking in her presence and fighting down the insane impulse to bend his head and slowly, endlessly, kiss the irreverent laughter from her soft, inviting lips, to carry her into the darkness and make love to her right there.

She was a natural temptress, alluring and provocative, with the smile of an angel, the slender, voluptuous body of a goddess, and an unspoiled charm that made him grin whenever he thought of her. And she had a sense of humor, an irreverent contempt for the absurd, that matched his own.

Clayton gave up trying to understand his reasons for the step he was about to take. He wanted her, that was reason enough. She was warm and witty and elusive as a damned butterfly. She would never bore him as other women had; he knew it with the wisdom born of years of experience with the fair sex.

His mind made up, he turned and strode briskly to the desk. "I will need some documents prepared, and there will have to be a transfer of a considerable amount of money when Stone accepts my offer."

"*If* Stone accepts it," Matthew corrected automatically.

The Westmoreland brow quirked in sardonic amusement. "He'll accept it."

Despite his nervousness today, Matthew was a respected legal advisor who had schooled himself never to show any emotion when dealing with delicate matters of a client. Nevertheless, when his grace began to dictate the terms under which a staggering sum of money was being offered to Martin Stone, Matthew raised his head and gaped in astonishment at the duke.

Clayton stood at the windows, absently watching the coach bearing Matthew Bennett back to Paris make its winding way down the hillside. Already he was impatient to have everything completed. He wanted Whitney, and he wanted her immediately, but he'd be damned if he'd court her in France, standing in line, playing the fop and bowing like an ass. That he would not do for any woman, even Miss Stone. Besides, he'd been away from England too long already. In order to manage his business affairs, he needed to be closer to London.

Since the Stone estate was only seven hours from the city, he could manage his business *and* his courtship very nicely from somewhere near her home. That being the case, he decided to have Whitney's father summon her back to England as soon as his signature was on the documents and the money had changed hands.

Not for one moment did Clayton think Martin Stone would refuse his offer, nor did he have the slightest doubt of his own ability to lure Whitney into his arms.

What *did* concern him was the reported dissension between Whitney and her father—there was a small chance that if she learned of the arrangement too soon, she might rebel against it merely to defy Martin Stone. Clayton's instincts warned him that if Whitney were ever forced into the position of opposing him, she could become a very determined young adversary. And he didn't want to do battle with her, he wanted to make love to her.

Then too, there was the added complication of his identity and the personal notoriety that went with it. He rather fancied the idea of a charming country courtship, but how could he manage that with everyone bowing and scraping and cautiously keeping their distance. And the moment the newspapers discovered he was living in a remote country shire, the conjecture over what he was doing there would create a furor, and the villagers would watch every move he made with fanatical curiosity, particularly when he began to pay attention to Whitney.

Since Whitney had such a low opinion of the nobility—and dukes in particular—Clayton began to wonder if it might be wise to keep not only the arrangement with her father, but his identity as well, a secret from her until he had won her over.

Seven days later, Matthew returned to the duke's country house in France and was shown out onto a wide veranda where Westmoreland was seated at an ornamental iron table, working on some papers, his back to the panoramic view. "Will you join me in a brandy, Matthew?" he said without looking up.

"Yes, thank you, your grace," murmured Matthew, pleased and amazed by the duke's use of his given name and the friendly offer of a brandy. The Duke of Claymore glanced over his shoulder at the manservant hovering near the stone balustrade, and the drinks were produced without a word being spoken. A few minutes later, his grace shoved his papers aside and regarded Matthew, who had taken the chair across from him at the table.

Like the servant, Matthew found himself responding to an unspoken command, retrieving the documents from his case and handing them over. "As you requested, I included the provision that you will assume financial responsibility for Miss

Stone's expenses. Did you wish to stipulate any maximum figure?"

"No, I'll assume complete responsibility for her," Clayton murmured absently, his gaze moving down the pages. After several minutes, he laid the documents aside and grinned at Matthew. "Well," he said, "what do you think?"

"What does *Miss Stone* think?" Matthew countered, grinning back at the duke.

"What Miss Stone thinks won't be known for a little time yet. She knows nothing of this. For that matter, she knows nothing of me."

Matthew concealed his shock by taking a fortifying swallow of the excellent brandy. "In that case, I wish you luck with the father *and* the young lady."

The duke waved the offer of luck aside as if he didn't need it, and leaned back in his chair. "I'll be leaving for England within the week to discuss this matter with Martin Stone. Assuming he agrees, I'll need a place to stay nearby. Notify your father in the London office to locate a comfortable one for me, will you? A modest place," he emphasized to Matthew's further astonishment. "If possible, no more than a half-hour's ride from the Stone estate. I don't want to spend any more time than necessary settling matters with Miss Stone, and I haven't any intention of wasting it travelling between her father's place and mine."

"A modest place, no more than a half-hour's ride from Stone's," repeated Matthew dazedly.

The man's obvious bewilderment brought a glint of amusement to Clayton's eyes. "Correct. And negotiate the lease in the name Westland, not Westmoreland. Once my staff and I are installed, we will keep to ourselves as much as possible, and I will pass myself off as a new neighbor, Clayton Westland."

"Surely not to Miss Stone?" Matthew said.

"Especially to Miss Stone," Clayton chuckled.

Chapter Eight

ONE MONTH LATER, WILSON, THE GILBERTS' DIGNIFIED BUTLER, padded down the hall to Lord Gilbert's study and handed him the mail. On the top of the stack was a letter from England. Five minutes later, the door to Lord Gilbert's study was flung open and he bellowed at the butler, "Have Lady Gilbert join me here at once! Don't dawdle, man. Hurry, I said," he called after the harassed servant who was already sprinting down the hall, his black coattails flapping behind him.

"What is it, Edward?" Anne said, flying into her husband's study in answer to his urgent summons.

"This!" said Edward, thrusting the letter from Martin Stone at her. Anne looked from her husband's white face to the signature on the single sheet of paper in her hand. "He's sent for Whitney?" she guessed in a tortured voice.

"He says he will reimburse me for all her expenses during the last four years, as soon as he receives an accounting from me," Edward said furiously. "And he's sent a blasted fortune along with this letter, for her to spend 'on clothing and trinkets' before she returns. Who the devil does he think he is? He hasn't sent a penny to cover her expenses in all this time. That bastard! He'll get no accounting from me, and *I* will see that she returns in style. He can shove his money precisely—"

"Whitney is going home," Anne whispered brokenly,

sinking into a chair. "I—I had deluded myself into thinking he'd forgotten about her." She brightened. "I have it! Wr-write Martin at once and hint of a match with Nicolas DuVille. That would buy us time."

"Read the letter, Madame. He says as plainly and as rudely as can be that she's to leave here in one month to the day, without excuses or delay."

Anne did as he said, her eyes moving dully over the lines. "He says she is to spend the remaining time saying farewell to her friends and visiting her favorite modistes and milliners." She tried to look encouraged. "He must have changed in the last four years—he'd never have thought of Whitney requiring time to order her clothing here in Paris, where fashions are so far advanced. Edward," she said, "do you suppose that he could have received an offer for Whitney from that young man she adored so much when she was a girl?"

"He's received no marriage proposal," Edward snapped, "or he would have been gloating about it in this damned letter, thinking he had succeeded where he believes we've failed." He turned his back to his wife. "You may as well tell her now and have done with it. I'll be up in a bit."

Whitney stood numbly, trying to assimilate the news she thought she'd longed to hear. "I—I'm happy to be going home, Aunt Anne," she managed finally. "It's just that . . ." Her voice trailed off.

Happy to be going home? Terrified of going home! Terrified that now the chance was being given to her, she might fail. It was one thing to languish in Paris, surrounded by men who flattered and admired her, another to go home and try to make Paul see her with their eyes. There was her father to cope with, and Margaret Merryton, and everyone's mothers, who had always made her feel lower than an insect. But here, there was Aunt Anne and Uncle Edward who loved her and laughed with her, who made her life warm and happy.

Her aunt turned her face to the windows, but Whitney saw a tear trickle down her cheek. She bit her lip; if Aunt Anne had misgivings about her returning to England, then surely it was too soon to go. She wasn't *ready* to confront everyone yet. She turned to the mirror, hoping to find some reassurance in her appearance. In Paris, gentlemen said she was beautiful. Would Paul think so? The mirror promptly quashed that idea! It was happening already, she realized in panic. Before she even left, she could feel her facade falling away. She was plain, awkward, too tall—even her fingers were fidgeting nervously as they used to do. And there—on the bridge of her nose—she could still see faint traces of the freckles she loathed. *Oh the devil!* Whitney thought, suddenly impatient with herself. Freckles do not reappear before one's eyes; fingers do not *have* to fidget, and she would not, *would not,* begin inventorying her faults and shortcomings as she had in the old days!

Her stomach ceased its frantic churning. Inside of her, something else began to blossom: hope. Her lips curved into a soft smile. I am going home, she thought. I am going home to Paul—home to show everyone how much I've really changed. I am actually going home!

But going home also meant leaving her beloved aunt and uncle.

She turned away from the mirror and saw her aunt's shoulders shaking with silent weeping. "I feel as if I'm being severed in half," Anne choked.

"I love you, Aunt Anne," Whitney whispered, hot tears rushing to her eyes and streaming down her cheeks. "I love you so much." Aunt Anne opened her arms, and Whitney fled into them, trying to comfort and be comforted.

Pausing outside Whitney's bedroom, Edward squared his shoulders and carefully schooled his desolate features into a fixed, bright smile. Clasping his hands behind his back, he strolled into the room. "Having a good time, ladies?" he ventured with forced joviality, glancing from one weeping woman to the other.

Two teary, anguished faces gaped at him in utter disbelief. "*Having a good . . . ?*" Anne echoed incredulously. She looked at Whitney and Whitney looked at her. Suddenly they began to giggle, then the giggles burst into great, gusty laughs.

"Yes . . . er . . . well, good. Glad to see it," Edward

murmured, bewildered by his ladies' excessively unstable behavior. Then he cleared his throat. "We'll miss you, child. You've been a blessing and a joy to us both."

Whitney's gaiety fled, and fresh tears stung her eyes. "Oh Uncle Edward," she whispered brokenly, "I shall never, never love any man as much as I love you."

To his acute dismay, Edward felt his eyes misting. He opened his arms wide, and his niece came into them. When at last the storm of emotions had passed, the three of them stood looking sheepishly at one another, each clutching a handkerchief. Edward was the first to speak. "Well now, England isn't the end of the world, is it?"

"It—it isn't exactly next door, either," Whitney said, dabbing at her eyes.

"You have friends there," Edward reminded her. "And of course, that young man you admired so much is there too—the blond fellow who didn't have brains enough to recognize a jewel when she was right under his nose. What was his name?"

"Paul," Whitney provided with a teary smile.

"The man's a fool—he should have snatched you up before." Edward paused, then watching her very closely, he said, "I expect he will now."

"I hope so," Whitney said fervently.

"I rather thought you did, child," he said with an I-told-you-so look at Anne. "In fact, I've often wondered if the reason you've never found any of your suitors here acceptable is because you've always wanted to go back to England and bring *him* up to scratch. That's what you're going to do, isn't it?"

"I intend to try," Whitney admitted, puzzled because her uncle suddenly looked like a small mischievous boy.

"In that case," he continued, "I expect you'll get yourself betrothed before the snow falls."

"If I can," Whitney said, smiling eagerly.

Jamming his hands into his pants pockets, he seemed to consider an idea. "I rather think at a time like that, a lass should have a woman to advise her. It might take a lot of planning to snare such a laggard as . . . er . . . ?"

"Paul," Whitney provided breathlessly.

"Right, Paul. You know my dear," he said thoughtfully, "you might like to have your aunt come with you." He peered over his spectacles at Whitney. "Would that please you?"

"Yes!" she shrieked, laughing. "Yes, yes, yes!"

Edward hugged her and looked over her shoulder at his beaming wife. The smile of gratitude that she gave him was compensation enough for his sacrifice. "I've been postponing a journey to Spain," he said. "When the two of you leave, I'll be about the kingdom's business there. After a stop or two along the way, I'll come to England to congratulate that laggard you'll be betrothed to, and I'll bring your aunt back home with me when I leave."

Now that he had the satisfaction of outmaneuvering Martin Stone by sending Anne along to be certain Whitney got off to the right start, Edward relented on his original decision about the extravagant sum Martin had sent for Whitney to spend. Accordingly, his ladies set out on a round of shopping excursions which began in the morning and ended with just enough time to dress for the evening's festivities or collapse in bed.

Nicolas DuVille's parents held a lavish party in Whitney's honor the night before Lady Anne and Whitney were to leave. All evening, Whitney dreaded saying goodbye to Nicki, but when the time came, he made it relatively easy.

They had stolen a few moments alone together in one of the anterooms of his parents' spacious house. Nicki was standing by the fireplace, one shoulder propped against the mantle, idly contemplating the drink in his hand. "I'll miss you, Nicki," Whitney said softly, unable to endure the silence.

He looked up, his expression amused. "Will you, cherie?" Before she could answer, he added, "I shall not miss you for very long."

Whitney's lips trembled with surprised laughter. "What a perfectly unchivalrous thing to say!"

"Chivalry is for callow youths and old men," Nicki told her with a teasing inflection in his voice. "However, I shan't miss you for long, because I intend to come to England in a few months."

Whitney shook her head, and in sheer desperation said, "Nicki, there is someone else. At home, I mean. At least, I think there is. His name is Paul and . . ." She trailed off, bewildered by Nicki's slow grin.

"Has he ever come to France to see you?" he asked carefully.

"No, he wouldn't even think of such a thing. You see, I was different then—you know, childish, and he only remembers me as a reckless, unruly, inelegant young girl who . . . Why are you grinning like that?"

"Because I am delighted," Nicki said, laughing softly. "Delighted to learn, after so many weeks of wondering who my rival is, that he is some English idiot whom you haven't seen in four years, and who hadn't sense enough to anticipate the woman you would become. Go home, cherie," he chuckled, putting his glass down and drawing her tightly against him. "You will soon discover that in matters of the heart, memories are much kinder than reality. Then, in a few months, I will come, and you will listen to what I wish to say."

Whitney knew he intended to declare himself, just as she knew it would be futile to argue the point now. Her memories would not prove better than reality, because none of her memories were good ones. But she didn't want to explain to Nicki how shockingly she had behaved, and *why* Paul couldn't possibly have imagined she would turn out to be a presentable young woman.

Besides, Nicki wouldn't have listened; he was already bending his head to claim her lips in a long, violently sweet kiss.

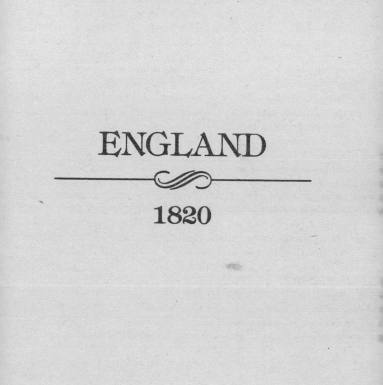

ENGLAND

1820

Chapter Nine

IN THE DEEPENING DUSK OF A SPLENDID SEPTEMBER DAY, Whitney gazed out the coach window at the achingly familiar scene. She was only a few miles from home.

Uncle Edward had insisted that they travel in style, which meant that, in addition to their coach, there were two more, heavily loaded with trunks and valises, and a fourth carrying Aunt Anne's maid and Clarissa, Whitney's own maid. Besides the four coachmen and four postillions, there were six outriders, three in front and three bringing up the rear. Altogether they combined to make a rather spectacular caravan, and Whitney wished that Paul could see her returning in such grand style.

The coach swayed as they turned north onto the private drive leading up to her home. Whitney's hands shook as she drew on her lilac gloves so that she would look absolutely perfect when she saw her father.

"Nervous?" Anne smiled, watching her.

"Yes. How do I look?"

Lady Anne gave her a thorough appraisal from the top of her head where a fragile filigree clip held her heavy mahogany tresses off her forehead, past her glowing face, to the fashionable lilac travelling costume she was wearing. "Perfect," she said.

Lady Anne pulled on her own gloves, feeling almost as

nervous as Whitney looked. In order to eliminate the possibility that Martin Stone might somehow object to her accompanying Whitney home, Edward had decided the best course was for her to arrive unexpectedly with Whitney, leaving Martin with no choice but to make her welcome. At the time, Anne had recognized the wisdom in her husband's thinking, but as her confrontation with Martin approached, she was miserably uncomfortable at being an uninvited houseguest.

Their coaches drew up before the wide steps at the front of the house. The footman opened the door and let down the steps, and both women watched Martin making his decorous way toward the coach. Whitney gathered her skirts so that she could step down and threw a smiling look at Anne.

From within the coach, Anne watched eagerly as Martin came face to face with the gorgeous, elegant young woman who was smiling dazzlingly at him. In a stiff, self-conscious voice, he spoke to the daughter he hadn't seen in four years. "Child," said he, "you've grown even taller."

"Either that, Papa," Whitney returned gravely, "or you have shrunk."

Lady Anne's muffled laugh announced her presence in the coach, and she reluctantly climbed down to confront her host. She had not expected effusive cordiality—Martin was never effusive, and rarely cordial—but neither had she expected him to gape at her, while his expression went from thunderstruck to alarmed to irritated. "Good of you to see Whitney home," he managed finally. "When d'you plan to leave?"

"Aunt Anne is going to remain with me for two or three months, until I'm settled again," Whitney interjected hastily. "Isn't that kind of her?"

"Yes, kind," he agreed, looking definitely irked. "Why don't you both relax before supper . . . have a rest, or supervise the unpacking, or something. I have a note to write. I will see you later," he added, already starting for the house.

Whitney was torn between mortification over the way her father was treating her aunt, and a nostalgic joy at being home again. As they mounted the staircase, she let her gaze wander over the familiar old house with its mellow, oak-panelled walls lined with English landscapes and framed portraits of her ancestors. Her favorite painting, a lively hunt scene in the cool morning mist, was in its place of honor on the balcony, hanging between a pair of Chippendale sconces. Everything was the same, yet different. There seemed to be three times as many servants as they'd ever had before, and the house shone from the painstaking labor of many extra hands. Every inch of parquet floor, every bit of panelled wall was glowing with newly applied polish. The candleholders lining the hall were gleaming, and the carpet beneath her feet was new.

In the doorway to her old bedroom, Whitney stopped and caught her breath. Her room had been completely redone in her absence. She smiled with pleasure as she looked at her bed, its canopy and coverlet of ivory satin with threads of gold and pale orange. Matching draperies hung at the windows. "Clarissa, doesn't it look wonderful?" she exclaimed, turning to her maid. But the plump, gray-haired woman was busily directing the footmen who were carrying in the trunks from the coaches. Whitney was too excited to rest, so she helped Clarissa and a new maid with the unpacking.

By mealtime, she had bathed and changed clothes, and the maids were nearly finished unpacking. Whitney went down the hallway to her aunt's room. The large guest suite had not been redone and looked shabby in comparison to other parts of the house. Whitney wanted to apologize to her aunt for it, and for her father's rude reception, but Aunt Anne stopped her with an understanding smile. "It doesn't matter, darling," she said. Linking her arm through Whitney's, they went downstairs.

Her father was waiting for them in the dining room, and Whitney vaguely noted that the chairs at the table had been reupholstered in rose velvet to match the new draperies that were pulled back with heavy tassels. Two footmen in immaculate uniforms were hovering near the sideboard, and another was pushing in a silver cart laden with covered dishes from the kitchen.

"There seems to be a score of new servants in the house,"

Whitney remarked to her father as he politely seated Anne at the table.

"We always needed them," he said brusquely. "The place had begun to look run down."

It had been four years since anyone had spoken to her in that tone, and Whitney stared at him in bewilderment. It was then, with the bright light from the chandelier above the table illuminating him, that she realized his hair had turned from black to gray in her absence, and that deep crevices now marked his forehead and grooved the sides of his mouth and eyes. He looked as if he had aged a decade in four years, she thought with a sharp pang.

"Why are you staring at me?" he said shortly.

He had always been this sharp with her in the old days, Whitney remembered sadly, but then he had had reason to be. Now that she was home, however, she didn't want them to fall into their old pattern of hostility. Softly she said, "I was noticing that your hair has turned gray."

"Is that so surprising?" he retorted, but with less edge to his voice.

Very carefully, very deliberately, Whitney smiled at him, and as she did so, it occurred to her that she couldn't remember ever smiling at him before. "Yes," she said, her eyes twinkling. "If *I* didn't give you gray hair while I was growing up, I'm amazed mere years could do it."

Her father looked startled by her smiling reply, but he unbent a bit. "Suppose you know your friend Emily got herself a husband?" Whitney nodded, and he added, "She'd been out three seasons, and her father told me he'd all but despaired of ever seeing her suitably married. Now the match is the talk of the whole damn countryside!" His gaze levelled accusingly on Lady Anne, rebuking *her* for having failed to see Whitney suitably married.

Lady Anne stiffened and Whitney hastily tried to interject a teasing note into her voice. "Surely you haven't despaired of seeing *me* suitably married?"

"Yes," he said bluntly. "I had."

Pride demanded that Whitney tell him of the dozen splendid offers Uncle Edward had received for her hand; reason warned that her father would react violently to the discovery that, without consulting him, Uncle Edward had rejected those offers. Why was her father so cold and unapproachable? Whitney wondered unhappily. Could she ever hope to bridge the gulf between them? Putting her cup down, she gave him a warm, conspiratorial smile and said lightly, "If it would lessen your mortification at having an unwed daughter already out four seasons, Aunt Anne and I could have it whispered about that I declined offers from two baronets, an earl, a duke, and a prince!"

"Is this true, Madam?" he snapped at Aunt Anne. "Why wasn't I informed of these offers?"

"Of course, it isn't true," Whitney interceded, trying to keep the smile pasted on her face. "I've met only one real duke and one imposter—and I detested them both equally. I did meet a Russian prince, but he was already spoken for by the princess, and I doubt she'd give him up so that I could outdo Emily."

For a moment he stared at her, then said abruptly, "I'm having a little party for you tomorrow night."

Whitney felt a glow of warmth tingle through her that remained even when he irritably corrected: "Actually, it's not a *little* party, it's a damned circus with every Tom, Dick and Harry for miles around coming—an orchestra, and dancing, and all that rubbish!"

"It sounds . . . wonderful," Whitney managed to say, keeping her laughing eyes downcast.

"Emily is coming from London with her new husband. *Everybody* is coming."

His shifts of mood were so unpredictable that Whitney stopped trying to converse with him, and the rest of the meal progressed in wary silence. Not until dessert was nearly finished did he break the silence, and then his voice was so unnaturally loud that Whitney started. "We have a new neighbor," he almost boomed, then checked himself, cleared his throat, and spoke more naturally. "He'll be coming to your party too. I want you to meet him. Good-looking chap—a bachelor. Excellent man with a horse. Saw him out riding the other day.''

Understanding dawned, and Whitney burst out laughing. "Oh Papa," she said, shaking her long, shining hair, "you don't have to start matchmaking—I'm not *quite* at my last prayers yet." Judging from his expression, her father didn't share her humor in the matter, so Whitney tried to look dutifully solemn as she asked the name of their new neighbor.

"Clayton Westmor . . . Clayton Westland."

Lady Anne's spoon clattered to her plate and onto the table. She gazed with narrowed eyes at Martin Stone, who glared at her in return while his face turned a suspicious red.

After considering her father's stormy countenance, Whitney decided to rescue her aunt from his trying moods. Putting down her own spoon, she stood up. "I think Aunt Anne and I would both like to retire early after our journey, Father."

To her surprise, Lady Anne shook her head. "I would like to spend a few minutes with your father, dear. You go ahead."

"Yes," Martin echoed instantly. "Run along to bed, and your aunt and I will have a friendly chat."

When Whitney left, Martin curtly dismissed the footmen, then regarded Anne with a mixture of caution and annoyance. "You reacted very queerly to the mention of our neighbor's name, Madam."

Lady Anne inclined her head, watching him intently. "Whether or not my reaction was 'queer' depends upon whether or not his name is Clayton Westland—or Clayton Westmoreland. I warn you that if the man *is* Clayton Westmoreland, I shall recognize him the moment I see him, even though we've never been introduced."

"It is Westmoreland, if you must know," Martin snapped. "And there's a very simple explanation for his being here: He happens to be recovering from exhaustion—the result of an old ailment that sometimes troubles him."

That explanation was so ludicrous, Anne stared at him open-mouthed. "You're joking!"

"Dammit, do I *look* like I'm joking?" he hissed furiously.

"Do you actually believe that Banbury tale?" Anne exclaimed, not sure whether he might. "There are countless places where the Duke of Claymore would go, were he in need of a rest. The very last I can think of is here, with winter coming on."

"Be that as it may, I can only tell you what he told me. His grace feels the need to escape from the pressures of his life, and he has chosen to do it here. Since only I—and now you—know who he is, I trust that neither of us will deprive him of his privacy by giving his identity away."

Upstairs in the solitude of her rooms, Lady Anne sought to come to grips with the furor in her mind. Feverishly, she thought back to the night of the Armands' masquerade when Whitney had asked the name of the tall, gray-eyed man with Marie St. Allermain. Anne was absolutely positive the man had been the duke; it was common knowledge that the gorgeous St. Allermain was Claymore's mistress, and that she never honored any other man with her company. The duke, of course, was not so singular in his attentions, and frequently escorted other beautiful women when St. Allermain was on tour in Europe.

Very well, Anne thought, dismissing St. Allermain from her mind, Claymore had been at the masquerade, and Whitney had asked about him. But they couldn't have spent any time together, or Whitney would have known who he was without having to ask. And Claymore could not have followed Whitney here—he was here *before* she arrived. Therefore, it must be mere coincidence that Whitney had inquired about him at the Armands', and he was now in quiet seclusion here.

Lady Anne felt much better, but only for an instant. Tomorrow night Clayton Westmoreland and Whitney would be introduced to each other. Whitney would attract him, of that Anne had no doubt. What if he chose to pursue her? Anne shuddered, then stood up, and her feminine jaw was hardened with resolve. She had no desire to make an enemy of the powerful Duke of Claymore by giving his identity away, but if she suspected that Whitney might be falling victim to his legendary charm and good looks, she would reveal not only his identity to Whitney, but a full accounting of his past female conquests and behavior!

Not for one moment would Anne allow herself to hope that Claymore might meet Whitney and tumble into love with her, ignore the fact that she was neither wealthy (by his standards) nor of aristocratic lineage, and offer her marriage. No indeed! There were hundreds of embarrassed mamas with heartbroken daughters who'd been foolish enough to hope that!

Lady Anne undressed and went to bed, but Clayton Westmoreland's presence in the district kept her lying awake for hours. Nor could Whitney sleep. She was dreamily contemplating tomorrow night's party, when Paul would see her for the first time, elegantly gowned and grown to womanhood.

Three miles away, the objects of both their thoughts were together at Clayton's temporary home, relaxing over a brandy after a game of cards. Stretching his legs toward the fire, Paul savored the taste of the amber liquid in his glass. "Are you planning to attend the Stone affair tomorrow night?" he asked.

Clayton's expression was guarded. "Yes."

"Wouldn't miss it, myself," Paul chuckled. "Unless Whitney's done a complete turnabout, it should be an entertaining evening."

"Unusual name—Whitney," Clayton remarked with just the right degree of mild curiosity to encourage his guest to continue.

"It's a family name. Her father was bent on having a boy, as I understand it, and he hung the name on her anyway. He nearly got his wish, too. She could swim like a fish, climb like a monkey, and handle a horse better than any female alive. She showed up in men's pants one day—another, she set off on a raft saying that she was sailing for America on an adventure."

"What happened?"

"She came to the end of the pond," Paul said, grinning. "To give her credit, the chit has—had—a pair of eyes that were something to behold, the greenest green you'll ever see." Paul gazed into the fire, smiling with an old memory. "When she left for France four years ago, she asked me to wait for her. First proposal I ever got."

Dark brows lifted over inscrutable gray eyes. "Did you accept?"

"Hardly!" Paul laughed, taking a long swallow of brandy. "She was barely out of the school room and determined to compete with Elizabeth Ashton. If Elizabeth came down with a case of mumps, Whitney wanted a worse case. God! She was a tangle-haired ruffian. Never conformed to a single rule of propriety in her life." Paul fell silent, remembering the day she had left for France, when he had brought her the little pendant. *But I don't want to be just your friend,* she had pleaded desperately. The smile faded from his face. "For her father's sake," he said with feeling, "I hope she's changed."

Clayton eyed Sevarin with amusement, but said absolutely nothing.

After his guest had left, Clayton relaxed back in his chair and thoughtfully swirled the brandy in his glass. At best, this masquerade of his was risky, and the more people he came into contact with, the greater his chances of being discovered.

Yesterday, he had received a jolt when he learned that the Emily Archibald he'd been hearing so much about was married to a remote acquaintance of his. That problem had been handled with a five-minute private meeting with Michael Archibald. Not for a moment had the baron believed his explanation about "needing a rest," Clayton knew, but Michael was too much of a gentleman to pry, and honorable enough to keep Clayton's identity secret.

Lady Anne Gilbert's arrival with Whitney today was another unforeseen complication, but according to Martin Stone's note, Lady Anne had accepted the explanation that he was here for a rest.

Clayton stood up and dismissed those incidents. If his

identity was revealed, he would be deprived of the pleasure of pursuing Whitney as an ordinary country gentleman, but the legal agreement was already signed, and the money accepted by Stone who, from the looks of things, was busily spending as much of it as he could. Therefore, Clayton's ultimate objective was absolutely secure.

Chapter Ten

WHITNEY THREW OPEN THE WINDOWS AND INHALED THE WON-
derful fresh country air. While Clarissa helped her into a chic
turquoise riding habit, Whitney's traitorous mind suggested
again and again that she pay a morning call on Paul. Each
time, she firmly thrust the notion aside. She would ride over
and see Emily.

The stables where the horses were kept was situated down
a path and off to the left, screened from view of the main
house by a tall boxwood hedge. Twenty stalls ran the length
of the building on both sides. A wide, overhanging roofline
provided shade and protection to the building's equine occupants. Halfway there, Whitney stopped to let her gaze rove
appreciatively over the lovely, familiar landscape.

In the distance a newly whitewashed fence stretched in a
broad oval, marking the boundary of the timing track where
her grandfather used to test the speed of his horses before
deciding which to take to the races. Behind the track, hills
rolled gently at first, dotted with oak and sycamore trees,
then became steeper, ending in a densely wooded rise along
the northeast boundary of the property.

As Whitney approached the stable, she was amazed to see
that every stall along this side was occupied. A brass name-
plate was bolted to each door, and Whitney stopped at the
last stall on the corner, glancing at the name on the plate.

"You must be Passing Fancy," she said to the beautiful bay mare as she stroked her satiny neck. "What a pretty name you have."

"Still talking to horses, I see," chuckled a voice behind her.

Whitney swung around, beaming at the ramrod-straight figure of Thomas, her father's head groom. Thomas had been her girlhood confidant and a sympathetic witness to some of her most infamous outbursts of temper and unhappiness. "I can't believe how full the stable is," she said after they had exchanged greetings. "What on earth do we do with all these horses?"

"Exercise them mostly. But don't stand out here. I've something to show you." Wonderful smells of oil and leather welcomed Whitney as she stepped into the cool stable, blinking to adjust to the dim light. At the end of the corridor, two men were attempting to soothe a magnificent black stallion who was crosstied, while a third tried to trim his hooves. The stallion was a flurry of movement, shaking and tossing his head, rearing the few inches off the ground that the slack in the ropes allowed. "Dangerous Crossing," announced Thomas proudly. "And a right fitting name for him, too."

Already Whitney could feel those splendid muscles flexing beneath her. "Is he broken to ride?"

"Sometimes," Thomas chuckled. "But most of the time he tries to break the rider. Moodiest animal in the world. One day you think he's ready to give in and start responding, the next he'll try to rub you off on the fences. Gets himself all worked up over something, and he'll charge like he's half bull." Thomas raised his crop to point to another stall and the frenzied horse tripled his efforts to break free.

"Whoa! Easy now. Easy," gasped one of the struggling stableboys. "Master Thomas, could you put that crop behind you?"

Quickly tucking the crop behind him with an apologetic look at the sweating stableboy, Thomas explained to Whitney, "This animal hates the sight of the crop. George there tried to back him off a fence with it last week and nearly ended up making the acquaintance of his Creator. Never mind the stallion, I've got something else to show you." Thomas steered Whitney toward the opposite entrance to the stable where another stable boy was leading—or being led by—a magnificent chestnut gelding with four snowy white feet.

"Khan?" Whitney whispered. Before Thomas could answer, the chestnut nuzzled her at the hip, looking for the pocket where she used to hide his treats when he was a colt. "Why you beggar!" she laughed. She smiled over her shoulder at Thomas. "How does he go? He was much too little to saddle when I left."

"Why don't you try him out and see for yourself?"

Whitney needed no more encouragement. With her crop clenched between her teeth, she reached up to tighten the turquoise ribbon that held her hair at the nape. Dangerous Crossing lunged backward, kicking out at the men, creating a furor. "Hide the crop!" Thomas warned sharply, and Whitney quickly complied.

Khan pranced sideways with anticipation as he was led outdoors. Thomas gave Whitney a leg up, and she landed gracefully in the sidesaddle. Turning Khan toward the open gate, she said, "I'm a little out of practice. If he comes back without me, I'll be between here and Lady Archibald's father's house."

As Khan trotted up the drive to Emily's house, a curtain shifted at a wide bow window. A moment later the front door opened, and Emily came flying outside. "Whitney!" she cried joyously, flinging her arms around her and returning Whitney's hug. "Oh Whitney, let me see you." Laughing, Emily backed up, still clasping both Whitney's hands in hers. "You're absolutely beautiful!"

"You're the one who looks wonderful," Whitney said, admiring Emily's light brown hair cut fashionably short and threaded with a ribbon.

"That's because I'm happy, not because I'm beautiful," Emily argued.

Arm in arm the girls strolled into the drawing room. A

slender, sandy-haired man in his late twenties stood up, his hazel eyes smiling as Emily breathlessly began the introduction. "Whitney, may I present my husband—"

"Michael Archibald," he finished before his wife put the barrier of his title in Whitney's way. It was a simple, unaffected gesture of open friendliness, and Whitney appreciated the subtle thoughtfulness, as did his beaming wife.

Shortly thereafter, he excused himself and left the girls to talk, an activity in which they engaged eagerly for two hours.

"Paul was here this morning," Emily said as Whitney reluctantly rose to leave. "He came over to speak to my father about something." A guilty smile flitted over Emily's pretty features. "I . . . well . . . I didn't think it would hurt if I—very casually, you understand—repeated some of the things Monsieur DuVille had mentioned about how popular you are in France. Although," Emily added as her smile vanished, "I'm not sure Monsieur DuVille did you a favor talking about you like that in front of Margaret Merryton. He flayed her alive with tales of your conquests, and now she hates you even more than she ever did."

"Why?" Whitney asked as they walked down the front hall.

"Why has she always hated you? I suppose because you were the wealthiest of all of us. Although, now that she's preoccupied with your new neighbor, maybe she'll be nice for a change, instead of so hateful." At Whitney's puzzled look, Emily explained. "Mr. Westland, your new neighbor. From what Elizabeth was telling me yesterday, Margaret considers him her exclusive property."

"How is Elizabeth?" Whitney asked, forgetting about Margaret entirely at the mention of her rival for Paul's love.

"As pretty and sweet as ever. And you may as well know that Paul escorts her practically everywhere."

Whitney thought about that as she galloped diagonally across an unplanted field belonging to Emily's father. Elizabeth Ashton had always been everything Whitney wanted to be—ladylike, demure, blond, petite, and sweet.

The wind tore at her hair, tugging it loose from the velvet ribbon, tossing it wildly about. Beneath her, Whitney could feel Khan gathering and flexing gracefully as he flew over the ground with amazing speed. Regretfully, she eased him back into a canter, slowing him to a walk as they entered the woods to follow a path that existed now only in Whitney's memory. Rabbits scampered in the underbrush, and squirrels darted up the trees as they wound their way through the dense growth. A few minutes later, they crested the hill, and Whitney guided Khan carefully down the steep slope where a small meadow was bordered by a wide brook that ran through the northern section of her father's property.

Dismounting, Whitney looped Khan's reins around a sturdy oak, waited a minute to be certain that he would stand quietly, then patted his sleek neck and struck out across the meadow toward the stream. As she walked, she stopped now and then to gaze around her with older, more appreciative eyes, and to savor the scent of late summer wildflowers and fresh clover. She did not, however, look up and over her shoulder, and so she didn't notice the solitary horseman who was motionless atop a great sorrel stallion, watching every step she took.

Clayton grinned when Whitney stripped off her turquoise jacket and slung it jauntily over her right shoulder. Free of all the restrictions of Parisian society, her walk was an easy, swinging gait that was both lively and seductive, sending her luxuriant mane of hair swaying to and fro as she strolled toward the stream. She sauntered up a gentle knoll that sloped toward the water's edge. Seating herself beneath an ancient, gnarled sycamore standing sentinel atop the knoll, she pulled off her riding boots, peeled her stockings down, and tossed them over by the boots.

His horse moved restlessly beneath him while Clayton debated whether or not to approach his quarry. When she hitched her skirts up and waded into the stream, he chuckled and made his decision. Angling his horse back into the trees, he descended through the woods toward the meadow below.

Wading in this stream, Whitney quickly decided, was not quite as enjoyable as she remembered it. For one thing, the water was freezing cold, and beneath her feet the rocks were sharp and slippery. Gingerly, she waded back to the bank, then stretched out on the grass. Her hair tumbled to the sides, floating on the water's rippling surface as she lay propped up on her elbows, her chin cupped in her hands, lazily raising and lowering her wet calves, letting the breeze dry them. She was watching the minnows darting in the shallows and trying to imagine the moment when Paul would see her for the first time tonight, when a slight movement near the sycamore tree to her left drew her attention.

From the corner of her eye, Whitney glimpsed a pair of expensive brown riding boots polished to a mirror shine. She froze, then rolled over and quickly raised herself to a sitting position, drawing her knees up against her chest, hastily tugging her sodden skirts down around her bare ankles.

The man was standing with one shoulder negligently propped against the sycamore tree, his arms crossed loosely over his chest. "Fishing?" he inquired, as his gaze roamed over every warm curve of her body, lingered momentarily on her bare toes peeping out from beneath the wet hem of her riding skirts, then moved upward in a leisurely inspection of her feminine assets that left Whitney feeling as if she'd just been stripped of all her clothing.

"Spying?" she countered coldly.

He didn't deign to reply, but looked at her in ill-concealed amusement. Whitney lifted her chin and haughtily returned his gaze. He was very tall, easily 6 feet 2 inches, lean and superbly fit. His jaw was firm and well carved, his nose straight. The breeze lightly ruffled his hair which was a thick, coffee-brown. Beneath dark brows, his gray eyes observed her with frank interest. His clean-shaven face was very handsome—Whitney allowed him that—but there was an aggressive virility in his bold gaze, and an uncompromising authority, an arrogance, in the set of his jaw, that was not at all to Whitney's liking.

His mouth quirked in a half smile. "Were you going for a swim?"

"No, I was trying to be alone, Mr. . . . ?"

"Westland," he provided, his gaze dipping to touch the rounded fullness of her breasts where they pressed against her sheer white shirt.

Whitney crossed her arms protectively over her bosom, and

his smile widened knowingly. "Mr. Westland!" she snapped angrily, "your sense of direction must be nearly as poor as your manners!"

Her tart reprimand only seemed to push him nearer the brink of outright laughter. "Really, why is that, Ma'am?"

"Because you are trespassing," Whitney said. When he still showed no inclination to leave or apologize, Whitney knew *she* would have to be the one to go. Gritting her teeth, she glanced disgustedly toward her stockings and boots.

He straightened from his lounging position and stepped over to her, extending his hand. "May I help you?" he offered.

"You certainly may help me," Whitney replied, her smile deliberately cold and ungracious. "Get on your horse and go away."

Something flickered in his gray eyes, but his smile remained, and his hand was still outstretched. "Here is my hand, take it." Whitney ignored it and rose to her feet unassisted. It was impossible to put on her stockings without exposing her legs to the man who was leaning against the tree watching her, so she pulled on her boots and stuffed the stockings in her jacket pocket.

Walking quickly over to Khan, she picked up her crop and, stepping onto a fallen stump, hoisted herself into the saddle. His horse, a beautifully muscled sorrel, was tied beside her. She turned Khan in a tight circle, urging him into a lunging gallop around the woods.

"A pleasure meeting you again, Miss Stone," Clayton chuckled aloud. "You little hellcat," he added appreciatively.

Once out of sight, Whitney slowed Khan to a loping canter. She could hardly believe Mr. Westland was the neighbor her father held in such high esteem. She grimaced, recalling that he was invited to her party tonight. Why, the man was insufferably rude, outrageously bold, and infuriatingly arrogant! How could her father like him?

She was still wondering about that when she wandered into the sewing room and sat down beside her aunt. "You will never guess who I have just met," she was telling her aunt when Sewell, the old family butler, circumspectly cleared his throat and announced, "Lady Amelia Eubank asks to see you."

Whitney blanched. "Me? Dear God, why?"

"Show Lady Eubank into the rose salon, Sewell," Lady Anne said, curiously studying Whitney, who was looking wildly around the room for a place to hide. "What on earth has you looking so alarmed, darling?"

"You just don't know her, Aunt Anne. When I was little she used to shout at me not to chomp my nails."

"Well, at least she cared enough about you to want to correct you, which is more than I can say of anyone else here."

"But we were in *church*," Whitney cried desperately.

Anne's smile was sympathetic but firm. "I'll admit she's a trifle deaf and very outspoken. But four years ago, when all your neighbors came to see me, Lady Eubank was the only person who had a kind word to say about you. She said you had spunk. And she has a great deal of influence with everyone else hereabouts."

"That's because they're all frightened to death of her," Whitney sighed.

When Lady Anne and Whitney walked into the salon, the dowager Lady Eubank was examining the workmanship of a porcelain pheasant. Grimacing to show her distaste, she replaced the object atop the mantle and said to Whitney, "That atrocity must be to your father's liking. Your mother wouldn't have had it in her house."

Whitney opened her mouth to speak, but couldn't think of a reply. Lady Eubank groped for the monocle dangling from a black ribbon over her ample bosom, raised it to her eye and scrutinized Whitney from the top of her head to the tip of her toes. "Well, miss, what have you to say for yourself?" she demanded.

Fighting down the childish urge to wring her hands, Whitney said formally, "I am delighted to see you again after so many years, my lady."

"Rubbish!" said the dowager. "Do you still chomp your nails?"

Whitney almost, but not quite, rolled her eyes. "No, actually, I don't."

"Good. You have a fine figure, nice face. Now, to get down to the reason for my visit. Do you still mean to get Sevarin?"

"Do I—I what?"

"Young woman, I am the one who's supposed to be deaf. Now do you, or do you not, mean to get Sevarin?"

Whitney frantically considered and cast aside half a dozen responses. She glanced beseechingly at her aunt, who gave her a helpless, laughing look. Finally, she clasped her hands behind her back and regarded her tormentor directly. "Yes. If I can."

"Ha! Thought so!" said the dowager happily, then her eyes narrowed. "You aren't given to blushing and simpering, are you? Because if you are, you may as well go back to France. Miss Elizabeth has tried that for years, and she's yet to snare Sevarin. You take my advice, and give that young man some competition! Competition is what he needs—he's too sure of himself with the ladies and always has been." She turned to Lady Anne. "For fifteen years, I have listened to my tiresome neighbors foretelling a dire future for your niece, Madam, but I always believed there was hope for her. Now," she said with a complacent smirk, "I intend to sit back and laugh myself into fits watching her snap Sevarin up right in front of their eyes." Raising her monacle to her eye, she gave Whitney a final inspection, then nodded abruptly. "Do Not Fail Me, Miss."

In amazed disbelief Whitney stared at the empty doorway through which the dowager had just passed. "I think she's a little mad."

"I think she's as wily as a fox," Lady Anne replied with a faint smile. "And I think you'd be wise to take her advice to heart."

Trancelike, Whitney sat before her dressing table mirror, watching Clarissa deftly twist her heavy hair into elaborate curls entwined with a rope of diamonds—her last, and most extravagant purchase made with the money her father sent her to spend in Paris. As Clarissa teased soft tendrils over her ears, the night breeze wafted the curtains, raising bumps on Whitney's arms. Tonight was going to be unseasonably cool, which suited Whitney perfectly, for the gown she wanted to wear was of velvet.

As the gown was being fastened up the back, Whitney heard the sound of carriages making their way along the drive, the echo of muted laughter, distant but distinct, drifting through the open windows. Were they laughing as they recounted her old antics? Was that Margaret Merryton or one of the other girls, sniggering about the shameful way she used to behave?

Whitney didn't notice when Clarissa finished and quietly left the room. She felt cold all over, frightened, and more painfully unsure of herself than ever before in her life. Tonight was the night she had been practicing for and dreaming of all these years in France.

She wandered over to the windows, wondering distractedly what Elizabeth would wear tonight. Something pastel, no doubt. And demurely fetching. Parting the ivory and gold curtains, she stared down, watching the carriage lamps twinkling as they approached along the sweeping drive. One after another, in amazing numbers, they rolled to a stop at the steps. Her father must have invited half the countryside, she thought nervously. And of course, they had all accepted his invitation. They would all be eager to look her over, to search for some flaw, some sign of the unruly girl she'd been before.

Two steps into Whitney's room, Anne came to an abrupt halt, a slow, beaming smile working its way across her face. In profile, Whitney's finely sculpted features looked too lovely to be real. Anne took in everything, from the shadows of thick lashes on glowing magnolia skin, to the diamonds glittering amidst her shiny mahogany curls and peeping from beneath the soft tendrils at her ears. Her curvaceous form was draped in an emerald-green velvet gown with a high waist. The bodice was molded firmly to her breasts, exposing a daring amount of flesh above the square neckline. As if to atone for the gown's immodest display of bosom, the sleeves were fitted tubes of emerald velvet which did not allow so much as a glimpse of skin from shoulder to wrist, where they ended in deep points at the tops of her hands. Like the front, the back of the gown was elegant in its simplicity, falling in velvet folds.

A carriage drew up below, and Whitney watched a tall, blond man bound down and offer his hand to a beautiful blond girl. Paul had arrived. And he had come with Elizabeth. Jerking away from the window, Whitney saw her aunt and visibly jumped.

"You look positively breathtaking!" Lady Anne whispered.

"Do you really like it—the dress, I mean?" Whitney's voice was raspy and tight with mounting tension.

"Like it?" Anne laughed. "Darling, it's you! Daring and elegant and special." She extended her hand from which dangled a magnificent emerald pendant. "Your father asked me this morning what color your gown was, and he just brought me this to give to you. It was your mother's," Anne added when Whitney stared at the glittering jewel.

The emerald was easily an inch square, flanked by a row of glittering diamonds on all four sides. It was *not* her mother's; Whitney had spent hours, long ago, lovingly touching all the little treasures and trinkets in her mother's jewel case. But she was too nervous to argue the point. She stood rigidly still while her aunt fastened the pendant.

"Perfect!" Anne exclaimed with pleasure, studying the effect of the glowing jewel nestling in the hollow between Whitney's breasts. Linking her arm through Whitney's, Anne took a step forward. "Come, darling—it's time for your second official debut." Whitney wished with all her heart that Nicolas DuVille were here to help her through this debut, too.

Her father was pacing impatiently at the foot of the stairs, waiting to escort her into the ballroom. When he saw her coming down the steps toward him, he halted in mid-stride, and the stunned admiration on his face bolstered Whitney's faltering confidence.

Under the wide arched entrance to the ballroom, he stopped and nodded at the musicians in the far alcove, and the music ground to an abrupt halt. Whitney could feel the eyes swerving toward her, hear the roar of the crowd dying swiftly as the babble of voices trailed off in ominous silence. She drew a long, quivering breath, focused her eyes slightly above everyone's heads, and stepped down the three shallow steps, allowing her father to lead her toward the center of the room.

Staring, watchful silence followed her and, at that moment, had she been able to find the strength, Whitney would have picked up her skirts and fled. She clung to the memory of Nicolas DuVille, of his proud, laughing elegance, and the way he had escorted her everywhere. He would have leaned over and whispered in her ear, "They are nothing but provincials, chérie! Just keep your head high."

The crowd parted as a young, red-haired man shoved his way through—Peter Redfern, who had teased her unmercifully as a child, but had also been one of her few friends. At five and twenty, Peter's hairline had receded slightly, but the boyishness that was so much a part of him was still there. "Good God!" he exclaimed with unconcealed admiration when he was standing directly in front of her. "It *is* you, you little ruffian! What have you done with your freckles?!"

Whitney gulped back her horrified laughter at this undignified greeting and put her hand in his outstretched palm. "What," she countered, beaming at him, "have *you* done with your hair, Peter?"

Peter burst out laughing, and the silent spell was broken. Everyone started talking at once, closing in on her and exchanging greetings.

Anticipation and tension were building apace, but Whitney restrained the urge to turn and look for Paul as the minutes ticked past and she continued making the same mechanical responses, over and over again. Yes, she had enjoyed Paris. Yes, her Uncle Edward Gilbert was well. Yes, she would be pleased to attend this card party or that dinner party.

Peter was still beside her a quarter of an hour later while Whitney was speaking with the apothecary's wife. From her left, where all the local girls and their husbands were standing, Whitney heard Margaret Merryton's familiar, malicious laugh. "I heard she made a spectacle of herself in Paris and is all but shunned from polite society there," Margaret was telling them.

Peter heard her too, and he grinned at Whitney. "It's time to face Miss Merryton. You can't avoid her forever. And anyway, she's with someone you haven't met yet."

At Peter's urging, Whitney reluctantly turned to face her childhood foe.

Margaret Merryton was standing with her hand resting possessively on Clayton Westland's claret-colored sleeve. This afternoon, Whitney would have sworn that nothing, *nothing* could make her dislike Clayton Westland more than she did, but seeing him with Margaret, knowing he was listening to her vituperative comments, turned Whitney's initial dislike into genuine loathing.

"We were all so disappointed that you weren't able to find a husband in France, Whitney," Margaret said with silken malice.

Whitney looked at her with cool disdain. "Margaret, every time you open your mouth, I always expect to hear a rattle." Then she picked up her skirts, intending to turn and speak to Emily, but Peter caught her elbow. "Whitney," he said, "allow me to introduce Mr. Westland to you. He has leased the Hodges place and is just back from France."

Still stinging from Margaret's cruel remarks, Whitney jumped to the conclusion that if Clayton Westland had just returned from France, he must be the one who had provided Margaret with the lie that Whitney was an outcast there. "How do you like living in the country, Mr. Westland?" she inquired in a voice of bored indifference.

"*Most* of the people have been very friendly," he said meaningfully.

"I'm certain they have." Whitney could almost feel his eyes disrobing her as they had at the stream. "Perhaps one of them will even be 'friendly' enough to show you the boundary of your property, so that you don't embarrass yourself by trespassing on ours, as you did earlier today."

A stunned silence fell over the group; the amusement vanished from Clayton Westland's expression. "Miss Stone," he said in a voice of strained patience, "we seem to have gotten off on a rather bad foot." Inclining his head toward the dance floor, he said, "Perhaps if you will do me the honor of dancing . . ."

If he said anything more, Whitney didn't hear it, because directly behind her and very close to her ear an achingly familiar, deep voice said, "I beg your pardon, I was told Whitney Stone was to be here tonight, but I don't recognize her." His hand touched her elbow, and Whitney's pulse went wild as she let Paul slowly turn her around to face him.

She lifted her eyes and gazed up into the bluest ones this side of heaven. Unconsciously, she extended both her hands, feeling them clasped firmly in Paul's strong, warm ones. In the last four years, she had rehearsed dozens of clever things to say when this moment finally arrived; but looking up at his beloved, handsome face, all she could say was, "Hello, Paul."

A slow, appreciative smile worked its way across his face as he tucked her hand in the crook of his arm. "Dance with me," he said simply.

Trembling inside, Whitney stepped into Paul's arms and felt his hand glide around her waist, gathering her closer. Beneath her fingertips, his beautiful dark blue jacket seemed to be a living thing that her fingers ached to slide over and caress. She knew that *now* was the time to be the poised, light-hearted female she'd been in Paris, but her thoughts were jumbled and erratic, as if part of her was fifteen years old again. All she wanted to say was, "I love you. I have always loved you. *Now* do you want me? Have I changed enough for you to want me?"

"Did you miss me?" Paul asked.

Warning bells went off in Whitney's head as she heard the thread of confidence in his tone. Instinctively, she gave him a provocative sidewise smile. "I missed you *desperately!*" she declared with enough extra emphasis to make it seem a gross exaggeration.

"How 'desperately'?" Paul persisted, his grin widening.

"I was utterly desolate," Whitney teased, knowing full well that Emily had regaled him with stories of her popularity in Paris. "In fact, I nearly wasted away in loneliness for you."

"Liar." He chuckled, his hand on her waist tightening

possessively. "That's not what I heard this morning. Did you, or did you not, tell some French nobleman that if you were as impressed with his title as you were with his conceit, you'd be tempted to accept his offer?"

Whitney nodded slowly, her lips twitching with laughter. "I did."

"May I ask what his offer was?" Paul said.

"No, you may not."

"Should I call him out?"

Whitney felt as if she was dancing on air. Should he call him out? Paul was flirting with her, actually flirting with her!

"How is Elizabeth?" Before the words were past her lips, she cursed herself in French *and* English. And when she saw the satisfied smile sweeping across Paul's face, she felt like stamping her foot in self-disgust.

"I'll find her and bring her over, so you can see for yourself," Paul offered, the knowing smile lingering in his eyes as the music wound to a close.

Whitney was still trying to recover from the humiliation of her hideous blunder when she realized that Paul was guiding her directly toward Clayton Westland's group. Until that moment, she'd entirely forgotten that she'd turned her back on him when he was asking her to dance, and had strolled off with Paul.

"I believe I stole Miss Stone away when you were about to request a dance, Clayton," Paul said.

Considering her earlier rudeness, Whitney couldn't see any way to avoid dancing with her loathsome neighbor now. She waited for Clayton to repeat the invitation, but he did nothing of the sort. With everyone witnessing her chagrin, Clayton let her stand there until she flushed with angry embarrassment. Then he offered his arm and said in a bored, unenthusiastic voice, "Miss Stone?"

"No, thank you," Whitney said coldly. "I don't care to dance, Mr. Westland." Turning on her heel she walked off toward the opposite end of the room, putting as much space as possible between herself and that boorish clod, and joined a group of people that included Aunt Anne. She had been standing there for perhaps five minutes when her father appeared at her elbow and drew her away. "There is someone I want you to meet," he said with gruff determination.

Despite his tone, Whitney could tell that he was very proud of her tonight, and she accompanied him gladly as he skirted around the perimeter of the ballroom . . . until she realized where he was taking her. Directly ahead, Clayton Westland was engaged in laughing conversation with Emily and her husband. Margaret Merryton still clung to his arm.

"Father, please!" Whitney whispered urgently, drawing back. "I don't like him."

"Don't be absurd!" he snapped irritably, forcibly pulling her the rest of the way. "Here she is," he told Clayton Westland in a booming, jovial voice. He turned to Whitney and said, as if she were nine years old, "Make your curtsy and say 'how do' to our friend and neighbor, Mr. Clayton Westland."

"We've already met," Clayton said drily.

"We've met," Whitney echoed weakly. Her cheeks burned as she endured Clayton's mocking gaze. If he said or did anything to embarrass her in front of her father, Whitney thought she would murder him. For the first time in her life, her father was seeing her as an accepted, and acceptable, human being, and he was *proud* of her.

"Well good. Good," her father said, looking expectantly from Whitney to Clayton. "Then why don't you two dance? That's what this music is for—"

The reason they weren't going to dance, Whitney instantly realized, was because it was obvious from Clayton's aloof expression that he wouldn't ask her to dance again if someone held a gun to his head. Feeling lower than an insect, Whitney made herself look imploringly at him, and then at the dance floor, in an unmistakable invitation to *him*.

His brows arched in ironic amusement. For one hideous moment, Whitney thought he intended to ignore her invitation, but he shrugged instead and, without so much as offering her his arm, he strolled toward the dance floor, leaving her to follow or remain standing there.

Whitney followed him, but she loathed him every single step of the way for making her do it. Trailing along in his wake, she stared daggers at the back of his wine-colored jacket, but until he turned toward her, she didn't realize that he was laughing—actually *laughing* at her mortification!

Whitney stepped toward him, then right past him, fully intending to leave him standing there in the middle of the dancers.

His hand shot out and captured her elbow. "Don't you dare!" he growled, laughing as he drew her around to face him for the waltz.

"It was excessively kind of you to ask me to dance," Whitney remarked sarcastically as she stepped reluctantly into his arms.

"Wasn't that what you wanted me to do?" he asked with mock innocence, and before she could answer, he added, "If I had only realized that *you* prefer to do the asking, I'd not have wasted my other two attempts."

"Of all the conceited, rude—" Whitney caught her father's anxious stare and smiled brilliantly at him, to show what a marvellous time she was having. The moment he looked away, she glared murderously at her dancing partner and continued, "—unspeakable, insufferable—" Clayton Westland's shoulders began to rock with laughter, and Whitney choked on her ire.

"Go on," he urged with a broad grin. "I haven't had such a trimming since I was a small boy. Now, where were you? I am 'unspeakable, insufferable'—?"

"Outrageously bold," Whitney provided furiously, and then for want of anything better, "—and ungentlemanly!"

"Now that puts me in a very difficult position," he mocked lightly. "Because you've left me no alternative except to defend myself by pointing out that your behavior to me tonight has been anything but ladylike."

"Smile, please. My father is watching us," Whitney warned, forcing her mouth into a smile.

Clayton complied immediately. His teeth flashed white in a lazy grin, but his gaze dipped lingeringly to her soft lips.

The focal point of his gaze did not escape Whitney, who stiffened in his arms. "Mr. Westland, I think this brief, unpleasant encounter has gone on long enough!"

She jerked back, but his arm tightened sharply, preventing her from pulling free. "I haven't any intention of either of us becoming a spectacle, little one," he warned. Since Whitney had no choice except to move where he led her, she ignored his improper endearment, shrugged, and looked away. "Lovely evening, isn't it?" he drawled, and then in a stage whisper, he added. "Your father is watching us again."

"It *was* a lovely evening," Whitney retorted. She waited for Clayton's rejoinder and when, after several seconds, there was none, she glanced uncertainly at him. He was watching her intently, but without a trace of rancor over her jibe. Suddenly Whitney felt foolish and bad-tempered. True, he had behaved outrageously this afternoon at the stream but, considering the things *she* had done and said to him tonight, she had not behaved any better. A rueful smile lit her eyes to glowing jade as she looked at him. "I think it is your turn to be rude to me now," she offered fairly. "Or have I lost count?"

His eyes smiled his approval at her sudden change of attitude. "I think we're about even," he said quietly.

Something about his deep voice and gray eyes, about the effortless ease with which he danced the waltz, stirred the ashes of some vague memory. Forgetting that his eyes were locked to hers, Whitney gazed at him, trying to grasp what was niggling at the back of her mind. "Mr. Westland, have we ever met before?"

"If we had, I hate to think that you could forget it."

"I'm certain that if we had, I would remember," Whitney said politely, and dismissed the idea.

True to his promise, Paul brought Elizabeth over when Clayton and Whitney strolled off the dance floor. Elizabeth Ashton, Whitney thought despairingly, looked like a beautiful, fragile china doll. She was wrapped in a gown of ice-blue satin that complemented the pink of her cheeks and the shining gold of her curls, and her voice was soft with amazed admiration as she said, "I can't believe it's you, Whitney."

There was the implication, of course, that Whitney had been so unpresentable before that Elizabeth couldn't believe the change, but watching her stroll away on Clayton's arm, Whitney didn't think Elizabeth had meant to be insulting.

Since Elizabeth was dancing with Clayton Westland, Whitney waited, hoping that Paul would ask *her* to dance again. Instead he frowned and said abruptly, "Is it the custom in Paris for a man and woman who have just been introduced to gaze into one another's eyes while they dance?"

Whitney looked at him in startled surprise. "I—I wasn't gazing into Mr. Westland's eyes. It was just that he seemed familiar to me, and yet, I don't know him at all. Hasn't that ever happened to you?"

"It happened to me tonight," Paul said curtly. "I thought *you* were someone I knew. Now I'm not certain I know you at all." He turned on his heel and walked away, leaving Whitney staring after him. In the old days, Whitney would have run after him to reassure him that it was *him* she wanted, only him, and not Clayton Westland. But these weren't the old days and she was much wiser, so she smiled to herself and turned in the opposite direction.

Even though Paul never approached her again, she was perfectly happy to dance the night away with the local swains. Given a choice between an overconfident Paul and an aloof, jealous one, Whitney definitely preferred the latter. Lady Eubank was right, Whitney decided. Competition was what Paul needed.

It was nearly noon when Whitney awoke the following day. She threw back the covers and jumped out of bed, positively certain that Paul would come to call.

Paul didn't come, but several of her other neighbors did, and she spent the afternoon trying to be charming and gay while her spirits sank along with the setting sun.

When she went to bed that night she told herself that Paul would surely come tomorrow. But tomorrow came and went without a sign of him.

It was not until the day after, that Whitney saw him, and then it was purely by chance. She and Emily were riding back from the village, their horses kicking up little puffs of dust as they walked along the road. "Did you know that Mr. Westland was called away to London the day after your party?" Emily asked.

"My father said something about it," Whitney said, her mind on Paul. "I think he is expected back tomorrow. Why?"

"Because Margaret's mama told mine that Margaret has been counting the hours until he returns. Apparently, Margaret's affections are absolutely fixed on him and—" Emily stopped talking and squinted down the road. "Unless I mistake my eyes," she said with a teasing glance at Whitney, "we are about to encounter your prey."

Leaning forward, Whitney made out an elegant phaeton tearing along at a spanking pace in their direction. There was scarcely time for her to smooth the skirt of her riding habit before Paul was upon them. He pulled up, greeted Whitney politely, and then devoted his complete attention to Emily, flattering her with teasing gallantries until she laughingly ordered him to desist because she was now a married woman.

Khan had taken an instant aversion to Paul's showy black horse, and Whitney listened to their conversation while trying to keep Khan under control. "Are you going to Lady Eubank's affair tomorrow?" she heard him ask. When there was a lengthening moment of silence, she looked up to find Paul's attention on her.

"Are you going to Lady Eubank's affair tomorrow?" he repeated.

Whitney nodded, her heart doubling its tempo.

"Fine. I'll see you there." Without another word, he flicked the reins, and the phaeton bowled off down the road. Emily turned, watching the vehicle until it vanished from view. "If that wasn't the most extraordinary encounter I have ever had in my life, I can't imagine what was!" she said. A slow smile dawned across her features as she looked at Whitney. "Paul Sevarin just went to great pains to completely ignore you. Whitney!" she said excitedly, "doesn't that strike you as rather odd?"

"Not at all," Whitney said with a disheartened sigh. "If you remember, Paul *always* used to ignore me."

"Yes, I know," Emily said, laughing softly. "But back

then, he wasn't watching you the entire time he did it. The whole time he was talking to *me* just now, he was watching *you*. And at your party the other night, he watched you constantly when you weren't looking."

Whitney jerked Khan to a halt. "Did he truly? Are you certain?"

"Of course I'm certain, silly. *I* was watching him, watching you."

"Oh, Emily," Whitney laughed shakily. "I wish you didn't have to go back to London next week. When you're gone, who will tell me the things I want to hear?"

Chapter Eleven

By the night of Lady Eubank's party, Whitney had worked herself into a knot of anticipation and foreboding. She was ready early, waiting for her aunt in the hall in a gown of midnight-blue chiffon spangled with glittering silver flecks. Diamonds and sapphires twinkled at her ears and throat, and winked from her elegant Grecian curls.

"Aunt Anne," she said in the carriage on the way to Lady Eubank's, "do you think Paul truly loves Elizabeth?"

"If he did, I believe he would have offered for her long ago," Anne replied, pulling on her gloves as their carriage turned into the long drive at Lady Eubank's great old mausoleum of a house. "And your friend Emily is absolutely correct—he watched you constantly the night of your party, when he thought no one was looking."

"Then *why* is he taking so long to *do* something about it?"

"Darling, only consider the awkward position he is in. Four years ago, everyone knew that he barely tolerated your devotion. Now he is faced with the problem of reversing himself completely and openly courting you." She smiled at Whitney's glum look. "If you want to speed things up, I think you ought to take Lady Eubank's advice and give him some competition."

Three hours later, Whitney was beginning to agree. She

was popular and sought after by every eligible man present
. . . except the one who mattered.

Across the room from Whitney, surrounded by several of
the local girls, Clayton bent his head toward Margaret
Merryton, smiling to conceal his impatience with her ceaseless chatter.

After spending the past few days in London on an emer-
gency business matter, he'd returned just in time tonight to
change and come to this little gathering of Amelia Eubank's.
And that outrageous old harridan had greeted him in the
entryway and announced that she would appreciate it if he
would be especially attentive to Miss Stone tonight, and thus
provide some romantic competition for Sevarin. As a result,
Clayton was not in the best of moods.

Rudely turning her back on the woman who was talking to
her, Amelia Eubank raised her monocle and scanned the
knots of guests until her gaze fell upon the Duke of Claymore,
who was surrounded by several of the local girls, all vying for
his attention. Claymore, she noted, was treating them with
amused tolerance, but his attention was on the only female in
the room who seemed immune to his magnetism—Whitney
Stone.

Amelia dropped her monocle, letting it dangle from its
black ribbon over her ample bosom. Through a distant
connection of her deceased husband, Amelia could claim a
slight kinship with the duke, and when Claymore had arrived
at her home several weeks ago, announcing his intention to
take up residence five miles from her under the name
Westland "in order to take a much needed rest," she had
immediately assured him of her discretion.

Now, however, an intriguing idea occurred to her, and her
eyes took on a speculative gleam as she watched the duke
watching Miss Stone. She paused a moment to contemplate
how utterly unethical and devious her scheme was, and then,
with a pleased little smile, she leaned back and instructed a
footman to bring Miss Stone to her immediately, and then to
ask Mr. Westland to join them.

Whitney was dancing with Emily's husband when a footman appeared at her elbow and said that Lady Eubank

wished to see her *at once*. Excusing herself to Lord Archibald, Whitney obeyed Lady Eubank's imperative summons with feelings of distinct apprehension, an apprehension which immediately turned to alarm when the dowager hoisted herself out of her chair and said irritably, "I told you *competition* is what Sevarin needs, and your best friend's husband is *not* competition. I want you to make up to Mr. Westland. Bat your eyes at him, or whatever it is you young gels do to attract a man."

"No, I can't. Really, Lady Eubank, I'd rather—"

"Young woman," she interrupted, "I will have you know that I'm giving this party for the sole purpose of helping you secure Sevarin. Since you seem so foolish about how to go about it, you've left me no choice but to step in. Clayton Westland is the only man here whom Sevarin will consider a rival, and I've sent a footman for him." Whitney blanched, and Lady Eubank glowered at her. "Now, when Mr. Westland comes, you can either look at him the way you're looking at me—in which case, he will probably offer to take you to a physician—or you can smile at him, so that he will offer to take you out on the balcony instead."

"I don't want to go out on the balcony!" Whitney hissed desperately.

"You will," her ladyship predicted, "when you turn around and observe how charmingly Elizabeth Ashton is strolling in that direction on Sevarin's arm."

Whitney turned and saw that Paul and Elizabeth were indeed strolling toward the balcony doors. Discouraged, Whitney recognized the sense in what Lady Eubank was trying to force her to do, but she was reluctant to stoop to outright scheming. Not that her hesitancy mattered, because Lady Eubank had neatly taken the choice out of her hands and was already saying to a faintly smiling Clayton, "Miss Stone was just mentioning that she is excessively overheated from all her dancing, and that she would enjoy a stroll on the balcony."

Clayton Westland glanced toward the balcony doors, and in the space of an instant, Whitney watched his lazy smile harden into a mask of ironic amusement. "I'm sure she would," he said sarcastically.

He took her elbow in a none too gentle grasp, and said, "Shall we go, Miss Stone?" Whitney let him guide her through the throngs of chattering guests and around the perimeter of the buffet table. So lost was she in thoughts of Paul that she didn't notice that she was being led toward the French doors that stood at right angles to the ones Paul and Elizabeth had used. If they went this way, Whitney realized that they would emerge around the corner—and out of sight—of Paul and Elizabeth.

"Where are we going?" Whitney asked quickly, starting to draw back.

"As you can see, we are going out onto the balcony," her escort said coolly. Tightening his hold on her elbow, he opened the French doors with his free hand, propelled her outside and closed them behind her. Without a word, he dropped her arm and strolled over to the stone balustrade. Perching his hip on it, he regarded her in silence.

Whitney stood there, miserable because Lady Eubank's plan had failed, embarrassed because she had participated in it, and still determined to somehow carry it off if possible. "Perhaps we could stroll around to the other side?" she suggested.

"We could, but we aren't going to," Clayton almost snapped. He gazed at her, knowing she was trying to use him as a decoy and growing more impatient and annoyed with her as each second passed. She looked like a wild young temptress with the moonlight gleaming on the silver spangles of her gown as it blew gently in the midnight breeze. And she was his, dammit! He had even paid for the gown she was wearing.

After a few moments, an idea occurred to him. Leaning back, he looked around the corner of the balcony, ascertained that Sevarin and Elizabeth Ashton were standing at the balustrade, then returned his undivided attention to the lovely young woman who was now nervously fingering the folds of her gown. "Well, Miss Stone?" he drawled in a voice just raised enough to carry around the corner.

Whitney jumped at the sound of her name. "Well what?" she questioned, starting to move forward in the hope of peeking around the corner and seeing what Paul and Elizabeth were doing. In this she was instantly thwarted, because Clayton abruptly stood up and strolled toward her, effectively blocking her view of everything but his chest and shoulders. "Well what?" Whitney repeated, automatically stepping back in an effort to widen the space between them. Before she realized what was happening, she had backed into the shadowy stone wall of the house.

"Now that I've brought you out here," Clayton began conversationally, "what do you want me to do next?"

"Next?" Whitney repeated cautiously.

"Yes, next. I want to be certain I understand my part in this little game we're playing. I imagine I'm suppose to kiss you, in order to make Sevarin jealous, is that it?"

"I wouldn't let you touch me to save me from drowning!" Whitney retorted, too angry to be humiliated.

Ignoring that completely, he said thoughtfully, "I don't mind playing my part, but I can't help wondering if I'm going to enjoy it. Am I going to kiss an amateur, or have you been kissed often enough to know how it's supposed to be done? How may times *have* you been kissed?"

"I'll wager you live in constant terror of being mistaken for a gentleman!" she snapped to cover her growing alarm. His hands locked on her arms and he began drawing her toward his chest. Giving up her futile struggle, she glared murderously at the laughter glinting in his eyes. "Take your hands off me!"

"Are the times you've been kissed too numerous to count? Or were they all so meaningless that you can't recall them?"

Whitney thought she was going to explode. "I have been kissed often enough not to require lessons from the likes of you, if that's what you have in mind!"

He chuckled as his arms encircled her rigid body. "So vou've been kissed that often, have you, little one?"

Whitney stared at his chest, refusing to look up at him. Screaming was out of the question; her reputation would be destroyed if anyone saw her in such a compromising situation. She could not, *could not* believe this was actually happening to her. Torn between the urge to burst into tears, or hit him, she said as calmly as possible, "If you are quite through trying to frighten and humiliate me, please let me go."

"Not until I discover how much you've learned from all your 'experience,'" he whispered.

Whitney snapped her head up, intending to launch into a tirade, only to have her words smothered by his mouth. She froze at the initial shock of the contact, then forced herself to be perfectly still beneath the pressure of his lips. Although she had little experience in kissing, she had considerable experience in avoiding it, and she knew that by neither struggling nor responding, a woman could reduce an over-ardent male to a state of apologetic chagrin.

When Clayton finally drew back, however, he looked neither chagrined nor apologetic. Instead he regarded her with an infuriating grin. "Either you had very poor teachers, my lady, or you are sorely in need of more lessons."

His arms loosened, and Whitney stepped back. Pivoting on her heel, she vengefully fired a parting remark over her shoulder, "At least *my* lessons weren't learned in a brothel!"

It happened so quickly, there was no time to react. A hand like a vice shot out and seized her wrist, spinning her around back into the shadows, and jerking her into his arms. "I think," he enunciated in an awful voice, "that your problem is purely a matter of inexperienced teachers."

His mouth crushed down on hers, mercilessly bruising her lips, forcing them to part from sheer, cruel pressure and when they did, his tongue plunged into her mouth, ravaging its softness.

Whitney writhed futilely in his iron embrace while tears of impotent rage raced down her cheeks. The more she struggled, the more insolent and punishing his mouth became, until she finally grew still, defeated and trembling in his arms. The moment she stopped fighting, he lifted his head and cradled her face between his two hands. Gazing into her stormy, tear-brightened eyes, he said quietly, "That was your first lesson, little one. Never, ever play games with me. I've played them all before, and you can't win. This is the second lesson," he murmured as his mouth descended toward hers.

Whitney drew a sharp breath and started to scream, but his mouth throttled the scream to an hysterical whimper, and so gently this time that she was stunned into silent quiescence. His hand curved around her nape, his fingers stroking and soothing, while the other drifted over her back in a slow, restless caress, moving her closer to his length. And all the while, his lips were moving on hers with fierce tenderness, shaping and fitting their soft curves to his own.

He touched his tongue to her lips, coaxing them to part, and when they did, his tongue slid gently between them, sending wild jolts through Whitney's body. She reached her arms around his neck, clinging to him for support. His arm tightened protectively around her, and his tongue fully invaded the soft recesses of her mouth, tasting and exploring, filling her, until her whole body was a rioting mass of dizzying sensations.

He deepened the kiss, and his hand moved from her back to her midriff, sliding upward to her breast, boldly cupping its soft, enticing fullness.

Outrage at that intimate fondling banished every other emotion in a blinding flash of fury. With a strength she didn't know she possessed, Whitney tore free, flinging his arms furiously away. "How dare you!" she hissed at the same time that she lifted her hand and slapped him as hard as she could.

In utter disbelief, Whitney watched a slow, satisfied grin sweep across his face. So incensed that she could scarcely draw enough air to speak, she said, "If you ever, *ever* touch me again, I'll kill you!"

Her threat only seemed to please him more, and there was no mistaking the silent chuckle that preceded his next words. "That won't be necessary, my lady. I already have the answers I sought."

"Answers!" Whitney gasped. "If I were a man, I'd give you an answer at the point of a pistol."

"If you were a man, you'd have no reason to."

Whitney stood there, shaking with thwarted outrage, yearning to do or say something that would penetrate his cool, imperturbable exterior. The tears filling her eyes were tears of fury, but the moment he saw them he was contrite. "Dry your eyes, little one, and I'll return you to your friends inside." So saying, he produced a white handkerchief and held it toward her. Whitney thought she would splinter apart from the turbulence of her hatred and animosity. She snatched the handkerchief from his hand and flung it to the ground, spinning on her heel with every intention of stalking into the ballroom alone.

"Excuse us," Paul said with a curt nod as he escorted Elizabeth past them, toward the doors into the ballroom.

"How long has Paul been there?" Whitney demanded wrathfully, facing Clayton with her fists clenched. "You vile, contemptible . . . you did all that deliberately, for his benefit, didn't you? So that he would see it. You *wanted* him to see it!"

"I did it deliberately, for *my* benefit," Clayton corrected her blandly, placing his hand under Whitney's elbow and guiding her toward the French doors.

They stepped into the safety of the brightly lit house, and Whitney jerked her arm away, her voice a furious whisper. "You must be Satan's own son!"

"My father would have been disappointed to think so," Clayton replied with an infuriating chuckle.

"Your father?" Whitney scoffed, stepping away from him. "If you think your mother even knew his name, you deceive yourself!"

There was a moment of stunned silence while it registered on Clayton that he had just been called a bastard, followed by a shout of laughter as her ladylike slur on his legitimacy sank in. He was still grinning as he strolled along in her indignant wake, admiring the sway of her slender hips.

Blind with anger, Whitney stormed up to a group of middle-aged guests, which included her aunt, and stared past them, oblivious to their conversation. How she loathed and despised Clayton Westland! If it was the last thing she ever did, she would repay him for this night, for putting his filthy, debauched hands on her, for causing her to appear a harlot in front of Paul.

It was at least an hour later when Paul's deep voice said very quietly near her ear, "Come and dance with me." His hand had already taken possession of her elbow, and Whitney walked beside him. She was so afraid of seeing condemnation on his face that even when they were dancing she couldn't bring herself to look at him. "Does a man have to take you out to the balcony to get your attention, Miss Stone?" he taunted.

Whitney's gaze flew to his, and she discovered to her intense relief that the scene he had witnessed on the balcony had obviously annoyed him, but there was no disgust in his expression.

"Would you prefer a stroll in the night air?" he mocked.

"Please don't tease me about that," she half pleaded, half sighed. "It's been a long evening, and I'm exhausted."

"I'm not surprised," he said with heavy irony, but when Whitney flushed with embarrassment, he relented. "Do you think you could recover from your 'exhaustion' by tomorrow morning—in time for a picnic with, say, ten people, in your honor?"

Lady Eubank and Aunt Anne had been right! Whitney realized jubilantly. "I would love it," she admitted with a bright, happy smile.

When the dance ended, Paul led her to a relatively quiet corner of the room. He stopped a footman bearing a tray of champagne, took two glasses, and gave one to Whitney. Leaning his shoulder against a pillar, he grinned down at her. "Shall I invite Westland?"

Whitney's first instinct was to grab his lapels and scream no! But one look at that confident grin of his, and she chose a wiser course. She shrugged and even managed to smile. "By all means, invite him if you wish."

"You wouldn't object?"

Whitney gave him an innocent stare. "I can't think why I should. He's, well, very handsome . . ." She looked down at her glass to hide her grimace of revulsion. "And charming, and . . ."

"Miss Stone," Paul said, subjecting her to an amused scrutiny, "you wouldn't by any chance be trying to make me jealous, would you?"

"Are you?" Whitney countered with a flirtatious smile.

He didn't answer, but Whitney was almost certain that he was. Either way, the balance of the evening was the way she used to dream it would be. Paul remained at her side most of the time, and when he did leave her, it wasn't to return to Elizabeth.

Dismissing his valet, Clayton poured himself a light brandy. Inwardly, he smiled at the bizarre turn his courtship had taken tonight. Never in his wildest imaginings had he visualized anything quite like this! Nevertheless, he was extremely pleased by what he had learned on Amelia Eubank's balcony a few hours ago. None of Whitney's suitors in France had been permitted the liberties he had taken; she had been shocked by his intimate kiss and outraged when his hand touched her breast.

God, what an enchanting creature she was—part angel, part spitfire; artlessly sophisticated, with a ripe, opulent beauty that made his blood stir hotly.

Lifting his glass, he frowned into the contents. He had treated her badly tonight. Tomorrow, he would have to find a way to make amends.

Chapter Twelve

THE MORNING OF THE PICNIC DAWNED BRILLIANT BLUE, WITH A fresh cool breeze that carried the scent of fall.

Whitney bathed and washed her hair, then debated what to wear. Paul would undoubtedly call for her in the carriage, but Whitney had a deep yearning to ride beside him on horseback, as they occasionally had in years past. Her mind made up, she snatched a buttercup-yellow riding habit from the wardrobe.

She was ready when she heard Paul's carriage coming to a stop directly below her open bedroom window, but she made herself pace the length of her room ten times before she hurried out into the hallway and across the balcony.

Paul watched her coming down the stairs, a look of unconcealed appreciation on his handsome face as he surveyed her jaunty yellow riding habit and the yellow-and-white dotted silk shirt that peeked from beneath her open jacket. Around her neck she had tied a matching dotted scarf, knotting it on the side, with the ends flipped over her right shoulder. "How can you look so lovely so early?" he asked, taking both her hands in his as she stepped onto the polished foyer floor.

Whitney suppressed the urge to fling herself into his arms and smiled up at him instead. "Good morning," she said softly. "Shall we ride, rather than take the carriage? The stable is filled with horses, and you may have your choice."

"I'm afraid you'll have to ride over without me. I'll need the carriage to escort those females who seem to live in constant terror of falling from a horse." He inclined his head toward a dark shadow near the front door. "Clayton will ride with you and show you where we'll be."

Whitney panicked at the lump of disappointment and alarm swelling in her throat. She couldn't believe Paul was doing this. Since he'd invited her, and since the picnic was in her honor, his first obligation was to escort her there. Besides, only one of the girls in the neighborhood was afraid of horses—Elizabeth Ashton. She had a terrible feeling that appointing Clayton Westland as her substitute escort was Paul's way of demonstrating to her that he would not play the part of jealous suitor. Last night he had realized that she was trying to make him jealous, and this morning he was showing her that it hadn't worked.

With a sublime effort, Whitney forced herself to shrug lightly and smile. "You'll miss a lovely ride then. It's much too fine a day to be cooped up in a carriage."

"Clayton will show you the place," Paul repeated, studying her composed features. Drily, he added, "I gather that you two know each other well enough to be on a first-name basis?"

Whitney dragged her gaze toward the tall figure lounging in the doorway, and gritted her teeth to hide her loathing.

"I'm sure your father won't object if Clayton rides one of your horses," Paul said, already starting to leave.

Outside on the fourth step, he turned. "Take good care of my girl," he called to Clayton, and then he was gone, leaving Whitney slightly pacified and thoroughly mystified at being first cavalierly handed over into Clayton's custody, and then called "my girl."

Her bemused thoughts were interrupted by the deep voice she despised saying a quiet, "Good morning." Resentfully, Whitney snapped her attention to Clayton, who was still standing in the doorway. Biting back three nasty responses to his simple greeting, she passed a disdainful glance over his immaculate white shirt, which was open at the collar, his gray riding breeches, and his gleaming black boots. "Can you ride?" she asked icily.

"Good morning," he repeated with calm emphasis, still smiling at her.

Whitney clamped her mouth shut and brushed past him into the brilliant sunlight, leaving him to follow her or stay in the house, she didn't care which.

As she marched down the path leading around the back of the house toward the stable, he remained a pace behind her, but halfway there, he stepped in front of her, blocking her way. Smiling down at her, he said, "Do you treat every gentleman who steals a kiss from you with such animosity—or only me?"

Whitney looked at him with withering scorn. "Mr. Westland, in the first place, you are no 'gentleman.' In the second, I don't like you. Now, please get out of my way."

He remained there, studying her stormy face in thoughtful silence. "Kindly move out of the way and let me pass," Whitney repeated.

"If you will keep still long enough to allow me to do it, I would like to apologize for last night," he said calmly. "I can't remember the last time I apologized for anything, so I may be a bit awkward about it."

What an arrogant, conceited beast he was to think he could take liberties with her and then placate her with a few lukewarm words of apology. By telling her to "keep still" he completely banished Whitney's momentary inclination to hear him out anyway, and get it over with. "I won't accept any apology from you, awkward or otherwise. Now get out of my way!"

His face darkened with annoyance, and Whitney could almost feel his struggle to hold his temper in check. She glanced toward the stable to see if anyone would be within hearing if she needed help. Thomas was there, trying to hold a furious Dangerous Crossing who was lurching and trying to rear.

And revenge took the shape of a fiery black stallion.

The smile Whitney turned upon the angry man before her

was dazzling and genuine. "My manners have not been entirely beyond reproach either," Whitney said, trying desperately to look ruefully apologetic when she felt like laughing. "If you wish to apologize, I shall be most willing to accept it." Instantly, he looked suspicious, so Whitney prodded, "Or have you changed your mind?"

"I haven't changed my mind," he said quietly. Putting his hand beneath her chin, he tipped it up and said, "I am truly sorry if I frightened you last night. It was never my intention to hurt you, and I would like for us to be friends."

Whitney resisted the urge to slap his hand away and appeared to consider his offer. "If we're going to be friends, we should have something in common, should we not? I particularly love to ride. Are you an adequate horseman?"

"Adequate," he confirmed, subjecting her to a cool, appraising look.

Eager to be free of his scrutiny, Whitney pulled away and started down the path toward the stable. "I'll see to a horse for you," she called over her shoulder. Clayton Westland was going to have to ride that stallion, or else admit he was afraid to try it. Either way, his monstrous ego was going to take a beating, and Whitney felt he deserved every bit of what was in store for him.

By the time she reached Thomas, she was breathless from running. She threw a furtive glance over her shoulder, saw that Clayton was less than five paces behind her, and dropped her voice to an urgent whisper. "Have Dangerous Crossing saddled immediately, Thomas. Mr. Westland insists on riding him."

"What?" Thomas gasped, staring at Westland. "Are you certain?"

"Positive!" Whitney said, laughing silently as Thomas turned and walked into the stable. Feeling extremely pleased with herself, Whitney clasped her hands behind her back and strolled over to the white corral fence to stand beside Clayton. "I've arranged for you to ride our very finest horse," she told him.

Clayton studied her bright smile, but his attention was diverted by the sound of a scuffle from within the stable. Two violent oaths from a groom were followed by a yowl of pain, and Dangerous Crossing erupted into the enclosure, flinging one groom against the fence, then kicking savagely at the other.

"Isn't he wonderful?" Whitney rhapsodized, casting a mirthful sidewise glance at her intended victim. At that moment, the horse changed direction, charging for the rail where they stood, then swung around. Whitney jumped back just as his rear feet punched out, exploding against the fence like the crack of a cannon. With a tremor in her voice, she explained, "He's . . . ah . . . very spirited."

"So I see," Clayton agreed, shifting his impassive gaze from the nervous, sweating stallion to Whitney.

"If you're afraid to ride the stallion, simply say so," Whitney generously suggested. "I'm sure we can find you a more suitable mount . . . like Sugar Plum." Fighting back her laughter, she nodded sweetly toward the old brood mare who was nibbling contentedly at grass, her belly hanging down, and her backbone sticking up. Clayton followed her gaze, and a look of cold revulsion crossed his features. Instantly, Whitney decided it would be much more satisfying if Clayton Westland had to jog up to the picnickers on the ancient mare. "Thomas!" Whitney called, "Mr. Westland has decided to ride Sugar Plum instead, so—"

"The stallion will do," Clayton snapped at Thomas, then he swung his icy gaze on Whitney.

Defensively, she said, "Why don't you just tell me where the picnic is, and I'll go on ahead."

"I have no intention of doing that, nor do I intend to gratify your wish to see me lying on the ground under the stallion's hooves." Jerking his head toward Khan, who was being led out of the stable, he said curtly, "Get on your horse and keep him at the rail out of my way. I'm going to have enough on my hands without having to worry about you."

His arrogant assumption that he could ride the stallion wiped out Whitney's momentary trace of guilt. She mounted Khan and guided him to the rail at the far end of the enclosure. Transferring Khan's reins to her teeth, she reached up behind her neck, gathered her hair into a fist at her nape and then tugged her scarf loose, using it to tie her hair back.

Grooms and stablekeeps and three gardeners hurried to the enclosure, positioning themselves along the fence for the best view. Thomas and two grooms held the stallion's head while Clayton ran his hand along the horse's sleek neck, speaking quietly to him. The remembered feel of that same hand fondling her breast made Whitney flush with anger.

Clayton put his foot in the stirrup, then eased up and over, settling slowly, carefully into the saddle, avoiding any sudden movement that might add to the stallion's alarm. In spite of his caution, Dangerous Crossing snorted and jerked wildly at the men holding him. The last man who had used that particular saddle was shorter than Clayton and, for a moment, it looked to Whitney as if Crossing were going to rid himself of his unwelcome burden while the stirrup leathers were being lengthened.

Whitney laughed at the way the stallion was turning and twisting about. At any second, she expected Clayton to give up and dismount. Instead he gathered the reins and the grooms turned the stallion loose, then leapt out of the way.

All Clayton's attention was concentrated on the nervous, sweating stallion beneath him. "Easy now," he soothed, loosening the reins very slightly. Dangerous Crossing jerked his head furiously, trying to get the bit between his teeth as he danced sideways across the enclosure, threatening first to rear and then trying to get his head down to buck. "Easy now . . . Easy . . ." The voice calmed the horse's ragged nerves; the light contact on his reins held him firmly but not harshly under control.

Whitney watched in wide-eyed astonishment as the stallion fretted a bit and then smoothed out, easing into a flashy trot across the length of the enclosure. The stallion's ears were forward, and he looked as if he were almost enjoying himself, proud to be bearing the burden of the tall man atop him— until Clayton brushed the stallion's flank with the crop, signaling for a canter. Instantly Crossing jerked his head, bunching his hindquarters to buck.

"It's the crop, sir," Thomas called happily. "Drop it—that's all that's worrying him now."

For the moment, Whitney dismissed her grievances against the man. She was too fine a horsewoman herself to pretend to be unimpressed by what she had just witnessed. Clayton's expert handling of Dangerous Crossing filled her with admiring respect, and she made no effort to conceal it as the stallion trotted toward her. Her mouth curved into a smile as she started to pay him the tribute he deserved—only to have Clayton slap the crop into her outstretched hand and snap, "Sorry to disappoint you. Find someone else to play your nursery games with next time."

"You monster!" Whitney hissed, raising her arm; the crop sliced the air, missed Clayton's shoulder, and bit into the stallion's flank. Raging and violent, the stallion threw himself into the air, broke for the fence as if he were going to crash through it, and at the last possible moment, leapt it instead with the bit in his teeth—completely out of control.

"Oh dear God," Whitney whispered, watching horse and rider tearing across the rolling landscape. In belated shame, she looked away. The silent punishment she was heaping on herself for her childish attempt at vengeance was reinforced by Thomas, who flung himself across the corral, his face purple with fury. "Is this what you learned in France—to bring injury to strangers! Is it?" he roared. "No one will ever mount that horse again, you little fool!" He turned and ran for a mount to pursue the stallion.

It was all Whitney could do not to go after Thomas and explain that she'd intended to hit the rider, not the horse. Never the horse. Off to her distant left, the stallion was rapidly diminishing to a speck on the horizon, and there was no way to tell if the rider was still up. Glancing about her, Whitney saw disapproval on every servant's face before their eyes slid away from her.

She couldn't bear to remain here and suffer their silent accusation. She turned Khan and cantered from the enclosure, but once outside its boundary, she realized she hadn't any idea where to go. She drew Khan to a halt and hesitated.

She really ought to stay here and face the results of her wretched conduct. Would they bring Clayton back on a litter? If so, she must remain to lend whatever assistance she could.

She turned Khan back toward the stable, then brought him up short again. Could Clayton possibly remain on Dangerous Crossing and bring him back? She hoped so, but if that should be the case, Whitney had no desire to be present when he did return. Just imagining his righteous wrath made her hands tremble with fear. "Coward!" she hissed at herself, turning Khan and starting for the Sevarin house where she could inquire about the location of the picnic.

Khan tossed his head, tugging at the reins, eager for a run, but Whitney had no heart for speed, and she kept him at a sedate walk. Never had she felt so thoroughly obnoxious. Why, she wondered miserably, had she made a mess of her life the moment she set foot in England? How she hated herself for lapsing into the childish tempers she'd indulged in as a girl. After several minutes of harsh self-recrimination, her present predicament again intruded on her thoughts. How to atone for this calamity? Would the horse hurt himself and have to be destroyed? Whether the animal was injured or not, her father would never forgive her for her actions.

Her father! For the first time in her life, she'd seen approbation in his eyes when he looked at her, and now everything would be ruined. He would despise her for mistreating the horse, and if she tried to explain that she had meant to hit the man, he'd be even more furious. Somehow, she had to keep the tale from him. None of the servants would tell him, of that Whitney was reasonably certain. Clayton Westland might, but perhaps if she begged him not to, pleaded with him not to . . .

Her unhappy reflections were interrupted by the sound of hooves beating a quick staccato behind her, and Whitney looked over her right shoulder, gaping at the sight of Clayton atop a lathered Dangerous Crossing who was closing rapidly on her.

Out of pure reflex, Whitney raised her crop to send Khan bolting ahead, then checked herself and dropped her arm.

She would stay here and face the man, admit her fault—a lot of good it would do to deny it anyway!

As Clayton drew abreast, Whitney beheld a face of such dark, menacing rage that she shuddered. In one fluid motion, Clayton swooped down, grabbed Khan's right rein, and hauled both horses to a sharp stop. "You can let go of my rein," Whitney said softly. "I'm not going to run."

"Shut up!" he hissed. Since he maintained his hold on Khan's rein, Whitney had no choice but to ride quietly beside him while he let Dangerous Crossing cool. In the oppressive silence, she tried to think of something to say to break the tension, but the only thing she could think of was to comment on how well Clayton had managed the stallion. Under the circumstances, however, she didn't think this was an appropriate time to say, "Well done, Mr. Westland!"

At the remains of an old stone wall a few yards from where they'd first met beside the stream, Clayton halted the horses and dismounted. He tied the stallion with swift, precise movements then strode to Whitney, jerked Khan's left rein from her hand, and tied him on the opposite side of the wall from the stallion. He turned on his heel, snapped, "Get down!" to Whitney, and stalked toward the old sycamore tree atop the knoll.

Whitney took judicious note of the taut set of his jaw, his long, purposeful strides, and felt the first tendril of fear coil in the pit of her stomach. "I prefer to stay here," she said unsteadily, watching him over her shoulder.

As if he didn't hear her, he flung his riding gloves to the grass and jerked off his jacket. He sat down with his back against the tree and drew one leg up at the knee, resting his arm across it. In a voice like the crack of a whiplash, he said, "I told you to get down off that horse."

Whitney reluctantly did as she was bidden and slid awkwardly down from Khan, stepped onto the boulder next to her, then gingerly to the ground. She waited there beside her horse, enduring the icy blast of his gaze. It dawned on her that he was striving for control of his anger, and Whitney prayed he would gain it. His eyes raked over her, riveting on a spot just below her right hand. Following his stare, Whitney realized she still held the crop. It slid from her numbed fingers.

"I believe there are several things which you enjoy as much as riding," he remarked with scathing sarcasm.

Whitney nervously clenched and unclenched her hands.

"Come, come, don't be shy," he prodded in a soft, menacing voice. "You're a young woman of many pleasures —you enjoyed humbling me into an apology, did you not?"

Whitney nodded, then winced at the blaze of fury her answer ignited in his hard features. Quickly she tried to shake her head to cover the admission she'd just made.

"No, don't deny it. You enjoyed it tremendously. And I think we can assume that besides riding and apologies, you also enjoy using the crop. Correct?"

How could she answer these questions? Whitney thought frantically. She flicked a glance at Khan, longing to flee.

In a silky, dangerous voice, he warned, "Don't try it."

Whitney stayed where she was. She didn't think she could get away, knew, in fact, that if she tried, she'd only enrage him further. Besides, if she didn't let him vent his wrath now, he'd undoubtedly go to her father. She steeled herself to endure the rest of his verbal assault.

"You wanted us to have something in common if we were going to be friends. You wanted us to enjoy the same things, didn't you?"

Whitney swallowed convulsively and nodded.

"Pick up the crop!" he clipped.

Cold fear raced down Whitney's spine, and her pulse accelerated wildly. In all her life, she'd never encountered such controlled, purposeful rage. She bent down and picked up the crop with shaking fingers.

"Bring it to me," he rapped. Whitney froze at the sudden, blinding realization of what he intended, and he said in a terrifyingly pleasant tone, "Which will you have, your father or me? Do we settle this between us now, or would you prefer that I take it up with him?"

Whitney frantically considered her choice: physical punishment meted out by this man whom she despised, or the mental anguish of reopening old hostilities with her father. Her choice was really no choice at all.

Rather than give her tormentor the satisfaction of seeing her quaking fear, Whitney reverted to an old girlhood habit of putting her chin up and assuming an appearance of remote indifference. Haughtily, she walked over and held the crop out to him like a queen bestowing the sword of knighthood, her disdainful green eyes clashing with his icy gray ones.

"Now we are both going to share your favorite amusements: Riding, using the crop, and apologizing. You will 'ride' my knee, I will use the crop, and you are going to apologize. Do you understand the rules of our little game?"

Whitney's gaze slid unwillingly to the black riding crop in his hand, then jerked back to his tanned face. She did not deign to reply.

"Lie across my lap, Whitney." He politely extended his hand to assist her, and in her terror, Whitney unthinkingly accepted it. She knelt beside him, glaring at him in stiff hatred. Cocking a dark eyebrow, he nodded meaningfully at his lap.

Drowning in an ocean of mortification, Whitney lowered herself into the humiliating position. His hard thighs pressed against her churning stomach; a beetle scurried through the blades of grass inches from her nose.

Above her, she heard his voice. "I will stop when you apologize. Not before." He raised his arm and Whitney wondered wildly how much protection her riding habit would provide, then had her answer as the crop whined through the air, slicing against her clothing, welting her tender flesh. He paused, waiting. For her apology.

Whitney gritted her teeth; he could beat her senseless but she'd never give him the satisfaction of an apology. Never! His arm came up another time, the crop landed mercilessly across her buttocks. Another pause . . .

Whitney counted through streaks of vivid pain—three times, four, five. By now she was sobbing. The sixth time her body jerked and a strangled cry wrenched from her. His arm lifted, and she screamed "Stop!" then cursed herself because he had already flung the crop away.

He grasped her roughly by the shoulders and turned her in his arms to sit across his lap. Whitney tried to pull away, but his arms tightened, and his hand lifted to hold her face pressed to his chest. Her ribs heaved and scalding tears raced down her cheeks, soaking through the front of his shirt as she wept, more from impotent fury than from pain. As if he were soothing a child, he began to stroke her hair. Whitney angrily shoved his hand away, but he ignored her and continued.

The minutes passed, and Whitney had just gotten control of herself when his hand touched her chin, tipping her face up to his. Glaring at him through a haze of wrathful tears, she whispered, "I hate you!"

"I know you do," he said quietly. It registered on Whitney that there was neither triumph nor satisfaction on his face and, since she could find nothing else in his expression to stoke the flames of her animosity, she looked away, staring fixedly off to the left, occasionally wiping at her tear-streaked face with her fingertips.

"Look at me," he ordered gently.

"No!" Whitney retorted. "If I do, I'll scratch your eyes out, so help me!"

"You're not nearly so angry with me as you are with yourself."

"How much would you care to bet?" Whitney snapped, but she could feel her anger ebbing as she looked at Dangerous Crossing, whose satin blackness was now splashed with huge, sweaty white patches. It was a miracle that the horse hadn't injured himself, that the rider had been expert enough to stay on him, and wise enough to continue riding him instead of returning him to the stable. It was a double miracle that both horse and rider hadn't been seriously injured.

He was right: she was bitterly angry with herself for what she had done even if her regret was more for the sake of the horse than the man. She finally realized that Clayton was waiting for her to apologize, and since she wanted nothing more than to get away from him, she said tonelessly, "I never meant to hit the horse, I meant to hit you. But either way, I suppose it was irresponsible and dangerous, a childish act deserving of a child's punishment."

"Thank you for that," he said almost tenderly.

To be guilty and punished, to feel remorse and then be forgiven was a sequence of events totally missing from Whitney's childhood experience. Whenever she had apologized to her father, he had listened and then launched into a fresh tirade about her misbehavior, and Whitney had expected about the same from Clayton. She stared at him, hardly able to believe what she saw and felt. His gray eyes were full of warmth, and he was smiling at her with gentle understanding.

Suddenly, Whitney felt as if they were the best, the closest, of friends—as if there was some special bond between them now. The feeling stunned her, then surged through her, sweeping everything away in its path. "I'm terribly sorry about . . ."

"No more," he interrupted softly. "It's forgotten."

Whitney knew, as he slowly bent his head to her, that he was going to kiss her, but instead of drawing away she shyly lifted her face and met him halfway, somehow seeking proof of forgiveness. His lips came down to caress hers in a long, tender, undemanding kiss.

Even when the kiss deepened and her lips were being sensually shaped and molded to his, Whitney knew he would let her pull away if she tried. Instead her hands crept up his chest, twining around his neck, and everything changed.

His hands tugged the scarf loose from her hair and tangled in the luxuriant tresses. Tenderly cupping her face between both his hands, he gazed down into her melting green eyes. "My God, you are sweet," he whispered. Whitney's heart skipped a beat, then began to hammer as he slowly, deliberately buried his lips in hers once again. He kissed her long and lingeringly, slow, compelling kisses that made her head swim. His tongue flicked over her lips, teasing at first—then urging, insisting that she part them and, the moment she did, plunging inside to intimately explore her mouth while his hands moved down her back, finding the place where the crop had welted, lifting her up and tighter to him, then gently soothing away the sting.

Jolt after jolt of wild sensation rocketed through Whitney from her neck to her knees, leaving her trembling violently and clinging to him. The world tilted as he twisted her halfway around to lie in the grass beside him, wrapped in his strong arms. He leaned over her, and Whitney shook her head in feeble protest: "We can't . . ."

His mouth came down hard on hers, silencing her objection, taking her lips in a fierce, devouring kiss. He parted her lips, teasing and tormenting her with his tongue as it plunged gently, then retreated, until Whitney, in a fever of longing, touched her own tongue to his lips.

He groaned and crushed her tighter to the hard length of his body, drawing her tongue into his mouth and caressing it with his own. When his mouth left hers it was to explore her ear before tracing its way across her cheek and covering her lips again. His hand left a trail of glowing warmth as it slid down her throat, across her breasts, and he began unfastening her thin shirt, seeking the soft swells beneath.

The touch of his strong fingers on her naked flesh penetrated Whitney's passion-drugged senses, jerking her back to reality. Frantically, she shook her head, trying to tear her mouth from his as he pulled down her chemise, baring her swelling breasts to his hand.

"Don't," he commanded in a throbbing whisper, deepening the wildly consuming kiss while his hand fondled her breasts, pushing them upward, teasing the sensitive nipples until they stood erect and proud against his palm.

And then, without warning, he stopped.

Kissed and caressed into dazed insensibility, Whitney watched his smoldering gaze lift from her ivory breasts to her face. "If we don't stop now, little one," he murmured in an odd, strained voice, "I'm going to be too caught up in finishing what I began, to turn back." Bending his head, he kissed the top of each soft breast before reluctantly drawing up her chemise.

Lying beside her, propped up on an elbow, Clayton touched her cheek with a forefinger, lightly tracing the elegant curve of her cheekbone. He adored her spirit, her freshness; she was warmth and awakening passion, ready to be taken—as the throbbing ache in his loins reminded him. She was everything he had known she would be and much, much more: Headstrong, sweet, fiery-tempered, impertinent and witty . . . a treasure of exciting contrasts. *His* treasure!

Whitney basked in the warmth of his slow, lazy smile and reached up, laying her hand against his hard chest. He covered her hand with his, holding it pressed against his shirt over the steady thudding of his heart.

Dreamily, she heard the sounds of the early fall day drifting about them. A squirrel skittered up a tree with a nut to be stored for the winter. Crickets serenaded in hoarse harmony. One of the horses stamped fitfully. Whitney lay there, wondering why she'd never really noticed how extraordinarily handsome he was.

His next words brought her floating spirit plummeting back to earth: "It's time to go—there'll be explanations due everyone as it is." He chuckled at the look of disappointment that crossed her lovely forehead and pressed a bold kiss on the peak of her breast. "Brazen little hussy!" he teased.

Whitney lurched to a sitting position, her face flushed, and he began smoothing her hair. "Of course," she said, surging to her feet. "We—we should have left long ago."

Clayton reached for her but she turned on her heel and walked swiftly away. As she started to climb on her horse, he caught her at the waist and drew her back against his chest, wrapping his arms around her from behind. "Little one," he chuckled, nuzzling her neck, "there will be many times to come when I will hold you much longer, and much closer." Soothingly, he added, "I promise."

Whitney could hardly believe her ears! After calling her a brazen hussy, he had sympathetically promised to provide further intimacies to satiate her lust! How could she have forgotten how utterly amoral, how supremely conceited he was? She pulled away and glanced at him over her shoulder. With as much disdain as she could muster in her humiliated confusion, she said, "Do you think so?"

Clayton's grin was tigerish. "Indeed I do."

"Don't depend on it," she said, turning her face away and gathering Khan's reins. He lifted her effortlessly into the sidesaddle and let his hand boldly rest on her thigh. Whitney's voice shook as she asked, "Where is the picnic?"

"At the little clearing between Sevarin's place and mine," he replied, swinging up onto Dangerous Crossing's back.

More than anything, Whitney wanted to gallop Khan away, to put as much distance between herself and Clayton Westland as possible. At the same time, she wanted to conceal how deeply she was hurt. So, with brittle gaiety, she called, "See you there," and turned Khan into a tight circle, urging him into a lunging gallop. She rode with her hair tossing wildly behind her, letting the wind cool her flushed face.

She could have wept with shame. "Brazen little hussy" he'd called her, and hussy she'd been! Letting him kiss her in such a way—and oh, God, touch her like that. And that *bastard* thought he was rewarding her by promising to hold her much closer and much longer in the future! Where was her pride, her sense of right and wrong, to have allowed him such liberties? She felt like such a horrid fool for lying there desiring him. And he had known exactly how she felt. He was undoubtedly an expert at making women desire him.

In the distance ahead the picnickers came into view, their gaily colored garments dotting the gently rolling hillside behind them. Even from so far away, Whitney could almost pick out Paul's silhouette. Paul! She groaned aloud thinking of how he would despise her if he ever learned what had just happened at the stream. She'd be ruined in Paul's eyes. In everyone's eyes.

Whitney glanced behind her and saw that Clayton was about ten lengths away. In a sudden frenzy to get to the picnic as quickly as possible, without appearing to be fleeing in panic, Whitney raised her crop in a gesture of challenge and called over her shoulder, "Shall we?"

"If you think you have a chance," Clayton laughed, then shouted, "I'll give you ten lengths. Go ahead."

Whitney considered rejecting his offer of a handicap, but

decided that where *he* was concerned, winning by any means available was acceptable. Leaning forward over Khan's neck, she tapped him with her heel, and he bolted forward. His strides lengthened out, and the ground flew by beneath her.

As she neared the picnickers, Whitney looked over her shoulder to see what kind of a lead she was holding. Disgust mingled with surprise, for the stallion had gained back nine of the ten paces. For a few seconds, Whitney thought she was still going to win, but at the very last moment, the stallion closed the gap and finished a nose in front of Khan.

The horses leapt about beneath them as a groom ran forward to take the reins, then help her dismount. Whitney settled her skirts and, pretending complete indifference to Clayton's existence, started to walk past him.

He leaned down from his horse and chucked her familiarly under the chin. "I won." He grinned.

The groom, who had bent to examine Khan's right front foot, glanced up and politely said, "The lady's horse was running with a stone in his hoof, sir."

Whitney was about to pounce on that excuse, but Paul's arrival interrupted her. "Where the deuce have you two been?"

"We had some trouble with the stallion," Clayton calmly replied as he dismounted.

Paul glanced skeptically from the docile black horse to Whitney's flushed, angry face. "I was worried about you," he said.

"Were you? There was no need," Whitney murmured, positive she looked as guilty as she felt.

He led her over to a light blue blanket, seated her beside Emily and Michael Archibald, then sat down next to her, with Elizabeth and Peter across from them.

Clayton accepted a glass of wine from a servant and sauntered over to the blanket directly across from theirs, seating himself beside Margaret Merryton and another couple. Whitney saw the bright smile that Margaret beamed on him as he settled beside her. If Margaret's eyes weren't perpetually narrowed with malice, Whitney thought, she would be a very pretty girl. Right now, however, the hazel eyes were slits of hatred as they turned toward Whitney. "If you were racing, you lost, Whitney." She smirked.

"We were, and she did," Clayton confirmed promptly, his laughing gaze daring Whitney to deny it.

"In the first place, my horse was running with a bad foreleg," Whitney retorted "Secondly, if I'd been riding the stallion, I think I'd have won by a greater margin."

"If you'd been riding that stallion, young lady, we'd be summoning your relatives to your bedside," he contradicted, grinning.

"Mr. Westland," Whitney said, "I could handle that stallion *and* get a better performance from him than you did."

"If you think so, I'll ride one of my own horses, and you may test your skill with the stallion any time you want a rematch."

Goaded by the mocking amusement in his eyes, Whitney snatched up the gauntlet of challenge. "A flat course," she specified. "No high jumps. The stallion knows nothing about jumping yet."

"He did rather well in clearing several fences today, as I recall," Clayton reminded her drily. "However, it will be as you wish. You choose the course."

"Aren't you taking on a little more than you can handle?" Paul asked, his forehead furrowed in concern.

Whitney tossed a vengeful glance at Clayton and said with more conviction than she really felt, "Certainly not. I'll win easily."

"Are you planning to wear men's breeches and ride astride? Or will you go barefoot and try to stand on his back?" Margaret taunted viciously.

As if by mutual agreement, everyone else began talking at once, drowning out Margaret's voice, but Whitney heard snatches of what she was saying to Clayton and the other couple: ". . . disgraced her father . . . scandalized the village . . ."

The servants began to distribute baskets of cold chicken, ham, cheese, and apples and pears. Whitney determinedly shook off the pall of Margaret's spite and strove to make something enjoyable of what was left of her day. She listened to the light raillery Emily was exchanging with her husband, Michael. "Whitney and I made a bet when we were very young," she was telling him. "The first of us to marry had to pay the other a forfeit of £5."

"That's absolutely right!" Whitney smiled. "I had forgotten."

"Since it was I who influenced her to marry me," Michael Archibald said, winking at Whitney, "I suppose I am honor-bound to pay her forfeit."

"Indeed you are," Whitney returned. "And I hope that won't be the last time Emily allows you to influence her, my lord."

"So do I!" Baron Archibald replied with such exaggerated despair that Whitney burst out laughing.

Paul leaned close, and Whitney looked up at him, traces of laughter still lingering in her eyes. "Are you planning to allow *me* to influence *you?*" he asked.

It was so near to a declaration of his intentions that Whitney could hardly believe she'd heard him correctly. "That depends," she said in a whisper, unable to tear her gaze from his compelling blue eyes. A fierce gust of wind blew up, tossing her hair wildly about her face and shoulders. Absently, Whitney reached behind her for the yellow and white dotted scarf that should have been holding her hair back.

"Are you looking for this?" Clayton drawled, pulling her scarf from his pocket and holding it toward her.

Paul's jaw tightened, and Whitney snatched the scarf out of Clayton's hand. She knew that Clayton had just deliberately caused everyone to wonder not only about how her scarf came to be in his pocket, but about their delayed arrival at the picnic as well, and to her consternation, she felt a guilty flush creeping up her cheeks. The idea of doing him bodily harm filled Whitney with morbid delight. She would have thoroughly enjoyed running him through with a sword or blowing his head off with a gun or seeing him hanging from a tree.

Late in the afternoon when the last of the picnickers had departed, Paul instructed a groom to ride Khan, and he took Whitney home in his gleaming carriage. The horses pranced down the dry, dusty lane with Paul handling the reins in preoccupied silence.

"Paul, are you angry with me?" Whitney ventured cautiously.

"Yes, and you know *why* I am."

Whitney did know, and she was torn between worry and happiness. It was possible, just possible, that Clayton Westland was providing the impetus Paul needed to declare himself without delay. All day, Paul's loverlike jealousy had been unmistakable.

In the drive at the front of her house, Paul pulled the horses to a stop and turned toward her, resting his arm on the back of the seat behind her. "I don't remember telling you how beautiful you look today," he said.

"Thank you," Whitney replied with surprised pleasure.

He grinned suddenly. "I'll call for you at eleven tomorrow morning. We'll talk about it then."

"About how beautiful I looked today?" Whitney teased.

"No, about why I'm angry."

She sighed. "I'd rather talk about the other."

"I'm sure you would," Paul said with a chuckle as he climbed down and came around to help her alight.

Paul arrived at precisely eleven the following morning. In the doorway of the drawing room, Whitney stopped, scarcely able to believe he was actually here, calling for her, exactly as she used to dream he would be! He looked incredibly handsome as he laughed at some remark of Lady Anne's.

"I like your young man," Anne whispered to Whitney as she left.

"He isn't mine yet," Whitney whispered back, but she was smiling optimistically.

The sky was bright blue with a fresh breeze that gently ruffled Paul's blond hair as they toured the country roads in

Paul's well-sprung carriage, talking and laughing, stopping occasionally to admire a particularly pleasing view of the hilly terrain stretching out on both sides of the road. A few of the trees were already exchanging the lush green leaves of summer for the bright golds and oranges of early fall, and for Whitney, it was a halcyon day.

Paul was charming and entertaining, treating her as if she were made of fragile porcelain, as if she weren't the same female who used to catapult from one misadventure to the next near calamity. And Whitney was scrupulously careful to say nothing which might remind him of the young girl she had been. Even now, years later, it still made her cringe with embarrassment when she recalled how she had tried to kiss him and begged him to wait for her.

They had luncheon with Paul's mother, and although Whitney had dreaded the idea at first, it turned out to be a very pleasant meal.

Afterward, they strolled across the lawn to the edge of the woods. At Paul's suggestion, Whitney sat on a swing suspended from a stout oak branch.

"Why were you and Westland so late getting to the picnic yesterday?" he demanded without preamble.

Whitney started, then shrugged, trying to appear bewildered and unconcerned, when she was neither. "We took the stallion and he gave us trouble."

"Whitney, I find that very difficult to believe. I've ridden with Westland; he's no novice around horses. And yesterday he seemed perfectly docile and well-mannered."

"Who seemed docile?" Whitney teased, trying desperately to lighten his mood. "The stallion? Or Mr. Westland?"

"I was referring to the stallion's behavior, but now that you've mentioned it, I would rather hear about Westland's."

"Paul, for heaven's sake!" she almost pleaded. "You know perfectly well that some horses are completely unpredictable and can give even the most experienced horsemen trouble managing them."

"Then perhaps you will explain to me why, if that horse is

so damned difficult to handle, you agreed to ride him in a race against Westland?"

"Oh that. Well, he taunted me until I could hardly refuse." Through her lowered lashes, Whitney stole a glance at Paul's grim, dubious expression. Under the circumstances, she thought it might be wise—even expected—for her to display a degree of righteous indignation. "Paul, I can't abide the man, and I—I don't think it's nice of you to quiz me like this. It's unfair and improper."

Unexpectedly, he grinned. "I never thought I'd see the day when you were conscious of propriety." Without warning, he pulled her off of the swing and into his arms. "God, you are beautiful!" he whispered.

Whitney caught her breath and held it, thinking stupidly over and over, *He's going to kiss me!* She was so nervous that she felt a giggle welling up inside of her as his head slowly descended to hers. But at the first brush of his warm, smooth lips on hers, all traces of laughter vanished.

She tried to keep her hands at her sides, but they slid of their own volition part way up his chest. She held back as best she could, afraid to abandon herself to the kiss for fear that Paul might somehow be offended by the depth of her feeling.

But Paul wouldn't let her remain uninvolved. He tightened his arms, holding her imprisoned against the hard wall of his chest, kissing her expertly, his mouth moving insistently over hers, sometimes teasing and gentle, then hungry and demanding. By the time he finally let her go, Whitney's legs were weak. With a sinking heart, she realized that she had just been kissed by someone who knew a great deal about kissing and who undoubtedly had stored up a wealth of practice. No wonder he had always been so popular, so sought after and dreamed about, by the girls in the neighborhood.

He was watching her, his expression pleased and confident. "You do that very well," Whitney complimented, hoping to sound as if she were competent to judge.

"Thank you," Paul said, looking mildly irritated. "Is that conclusion based upon your vast experience in France?"

Whitney sat down on the swing, smiled at him, and said absolutely nothing. Pushing hard with the toe of her slipper, she sent the swing backward. On the second sweep, Paul's strong hands shot out, caught her at the waist and plucked her unceremoniously off her moving chair and into his arms. "You infuriating, outrageous brat." He chuckled. "If I don't watch myself I'll be more insane about you than those mincing fops in Paris were."

"They weren't," Whitney protested weakly as his mouth covered hers, "mincing fops."

"Good," he murmured huskily, "because I would hate being in such poor company."

Whitney's heart somersaulted. "Meaning?" she whispered against his lips.

"Meaning," Paul answered, his arms tightening around her, his mouth beginning to move hungrily over hers, "I already am insane about you."

Two hours later, Whitney floated dreamily into the house, inquired after her aunt and was informed by Sewell that her aunt, her father, and Mr. Westland were together in her father's study. She shot a cautious glance down the hall to be certain she hadn't been seen, then hurried up the stairs to her room. Nothing, absolutely nothing, would spoil her happiness, and seeing Clayton Westland was about the only thing that could do it. With a sigh of relief, Whitney closed the door to her room and flopped across the bed, hugging her memories of the afternoon to her heart.

Tears sparkled in Lady Anne's eyes as she curtsied stiffly to the Duke of Claymore in Martin's study. With long, determined strides he turned and left the room, and still she stood there, her chest painfully constricted around a knot of emotion.

Chair legs scraped against the floor as Martin Stone stood up and came around from behind his desk. "I would not have told you about all this yet; however, his grace felt that you should be made aware of the arrangements. I hope I don't have to remind you that you gave your solemn word to remain silent about everything we discussed?"

Anne stared at him, her throat filled with tears. She started to raise her hand in a helpless, beseeching gesture, then let it drop to her side.

Apparently encouraged by her silence, Martin softened his tone slightly. "I will admit to you that I was not best pleased when I saw that you had accompanied Whitney, but since you're here, you could be of great assistance. I want you to express approval of the duke to Whitney. She respects your opinion, and the sooner she develops a fondness for him, the better off we'll all be."

At last, Anne found her voice. *"Develops a fondness for* him?" she echoed in terse disbelief. "Whitney loathes the air he breathes!"

"Rubbish! She scarcely knows him."

"She knows him well enough to despise him. I have it from her own lips."

"Then I shall rely upon you to change her opinion."

"Martin, are you blind? Whitney is in love with Paul Sevarin."

"Paul Sevarin is hard put to hold his own place together," Martin snorted. "All he could offer her is a life as a house drudge."

"Nevertheless, it is still Whitney's decision to make."

"Poppycock! The decision was mine to make, and I made it."

Anne opened her mouth to argue, but Martin cut her off in a savage voice. "Let me explain something to you, Madam. I signed a legal agreement drawn up by Claymore's attorneys, and I accepted £100,000 from the duke as his part of the bargain. I have already paid off my creditors and spent more than half the money. *Half,*" he emphasized. "If Whitney should refuse to honor the agreement, I can't return the man's money. In which case, Claymore could, and would, bring me up on charges of fraud, theft, and God knows what else. And if *that* doesn't concern you, let me put it a different way: Just how happy do you think Whitney would be married to Sevarin, while everyone for a hundred miles sniggers and gossips about her father who is rotting away in a dungeon?"

Having delivered this diatribe, he stalked to the door. "I shall expect your cooperation in all this, for Whitney's sake, if not for mine."

Chapter Thirteen

WHITNEY GREETED THE NEWS THAT CLAYTON WAS TO DINE WITH them the following evening with all the enthusiasm she would have felt for a public flogging. Nevertheless, her father liked the man, and Whitney was prepared to endure him for her father's sake.

They dined at eight o'clock, with her father at one end of the long, damask-covered table and Lady Anne at the other. Which left Whitney sitting across from Clayton. Using the heavy silver candelabra in the center of the table as a barrier between herself and her unwanted dinner companion, she maintained a cool, formal silence. Several times during the meal, Clayton made inflammatory remarks which she knew were deliberately intended to rile her into entering the dinner table conversation, but she meticulously ignored him.

Surprisingly, the other three managed quite well without her, and the conversation became animated as the evening wore on.

As soon as dessert was cleared away, Whitney stood and excused herself, pleading an impending attack of the vapors. She thought she saw Clayton's lips twitch, but when her narrowed gaze searched his face, he seemed to be regarding her with polite concern and nothing else. "Whitney has the constitution of an ox," her father was reassuring his guest as Whitney walked out of the room.

During the next two weeks, Paul called for her every day. Her life took on a dreamlike quality, spoiled only by the frequency with which she had to endure Clayton's company in the evenings. However, she bore it without complaint for her father's sake. No matter what Clayton said or did, Whitney was unfailingly cool, polite, and distant. Her withdrawn formality pleased her father (who mistook it for ladylike reserve); irritated Clayton (who apparently never mistook anything); and, for no reason Whitney could understand, seemed to worry her aunt.

In fact, Whitney thought Anne was acting very peculiarly lately. She spent endless hours writing letters to every capital in Europe where she thought Uncle Edward might be, and her moods shifted constantly from nervous animation to dazed solemnity.

Whitney decided that the cause of her aunt's odd behavior was loneliness for her husband. "I know how dreadfully you must miss Uncle Edward," Whitney sympathized one evening two weeks later, when they were to dine with Clayton at *his* house for the first time.

Aunt Anne seemed not to have heard, as she concentrated on selecting a gown for Whitney to wear. Finally she chose a gorgeous peach-colored crepe, scalloped at the low neckline, with wider scallops at the hem. "I missed Paul dreadfully the entire time I was in France, so I know how you must feel," Whitney continued, her voice muffled by the peach gown which Clarissa was lowering over her head.

"Childhood romances," her aunt replied, "always seem so real, so enduring, when we are separated from the object of our affection. But usually, when we return, we find that our dreams and memories quite surpassed reality."

Whitney jerked around without a thought for poor Clarissa, who was busily applying a brush to Whitney's long hair. "You can't think Paul is a 'childhood romance.' Well, he was of course, but not any longer. We are going to be married, precisely as I always dreamed we would be. And very soon."

"Has Paul mentioned marriage to you?"

When Whitney shook her head and started to reply, Anne drew a long breath and interrupted her. "I mean, if it was his intention to offer for you, he's surely had sufficient time by now to do so."

"I'm certain he's only waiting for the right moment to declare himself. And I haven't really been home very long, a few weeks only."

"You've known each other for years, darling," Aunt Anne contradicted gently. "I've seen matches between two perfect strangers arranged in the length of time we've been back here. Perhaps Mr. Sevarin merely enjoys paying court to a lovely young woman who is all the rage, right now. Many men do, you know."

Whitney smiled confidently and planted a kiss on her aunt's cheek. "You worry too much for my happiness, Aunt Anne. Paul is on the verge of offering, you'll see."

But as their open carriage rocked along beneath the shadowy oaks toward Clayton's house, Whitney's optimism began to ebb. Idly, she toyed with a long strand of her hair which hung in gentle waves over her shoulders and midway down her back where it curled at the ends. Could it be that Paul merely enjoyed escorting the current neighborhood beauty? she wondered. Unemotionally, Whitney knew she had usurped that title from Elizabeth Ashton, although she didn't derive nearly as much satisfaction from the knowledge as she once thought she would. Invitations to local card parties and soirées were arriving with flattering regularity, and whenever Whitney accepted, Paul either escorted her or spent most of the evening at her side. In fact, the only person in the neighborhood who rivaled Whitney's popularity was Clayton Westland, and she saw him everywhere she went.

Whitney shrugged the thought of her despised neighbor aside. Why *didn't* Paul declare himself? she wondered. And why didn't he ever speak of love, if not marriage? Whitney was still searching for answers to those troublesome questions when they arrived at Clayton's home.

The front door was opened by a stiff-backed butler who eyed the trio down the length of his nose. "Good evening," he intoned majestically. "My master is expecting you." Whitney was at first shocked, then secretly amused by his lofty manner, which would have been far more appropriate if he were the butler of some grand personage, opening the front door of a magnificent mansion.

As Aunt Anne and her father were being divested of their outer garments, Clayton came striding down the hall into the small foyer. He went directly to Whitney. "May I?" he inquired politely, stepping behind her, his long fingers resting lightly on the peach-colored satin cape covering her shoulders.

"Thank you," Whitney said civilly. Pushing back the wide hood, she unfastened the satin frog closing at her throat, releasing the cape with as much speed as possible. The touch of his hands reminded her of the way he had held and caressed her the day of the picnic, the way he had promised to hold her much closer for far longer as if he were offering a sweet to a child. Conceited ass!

Her father detained her aunt to admire some carved ivory objects adorning a hall table while Clayton showed Whitney to a medium-sized room that apparently served as a combined salon and study.

A fire burned cheerily on the wide hearth, chasing away the night chill and adding its lively glow to the light of the candles in sconces above the mantle. The room was sparsely but rather grandly furnished to suit masculine tastes. One wall was taken up by a long, richly carved oak cabinet which bore a pair of massively splendid sterling silver candelabra, one at each end. The top of the cabinet was inlaid with marble squares, each of which was surrounded by strips of intricately carved wood. In the center stood an enormous sterling tea service unlike any Whitney had ever seen. It was so immense that Sewell, their butler, would never be able to lift it, let alone carry it with dignity. Whitney smiled a little as she visualized the ever-correct Sewell staggering into a room, laboring beneath the weight of the tray.

"Dare I hope that smile denotes a softening in your opinion of me?" Clayton drawled lazily.

Whitney snapped her head around. "I have no opinion of you," she lied.

"You have a very strong opinion of me, Miss Stone," he said, chuckling as he seated her in a comfortable wingback chair upholstered in soft burgundy leather. Instead of sitting down across from her in the other wingback chair, the man had the unmitigated gall to perch atop the arm of hers and casually stretch his right arm across the back of it.

"If there is a shortage of comfortable seating, I will be happy to stand," Whitney said coldly, already starting to rise.

Clayton's hands caught her shoulders, pressing her back into the chair as he compliantly stood up. "Miss Stone," he said, grinning, and gazing down into her angry upturned face, "you have the tongue of an adder."

"Thank you," Whitney said calmly. "And you have the manners of a barbarian."

Inexplicably, he threw back his head and shouted with laughter. Still chuckling, he reached down and affectionately rumpled the shining hair atop her head, which brought Whitney surging to her feet, torn between slapping his face and giving him a swift kick in the shin. Her father and aunt found them still standing face to face, Clayton's expression boldly admiring, while Whitney glared at him in frigid silence.

"Well, I see you two are having a devilish pleasant chat," her father announced jovially, which made Clayton's lips twitch and Whitney almost, but not quite, burst out laughing.

Dinner was a feast that would have done credit to a royal chef. Whitney toyed with the delicious lobster in light wine sauce, feeling vastly uncomfortable seated at the opposite end of the table from Clayton, as if she were mistress of his home. He was playing the host tonight with a natural, relaxed elegance that Whitney reluctantly admired, and even Lady Anne had unbent completely as she carried on an animated political discussion with him.

During the fifth course, Whitney broke her long-enduring, self-imposed silence. Clayton had taunted and goaded her all evening until she finally jumped into the conversation in order to argue in favor of educating females in the same manner as males. "What use is geometry to a woman who will spend her time embroidering handkerchiefs for her husband?" he had challenged.

Whitney accused him of thinking like his grandfather, and he laughingly retaliated by calling her a bluestocking.

"Blasted bluestocking," Whitney amplified with an amused smile. "It is what gentlemen such as you, who cherish antiquated ideas, call any female whose vocabulary contains more than the three acceptable phrases."

He grinned. "And what three phrases would those be?"

"The phrases are 'yes, my lord'; 'no, my lord'; and 'as you wish, my lord.'" She lifted her chin and said, "I find it sad that most of my sex have been trained from babyhood to sound exactly like witless female butlers."

"So do I," Clayton admitted quietly. Before Whitney had recovered from her astonishment, he added, "However, the fact remains that no matter how well-educated a woman is, she will someday have to submit to the authority of her lord and master."

"*I* don't think so," Whitney said, ignoring her father's anguished, quelling looks. "And what's more, I shall never, *ever* call any man my lord and master."

"Is that right?" he mocked.

Whitney was about to answer when her father suddenly launched into a monologue on the merits of irrigating farms, which surprised Whitney and visibly annoyed Clayton.

During dessert, Clayton again returned his attention to her. "I was wondering if there is any particular game you would enjoy playing after dinner." His gray eyes locked onto hers in silent, laughing communication as he added meaningfully, ". . . other than those little 'games' you and I have already played together?"

"Yes," Whitney said, boldly returning his gaze. "Darts."

A ghost of a smile flickered across his features. "If I had any darts, which I don't, I wouldn't care to be within your range, Miss Stone."

"For a mere female, I have an excellent aim, Mr. Westland."

"Which is why," he said pointedly, "I would not care to be within your range." Grinning, Clayton lifted his glass to her in a gesture of salute. Whitney accepted his tribute for their verbal swordplay with an exaggerated nod of condescension, then favored him with an irrepressible sidewise smile.

Clayton watched her, wanting more than anything to thrust his other two dinner guests out the front door and snatch Whitney into his arms, to kiss the laughing mischief from her lips until she was clinging to him, melting with desire. He leaned back in his chair, absently fingering the stem of his wineglass, while he relished the knowledge that tonight he had finally battered down her wall of cold indifference. Just why Whitney had retreated behind it the day of the picnic, and remained aloof and distant until an hour ago, was still a question to which he would someday demand an answer. Darts! he thought with an inward grin. He ought to wring her lovely neck.

After the meal, a servant escorted Martin and Lady Anne from the dining room, but Clayton placed a restraining hand on Whitney's arm when she started to follow them. "Darts!" he chuckled. "What a bloodthirsty wench you are!"

Whitney, who had been on the verge of smiling back at him, went scarlet. "Your way with words must make you the envy of all your friends," she flared. "In our brief acquaintance you've referred to me first as a hussy and now as a wench. Think what you will of me, but in future, I'd appreciate it if you'd keep your opinions to yourself!" Shamed and guilt-stricken because she felt she had earned both names, Whitney tried to pull her arm free, but his hand tightened.

"What the devil are you talking about? Surely, you can't think I meant an insult with either name?" He saw the flushed, hurt look which she tried to hide by turning her face away. "My God, that is exactly what you think," he said softly. Putting his hand against her cheek, he forced her to look at him. "I beg your forgiveness, little one. I've moved too long in circles where it is fashionable to speak boldly, and where the women are as frank as the men with whom they flirt."

Although she'd never been exposed to the daringly fast set, evidently he had, and Whitney knew that the women were shockingly outspoken and behaved with wanton abandon, flirting openly, and even taking lovers. Suddenly she felt foolish and unsophisticated. "It isn't just the names," she protested defensively. "It's the day of the picnic, too, and the way you . . ." Her voice faltered when she recalled that she had been a willing participant in the heated kisses they exchanged. "I'll strike a bargain with you," she offered after a moment. "You forget everything I've done, and I'll forget what you've done, and we'll start again. Providing, of course, that you give me your solemn word that you won't try to do what you did to me by the stream."

His brow furrowed in puzzlement. "If you're referring to the crop, surely you don't think—"

"Not that. The other."

"What? Do you mean kiss you?"

When Whitney nodded, he looked so utterly astounded that she burst out laughing. "Now, don't tell me I'm the first female you've ever met who didn't want you to kiss her?"

He lifted his shoulders in a brief shrug that dismissed her question. "I admit to being somewhat spoiled by women who seemed to enjoy my . . . attentions. And you," he added, smashing her momentary sense of triumph, "have been too long surrounded by besotted fools who kiss the hem of your skirts, begging your permission to be your lord and master."

Whitney's smile was filled with confident amusement. "I told you, I will never call any man my lord. When I marry, I shall be a good and dutiful wife—but a full partner, not an obedient servant." In the doorway of the salon, he glanced down at her with an odd combination of humorous skepticism and absolute certainty. "A good and dutiful wife? No, little one, I'm afraid not."

Shaken by an inexplicable sensation of prickling alarm, Whitney looked away. It was as if he believed he had some sort of power over her. From the very first moment she'd seen him watching her at the stream, from the first words he'd spoken to her there, she'd had this same peculiar feeling. Perhaps that was why it always seemed so important, so necessary to avoid or outmaneuver him whenever possible. With a start, Whitney realized that he was speaking to her.

"I asked if you would enjoy a game of whist, or if you'd prefer something else. Other than darts," he joked.

"I suppose we could play whist," Whitney said with more politeness than enthusiasm. Her gaze fell on the chess set in front of the fireplace, and she wandered closer to inspect it. "How beautiful," she breathed. Half the set was cast in a burnished gold, the other in a silvery metal. Each piece was nearly as tall as her hand, and when she picked up the heavy king and held it to the light, she caught her breath sharply. There in her hand she held the figure of King Henry II, his face so real and lifelike that Whitney could only marvel at the genius of the craftsman who had created it. The queen was Henry's wife, Eleanor of Aquitane. With a smile, Whitney put the queen down and picked up the bishop. "I knew it would be Becket." She smiled at Clayton over her shoulder. "Poor Henry, even on a chessboard the image of the Archbishop of Canterbury still plagues him." Gently and reverently, she put the piece down.

"Do you play?" Clayton asked, surprise and doubt in his voice.

He sounded so incredulous that Whitney immediately decided to entice him into playing with her. "Not very well, I'm afraid," she replied, lowering her eyes to hide her mischievous laughter. Only so well that Uncle Edward stoutly rued the day when he'd decided to teach her. Only so well that he used to challenge his most skilled opponents from the Consulate to come to the house and try to take a victory from her. "Do you play often?" Whitney inquired innocently.

Clayton was already drawing the burgundy leather wingback chairs into place on opposite sides of the chess table. "Very infrequently."

"Good," Whitney said with a bright, vivacious smile as she sat down. "In that case, this won't take very long."

"Planning to trounce me, Ma'am?" he drawled, one brow arrogantly raised.

"Soundly!" Whitney told him.

She made her moves skillfully, confident she could best him, but careful not to underestimate his ability. He was bold at first, decisive and quick, but after forty-five minutes, the play had slowed considerably.

"It seems you mean to make good your threat," he chuckled, eyeing her in frank admiration as she captured his rook.

"Not nearly as easily as I'd hoped," Whitney said. "And I recognized your skill three moves before you became aware of mine. That alone should have cost you the game."

"I apologize for disappointing you," he mocked.

"You are absolutely delighted to 'disappoint me' and you know it!" Whitney laughed. She was just reaching for her bishop when her father suddenly stood up and announced that, inasmuch as his gout was troubling him, he would be grateful if Mr. Westland would escort Whitney home when their game was finished. With that, he seized his sister-in-law's hand and strode swiftly toward the door on what were obviously two perfectly healthy legs, hauling Anne in his wake.

Whitney was already on her feet. "We can have our game another time," she said hastily, hiding her wistful regret over being unable to go on playing.

"Nonsense!" her father declared stoutly, hurrying over and pressing a clumsy kiss on her forehead, while forcing her back into her chair. "Nothing improper about the two of you going on with your game—there's a house full of servants for chaperones."

Having once been the object of scorn and ridicule in this neighborhood, Whitney had no desire to bring censure down on herself over such a trifling thing as a game of chess. "No, really, I couldn't, Father." Unable to rise with her father's restraining hand on her shoulder, she looked beseechingly to her aunt, who shrugged helplessly, then levelled her rapier gaze on Clayton. "I trust you will remember to conduct yourself as a gentleman, Mr. Westland?"

"Whitney will be treated with all the deep respect and affection I have for her," Clayton replied with tolerant amusement.

The second game was begun, the first having ended in a stalemate. For a while after her father and Aunt Anne departed, Whitney felt ill at ease, but she soon relaxed, and by the time they were well into the second game, both opponents were heckling one another outrageously.

With her elbows propped on the huge chess table and her chin cupped in her hands, Whitney watched Clayton reach for his knight. "Most imprudent," she advised him.

Clayton gave her a wicked grin, ignored her advice, and advanced his knight. "You are hardly in a position to counsel me on strategy after your last reckless move, Miss."

"Then don't ever complain that I didn't warn you," Whitney mused, tapping her long, tapered fingernail on an empty square, while she pondered his wily move of the knight. Leaning forward, she plunked her rook into position, then rested her chin on her hands again.

Each time she reached across the board, she unwittingly afforded Clayton glimpses of the thrusting fullness of her breasts above the scalloped bodice of her dress, until it required every ounce of his self-control to concentrate on the game. Long ago, she'd abandoned her slippers and now sat curled up in her chair with her legs tucked beneath her. With her luxuriant hair tumbling over her shoulders and her green eyes glowing with devilment, she presented such a captivating picture that Clayton was torn between the urge to shove the chess table aside, draw her onto his lap, and let his hands revel in the richness of his prize—and the equally delightful desire simply to lean back in his chair and feast his eyes on her.

At one and the same time, she managed to be an alluringly beautiful woman and a bewitchingly innocent girl. She was a study of intriguing and beguiling contrasts. In the course of one evening, she had treated him with cool disdain, tempestuous rebellion, blazing anger and now, with a jaunty impertinence and breezy impudence that he found utterly exhilarating. And to top it all off, she played one hell of a chess game.

In the spirit of bald needling and relaxed affability which they'd been enjoying, Whitney raised her eyes to his and inquired with a radiant smile, "Are you contemplating your next move—or regretting your last, my lord?"

Clayton chuckled. "Aren't you the same young woman who informed me only hours ago that you'd call no man 'my lord'?"

"I only called you that," she informed him lightly, "to distract you so that you'd forget your strategy. However, you didn't answer my question."

"If you must know," he said, reaching for his king and attacking from an unexpected position on the board, "I was wondering what possessed me to play chess with a woman, when everyone knows chess is a game which requires a man's superior logic."

"You conceited beast!" Whitney laughed, cleverly side-stepping his attack on her bishop. "I can't imagine why I'm wasting my skill on such a weak opponent."

An hour later, Whitney's dark head was bent over the chessboard as she contemplated the success of her strategy. Three more moves, four possibly, and the game would be hers. "How perverse of you to maneuver me into such an impossible position," she complained, smiling to herself as he made the very move she'd anticipated he would.

"You think you have me trapped, I presume?" he observed with alacrity.

While Whitney carefully considered her next move, Clayton leaned around and nodded over his shoulder to a manservant who'd been standing at stiff attention near the door from the moment her aunt and father had left.

In response to the duke's silent command, the servant went to a table on which stood several crystal decanters and poured an amber liquid from one of them into a glass. He paused and looked inquiringly toward the duke for instruction as to the young lady's beverage. Clayton lifted two fingers, indicating that two brandies were to be served.

The servant arranged the two glasses on a small silver tray

and brought it over to the table beside the chessboard. He put it down, and at Clayton's brief nod of dismissal, bowed, and quietly withdrew from the room, closing the door behind him.

Whitney was oblivious to all this, but she looked up as Clayton politely handed a glass to her. The color was obviously not that of wine, and she glanced suspiciously from the amber liquid in her glass to Clayton's face.

Watching her with tranquil amusement, he explained, "At dinner tonight, you argued so eloquently against the restrictions placed upon females by society, that I presumed you would prefer to have whatever I drink."

He really was the most provoking man alive, taunting her this way, Whitney thought with a smile. Determined to brazen it out for as long as possible, she sniffed the pungent odor emanating from her glass. Uncle Edward's favorite drink. "Brandy," she said, favoring Clayton with a bland smile. "Perfect with a good cigar, is it not?"

"Most assuredly," he agreed straight-faced. Reaching out, he lifted an enameled metal box from the table beside them and snapped the lid open with his thumb. Holding the box toward her, he offered Whitney her choice of the cigars within it.

He was so supremely blasé about it that Whitney's composure slipped another notch closer to laughter. Catching her lower lip between her teeth to still its treacherous trembling, Whitney studied the cigars as if trying to decide which she preferred. What would he do if she actually selected one from the box? Light it, no doubt! she thought with a silent giggle.

"May I suggest the longer one to your left?" he murmured courteously.

Whitney crumpled back into her chair, convulsed with silent mirth.

"A pinch of snuff perhaps?" he urged solicitously, sending Whitney into gales of musical laughter. "I keep it on hand for particularly discriminating guests such as yourself."

"You are impossible!" she laughed. When she finally caught her breath, she lifted her glass and, under his amused gaze, gingerly sampled her brandy. It burned a path straight down to her stomach. The second and third sips were not quite so awful, and after a few more, she categorized brandy as one of those things for which one must acquire a taste. Very soon after, she became aware of an unaccustomed, delicious warmth seeping through her, and she firmly put the glass aside, wondering just how potent a few sips of brandy could be.

"Who taught you to play?" Clayton asked.

"My uncle," Whitney replied. Leaning forward, she picked up her king and held it to the light to admire the splendid craftsmanship. "If one didn't know better, one would think these pieces were actually cast in gold and silver."

"If one didn't know better," Clayton said blandly, removing the solid gold king from her graceful fingers to prevent her from inspecting it any closer, "one would think you were trying to extricate yourself from my clever trap by contriving to place him in a safer position on the board."

Whitney was instantly alert. "Extricate myself? A safer position? Whatever are you talking about? My king isn't in jeopardy!"

A slow, roguish grin dawned across his features. Reaching out, he moved his bishop into position. "Check," he said.

"Check?" Whitney repeated in disbelief, staring at the board, trying to reassess her vulnerability. She *was* in check! And no matter which of the available moves she made, one of his men was poised to attack.

Slowly she raised her eyes to his, and Clayton basked in the unconcealed admiration lighting her beautiful face. When she spoke her voice was soft and filled with awe. "You blackhearted, treacherous, conniving scoundrel."

Clayton threw back his head and laughed at the contrast between her tone and her words. "Your flattery warms my heart," he chuckled.

"You have no heart," Whitney quipped, smiling dazzlingly at him. "If you did, you'd never abuse a helpless female by luring her into a game at which you are obviously a master."

"You lured *me,"* he reminded her, grinning. "Now, shall we finish the game, or do you plan to deny me my triumph by claiming the game was incomplete?"

"No," Whitney said good-naturedly. "I surrender completely."

Her words seemed to hang portentously in the silence that followed. "I was hoping you would," he said quietly.

He unbuttoned his dark blue jacket, leaned back in his chair, and stretched his long legs out beside the table. Relaxed and comfortable, he turned his head slightly and gazed into the fire.

Whitney studied him surreptitiously as she sipped from her brandy. Sitting like that, he looked like an artist's portrait of the "gentleman of leisure." And yet, she had the strangest feeling that beneath his relaxed exterior there was a forcefulness, a power, carefully restrained now, but gathered. Waiting. And if she made a wrong move, a mistake, he would unleash that force, that power on her. Mentally, she gave herself a hard shake. She was being foolish and fanciful. "I can't make out the time," she said softly, a while later, "but it's surely long past the hour for me to leave."

His gaze shifted from the fire to her. "Not until I hear you laugh again."

Whitney shook her head. "I haven't laughed *that* hard since the day of our spring musicale when I was twelve years old."

When he realized that she had no intention of elaborating, Clayton said, "Since you're obviously reluctant to share it with me, I claim the retelling of that story as my victory prize."

"First you lure me into a chess game," Whitney berated him, smiling. "Then you outwit me, and now you want to claim a reward from me for doing it. Have you no mercy?"

"None. Now go on."

"Very well," she sighed. "But only because I refuse to further flatter your vanity by pleading to be let off." Her voice softened as she looked back into the past. "It was a long time ago, yet it seems like yesterday. Mr. Twittsworthy, our local music instructor, decided that the village should have a spring musicale. All the females whose musical education was entrusted to his tutelage were to display their accomplishments by playing or singing a short piece. There were about fifteen of us, but Elizabeth Ashton was the most gifted performer, so Mr. Twittsworthy bestowed the honor of hosting the musicale on her mama and papa. I didn't even want to go, but . . ."

"But Twittsworthy insisted that you must, or the musicale would be a dismal failure?" Clayton speculated.

"Good heavens, no! Mr. Twittsworthy would have been delighted if I'd stayed away. You see, whenever he came to the house to listen to me play the pianoforte, his eyes began to burn and water. He complained to everyone that my playing was so offensive to his ears that it actually made him weep."

Clayton felt an unexplainable surge of anger at the music instructor. "The man must have been a fool."

"Indeed he was," Whitney agreed with a breezy smile. "Otherwise, he would have realized that I was sprinkling pepper in his snuffbox whenever he came to give me lessons. Anyway, the morning of the musicale, I pleaded and argued with my father that I shouldn't have to go, but he would have it to the very last hour that I absolutely must!

"Looking back, I think Father would have relented if I hadn't been seized with the unfortunate inspiration of sending Clarissa, my maid, down with a note for him."

Clayton grinned at her over the rim of his glass. "What did you say in the note?"

"I said," Whitney confessed with twinkling eyes, "that I had taken to my bed with a case of cholera, but that he should go to the musicale without me and ask everyone to pray for my recovery."

Clayton's shoulders began to lurch and Whitney said severely, "I've not yet come to the humorous part of the story, Mr. Westland." He smoothed the laughter from his face and Whitney continued, "Father gave poor Clarissa a thundering scold for having failed to instill in me a grain of respect for truth. The very next thing I knew, Clarissa was thrusting me into my best dress which was much too short, because I'd told her I wasn't going and she didn't need to let the hem down, and Father was marching me into the carriage.

Of course, I hadn't learned my piece for the musicale, which was nothing out of the ordinary, since I never had the patience to plink and plank my life away at the pianoforte, and I pleaded with Father to let me go back into the house and get my music, but he was too angry with me to listen.

"Every neighbor for miles was gathered in the music room at Elizabeth's house. Elizabeth played like an angel, which was always the way, and Margaret Merryton's piece was judged quite agreeable. I was saved for last." Whitney lapsed into pensive silence. For one brief moment, she was again sitting in the third row of the crowded music room, just behind Paul, whose eyes were riveted on Elizabeth's dainty, angelic profile as she played the pianoforte. Paul had leapt to his feet, with everyone else, to applaud Elizabeth's performance while Whitney stood behind him, tugging at her short, unbecoming pink dress and hating her own awkward body which was all arms and legs and knees and elbows.

"You were the last to play," Clayton prodded, his teasing voice rousing Whitney from her unhappy recollections. "And even without your music, you played so well that they all cheered and called for an encore?"

"I would say," Whitney corrected him with a tinkling laugh, "that their reaction was more one of dazed silence."

Despite Whitney's offhand manner of telling the story, Clayton found it more poignant than funny. At that moment, he could have cheerfully strangled every one of these small-minded country bumpkins who had ever embarrassed her, beginning with her music instructor and ending with her stupid father. Deep inside, he felt a stirring tenderness, a protectiveness toward her, that surprised and disturbed him, and he lifted his glass, drinking from it to cover his own bewildering emotions.

Afraid that he might somehow feel sorry for her, Whitney smiled and waved her hand dismissively. "I've only told you this to give you the background. The reason for my hilarity occurred later, while everyone was enjoying a light luncheon out on the lawn. You see, a prize was to be awarded after lunch for the best performance, and Elizabeth Ashton was to receive it. Unfortunately, the prize vanished, and a rumor was circulated that it had been hidden up in the largest tree on the lawn."

Clayton studied her, and his gray eyes lit with amused speculation. "Did *you* put it there?"

Whitney pinkened. "No, but I started the rumor that it was up in the tree. Anyway, everyone had just begun to eat when suddenly Elizabeth came tumbling from the tree, crashing like a rock onto the table. I thought she made a *very* fetching centerpiece, reclining amidst the sandwiches and pudding in her pink and white ruffles, and I started to laugh." Whitney smiled as she recalled the scene, then she remembered the way Paul had run to Elizabeth's rescue, drying her tears with his handkerchief, while he glared furiously at Whitney.

"I assume that when the adults saw you laughing, they blamed you for hiding the prize in the tree?"

"Oh, no, the adults were much too busy trying to remove Elizabeth from their lunch to notice that I was laughing myself into fits. Peter Redfern *did* notice, though, and he assumed I was guilty, particularly since he knew I could climb a tree faster than even he could. He threatened to box my ears then and there, but Margaret Merryton told him I deserved a whipping from my father instead."

"Which was your fate?" Clayton asked.

"Neither one," Whitney said, and her laughter reminded Clayton of wind chimes. "You see, Peter was too angry to listen to Margaret, and I was so positive that he wouldn't dare to hit me, that I didn't think to duck until the very last moment. He hit Margaret instead," Whitney finished merrily. "Oh lord! I shall never forget the look on poor Peter's face when Margaret rolled over in the grass and sat up. She had the most heavenly purple eye you could imagine."

Across the chess table, their laughing gazes held, the happy silence punctuated by the cheery crackling of the logs burning on the grate. Clayton put his glass down, and Whitney's smile began to fade as he purposefully came to his feet. Darting a glance toward the door where the servant had been standing earlier, Whitney realized that he was no longer there. "It's dreadfully late," she said, hastily standing up as Clayton came toward her. "I should be leaving at once."

He stopped an inch from her and said in a deep, velvety voice, "Thank you for the most delightful evening of my life."

She saw the look in his eyes, and her heart began to hammer uncontrollably while a warning screamed along her nerves. "Please don't stand so close," she whispered desperately. "It makes me feel like a rabbit about to be pounced upon by a—a ferret!"

His eyes smiled, but his voice was quiet, seductive. "I can hardly kiss you if I'm standing across the room, little one."

"Don't call me that, and don't kiss me! I've just barely forgiven you for the last time at the stream."

"Then I'm afraid you're going to have to forgive me again."

"I warn you, I won't," Whitney whispered, as he drew her into his arms. "This time I'll never forgive you."

"A terrifying possibility, but I'll risk it," he murmured huskily, and his mouth opened hungrily over hers. The shock of the contact was electrifying. His hands moved down her shoulders and back, molding her tighter and tighter to the hard length of his body. He kissed her thoroughly, insistently, endlessly, and when her quivering lips parted for his probing tongue, he crushed her into himself. His tongue plunged into her mouth, then slowly retreated to plunge again and again, in some unknown, wildly exciting rhythm that produced a knot of pure sensation in the pit of Whitney's stomach.

The provocative caresses of his hands, the feel of his mouth sensuously joined with hers, the hard strength of his legs pressing intimately against her, brought Whitney's body to vibrant life in his arms. She surrendered helplessly to the inflaming demands of his hands and mouth, and as she did, her mind went numb. Dead. The longer the kisses continued, the more splintered apart she became. It was as if she were two people, one warm and yielding, the other paralyzed with alarm.

When he finally drew back, Whitney let her forehead fall against his chest, her hands flattened against the crisp, starched whiteness of his shirt. She stood there in a kind of disoriented, bewildered rebellion, furious with herself and with him.

"Shall I implore your forgiveness now, little one?" he teased lightly, tipping her chin up. "Or should I wait?" Whitney lifted her mutinous green eyes to his. "I think I'd better wait," he said with a rueful chuckle. Pressing a brief kiss on her forehead, he turned and strode from the room, returning a moment later with her satin cape. He put it around her shoulders, and she shivered when his hand touched her skin. "Are you cold?" he murmured, folding his arms around her from behind and drawing her back against his chest.

Whitney could not drag a sound through her constricted throat. She was a roiling mass of shame, bewilderment, anger, and self-loathing.

"Surely I cannot have rendered you speechless," he whispered teasingly, his breath touching her hair.

She spoke, but her voice was a strangled whisper. "Please let go of me."

He did not attempt to talk to her again until they drew up beneath the arched carriage entrance at the side of her house. "Whitney," he said impatiently, grasping her arm when she opened the door and started to go inside. "I want to talk to you. There are some things that should be understood between us."

"Not now," Whitney said tonelessly. "Another time perhaps, but not tonight."

Whitney lay awake until dawn, trying to understand the turbulent, consuming emotions Clayton was able to arouse in her; how he managed to take her in his arms and sweep away her plans and dreams of Paul, her sense of decency and honor.

She rolled over, burying her face in her pillow. From this night forward, she would scrupulously avoid being alone with him again. Any future contact with him would have to be brief, impersonal, and public. Her mistake—and she would never, never make it again—was that she'd enjoyed his company so much tonight, been so disarmed by his relaxed charm, that she had started thinking of him as her friend.

Friend! she thought bitterly, rolling over onto her back and staring up at the canopy. A boa constrictor would make a more trustworthy friend than that man! Why, that lecherous libertine would try to seduce a saint in church. He would go to any lengths to make another conquest. The harder he had to try, the more difficult his prey made it for him, the better he seemed to enjoy it. And Whitney knew now, beyond a doubt, that *she* was his prey. He intended to seduce her, to dishonor her, and nothing was going to deter him from trying.

For her sake, and for Paul's, the sooner their betrothal was announced, the better, because even Clayton Westland wouldn't dare to pursue a woman who was promised to another man. A man who happened to be an outstanding shot!

Chapter Fourteen

Whitney smoothed her hair, cast a last critical appraisal over her soft green wool dress with white ruffles at the throat and wrists, then straightened the velvet bow which held her dark hair demurely caught at the nape of her neck. Her sleepless night had left shadows beneath her eyes, but otherwise she looked pretty and young and girlish. Not at all the sort, Whitney thought wryly as she turned away from the mirror, to plan to entrap a man with a falsehood designed to force him into declaring himself. Now—today.

Mentally she rehearsed her strategy as she walked downstairs to the drawing room where Paul was waiting for her. She would make him think she was returning to Paris with Aunt Anne when Uncle Edward came for her. If *that* didn't prod Paul into offering for her, then nothing ever would.

In the doorway of the drawing room, she hesitated. Paul looked so wonderful, so handsome, that she was sorely tempted to throw propriety to the winds and offer for *him*. Instead she said brightly, "It's a lovely afternoon. Shall we walk in the garden?"

The moment they were within the sheltered seclusion of the high, clipped hedges that surrounded the last of the blooming roses, Paul took her in his arms and kissed her. "I'm trying to atone for all my years of neglecting you," he teased.

It was exactly the sort of opening she needed. Stepping

back, she smiled gaily and said, "Then you'll have to hurry, because you have a great many years to atone for and only a few weeks left in which to do it."

"What do you mean, 'only a few weeks left?'"

"Before I go back to France with my aunt and uncle," Whitney explained, almost sagging with relief at the swift scowl that darkened his face.

"Before you go back to France? I thought you were home to stay."

"I have a home there too, Paul. In some ways, more of a home than I have here." He looked so upset that Whitney felt guilty, yet all he had to do to prevent her from going to France was propose, and he knew it.

"But your father is here," he argued. *"I'm* here. Doesn't that mean something?"

"Of course it does," Whitney whispered, looking away so he'd not see just how much it did mean. Why couldn't he, why didn't he, simply say "Marry me," she wondered. Turning her back on him, she pretended to admire a scarlet rose.

"You can't leave," he said in a strained voice. "I think I'm in love with you."

Whitney's heart stopped beating, then began hammering wildly. She wanted to hurl herself into his arms, but it was too soon; his declaration was lukewarm, inconclusive. She took a step down the path and smiled flirtatiously over her shoulder. "I hope you'll write and let me know—when you decide for certain."

"Oh no, you don't!" Paul laughed, capturing her arm and drawing her back. "Now, Miss Stone, do you, or do you not, love me?"

Whitney stifled her wild avowal of eternal love. "I *think* I do," she said, twinkling.

Instead of pursuing the issue, as she expected, Paul abruptly dropped her arm, his expression turning remote, shuttered. "I have some things to do this afternoon," he said coolly.

He was going to leave, she realized in shocked despair. She had the most horrible, humiliating feeling that he had seen through her ploy, that he knew she was trying to manipulate him, to force him.

They walked to the front of the house where his sleek new carriage waited on the circular drive below. Paul stayed only long enough to press a brief, formal kiss on her fingertips, then he turned and started to leave. One step away, he turned back again. "Exactly how much competition do I have, besides Westland?" he demanded.

Whitney's spirits soared crazily. "How much would you like?" she smiled.

His eyes narrowed; he opened his mouth to speak then changed his mind, turned on his heel, and left.

Whitney's smile faded. In tortured misery, she watched him bounding down the steps, her heart beating a funeral dirge in time to each long stride he took. She had forced him to reveal his intentions, and now she knew what they were. He intended to have a light, meaningless flirtation with her, and nothing more. He hadn't wanted her before she went away, and he didn't want her now.

Beside his carriage, Paul paused, reached to take the reins from the groom, then paused again. He stood motionless, his back to her, and as Whitney watched him, she began uttering feverish, pleading, disjointed prayers.

In tense silence, afraid to hope and unable not to, she watched Paul slowly turn and gaze up at her . . . and then begin retracing his steps. By the time he was near enough for Whitney to see his face, her knees were quaking so badly that she could scarcely stand.

"Miss Stone," he said in a laughter-tinged voice, "it has just occurred to me that I have only two choices where you are concerned. I can either avoid all future contact with you, and thus put an end to my torment—or I can marry you in order to prolong it."

Gazing into his teasing blue eyes, Whitney realized he had already made his choice. She tried to smile at him, but she was so relieved that her voice filled with tears. "You know you would never be able to forgive yourself if you took the coward's way out."

Paul burst out laughing and opened his arms, and Whitney collapsed against him, laughing and crying at the same time. She pressed her cheek against the steady, rhythmic thudding of his heart, revelling in the feel of his strong arms holding her tightly, possessively to him.

She felt as if she were encased in a golden haze of security, for Paul had just given her a gift as priceless as his love, and she was so grateful to him that she could have sunk to her knees and wept with gratitude: Paul loved her, he wanted to marry her—and that was *proof*, real, incontrovertible proof, that she had really changed in France. She wasn't just a polished counterfeit dressed in the height of fashion and masquerading as a young lady of refinement, as she had often feared. She wasn't a hopeless misfit anymore. She was real. She was worthy. The villagers would no longer snigger about the fool she had made of herself over Paul Sevarin; they would smile now and say Mr. Sevarin had always liked her, they would say he'd merely been biding his time, waiting for her to grow up. She could live here among the people she had always wanted to like her. She had redeemed herself in their eyes, and in her father's too. She was so relieved that she felt like sobbing.

"Let's find your father," Paul said.

Whitney lifted her head and stared at him in happy incomprehension. "Why?"

"Because I would like to get the formalities over with and I can hardly ask your aunt for your hand in marriage. Not," he added ruefully, "that I wouldn't prefer to do it that way if I could."

"Sewell, where is my father?" Whitney said anxiously as they stepped into the house.

"On his way to London, Miss," the butler replied. "He left a half hour ago."

"London?" Whitney gasped. "But I thought he wasn't planning to leave until tomorrow? Why did he leave today instead? Is he returning any sooner?"

Sewell, who always knew everything, claimed to know

nothing. Whitney watched him pad away down the hall, his long coattails flapping, and felt like the sun had just set on her happiness.

Paul looked like a man who had braced himself to face an unpleasant confrontation and having been granted a temporary reprieve, didn't know whether he was relieved or disappointed that he couldn't get it over with. "When is he coming back?"

"Not for five whole days," Whitney said, her slender shoulders drooping. "Just in time for a surprise party in honor of his birthday." She groaned in dismay. "The cards have already been sent to those of my relatives who have a distance to travel. Unless he returns earlier in the afternoon than we expect, you won't be able to speak to him until the following day. Sunday, after church?" she ventured, brightening a little.

Paul slowly shook his head, deep in thought. "I want to settle the deal on a matched pair of Ainsleys—two splendid purebreds, you'll love them. And if I'm going to have enough time to reach the auction at Hampton Park, I've got to leave on Saturday, the day your father returns."

Whitney tried not to sound as disappointed as she felt. "How long will you be gone?"

"Less than a fortnight—nine or ten days, no more."

"That seems like forever."

Paul took her in his arms. "To prove how honorable my intentions are, I'll be on hand all day Saturday, in case your father should return early enough for me to speak to him. That's only five days away. And," he added, chuckling at her desolate look, "I'll even delay my departure so that I can spend a few hours at his birthday party—assuming that you intended to invite me?"

Whitney nodded, smiling.

"Then, if there isn't an opportunity to speak with him during his party, and I rather doubt there will be, you can tell him after the party that I'm going to pay the formal call as soon as I return. Now"—he grinned—"does that sound like a man who wants to escape wedlock?"

After Paul left, Whitney deliberated over telling Aunt Anne the news and tentatively decided against it. She wanted to clasp her joy to herself for now, and she felt a superstitious fear of telling anyone of her forthcoming betrothal to Paul before Paul himself had actually asked for her hand. Besides, her father would undoubtedly return early enough on Saturday for Paul to speak with him. Then they could announce their betrothal at the birthday party that very night.

Feeling vastly cheered by the thought, Whitney went into the house to join her aunt for lunch.

As was his habit, Clayton was perusing his mail while he ate his lunch. In addition to the usual business correspondence and invitations, there were letters from his mother and brother. Clayton grinned, thinking of the surprise in store for his mother when she learned that he was finally going to marry and provide her with the grandchildren she'd been plaguing him to give her. He would give her about six of them, he decided with a silent chuckle, and he hoped they would all have Whitney's green eyes.

He was still smiling as he initialed the ticket from the London jeweler for the emerald pendant Whitney had worn the night of her homecoming party.

Laying that aside, he began reading a long missive from his secretary requesting instructions on how to proceed on matters as diverse as the pensioning off of an old family retainer, to the divestiture of a large block of shares in a shipping company. Beneath each inquiry, Clayton wrote precise, detailed instructions.

In the doorway, the butler cleared his throat. "Mr. Stone is here to see you, your grace," he explained when Clayton looked up. "Naturally, I informed him that you were dining, but the man insists his reason for calling is extremely urgent and cannot wait."

"Very well, show him in here," Clayton said with an irritated sigh. With Whitney, Clayton had all the patience in the world; with his future father-in-law, he had none. In fact, it was all he could do to stomach the man.

"I had to come before I started for London," Martin explained as he hastened across the room and seated himself at the table across from the duke. "We've got a beastly mess on our hands, and it's going to get messier if you—we—don't do something about it at once."

Clayton nodded a curt dismissal to the footman who had been serving him his lunch and waited until the servant had closed the door behind him, before shifting his impassive gaze to his unwelcome visitor. "You were saying, Martin?"

"I was saying that something has come up. A complication. It's Sevarin. He was with Whitney when I left."

"I told you I'm not worried about Sevarin," Clayton said impatiently.

"Then you'd better *start* worrying about him," Martin warned, looking anguished and angry at the same time. "When Whitney was fifteen years old, she got some bee in her bonnet about snatching Sevarin away from the Ashton girl, and even though it's taken her five years—five years!—she's still hell-bent on pulling it off. And she's about to. You mark my words, that poor devil is thinking of marrying her. He's only a hair's breadth from offering for her. God knows why, because she'd drive him mad. She drives *me* mad."

Clayton's voice was heavy with ironic amusement. "Speaking as the 'poor devil' who has already offered for her, I can only applaud Sevarin's taste. However, as I've told you several times, I can handle Whitney and—"

Martin looked as if he were going to explode from frustration. "You *can't* handle her. You *think* you can, but you don't know her as I do. Dammit, she's a stubborn, willful chit and always has been. Once she gets some maggot in her head—like marrying Sevarin—she'll follow through with it no matter what."

Reaching into his pocket, Martin found a handkerchief and swiped at the film of nervous perspiration standing on his forehead, then he continued, "Once she brings Sevarin to the point of wanting to marry her, she may feel she's accomplished her goal, and forget all about him after that. On the other hand," he emphasized in a dire tone, "if that hellion of mine takes it into her head to actually *marry* him, you'll end up dragging the chit to the altar while she fights you every step of the way. Do you understand what I am trying to say?"

A pair of cool gray eyes regarded him dispassionately. "Yes."

"Good, good. Then the thing to do is prevent Sevarin from mentioning marriage to her, and the way to do it is to tell Whitney at once that she's been betrothed to you since July. Tell Sevarin that. Tell *everyone* that. Announce your engagement immediately."

"No."

"No?" Martin repeated in bewilderment. "Then what are you going to do about Sevarin?"

"What do you suggest I do?"

"I told you!" said Martin desperately. "Order Whitney to give up whatever scheme she has in mind for Sevarin and command her to prepare herself to be wed to you at once!"

Clayton had a difficult time keeping his face straight. "Martin, have you ever actually 'commanded' your daughter to do something she didn't want to do?"

"Of course I have. I'm her father."

Amusement tugged at the corner of Clayton's lips. "And when you 'commanded' her, did Whitney dutifully accept your authority, and do as she was bidden?"

Martin slumped back in his chair, his face flushed with chagrined defeat. "The last time I 'commanded' my daughter to do my bidding she was fourteen years old," he admitted. "I ordered her to emulate the Ashton girl, and for two months afterward, Whitney curtsied me to death. She curtsied into and out of every room in the house. She curtsied to the butler and the cook, she curtsied to the horses. Every damn time I looked at the chit, she dropped whatever she was doing and curtsied to me. The rest of the time she did that ridiculous thing with her eyelashes . . . you know, fluttering them. She said she was obeying my order to emulate the Ashton girl."

"Whitney will do my bidding," Clayton said in a tone that brooked no further debate. "But until I am ready to tell her about our betrothal, no one is to tell her about it. When I think the time is correct, *I* will do so. Is that perfectly clear, Martin?"

Martin nodded resignedly.

"Fine," Clayton said, picking up an envelope from the stack of correspondence and opening it.

Running a nervous finger between his neckcloth and throat, Martin said, "There's just one more thing. A small thing."

"Yes, go on," Clayton said without looking up from his correspondence.

"It's Lady Anne Gilbert. She has some ridiculous notion that Whitney dislikes you. I'd like you to convince her that you can overcome that problem."

"Why?"

"Because my servants inform me that she is sending letters directed to her husband at consulates all over Europe. I assume she wants to find him and bring him here at once."

The duke's face hardened with such cold displeasure that Martin pressed back in his chair. "Are you telling me that she is opposed to the marriage?"

"My God, no! I didn't mean that," Martin exclaimed desperately. "Anne Gilbert's a sensible woman, but she's soft where Whitney's concerned. After you told her what we'd done—you and I—and her shock had passed, she admitted that it was a brilliant match. She said you were the best catch in all Europe, and that there is no more aristocratic, important family in England than the Westmorelands."

"I'm delighted that Lady Gilbert is so sensible," Clayton said, somewhat mollified.

"Not *that* sensible!" Martin contradicted. "She's up in the boughs over the way we went about the matter without Whitney's knowledge." Bitterly, he added, "She accused me of being a cold, heartless father without a grain of human sensitivity!" Stung by the look of agreement on the duke's face, Martin burst out defensively, "She accused *you* of being dictatorial and autocratic. She said she doesn't like your reputation with the ladies above half, and that you are entirely too good-looking for comfort. In short, Lady Gilbert thinks Whitney is too good for both of us."

"I'm surprised my little gift to you of £100,000 didn't soften her feelings," Clayton drawled cynically.

"She called it a bribe," Martin announced, then shrank back at the frigid look in the duke's eyes. "Lady—Lady Gilbert needs assurance that you won't force Whitney to marry you without first giving her ample time to develop a *tendre* for you. If she doesn't receive this assurance from your own lips, I think she means to urge her husband to use his influence to block the marriage. He has contacts in the highest circles, and his opinions carry much weight with people who count."

Unexpectedly, the duke's ominous expression lightened with genuine amusement. "If Lord Gilbert wants to *maintain* his influence in those circles, he won't want to make an adversary of me. At the risk of sounding immodest, Martin, I *am* one of those 'people who count.'"

After Martin had left, Clayton got up and walked over to the window. Leaning his shoulder against the frame, he gazed at workmen constructing a small rustic pavillion at the far end of the lawn near the woods.

If Martin had come to him yesterday, rather than today, and urged him to order Whitney to marry him, he might have given the idea more consideration. Until last night, Whitney had simply been a possession he had acquired—a valued possession, perhaps even a treasured one, but a possession nonetheless.

On the night of the Armands' masquerade, he'd briefly considered making Whitney his mistress, but deflowering a gently reared virgin violated even his relaxed code of honor where women were concerned. Then, too, it was his duty to marry and provide an heir, a responsibility of which he had been constantly reminded from the day he came of age. And so, as he gazed down into her radiant, laughing face in the Armands' garden, he had arrived at a highly satisfactory solution to the dual problem of his duty and his desire: He would marry Whitney Stone.

Until last night, Whitney had merely been the delightful object of his lustful thoughts, and the future mother of his needed heir. But last night, that had changed. Last night, she had touched a tenderness, a protectiveness, within him that he never knew existed.

He had listened to her laughingly telling a story that seemed more sad than funny to him, a story about a motherless young girl who was made to play at a stupid musicale in front of a roomful of thoughtless people and, for the first time, he had realized the pain and frustration, the angry humiliation, she must have felt as a girl.

He didn't like most of her neighbors; they struck him as small-minded, gossipy country bumpkins, and from the moment word had reached them that Whitney was returning from France, they had regaled each other—and him—with endless tales of her girlish antics and her youthful pursuit of Paul Sevarin.

If showing them all that she could bewitch Sevarin was the only way Whitney could regain her pride, then Clayton was willing to allow her to do it. Let her show the villagers she had captivated Sevarin for a few days more. Clayton could wait that long . . . provided that Sevarin didn't actually screw up the courage to ask her father for her hand. Clayton's leniency toward Whitney did *not* extend to allowing her actually to betroth herself to another man. That he would not tolerate.

His mind made up, Clayton went back to the table. Martin was going to be gone for five days, and that was too long to wait to see Whitney again. He needed some excuse to see her in the meantime, some ploy to make her agree to see him. He considered the possibilities and, with a satisfied grin, remembered she had challenged him to a race in which she would ride Dangerous Crossing against him.

He picked up a sheet of plain stationery, then deliberated over the correct phrasing; it had to be worded as a challenge, not an invitation which she would only turn down.

"Dear Miss Stone," he wrote quickly. "I believe you indicated a desire to test your skill with the stallion. I can be available Wednesday morning for a race over any course you choose. If, however, you regret your hasty challenge, be assured I shall attribute your change of heart not to cowardice, but to a justifiable fear that the horse is too much for you to handle. Yours, etc." He sprinkled fine sand over it and sealed it with wax. With an elated sense of accomplishment, he gave instructions to have it brought round to Miss Stone and to await a reply.

His footman returned a quarter hour later with Whitney's response, written in the beautiful, curving hand of a scholarly monk, not the illegible scrawl typical of so many well-bred but under-educated females. There was no salutation. "Wednesday is perfectly agreeable," she wrote. "I shall meet you at 10:00 in the morning at the northwestern edge of Mr. Sevarin's property near the grove." That was all. But it was enough to make Clayton grin as he got up and stretched. Whistling, he strolled through the quiet house and went upstairs to change into riding breeches.

Chapter Fifteen

THE SPECTACLE THAT GREETED CLAYTON ON WEDNESDAY MORNing when he crested the hill overlooking Sevarin's grove made him rein his horse in sharply. Curricles were scattered everywhere below, occupied by women holding brightly colored parasols and men in their Sunday best. Those less affluent spectators who had no curricle were either mounted on horseback, standing atop wagons, or milling about on foot.

All the scene below lacked to make it appear a full-fledged country fair were a few acrobats in bright silk tunics, and a juggler or two. Even as he thought it, someone raised a trumpet and blew two long blasts, and the crowd turned in unison to watch him descend the slope.

Beneath carefully lowered lids, Whitney slanted a long, considering look at Clayton's horse as he approached. She saw four finely conformed legs and the muscled chest and rump of a strong hunter but, since her view from this angle was restricted, the only other information she could garner was that the rider of the horse was wearing gleaming brown leather riding boots and a pair of buckskin riding breeches which fit him to perfection.

"Are you wishing this was pistols at twenty paces, Miss Stone?" Clayton teased as he moved his horse into position at the starting line beside her.

Whitney lifted her head, intending to treat him with cool formality, but his grin was so boyishly disarming that she nearly smiled. Two of the neighborhood men rushed up to offer him good wishes, distracting his attention from her.

Whitney watched him as he talked and joked with them. He looked so relaxed atop his great, powerful horse, and he spoke to the men with such lazy good humor that she could hardly believe he was the same relentless, predatory seducer who had stalked her at his house, who had held her clasped to him while his hungry mouth devoured hers. It was as if he were two people, one she could like very much, and one she feared and mistrusted—with excellent reason.

Elizabeth's father blew another blast on the trumpet and beneath her, Dangerous Crossing gave a frantic lurch. "Are you ready?" Paul called to Whitney and Clayton. As he raised his pistol in the air, Whitney leaned toward Clayton, smiled warmly into his surprised gray eyes, and said very gently, "If you would care to follow me, sir, I shall be happy to show you the way."

Clayton gave a shout of laughter, the pistol fired, and his horse bolted. He had to swoop down to recover the rein he had dropped in his surprised mirth and, by the time he had brought his bolting animal around, Whitney had gained a considerable lead on him.

His horse's hooves thundered over the hard green turf as Warrior fought to close the gap, but Clayton held him slightly back, biding his time as they turned west, galloping alongside the stream. "Easy now," Clayton soothed his lunging mount. "Let's see what she can do before we make our move."

Ahead of them, Dangerous Crossing vaulted over a low stone wall in perfect stride, and Clayton grinned approvingly. Whitney was light and lovely in the saddle, managing her novice hunter with expert skill.

By the time they made the turn for the last leg of the race, Clayton could tell that Dangerous Crossing was beginning to tire. Deciding to overtake Whitney when he rounded the next sharp bend of the woods, Clayton eased up and forward in the saddle, relaxing all tension on the reins. Instantly, Warrior shot forward in long, ground-devouring strides.

They galloped wide around the next curve—and Clayton's breath froze in his chest. The black stallion was veering across his path . . . without a rider. Hauling back viciously on Warrior's reins, Clayton looked for her, his heart thundering in alarm.

And then he saw her. She was lying in a crumpled heap beneath a large oak at the perimeter of the woods. Above her was a thick, jutting limb which must have unseated her when she took the corner too sharply.

Vaulting down from the saddle, he ran to her, more frightened than he had ever been in his life. Frantically, he felt for a pulse and found it throbbing steadily in her slim throat, then he began searching her scalp for sign of a head wound. Panic shot through him as he recalled stories of people who had suffered blows to the head, never to regain consciousness.

When he found no cut or bump on her head, he ran his hands over her arms and legs, looking for broken bones. Nothing seemed to be broken, so he jerked off his jacket and placed it beneath her head. Sitting back on his heels, he began chafing her wrists.

Her eyelids fluttered, and Clayton almost groaned with relief. Gently smoothing the heavy, rumpled hair away from her forehead, he leaned close to her. "It's all right now, little one. Where are you hurt? Can you speak?"

Sea-green eyes opened, regarding him calmly and steadily. She had such beautiful eyes, he thought as she gave him a shaky, reassuring little smile. But her first words banished all tenderness from his mind. "You will recall," she whispered, "that at the time of the mishap, *I* was in the lead."

Clayton could hardly believe his ears. He stood up on unsteady legs and leaned against the trunk of the tree, staring at her in amazed silence.

"Will you help me up?" she asked after a minute.

"No," he said implacably, crossing his arms over his chest. "I will not."

"Very well," she sighed, rising somewhat stiffly to a standing position and straightening her skirts, "but it's most ungracious of you."

"No more ungracious than it was of you to fake a fall when you realized you couldn't hold the lead."

Giving him a queer look, she reached down and plucked his jacket from the leaves, then she brushed it off and handed it to him. Remorsefully, she shook her head, but Clayton saw the tiny smile that touched her lips. "It has always been one of my most tiresome faults," she admitted with an exaggerated sigh. "And it has caused me a deal of regret, I assure you."

"What has?" Clayton asked, stifling a grin at the complete absence of contrition on her lovely, upturned face.

"Cheating," she solemnly replied. "I do it when I cannot win." She raked her fingers through her hair, grimacing at the leaves that fell from the tousled tresses, and Clayton chuckled to himself. She could turn her faults into virtues and her virtues into faults with a shrug of her shoulders or a shake of her pretty head.

While Whitney searched amidst the leaves for her riding crop, Clayton stalked over to his horse and swung up into the saddle. Trotting over to Dangerous Crossing, he caught the stallion's reins and led him back to Whitney, but when she reached for Crossing's reins, Clayton deliberately led the horse a pace forward, out of her reach. "I am so impressed by your honest confession, young lady," he explained when she dropped her arms and frowned at him, "that I feel I ought to make a confession of my own. You see, I am one of those perverse people who will go to extraordinary lengths to prevent a cheater from winning. In fact, I myself will cheat, to prevent it from happening."

Leading her horse, he trotted a few paces away, then he turned and looked at her over his shoulder. Whitney was staring at him in speechless indignation. "It isn't a long walk back," Clayton reminded her in a laughing voice. "However, if you prefer to ride, someone is bound to come along any moment now to see what has delayed us. But either way, you are not going to remount your rested horse and attempt to finish the race."

Whitney watched through narrowed eyes as he trotted away, leading her horse. In frustrated dismay, she slapped her leg with the crop, then yelped at the sting she received. She sank dejectedly to the ground to await rescue, but the longer she sat there, the funnier it all seemed. She hadn't purposely fallen from her horse at all. If she was guilty of anything, it was of foolishly looking over her shoulder to determine how long it would be before Clayton overtook her tiring mount. When she turned back around, a low limb was jutting out in front of her chest.

Whitney tried to stay angry with Clayton for leaving her so ignominiously behind, but she couldn't sustain her ire. She kept remembering how deeply alarmed he'd seemed as he bent over her. His voice had been hoarse with concern, and his face ravaged with worry as he whispered, "It's all right now, little one."

Whitney pulled out a fistful of grass and tossed it away with a sigh. How she wished Clayton would settle for just being her friend. He would make such a wonderful friend, she thought. He could be so charming and entertaining, and he made her laugh. Perhaps when she was a married woman, Clayton would stop looking at her as a possible conquest and *then* they could be friends. Perhaps—

Whitney forgot about Clayton as Paul came galloping around the bend and reined to a sharp halt beside her. When he saw her sitting there, his expression changed from worry to annoyance. "Do you suppose you could explain to me why it is that every time you and Westland are together, the pair of you seem to vanish?" he demanded irritably.

The moment Clayton trotted into the grove leading Dangerous Crossing, a cry of alarm went up from the spectators. They surged forward with Lady Gilbert in the lead. "What happened?" Whitney's aunt cried. "Where is Whitney?"

"She'll be along," Clayton called to her. Turning in his saddle, Clayton watched Whitney coming into the grove, mounted sideways in front of Sevarin. As he looked at her, he suddenly reversed his earlier opinion of how she had become separated from her horse during the race. However she'd come unhorsed, it hadn't been deliberate, he decided. It simply wasn't in Whitney to quit.

At the finish line, Whitney slid down from Paul's horse and glanced uncertainly at Clayton, wondering what he had told everyone. The spectators converged on her while those who had placed wagers on the outcome of the race shouted for her to give them the results.

Leaning over, Clayton caught her under the arms and swung her up onto his horse so that she was sitting sideways in front of him. "They are waiting for you to tell them who won the race," he pointed out, ignoring her indignant expression at being so familiarly handled.

"My horse was winded over a mile back," Whitney called out. "Mr. Westland won." She turned to Clayton and said under her breath, "Actually, there was no winner."

His brows lifted mockingly. "Your horse was tiring and you were going to lose," he told her. "And you are a fine enough rider to have realized that long before you fell."

"I'm delighted that you are at least willing to give me credit for taking an honest fall," Whitney retorted primly.

Clayton chuckled. "If you had the slightest notion of how much credit I *do* give you, it would astonish you."

Before Whitney could consider that staggering pronouncement, he lifted her effortlessly down from the saddle. Standing beside Paul, she watched Clayton turn his horse and gallop over the crest of the hill.

Thursday dragged by with little to occupy Whitney's time. Paul was busy with preparations for his trip, so she spent her day helping with the arrangements for her father's birthday party on Saturday and catching up on her correspondence with friends in Paris.

Friday morning, she wrote a long letter to Emily, who was back in London. The temptation to break her self-imposed, almost superstitious silence about Paul was nearly past bearing, so she hinted that she would soon have some very exciting news for her friend. She ended with a promise to visit Emily in London, a promise Whitney knew she would keep very soon, because she would need to go there in order to purchase her wedding gown and trousseau. When she was there, she would ask Emily to be matron of honor at the wedding, she decided happily.

She brought the letter downstairs to be sent off, and discovered that Clayton Westland had just arrived. He was chatting amiably with Anne in the rose salon, and he politely rose when Whitney joined them.

"I came to reassure myself that you've fully recovered from your accident the other day," he told her, and there was none of his usual mocking irony in his tone.

Whitney knew this was his way of apologizing for thinking she had faked her fall. "Completely recovered," she assured him.

"Excellent," he said. "Then you won't be able to claim fogged thinking or ill health if I beat you soundly at chess again. This afternoon?"

Whitney rose to his bait like a trout for a fly—which is why she ended up spending the better part of the day pleasurably engaged in battling and bantering with him across the chessboard, with her aunt ensconced on the settee, acting as smiling chaperone while her fingers flew nimbly over her embroidery.

Lying in bed that night, Whitney courted sleep, but it refused to come. She lifted her left hand and looked at her long fingers in the darkness. Would there be a betrothal ring there tomorrow? It was possible, if only her father would return early enough tomorrow afternoon for Paul to speak to him. And then they could announce their engagement at the party tomorrow night.

Whitney was not the only one unable to sleep. With his hands linked behind his head, Clayton stared at the ceiling above his bed, pleasurably contemplating their wedding night. His blood stirred hotly as he imagined Whitney's silken, long-limbed body beneath his, her hips rising to meet his thrusts. She was a virgin, and he would take care to arouse her gently until she was moaning with rapture in his arms.

With that delightful thought in mind, he rolled over onto his side and finally drifted off to sleep.

Chapter Sixteen

LADY ANNE WAS AWAKENED BY THE BABBLE OF VAGUELY familiar voices calling cheerful greetings to one another in the halls. She blinked at the dazzling sunlight and realized her head was pounding, while a feeling of foreboding crept over her.

Martin's surprise birthday party had been Whitney's idea and, at the time, Anne had immediately supported it, hoping it might help bring Martin closer to his daughter. But she hadn't known then of Whitney's betrothal to the Duke of Claymore. Now, she worried that one of the thirty visiting guests might recognize the duke, and then God knew what would happen to all the careful plans hatched by Martin and the duke.

Reaching behind her, she tugged on the bellpull to summon her maid and reluctantly climbed out of bed, unable to shake the feeling of impending doom.

Dusk had fallen when Sewell finally tapped at Whitney's bedroom door and informed her that her father had returned.

"Thank you, Sewell," Whitney called dejectedly. Tonight would have been such a perfect occasion for announcing her betrothal; the Ashtons and the Merrytons and everyone else of any consequence in the neighborhood would be at the party. How she wanted to see their collective reaction to the news that Paul and she were going to be married.

Still, she reasoned hopefully as she lathered herself with carnation-scented soap, there was a chance that Paul might find an opportunity to draw her father aside during the party. Then they could still announce their betrothal tonight.

Three quarters of an hour later, her maid, Clarissa, stood back to survey Whitney's appearance while Whitney dutifully turned around for her inspection.

Whitney's elegant ivory satin gown shimmered in the candlelight, and its low, square-cut bodice molded itself to her breasts, displaying a tantalizing glimpse of the shadowy hollow between them. The wide bell sleeves were trimmed with rich topaz satin from her elbows to her wrists, and a matching band of topaz adorned the hemline. From the front, the gown fell in straight lines, widening slightly at the hem, but viewed from the back, it flared out into a graceful, flowing half train. Topaz and diamonds glittered at her throat and ears, adding their fire to the matching strand of jewels twined in and out among the thick, shining curls of her elaborately coiffed hair.

"You look like a princess," Clarissa announced with a proud smile.

From below and along the halls, Whitney heard the guests stealthily moving about. Her father's valet had been instructed to inform his master that "a few guests" had been invited for dinner, and that he was requested to come downstairs at seven o'clock. Whitney glanced at the clock on her mantel; it was six-thirty. Her spirits lifted as she imagined her father's happy surprise at finding relatives who had travelled from Bath, Brighton, London, and Hampshire to celebrate his birthday. With the intention of asking Sewell to try to keep the guests a little quieter, Whitney slipped out of her room and into the hall.

There on the balcony, leaning over and peering down into the entrance foyer, stood her father, his neckcloth hanging loosely over his starched white shirt. So much for the "surprise," Whitney thought ruefully as she walked over and stood beside him. Below, the local guests were arriving in a steady stream, exchanging greetings in boisterous whispers while a harassed Sewell shepherded them toward the drawing room, admonishing, "Ladies and Gentlemen—Madam, Sir—I must request that you lower your voices."

Her father's puzzled grimace swung from the guests below, to the long hall beside him where two bedroom doors were opened and quickly banged shut again, as the relatives spied their guest of honor standing on the balcony. Whitney pressed a self-conscious kiss on his bristly cheek. "They've come to celebrate your birthday, Papa."

Despite his stern, disgruntled expression, Whitney could tell that he was touched. "I take it that it's to be a surprise, and I'm not supposed to notice this clamor in my house?"

"That's right." Whitney smiled.

"I shall try, my dear," he said, awkwardly patting her arm. Suddenly there was the ear-splitting sound of glass shattering on the floor. "Oh my goodness, *goodness* gracious!" trilled an agitated female voice.

"Letitia Pinkerton," Martin identified the voice with his head tilted slightly to the side. "That is her favorite and *only* expression of dismay." With an odd catch in his voice, he looked at Whitney and added, "I used to send your dear mother into spasms by threatening to teach Letitia to say 'Goddamn!'" With that, he turned and strolled off toward his bedchamber, leaving Whitney staring after him in silent laughter.

Half an hour later, with Whitney on one arm and Lady Anne Gilbert on the other, Martin made his way toward the drawing room. At Whitney's nod, Sewell threw the doors wide and Martin was greeted by exuberant cries of "Surprise!" and "Happy Birthday!"

Anne started forward to begin performing her duties as hostess, but a footman forestalled her. "Pardon me, my lady, but this letter was just delivered by special messenger, and Sewell instructed me to bring it to you directly."

Anne glanced at the letter, saw the familiar, beloved scrawl that was Edward's hand, and with a quick gasp of joyous relief, she took it from him and hurriedly broke the seal.

Whitney looked for Paul, and when she didn't immediately

see him, she made her way to the dining room to make certain that everything was exactly as Aunt Anne and she had planned.

The doors dividing the salon from the dining room had been pushed back, creating one vast area of small tables, each seating six. Enormous clusters of red, white and pink roses reposed in gigantic silver bowls and atop tall floor stands. Silver and crystal gleamed in the candlelight, and her mother's finest linen, in a soft shade of pale pink, was spread on all the tables.

She walked through the salon and peered into the ballroom. Like the other two rooms, the ballroom was lavishly decorated with bouquets of roses that lent color and drama to what had been a cold, austere room.

From behind her she heard Paul's deep voice, and she smiled softly as she turned.

"I missed you today," he said. His gaze drifted appreciatively over her elegant ivory satin gown then lifted to her glowing features. "Who would have guessed," he whispered, drawing her into his arms for a long, tender kiss, "that you were going to turn into such a beauty?"

Anne's eyes were still devouring the contents of Edward's missive as she walked into the dining room. Glimpsing Whitney's ivory gown at the opposite end of the long room, Anne began at once in a happy voice, "Darling, I have finally had word from that laggard uncle of yours! He has been on holiday . . ." She glanced up just in time to witness the hastily broken embrace, and her eyes widened in shock.

"It's all right, Aunt Anne," Whitney explained, blushing gorgeously. "I've been dying to tell you for days, and I can't wait any longer. Paul and I are going to be married as soon as he has Papa's permission. He's going to try to speak to him tonight, so that we— Aunt Anne?" Whitney said as her aunt abruptly turned on her dainty, satin-shod heel and marched away. She apparently had not heard a word Whitney had said. "Where are you going?"

"I am going over to this table, and I am going to pour myself a very large glass of this burgundy," her aunt announced.

In amazed silence, Whitney watched Anne pluck a crystal goblet from the table, snatch up a bottle of burgundy, and fill the glass to the brim.

"And when I have finished this glass," her aunt added, transferring the glass to her left hand and picking up her mauve silk skirts with her right, "I am going to have another." With that she swept regally from the room. "Good evening, Mr. Sevarin," she said, graciously inclining her dark, silver-streaked head at Paul as she passed him. "So nice to see you again."

"She'll have the devil of a head in the morning, if she plans to keep that up," Paul observed wryly.

Whitney looked up at him, her face full of confusion and concern. "Head?"

"Yes, head. And you, my girl, are going to have your *hands* full tonight." Placing his fingers beneath her satin-sleeved elbow, he reluctantly guided Whitney toward the drawing room. "Unless I miss my guess, your aunt isn't going to be of much help entertaining your guests."

Paul's prediction was certainly accurate, Whitney thought with an inward sigh an hour later, as she stood at the entrance to the drawing room, welcoming latecomers. In France, Aunt Anne had always performed the endless duties required of a hostess; now, bearing the full burden of responsibility herself, Whitney felt as if she needed another pair of eyes and ears.

She signalled to a servant for more trays of drinks to be passed among the guests, then turned to greet Lady Eubank. Whitney's eyes riveted in horror on the dowager's startling combination of purple turban and red gown. "Good evening, Lady Eubank," she managed, fighting to keep her face straight.

Ignoring her greeting entirely, the dowager raised her monocle and looked about the room. "It doesn't look like a 'good evening' to me, Miss," Lady Eubank snapped. "I perceive Mr. Sevarin standing over there with Elizabeth Ashton on one arm, and the Merryton girl on the other, and I don't even see Westland in the room." She dropped her monocle and directed a disgusted scowl on Whitney. "I credited you with spunk, girl, and you've let me down. I thought you were going to snare the most eligible bachelor alive right in front of these tiresome neighbors of ours. I've half expected to hear a betrothal announcement, and instead, I find you standing by yourself and—"

Whitney couldn't stop the beaming smile that lit her face. "I have snared him, my lady, and you *are* going to hear an announcement. If not tonight, then as soon as Paul returns from his trip."

"Paul?" Lady Eubank echoed blankly, and for the first time since Whitney had known her, the dowager seemed at a loss for words. "Paul Sevarin?" she repeated. Suddenly a look of unabashed glee danced in her eyes as she again scanned the crowd. "Is Westland coming tonight?" she demanded.

"Yes."

"Good, good," her ladyship said, and she began to chuckle. "This should be a most diverting evening. *Most* diverting!" she chuckled, and strolled away.

By half past nine, the stream of arrivals had dwindled to a trickle. Standing near the entry where she was greeting latecomers, Whitney heard one of them speak to Sewell out in the hall. A moment later, Clayton Westland appeared in the doorway.

Whitney watched him coming toward her. He looked almost breathtakingly handsome in fastidiously tailored black evening attire that hugged his wide shoulders and long legs, and contrasted beautifully with his dazzling white ruffled shirt and neckcloth.

In the spirit of relaxed friendship that had sprung up between them during their afternoon of chess two days ago, Whitney smiled and extended both her hands to him in a cordial gesture of greeting. "I was beginning to think you weren't coming," she said.

Clayton grinned with satisfaction as he took her hands in his. "That sounds very much as if you've been watching and waiting for me."

"If I *had* been, I'd never admit it, you know," Whitney laughed. Looking at him now, she could scarcely credit her belief that he was an unprincipled libertine bent on her seduction, and then she realized that he still retained both her hands in his, and that he was standing so close to her that the starched ruffles at his shirtfront lightly brushed against the bodice of her gown. Self-consciously withdrawing her hands, Whitney took a small step backward.

His eyes mocked her cautious retreat, but he made no comment on it. "If losing two games of chess to you on Thursday has finally put me in your good graces," he teased, "then I promise to let you defeat me in all future contests."

"You did not *let* me defeat you at chess," Whitney reminded him with an exasperated sidewise glance. Catching the eye of a footman, she signalled him to approach. With the finesse of a natural hostess, she asked him to fetch a whiskey for Mr. Westland. When she turned back to Clayton, she glimpsed his surprised pleasure at the fact that she remembered his preference in drink.

It showed in his eyes as he said, "We seem to be at a stalemate. I won our race, but you've won a majority of our chess games. How will we ever prove which of us is the better man?"

"You are impossible!" Whitney berated him, smiling. "Merely because I think that a female should be as well-educated as a man, does not mean I wish to *be* a man."

"It's just as well," he said, and his gaze drifted meaningfully over her exquisite features and provocative figure. His warmly intimate appraisal made Whitney's pulse leap in a bewildering combination of excitement and alarm. "At any rate," he continued, "I doubt there's any other contest of skill in which we could compete evenly. As a male, my youthful pursuits were naturally more vigorous, while yours were sedate and ladylike."

Whitney flashed him a jaunty smile. "How are you with a slingshot?"

His hand stilled in the act of reaching for the drink the footman was handing him. "*You* can use a slingshot?" he said with such exaggerated disbelief that she burst out laughing.

"I wouldn't tell just everyone this," she said, leaning a

trifle closer, while she resumed her vigilant surveillance of her guests' well-being. "But I used to be able to snap the petals off a daisy at seventy-five paces." Across the room, she saw Paul start toward her father and for one moment, it looked as if he would be able to catch him alone, but two of her relatives were already bearing down on him from the other side. Inwardly, Whitney sighed.

Clayton knew she was preoccupied with her guests and that he was monopolizing her time, but she looked so damned beautiful that he was loath to leave her side. Besides, she was practically flirting with him, and he was enjoying every moment of it. "I'm very impressed," he murmured.

Whitney scarcely noticed the betraying huskiness in his tone. She was watching one of her elderly uncles approach a gaily laughing group. "Do any of you know about prehistoric rocks?" Hubert Pinkerton demanded loudly. "Devilish interesting topic. Let me tell you about them. We'll start with the Mesozoic era . . ." In growing dismay, Whitney watched the gay atmosphere of the group deteriorate to polite attention, then restrained antagonism. And she'd so wanted her father's party to be gay and lively!

She turned to Clayton, intending to leave him and try to divert her uncle. "Will you excuse me, I—" She turned her head as a harried-looking footman approached and said that they were running low on champagne. He was immediately followed by another servant requesting instructions about supper. After handling both minor calamities, Whitney turned apologetically to Clayton and saw him frowning as he looked about the room. "Where is your aunt this evening? Why isn't she helping you attend to these details?"

"She's feeling a trifle indisposed," Whitney explained lamely, watching his piercing gaze rivet on Anne, who was clutching a wine goblet and staring trancelike out a window.

"Please excuse me," Whitney said, tipping her head toward Uncle Pinkerton. "I have to rescue those people from my Uncle Hubert. He will bore everyone to distraction talking about prehistoric rock formations, and they already look antagonized enough to do him an injury."

"Introduce me to your uncle," Clayton said. She looked so

astonished that he added, "I will divert him so that you can look after the rest of your guests."

Whitney gratefully brought him over and performed the introductions, then watched in fascinated admiration as Clayton bowed to the elderly man and said smoothly, "I was just now telling Miss Stone how much I would enjoy discussing our mutual interest in the rock formations of the Mesozoic period." Positively emanating enthusiasm, Clayton turned to Whitney and said, "Will you excuse us, Miss Stone? Your uncle and I have much to discuss."

He carried off his flagrant deception with such skill that Whitney could hardly tear her eyes from him as he guided Uncle Hubert off to a deserted corner and appeared to become instantly absorbed in whatever her uncle was saying to him.

The long day of undiluted tension and anxiety as Whitney waited for her father to return had taken its toll. By half past ten, as she gently urged the stragglers into the dining room, Whitney could think of nothing as inviting as finding a quiet corner where she could relax. The guests were making their way along the banquet table, filling their plates from the sumptuous array of foods, when Elizabeth Ashton's father's sudden exclamation halted the line and stopped conversations in mid-sentence. "You say the Duke of Claymore is missing?" he demanded of a visiting relative from London. "You mean Westmoreland?" He clarified as if unable to believe he'd heard right.

"Yes, I thought everyone knew," the relative replied, raising his voice for the benefit of the people who had turned to stare at him. "It was in the papers yesterday, and London is buzzing with speculation over where he is."

The level of conversation in the room soared to a fever pitch. Whitney's neighbors picked up their plates and crowded together at tables where better informed guests from out of town could impart their news. After supper, it was impossible to thread one's way through the people who were clustered between the tables, speculating over the Duke of Claymore's disappearance. Whitney was standing with a large group which included her aunt, Lady Eubank, and Clayton Westland, while Paul was hopelessly trapped across the room, wedged between Elizabeth Ashton and Peter Redfern, unable to make his way to her.

"Claymore's in France this time of year, if you want my guess," someone said.

"Oh? Do you think so?" Lady Anne asked, her face flushed with a vivacious interest that Whitney attributed to too much wine. At the first mention of the Duke of Claymore, her aunt's distraction and lethargy had vanished. But while her aunt was obviously enjoying the gossip and speculation about the man, the subject made Whitney's father fidgety and nervous, and he was periodically slaking an uncharacteristic thirst for whiskey.

Personally, Whitney found the subject excessively boring and she stifled a yawn.

"Tired, little one?" Clayton whispered beside her.

"Yes," Whitney admitted as Clayton drew her hand through the crook of his arm, covering it with his own strong fingers as if he were trying to infuse some of his stamina into her. He shouldn't call her "little one," she thought, and he shouldn't be holding her hand in such a familiar way, but she was too grateful for his assistance tonight to cavil over such trifles.

"I heard that his mistress took her own life in Paris last month," Margaret Merryton said, turning to address her stunned audience. "Apparently Claymore cast her aside, and she went all to pieces. She cancelled her European tour, went into seclusion, and—"

"—And," Amelia Eubank put in frigidly, "she is now spending a fortune renovating a country estate she just purchased. Do you expect us to believe she's a ghost, you henwit!"

Flushing furiously under the assault of Lady Eubank's sharp tongue, Margaret wedged herself around and looked appealingly to Clayton. "Mr. Westland has lately been in Paris and London. Surely *you've* heard the news of her suicide?"

"No," Clayton replied curtly. "I've heard nothing of the kind."

Margaret's papa's thoughts had taken another twist. Stroking his goatee, he said thoughtfully, "So St. Allermain's bought a country estate and is spending a fortune renovating it, is she?" Laughter rumbled in his belly as he turned a slow, knowing leer on the gentlemen. "It sounds to me as if Claymore has pensioned her off—with a bit extra for good behavior!"

Beneath her fingertips, Whitney felt the muscles in Clayton's forearm harden. Tipping her head to see his face, she found him looking at Mr. Merryton and the others with an expression of such excruciating distaste and cold boredom that she almost flinched. Unexpectedly, his gaze slid to her and his expression softened into a faint smile.

Inwardly, however, Clayton was *not* smiling. He was furious at his secretary for failing to put a stop to the speculation over his whereabouts by giving out the story that he was *somewhere!* He was mentally dictating a sharp note of reprimand to the man when he realized, to his infinite disgust, that the guests were now wagering on the identity of his next mistress.

"I'll wager £5 on the Countess Dorothea," Mr. Ashton put in. "Do I have a taker?"

"Indeed you do, sir," Mr. Merryton declared with a sly laugh. "The countess is old news! She's been dangling after Claymore these past five years, even followed him to France with the poor old earl still on his deathbed. And what happened?—I'll tell you what: Claymore cut her dead in front of half of Paris. Lady Vanessa Standfield will be his next choice, but the duke will marry her. She's been waiting patiently for him since her come-out. My £5 says his grace's attention will next turn to Lady Standfield and that he'll marry the young woman. Can I interest anyone in that sporting wager?"

The entire conversation was excessively improper in the presence of ladies and, with great relief, Whitney saw that her aunt was going to intervene at last. "Mr. Merryton," Aunt

Anne said, waiting until she had his full attention. "Would you care to make it £10?"

A shocked silence followed her aunt's unladylike proposition, and Whitney was grateful when Clayton's choked laugh made it seem as if it was all in good fun. Aunt Anne then turned to Clayton. "And you, Mr. Westland?" she asked brightly. "Would *you* care to wager on Lady Standfield being the future Duchess of Claymore?"

Clayton's lips twitched with amusement. "Certainly not. I have it from an unimpeachable source that Clayton Westmoreland has decided to wed an enchanting brunette he met in Paris."

Whitney caught the sly, piercing look that Lady Eubank passed over Clayton, then forgot about it when someone else said, "There's a remarkable similarity in your names, Mr. Westland. Are you by chance related to the duke in some way?"

"We're closer than brothers," Clayton answered promptly, with an arch grin to make it seem an outrageous jest. From there, the conversation drifted to inaccurate descriptions of the duke's lavish estates, to the horses in his famous stables, and inevitably returned to more tales of his mistresses and conquests.

Clayton glanced at his future wife to see how attentively she was listening (and therefore how much further he was sinking in her estimation, by virtue of what she was hearing) and saw Whitney concealing a yawn behind her slender fingertips. Under cover of the group's boisterous banter, Clayton leaned toward her and teased in a low voice, "Aren't you concerned about the future Duchess of Claymore, my lady?"

Caught in the act of yawning, Whitney's gaze flew guiltily to his face. She smiled that slow, unconsciously provocative smile of hers that sent a fresh surge of pure lust firing through Clayton's veins, while smoothing the satin skirt of her gown, preparatory to leaving. "Of course I'm concerned about her," she whispered gravely. "I have the deepest sympathy for anyone who marries that disgusting, dissolute, amoral, lecherous seducer of women!" With that, she turned and headed for the ballroom to instruct the musicians to begin.

There hadn't been the slightest opportunity for Paul to speak to Whitney's father, and with a sinking heart, Whitney watched the hands on the clock lurch toward twelve midnight. During their only dance together, Paul and she had carefully chosen the precise moment of his departure, so that they might snatch a few stolen minutes to say goodbye. Excusing herself, Whitney picked up her skirts and discreetly followed well behind Paul as he strode from the room.

With a shoulder propped against a Gothic pillar, Clayton raised his glass to his lips and watched with a mixture of possessive pride and irritation as Whitney glanced secretively around, then started to follow Sevarin from the room. One of the guests waylaid her, and while Clayton looked on, Sevarin returned to the ballroom and, abandoning all pretense at discretion, took her by the arm and drew her away.

That particular proprietary gesture of Sevarin's sent a stab of sharp anger through Clayton. Why, he wondered, was he standing here like a damned fool, tolerating the Merryton girl's flirtatious advances, when his own betrothed was strolling away on another man's arm? With a sardonic smile, he contemplated the satisfaction he could have by crossing the room in a dozen quick strides and informing Sevarin that he did not like another man's hands on his betrothed. Then, in a few sentences, he could inform Whitney that his "disgusting, lecherous" attentions were permanently fixed on her and that she should prepare herself to be wed within the week!

He was seriously considering doing exactly that when Amelia Eubank bore down on him. "Margaret," Amelia barked heartlessly, "stop hanging on Mr. Westland and go attend to your hair."

Without a trace of sympathy, she watched the young woman blush furiously, then turn and leave. "Nasty chit," Amelia said, directing her attention to Clayton. "The girl is nothing but malice and spite, held together by a core of viciousness. Her parents spend every penny they can scrimp together to send her to London and keep her in society. They can't afford it, and she doesn't belong there. She knows it too, and that makes her envious and mean."

Realizing that he wasn't paying any attention to her, Amelia craned her turbaned head in an effort to discover the object of his unwavering interest. Whitney Stone, she noticed with a tiny smile, was just returning to the ballroom, directly in his line of vision. "Well, Claymore," she said, "if the 'enchanting brunette' you've decided upon is who I think it is, you've taken too long. Her betrothal to Sevarin is to be announced as soon as Sevarin returns."

The duke's eyes turned cold and cynical. "Excuse me," he said in a dangerously soft voice. Putting his glass down, he walked away, leaving Amelia gazing after him with gleeful satisfaction.

Whitney felt Clayton's light touch at her elbow and turned, her warm smile filled with gratitude. From the moment he'd diverted Uncle Hubert at the beginning of the evening, Clayton had carefully placed himself wherever a conversant, amiable, unattached gentleman was most needed. Without being told, he had recognized her need for help and come to her aid. "You must be exhausted," he murmured in her ear. "Can't you slip away and get some sleep now?"

"Yes, I think I will," Whitney sighed. Nearly all the guests had already departed or retired upstairs for the night, and Aunt Anne seemed perfectly willing and able to function as hostess to those remaining. "Thank you for all your help tonight," she said as she turned to leave. "I'm very grateful."

Clayton watched her until she disappeared down the hall, then he strode purposefully toward Martin Stone. "I want a word with you and Lady Gilbert after your guests leave tonight," he said curtly.

Just climbing the stairs was an effort for Whitney's tired legs. Once she was in her room, it took ten minutes of struggling with the long row of tiny satin buttons down her back to unfasten her gown. She leaned forward to step out of it, and a shiny object tumbled from the gaping bodice of her chemise.

With infinite tenderness, Whitney picked up the opal ring

from the carpet and looked at it. Paul's ring, given to her as he left tonight. "To remind you that you're mine," he had whispered, pressing the ring into her palm.

A wild thrill of excitement shot through her now as she slowly placed the opal ring onto her finger. All the exhaustion she'd felt but a moment before seemed to melt away in a burst of joy.

She hummed softly as she wrapped herself in an oriental dressing gown of red silk and sat down at her dressing table to unpin and brush her hair. With each stroke of her ivory-handled brush through her long hair, the glittering opal seemed to catch fire and sparkle in the mirror. Laying the brush aside, Whitney held her hand out in front of her to better admire her betrothal ring. Her betrothal ring! "Mrs. Paul Sevarin," she said softly, smiling at the sound of the wonderful words. "Whitney Allison Sevarin." Something about that tickled her memory, and Whitney said it again, trying to recall . . .

With a joyous laugh, Whitney remembered and hurried over to her bookshelves. Taking down the leather-bound Bible from the shelf, she quickly fanned through the pages, but found nothing. Finally she grasped the book by its covers and turned it upside down, giving it a hard shake. A small scrap of paper, smudged and folded several times, drifted to the floor. Picking it up, Whitney smiled as she began to read:

"I, Whitney Allison Stone, being fifteen years of age and in full possession of my mind and all my faculties (despite what Papa says) do hereby Vow, Swear and Promise that I shall someday manage to make Paul Sevarin marry me. I shall also make Margaret Merryton and everyone else take back every single horrid thing they have said about me. Sworn this day and duly signed by the future Mrs. Paul Sevarin."

Beneath the signature, she'd written "Whitney Allison Sevarin" and then, apparently carried away by her longing, had practiced the wished-for name at least a dozen more times.

Reading that note after so many years, remembering the despair that had driven her to write it, made her joy at possessing Paul's ring swell within her until Whitney thought she would burst if she couldn't show her ring to someone and share her glad tidings.

Going to bed when she felt like this would be hopeless; she was more in the mood for singing and dancing! She had to tell someone, she just had to . . .

Whitney hesitated for a few minutes, and then happily decided to tell her father that Paul was going to offer for her. He would remember how she had chased after Paul years ago, and he would be gratified to know that at last, the villagers would no longer have any reason to ridicule her antics. Now, it was Paul Sevarin who was pursuing *her*. He wanted to marry her!

Whitney checked her appearance in the mirror, straightened the high mandarin collar of her red dressing robe, tightened the sash around her slender waist, and tossing her glossy hair off her shoulder, marched to her bedchamber door.

Trembling with anticipation and a bit of apprehension, she walked along the hall, her robe rustling behind her. In the aftermath of so much laughter and gaiety there was something almost melancholy about the silence now, but Whitney ignored the feeling as she raised her hand to tap on her father's door.

"Your father is in his study, Miss." The footman's voice echoed hollowly from the darkened entrance foyer below.

"Oh," Whitney said softly. Perhaps she ought to show her ring to Aunt Anne tonight, and wait until tomorrow to tell her father everything. "Has my aunt retired yet?"

"No, Miss. Lady Gilbert is with your father."

"Thank you. Good night."

Whitney hastened downstairs, knocked on the study door, and in response to her father's call to enter, she swirled into the room, closing the door behind her. Flattening her palms against the thick oaken panel, she leaned against it. Her smiling gaze took in her father, seated behind his desk directly in front of her and, over to her left, Aunt Anne, who was watching her alertly from a wingback chair at right angles to the fireplace. With only the glow from the cheery little fire to illuminate the room, Whitney completely overlooked the shadowy form seated in the wingback chair opposite her aunt's, with its high back concealing its occupant.

Her father's voice was faintly slurred but friendly as he splashed brandy into his glass. "Yes, Daughter, what is it?"

Drawing a long, deep breath, Whitney plunged in. "I have something wonderful to tell you, Papa, Aunt Anne, and I'm so happy that you're here together, so that I can share it with you both at the same time."

Strolling over to her father, Whitney moved the brandy glass aside and perched a hip on his desk. For a moment she gazed fondly into his glassy-eyed, upturned face, then she leaned forward and planted a kiss on his forehead. "I, Whitney Stone, love you very much, Papa," she said softly. "And I am deeply sorry for the grief I brought you when I was growing up."

"Thank you," he murmured, flushing.

"And," Whitney continued, getting up and coming around the front of the desk so that she could face Aunt Anne, "I love you too, Aunt Anne, but then you've *always* known that."

She drew another long, quavering breath, and suddenly her words came tumbling out, gathering excited momentum. "And I also love Paul Sevarin. And Paul loves me and wants to marry me! And, Papa, when he returns, he's going to ask your permission to do so. I know how— Is something wrong, Aunt Anne?"

Bewildered, Whitney stared at her aunt who had half-risen from her chair and was staring straight ahead with a look of such horrified alarm that Whitney leaned forward and peered into the shadows. She gasped when she saw Clayton Westland sitting there. "I—I beg your pardon! I'm sorry to have interrupted the three of you. As you've probably guessed, Mr. Westland, I had no idea you were sitting there. But since you are," Whitney persevered, determined to finish now that she'd begun, "I hope I can depend upon you not to mention my forthcoming betrothal to anyone. You see . . ." The screech of chair legs on the planked floor as her father heaved himself to his feet, checked Whitney in mid-sentence. The fury in his voice brought her whirling around to face him.

"How dare you!" he bellowed. "What is the meaning of this?"

"The meaning?" Whitney echoed in bewilderment. Her father was standing with palms flat against the top of his desk, his arms trembling. "Paul Sevarin has asked me to marry him, that's all." In defiance of his thunderous glower, which she recalled so well as a child, Whitney added, "And I am going to do it."

Slowly, distinctly, as if he were addressing an idiot, her father said, "Paul Sevarin hasn't a pittance to his name! Do you understand me? His lands are mortgaged, and his creditors are hounding him!"

Despite her shock, Whitney managed to make her voice sound calm and reasonable. "I had no idea Paul was pressed for funds, but I can't see why it should signify one way or another. I have money of my own from my grandmother. And there's my dowry, besides. And whatever I have will be Paul's."

"You have nothing!" her father hissed. "I was in worse straits than Sevarin. The duns were after me. I used your inheritance and dowry to pay them."

Recoiling as much from the vicious tone of his voice as the words he said, Whitney turned to her aunt, expecting her support. "Then Paul and I will have to live simply, without the luxuries my dowry and inheritance could have provided."

Aunt Anne just sat there, clutching the arms of her chair.

In helpless confusion, Whitney turned back to her father. "Papa, you should have told me that you were in such trouble! Why, I—I spent a fortune on clothes and jewels and furs before I came home from France. If only I'd—"

It penetrated through the wave of guilt and alarm sweeping over her that there was something amiss in all of this, something that didn't make any sense. Then it dawned on Whitney what it was. Cautiously, she said, "The stables are filled with new horses. The house and grounds are swarming with more servants than we could possibly need. If you are in such dire circumstances, why are we living in this extravagant manner?"

Her father's face took on a frightening purple hue. He opened his mouth, then clamped it shut.

"Surely I have a right to an explanation," Whitney persisted carefully. "You have just told me that I must marry Paul as a pauper, without dowry, and that my inheritance is gone. If all this is true, how do we manage to live like this?"

"My circumstances improved," he hissed.

"When?"

"In July."

Unable to keep the accusation from her voice, Whitney said, "Your circumstances improved in July, yet you aren't going to replace my inheritance or my dowry?"

His fist crashed against the desktop; his roar reverberated through the room. "I'll tolerate no more of this farce. You're betrothed to Clayton Westmoreland. The arrangements have been made. The settlement has already taken place!"

The subtle difference in Clayton's surname momentarily escaped Whitney's notice as she groped frantically through the tumult in her mind. "But how—why—*when* did you do this?"

"In July!" he hissed. "And it's settled, do you understand? It's final!"

Whitney stared at him through eyes huge with horror and disbelief. "Are you telling me that you made a settlement on this man without ever consulting me? You pledged my dowry and my inheritance to a perfect stranger, without considering my feelings?"

"Damn you!" her father hissed between his clenched teeth. "*He* made the settlement on *me!*"

"You must have been a very happy man in July," Whitney whispered brokenly. "You finally managed to rid yourself of me forever, and this 'gentleman' actually paid you for me, and—oh God!" she cried. With sudden, heartbreaking clarity, all the pieces of the bizarre puzzle fell into place, presenting the whole gruesome picture, complete in every profane detail.

Closing her eyes against the scalding tears that threatened, she braced her hands on the desk for support. When she opened them, she saw her father through a bleary haze. "He has paid for all of this, hasn't he? The horses, the servants, the new furniture, the repairs to the house . . ." She choked on her next words. "The things I bought in August in France. What I'm wearing now, he paid for that too, didn't he?"

"Yes, dammit! I had lost everything. I had sold everything I could."

A boulder settled where Whitney's heart had been; cold fury dwelled where there had been love. "And when there was nothing else you could bear to part with, you sold me! You sold me to a perfect stranger for a lifetime!" Whitney stopped, drawing a long, anguished breath. "Father, are you *certain* you got the best price for me? I hope you didn't take his first offer. Surely you haggled a little—"

"How dare you!" he thundered, slapping her across the face with a force that nearly sent her to her knees. His hand lifted to strike her again, but the biting fury in Clayton Westmoreland's voice checked him in mid-motion. "If you touch her again, Martin, I'll make this the sorriest day of your life."

Her father's face froze, then sagged with defeat as he sank back into his chair. Whitney swung around on her "rescuer," her voice shaking with fury. "You low, vile snake! What sort of man are you that you have to purchase a wife? What sort of animal are you that you had to buy her without ever having seen her? How much did I cost you?" she demanded.

Despite her haughty stance, Clayton saw that her beautiful eyes, which were hurling scornful daggers at him, were also glittering with unshed tears. "I am not going to answer that," he said gently.

Whitney's thoughts circled, looking for some crack in his armor of implacable calm, some spot where she could thrust the blade of her anger. "You couldn't have paid much," she taunted. "The house you live in is no more than modest. Did you squander your entire pitiful fortune on acquiring me? Did my father drive a hard bargain or—"

"That's enough," Clayton interrupted quietly, coming to his feet.

"He can give you everything . . . everything," her father rasped behind her. "He's a duke, Whitney. You'll have everything you—"

"A duke!" Whitney scoffed contemptuously, glaring at Clayton. "How did you manage to convince him of that, you lying, conniving . . ." Her voice broke, and Clayton tipped her chin up, forcing her rebellious gaze to meet his.

"I am a duke, little one. I told you that months ago, in France."

"Why you . . . You Human Pestilence! I wouldn't marry you if you were the King of England." Jerking her head away, she hissed furiously. "And I never had the misfortune to lay eyes on you in France."

"I told you I was a duke at a masquerade in Paris," he persisted quietly. "The Armands' masquerade."

"You liar! I didn't meet you there. I had *never* met you until I came home!"

"Darling," Aunt Anne said with gentle caution. "Think back to the night of the masquerade. Just as we were leaving, you asked me if I could identify one of the guests—a very tall man with gray eyes, wearing a long black cloak and . . ."

"Aunt Anne, please!" Whitney expelled her breath in an uncomprehending rush of frustrated impatience. "I didn't meet this man that night or any . . ." A strangled gasp emitted from Whitney as a kaleidoscope of images chased themselves across her mind. A pair of now familiar gray eyes glinted down at her in the Armands' garden. A deep voice tinged with laughter said, *"Suppose I told you that I am a duke . . ."*

In the space of ten seconds, all these memories collided head on with the reality of the present, bringing her whirling around on Clayton in a tempestuous fury. "That was you! That was you, skulking behind that mask!"

"Without a quizzing glass," Clayton confirmed with a grim smile.

"Of all the treacherous, despicable, underhanded . . ." Whitney ran out of words to express her turbulent animosity at approximately the same time another blinding realization

207

dawned, bringing with it a fresh rush of scalding tears. "My Lord Westmoreland"—she spat his correct surname with all the contempt she could summon—"I should like to inform you that I found the endless conversation about you this evening—about your estates, your horses, your wealth, your women—not just boring, but utterly *nauseating!*"

"So did I," Clayton agreed sardonically.

The amusement Whitney thought she heard in his voice was like acid on a burn. Clutching a fold of her dressing robe, she twisted it until her knuckles turned white, while she tried to drag enough air through the thick knots of emotion in her chest to speak. All she could manage was a painful constricted whisper. "I'll hate you for this until the day I die!"

Ignoring her threat, Clayton said gently, "I want you to go to bed now and try to get some sleep." He slid his hand under her elbow, tightening his hold when she tried to pull free. "I'll come back in the afternoon. There are a great many explanations to be made, and I'll make them, when you're in a better frame of mind to listen."

Not for one second was Whitney deceived by his pretense of tender concern. The moment Clayton finished speaking, she snatched her arm away and stalked to the door.

As she reached for the brass handle, he added in a flat, authoritative voice, "Whitney, I expect you to be here when I arrive." Whitney's hand froze on the handle; her heart shrieked her resentment of his commands, his directives, his existence! Without so much as a backward glance to indicate she'd heard, she wrenched the door open, barely restraining the wild urge to jerk the oak panel shut behind her with a crash.

So long as they could hear her footsteps in the hall, Whitney walked slowly, refusing to give them the satisfaction of hearing her flee like a terrified hare. At the end of the hall she turned, her pace quickening with every step until she was rushing headlong, tripping on a stair, then running down the hall toward the safety, the sanity, of her room. Once inside it, she leaned against the door in a cold, trembling paralysis . . . staring at the cheerful, cozy room she'd left so excitedly but a half hour ago, her mind unable to cope with the disaster that had just occurred.

Downstairs in the study, the awful, ominous silence lengthened until even the air seemed to crackle with tension. Clayton stood with his hands braced against the fireplace mantel, staring into the fire with murderous rage emanating from every inch of his taut, powerful frame.

Martin dropped his hands from his face so abruptly that his fists thudded against the desktop, making Anne jump. "It was the liquor, I swear it," Martin whispered, his face ashen. "I've never raised a hand to her before. What can I do to . . ."

Clayton's head jerked around. "What can you do?" he snapped savagely. "You've done enough! She'll marry me, but she'll make you pay for what happened tonight and, in doing so, she'll make me pay as well." His tone changed, his words coming slowly, like uncoiling whips. "From this night forward, no matter what she says, you are going to keep your mouth shut! Is that clear to you, Martin?"

Martin swallowed hard and nodded. "Yes. Clear."

"If she tells you she's just put poison in your tea, you are going to drink it, and you'll . . . keep . . . your . . . god damned . . . mouth . . . shut!"

"Yes. Shut."

Clayton started to say more, then stopped, as if he could no longer trust himself to speak. With a curt bow to Anne, he strode swiftly to the door and jerked it open. He paused, his icy gaze swinging back to Martin. "When next you're counting your blessings, give thanks to Almighty God that you have twenty years on me, for I swear that if you didn't—" With a superhuman effort, Clayton bit off the rest of his threat and stalked from the room, his rapid footsteps echoing sharply down the hall.

In front of the house, the coach lamps on the duke's carriage flickered and wavered in the breeze, conjuring eerie shapes that crept forward, then pirouetted away beneath the rustling, swaying branches of the elms that lined the drive.

James McRae, Clayton's coachman, shifted patiently on his perch. All the guests had left, with only the duke remaining behind, but McRae didn't mind waiting. In fact, he could not have been more pleased that his master was prone to linger in Miss Stone's company, for he had wagered a rather large sum of money with Armstrong, the duke's valet, that Miss Stone was destined to be the next Duchess of Claymore.

The front door of the house opened and the Duke of Claymore bounded down the front steps. From the corner of his eye, McRae observed the duke's long, ground-devouring strides, which were eloquent of either rage or exhilaration. McRae wasn't certain which, nor did he think it much mattered; so long as Miss Stone continued to provoke such unprecedented emotional reactions in the duke, the odds continued to grow in McRae's favor.

"Let's get the hell out of here!" the duke growled, flinging himself into the open carriage and slamming the door behind him.

Something's amiss with the lass, McRae concluded with a chuckle, sending the magnificent grays bowling down the drive. So delighted was he, that not even the persistent throbbing of his abscessed wisdom tooth could dull his spirits. Mentally visualizing a variety of pleasant ways to spend the proceeds from his wager, McRae began to hum a lilting Irish melody. After a few bars, the duke leaned forward and demanded furiously, "Are you in pain, McRae?!"

"No, your grace," McRae hurriedly replied over his shoulder.

"In mourning?" the duke snapped.

"No, your grace."

"Then cease that goddamn moaning!"

"Aye, your grace," McRae said, carefully concealing his happy expression from his infuriated master.

Chapter Seventeen

WHITNEY SLOWLY OPENED HER EYES, BLINKING IN CONFUSION AT the late morning sunlight filtering through the draperies. Her head ached dully, and she felt strangely, unaccountably melancholy. Her benumbed mind refused to function, preferring instead the anesthesia of watching the shadows creeping across the gold carpet as the sun was slowly obliterated by a heap of dark clouds rolling past. She frowned, trying to understand the bitter desolation that seemed to be weighting her down, and in that instant, the scene in the study last night penetrated her sleep-fogged consciousness.

In a panic, Whitney squeezed her eyes closed, trying to shut out the reality of the Cheltenham Tragedy that had been enacted, with all its macabre plots and twisted subplots, but it was too painfully sinister to be ignored.

Dragging herself up into a sitting position, she twisted around and arranged the pillows behind her, then fell back against them. She knew she had to think, to plan, and with grim determination she set about systematically reviewing what facts she had. First, the man who occupied the Hodges' place was Clayton Westmoreland, the "missing" Duke of Claymore. Which, she thought listlessly, finally explained his expensive clothes and those monstrously aloof servants of his.

He was also the man she'd met at the Armands' masquerade, the same arrogant, lecherous . . . With an effort, Whitney set aside her boiling animosity and made herself return to the facts at hand. After they met at the masquerade, Clayton Westmoreland must have come directly to her father to purchase her for his wife. Her father said last night that everything was "arranged," which undoubtedly meant that a preliminary marriage contract was already signed.

Once Clayton had accomplished that, the unspeakable cad had evidently installed himself and his servants in his lair, not two miles from her front door.

"Unbelievable!" Whitney whispered aloud. It was more than that, it was ridiculous, absurd! But, whether it was or not, it was also true. She was technically . . . obscenely . . . unwillingly betrothed to the Duke of Claymore. Betrothed to a notorious libertine, a profligate rake!

Why, he was as hateful as her father! Her father . . . The agonizing recollection of her father's heartless treachery was more than Whitney could bear. She drew her knees up against her chest, wrapping her arms tightly around her legs in a sort of protective cocoon, and rested her forehead on her knees. "Oh, Papa," she whispered brokenly, "how could you have done that to me?" The lump in her throat grew and grew until it was suffocating her; unshed tears burned her eyes and made her throat ache unbearably. But she didn't let go, would not break down.

She had to be strong. Her opponents outnumbered her two to one—three to one, if Aunt Anne were a party to this monstrous scheme. The thought that her beloved aunt might have betrayed her too, very nearly broke the dam of her control. Swallowing convulsively, Whitney stared out the window across the room. She might be outnumbered now, but when Paul returned, he would stand against them too.

In the meantime, she reminded herself sternly, she would have to rely on her own courage and determination, but she had plenty of both, and a stubborn nature that Clayton Westmoreland heretofore had only glimpsed! Yes, she could manage perfectly well on her own until Paul returned.

Almost gleefully, Whitney began planning ways to thwart and foil and exasperate the duke. By the time she was finished with him, his grace would know that if he wished to have either peace or joy in his remaining years, she was not the wife for him! Perhaps if she was clever enough, she might even maneuver him into crying off and, by the time Paul returned, this vile betrothal could be nothing more than an unpleasant memory.

There was a light tap on the door, and Aunt Anne walked in, her features composed into a sympathetic, encouraging smile. Friend or foe? Whitney wondered, watching her warily. Forcing herself to sound calmly unemotional, Whitney said, "When were you informed of this, Aunt Anne?"

Her aunt settled herself on the bed. "On the same day you saw me send letters to your uncle in four different countries and cancel my trip to London."

"Oh," Whitney whispered hoarsely. Aunt Anne had been trying to locate Uncle Edward to come to their aid; she hadn't betrayed her. A piercing sweetness flooded through Whitney, washing away her defenses until her chin quivered. Her shoulders began to shake with relief and misery and, as Aunt Anne's arms went around her, Whitney surrendered to the harsh, racking sobs that had been screaming for release since the moment she'd awakened.

"Everything is going to be fine," her aunt soothed, smoothing the soft tangles from Whitney's hair.

When the last rush of tears subsided, Whitney found she felt immensely better. She dried her eyes and smiled ruefully. "Isn't this the most wretched coil, Aunt Anne?"

Her aunt fervently agreed that it was, then disappeared into the adjoining bathroom, returning with a soft cloth wrung out in cold water. "Here, darling, press this against your eyes so they won't be swollen."

"I am going to marry Paul," Whitney said in a muffled voice, obediently holding the damp cloth to her face. "I have planned to since I was a child! But even if I hadn't, I wouldn't wed that . . . that degenerate lecher!" Whitney pulled the cloth away in time to see her aunt quickly smother a frown. "You *are* on Paul's side, aren't you, Aunt Anne?" she questioned anxiously, scrutinizing her aunt's noncommittal face.

"I'm on *your* side, darling. Only yours. I want what's best for you." Anne started for the door. "I'll send Clarissa in to you. It's nearly noon, and his grace sent word he would arrive at one o'clock."

"'His grace!'" Whitney repeated, infuriated by this reminder of Clayton's lofty rank. All other noblemen were referred to merely as "his lordship" and addressed as "my lord," but not a duke. Because a duke outranked all other noblemen, he must be addressed much more respectfully—as "your grace."

"Whitney, shall I have your new challis pressed?" Anne persisted.

Whitney glanced bleakly out the window. Half the sky promised a bright, sunny day, while the other half was dark and overcast. The wind was up and the trees were swaying fitfully. She didn't think this was the time to look her best; in fact, since she didn't *want* Clayton Westmoreland's admiration, she ought to look her worst! She would wear something drab and, more important, something *he* hadn't paid for. "No, not the challis. I'll think of something else."

By the time Clarissa came in, Whitney had decided what to wear, and the idea filled her with grim, perverse satisfaction. "Clarissa, do you remember the black dress Haversham used to wear when she scrubbed the stairs? Will you see if you can find it."

Clarissa's kindly face was furrowed with bewildered sympathy. "Lady Gilbert told me what happened last night, child," she said. "But if you mean to antagonize the man, you may be making a terrible mistake."

The compassion Whitney saw in her faithful maid's plump face almost reduced her to tears again. "Oh, Clarissa, please don't argue with me," Whitney begged. "Just say you'll help me. If I look ugly enough, and if I'm very strong and very clever, I may be able to make him decide to give up and go away."

Clarissa nodded, her voice gruff with repressed tears. "I've never failed to stand by you, and I have the white hairs to prove it. I'll not abandon you now."

"Thank you, Clarissa," she whispered humbly. "Now I

know I have at least two friends to stand by me. Three with Paul."

An hour and fifteen minutes later, bathed and seated at her dressing table, Whitney flashed an approving smile in the mirror as Clarissa twisted her heavy hair into a thick knot and secured it with a slender black ribbon. The severe hairdo accented Whitney's classically sculpted features and high cheekbones. Her wide green eyes, with their heavy fringe of sooty lashes, seemed enormous in her pale face and added to the overall effect of fragile, ethereal beauty. Whitney, however, thought she looked ghastly. "That's perfect!" she said. "And you needn't rush so—his grace can cool his heels and wait for me. That's part of my plan. I intend to teach him some distasteful lessons about me, and the first one is that I'm not the least impressed by his illustrious name and title, nor have I any intention of leaping to his commands."

At one-thirty, Whitney went down to the small salon where she had deliberately instructed the butler to install Mr. Westland when he arrived. Pausing with her hand on the brass door handle, she lifted her chin and swept silently inside.

Clayton was standing with his back partially to her, impatiently slapping his tan gloves against his muscular thigh, while he gazed out the windows overlooking the front lawns. His broad shoulders were squared, his jaw set with implacable determination, and even in this pensive pose, he seemed to emanate the restrained power and unyielding authority she had always sensed—and feared—in him.

Drop by precious drop, Whitney felt her confidence draining away. How could she have deluded herself into believing she could sway him from his purpose? He was no foppish, romantic young gallant to be put off with a cool smile or polite indifference. Not once since she'd met him had she ever emerged the victor in any conflict with him. Bracingly, Whitney reminded herself that she only had to cope with him alone until Paul came back.

She closed the door behind her, and the latch clicked into place. "You sent for me?" she said in a flat, emotionless voice.

For the past twenty minutes, Clayton had been struggling with his mounting annoyance at being made to wait in a small stuffy room like a beggar hoping for a handout. He had told himself a dozen times that Whitney had been hurt and humiliated last night, and that today she would undoubtedly demonstrate her rebellion against him by doing whatever she could to defy and provoke him.

As he turned at the sound of her voice, he reminded himself that no matter what she said or did, he would be patient and understanding. But when he looked at her, it was all he could do to bridle his temper. Her chin held defiantly high, she stood before him, decked out like a servant in a long, shapeless, threadbare black dress. A white apron was tied around her slender waist, and her lustrous hair was hidden beneath a mob cap. "You've made your point, Whitney," he told her curtly. "Now I'll make mine. I will not have you dressed like that ever again!"

Whitney bristled at his tone. "We are all your servants in this house. And *I* am the lowliest servant of all, for I'm nothing but a bondservant whom you purchased from the debtor's block."

"Don't use that tone of voice with me," he warned. "I'm not your father."

"Of course you aren't," she mocked. "You're my *owner.*"

In three long strides, Clayton closed the distance separating them. Furious that her anger was ricocheting off her stupid father onto him, he grasped her hard by the upper arms, longing to shake her until her teeth rattled. Beneath the harsh grip of his hands, he could feel her body tense, bracing for violence.

She lifted her head, and his anger slowly drained away. Although her glorious green eyes were glaring defiance at him, they were sparkling with suppressed tears, shining with pain that *he* had caused. The translucent skin beneath them was smudged with dark shadows, and her normally glowing complexion was drained of color. Gazing down at her lovely, rebellious face, he asked quietly, "Does the mere thought of being my wife bring you such misery, little one?"

Whitney was shocked by his unexpected gentleness and, worse, completely at a loss as to how to answer. She wanted to appear haughty, coldly remote—anything but "miserable," for that was tantamount to "weak" and "helpless." On the other hand, she could scarcely say *No, the idea doesn't make me miserable.*

A discordant note of laughter echoed through the hall, followed by footsteps and chattering voices as three of the Stones' houseguests passed the salon on their way to the dining room. "I want you to come outside with me," Clayton said.

He didn't ask, he *stated,* Whitney noted angrily. Outside, they crossed the drive and walked across the sloping front lawn toward the pond in the center. Beneath a graceful old elm near the edge of the pond, Clayton stopped. "At least we can hope for some privacy out here," he said.

It was on the tip of Whitney's tongue to retort that the *last* thing in the world she wanted was privacy with him, but she was in such an emotional turmoil that she couldn't trust herself to speak.

Stripping off his jacket, he placed it on the grass beneath the tree. "I think we could discuss this better if we sat down," he said, inclining his head toward the jacket.

"I prefer to stand," Whitney said with cold hauteur.

"Sit!"

Infuriated by his imperious tone, Whitney sat—but not on his jacket. Instead, she dropped to the grass, curled her legs beneath her, and stared straight ahead at the pond.

"You're quite right," Clayton observed drily. "The damage to those rags you're wearing is much less important than soiling one of my favorite jackets." So saying, he picked up his jacket and put it around her stiff shoulders, then settled himself beside her.

"I'm not cold," Whitney informed him, trying to shrug his jacket off.

"Excellent. Then we can dispense with this absurd cap you're wearing." He reached up and snatched the little mob cap from her hair, and Whitney's temper ignited, sending a flush of hot color to the soft curve of her cheek. "You rude, overbearing . . ." She clamped her mouth closed in frustrated rage at the glint of laughter in his gray eyes.

"Do go on," Clayton encouraged. "I believe you left off at 'overbearing.'"

Whitney's palm positively itched to slap that mocking grin from his face. She drew a long, rasping breath. "I wish I could find the right words to tell you just how much I loathe you, and everything you represent."

"I'm sure you'll go on trying until you do," he remarked agreeably.

"Do you know," Whitney said, staring fixedly at the pond, "I hated you from the first moment I met you at the masquerade, and the feeling has intensified with every encounter since then."

Pulling his knee up, Clayton rested his wrist on it and studied her impassively for a long, silent moment. "I'm very sorry to hear that," he said softly. "Because I thought that you were the loveliest, most enchanting creature God ever created."

Whitney was so startled by the gentle caress in his voice that she snapped her head around and searched his face for signs of sarcasm.

Reaching out, he traced his forefinger along the curve of her cheek. "And there have been times, when you were in my arms, that you gave no sign of this hatred you insist you've always felt. In fact, you seemed to *enjoy* being there."

"I have *never* enjoyed your attentions! In fact I've always found them . . ." Whitney groped desperately for the right word, hampered by the knowledge that they both knew her traitorous body *had* responded to his caresses. "I've always found them—most disturbing!"

He slowly brushed his knuckles along her chin, up to her earlobe, sending shivers down her spine. "Those times were 'disturbing' for me as well, little one," he murmured quietly.

"Yet you persisted in doing it, although I told you not to!" she blazed. "Even now, this very minute, I can tell you're just waiting for another opportunity to—to pounce on me!"

"True," he admitted with a throaty chuckle. "I'm drawn to you like a moth to a flame. Just as you are to me."

Whitney thought she was going to explode. "Why you conceited bas—"

His forefinger pressed against her trembling lips, silencing her. Grinning, he shook his head. "It grieves me to deprive you of one of your epithets, but I have it on the best authority that there is no question of my legitimacy."

Her life was in tatters and he was laughing! Flinging off his restraining hand, Whitney scrambled to her feet and said woodenly, "If you don't mind, I'm tired. And I'm going inside. I can't share your humor in all of this. I have been sold by my own father to a stranger, an arrogant, cold-hearted, selfish fiend, who, without a care for my feelings—"

Panther-quick, Clayton rolled to his feet, his hands locking like slave manacles on her arms as he pulled her around to face him. "Allow me to help you itemize my crimes against you, Whitney," he said with cool calm. "I am so cold-hearted that I saved your father from debtor's prison by paying all his debts. I am so selfish that I've stood by, watching you flirt with Sevarin, so arrogant that I let you sit next to him at that goddamned picnic and snipe at me, when the taste of your mouth was still warm on mine. And why have I done this? Because in my cruel, fiendish way, I want to give you the protection of my name, an unassailable position at the pinnacle of society, and a pampered life replete with every luxury within my power to grant you." He looked at her levelly. "For this, do you honestly think I deserve your bitterness and animosity?"

Whitney's shoulders drooped. She swallowed and looked away, her spirit shattered. She felt confused and miserable, no longer entirely right—yet not completely wrong either. "I—I don't know what you deserve."

He tipped her chin up. "Then I'll tell you," he said quietly. "I deserve nothing—except to be spared the hatred and blame for your father's drunken blundering last night. That's all I ask of you for now."

To Whitney's mortification, tears welled up in her eyes.

Brushing them away with her fingertips, she shook her head, declining his proferred handkerchief. "It's only that I'm tired. I didn't sleep very well last night."

"Nor did I," he said feelingly, escorting her back to the house. Sewell opened the front door, and from the salon came peals of laughter and loud, jesting remarks on the progress of the whist games apparently in progress. "We'll ride tomorrow morning. But if we aren't going to provide the main topic of conversation for your houseguests, I think it would be best if I met you down at the stables. At ten o'clock."

In her room, Whitney untied the white apron and pulled off the ugly black dress. Even though it was not yet two, she felt limp and exhausted. She knew she should put in an appearance downstairs, but she recoiled from the thought of the false smile she would have to wear and the gay chatter she would have to listen to; besides, if just one person said so much as a word about the Duke of Claymore, she was positive she would have hysterics!

The gold coverlet had been neatly turned down, and the bed beckoned to her. A nap might restore her spirits and enable her to think more clearly, she decided. She slid between the cool covers, and, with a heavy sigh, she closed her eyes.

When next she awoke, the moon was riding high in a black velvet sky. She rolled over onto her stomach, seeking the peace of slumber before she lost it to wakefulness and the torturous thoughts that would surely come.

Chapter Eighteen

CLAYTON WAS LEANING AGAINST THE FENCE, LAUGHING WITH Thomas when Whitney arrived at the stables the next morning. Whitney managed a smile for Thomas, but it died on her lips when she looked at the lazily relaxed man beside him.

When she didn't reply to his "Good morning," Clayton sighed resignedly and straightened. Tipping his head toward Khan, who was being led out of the stable, he said, "Your horse is ready."

They raced side by side across the rolling countryside. Soon the hell-for-leather speed and the fresh autumn breeze revived Whitney's flagging spirits, making her feel more alive than she had in two days.

At the edge of the woods where the meadow sloped down to the stream, Clayton drew up and dismounted, then walked over to lift Whitney down from Khan. "The ride has done you good," he said, noting the blooming color in her cheeks.

Whitney knew he was trying to break the ice and carry on a reasonably normal conversation with her. Sullenness was foreign to her nature, and she felt horribly churlish for remaining silent, yet it was impossibly awkward trying to talk to him. Finally she said, "I do feel better. I love riding."

"I like watching you," he said as they strolled over to the bank of the stream. "You are without question the finest horsewoman I have ever seen."

"Thank you," Whitney said, but her alarmed gaze was riveted on the old sycamore perched atop the knoll beside the stream, its ancient gnarled branches sheltering the very spot where she had lain in his arms the day of the picnic. It was the last place on earth she wished to be with him now. Clayton shrugged out of his jacket and started to put it on the grass, precisely where they had lain the last time. Hastily, she said, "I'd rather stand, if you don't mind." To illustrate her point, she retreated a step and leaned her shoulders against the sycamore's trunk, as if it were the most comfortable place in the world to be.

With a noncommittal nod, Clayton straightened and walked two paces away, propping his booted foot upon a large rock beside the stream. Leaning his forearm on his bent knee, he studied her impassively, without speaking.

For the first time, it really penetrated Whitney's bemused mind that this man was her affianced husband! But only for the time being, she told herself—just until Paul returned and they could carry through with the plan she had in mind. For now, all she could do was tread carefully and bide her time.

The bark of the tree dug into her shoulder blades, and Clayton's unwavering gaze began to unnerve her. For lack of anything better to say, and anxious to break the tense silence, Whitney nodded toward the place where he had tied his chestnut stallion. "Why didn't you ride that horse against me in the race? He's much faster than the sorrel you rode."

Her chosen topic of conversation seemed to amuse him as he glanced at the horses. "Your black stallion tired too easily when I rode him the day of the picnic. I rode the sorrel because he's about equal in stamina and speed to your stallion, and I was trying to give you a fair chance to win. If I'd ridden this brute against you, you wouldn't have had a prayer. On the other hand, if I'd ridden a vastly inferior horse against your stallion, you wouldn't have enjoyed winning."

Despite her dire predicament, Whitney's lips twitched with laughter. "Oh yes, I would. ¹ would have enjoyed beating you in that race, even if you were riding a goat!"

Chuckling, he shook his head. "In the three years I've known you, you've never failed to amuse me."

Whitney's eyes narrowed suspiciously. "Three years? How could that be? Three years ago, I'd only just made my come-out."

"You were in a millinery shop with your aunt, the first time I saw you. The proprietress was attempting to foist off on you a hideous hat covered with little grapes and berries, by convincing you that if you wore it for a stroll in the park, the gentlemen would fall at your feet."

"I don't recall the time," Whitney said uncertainly. "Did I buy the hat?"

"No. You informed her that *if* the gentlemen fell at your feet, they would only be trying to avoid the swarm of frenzied bees who were attracted by a fruit platter wearing a female."

"That rather sounds like the things I say," Whitney admitted, self-consciously toying with her gloves. She could almost believe there was tenderness in the way Clayton spoke of the incident, and it flustered her. "Is that when you decided you . . . ah . . . wanted to know me better?"

"Certainly not," he teased. "I was relieved that the proprietress, and not I, had to withstand those flashing green eyes of yours."

"What were you doing in a millinery shop?" Before the question was out, Whitney could have bitten her foolish tongue! What *would* he be doing there, except waiting for his current mistress?

"I can see from your expression that you've arrived at the answer to that," he remarked blandly.

Repressing her irrational annoyance over his being in the shop with another woman, Whitney asked, "Did we meet again after that— I mean, before the masquerade?"

"I saw you occasionally that spring, usually driving in the park. And then I saw you again a year later, quite grown up, at the DuPres' ball."

"Were you alone?" The question just seemed to pop out, and Whitney clenched her fists in self-disgust.

"I was not," he admitted frankly. "But then, neither were you. In fact, you were surrounded by admirers—a snivelling lot, as I recall." He chuckled at Whitney's indignant glare. "There's no reason to glower at me, my lady. You thought they were too. Later that evening, I overheard you telling one of them who was nearly killing himself with rapture over the scent of your gloves, that if the smell of soap affected him so, he was either deranged or very dirty."

"I would never have been so rude," Whitney protested, uneasily aware that he had called her "my lady" as if she were already his duchess. "He sounds only silly and not at all deserving of such a setdown, and . . ." Forgetting what she was about to say, she stared past Clayton, trying to bring a hazy recollection into focus. "Did he walk with absurd little mincing steps?"

"Since I was far more interested in your face than his feet, I wouldn't know," Clayton responded drily. "Why?"

"Because I do remember saying that now," she breathed. "I remember watching him mince away, thinking how thoroughly I disliked him. Then I turned around and saw a tall, dark-haired man standing in the doorway, smiling as if the entire scene had amused him. *It was you!*" she gasped. "You were spying in that doorway!"

"Not spying," Clayton corrected. "I was merely preparing to lend a hand to the poor besotted devil in case you drew blood with that razor tongue of yours."

"You shouldn't have bothered, for he more than deserved anything I said. I can't recall his name, but I do remember that the evening before, he'd tried to kiss me, and that his hands had a nauseating tendency to wander."

"A pity," Clayton drawled icily, "that you can't recall his name."

Beneath demurely lowered lashes, Whitney stole a peek at his ominous expression and realized with satisfaction that now he, and not she, was the jealous one. It dawned on her then that if she could appear fickle, perhaps even a little fast, he might have second thoughts about wanting to marry her. "I think I ought to tell you that he wasn't the only gentleman in Paris who tried to win my affections and became . . . overeager. I had dozens of serious suitors in Paris. I can't even remember all their names."

"Then allow me to assist you," Clayton offered calmly. While Whitney stared at him in shock, he rapped off the names of every man who had offered for her. "I left out DuVille," he finished, "because he is still biding his time. But I suppose I ought to include Sevarin, since he is *trying* to offer for you. It appears to me, Madam," he continued conversationally, again addressing her as if she were already a married woman, "that for a sensible young woman, you are extremely foolish about the men you allow to court you."

To avoid discussing Paul, Whitney seized upon Clayton's implied criticism of Nicki. "If you are referring to Nicolas DuVille, his family happens to be one of the oldest and most respected in France!"

"I am referring to Sevarin, and you know it," he said in a coolly authoritative tone that Whitney particularly resented. "Of all the men I mentioned, Sevarin is the least suitable, yet if it had been left to you, he would be your choice. He is no match for your intelligence or your spirit or your temper. Nor," he added meaningfully, "is he man enough to make a woman of you."

"And just what do you mean by that remark?" Whitney demanded.

His glance slid meaningfully to the grassy spot near her feet where he had used the crop on her tender backside, then held her in his arms, soothing her. "I think you know *precisely* what I mean," he said, watching the pink tint creeping up her cheeks.

Whitney wasn't completely certain, but she did know it was not a subject she wished to pursue. She switched to an earlier, less inflammatory one. "If you were so 'taken' with me in France, why didn't you do the proper thing and approach my uncle to make your offer?"

"So that he could fob me off with that nonsense about your being too young to marry, and your father not being ready to part with you yet?" he said with sardonic amusement. "Hardly!"

"What you really mean," Whitney retorted, "is that it was beneath your exalted position in life to bother being introduced to me, and then to—"

"We *were* introduced," Clayton interrupted. "We were introduced that same night, by Madame DuPre. You didn't pay enough attention to hear my name, and you accorded me a brief nod and one shrug before you returned to the more pressing business of accumulating as many fawning admirers as you could squeeze around your skirts.''

How that cool reception must have deflated him, Whitney thought with secret pleasure. "Did you ask me for a dance?" she needled sweetly.

"No," he replied drily. "My card was already full."

Under other circumstances, Whitney would have laughed at the joke, but she knew that it was intended as a barbed reminder that he, too, was popular with the opposite sex. As if she needed to be reminded! She threw him a derisive look that matched her tone. "I imagine that if men did have dance cards, *yours* would always be full! Now that I think about it, what does a man do with his mistress when he desires to dance with someone else?"

"I don't recall having found that an insurmountable obstacle the night you and I danced at the Armands' masquerade."

The gloves Whitney had been holding dropped to the grass. "How *dare* you be so crude as to—"

"—as to even bring up such a thing?" he countered smoothly. "Isn't the saying 'an eye for an eye'?"

"I can hardly believe my ears!" Whitney scoffed furiously. "If you aren't a living example of 'the devil quoting scripture.'"

"Touché." He grinned.

His amusement only made Whitney angrier. "You may be able to dismiss your scandalous conduct with a laugh, but I can't. In the time I *remember* knowing you, you've made lewd suggestions to me at the Armands', insulted me at Lady Eubank's, and assaulted me in this very spot." Whitney bent down and snatched her gloves from the grass. "God alone knows what you'll try to do next."

Her last sentence brought a warm gleam to his eyes, and Whitney warily decided it was time to leave. She started to stalk past him toward the horses, but he reached out and caught her wrist, pulling her toward him. "With the exception of the Armands' masquerade, I have always treated you precisely as you've deserved to be treated, and that's the way it will always be between us. I have no intention of letting you walk all over me. If I did, you'd soon have no more respect for me than you would have had for Sevarin, had you been unfortunate enough to marry him."

Whitney was thunderstruck by his monumental gall in presuming to know *how* she would feel, and she was stricken by the awful finality with which he dismissed her plan to marry Paul as an unfortunate whim, entirely beyond the realm of possibility. And to make everything worse, his arms were encircling her at that very moment. "Don't you care that I don't love you?" she asked despairingly.

"Of course you don't," Clayton teased, "You hate me. You've told me so at least half a dozen times. Right here, in this very spot, as a matter of fact. And just a few moments before you became a warm, passionate woman who held me in her arms."

"Stop reminding me of what happened that day! I want to forget it."

He gathered her closer against his muscular frame and gazed down at her with tender amusement. "Little one, I would give you anything within my power, but I will never let you forget what you were that day. Never. Ask anything else of me, and it's yours."

"Ask anything else of you and it's mine?" she scoffed, wedging a space between them by forcing her hands up against his chest. "Very well. I don't want to marry you. Will you release me from my father's bargain?"

"No, I'm afraid not."

Whitney could hardly contain her bitterness and animosity. "Then don't insult my intelligence by pretending to care about my wishes! I don't want to be betrothed to you, but you won't release me. I don't want to marry you, but you fully intend to drag me to the altar anyway. I—"

He let go of her so abruptly that Whitney staggered back a step. "Had I any intention of 'dragging you to the altar,'" he said tersely, "you would have been ordered home from France to be fitted for your wedding gown. However, the simple fact is that I don't want a cold, unwilling wife in my bed."

Whitney was so relieved and overjoyed that she completely forgave his suggestive reference to his bed. She threw up her hands. "Good heavens, *why* didn't you tell me that before? Since that's the way you feel, there's no need for you to trouble yourself with me any longer."

"Meaning?"

"Meaning that I would make you the coldest, most unwilling wife imaginable."

One dark eyebrow flicked upward in a measuring look. "Are you threatening me?"

Whitney hastily shook her head, smiling. "No, of course not. I'm only trying to explain that my feelings toward you won't change."

"You're quite certain?"

"Absolutely positive," Whitney said brightly.

"In that case, there's very little point in delaying the wedding any longer, is there?"

"What?" Whitney gasped. "But you said you wouldn't marry me if I was cold and unwilling."

"I said that I didn't *want* to do so. I did not say that I wouldn't, if that's the way it has to be." With that he nodded curtly toward the horses and started to turn, leaving Whitney petrified that he intended to go straight back to the house and summon a cleric to officiate at their wedding. No doubt he already had a special license! Her mind sought frantically for some way to save herself. If she fled, he'd overtake her; if she threatened him, he'd ignore her; if she refused, he'd make her.

She chose the only solution open to her, humiliating though it was to have to plead and wheedle. Reaching out, she laid her hand upon his sleeve. "I have a favor to ask of you, and you did say that you would give me anything within your power—?"

"Within my power," he stated coolly, "and within reason."

"Then will you give me time? I need time to get over this awful feeling I have of being a helpless pawn in a chess game

228

being played by you and my father, and I need time to become adjusted to the idea of our marriage."

"I will give you time," he agreed evenly, "provided that you use it with discretion."

"I will," Whitney assured him, lying more easily now. "Oh, and there's one more thing: I'd like to keep both your identity and our betrothal a secret between us for a while."

His expression turned coolly speculative. "Why?"

Because when she eloped with Paul next week, Clayton was going to be furious. But if she made a complete fool of him by publicly scorning him in front of villagers who knew of their betrothal, God alone knew what form his vengeance might take.

"Because," she said cautiously, "if everyone knows about you—us—they'll want to talk about who you are and how we met and when we're getting married, and I'll feel more pressed than I already do."

"Very well, we'll keep it a secret for now." He walked her to her horse and lifted her effortlessly into the saddle. Thinking the subject was closed and their meeting at an end, Whitney gathered up Khan's reins, eager to get away. But he wasn't finished yet, and her entire body tensed at the threat disguised beneath the smooth politeness of his tone. "I've granted you the time you asked for because you said you want to become accustomed to the idea of our marriage. If I ever have reason to think you want the time for some other purpose, you will not like the consequences."

"Are you through?" Whitney asked, hiding her fright behind hauteur.

"For now," he sighed. "We'll talk more tomorrow."

Whitney spent the rest of the day with her relatives. With her entire future hanging by a thread, it took a supreme effort to smile and converse with these cheerful, well-meaning people, and to ignore her father's apprehensive glances. The moment the evening meal was over, she excused herself and escaped to the quiet of her room.

Late that evening, Anne came up to see her. Whitney, who had been dying to confide in her all day, jumped up from the settee, wringing her hands in pent-up frustration. "Aunt Anne, that arrogant, ruthless tyrant actually intends to force me to marry him. He said as much this morning."

Settling herself on the settee, Anne drew Whitney down beside her. "Darling, he can't force you to marry him. I'm certain England has laws which would prevent him from doing so. As I see it, your problem is not whether he can force you to marry him, but rather, what will happen to your father if you don't."

"My father didn't consider the consequences to me when he agreed to the betrothal, so I don't feel the slightest need to consider the consequences to him, if I don't agree to the marriage. He has never loved me, and I no longer love him."

"I see," Anne said, watching her closely. "Then it's probably best that you feel that way."

"Why do you say that?"

"Because your father has already spent the money Claymore gave him. If you refuse to honor the betrothal agreement, his grace will naturally demand the return of his money. Since your father can't give it back, he will very likely spend his declining years in a rat-infested cell in debtors' prison. If you had any love left for him, it might be very difficult for you to be happy with Paul, knowing that you were responsible for your father's plight. But so long as you're completely certain that you'd feel no guilt, we really needn't concern ourselves one way or another with your father, need we?"

The door closed behind her aunt, leaving Whitney haunted with gruesome images of her father, ragged and filthy, rotting away in a wretched, dank cell.

There had to be some way to repay Clayton Westmoreland the money he had settled on her father. Perhaps if she and Paul lived very carefully, they could repay the debt on her father's behalf over a period of years. Or better yet, there might be some way to goad the duke into crying off from the engagement himself, so that the money wouldn't have to be returned. Or would it? How had the preliminary marriage contract been worded? Whitney wondered.

"Uncle Edward!" she breathed suddenly. Uncle Edward

would never stand idly by, knowing Whitney was being forced to exchange her life for her father's debts. Perhaps Uncle Edward could advance her father the funds to repay Clayton —a purely business arrangement, of course. She herself would see that the estate was put up as collateral.

But did Uncle Edward have sufficient capital to repay Clayton? If only she knew how much money had changed hands. It must have been a great deal, because it had paid for all the extensive repairs to the house, two dozen new horses, a dozen servants, and her father's debts, too. £25,000? £30,000? Whitney's heart sank; Uncle Edward wouldn't have so much as that.

When Clarissa came in to awaken Whitney the next morning, she found her seated at her writing desk, thoughtfully nibbling on the end of a quill.

After a minute's deliberation, Whitney began to write. Her eyes sparkled with triumphant satisfaction as she politely explained to Clayton that she had wrenched her knee and had to remain abed. She ended with a sugary statement that she would look forward to seeing him on the morrow—if her pain lessened. She signed it simply, "Whitney," then sat back, congratulating herself.

The idea of an injured knee was an absolute inspiration, for such injuries were not only painful, but unpredictably long in mending. Tomorrow she could send him another sorrowful note, and add a few convincing details about how the imaginary injury had occurred. With any sort of luck, she might be able to avoid seeing him until after Paul returned!

"What would you like to wear when you see the duke today?" Clarissa asked.

A beaming smile dawned across Whitney's features. "I'm not going to see him today, Clarissa. Or tomorrow, or the day after. Listen to this," Whitney said, and quickly read the note to her.

"Well, what do you think?" she asked, folding it and sealing it with a few drops of wax.

Clarissa's voice was tight with alarm. "I think he'll realize what you're up to, and he'll bring the house down around our ears. ı don't want any part of it. You should ask Lady Anne before you send it."

"I can't wait for my aunt to arise, and you *have* to take part in it," Whitney explained patiently. "You must bring the note to him."

Clarissa paled. "Me? Why do I have to do it?"

"Because I need to know exactly how he reacts to it, and I can't depend upon anyone else to tell me."

"I get palpitations of the heart just thinking of what could go wrong," Clarissa complained, but she took the note for delivery. "What if he asks me questions about the injury?"

"Just make up answers," Whitney advised cheerfully. "Only remember to tell me what you say to him so that I don't accidentally contradict you."

When Clarissa left, Whitney felt as if an enormous weight had been lifted from her shoulders. Humming gaily, she went over to the wardrobes to select a gown to wear.

Clarissa returned twenty minutes later, and Whitney rushed out of the dressing room. "What did he say?" she asked eagerly. "How did he look? Tell me everything."

"Well, his grace was at breakfast when I arrived," Clarissa said, nervously fingering the starched collar of her dress. "But the butler showed me directly to him as soon as I said who I was. Then I gave his grace the note and he read it."

"He wasn't angry, was he?" Whitney prompted, when Clarissa fell silent.

"Not that I could tell, but I don't think he was pleased either."

"Clarissa, for heavens sake! *What did he say?*"

"He thanked me for bringing the note, then he nodded toward one of those uppity servants of his, and I was shown out."

Whitney wasn't certain whether she should feel relieved or apprehensive about his reaction, and as the day wore on, she discovered that her respite was not so blissful as she'd expected it to be.

By noon, she jumped every time she heard footsteps in the hall, thinking that she was going to be informed that Clayton had come to call. It would be just like the man to insist that her aunt accompany him to her bedchambers, even though that would be an unforgivable breach of propriety.

Dinner was brought up to her on a tray, and Whitney ate in bored solitude. For the first time all day, her thoughts drifted to Paul. Poor Paul, she thought contritely. She'd been so caught up in this web of intrigue, trying to outmaneuver and second-guess Clayton Westmoreland, that she hadn't devoted any thought at all to the man she loved.

Chapter Nineteen

THE NEXT MORNING, WHITNEY DASHED OFF A SECOND NOTE TO her betrothed, going into more detail about the agonizing pain she was suffering from her clumsy tumble down the staircase, and begging rather prettily to be excused from seeing him today. Although it meant having to spend another long day alone in her room because she couldn't risk being caught downstairs with her relatives should Clayton decide to inquire personally about her ankle, Whitney felt the enforced solitude was more than worth it—not only because she could avoid Clayton, but because she had the equally great satisfaction of outwitting him!

"Do you really think this is wise, darling?" Anne frowned, reading Whitney's clever note. "If you anger him needlessly, I can't think what he'll do."

"There's nothing he *can* do, Aunt Anne," Whitney reassured, sealing the note and handing it to Clarissa to deliver. "You've already written to Uncle Edward asking him to come quickly. When he arrives, he'll help me think of some way out of this. In the meantime, I'll continue with this farce about my knee for as long as I can, then I'll think of something else. Maybe I can *bore* his grace into going away," Whitney laughed.

Clarissa returned to report in a harassed voice that the

duke had scanned the note, and looked at her in an exceedingly odd way.

"Clarissa, please, can't you be more specific than that?" Whitney begged impatiently. "What sort of 'odd' way?"

"Well, he read it," Clarissa recounted. "Then he looked as if he were about to smile. But he didn't exactly smile, and he asked another one of his high-and-mighty servants to show me out."

Whitney bit her lip as she puzzled over Clayton's baffling reaction, then with a smiling shrug, she dismissed the entire matter. "The three of us really should stop worrying about his every word and gesture. After all," she said breezily, flopping down on the settee, "whether he thinks I'm lying or not, what can he possibly do about it?"

The answer to that question arrived shortly after luncheon in a sleek, black-lacquered Westmoreland travelling coach drawn by four prancing black horses in silver harnesses. A somberly garbed, portly gentleman alighted from the conveyance and proceeded briskly toward the house. In his left hand he carried a large black leather bag; in his right a small engraved card which he handed to Sewell. "I am Dr. Whitticomb," he said to the butler. "I have been brought here from London and instructed to ask for Lady Gilbert."

When Anne greeted him in the salon, Dr. Whitticomb smiled politely into her puzzled eyes and explained, "His grace, the Duke of Claymore, has sent me to examine Miss Stone's knee."

Lady Gilbert turned so white that Dr. Whitticomb feared she might be ill, but after bidding him to wait, she left the room, snatched up her skirts, sprinted down the hallway, and vaulted up the staircase with a speed and agility that would have been remarkable in a healthy female half her years.

"He's done what?" Whitney shrieked, jumping to her feet and sending the volume of *Pride and Prejudice* in her lap thudding to the floor. "Why that low, vile . . ."

"There'll be time enough for all that later, if we survive this," Anne panted, already unfastening Whitney's dress with shaking fingers and jerking it unceremoniously over her head.

Clarissa was hauling back the bedcovers, then flying to the wardrobe from which she snatched a fleecy dressing robe.

"Couldn't you have told him that I was asleep or something, and sent him back to London?" Whitney implored as she dived into bed and pulled up the covers.

"Dr. Whitticomb," Anne said, trying to catch her breath, "is no fool, believe me. He's been sent here to treat your knee, and he intends to do exactly that." Casting a quick, critical eye over Whitney, she said, "Clarissa, bring two pillows and place them beneath Whitney's knee. Then fetch some hartshorn from my room and put it on the bedside table. That will be a nice touch, I think." She started for the door. "I'll forestall Dr. Whitticomb for as long as I can to give you time, but don't count on more than a few minutes."

Clarissa remained rooted to the floor, her eyes glassy, her hands gripping the back of a chair. "Clarissa!" Lady Anne said sharply. "Do not even *consider* fainting!"

"I thank you, Lady Gilbert, but no," Dr. Whitticomb said, refusing for the third time the refreshments which, in an apparent excess of polite solicitude, Lady Gilbert was again trying to press upon him. He had already replied to her inquiries about the weather in London, the weather outside, and the pleasantness of his journey from London. When she tried to engage him in a discussion over how much snow they ought to expect this winter, Dr. Whitticomb said bluntly, "I wonder if I might see Miss Stone now."

Lady Gilbert led him upstairs and down the hall to the fourth door on the left. After a curiously long interval, the door was finally opened by a stout, elderly maid whose mob cap sat crazily askew atop her wiry gray head. Dr. Whitticomb, who was no stranger to the temperaments of wealthy, pampered young ladies, immediately assumed that Miss Stone was spoiled and had harassed her poor maid until that woman looked ready to swoon dead away.

This conclusion was reinforced by the appearance of the patient herself, a young lady of stunning good looks and high color who was reclining upon a large canopied bed, eyeing his approach with ill-concealed antagonism. A pair of jade-green eyes narrowed briefly on his face, wandered indifferently along his black frockcoat, then riveted in alarm on the black bag he carried.

Trying in his compassionate way to distract his patient from her terrified preoccupation with his instrument case, Dr. Whitticomb put it down beside her bed and said soothingly, "His grace, the Duke of Claymore, is most deeply concerned about you."

Two bright spots of color appeared on her high cheekbones. In a strangled voice, she whispered, "He is the embodiment of kindness and solicitude."

"Quite so," Dr. Whitticomb agreed, not able to believe the sarcasm he thought he heard. "As I understand it, Miss Stone," he began briskly, "you took a nasty fall down the staircase." Reaching for the bedcovers, he said, "Let's just have a look at that knee, shall we?"

"Don't!" she yelped, clutching the bedcovers to her pretty chin and eyeing him mutinously.

For a moment he stared at her in amazement, but then he realized what was distressing her and his expression gentled. Drawing up a chair beside the bed, he sat down. "My dear girl," he said kindly, "we are no longer in the dark ages when a female denied herself the ministrations of a competent physician merely because he was a man and she a woman. I applaud your modesty—God knows we see it all too seldom in young ladies these days—but this is *not* the proper time for it, as I am sure your aunt would tell you. Now then . . ." Reaching out, he tried to draw the sheets back, but his patient's tightly clenched fists exerted equal pressure to draw them in the opposite direction.

Dr. Whitticomb reared back and frowned with frustrated annoyance. "I am a competent physician with a score of female patients, including Her Majesty, if that will reassure you, Miss Stone."

"Well, it doesn't reassure me in the least!" his patient fired back in a voice remarkably strong for one supposedly in excruciating pain.

"Young woman," he warned, "I am under specific orders from his grace to examine your knee and prescribe the proper care. *And,*" he added ominously, "he instructed me to have you restrained, if necessary, in order to do so."

"Restrained!" Whitney burst out. "Of all the unmitigated, unbelievable gall! Just who does he think would *dare* to do such a . . ." She choked back her outburst, already visualizing Clayton striding into her bedchamber in defiance of every law of decency and propriety, and forcibly pinning her to the bed, so that Dr. Whitticomb could examine her knee.

Frantically, she groped for some way to deter the physician from examining her. Excessive modesty was her only hope. Her lids fluttered closed, then opened to regard the man in charming embarrassment. Shyly, she plucked at the sheets. "I know how silly and foolish I must seem to you, Dr. Whitticomb, but I would simply die of mortification to be so . . . exposed . . . to a perfect stranger, no matter how fine a doctor you are."

"My dear girl, we are only talking about 'exposing' your knee, after all."

"But I can't help the way I feel," Whitney protested virtuously. "You don't know me, but surely his grace, who does know me, should have considered my tenderest feelings in this. I'm quite shocked by his callous disregard of my . . . my . . . ?"

"Maidenly sensibilities?" the doctor offered automatically, thinking to himself that Claymore was going to have his work cut out for himself on his wedding night with this young woman, and that it was a very good thing that the duke was no novice where females were concerned.

"Exactly! I knew you would understand."

Reluctantly Dr. Whitticomb capitulated. "Very well, Miss Stone, I will not examine your knee on one condition: You must permit a local physician to examine it."

"Immediately!" Whitney agreed, beaming a bright smile on him.

Leaning over, he snapped his bag shut and picked it up. "Do you know of someone who has experience with sprains and breaks—someone with whom you could feel comfortable?"

"Someone with experience with sprains and breaks?"

Whitney repeated, searching madly for some name to give him. "Why yes. Yes, I do," she announced triumphantly.

"Who?" Dr. Whitticomb persisted, standing up. "What is his name?"

"Thomas," Whitney provided promptly, smiling widely at her own inspiration. "I trust him implicitly, as does everyone for miles around—whenever there's a sprain or a break, it is always brought to Thomas for treatment." With a gracious smile, she said, "Goodbye, Dr. Whitticomb. I do thank you for coming, and I'm most dreadfully sorry for the inconvenience you've been caused. Clarissa will show you out."

"No need to bid me farewell just yet," Dr. Whitticomb assured. "I'll be up to see you after I've spoken with Dr. Thomas."

"Oh dear God!" Clarissa gasped, blindly clutching the bedpost for support.

Dr. Whitticomb ignored her outburst. Reaching into his waistcoat pocket, he withdrew a heavy gold timepiece, glanced at the time, then snapped it shut. "His grace's driver and coach are waiting, so if someone will be so kind as to direct me to Dr. Thomas, I'll meet with him and assure myself of his credentials, then bring him back with me."

Whitney levered herself up on both elbows. "Whatever for? I mean, I've just assured you that he's qualified. You can take my word for it."

"No, I'm sorry, but I can't. Even if I were willing to entrust your health to some unknown colleague, which I'm not, I can assure you that the duke would never permit it. Actually, we discussed calling in Grundheim from Germany; he's a good man with injuries to the joints. And there's Johannsen in Sweden—"

"He wouldn't dare!" Whitney retorted.

"Actually," Dr. Whitticomb admitted ruefully, "it was *my* idea to have them come to examine your knee. Claymore thought it best if I saw you first. He had certain—ah—doubts about the severity of your injury. Lady Gilbert," he said, "would you be so kind as to give me directions to Dr. Thomas?" He started for the door, but stopped in his tracks when, from the occupant of the bed, there came a stifled moan, followed by a series of blistering remarks about someone's character and integrity, liberally salted with words such as "scoundrel, wretch, blackguard, and hypocrite."

Dr. Whitticomb turned in surprise. Gone was the shy, demure young lady who'd sighed and languished in her bed but a moment before. His lips twitched with laughter and admiration as he beheld the tempestuous beauty who was now sitting bolt upright against the pillows, positively emanating stormy wrath.

"Dr. Whitticomb," the beauty snapped at him, "I really cannot endure another moment of this. For the love of God, look at my knee before *that man* has every leech in Europe at my bedside!"

"I personally do not condone leeching," Dr. Whitticomb remarked as he walked back to the bed and put his instrument case down. This time there was no resistance when he drew back the bedcovers. He parted her dressing robe well below the thigh, exposing a pair of long, shapely limbs, one of which was propped upon a pile of pillows.

"That's odd," he said, suppressing a smile as he glanced at his rebellious patient. "Yes indeed—I wondered about the lump created by this pile of pillows."

Whitney frowned at him. "I can't see anything the least bit 'odd' about two pillows propping up an injured knee."

"I quite agree with you there." Dr. Whitticomb's eyes twinkled. "But unless I misread your note to his grace, it was your *left* knee which was injured. Yet it is your right knee which we see here upon these pillows."

His finger pointed accusingly to the wrong leg and Whitney pinkened. "Oh that," she said hastily. "We propped the right leg up to keep it from bumping the left."

"Very quick thinking, my dear," Dr. Whitticomb said with a chuckle.

Whitney closed her eyes in chagrin. She wasn't fooling him at all.

"There doesn't appear to be any swelling." His fingers gently felt first her right knee, then her left, then the right again. "Do you feel any pain here?"

"Dr. Whitticomb," Whitney said with a resigned smile trembling on her lips, "would you believe, even for one second, that I am in any pain?"

"No. I'm afraid not, actually," he admitted with equal candor. "But I must say I admire your knack for knowing when the time has come to throw in your cards and call the game lost." He replaced the bedcovers and leaned back in his chair, gazing at her in thoughtful silence.

He couldn't help admiring her spirit. She'd concocted a scheme and she'd done her level best to see it through. And now, when she was defeated, she conceded the victory to him without rancor, no missish sulks and sullens, no tears or begging. Damned if he didn't like her for it! After a moment, he straightened and said briskly, "I expect we should discuss what I am going to do next."

Whitney shook her head. "There's no need to explain. I know what you're obligated to do."

Dr. Whitticomb gave her an amused look. "First of all, I'm going to prescribe absolute, undisturbed bedrest for the next twenty-four hours. Not for you"—he laughed at Whitney's joyous expression—"but for your poor, beleaguered maid behind me, who's been torn between grabbing the nearest heavy object and bludgeoning me unconscious or swooning dead away." Plucking the hartshorn bottle from the bedside table, he passed it to Clarissa. "If you will take some free advice from an extremely expensive physician," he told her severely, "you will not involve yourself in any more of this lovely hoyden's intrigues. You haven't the constitution for it. Besides, your face quite gave your mistress away."

When Clarissa closed the door behind her, Dr. Whitticomb turned his gaze upon Lady Gilbert, who'd gone round the bed and was standing beside Whitney, waiting like a condemned man in the box to share her niece's sentence. "You, Lady Gilbert, are not in much better condition than that maid. Sit down."

"I'm quite all right," Lady Anne murmured, but she sank to the bed.

"Much better than all right," Dr. Whitticomb chuckled.

"Quite splendid, I should say. You never betrayed your niece by even the flicker of an eye." Whitney was the next object of the doctor's penetrating gaze. "Now then, how do you think your future husband is going to react to this deception of yours?"

Whitney closed her eyes against the frightening image of an enraged Clayton, his gray eyes icy and his voice vibrating with cold fury. "He'll be furious," she whispered. "But that was the risk I took."

"Then there's nothing to be gained by confessing the deception, is there?"

Whitney's eyes snapped open. "Me confessing? I thought *you* were going to tell him the truth."

"The truth I have to tell, young lady, is this: An injury to a joint, any joint, can be difficult, even impossible, to diagnose. Despite the absence of swelling, I could not definitely rule out the possibility that your knee was injured precisely as you claimed. Beyond that, any further revelations will have to come from you. I am here as a physician, you know, not an informant."

Whitney's spirits soared. She snatched a pillow from beside her and hugged it to her chest, laughing with relief and gratitude. After thanking him three times, she said, "I don't suppose that you could tell his grace that I should stay in bed?"

"No," Dr. Whitticomb said flatly. "I cannot and would not do so."

"I quite understand," Whitney said generously. "It was just a thought."

Reaching out, he took Whitney's hand in his and smiled gently. "My dear, I have been a friend of the Westmoreland family for many years. You are soon to become a Westmoreland, and I would like to think we are also friends. Are we?"

Whitney was *not* going to become a Westmoreland, but she nodded acceptance of his offer of friendship.

"Good. Then allow me to presume upon this new friendship of ours by telling you that denying your fiancé your company in order to gain whatever it is you want, is not only foolish but risky. It was obvious to me that his grace has a great affection for you, and I truly think he would give you anything you want if you simply gave him that lovely smile of yours and *asked* him for it."

More emphatically he said, "Deceit and deviousness do you no credit, my child, and what's more, they will get you absolutely nowhere with the duke. He has known females far more skilled in deception and trickery than you, and all those ladies ever got from him was the opportunity to amuse him for a very brief time. While you, by being direct and forthright as I sense that you are, have gained the very thing those other females most desired. You," he said, "have gained the offer of his grace's hand in marriage."

Fireworks exploded behind Whitney's eyes; bells clanged in her ears. *Why* did everyone act as if she'd just been offered the crown jewels because Clayton Westmoreland had stepped down from his lofty pinnacle and deigned to make poor little lucky her an offer of marriage? It was insulting! Degrading! Somehow she managed to nod and say, "I know your advice is well meant, Dr. Whitticomb. I—I'll think about it."

He stood up and smiled at her. "You'll think about it, but you don't plan to follow it, do you?" When Whitney made no reply, he reached down and patted her shoulder. "Perhaps you know best how to deal with him. He's quite taken with you, you know. In fact, I never thought to see the day anything or anyone would unnerve him. But you, my dear, have come very close. When I arrived from London this morning, I found him wavering between anger and laughter. One moment, he was quite prepared to break your pretty neck for pulling this 'stunt,' I believe he called it. The next minute he was laughing and regaling me with stories about you. The man is torn between merriment and murder."

"So when he couldn't choose between the two, he sent you here to teach me a lesson," Whitney concluded darkly.

"Well, yes," Dr. Whitticomb said, chuckling. "I rather think that was his intent. I confess that I felt a certain annoyance when I discovered that the patient I'd been hauled out of my house and bounced across half of England to treat was most likely shamming. But now that I've been here, I daresay I wouldn't have missed it for the world!"

Gaiety, Whitney thought testily as she dined with her houseguests that evening, was not a balm for misery, it was an irritant. But then, nothing seemed to help. In an attempt to bolster her drooping spirits, she had taken extra care with her appearance and had even worn one of her new gowns—a soft powder-blue confection. At her throat and ears were blue sapphires encircled with diamonds which she'd bought her last day in Paris. Her hair was pulled back off her forehead and fastened with a diamond clip, leaving the rest to cascade naturally over her shoulders and down her back.

I am a kept woman, she thought as she listlessly pushed at a stuffed oyster with her fork. *He* had paid for the clothes she was wearing, the jewels, even her underthings. To add to her unwholesome feelings about herself, her cousin Cuthbert's slavering gaze kept slithering sideways as he tried to steal a glimpse of what her bodice concealed.

Her father, she noted, was behaving with artificial joviality, proclaiming to his guests how happy he was that they'd come, and how sad he was that they were departing tomorrow. Whitney thought that he probably *was* sorry to see them go. After all, he had been using them as a shield to insulate himself from her impending wrath. So much the better, Whitney thought. She didn't want a confrontation with him. All she felt for him now was a frigid core of . . . nothingness.

After the gentlemen had enjoyed their port and cigars, they joined the ladies in the drawing room, where tables were set up for whist. The instant Cuthbert saw her, he started toward her table. He was pompous, balding and, to Whitney, wholly repulsive. Mumbling a quick excuse to Aunt Anne about not wanting to play whist, Whitney hastily stood and left the room.

She wandered down the back hall and into the library, but could not find anything of interest among the hundreds of books lining the shelves there. The salons were being used for parlor games, and Cuthbert was in the drawing room. Under no circumstances could Whitney endure another moment near him, which left her the choice of either returning to her bedroom and the plaguing problems that would haunt her there, or else going into her father's study.

She chose the latter and, after Sewell brought her a pack of cards and added a log to the cheerful fire burning in the grate, Whitney settled into a high-backed chair beside the fire. I am becoming a hermit, she thought, slowly shuffling the deck, then laying the cards, one at a time, on the parquet table in front of her. Behind her, she heard the door open. "What is it, Sewell?" she asked without looking around.

"It isn't Sewell, Cousin Whitney," chanted a singsong voice. "It is I, Cuthbert." He sauntered over and stood beside her chair where he could avail himself of this new view of the creamy swells above her bodice. "What are you doing?"

"It's called solitaire," Whitney explained in a cool, ungracious voice, "or Napoleon at St. Helena. It can only be played by one person."

"I never heard of it," said Cuthbert, "but you must show me how."

Gritting her teeth, Whitney continued to play. Every time she leaned forward to place a card on the table, Cuthbert leaned forward too, feigning interest in the play while his gaze delved into her bodice. Unable to endure it a moment longer, Whitney slapped the cards down and leapt to her feet in irritated resentment. "Must you stare at me?" she snapped.

"Yes," Cuthbert rasped, grasping her arms and trying to pull her toward him, "I must."

"Cuthbert," Whitney warned ominously, "I'll give you just three seconds to take your hands off of me before I start screaming the house down."

Unexpectedly, Cuthbert did as she commanded, but as his arms dropped, his body followed. Falling to one knee, he placed a hand over his heart, preparatory to proposing matrimony. "Cousin Whitney," he murmured hoarsely, indulging himself in a visual fondling of her from the tips of her toes to the top of her head and back down. "I must tell you what is in my heart and mind—"

"I *know* what is in your mind," Whitney interrupted

scathingly. "You've been ogling me for hours. Now get to your feet!"

"I have to say it," he persisted in rising tones. His pudgy hands felt the hem of her blue gown and Whitney snatched her skirt away, half convinced that he intended to lift it and peak beneath it. Deprived of her hem, his hand returned to cover his heart. "I admire you with every fiber of my being. I have the deepest regard for—" Gulping, he broke off, his widened eyes riveted on a point behind her.

"I sincerely hope," drawled a lazily amused voice from the doorway, "that I am not interrupting a devoted man at his prayers?" Strolling to Whitney's side, Clayton looked down at an angry Cuthbert until Whitney's cousin finally staggered to his feet.

"My cousin was teaching me a new game of cards, and only one can play," he said.

The indulgent amusement in Clayton's expression vanished. With a curt nod toward the door, he said, "Now that you have learned, go and practice."

Cuthbert clenched his fists, hesitated, took a second look at the coldly determined line of his opponent's jaw, and left. Whitney watched the door close behind him and looked up at Clayton with relieved gratitude. "Thank you, I—"

"I ought to break your neck!" Clayton interrupted.

Too late, Whitney realized that she shouldn't have been standing all this time on her "injured" knee.

"Allow me to congratulate you on a fine day's work, Madam," he said sternly. "In less than twelve hours, you've brought Whitticomb to your side and Cuthbert to your feet."

Whitney stared at him. Although his tone was very grave, one corner of his mouth was quirked into something that looked suspiciously like a grin. To think she'd been quaking with fear because she thought he was furious! "You devil!" she whispered, torn between laughter and anger.

"I would hardly describe you as an angel," Clayton mocked.

All day, Whitney's emotions had been careening crazily between anger, dread, fear, and relief, rebounding from one near calamity to the next narrow escape. And now, gazing up at the darkly handsome man who was amused instead of enraged, as she'd expected, the last vestige of her control slipped away. Tears of exhausted relief sprang to her green eyes. "This has been the most *awful* day," she whispered.

"Probably because you've been missing me," he said with such ironic derision that Whitney's shoulders trembled with mirth.

"Missing you?" she giggled incredulously. "I could cheerfully *murder* you."

"I'd come back to haunt you," he threatened with a grin.

"And that," she said, "is the only reason why I haven't tried." Without warning, what had started as a giggle became a choked sob, and tears came spilling down her cheeks.

Clayton's arm slid gently around her. He was offering her comfort, and Whitney accepted it. Turning into his arms, she buried her face against his dove-gray jacket and wept out her troubles in the embrace of the man who was responsible for causing them. When the tears finally subsided, Whitney remained where she was, her cheek resting against the solid, comforting wall of his chest.

"Feel better now?" he murmured.

Whitney nodded sheepishly and accepted his proffered handkerchief, dabbing at her eyes. "I can't remember crying after I was twelve years old, but since I came back here a few weeks ago, it seems as if I'm forever weeping." Glancing up, Whitney surprised a look of pained regret in his eyes. "May I ask you something?" she said softly.

"Anything," Clayton replied.

"Within your power, and within reason, of course," Whitney reminded him with a teary half smile.

He accepted her mild jibe with an amused inclination of his head.

"Whatever made you do this Gothic thing?" she asked him quietly, without rancor. "Whatever made you come to my father, without speaking to me first, scarcely knowing me?" Although there was no change in his expression, Whitney felt his muscles tense, and she quickly explained, "I'm only trying to understand what you could have been thinking of. We didn't get along well at the Armands' masquerade. I mocked your title and rebuffed your advances, yet you decided you wanted to marry *me,* of all people. Why *me?*"

"Why do you think I chose you?"

"I don't know. No man offers for a woman merely to make her miserable and ruin her life, so you must have had another reason."

Despite the unintended insult in her words, Clayton grinned. She was letting him hold her, and he was feeling extremely tolerant. "You can't condemn me for wanting you, unless you condemn every other man who has. And arranged marriages may be Gothic, but they have been a custom in the best families for centuries."

Whitney sighed. "In yours perhaps, but not in mine. And I can't believe that in those marriages there wasn't at least a chance that both people would eventually come to like one another, even to develop an affection for each other."

"Can you honestly say that you haven't occasionally felt a liking for me?" he persisted gently. "Even against your will?"

There was no mockery or challenge in his tone to justify an argumentative denial, and Whitney's innate fairness prevented her from attacking without provocation. She shrugged uncomfortably and looked away. "Occasionally."

"But always against your will?" Clayton teased.

In spite of herself, Whitney smiled. "Against my will, *and* against my better judgment." His eyes warmed and Whitney cautiously changed the subject. "You promised to tell me why you wanted to marry me, and you haven't."

"How could I have known when I came here that you would set out to despise me the moment you saw me?" he countered.

"Clayton!" Whitney burst out, then froze in surprise at the sound of her voice using his given name. Hastily, she corrected her error. "My lord duke—"

"I liked it much better the other way."

"My lord duke," she persisted stubbornly as the quiet intimacy of their truce began to crumble, "you answer all my questions with questions! What in heaven's name possessed you to come here and offer for me?" At last Whitney realized that his arms were around her, and she jerked away. "And don't bother trying to tell me that you thought you loved me."

"I didn't," Clayton agreed equably. "As you have just pointed out, I hardly knew you at the time."

Whitney turned her back on him, unable to understand why his answer hurt her. "Wonderful!" she said bitterly. "Now it is all perfectly clear. You met me a time or two and, knowing nothing about me—caring nothing about me—you came to England and purchased me from my greedy, penniless father, who drove a sound bargain and then sent for me to hand me over to you!" She swung around, ready—eager— for battle, but Clayton simply stood there, calm and impervious, refusing to take up the gauntlet.

In angry despair, Whitney sank back down into the chair she'd occupied earlier, and picked up the cards. "This is solitaire," she said, dismissing him as she resumed the game she'd left unfinished. "It's all the rage in France, but it can only be played by one person."

Clayton watched her. "In this instance, my lady, it would seem to require two." Leaning down he deftly made four obvious plays which Whitney had overlooked because Cuthbert had been hanging over her shoulder.

"Thank you," Whitney said. "But I would rather play this alone."

Turning, he went to the door, and Whitney thought he was finally leaving. Instead he spoke to a servant in a low tone, and a moment later he came back to the table and placed an intricately carved rosewood box, belonging to her father, before her. Flipping up the lid, he exposed stacks of wooden chips. Whitney recognized them as the same sort of chips which Uncle Edward and his friends used when they gambled at cards.

A quiver of excitement shot through her as she realized that Clayton apparently intended to teach her how to use them. What a shocking, scandalous thing for him even to contemplate . . . but it was such an intriguing idea that Whitney made no protest. She watched as Clayton shrugged out of his jacket and draped it carelessly over her father's desk. Sitting down across from her, he unbuttoned his gray waistcoat, leaned back in his chair, and inclined his head toward the deck of cards. "Deal," he said.

Whitney was so nervous about the severe breach of propriety she was committing, that she knew she'd never be able to shuffle the cards properly. She gathered them together and pushed the deck toward Clayton. Fascinated, she watched the cards spring to life in his hands, flying into place with a whoosh and a snap as he shuffled them. Her voice was tinged with reluctant admiration. "I'll bet you're acquainted with every gaming hall in London."

"Intimately," he agreed. Palming the deck face down on the table, he raised a dark, challenging brow at her. "Cut the cards," he said.

Whitney hesitated, trying unsuccessfully to maintain a cool, disdainful attitude toward him, but how *could* she when he looked so outrageously handsome and elegantly dissolute? Lounging nonchalantly in that chair, with his waistcoat open at the front, he was the personification of the well-bred gentleman at the gaming table—and he was going to teach her how to play. Besides, she knew in her heart that he was trying to cheer her and distract her from her troubles. "I hope you know," she said, leaning forward, her hand hovering uncertainly over the deck, "that if anyone sees me doing this, my reputation will be destroyed."

Clayton gave her a long, meaningful look. "A duchess can do as she pleases."

"I am not a duchess," Whitney returned.

"But you're going to be," he said with absolute finality.

Whitney opened her mouth to argue, but he nodded toward the deck. "Cut the cards."

Gambling, Whitney thought two hours later as she stacked the chips away, made one feel deliciously wicked and decadent. Despite her unfamiliarity with the games, she had played very well and lost only a little money. She sensed that Clayton was proud of how quickly she learned, yet any other gentleman of her acquaintance, even Nicki, would have been horrified that she seemed to possess such a penchant for gaming. Why, she wondered absently, watching Clayton button his waistcoat and pull on his jacket, did he admire in her the very things that would shock or intimidate her other suitors? When she was with Paul, she had to be very careful to stay well within the bounds of feminine propriety, yet Clayton seemed to like her best when she was being her most outrageously impertinent self. If Paul knew she had gambled at cards, he would be shocked and displeased, yet Clayton had taught her to play and grinned at her in open admiration when she did it well.

Her thoughts scattered as Clayton leaned over her chair and pressed a light kiss on her upturned forehead. "We'll go for a drive tomorrow at 11 o'clock if the weather permits," he said. And he left.

Dr. Hugh Whitticomb was seated before the fire enjoying a glass of his host's excellent brandy when Clayton returned. "How did you find my young patient?" he asked with pretended casualness as Clayton poured himself a nightcap.

Sitting down, Clayton propped his feet on the low table between them, and gazed dispassionately at the physician. "I found her much the same as you probably did this afternoon —standing on her own two feet."

"You don't sound very pleased about it," Dr. Whitticomb remarked evasively.

"I found her," Clayton clarified with a grim smile, "receiving a proposal of marriage from one of her cousins."

Dr. Whitticomb made an impressive show of choking upon his brandy while he struggled to keep his face straight. "I can understand how that might have surprised you."

"I have long passed the point where anything Whitney does surprises me," he said, but his irritated tone completely denied his philosophical words.

After a moment's hesitation, Dr. Whitticomb said, "I am a detached observer and not inexperienced in dealing with the female mind. If you will pardon the presumption of an old family friend, perhaps I might be able to offer some advice?" Taking the duke's silence for consent, Dr. Whitticomb continued, "I have already gathered that Miss Stone wants something you aren't willing to give her. What is it that she wants?"

"What she wants," Clayton replied sardonically, "is to be released from the betrothal contract."

Dr. Whitticomb gave a bark of horrified laughter. "My God! No wonder she glowered at me when I offered subtle suggestions on how she ought to comport herself in order to keep you." Conflicting thoughts chased across his mind—amazement that the young lady could find fault with an offer from England's most eligible, most sought after bachelor; admiration for Clayton's patience in dealing with her rebellion; and bewilderment over why the most eagerly awaited betrothal announcement in a decade was being kept hushed. "What objection does the lovely widgeon have to your offer?" he said finally.

Leaning his head against the back of his chair, Clayton closed his eyes and sighed. "That I neglected to consult her first."

"I can't see why she should fault you for that. But then, knowing her independent temperament as you must have done, why didn't you consult with her first?"

Clayton opened his eyes. "Since she didn't even know my name at the time, I felt that it might be awkward to discuss marriage with her."

"She didn't know your . . . You can't mean to tell me that with half the females in Europe throwing themselves at you, you offered for a young woman you didn't even know!"

"I knew *her*. She did not know me."

"And you automatically assumed that once she learned of your wealth and title, she would naturally consent," Dr. Whitticomb speculated, his eyes dancing with amusement. The duke's quelling frown temporarily silenced him. "Who," he asked as a sudden, unsettling recollection struck him, "is Paul Sevarin?"

Clayton scowled. "Why do you ask?"

"Because I stopped in the village this afternoon after seeing Miss Stone, and spoke with the apothecary. He's a chatty fellow—the sort who tells you everything you didn't ask before he answers a simple question, and follows that with half a dozen questions of his own. Eventually he discovered the name of my patient, and he said some things which at the time I dismissed as nonsense."

"Such as?"

"Such as the fact that this Sevarin has been dangling after Miss Stone in earnest, and the village seems to be hanging on tenterhooks in expectation of a betrothal announcement. They seem to think the betrothal has already been arranged, and is entirely pleasing to Sevarin and your future wife."

"Frankly," Clayton drawled, "I don't give a blessed damn."

"About the gossip?" Hugh Whitticomb persisted carefully. "Or about Sevarin? Or about the girl?" When Clayton didn't answer, Hugh leaned forward and asked bluntly. "Are you, or are you not, in love with that young woman?"

"I am going to marry her," Clayton said stonily. "What else is there to say?" With that, he bid his guest good night and in four long strides, quit the room, leaving Hugh Whitticomb gazing at the fire in amazed alarm. After a moment, however, the physician's expression cleared. He began to chuckle and then he laughed aloud. "God help him." He chortled. "He doesn't realize he loves her. And even if he did, he wouldn't admit it."

In his small bedroom, Clayton jerked off his jacket, flinging it onto a chair. His waistcoat followed. Loosening the top buttons of his shirt, he stalked over to the window and jammed his hands into his pockets.

He was furious that the villagers believed a betrothal had already been arranged. True, he had wanted Whitney to have the satisfaction of showing them that she could make Sevarin pursue her, but he had never dreamed things would go this far. Whitney had never been betrothed to any man but him, and he would not allow anyone to think otherwise. She didn't *love* Sevarin, regardless of what she thought. She simply had some idiotic notion, some girlish dream, of winning him away from the Ashton girl.

She didn't love *him* either, but Clayton wasn't concerned about that. "Love" and all the obsessive behavior associated with it, was an absurd emotion. He was amazed that Hugh

Whitticomb had mentioned the word to him tonight. No one in his set ever professed to feeling anything stronger than a "tendre" or a lasting attachment even for their spouses. Love was a silly, romantic notion that had no place in his life.

Much of his anger evaporated as he considered the last few hours with Whitney. He could sense that she was slowly yielding to him. She had sought the comfort of his embrace of her own accord, and she had even admitted to a fondness for him. All that really stood between them now was her fading absorption with Paul Sevarin, and her understandable resentment over the way her stupid father had told her of her betrothal to Clayton. Just thinking of that night infuriated Clayton. Because of Stone's callous insensitivity, Clayton had been deprived of the pleasure of courting and winning Whitney. Despite its turbulent ups and downs, he had been enjoying his bizarre courtship, including Whitney's haughty rejections. She made him work to gain an inch, but each gain was a heady victory, more meaningful because it was so hard-won.

Yet there were times lately when his patience almost lost out in the battle against his desire. When she sniped at him and sparred with him, it took his last ounce of restraint not to snatch her into his arms and subdue her rebellion with his hands and mouth. He was neglecting his estates and his business interests, yet just when he decided that she would have to accustom herself to their betrothal *after* they were married, she'd look at him with those unbelievably green eyes of hers, and he could not quite bring himself to exert the power he held over her by forcing her to marry him.

Sighing, Clayton turned away from the window. Not for a moment did he ever doubt that Whitney *would* marry him. She would marry him either willingly, or unwillingly. In the latter case, the balance of their courtship and combat would have to take place in his bed.

Chapter Twenty

FRESH, COOL BREEZES SCENTED WITH THE INVIGORATING AROMA of burning leaves floated into Whitney's room, and she sniffed appreciatively as she stepped from her bath. Wrapped in a dressing robe, she went over to the open window and perched her hip upon the sill. Autumn, that most glorious of all the seasons, greeted her with a golden morning. She gazed out across the topaz and ruby landscape splashed with yellow and amber, and she tingled with the exuberant optimism she always felt at this time of year.

Reluctantly, she left the window and deliberated over the matter of clothing, finally choosing a high-waisted gown of dusky pink wool with a square neckline, long narrow sleeves, and a wide flounce at the hem. Clarissa pulled her hair straight back and up, then wound it into curls entwined with velvet ribbons of the same muted pink as her dress.

Thoughts of Paul and her unwanted betrothal to Clayton hovered uneasily at the back of her mind, but Whitney refused to dwell on them. Tonight she could agonize over her confused status, but for now, she was eager to be out in the sunshine. Nothing was going to spoil the perfection of such a gorgeous day.

At five minutes past eleven, a servant tapped at the door and announced that Mr. Westland was waiting downstairs. Snatching up the printed shawl which matched her dress,

Whitney hurried downstairs. "Good morning," she said gaily. "Isn't it a beautiful day?"

Clayton took her hands in his and gazed down at her glowing features. Quietly and without emphasis, he said, "You have a smile that could light up a room."

It was the first time he had ever remarked on her appearance, and although his compliment was much milder than the lavish ones the Frenchmen had heaped on her, it made Whitney feel unaccountably shy. "You are late," she admonished him with laughing severity, unable to think of anything else to say, "and I have been pacing the length of my bedchamber these past five minutes, waiting for you."

He said nothing, and for a moment Whitney fell under the spell of those boldly seductive gray eyes. His hands tightened on hers, drawing her closer. She held her breath, excited and alarmed at the realization that he was going to kiss her.

"I'm early," he stated unequivocally.

Whitney swallowed back a gurgle of relieved laughter, and he added, "However, now that I know how eager you are to see me, I shall make it a point to be early all the time." The great hall clock began to chime the hour of eleven as they left the house, and Clayton shot her an I-told-you-so look.

She climbed into his carriage and leaned back against the moss-green velvet squabs, gazing up at the puffy white clouds skittering across an azure sky. She felt his weight settle into the seat beside her, and her sidewise gaze wandered admiringly over his shiny brown boots, his long, muscular legs clad in biscuit superfine, his rust-colored jacket, and cream-silk shirt.

"If what I'm wearing doesn't please you," he drawled, "we can go to my humble abode and you can decide which of my clothes you approve."

Whitney's head jerked up. Her first impulse was to retort that it didn't matter in the least to her what he wore. Instead she surprised them both by shyly admitting the truth: "I was thinking that you look splendid."

She caught his startled look of pleasure before he gave the spirited grays the office to start, sending them trotting away.

Trees marched along both sides of the country lane, their

branches meeting overhead like lines of partners in a country dance, forming an arch for the carriage which rocked along beneath. Leaves swirled and drifted down in slow motion, and Whitney reached up, lazily trying to catch a bright yellow one.

When Clayton guided the pair south at the fork in the road, however, she sat bolt upright, turning on him in bewilderment and panic. "Where are we going?"

"To the village, for a start."

"I—I don't need anything from the village," Whitney insisted urgently.

"But I do," he said flatly.

Falling back against her seat, Whitney closed her eyes in bleak despair. They would be seen together and, in that sleepy little village where nothing ever happened, much would be made of it. She knew that everyone, with the exception of the man beside her, was expecting the announcement that she and Paul were soon to be married. She felt ill just thinking of Paul stopping in the village on his way home and hearing an exaggerated version of today's outing.

Their carriage clattered across the stone bridge and down the cobbled streets of the village, between the long rows of quaint, shuttered buildings which housed a few inferior shops and a small inn. When Clayton pulled the horses to a smart stop before the apothecary's shop, Whitney could have screamed. The apothecary, of all people—the worst of the village tattlers!

Clayton came around to help her alight. Trying to make her voice sound normal, she said, "Please, I would rather wait here."

In the voice of one issuing a command, but politely phrasing it as a request, Clayton said, "I would like it very much if you accompanied me."

That particular tone of his never failed to raise Whitney's hackles, and the friendly atmosphere of their outing abruptly disintegrated. "That's very unfortunate, because I'm not going into that shop." To her consternation and fury, Clayton reached into the carriage, grasped her by the waist, and lifted her down. She was afraid to struggle or push his hands away for fear of creating even more of a scene than they undoubtedly had already. "Are you trying to make a public spectacle of us?" she gasped, the instant her feet touched the cobbles.

"Yes," he said unanswerably, "I am."

Whitney saw the florid, jowly face of Mr. Oldenberry peering curiously at them through the window of his shop, and all hope of escaping notice was shattered. Inside the tiny, dimly lit shop an odd array of medicinal scents mingled with the odors of herbs, over which there was the pervading sting of ammonia salts. The apothecary was all effusive greetings, but Whitney saw his eyes lock with fanatic curiosity upon Clayton's hand, which still cupped her elbow.

"How is Mr. Paul?" he asked her slyly.

"I believe he's expected to return in another five days," Whitney said, wondering what this little man would be saying six days from now if she carried through with her tentative plan to elope with Paul.

Clayton asked for a bottle of hartshorn and the apothecary handed it to Whitney. Grimacing with distaste, Whitney waved it away. "It's for Mr. Westland, Mr. Oldenberry," she said solemnly. "I fear he suffers quite terribly from the vapors and the headache."

Clayton accepted her slur upon his masculine vitality with an infuriating grin. "Indeed I do," he chuckled, while his hand left Whitney's elbow and swept possessively around her shoulders, drawing her close for an affectionate squeeze. "And I intend to continue 'suffering.'" He winced as Whitney ground her heel into his instep, then winked at the apothecary. "My suffering gains me a great deal of sympathetic attention from this enchanting neighbor of mine."

"Oh rubbish!" Whitney burst out.

Clayton turned a conspiratorial smile on the apothecary and observed admiringly, "She certainly has a temper, doesn't she, Mr. Oldenberry?" Mr. Oldenberry puffed up with importance and agreed that, indeed, Miss Stone had *always* had a temper, and that he, like Mr. Westland, preferred females with spunk.

Whitney watched Clayton pay for the hartshorn, and she

caught the subtle movement of his hand as he placed the bottle back on the counter. Certain now that he had invented this errand for the sole purpose of illustrating to every gossip within fifteen miles that he had some claim upon her affection, Whitney spun on her heel. Clayton caught up with her as she stepped from the shop into the sunlight. "You're going to regret this," Whitney promised in a furious undertone.

"I don't think so," he said, guiding her across the street.

Elizabeth Ashton and Margaret Merryton were emerging from one of the shops, the latter's arms laden with bundles wrapped in white paper and tied with string. Politeness dictated that they all stop and exchange civilities. For once, Margaret didn't greet Whitney with an insulting, vindictive remark. In fact, she didn't greet her at all. Turning her shoulder to Whitney, she smiled into Clayton's gray eyes while Clayton obligingly took her bundles from her. As they crossed the street toward Margaret's carriage, Margaret linked her arm through his and said just loudly enough for Whitney to hear, "I've been meaning to ask you if I left my parasol in your carriage the other evening."

The shock of his betrayal knocked the breath from Whitney. True, she herself didn't feel obligated to honor their betrothal agreement, but Clayton had willingly and legally committed himself to her in a contract almost as binding and solemn as marriage. The man was worse than a rake, he was . . . promiscuous! And of all the women for him to be seeing in secret, he had chosen to consort with her bitterest enemy. Pain and rage seeped through Whitney's system.

"Margaret hates you terribly," Elizabeth murmured to Whitney as they both watched Clayton deposit Margaret's parcels in her carriage, then walk over to his carriage, apparently to search for Margaret's parasol. They lingered there, talking and laughing. "I think she hates you more for Mr. Westland than she did for that gentleman from Paris— Monsieur DuVille."

It was the first time Elizabeth had ever addressed a voluntary comment to Whitney, and if she hadn't been so miserably preoccupied, Whitney would have made a more cordial response. Instead she said stiffly, "I would be very obliged to Margaret if she were to snatch Mr. Westland right from under my nose."

"That's just as well," Elizabeth said, her pretty face troubled, "because she means to have him."

After assisting Elizabeth and Margaret into their carriage, Clayton reclaimed Whitney's hand and tucked it in the crook of his arm, as if nothing at all had happened. Whitney walked beside him, her face frozen with anger. At the end of the street was a small inn which boasted only one private dining parlor, the public rooms, and a small courtyard concealed from the street by vine-colored trellises. The proprietor's daughter greeted Clayton as if she knew him, then hastened to show them to a table in the courtyard.

Whitney watched in mounting annoyance as Millie batted her big brown eyes at him, then bent over the table, smoothing the linen and rearranging the vase of flowers, while deliberately providing Clayton with an unimpaired view of the ample bosom spilling over her bodice. Seething, Whitney observed the girl's swaying hips as she went to get their meal. "If that is the way Millie conducts herself around men, her poor parents must be at their wits' end."

Clayton observed Whitney's indignant features with a gleam of knowing amusement, and Whitney's tenuous hold on her temper snapped. Raking him with a contemptuous look, she added, "Of course, you've probably given Millie reason to believe you find her very desirable."

"What the devil do you mean by that remark?" he demanded.

"I mean that you have a notorious reputation with women —a reputation which you've undoubtedly earned!"

"Not for dallying with serving wenches, I haven't."

"Tell that to Millie," Whitney retorted frigidly. When Millie brought their meals, Whitney attacked her meat as if it were still alive. The instant they were finished eating, she pushed her chair back and arose.

Neither of them broke the charged silence on the way home until Clayton turned into his own drive, rather than continuing past it to hers, and pulled the grays to a stop before his house. When he came around to help her alight, Whitney pressed back into her seat. "If you think for one minute that I am going to set foot in that house with you, you're sadly mistaken."

A look of sorely strained patience crossed his face, and for the second time that day, he caught her by the waist and lifted her down from the carriage. "God help me if I ever injure my back," he quipped.

"God help you if you ever *turn* it," she snapped, "for there'll surely be some heartbroken papa or cuckolded husband ready with a knife—if *I* don't murder you first."

"I have no intention of arguing with you *or* ravishing you," Clayton said with exasperation. "If you will only look around, you'll see why I brought you here."

Whitney did, irritably at first and then with surprise. The Hodges estate had always had a seedy look about it, but all that had changed. The bushes were pruned, and the grass neatly trimmed. Missing flagstones from the walk had been replaced, and rotted woodwork repaired. But the biggest change was brought about by the twin expanses of great mullioned windows on the first story, where before there had only been three gloomy little glass-covered holes. "Why have you gone to such expense?" Whitney asked when it was apparent that he was waiting for some reaction from her.

"Because I bought it," Clayton said, indicating that she should walk with him toward the newly erected pavilion at the far end of the front lawn.

"You bought it?" Whitney gasped. Just the thought of the cozy trio they would make—she and Paul, with Clayton for a neighbor—made her feel quite violently ill. Was there no end to the obstacles one single man could put in the way of her happiness?

"It seemed a reasonably sound idea. This land adjoins yours, and someday the two estates can be combined."

"Adjoins *your* land, not mine!" Whitney corrected him bitingly. "You paid for it, just as you paid for me."

She started to step blindly into the wooden pavilion but his hand shot out and captured her arm, jerking her around. He studied her flushed, angry face for a moment, and then he said calmly, "Margaret Merryton's carriage wheel was broken, and I offered to take her up with me, rather than leaving her there in the road. I brought her home, where her father thanked me profusely and invited me to dinner, which I declined. There was nothing more to it than that."

"I don't care in the least what you and Margaret did!" Whitney lied angrily.

"The hell you don't! You've been sniping at me ever since she asked if she left her parasol in my carriage."

Whitney looked away, trying to decide if he was telling the truth and wondering why it mattered so much to her.

"If you won't credit me with discretion," he added quietly, "at least credit me with taste." He paused. "Am I forgiven, little one?"

"I suppose so," Whitney said, feeling absurdly relieved and thoroughly foolish. "But the next time you see Margaret . . ."

"I'll run her down!" he chuckled.

A faint smile touched Whitney's lips. "I was merely going to ask that you not encourage her, for she'll only behave more horridly to me than she already does, if she thinks you're interested in her. Did she have a parasol that day?" Whitney asked, suddenly suspicious.

"No. Not that I recall."

Pretending to study the toes of her pink slippers, Whitney asked carefully, "Do you think Margaret is . . . well . . . pretty?"

"Now *that's* more like it!" Clayton laughed, possessing himself of her other arm and drawing her close to him.

"What do you mean?"

"I mean that it pleases me to have you thinking like a wife—even a jealous one."

There was enough truth in that observation to make Whitney flush hotly. "I am not in the least bit jealous, nor have I any reason to be, because you do not belong to me, any more than I belong to you!"

"Except by virtue of a signed, legal contract betrothing you to me."

"A *meaningless* contract, since I was not consulted."

262

"But one which you will nevertheless honor," Clayton predicted.

Whitney looked at him with a mixture of resentment and pleading. "I loathe this constant bickering. Why can't I make you understand that I love Paul?"

"You don't care for Sevarin. You've told me so yourself, and more than once."

"I've told you nothing of the sort! I—"

"You've told me," he persisted, "every time you've been in my arms, that Sevarin has no claim on your heart."

Whitney, who was desperate enough to try *anything,* tried to intimidate him by scoffing. "For a man of your vast experience with women, you certainly place an absurd amount of importance on our few kisses. I'd have thought that you, of all men, would have learned better."

"I am experienced," he agreed curtly. "I am experienced enough to know that you respond to me when I kiss you, and that you're terrified of what I make you feel. If Sevarin could make you feel the way I do, you'd have nothing to fear from me. But he can't, and you damn well know it."

"In the first place," Whitney retorted, drawing a long, suffocated breath while trying to calm herself, "Paul Sevarin is a gentleman, which you are not! And, as a gentleman, he would never dream of kissing me the way you do. He—"

Clayton's mouth twisted in sardonic amusement. "Wouldn't he indeed? Apparently, I've been giving Sevarin more credit than he deserves."

Whitney's palm positively itched to slap that self-satisfied, mocking grin off his face. Why bother arguing with him, she told herself furiously, when he would only twist her words around until they suited him! Of course she'd responded to the wild, forbidden passions Clayton so skillfully aroused within her. What gently reared, unsuspecting female wouldn't be momentarily carried away by the newness of his practiced caresses?

Gently reared, unsuspecting females! Why, half the most sophisticated flirts in Europe had apparently fallen victim to his skill at lovemaking! Compared to them, she was a mere babe in arms!

"What?" Clayton chuckled maddeningly. "No arguments?"

If she'd had a knife at that moment, Whitney would have plunged it into his chest. Instead she chose the only means available to her to retaliate. Looking at him with just the right degree of amused scorn, she said, "If I do respond to you, there's a very simple explanation for it, but you aren't going to like it. The truth is, I find your intimate caresses not only sordid but boring! The only way I can endure them is by pretending you're Paul and—don't!" she cried out in panic and pain as his hands tightened punishingly on her upper arms.

With a vicious jerk, he brought her crashing against his chest. Whitney's head snapped back from the impact, and she saw his eyes glittering down at her like shards of ice. Her throat muscles constricted, choking her frantic apology. "I—I didn't mean it! I—"

Ruthlessly, his mouth swooped down, slanting punishingly back and forth over her lips until they parted from the sheer, cruel pressure. When she tried to tear her mouth away, his hand clamped the back of her head, holding her against the bruising assault of his mouth. Tears of pain sprang to her eyes, and still the agonizing, endless kiss continued.

"Lie to anyone you please," he growled savagely into her mouth. "But never again lie to me! Do you understand?" His arm tightened sharply, underlining the warning and cutting off her breath at the same time.

Wildly, Whitney struggled, trying to draw enough air into her lungs to tell him *yes!* Her ribs felt as if they were being cracked; he was suffocating her and growing more enraged at her helpless, involuntary silence. She forced her hand up along his chest, futilely trying to wedge some space between them, until her fingers finally encountered the male lips locked fiercely to hers.

She didn't realize it was the unintentional tenderness of laying her hand against his face that made him release her so abruptly. All she knew was that she could finally draw great, gulping breaths of air into her aching lungs.

"I bow to your better judgment," he drawled with icy

contempt. "That was both 'sordid' and 'boring.' In fact, I would be hard put to decide which of us found it more distasteful."

Irrationally, Whitney was stung. She stiffened her spine, meeting his cold gaze with as much proud defiance as she could muster. "I don't suppose you found it distasteful and disgusting enough to consider letting me go?"

What Clayton felt was not disgust, it was fury! Her announcement that when he was kissing her, she pretended he was Sevarin, had so incensed Clayton that he actually considered yanking her into the pavilion and taking her right there on the floor. Since the day she'd returned to England, he'd been tolerating her rebelliousness and overlooking her temper. On the floor of the pavilion, she would learn the folly of pushing him too far. Unfortunately, she would also learn to hate him with a virulence that might sustain her for years.

With deliberate insolence, Clayton inspected her slender, voluptuous form and her classic profile with its flawless camellia-like skin; the color on her cheekbones was heightening because she knew he was looking at her. The sun shown on her mahogany-brown hair, gilding it with red-gold. She looked incredibly beautiful in that dusky pink gown, framed by the wide sweep of emerald lawns behind her: a single, breathtaking rose blooming in a garden of green. But for once, her vivid beauty annoyed, instead of pleased, him, particularly because she was now blithely examining her manicure as if he didn't exist.

Miss Stone, Clayton decided coldly, was in dire need of a lesson. He considered her spiteful inquiry as to whether he had found the last kiss distasteful enough to let her go home, and an idea took shape. He'd let her go home all right, but before he did, he was going to teach her that his passion was a gift to be shared and enjoyed—a gift that he could give or withhold, when and if he pleased. First he was going to make her kiss *him*, and then, when he had her desire fully aroused, he would simply disentangle himself from her arms and walk away.

As if there had been no interval of several minutes since she'd snapped the question at him, Clayton answered it. "As a matter of fact, you're wrong. With the proper incentive, I would let you go."

Whitney's head snapped around, her heart leaping with elation, even though her common sense warned her that he was too high-handed, and too confident, to give up the idea of marrying her and let her go. "What sort of incentive did you have in mind?" she asked cautiously.

"I want a kiss from you. A goodbye kiss to take the chill off our parting. And *if* it is good enough, I'll let you go. It's as simple as that."

"I'm not certain I believe you. Why should you suddenly decide to let me go?"

"Let's say that these last few . . . unrewarding . . . minutes have convinced me of the wisdom of the idea. On the other hand"—he shrugged indifferently—"my generosity is not without a price."

A price? Whitney thought joyously. Why, it was no price at all! To be free of this betrothal she'd be willing to kiss his *horse!* "I am to kiss you goodbye, nothing more?" she said, watching him very, very closely, while she restated the terms of the bargain. "And you are giving me your word that in return, you will let me go?"

He nodded curtly. "Yes. In fact, I won't even accompany you home. I'll have my man drive you." Impatiently, he added, "Well, have we a bargain?"

"Yes!" Whitney said quickly, lest he change his mind.

They were standing almost within arm's reach, but instead of reaching for her, as Whitney expected, he leaned his shoulder against the pavilion wall, folded his arms across his chest, and said, "As you can see, I am completely at your disposal."

Whitney blinked at him. "What do you mean?"

"I mean that the next move is yours."

"Mine?" she gasped. Dear God! Did he intend for her to take the initiative? She stared uncertainly at his arrogant features and mocking gray eyes. That was precisely what he meant for her to do. And how like him to take this last, final, petty revenge! The breeze ruffled his dark brown hair as he glanced tranquilly up at the trees overhead, then serenely contemplated the azure sky. Leaning lazily against the pavilion with his arms crossed over his chest, he looked so insufferably arrogant that she positively yearned to give him a swift kick in the shin, and the devil fly with his bargain!

Without warning, he straightened as if he were tired of waiting and were about to call the bargain off.

"Wait!" Whitney stammered quickly. "I—I—" She gaped at him in angry consternation, feeling unutterably self-conscious. "It's just that I—"

"—don't know how to begin?" he finished sardonically. "Permit me to suggest that you take a step closer."

Drowning in resentful embarrassment, Whitney complied.

"Very good," he mocked. "Now, if you will put your lips on mine, you can get it over with."

Whitney expelled her breath in a long, humiliated rush, glowered at him, and clutching his rust-colored jacket by the lapels, she levered herself up high enough to reach his mouth and pressed a chaste kiss on his lips. Then she stepped back, poised for flight to blissful freedom.

"If that's the way you kiss Sevarin, I can understand why it's taken you all this time to bring him to the point of offering," he remarked with lazy cynicism. "If that maidenly peck is your best effort, I'm afraid the bargain is off."

"Well!" Whitney burst out indignantly, plunking her hands on her hips and giving him a murderous look. "I can't help it when you just stand there without so much as moving a muscle to cooperate."

"Perhaps you're right. On the other hand, you're supposed to *inspire* me to cooperate."

"Oh shut up!" she snapped with blazing eyes. "You just do your part. I'll do mine!"

"I'll do no more than follow your lead," he warned coolly. "And I have no intention of trying to teach you what you should have learned already. I have better things to do with my time than play tutor to a tiresomely naive schoolroom miss."

Whitney felt as if he'd hit her across the face. With an effort, she bit back a vengeful retort, and forced herself to concentrate on finding some way to "inspire" this cold, withdrawn man into participating. And while she was about it, she wouldn't mind throwing his taunts about "tutoring a schoolgirl" and "maidenly pecks" right in his teeth! Bending her head, she tried to imagine herself as a bold temptress, a courtesan, as wise in the ways of passion and seduction as he was. Very slowly, she raised jade-green eyes so full of promise and warmth that when they met Clayton's she witnessed a momentary crack in his aloof composure.

Emboldened by her success thus far, Whitney slid her hands inside his jacket, upward along his silk shirt. Beneath her fingertips, she felt his chest muscles leap reflexively, then draw taut and hard. He was trying to resist her! Some primeval female instinct told her that if he had to try to resist her, she must have struck a very responsive chord, and the realization brought a knowingly seductive half smile to her lips as her hands glided over his shoulders and up behind his neck. Keeping her eyes locked to his, she slid her fingers through the soft hair at his nape, inexorably drawing his face nearer to hers. Tenderly, she brushed her lips over his mouth . . . his *smiling* mouth! Damn him, he was grinning! And even though her arms were locked around his neck, his arms were still diffidently at his sides.

"A definite improvement," he congratulated her impersonally, "but hardly—"

Outraged pride made Whitney silence this final rejection with her parted lips. She found him blindly, and lingered endlessly, trying to force him to respond. His warm breath mingled with hers, his mouth followed her lead, but the moment she began to draw back, he did the same. Slowly, her fear of retreating too soon was surpassed by her greater fear of continuing too long. Her heart was beating in unsteady lurches, and her body was stirring to life in a most alarming way. Dropping her arms, she stepped back, and for the first time she realized that Clayton's arms had never been around her. He hadn't been the least bit affected by the kiss. "I hate you for this," she whispered, too humiliated to look at his face, which she was certain would be gleaming with sarcastic amusement.

Clayton was not amused, he was furious. For the first time in his adult life he had not been able to control his own body's responses. Her innocent kiss and light caress had sent a tidal wave of instantaneous lust surging through him, very nearly sweeping away his restraint. And while *he* was still struggling for control, *she* was declaring her hatred of him.

His jaw tightened and he tipped her chin up. "That was much better," he said smoothly. "This time will be goodbye."

Goodbye? Whitney thought, immediately forgetting she hated him. They were saying goodbye. This would be the last time they ever saw each other.

Whitney gazed up into his recklessly handsome male face with a nostalgic sensation that bordered on sadness. His was such a compelling face. A face that could seem almost boyish when the firm jawline and finely carved mouth were transformed by one of his lazy, devastating smiles. She liked the aura of calm authority that always surrounded him, that vibrated in his deep voice and lent purpose to his long, agile strides. She admired his ability to seem forever at ease and relaxed. He was, she thought with an inward sigh of regret, all the things a man ought to be.

His mouth was slowly moving closer to hers. "Shall we continue where you left off?" he suggested softly.

Drawing a long, ragged breath, Whitney lifted her trembling lips to within an inch of his. Then a half-inch. Her mind screamed a warning as her emotions reeled crazily and sudden shock waves of longing racked her.

His mouth came down hard, silencing Whitney's objection with a demanding insistence that sent a jolt rocketing through her, exploding along every nerve until she was clinging to him, her arms wrapped fiercely around his neck.

"Am I boring you?" he taunted, kissing her harder, more deliberately than before. His tongue plunged suggestively into her mouth. "Would you describe this as sordid?"

Rage burst in Whitney's breast, enclosing her in a mist of blind fury. He was lashing her with her own words, coldly and deliberately humbling her. She dug her fingernails into his wrists, trying futilely to pry his hands away from her head.

His kiss deepened, devouring her and sending silky tendrils of desire curling down her spine.

"Are you pretending I'm Sevarin?" he jeered. "Are you?"

Stunned, Whitney let her hands slide from his wrists. She had actually *hurt* him with those things she'd said. Somehow Clayton had always seemed so utterly invulnerable, so completely self-assured, that she'd never dreamed anything she ever said or did could hurt him. But evidently she had.

"Tell me how much you hate my touch," he ordered furiously. Pulling his mouth from hers, he stared down at her with biting gray eyes. "You despise my touch," he hissed. "Say it now, or don't ever, *ever* say it to me again."

Whitney's chest tightened around an aching lump of poignant contrition and shattering tenderness. She swallowed painfully, tears filling her eyes. "I—I can't."

"You can't tell me you despise my touch?" he jeered in a silky, ominous voice. *"Why* can't you?"

"Because," she whispered, attempting a trembly smile, "you warned me not five minutes ago, never to lie to you again." Whitney watched his features harden into a mask of cynical incredulity and, before he could say anything else to hurt them both, she leaned up to silence his retort with her lips.

Swearing savagely, he grabbed her arms and started to pull them down from around his neck. "Clayton, don't!" she cried out brokenly, locking her fingers tightly behind his nape. "Oh please, please don't!" Tears slipped down her cheeks as she ignored his painful grip on her arms and kissed this angry, unyielding man, this powerful, dynamic man, who had endured her hostility and outbursts with patience and humor . . . until now, when she had hurt him.

His hands went to her waist to shove her away, but Whitney pressed closer. Timidly, she touched her tongue to his lips, hoping he would like it if she kissed him that way. He went rigid. Every muscle in his body drew taut, hardening against her. Her tongue slid between his barely parted lips, encountered his, recoiled in wild alarm—and then crept back for one more sweet, forbidden touch. And her world exploded with the violence of his response. His arms went around her, crushing her to him as his mouth opened over hers, slanting fiercely back and forth. His tongue plunged boldly into her mouth, probing, as if to verify its welcome there.

Dazed with passion and longing, Whitney gloried in the wild excitement of his mouth moving with hungry urgency against hers. She kissed him back while his hands shifted possessively across her back and down her spine, then lower to cup her buttocks, molding her closer against his hard legs and thighs, forging their two bodies into one.

An eternity later, he lifted his mouth from hers and cradled her face between his hands, his thumbs gently stroking her flushed cheeks. Tenderness and desire smoldered in his gray eyes as he gazed down into her languorous green ones. "You beautiful, infuriating, wonderful little fool," he whispered thickly, and then he slowly buried his lips in hers again, deepening the kiss until flames were shooting through Whitney's veins and she was straining to be closer to him. His hands cupped and caressed her breasts, branding them with his touch, then stroking downward, fitting her hips against his rigid thighs.

Without warning, it was over. He tore his mouth from hers and kissed her eyes and forehead, then rested his jaw against her head. Whitney stirred and his arms tightened around her. "Don't move, little one," he whispered. "Stay close to me a while longer." Leaves rustled in the breeze and birds fluttered overhead, while loneliness and despair began invading the bliss of the moment. Longing to feel his lips covering hers again, to have him drive away this aching sadness creeping over her, Whitney leaned her head back, her gaze lingering on his firmly molded lips.

Automatically, Clayton bent his head to accept her shy invitation, but an instant before his mouth touched hers, he checked himself. "No," he said with a throaty chuckle.

Bewildered by his refusal to kiss her when he obviously wanted to, Whitney looked at him, her wide, questioning eyes shadowed with hurt confusion.

"If you continue to look at me like that," he teased huskily, "you're going to find yourself being thoroughly kissed once more. And if that happens, there's an excellent chance that I'll not be able to keep my promise."

"Why?" Whitney whispered, still shamelessly yearning for his kiss.

"Why?" he repeated, his mouth hovering so near hers that their breaths were mingling. "I'll be happy to show you why . . ." he offered in a lusty whisper.

Reason at last returned, cooling her ardor and restoring her sense. She shook her head. "No, for it would only make our parting more difficult." With a weak smile, she stepped back and away from him. "Goodbye, your grace," she whispered, gravely offering him her hand. Her heart gave a lurch when he took it and turned it palm up.

"So formal?" he grinned, rubbing his thumb over her palm, then boldly raising it to his lips and touching his tongue to the sensitive center.

Whitney snatched it away, tucking her tingling hand safely behind her back. For a long moment, she simply gazed at him, unconsciously memorizing his face, then she said, "I'm sorry, truly sorry that I've put you to so much trouble."

Clayton's eyes glinted wickedly. "I hope you'll feel free to 'trouble' me like that whenever you like."

"You know that's not what I mean." There were things she wanted to say to him, nice things, and things she wanted to explain, but how could she be serious when he was treating their parting so lightly? Perhaps he wanted no explanations, no apologies; perhaps this was the best way to say goodbye. Even so, her voice shook as she said, "I shall miss you, I really will." Before she crumbled in front of him, which she was positive she would do if he continued to look at her with gentle understanding, she picked up her skirts and stepped away, intending to leave him there at the pavilion. Two steps further away, she turned and said hesitantly over her shoulder. "About my father—"

Why *she* should feel any guilt or responsibility for her harsh sire was a mystery, yet she did. "I hope you won't deal harshly with him. If you'll just be patient, I'm certain he'll eventually be able to repay you."

Clayton's dark brows drew together into a mild frown. "Considering that he has given me his daughter to wed, I count myself fully repaid."

A feeling of impending disaster seemed to crackle in the air. "But all of that has changed now that you've agreed to let me go."

Clayton closed the distance between them, grasping her by the shoulders and turning her around to face him. "What in the holy hell are you talking about?"

"You agreed to let me go and—"

"I agreed to let you go *home,*" he stated emphatically.

"No!" Whitney cried, shaking her head. "You agreed to let me go—to give up the idea of marrying me."

"You can't believe that," Clayton said shortly. "I meant nothing of the kind."

A crushing weight settled in Whitney's chest. She should have known he would never give in. She stared at him in desperation . . . while something strangely like relief tingled through her. There was no chance for her to examine this odd feeling, however, for his arms went around her, pulling her close to him.

"Never, not even in my weakest moment, have I considered letting you go, Whitney. And if I had," he added, bluntly reminding her of her passionate response to him minutes ago, "do you think that after what has just passed between us, I would ever consider it again?" Clayton tipped her chin up, forcing her rebellious gaze to meet his implacable one. "You asked me for time, and I gave it to you. Use it to face the inevitability of our marriage, because I assure you that the marriage is going to take place. If you want to convince yourself that I deceived you a while ago, then do it, but I'll not honor a promise I didn't make."

His flat conviction that she had no choice except to marry him, to yield her body and her life to him, was more than Whitney could bear right now. "Then honor the promise you did make. Let me go home." Jerking away from him, she walked blindly toward the driveway, her emotions in turmoil.

Clayton caught up with her, snapped an order to the footman, and helped her into the carriage. Whitney looked down at him, her voice deadly calm. "Has it ever occurred to you that you cannot *make* me marry you? You can drag me by the hair to the altar, yet all I have to do is refuse to say my vows. It's as simple as that."

His brows rose. "If those are the thoughts you've been entertaining during this time you asked me for, then there's nothing to be gained by waiting any longer, is there?" He glanced over his shoulder as if he were looking for someone, then turned to start toward the house.

"Where are you going?" Whitney demanded sharply, alarmed by the sudden, purposeful vitality in his movements and the determined set of his jaw.

"I am about to order my valet to pack my bags for a lengthy trip. After which, I will have the travelling chaise brought round and horses put to. We," he stated coolly, turning around to face her, "are going to Scotland. We're eloping."

"Eloping!" Whitney cried, clutching the side of the carriage. "You—you wouldn't dare! The tongues would never cease wagging, the gossips would—"

Clayton shrugged indifferently. "As you should have gathered by now, gossip doesn't matter to me. Since it does matter to you, I suggest you consider your choices: Once we're in Scotland, you can either marry me or you can refuse to say your vows. If you refuse to say them, we will return unwed from an absence together of several days and nights which will cause a scandal you will never live down. Your last choice is to have a proper wedding in London as a duchess. Now, which is it going to be?"

What choice was there? Whitney thought bitterly. An elopement was scandalous enough, but if she returned with him from Scotland unwed, mothers would drag their daughters to the other side of the street when she passed, to avoid the contamination of a soiled female, and Paul would despise her. "A wedding!" Whitney hissed angrily, flopping back against the velvet seat. There was one other choice open to her, she reminded herself: She could elope with Paul. Her mind quailed at the thought of an elopement, with all the attendant censure and disgrace. Once again, she would be an outcast from the village society, the recipient of open snubs and scathing criticism. But at least she would have the compensation of being Paul's wife.

"Whitney," Clayton said, looking at her as if he would like to shake her, "for once in your life, forget this obsession with Sevarin, and try to face what is really in your heart. If you weren't so damned stubborn, you'd have done it weeks ago!"

The coachman came dashing around the side of the house, and Whitney bit back her angry retort, but Clayton's words nagged at her all the way home. Staring dismally at the coachman's stiff back, she struggled to sort out her jumbled emotions, not because Clayton had accused her of refusing to face what was in her heart, but because she truly couldn't understand herself anymore.

How could she respond so wantonly to Clayton's caresses while planning, yearning to marry Paul? Why had she been so shattered a few minutes ago when she realized she had hurt Clayton? Why had she felt so desolate when she believed she was saying goodbye to him forever? Was it because a grudging friendship had grown between them, nourished by the banter and raillery they always indulged in?

Friendship? she thought bitterly. Clayton was no friend of hers; he cared nothing about her. He cared only about himself and what *he* wanted, and for some obscure reason known only to himself, he happened to want *her*. He refused to believe she loved Paul because it didn't suit him to believe it. Paul was meant to be her husband; that place in her heart, in her life, had long ago been set aside for him and only him.

Paul. Her conscience took over, tormenting her for her disloyalty to Paul, her scandalous, unprincipled behavior in his absence. Mentally, she cringed, thinking of the way she had let Clayton caress her, kiss her. Let him! she thought with self-loathing, *she* had kissed *him*. She had wanted to be in his arms; she had trembled with desire when his mouth had opened over hers.

It seemed to Whitney as she lay in bed that night, staring at the canopy above her, that she had never been so miserable. Tormented with guilt, she thought of the plans Paul had discussed with her during the days following his proposal. He was going to restore the master suite in the west wing of his house because it was nearer the nursery. She had blushed petal pink when he mentioned children, but she had joyously made plans right along with him.

And now she had betrayed him. She had taken his love and defiled it in Clayton Westmoreland's arms. She was unworthy of Paul. Dear God! she was unworthy of Clayton Westmoreland, too. Wasn't she, even now, after returning his kisses, planning to marry another man?

Dawn had lightened the sky when she arrived at a final, irrevocable decision. Since Clayton would never willingly give her up, she would elope with Paul the day he returned. Paul *loved* her, and he trusted her; he was counting on her. The shame of an elopement would be her penance for her lustful, wicked behavior in Paul's absence. Someday, somehow, she would again be worthy of his love and trust. She would *earn* it by being the most devoted, obedient, *faithful* wife on earth.

Now that she had resolved on a course of action, she should have felt much better, but when she awoke late the next morning, she felt positively wretched.

Massaging her temples with both hands, Whitney swung her feet onto the floor and cautiously edged to the small washstand, her head pounding with every step she took. Squinting from the pain, she poured herself a glass of cool water and rang for Clarissa to help her dress.

Pale and distant, she slid into her chair at the breakfast table, managed a wan smile for Aunt Anne and flatly ignored her father. Unfortunately, her father refused to be ignored any longer. "Well, Miss," he demanded in a curt, authoritative tone, "have you and his grace set the date yet?"

Laying her fork aside, Whitney perched her chin on her folded hands, deliberately goading him with her wide, blank stare. "What date?"

"Don't treat me like an imbecile! You know I'm referring to a wedding date."

"Wedding?" Whitney repeated. "Did I forget to tell you? There's not going to be a wedding." Tossing an apologetic glance at Aunt Anne, Whitney rose from the table and left the room.

"Really, Martin, you are the greatest fool to push her that

way. What choice do you leave her except to defy you?" Distastefully, Anne shoved her plate aside and followed Whitney.

After a moment, Martin also shoved his plate aside and sent for his carriage in order to pay a morning call on his future son-in-law.

By eleven o'clock Whitney's headache had abated, but her mood had not improved. Seated across from Aunt Anne in the sewing room, she listlessly worked at her embroidery frame. "I loathe needlework," she observed unemotionally. "I have always loathed it. Even if I could do it well, I'd still loathe it."

"I know," her aunt sighed, "but it keeps one's hands busy." They both looked up as a footman came in with the mail and handed a letter to Whitney. "It's from Nicki," Whitney said, brightening with fondness at the memory of him. Eagerly she broke the seal and began to read Nicki's bold, firm scrawl.

The smile faded from her face, and her head began to pound with renewed vigor. Slumping back in her chair, she gazed in numb horror at her aunt. "Nicki is arriving in London tomorrow."

Anne's embroidery needle froze in mid-stitch. "His grace will not be pleased to have Nicolas DuVille here on our doorstep, pressing his suit right beside Paul Sevarin."

Whitney was more concerned about sparing herself the humiliation of having Nicki here as a houseguest, where he would inevitably learn of her scandalous elopement with Paul next week. "It needn't come to that," she said firmly, taking charge of the matter. She left the room, returning a moment later with quill and parchment.

"What are you going to say?"

"Not to put too fine a point on it," Whitney announced, dipping the quill into the inkpot and beginning to write, "I am going to tell Nicki to *remain* in London. What sort of contagious disease do you prefer? Malaria? The plague?" Seeing that her aunt was not sharing her semi-hysterical humor, Whitney added more calmly, "I shall simply tell Nicki that I have commitments away from here and won't be able to see him this trip. I gather from what he wrote that he is only going to be in England for a short time to attend some social function at Lord Marcus Rutherford's—whoever that may be."

For want of any more helpful comment, Anne said, "Lord Rutherford is connected with several of the best families in Europe, including the DuVilles. Your uncle has often said he is the most astute man in the government, and one of the most powerful, as well."

"Well, he certainly chose an inconvenient time to ask Nicki to come to England," Whitney remarked as she sprinkled fine sand over the note and rang for a footman to have it sent off at once.

Now that she'd taken matters into her own hands and done something to help avert disaster, Whitney felt better. With great gusto she applied herself to her needlework, but she had never been any good at it, and the tiny perfect stitches she planned in her mind failed to materialize on the cloth. In a fit of frustrated impatience, she ignored the ghastly effect she was creating and simply enjoyed the act of stabbing at the cloth with the needle.

Long after her aunt had gone down to lunch, she continued. This stab was for fate, which out of sheer perversity, was thwarting her at every turn. This stab was for Lord Rutherford, who was responsible for Nicki coming to England. This stab was for her father—cruel, heartless, unloving. This stab was for . . . In her vengeful enthusiasm, Whitney missed the fabric and yelped in pain as the needle pierced her left index finger.

A throaty chuckle preceded a familiar, deep voice. "Are you embroidering that cloth or assaulting it?"

Whitney surged to her feet in surprise, sending her embroidery sliding to the floor. She had no idea how long Clayton had been standing in the doorway watching her. All she knew was that he seemed to fill the room with his compelling presence and that her spirits soared crazily at the sight of him. Embarrassed by her reaction, she hastily directed her attention to her finger where a minuscule drop of blood had appeared.

"Shall I send for Dr. Whitticomb?" he offered. A smile tugged at the corner of his handsome mouth as he added, "If you don't want Whitticomb, I can send for 'Dr. Thomas' but I understand that his specialty is more in the line of sprains and breaks . . ."

Whitney bit her bottom lip, trying desperately not to laugh. "Actually, Dr. Thomas is very busy with another patient right now—a sorrel mare. And Dr. Whitticomb was rather irritated over being sent here on a fool's errand the last time. I doubt he'd be quite so gracious about being summoned on a second one."

"Was it 'a fool's errand'?" Clayton asked quietly.

The laughter fled from Whitney's face and an inexplicable guilt assailed her. "You know it was," she whispered, averting her eyes.

Clayton studied her pale face with a slight, worried frown. Despite her momentary gaiety, he could tell that she was as tense as a tightly coiled spring. He wasn't concerned by her rebellious announcement at breakfast this morning that there was not going to be a marriage, which was what had sent her father scurrying to him in a state of wild agitation. Martin Stone was a stupid bastard who continued trying to bully her, even though it only made Whitney more hell-bent on defying him. For that reason, Clayton had decided to do something to ease her plight and remove her from her father's abrasive presence for a while.

He walked toward her, and she watched him warily. "I have a favor to ask of you," Clayton said with quiet firmness. "I would like you to accompany me to a ball in London. You can bring that peculiar little abigail of yours—the stout woman with white hair who always scowls at me as if she suspects I'm going to carry off the family silver."

"Clarissa," Whitney provided automatically, her mind already searching for a suitable excuse not to accompany him.

Clayton nodded. "She can play duenna, so there'll be no lack of a proper chaperone." Actually, Lady Gilbert would have been a far more suitable chaperone, but he wanted Whitney to himself for a while. "If we leave in the morning, the day after tomorrow, we can be in London by late afternoon. That will give you time to visit with your friend, Emily, and rest before the ball. I'm certain the Archibalds will be delighted to have you stay for the night, and we'll return the following day." Before she could refuse, which Clayton could see she was about to do, he added, "Your aunt is even now writing a note to advise Emily Archibald of your arrival."

Wildly, Whitney wondered what madness had made Aunt Anne agree to such a thing, and then she realized that her aunt was in no better position to deny the Duke of Claymore anything than she herself was. "You didn't have a favor to ask," Whitney corrected him irritably. "You had a command to issue."

Clayton ignored her lack of enthusiasm for the ball—an idea which he had only conceived after talking to her father this morning. "I was hoping very much that you would like the idea," he said.

His gentle reply made Whitney feel churlish and rude. Sighing, she accepted the inevitable. "Whose ball are we attending?"

"Lord Rutherford's." Clayton hadn't really expected any reaction to that, but even if he had, nothing would have prepared him for what happened next. Whitney's eyes widened until they were huge green saucers. "Whose?" she demanded in a choked whisper, and before he could answer, she gave a stunned shriek of horrified laughter and literally collapsed into his arms, convulsed with gales of mirth.

Her eyes swimming with tears of hilarity, she finally leaned back in his arms and said, "You see before you a demented female who is beginning to look upon life's tragedies as one great lark." Swallowing another giggle, she said eagerly, "Does my aunt know yet? Whose ball we are to attend?"

"No. Why do you ask?"

Whitney reached for Nicki's note and handed it to him. "I wrote Nicki this morning and told him not to come—that I had other commitments away from home."

Clayton skimmed the note and gave it back to her. "Fine," he said curtly, annoyed because she called DuVille "Nicki," yet she persisted in addressing him, to whom she was betrothed, only in formal terms. With grim satisfaction, he realized that Whitney would be at *his* side when DuVille saw her at the Rutherford's and his annoyance abated. Pressing a light kiss on her forehead, he said, "I'll call for you at nine in the morning, the day after tomorrow."

Chapter Twenty-one

TWO DAYS LATER, ON THE STROKE OF NINE O'CLOCK, WHITNEY watched two shiny black travelling chaises draw up in the front drive. Pulling on the aqua kid gloves that matched her travelling costume, she trooped down the stairs to the entrance foyer with Clarissa marching beside her. Aunt Anne and her father came to bid her farewell. Whitney ignored her father and gave her aunt a fierce hug while Clayton excused himself to escort Clarissa personally out to the chaise.

"Where is Clarissa?" Whitney asked a few minutes later as Clayton handed her into his empty chaise.

Clayton, who had unceremoniously dispensed with the irate, protesting chaperone by thrusting her into the other chaise with his valet, said smoothly, "She is comfortably ensconced in the coach behind us, undoubtedly browsing through the excellent books I took the liberty of providing for her."

"Clarissa adores romances," Whitney remarked.

"I gave her *The Successful Management of Large Estates* and Plato's *Dialogues*," Clayton admitted impenitently. "But then, I had already put up the stairs and slammed the door before she ever had an opportunity to see the titles."

Whitney burst out laughing and shook her head.

The chaises swayed gently as they turned from her drive

onto the rutted country road, and it occurred to Whitney that although the chaise looked, from the outside, like hundreds of similar conveyances, it was much more spacious and luxurious on the inside. The velvet squabs were deeper and more comfortable, and the coach was so well sprung that it seemed to float on its frame. Beside her, Clayton had ample room to stretch out his long buckskin-clad legs without being cramped by the opposite seat, and although his broad shoulders were almost touching hers, it was not a lack of ample room that caused him to sit so close to her on the seat. Her pulse stirred as the faint scent of his spicy cologne touched her nostrils, and she hastily turned her head to concentrate on the lovely fall landscape moving past.

"Where is your home?" she asked after a long, comfortable silence.

"Wherever you are."

The quiet tenderness in his deep voice took her breath away. "I—I mean where is your real home—Claymore?"

"An hour and a half's drive from London in good weather."

"Is it very old?"

"Very."

"Then it must be quite dismal," Whitney reflected. He shot her a quizzical look and she hastily explained, "I mean that most of the old noble houses look very large and spacious from without, but inside they seem dark and oppressive."

"There have been some modernizations and additions made to Claymore." Dry amusement vibrated in his voice. "I don't think you'll find it 'dingy.' "

Whitney instantly assumed that his ducal residence must be palatial and extravagantly beautiful, but then she realized she would never see it, and a strange depression settled on her. Clayton seemed to sense her change of mood, and to Whitney's surprised delight he began regaling her with hilarious stories of his boyhood and his brother, Stephen. In all the time she had known him, he had never been so open with her, and her mood lightened with every mile until they neared Emily's London townhouse.

The sun was descending, and Whitney grew increasingly

tense as she stared out at the cobbled London streets. "What's wrong?" Clayton asked beside her.

"I feel conspicuous, arriving at Emily's house with you," Whitney admitted miserably. "It's going to seem very odd to her and to Lord Archibald."

"Pretend we're going to be married," Clayton laughed. Gathering her into his arms, he kissed her so long and so thoroughly that Whitney almost believed it.

The Archibalds' townhouse was trimmed with ornamental wrought iron and grillwork. Emily greeted them in the entry hall with smiling graciousness, and although Whitney knew Emily must be shocked that she had come to London with Clayton, she was relieved that Emily gave no hint of it. After giving Whitney a warm hug, she escorted her quickly up to a guest room, then went back downstairs to join her husband and Clayton in the drawing room and fulfill her duties as a hostess.

When she returned a quarter of an hour later, her serenity was gone and her cheeks were flushed with excitement. Whitney, who was helping Clarissa unpack, took one look at Emily's overbright eyes, and braced herself. "It's him!" Emily burst out, leaning against the door, gaping at Whitney. "He just told me who he really is. Michael has known all along, but his grace had asked Michael to keep his identity a secret. Everyone in London talks about him constantly, but I'd never seen him. Whitney!" she exclaimed, her pretty face lit with unabashed pride in her friend. "You are going to the Rutherfords' ball with *the most eligible bachelor in all Europe!* The Rutherfords' ball," she repeated as if trying to inspire enthusiasm in her friend. "Invitations to their parties are as coveted as diamonds!"

Whitney bit her lip uncertainly, longing to confide in Emily, yet unwilling to burden her with her own problems. If she told Emily she was betrothed to "the most eligible bachelor in Europe" Emily would obviously be thrilled. If she told Emily she didn't *want* to be betrothed to him, Emily would automatically sympathize. If she told Emily she was going to elope with Paul a few days from now, Emily would fear the inevitable scandal and she would plead with her not to do it.

"How long have you known he is the Duke of Claymore?"

"Less than a week," Whitney said cautiously.

"Well?" Emily prompted eagerly, so excited that her sentences ran together. "Tell me everything. Are you in love with him? Is he in love with you? Weren't you surprised to discover who he is?"

"Astounded," Whitney admitted, smiling slightly at the memory of her shocked horror at learning Clayton was her betrothed.

"Go on," Emily prodded.

Her delight was so infectious that Whitney's smile warmed, but she shook her head and answered in a firm tone that at least temporarily discouraged her friend from further probing. "He isn't in love with me, nor I with him. I am going to marry Paul. It's all but settled."

Clayton glanced at the clock above the mantel of the Robert Adams fireplace in his spacious bedroom suite as his valet eased a crisp white evening shirt onto his muscular shoulders. It was nearly ten, and he felt almost irrationally eager to be on his way to the Archibalds'.

"If I may say so, my lord," Armstrong murmured, assisting him into a black brocade waistcoat, "it's very good to be in London again."

While Clayton was buttoning the waistcoat, Armstrong removed a black evening jacket from the wardrobe, flicked a nonexistent speck off the lapel, then held it up while Clayton plunged his arms into the sleeves. After adjusting the ruby shirt studs, Armstrong stood back to survey the full effect of his master's tall frame in impeccably tailored, raven-black evening attire.

Clayton leaned close to the mirror to assure himself that his shave was close enough and flashed a broad grin at the hovering valet. "Well, do I pass muster, Armstrong?"

Surprised and gratified by the duke's uncharacteristic informality, Armstrong swelled with pleasure. "Most assuredly, your grace," he said, but when the duke left, Armstrong's pleasure slowly gave way to dismay as he realized that Miss Stone must be the cause of the duke's extraordinary good humor. For the first time, Armstrong began to doubt the wisdom of his wager with McRae, the coachman, against the master marrying the girl.

"Have a pleasant evening, your grace," the butler intoned as Clayton shrugged into an evening cloak lined with crimson silk and bounded down the long sweep of stairs that paraded from his magnificent Upper Brook Street mansion to the street. McRae, in full Westmoreland livery now, swept open the door of the coach as Clayton approached. Grinning at the red-haired Irish coachman, Clayton jerked his head toward the horses. "If they can't get above a trot, McRae, shoot them."

Elated anticipation seemed to build inside of Clayton with every revolution of the coach's wheels clattering over the cobbled London streets. He was exhilarated at the prospect of appearing in London with Whitney at his side. The Rutherfords' ball, which he'd originally intended to be a diversion for her, was now a profound pleasure for himself. He'd been dreaming of showing her off as his own since the night of the Armands' masquerade—and what better place to present her to London society than at the home of his good friends?

With boyish enjoyment, he contemplated Marcus and Ellen Rutherford's reaction when he introduced Whitney to them tonight as his fiancée. By presenting Whitney to London society as his fiancée, he wouldn't be breaking his promise to her, for she could still have the secrecy she desired when they returned to her home, at least for another few days. Secrecy! he thought disgustedly. He wanted the world to know!

"He's here," Emily exclaimed, rushing back into Whitney's room after greeting her noble guest downstairs. "Just think of it," she laughed. "You are making your London debut at the most important ball of the year, and the Duke of Claymore is your escort. How I wish Margaret Merryton could see you tonight!"

Emily's delighted enthusiasm, which had been increasing

all evening, was so contagious that Whitney couldn't help smiling as she stood up to leave, nor could she suppress the unexplainable joy that surged through her when she saw Clayton talking with Lord Archibald at the foot of the stairs.

Clayton looked up automatically as she began descending the staircase, and what he saw stopped his breath and made his heart burst with pride. Draped in a Grecian gown of nugget-gold satin which left one of her smooth shoulders deliciously bare and hugged her slender, voluptuous curves until it ended in a swirl of gold, Whitney looked like a shimmering golden goddess. A rope of yellow tourmalines and white diamonds was entwined in her lustrous dark hair, and a radiant smile lit her face and glowed in her eyes. Clayton thought that she had never looked so provocatively lush, nor so regally sensual as she did tonight. She was beautiful, glamorous, bewitching—and she was his.

Long gloves of matching gold covered her bare arms to well above the elbows, and when she reached the bottom of the staircase, Clayton took both her gloved hands in his. His gray eyes were smoldering, and his voice was almost hoarse. "My God, you are beautiful," he whispered.

Caught in the spell of those compelling gray eyes, Whitney yielded to the sudden temptation to let herself truly enjoy the evening, which already held the promise of enchantment. Stepping back, she favored Clayton with a sweeping look of unabashed admiration that ran the length of his long, splendidly clad frame, then she raised her laughing green eyes to his. "Not nearly so beautiful as you, I fear." Her eyes twinkled as she feigned dismay.

Clayton put her gold satin cape over her shoulders then rushed her from the house, not realizing until the door had closed behind them that he had neglected to say good night to the Archibalds.

Staring at the closed door, Emily expelled her breath in a long, wistful sigh.

"If you are wishing for something," Michael warned her gently, placing his arm around her shoulders, "wish that Whitney keeps her head, and not that Claymore loses his heart, because he won't. You've heard enough London gossip about him to know that. Even if he did lose his heart, and was willing to overlook her lack of fortune, he would never marry a female whose lineage was less aristocratic than his own. He is obligated by family custom not to marry beneath himself."

Outside the night was foggy, and a chilly breeze sent Whitney's cape fluttering behind her. She paused halfway down the steps to pull up the wide satin hood in order to protect her coiffeur. In the act, her gaze fell on the coach waiting in the street beneath the gas lamp. "Good heavens, is that yours?" she gasped, staring at the magnificent burgundy-lacquered coach with a gold crest emblazoned on the door panel. "Of course it is," she said quickly, recovering her composure and walking alongside Clayton down the steps. "It's just that I don't think of you as a duke. I think of you as you are at home. My home, I mean," she explained, feeling thoroughly absurd and unsophisticated as she stopped again to stare, not at the coach, but at the horses who drew it—four glorious grays with snowy white manes and tails, who stamped and tossed their heads in a restless frenzy to be off.

"Do you like them?" Clayton said, helping her into the coach and settling down beside her.

"Like them?" Whitney repeated as she pushed back her hood and turned her head to smile shyly into his eyes. "I have never seen such magnificent animals."

He slipped an arm around her shoulders. "Then they're yours."

"No, I couldn't accept them. Really, I couldn't."

"Is it now your intention to deprive me of the pleasure of giving you gifts?" he asked gently. "It pleased me mightily to know I had paid for your gowns and jewels even though you had no idea they were from me."

Lulled by his tolerant good humor, Whitney asked the one question she had heretofore been afraid to voice. "How much did you pay my father for me?"

The mood was shattered. "If you will grant me nothing else," he said shortly, "at least grant me this. Stop persisting in this foolish determination to see yourself as something I purchased!"

Now that she'd asked the question and incurred his anger, Whitney wanted an answer. "How much?" she repeated obstinately.

Clayton hesitated and then snapped icily, "One hundred thousand pounds."

Whitney's mind reeled. Never in her wildest imaginings had she dreamt of a sum like that; a household servant only earned thirty or forty pounds a year. If she and Paul scrimped and saved for the rest of their lives, they could never pay back a fortune like that. She wished with all her heart that she hadn't asked the question. She didn't want to spoil their evening; tonight would be their first and last gala affair together, and for some reason it was terribly important to her not to ruin it. Trying desperately to recover some of their earlier gaiety, Whitney said lightly, "You were a fool, my lord duke."

Clayton threw his gloves onto the seat across from them. "Really?" he drawled in a bored, insulting voice. "And why is that, Ma'am?"

"Because," Whitney informed him pertly, "I don't think you should have let him fleece you out of a single shilling over £99,000!"

Clayton's stunned gaze shot to her face, narrowed on her smiling lips, and then he leaned back his head and laughed, a rich throaty sound that warmed Whitney's heart. "When a man sets out to acquire a treasure," he chuckled, drawing her closer and smiling at her, "he does not argue over a few pounds."

The silence between them lengthened and the amusement in his eyes was slowly replaced by a slumbering intensity. His silver gaze held hers imprisoned as he slowly bent his head to her. "I want you," he breathed, and his lips parted hers for a deep, violently sensual kiss that left Whitney shaken and flushed.

The Rutherford mansion was ablaze with lights, and the long drive leading up to it crowded with vehicles making their way toward the front of the house where they stopped to allow their resplendent passengers to alight. Footmen carrying torches met each vehicle, then escorted the guests up the terraced front steps to the main door.

In a reasonably short time, Whitney and Clayton were being escorted up the steps by a torch-bearing, liveried footman. In the entry foyer, a servant took their outerwear, and they proceeded up the carpeted staircase where enormous bouquets of white orchids in tall silver stands had been placed on each step.

They walked around the corner and out onto a balcony and Whitney paused to gaze down at the scene in the ballroom below. Her first London ball, she thought. And her last. The crowd seemed to dip and sway as the ladies moved about the floor, talking and laughing. Immense crystal chandeliers reflected the dazzling kaleidoscope of colorful gowns, which were multiplied over and over again in the two-story mirrored walls.

"Ready?" Clayton said, tucking her hand possessively in the crook of his arm and trying to draw her toward the wide curving staircase which lead from the balcony down to the crowd below.

Whitney, who had been casually looking for Nicki, suddenly realized that everyone down in the ballroom was beginning to look at *them,* and she pulled back in confused alarm while hundreds of curious gazes swivelled up to where they were standing. The roar of conversation began steadily winding down until it was reduced to whispers and murmurings, and then it soared to deafening heights. Whitney had the terrifying feeling that every person in that ballroom was either looking at them or talking about them. A woman looked up at Clayton, then hurried over to speak to a tall, distinguished-looking man, who immediately turned to gaze up at Clayton, then disengaged himself from the people surrounding him and strode purposefully in the direction of the balcony where they stood. "Everyone is staring at us," Whitney whispered apprehensively.

Completely impervious to the stir he was creating, Clayton flicked a glance down at the guests, then shifted his gaze to Whitney's lovely, upturned face. "I see that," he agreed drily as the distinguished-looking man, who Whitney assumed must be their host, bounded up the last stair onto the balcony.

"Clayton!" Marcus Rutherford laughed. "Where the devil have you been? I was beginning to believe the rumors that you'd dropped off the face of the earth."

Whitney listened as the two men, who were obviously close friends, exchanged greetings. Lord Rutherford was handsome, and looked to be about seven and thirty, with piercing blue eyes that spoke of perceptiveness. Without warning, those blue eyes levelled on her, inspecting her with unconcealed admiration. "And who, pray, is this ravishing creature beside you?" he demanded. "Must I introduce myself to her?"

Glancing uncertainly at Clayton, Whitney was startled to find him gazing down at her with a look of profound pride. "Whitney," he said, "may I present my friend, Lord Marcus Rutherford—" Directing a meaningful glance at Whitney's hand which was still firmly clasped in Lord Rutherford's, Clayton finished, "Marcus, kindly take your hands off my future wife, Miss Whitney Stone."

"Whitney?" Marcus Rutherford repeated. "What an unusual . . ." A slow, disbelieving smile broke across his face as he stopped in mid-sentence and stared at Clayton. "Have I heard you aright?"

Clayton inclined his head in a slight nod, and Lord Rutherford's delighted gaze returned to Whitney. "Come with me, young lady," he said, eagerly drawing Whitney's hand through his arm. "As you may have noticed, there are about six hundred people down there all on fire to know who you are."

When Clayton seemed perfectly agreeable to letting her go with Marcus Rutherford, Whitney hastily took matters into her own hands. "My Lord Rutherford," she said, her pleading gaze directed at Clayton. "We—we wish to keep our forthcoming marriage a secret for a while."

She looked so distressed that Clayton reluctantly relinquished his plan to present her to everyone as his betrothed. "It's to remain a secret for a while, Marcus," he said.

"You must be mad," Lord Rutherford returned, but he released Whitney's hand. "You'll never keep this prize of yours a secret for a day. In fact"—he glanced in the direction of the crowd below which was now openly watching what was transpiring on the balcony—"you'll never manage such a feat for even an hour." He waited a moment, obviously hoping that Clayton would relent, then turned to leave them, saying over his shoulder, "You will at least allow me to confide in Lady Rutherford? She's already charged me to discover who this beautiful young woman with you is."

Before Whitney could object, Clayton nodded his assent. With a feeling of impending disaster, she turned a despairing look on him and said, "Now watch what happens." Lord Rutherford strode directly to a stunning redhead, drew her aside and said something to her, and that lady turned to gaze in astonished welcome at Clayton and Whitney while flashing them a conspiratorial smile. Precisely as Whitney expected, the moment Lord Rutherford left her side, Lady Rutherford hurried over to another woman and bent low to whisper in her ear, and that lady's head swivelled to Clayton and Whitney, pausing for a split-second before she raised her fan and leaned close to speak to the lady beside *her*.

Cold terror strangled Whitney's voice. "So much for secrecy." She choked out the words, and searched for someone to ask where she could freshen up. Too stricken to care what Clayton would think of her actions, she fled to the designated room and closed the door, leaving him standing alone on the balcony.

Her eyes were glazed with panic as she stared blindly at her reflection in one of the mirrored walls. This was a calamity! A disaster! The guests at this ball knew Clayton; they were his friends and acquaintances. In another fifteen minutes, every one of them would know that he was betrothed to her, and within a week, everyone in London would know it. When she eloped with Paul, they would also realize that she had scorned Clayton, fled to escape him and their forthcoming marriage. Dear God! Before this was over, Clayton was going to be publicly humiliated. She couldn't bear to do that to him. Even if she could, she would be afraid to do it. If she publicly shamed him, his vengeance would surely crash down on her with a savagery that would be devastating. She shivered, thinking of Clayton's inevitable fury and the awesome power he possessed to retaliate against her and her family, even Aunt Anne and Uncle Edward.

Sternly, determinedly, Whitney fought to bring her rioting panic under control. She couldn't continue to hide in this room like an hysteric, and she couldn't leave the ball. Hugging her arms around herself, she began to pace slowly across the crimson carpet, struggling against her quaking fear and forcing herself to think logically, clearly. In the first place, she reminded herself, Clayton had avoided matrimony for years. If he didn't marry her, wasn't it likely that everyone would assume she'd lost whatever appeal she had for him, and that *he* and not *she* had cried off? Of course they would—particularly when they discovered that she had neither wealth nor aristocratic lineage.

The painful knot in her stomach began to dissolve. After a few minutes of additional contemplation, she realized that when Clayton had refused to allow Lord Rutherford to introduce her as his intended bride, he had relegated their betrothal to the status of an unconfirmed rumor. And wasn't London, like Paris, always buzzing with rumors that were soon forgotten? Emily said it was. She felt much, much better.

Her heart gave a funny little lurch when she remembered how very proud of her Clayton had seemed when he introduced her to Lord Rutherford as his fiancée. Never in all these weeks had Clayton mentioned love, or even that he cared for her, yet there was no mistaking that expression on his face tonight; he did care for her, and more than a little. She didn't want to repay him by embarrassing him. She owed him more than to shame him by cowering in this room. At least for this evening she could surely pretend that she returned his affection.

Having made that decision, Whitney composed her features and carefully studied her reflection in the mirror. A perfectly poised young woman looked back at her, her chin resolutely high.

Satisfied, she reached for the door handle just as female voices sounded from the adjoining room where champagne had been placed on a small gilded table between a pair of silk settees. "Her gown is Parisian," a woman pronounced.

"But with a name like Whitney Stone, she must be as English as we," a second voice reminded, adding, "do you believe the rumor that they're betrothed?"

"Absolutely not. If the girl had wits enough to wring an offer from Claymore, you can be certain she'd also be smart enough to make sure he sent a notice straight to the *Times*. I can't see Claymore crying off an engagement once it was announced."

Chiding herself for eavesdropping, Whitney started to leave but paused when the outer door again opened and a third voice chimed in. "They're betrothed, you may rely on it," the newcomer declared emphatically. "Lawrence and I have just had a word with his grace, and I'm absolutely convinced it's true."

"Do you mean," the first voice gasped, "that Claymore confirmed the betrothal?"

"Don't be silly. You know how maddeningly uninformative Claymore always is when he knows one *most* wants to pry into his affairs."

"Well then, what makes you so certain he's betrothed to her?"

"Two things. First of all, when Lawrence asked where they'd met, Claymore grinned in a way that made Vanessa Standfield positively livid—you do recall that Vanessa told everyone that he was on the verge of offering for her before he unexpectedly left for France? Well, now poor Vanessa looks an utter fool, because it's obvious that he left for France to join Miss Stone. He admitted he met her there several years ago. Anyway, when Claymore talks about Miss Stone, he positively beams with pride!"

"I can't credit the image of Claymore 'beaming,'" the second voice said skeptically.

"Then merely think of it as a gleam in his eye."

"*That* I can credit," laughed the voice. "Now, what was the second reason?"

"It was the look the duke gave Esterbrook when Esterbrook asked him for an introduction to Miss Stone. Believe me, there was enough ice in his grace's expression to send Esterbrook scurrying for a fire where he could warm himself."

Unable to remain any longer, Whitney opened the door. A secret smile touched her lips and eyes and, as she passed the three thunderstruck women, she graciously inclined her head.

Clayton was standing precisely where she had left him on the balcony, but surrounded now by two dozen men and women. Even so, Whitney had no trouble spotting him because he was taller than everyone else. She was trying to decide whether she should remain where she was, or go to Clayton's side, when he looked up and saw her standing there. Without a word of explanation, he merely inclined his head to those gathered around him, and strolled out of their midst to Whitney.

As they descended the curving staircase to the ballroom, the musicians on the raised dais broke into a majestic waltz, but instead of dancing, Clayton led her toward an alcove which was partially concealed from the ballroom by a curtain swept gracefully to one side. "Don't you want to dance?" Whitney asked curiously.

He chuckled and shook his head. "The last time we waltzed you tried to leave me in the middle of the dance floor."

"Which was no more than you deserved," Whitney teased, carefully ignoring the watchful stares of the guests.

They stepped into the alcove and Clayton picked up two glasses of sparkling champagne from the tray on the table beside her. Handing one to her, he inclined his head toward the smiling people who were already bearing down on the alcove. "Courage, my sweet." He grinned. "Here they come." Whitney drained the contents of her champagne glass and plucked another off the silver tray. For courage.

They converged on the alcove in a ceaseless stream, in groups of six and eight, demanding good-naturedly to know where Clayton had been and pressing invitations on him. They treated Whitney with a combination of carefully concealed speculation and extreme friendliness, yet there were several times when Whitney sensed a jealous malevolence in the attitudes of some of the women. And no wonder, she thought, smiling to herself as she admired Clayton over the rim of her fourth glass of champagne. He looked breathtakingly handsome in the elegant black evening attire that fit his tall, broad-shouldered frame to perfection. No doubt many of the women here had yearned to have him at their side, to bask in the aura of restrained power and masculine vitality that emanated from him, and to know the spell of those bold gray eyes capturing and holding theirs.

As she thought it, he glanced down at her in the midst of a conversation with his friends, and a glow of warmth and happiness surged through Whitney that had nothing to do with the champagne she had consumed. Seeing him like this, relaxed and laughing among these glittering members of London's *haute ton* who admired him and courted his friendship, Whitney could hardly believe this urbane, sophisticated nobleman was the same man who had raced after her on Dangerous Crossing and talked about prehistoric rocks with her tiresome uncle.

When at long last there was a brief moment of privacy, Whitney slanted an audacious smile at him. "I would say that the consensus is that I am probably your mistress."

"As it happens, you're wrong," Clayton said, his gaze dropping to the near empty champagne glass in her hand. "Have you eaten anything tonight?"

"Yes," Whitney said. She was puzzled by his concern, but she dismissed it because the music was beginning again and Lord Rutherford and five other men were bearing down on her with the obvious intention of asking her to dance.

Clayton followed her from the alcove and leaned a shoulder negligently against a pillar, raising his glass of champagne to his lips while he watched her making her graceful way toward the dance floor. Whitney might think these people believed she was his mistress, but Clayton was making certain they realized she was his fiancée. They all knew he was not in the habit of gazing fondly at the women he escorted to balls, or holding up pillars while he watched them dance. By doing that now, he was deliberately announcing their engagement as clearly and emphatically as if it had been printed in the *Times*.

Just why it was so important to claim Whitney as his tonight, was something that eluded him. He told himself that it was because he didn't want Esterbrook and the others panting after her, but it was more than that. She was in his blood. Her smile warmed his heart, and her most innocent touch sent desire raging through his veins. There was a provocative sensuality about her, a natural, unaffected sophistication and exhilarating liveliness that drew men to her, and he wanted every one of them to know, here and now, that she was his.

He watched her, his mind drifting to the night soon to come, when that glorious mantle of shimmering dark hair would be spilling over his bare chest and her silken body would writhe in sweet ecstasy beneath his. In the past, he had preferred his women to be experienced in the art of lovemaking; fiery, passionate creatures who knew how to give pleasure and receive it, women who could admit their desire to themselves and to him. But now he was outrageously pleased that Whitney was a virgin. In fact, it gave him intense pleasure to contemplate their wedding night when he would guide her gently, tenderly from girl to woman, until she was moaning with rapture in his arms.

Three hours later, Whitney had danced with more men than she could possibly remember and drunk more champagne than she had ever consumed. She was feeling decidedly gay and definitely light-headed—so much so that not even Clayton's frown of displeasure when she accepted this, her second dance with Lord Esterbrook, could dampen her spirits. In fact she was quite convinced that nothing could spoil her enjoyment of the evening, until she glanced over Lord Esterbrook's shoulder and saw that, for the first time all night, Clayton was dancing with someone other than her. The young woman in his arms, whose eyes were turned laughingly up to his was a lushly beautiful blonde whose slender, voluptuous curves were draped in an exquisite gown of sapphire-blue, with diamonds and sapphires twined in and out among her shining curls. A blinding streak of jealousy suddenly ripped through Whitney.

"Her name is Vanessa Standfield," Lord Esterbrook provided with a hint of malicious satisfaction in his voice.

"They make a very striking couple," Whitney managed.

"Vanessa certainly thinks so," Esterbrook replied.

Whitney's eyes clouded as she recalled the conversation she'd overheard much earlier between the three women in the withdrawing room upstairs. Vanessa Standfield had been expecting an offer from Clayton just before he left for France. No doubt, Clayton had given her very good reason to believe he cared, Whitney thought with a fresh stab of painful jealousy as she watched him grinning at the gorgeous blonde. But then she reminded herself that Clayton had offered for *her* and not Vanessa Standfield, and in a dizzying shift of mood she felt perfectly wonderful again. "Miss Standfield is very beautiful," she said.

Esterbrook's brows lifted in amused mockery. "Vanessa was not nearly so complimentary when she remarked about you a few moments ago, Miss Stone. But then, she is quite convinced that you have wrung an offer from Claymore. Have you?" he asked abruptly.

Whitney was so stunned by his monumental nerve that she didn't even consider getting angry. In fact, her eyes danced with laughter. "Somehow, I cannot conceive of anyone 'wringing' anything from him, can you?"

"Oh come now," Esterbrook said testily, "I am not naive enough to believe you misunderstood my question."

"And I," Whitney said softly, "am not naive enough to believe I have to answer it."

With the exception of Lord Esterbrook, all her other partners were lavishly attentive and outrageously flattering, but the dancing and animated conversation eventually began to wear on her. She found herself longing to be at Clayton's side. Declining her current partner's request for another dance, she asked him to return her to the duke instead.

As usual, Clayton was surrounded with people, but without looking up from the conversation, he reached out and firmly took her arm, drawing her into the circle of his friends, and keeping her close to his side. It was a casually possessive gesture that somehow added to Whitney's sense of euphoric well-being . . . as did the next two glasses of champagne.

"What happened to Esterbrook?" Clayton asked drily a while later. "I expected him to ask you for a third dance."

Whitney twinkled. "He did. But I refused."

"To prevent gossip?"

An unconsciously provocative smile curved her lips as she shook her head in denial. "I refused because I knew you didn't want me to dance with him the last time, and I was quite, quite certain that if I did it again, *you* would retaliate by dancing again with Miss Standfield."

"That's very astute of you," he complimented softly.

"And very perverse of *you*," Whitney admonished, laughing. And then it dawned on her that she had just admitted to being jealous.

"Cherie—" Nicki's deep chuckle brought her spinning around in joyous surprise. "Have you now decided to conquer London as you did Paris?"

"Nicki!" she breathed, beaming at the handsome face that had been so dear to her for so long. "It's wonderful to see you," she said as he took both her hands in his familiar warm grasp and held them. "I asked Lord Rutherford if you were here, but he said you had been delayed in Paris and might not arrive until tomorrow."

"I got here an hour ago."

Whitney turned to Clayton, intending to introduce Nicki to him, but evidently they had already met. "Claymore, isn't it?" Nicki interrupted her introduction, his tawny eyes surveying Clayton critically.

Clayton's response was an equally cool inclination of the head, followed by a lazy, mocking smile which Whitney sensed was deliberately intended either to infuriate or intimidate Nicki. Whitney, who had never seen either man act this way to anyone before, had a sudden urge to run for cover, and an equally strong impulse, induced by champagne, to giggle at the male hostility she had somehow provoked.

"Dance with me," Nicki said, arrogantly disregarding

etiquette, which required that he first ask Clayton if he objected.

Since Nicki was already exerting pressure to draw her with him to the dance floor, Whitney looked helplessly over her shoulder at Clayton. "Will you excuse us, please?" she asked.

"Certainly," came Clayton's clipped reply.

The moment Nicki took her in his arms, his features tightened with disapproval. "What are you doing with Claymore?" he demanded, and before she could possibly answer, he said, "Chérie, the man is a . . . a . . ."

"Are you trying to say he's a frightful rogue where ladies are concerned?" Whitney asked, struggling against her mirth.

Nicki nodded curtly, and Whitney continued teasingly, "And he *is* a trifle arrogant, isn't he? Also very handsome and charming?"

Nicki's eyes narrowed and Whitney's shoulders trembled with laughter. "Oh Nicki, he is very much like *you!*"

"With one important difference," Nicki countered, "and that is that *I* would marry you!"

Whitney almost clapped her hand over his mouth in laughing horror. "Don't say that to me, Nicki. Not here and not now. You would not believe the coil I'm in already."

"This is not a laughing matter," Nicki said sharply.

Whitney swallowed a giggle. "No one knows that better than I."

Nicki studied her flushed face in frowning silence. "I am going to stay in London," he announced. "I have business I can transact while I am here and friends with whom I will visit. You said in your note that you had social commitments for the next two weeks. At the end of those two weeks, you and I are again going to discuss the subject of marriage— when you are in a clearer frame of mind."

Caught between horror and hilarity, Whitney made no protest and allowed him to return her to Clayton where she downed more champagne and gaily contemplated her predicament, which was growing more complicated and perilous by the moment.

Clayton sent word to have his coach brought round; then

he took her in his arms for a last dance. "What amuses you so, little one?" he asked, smiling down at her and holding her much closer than was seemly.

"Oh, everything!" Whitney laughed. "For example, when I was a girl I was absolutely positive that no one would ever want to marry me. And now Paul wants to—and Nicki says he does—and of course, you do." After a moment's thought, she announced expansively, "I wish I could marry all three of you, for you are all very nice!" She peeked at him from beneath her long sooty lashes, and asked almost hopefully, "I don't suppose you are the least bit jealous, are you?"

Clayton watched her intently. "Should I be?"

"Indeed you should," Whitney said merrily, "if for no other reason than to flatter my vanity because *I* was jealous when you danced with Miss Standfield." She sobered a bit and lowered her voice to the barest whisper. "I had freckles when I was a girl," she confessed.

"Surely not!" Clayton said in exaggerated shock.

"Yes, thousands of them. Right here—" she jabbed a long tapered fingernail at the general vicinity of her nose and almost poked her eye out.

A throaty chuckle escaped Clayton as he quickly reclaimed her right hand to prevent its being jabbed at her other eye.

"And," Whitney continued in the tone of one admitting to a ghastly deed, "I used to hang upside down from tree limbs. All the other girls used to pretend they were royal princesses, but I pretended I was a monkey . . ." She tipped her head back, expecting to see condemnation on Clayton's face. Instead he was smiling down at her as if she were something very rare and very fine. "I am having a wonderful time tonight," she said softly, mesmerized by the tenderness she saw in his eyes.

An hour later, Whitney sighed with contentment and snuggled deeper into the burgundy velvet squabs of Clayton's coach, listening to the steady clip-clop of the horses' hooves on the cobbled, fog-shrouded London streets. Experimentally, she closed her eyes, but dizziness made her snap them open. She concentrated instead on the weak yellow light from the flickering coach lamps that sent shadows dancing within the cozy confines of the coach. "Champagne is very nice," she murmured.

"You won't think so tomorrow," Clayton laughed, putting his arm around her.

Clutching his arm to help maintain her fragile balance, Whitney trailed beside him up the steps toward the front door of the Archibalds' townhouse, her face turned up to the dawn-streaked sky. At the front door, Clayton stopped.

Whitney finally realized that he was evidently waiting for something and pulled her gaze from the sky to his face. Her eyes narrowed on the laughter tugging at his lips, and she drew herself up to her fullest height. In a voice of offended dignity, she asked, "Are you thinking that I have had too much to drink?"

"Not at all. I am hoping that you have a key."

"Key?" she repeated blankly.

"To the door . . ."

"Oh certainly," she proudly declared.

After several moments passed, he chuckled. "May I have it?"

"Have what?" Whitney asked, trying desperately to concentrate. "Oh yes, of course—the key." She glanced about, trying to remember where she'd left her elegant little beaded reticule, and discovered it hanging haphazardly from her left shoulder by its short golden chain. Grimacing to herself, she muttered, "Ladies do not carry their reticules thus," and pulled it down, rummaging clumsily within it until she finally found the key.

In the darkened entrance hall, Whitney turned abruptly to bid Clayton good night, misjudged the distance separating them and collided with his chest. His strong arm encircled her, steadying her. She could have drawn away, but instead she stood there, her heart beginning to hammer as his gray eyes slid to her lips, lingering on them for an endless moment. And then he purposefully lowered his head.

His mouth opened boldly over hers, his hands sliding intimately over her back and then her hips, molding her tightly to his muscular frame. Whitney stiffened in confused alarm at the hardening pressure of his manhood, then suddenly wrapped her arms around his neck and shamelessly returned his kiss, glorying in the feel of his tongue insistently parting her lips, then plunging into her mouth, slowly retreating and plunging again in a wildly exciting rhythm so suggestive that she felt as if his body were plunging into hers.

Dizzily, she finally pulled away, and then was disappointed that he released her so readily. Drawing a long, unsteady breath, she opened her eyes and saw two Claytons gazing down at her, one superimposed over the other on her swimming vision. "You are shockingly forward, sir," she admonished severely, then spoiled it with a giggle.

Clayton grinned impenitently. "Understandably so, since you seem to find my attentions less than repulsive tonight."

Whitney considered that with a hazy, thoughtful smile. "I suppose that's true," she admitted in a candid whisper. "And do you know something else—I believe that you kiss quite as well as Paul!" With that backhanded compliment she turned and started up the stairs. On the second step, she paused to reconsider. "Actually," she said, looking at Clayton over her shoulder, "I *think* you kiss as well as Paul, but I can't be perfectly certain until he returns. When he does, I shall ask him to kiss me the way you do, so that I may make a more objective comparison." On a stroke of brilliance, she added, "I shall make a scientific experiment of it!"

"The hell you will!" Clayton half growled, half laughed.

Whitney lifted her delicate brows in haughty challenge. "I will if I wish."

A hard smack landed familiarly on her derriere. Whitney lurched around, swinging her arm in a wide arc with every intention of slapping his grinning face. Unfortunately, her aim was off and her hand grazed the wall alongside the staircase instead, dislodging a small painting and sending it clattering to the polished floor. "Now look what you've done!" she hissed unfairly, "You're going to awaken the entire household!" Turning, she flounced up the stairs.

Three Archibald servants were stationed at the sideboard which was covered with steaming platters of buttered eggs, ham, bacon, wafer-thin sliced sirloin, fresh crusty rolls, three kinds of potatoes and several other tempting dishes which Emily had ordered last night after due consideration as to what was appropriate to serve a man of the Duke of Claymore's lofty rank. They were waiting for Whitney to come downstairs and join them for the meal, to which the duke had been invited since he was escorting Whitney back home that day. Stirring her tea, Emily furtively studied the duke as he conversed across the table with Michael, while a romantic daydream of Whitney becoming the Duchess of Claymore floated through her mind.

"It appears that our houseguest is going to sleep away the day," Michael remarked.

Emily saw the meaningful look which his grace directed at her husband as he said mildly, "Whitney may be suffering from the effects of her evening."

"I had no idea she might be ill," Emily exclaimed. "I'll go up and see her."

"No," Whitney croaked behind them. "I—I'm here."

At the sound of her hoarse voice, all three turned in unison. She was standing in the doorway, arms extended, her hands braced against the doorframe on either side of her, swaying slightly as if she couldn't support herself. Alarmed, Emily pushed back her chair, but the duke was already out of his and striding swiftly across the room.

A knowing smile touched Clayton's eyes as he studied her pale face. "How do you feel, little one?" he asked.

"How do you *think* I feel?" she whispered, focusing an anguished, accusing look on him.

"You'll feel better after you've had some breakfast," he promised, taking her arm to lead her toward the table.

"No," Whitney rasped. "I am going to die."

Chapter Twenty-two

SHE WAS STILL HALF CONVINCED OF IT WHEN THEIR COACH DREW away from Emily's London townhouse. "Do you know," she whispered miserably, "I never liked champagne."

With a throaty laugh Clayton put his arm around her and drew her throbbing head against his shoulder. "I'm rather surprised to hear that," he teased.

Sighing, Whitney closed her eyes and slept until they were almost at her home, occasionally clutching Clayton's arm when their coach gave a particularly sharp lurch.

She awakened feeling entirely restored and very sheepish. "I haven't been very good company," she apologized, smiling ruefully at Clayton. "If you would like to come for supper, I—"

"I have to start back to London tonight," he interrupted.

"Tonight?" Whitney repeated, sitting bolt upright. "How long will you be gone?"

"A week."

Elation began to pulse through Whitney's veins and she quickly turned her face from him. If Clayton was in London, Paul and she could elope to Scotland without having to fear that he would learn of their elopement in time to come after them. His going to London now was a stroke of luck beyond any she could have hoped for. It was a boon! It was a blessing!

It was a *calamity.*

The relief she'd been feeling turned to panic, and Whitney's head began to pound with renewed vigor. Dear God, Clayton was going back to London. As gentlemen did, he would probably spend his evenings at his clubs, dining or gambling with his friends and acquaintances. In those clubs there were bound to be men who had attended the Rutherfords' ball and heard the rumor of his betrothal. In the club's atmosphere of easy camaraderie, his friends would naturally press him to confirm or deny the rumor. And Whitney could almost imagine Clayton grinning and telling them that it was true. And if he did, he would look like an utter fool when she eloped with Paul instead.

Awash with misery, Whitney squeezed her eyes closed. As much as she feared Clayton's vengeance, which would now be far more awesome because he would feel publicly humiliated, she dreaded even more being the cause of that public humiliation. She couldn't bear the thought of this proud man becoming the object of derision and pity. He had done nothing to deserve that. Last night she had seen how respected and admired he was by everyone. Now, because of her, he would be humbled before them.

Whitney clasped her clammy palms together in her lap. Perhaps she could prevent a public scandal. Paul was due home tomorrow. If they eloped tomorrow night, she could notify Clayton in London almost at once, and the sooner he knew of her elopement, the fewer people he would tell that he had offered for her.

Naturally, she would make certain her message didn't reach him in time for him to come after her. Timing, she decided with a lump growing in her throat, was going to be essential. No matter how travel-weary Paul might be, they would have to leave within hours of his return. Once Clayton learned of her elopement, he wouldn't tell anyone he was betrothed to her. He could pass the betrothal rumor off with one of his mocking smiles and simply appear at some public function with one of those beautiful women who panted after him. And that would be that! Everyone would believe that his betrothal to a penniless nobody like Whitney Stone had merely been a joke, a ridiculous rumor.

Paul. Her heart sank when she thought of telling him they had to elope. He wouldn't want to do it; he would be concerned about the damage to her reputation that an elopement would cause. He had been so happy the night of her father's party, telling her about the plans he had for them, the improvements he would make to his house and lands to please her.

Clayton's hand cupped her chin and Whitney jumped nervously. "When Sevarin returns," he said in a tone that brooked no argument, "I want you to inform him at once that you aren't going to marry him. I will not tolerate people believing that my future wife has been engaged to another man. Give Sevarin any reason you wish for declining his offer, but tell him immediately. Is that understood?"

"Yes," Whitney whispered.

Clayton gave her a long, penetrating look. "I want your word on it."

"I—" Whitney swallowed, profoundly touched that he was crediting her with having a sense of honor as strong as his own. She dragged her eyes to his, feeling utterly vile for betraying his trust. "I give you my word."

His expression softened and he looked at her with unbearable gentleness. "I know how hard it will be for you to tell him, little one. I promise I'll make it up to you someday." Tears burned the backs of her eyes and the muscles of her throat constricted as he tenderly traced the elegant curve of her cheek. "Forgive me?" he asked her softly.

Forgive *him?* Whitney's emotions were warring so fiercely inside of her that for one second, she actually considered turning into his strong arms and sobbing out her confused sorrow. Instead she nodded and gazed at him, trying to memorize his handsome face as it was now—because if she ever saw him again, she knew his expression would be one of icy rage.

They were turning up the road toward her house, and Whitney numbly pulled on her gloves.

"Why are you going back to London so quickly?" she asked as the time to bid him a final, painful goodbye drew nearer with each moment.

"Because I met with my business managers early this morning and there are some decisions which I must make, once I've met with some people in the city. It's purely a matter of choosing which are the best investments in which to place a rather large sum of money," he reassured her, and with a grin he added, "Contrary to the gossip you heard about me at your father's party, I don't lead a life of leisurely debauchery. I have seven estates, a thousand tenants, and a hundred business interests, all of which are suffering from the lack of my attention—which has been devoted almost exclusively to you, my pet."

The coach drew to a stop in front of her house, and a footman came to open the door and let down the steps. Whitney began to turn toward the door, but Clayton's quiet voice stopped her. "My business affairs won't require that I remain in London for that long, but I thought you would want some time alone after you confront Sevarin. Unless you send word to me in London, I'll remain there until Sunday—a week from tomorrow."

As he told her how to reach him in London, Whitney heard the guarded hope in his voice that she would indeed send for him before the week was out, and she laid a trembling hand on his sleeve, aching to plead for his forgiveness and understanding. "Clayton, I—" She saw his pleasure at her voluntary touch and her use of his given name, and her voice broke. "Have a pleasant trip," she managed to say, pulling away and blindly climbing down from the coach.

As soon as she reached her room, Whitney sent a note round to Paul's house with instructions that no matter what time Mr. Sevarin returned, he was to be given it. In it, she asked him to send word to her that he was back and then to go immediately to the old gamekeeper's cottage where she would join him. There, at least, she would have some privacy so that she could explain her predicament. Explain her predicament! How in the world was she ever going to find the words to do that? she wondered dejectedly.

By nightfall there was still no word from Paul.

Twice as she dressed for bed, Whitney almost went down the hall to enlist her aunt's aid in the elopement. Each time, her better judgment warned that Aunt Anne would never consent to an elopement no matter how urgent Whitney's reasons might be. Aunt Anne would think only of the irreversible damage the elopement would do to Whitney's reputation. She would never understand that Whitney couldn't, she just couldn't take the coward's way out now and let Paul down, even if she wanted to—which she didn't, Whitney told herself without much conviction. He loved her. He was counting on her.

Since she couldn't trust Clarissa with her secret either, Whitney slowly packed her necessities and hid the case, then she climbed into bed and gazed at the ceiling. Of all the unpleasant tasks facing her, the one she dreaded most was writing the note she would have to send to Clayton in London.

Mentally she worded and reworded it. It preyed on her mind until she finally decided to get it over with and dragged herself out of bed. "Paul and I have eloped," she wrote. "I hope some day you will find it in your heart if not to forgive me, at least to understand."

Forgive? Understand? Never would Clayton do so. She sat at her desk and stared at the note, imagining Clayton's reaction to it. At first he would smile, thinking that she was sending word to him to return early, and then his smile would fade . . .

Shivering as if the blast from those glacial gray eyes were already levelled on her, Whitney crawled back into bed and huddled under the covers. She wasn't certain she had the courage to elope or even if she *wanted* to elope.

Tears trickled down her cheeks and dampened her pillow as she thought of the tall, gray-eyed man whom she would have to face when she returned from her elopement—a forceful, vital man who would turn away from her in disgust and loathing, who would never again laugh with her, never hold her in his strong arms, and never again call her "little one" in that tender way of his.

Paul's message arrived at eleven o'clock the following morning. Dressed warmly against the frosty chill of the cloudy day, Whitney raced Khan around the hillside and galloped into the overgrown yard of the deserted cottage. She tied Khan beside Paul's horse, then shoved open the creaky door of the cottage. The timid little fire Paul had built snapped and flickered on the hearth but did little to dispel the chilly gloom of the single empty room. At a movement behind her, Whitney whirled nervously. "Paul!"

"I believe you were expecting me," he teased. Straightening from his lounging position against the wall, he opened his arms and said, "Come here."

Whitney went to him and automatically turned her face up for his kiss, while her mind sorted through various ways to begin.

"I've missed you, brat," he murmured in her hair. "Have you missed me?"

"Yes," she answered absently, pulling away from his arms. She had to explain slowly, not heap all their tangled problems on him in the first minute. She moved toward the center of the room, then turned to face him. "Paul, I have some things to tell you which you are going to find"—she searched madly for the right word—"surprising."

"Go on," Paul urged, grinning. "I like surprises."

"Well, you aren't going to like this one!" she burst out helplessly. "You know Mr. Westland?"

Paul nodded.

"And do you recall at my father's party, how everyone was gossiping about the Duke of Claymore, Clayton Westmoreland?"

"I do," Paul said.

"Well, Mr. *Westland* is actually *Westmoreland.*"

"The duke who disappeared?" Paul said, his expression a mixture of amusement, curiosity, and disbelief. "The duke who owns fifty estates, four hundred of the best horses in Europe, and who is, if my memory of the party gossip is correct, on the verge of marrying no less than fifty ravishingly beautiful females? That duke?"

Temporarily sidetracked, Whitney said, "Actually he only has seven estates. He may have four hundred horses, I don't know. But I do know that he is on the verge of marrying only one female. Now Paul," she said soothingly, her voice shaky with nerves, "I know you will find this as disconcerting as I did at first, but *I* am the female he's on the verge of marrying."

Paul's lips twitched with laughter as he came forward to draw her into his arms. "If he persists in his suit," he teased, running his thumb along her chin, "I'll tell him what I've just discovered—that when you are left to your own company, you drink the cooking sherry."

"Are you implying that I'm foxed?" Whitney gasped in disbelief.

"Drunk as a wheelbarrow," he joked, then he sobered. "Stop trying to make me jealous. If you're angry because I've been gone so long, then simply say so."

In sheer frustration, Whitney lurched back and stamped her foot. "I am *not* trying to make you jealous! I am trying to make you understand that I've been betrothed to Clayton Westmoreland since this past June." There, it was out!

"I beg your pardon?" Paul said, staring at her.

"Actually, I think it was July," Whitney rambled on disjointedly. "Do you think it's important?"

For the first time Paul took her seriously. "You accepted Westland?"

"Not Westland, West*more*land," Whitney emphasized. "And I didn't accept him, my father did."

"Then tell your father to marry him," Paul said tautly. "You love me, it's as simple as that." His blue eyes narrowed on her in censurious irritation. "You're playing games and I don't like it. None of this makes sense."

"I can't help it," Whitney shot back, stung. "It's the truth."

"Then will you kindly explain to me how you happen to have been engaged since July to a man you didn't meet until September."

Now he was deadly serious and Whitney almost wished he weren't. Drawing a long, unsteady breath, she said, "I was introduced to him in France, but I didn't pay any attention to his name, nor did I remember his face. The next time I saw him was at a masquerade in May, and I couldn't see his face then either. At the masquerade, he decided he wanted to marry me, but he knew that my uncle was turning down all my suitors—because I wanted to come back here and marry you—so he came here and paid my father £100,000 for me, then he had my father send for me and he moved into the Hodges place."

"Do you really expect me to believe all that?" Paul snapped.

"Not really," Whitney said miserably, "but it's the truth. I had no idea what had been done until the night you left. I went downstairs to tell my father and aunt that you and I were going to be married, and Clayton was there. The next thing I knew, my father was shouting at me that I was betrothed to the Duke of Claymore, who turned out to be Clayton, and then everything got even worse."

"I find it impossible to see how this *could* get worse," Paul answered sarcastically.

"Well, it has. Clayton took me to London with him three days ago, and he told one of his friends that we were going to be married—"

"Then you have agreed to marry him?" Paul said icily.

"No, of course not."

Paul turned on his heel and walked over to the fireplace. Propping his booted foot against the grate, he stared down into the fire, leaving Whitney gazing helplessly at his back. Suddenly he stiffened, and when he turned his face was white with shocked alarm. "What do you mean he paid your father for you?" he demanded. "It is customary for the father to dower the daughter, and not the reverse."

Whitney realized at once where his thoughts had drifted, and her heart turned over in pity for Paul, and for herself. "I don't have any dowry, Paul. My father had lost that and my inheritance as well."

Paul leaned his head back against the stone wall and closed his eyes, his broad shoulders drooping despondently.

The time had come for Whitney to commit herself to the path she had chosen, and she went to him with legs that felt like lead. Her mind screamed that she didn't *have* to do this, but her heart wouldn't let her desert him. Not now, not after seeing this tortured expression on his face. "Paul, my father told me how difficult your circumstances are, and it doesn't matter to me, please believe that. I will marry you anyway. But we will have to act quickly. Clayton will be in London for six more days and in that time, we can elope to Scotland. By the time Clayton discovers what—"

"Elope!" Paul's voice lashed out and his fingers bit viciously into her arms. "Are you out of your mind? My mother and sisters would never be able to hold up their heads."

"No," Whitney whispered hoarsely. "The shame will be mine."

"Damn your shame!" he snapped, shaking her. "Don't you see what you've done? I have just spent a small fortune on five horses and a phaeton!"

How was that her fault? Whitney wondered, recoiling from the blaze in his eyes. And then she knew. Bitter resentment twined around her heart like sharp steel bands, wringing a ragged, choking laugh from her. "You spent the 'fortune' you thought *I* had—the dowry you imagined I would bring, didn't you?"

Paul didn't have to answer; she could see the truth in his flaring eyes. Angrily flinging his hands away, she stepped back. "Five minutes after I accepted you, you were mentally spending my money, weren't you? You couldn't even wait to talk to my father first! You 'loved' me so much that you didn't bother to stay here with me and ask his consent. All you cared about was the money, and you didn't even spend it on important things. Your lands are mortgaged, your house is in disrepair . . . Paul," she whispered, her green eyes glittering with tears, "what sort of man are you? Are you so spineless and so irresponsible that you would have married me just for money to spend on horses you don't even need?"

"Don't be an idiot!" Paul snapped, but his face was flushed with guilty embarrassment. "I loved you. I'd never have asked you to marry me otherwise."

"Love!" Whitney scoffed bitterly. "None of you know the

313

meaning of the word! My father 'loves' me and he sold me to save himself. All you care about is how much money I'm worth to you. At least Clayton doesn't insult my intelligence by claiming to love me. He bought me like a bondservant, and now he expects me to live up to the bargain, but he doesn't pretend to 'love' me."

Paul's breath came out in a ragged sigh. "I'll think of something, but eloping is out of the question. Will Westland . . . Westmoreland . . . give you up?"

Whitney looked at him and stubbornly lifted her chin. "No," she said proudly, and at that moment, she would have given him that answer even if she believed otherwise. Turning, she stalked to the door, then paused to look at him over her shoulder. "Elizabeth Ashton is still available," she said bitterly. "I'm certain her dowry could cover your extravagances on this last trip. You'd better start thinking of ways to regain her favor so that you can get your hands on *her* money."

"Shut up!" Paul snapped. "Or I'll do just that."

Whitney slammed the door on his last word, but not until she gained the privacy of her own room did she allow the tears to come. Sinking down onto her bed, she wept all her heartbroken disillusionment into her pillow. She cried for herself, for her empty dreams and the misplaced devotion she'd lavished on Paul all these years. She cried because *she* had been willing to destroy her reputation for Paul, and all he had cared about was his mother and sisters. But most of all, she cried with rage at her own stupidity.

When Clarissa brought a dinner tray to her room that night, Whitney's eyes were puffy and her chest ached, but the storm of misery and animosity was mostly past. She ate alone, her thoughts in a swirling, melancholy turmoil that began nowhere and ended nowhere.

By noon the next day, Whitney was no longer angry with Paul. In fact, she was feeling strangely guilty. She had always imagined him as her modern-day knight in shining armor, courageous, romantic, and gallant, and it really wasn't his fault that he couldn't live up to that illusion. She felt a growing sense of shame and responsibility for the unwitting part she'd played in his worsened financial circumstances. She had exerted every wile she possessed to make him offer for her, and by accepting his offer, she'd inadvertently caused him to spend money *she* didn't have.

Late in the afternoon, as she wandered aimlessly among the last blooms in the rose garden, Whitney's active mind turned from the contemplation of problems to the consideration of solutions. Soon a hazy plan took shape. Elizabeth loved Paul, of that Whitney was certain. Surely there must be something Whitney could do to smooth things over with Elizabeth, so that she would be receptive to Paul if he chose to renew his interest in her.

Whitney hesitated and pulled her silk shawl tighter around her shoulders. Considering the chaotic state of her own affairs right now, she was the *last* person on earth capable of taking a guiding hand in someone else's romance. Nevertheless, it was her responsibility, and besides, she had never been able to stand meekly by and hope that fate would make the right things happen.

With a vitality that had been dormant for many days, Whitney decided to take matters into her own hands. She went into the house and dashed off a note to Elizabeth, then she paced across her bedroom, wondering if Elizabeth would flatly decline her invitation. There had been so much competitive jealousy on Whitney's part in years gone by, so many pranks and tricks, that poor Elizabeth would be understandably suspicious of any overture by Whitney to befriend her at this late date.

Whitney was so convinced that Elizabeth would refuse to come that she jumped when Elizabeth's soft voice spoke from the doorway of the bedroom. "You—you asked me to come?" Her blue eyes were darting nervously around the room, and she looked ready to bolt.

Whitney fixed a reassuring smile on her face and said graciously, "Yes, and I'm so happy that you have. May I take your gloves and bonnet?" As she reached out, Elizabeth nervously clapped both her hands to the crown of her bonnet, clutching it protectively to her curls, and Whitney recalled another bonnet of Elizabeth's—a little straw confection with pink ribbons that Paul had once complimented years ago. Five minutes later, the bonnet was discovered beneath the treads of the chair in which Whitney was rocking. Elizabeth was thinking of it too, Whitney realized, and a flush crept up her cheeks when she remembered poor Elizabeth's shriek of dismay.

"I—I prefer to keep it on," Elizabeth said.

"I don't blame you," Whitney sighed. For the next half hour, Whitney served tea and kept up a one-sided conversation of trivialities in an attempt to put Elizabeth at ease, but Elizabeth replied in monosyllables and continued to perch on the edge of her chair as if she were going to fly from the room at the first loud noise.

Finally, Whitney went to the point. "Elizabeth," she said, finding it very awkward to confess her foibles to the female she had always viewed as her arch-rival. "I owe you an apology for a grave injustice I've done you recently, as well as for some horrid things I did to you when we were young. About Paul—" she blurted out. "I know how you must hate me, and I don't blame you, but I would like to help you."

"Help me?" Elizabeth repeated blankly.

"Help you marry Paul," Whitney clarified.

Elizabeth's blue eyes widened. "No! No, really, I couldn't," she stammered, blushing gorgeously.

"Of course you could!" Whitney declared, passing her a tray of little pastries. "You're a very beautiful girl and Paul has always . . ."

"No," Elizabeth contradicted softly, shaking her blond head. *"You* are more in the way of being beautiful. I am only, well, pretty, at best."

After taking this monumental step in befriending Elizabeth, Whitney wasn't about to have her generosity outdone. "You have beautiful manners, Elizabeth. You always do and say the proper thing at the proper time."

"The properly *dull* thing," Elizabeth argued prettily. "Not lively and interesting things like you say."

"Elizabeth," Whitney said, unable to suppress her amusement, "I was always perfectly outrageous, while you were always perfectly perfect."

Elizabeth relaxed back in her chair and giggled. "There, you see! I would have only said 'thank you' but you always say unusual things."

"Do not pay me another compliment," Whitney warned with a laughing look. "I won't be outdone, you know, and we will be here all night admiring one another."

Elizabeth sobered and said, "I'm very happy about you and Paul." At Whitney's stunned glance, she explained, "Everyone knows your betrothal is supposed to be a secret, but since everyone is talking about it, I didn't think you would mind if I mentioned it."

"What do you mean, everyone is talking about it?" Whitney said hoarsely. "Who else knows?"

"Well, let me think. Mr. Oldenberry, the apothecary, told Margaret and me. He said he heard it from Lady Eubank's maid, who heard it from Lady Eubank, who heard it from Paul's own mama. I suppose everyone in the village knows."

"But it isn't true!" Whitney cried desperately.

Elizabeth's pretty face fell. "Please don't say it isn't true!" she implored agitatedly. "Not now, not when Peter is almost to the point of offering."

"Who is Peter going to offer for?" Whitney asked, momentarily diverted.

"For me. But he won't if Paul is unattached. You see, Peter is shy, and he's always believed I have a secret *tendre* for Paul, which isn't in the least true. But even if it was, my papa would never permit me to marry Paul because he's a shocking spendthrift and his lands are mortgaged."

Whitney slumped back in her chair and gaped at Elizabeth. "Peter Redfern *shy?*" she echoed. "Elizabeth, are we talking about the same Peter Redfern? The one who tried to box my ears the day of the picnic when you fell out of the tree?"

"Well, he's shy around me," Elizabeth said.

In speechless disbelief, Whitney pictured Peter's freckled face and thinning red hair, and tried to imagine how he could have won the heart of a fragile, ethereal beauty like Elizabeth, who had always had Paul at her beck and call. "Do you

317

honestly mean to tell me," Whitney uttered, "that you've been in love with Peter all these years?"

"Yes," Elizabeth admitted brokenly. "But if you tell everyone that you and Paul aren't going to be married, then Peter will just stand back, the way he always has, and let Paul take his place. And then I'll—I'll—" Elizabeth groped for her lacy handkerchief and promptly trailed off into dainty tears.

Whitney cocked her head to one side. "However do you manage to cry like that?" she asked admiringly. "I always gasp and snort and my eyes spill over like fountains."

Elizabeth giggled tearily and dabbed at her eyes before lifting them pleadingly to Whitney. "You said you'd done me injustices and you were sorry. If you truly mean it, couldn't you wait just a few days before crying off with Paul? Peter is going to say he wants to marry me any moment now, I can tell."

"You don't realize what you're asking of me," Whitney said, tensing. "If a certain person were to hear the gossip and believe I've truly betrothed myself to Paul, my life wouldn't be worth a farthing." Elizabeth looked on the verge of a fresh bout of tears and Whitney stood up, torn between the certainty that a few days really wouldn't make a difference and the inexplicable fear that they could result in disaster. "I'll give you three days before I put a stop to the gossip," Whitney reluctantly conceded.

Long after Elizabeth's departure, Whitney sat in her room, thinking and worrying. If everyone, including the servants, was openly gossiping about her "betrothal" to Paul, Clayton would certainly hear of it as soon as he returned. He had made it very clear that he wouldn't tolerate people believing she had ever been betrothed to anyone but him, and Whitney tried to think of some proof she could offer him that none of this was her fault—that she had, in fact, told Paul she wouldn't marry him, exactly as she had promised Clayton she would.

He had accepted her word and trusted her to keep it, and Whitney wanted him to believe she had, but the only one who could prove it was Paul, and Paul was in no mood to aid her.

Whitney bit her lip, concerned with more than just the loss of her honor. Without the incentive of marrying Paul to give her courage, she now felt a deep-rooted, genuine fear of Clayton's wrath. The more she pondered it, the more convinced she became that the best way to avert certain disaster was to go to London and explain to Clayton what was happening here. He would be far less angry hearing it from her than from strangers, and he would know she wasn't to blame. After all, if she was truly planning to marry Paul, as the gossip had it, why would she return to London to see Clayton?

Resolutely, Whitney got up and went down the hall to her aunt's room. She poured out the entire story, including the gossip about her betrothal to Paul and her abandoned plan to elope. Aunt Anne blanched but she remained silent until Whitney was finished. "What do you intend to do now?" she asked then.

"I think it would be best if I went to London and stayed with Emily. As soon as I arrive, I'll notify his grace I'm there, and he'll naturally come to see me. Then I'll choose exactly the right moment to tell him about the gossip here. I don't think he'll care so much about the talk, so long as he believes it isn't my fault."

"I'll come to London with you," her aunt instantly volunteered.

Whitney shook her head. "I wish you could, but there's a slim chance that he might return to the village without my having been able to see him in London. If he does, he'll hear the gossip and undoubtedly come straight here to the house. I need you here to explain and calm him down."

"What a cheerful prospect," Lady Anne said drily, but she was smiling. "Very well, I'll stay here. Now, assuming you reach him in London, what reason will you give him for being there?"

Whitney's smooth forehead knitted into an irritated frown. "I suppose I'll have to tell him the truth—that I was afraid he would come back to the village and believe that despite his warning, I hadn't refused Paul. Although, I find it excessively galling to have to tear off to London like a rabbit frightened of incurring his wrath. That man walked into my life a few months ago, and I've been like a puppet obliged to dance to his tune ever since. I think I shall tell him that too!" Whitney finished mutinously.

"While you're bent on being so honest about your feelings," Aunt Anne suggested with a knowing gleam in her eyes, "why don't you also tell him that you have developed a sincere affection for him and you are willing now to honor the betrothal contract? It will please him immensely to hear you say it."

Whitney shot up off the sofa as if she'd been scorched. "I most certainly will not!" she declared hotly. "Considering that he never cared whether I *wanted* to marry him, and has never doubted for a minute that I *would* marry him, I fail to see why I should flatter his vanity now by professing to *want* to marry him. Besides, I haven't made up my mind to marry him."

"I think you have, darling."

Her aunt's quiet voice checked Whitney in mid-stride as she headed for the door. "And if it will make it easier for you to admit your own feelings, I will tell you that, in my opinion, that man loves you with an intensity that would astonish him if he but recognized it—and very likely flatter *your* vanity."

"You're wrong, Aunt Anne," Whitney said tonelessly. "He has never even said he cares for me. I'm a possession he's acquired, nothing more. Don't ask me to crawl to him; I have very little pride left as it is, and I won't sacrifice it to soothe his temper or flatter his ego."

Elizabeth Ashton appeared at the house each afternoon to report her progress, but by the end of the third day, there was still no cause for celebration. Clarissa and Whitney were packing for the next day's trip to London when Elizabeth trailed into the bedroom, a soldier returning in defeat from a battle that should have been easy for her to win. "Peter is no nearer declaring himself now than he was ten years ago," she said glumly, flopping into a chair.

Whitney thrust an armload of underclothing into a trunk

and gazed at Elizabeth in perplexed dismay. "Are you certain?"

"Positive," Elizabeth said morosely. "I suggested we dine at my house tonight, without my parents, and do you know what he said? He said"—Elizabeth sighed heavily—"that he *likes* dining with my parents."

"That idiot!" Whitney burst out irritably. Slowly she began to pace back and forth. "You may be ready to accept defeat, but I'm not—at least not from Peter Redfern, of all people! That dolt has worshiped you since we were children. What he needs is some sort of motivation to force him into declaring himself without delay." Idly, Whitney shoved the fully packed portmanteau out of the way with her foot and frowned at the luggage scattered everywhere around the room. "I have it!" she burst out, whirling on Elizabeth with an impetuous, daring gleam in her green eyes that Elizabeth well remembered from days gone by. Terrified, she shrank back into her chair: "Whitney, whatever you're thinking, we aren't going to do it."

"Oh yes, we are!" Whitney hooted triumphantly. "Miss Ashton, I hereby invite you to come to London with me."

"But I don't *want* to go to London," Elizabeth sputtered desperately. "I want *Peter*."

"Good, and you're going to get him tonight. Now repeat after me, 'Yes, I will go to London with you.'"

"Yes, I will go to London with you," Elizabeth parroted. "But I don't want to."

"Perfect, because you aren't going to. But I have just asked you and you've accepted. This way, when you tell Peter you've agreed to come with me, you won't be lying to him." Advancing purposefully on a bewildered Elizabeth, Whitney caught her hand and pulled her over to the writing desk. "Now, write and tell Peter to join you here for dinner with me tonight. Tell him . . ." Whitney hesitated, her forefinger pressed to her lips, then chuckled at her own stroke of genius. "Tell him that you and I are planning to do the most extraordinary thing together. *That* should petrify him."

"Peter isn't going to like our going to London together," Elizabeth said.

"He'll *detest* the idea!" Whitney agreed proudly. "Even though I've grown up, Peter still watches me as if he expects me to do something outrageous at any moment."

For the first time in her sweet, acquiescent life, Elizabeth displayed a stubborn streak. "If Peter won't approve, I won't go."

Stung by Elizabeth's lack of appreciation for her brilliant plan, Whitney said, "You *aren't* going. Don't you see, Peter will be appalled at the idea of our going off together. He doesn't think I've truly changed. He still thinks of me as the same hoyden who used to smite Reverend Snodgrass's old mare on the rump with a slingshot."

"You did *that?*" Elizabeth gasped.

"That, and a great many other things Peter knows about," Whitney admitted impenitently. "He'll try to dissuade you from coming with me, but you are to tell him that *I* am insisting. I'll be right there to insist, and when Peter can't talk either of us out of it, he'll do the only thing he can do."

"What?" Elizabeth asked, looking intrigued but dubious.

Whitney threw up her hands. "Why, he'll propose, you widgeon!" Taking Elizabeth's trembling hand in an affectionate, reassuring grasp, Whitney said, "Please, please trust me. Nothing wrings an offer so quickly from a man as the fear that you are going to leave him. And nothing makes a man quite so brave and bold as the opportunity to rescue an innocent female from 'unsuitable companions,'—in this case, the unsuitable companion is me. Nicolas DuVille scarcely paid any attention to me unless he objected to some gentleman who was courting me, then he swooped down like an avenging angel to protect me from some man who was not nearly as dangerous a flirt as *he!* It was vastly amusing, I can tell you. Now please write that note. Before this night is over, Peter will propose, you just wait and see."

Reluctantly Elizabeth did as she was bidden and the note was dispatched to Peter with a footman.

Three hours later, against her protests, Elizabeth was draped in Whitney's most daring gown, which had been temporarily shortened, and her golden curls had been tamed into a sleek chignon. Still objecting, she was led to a mirror by Clarissa and Whitney.

"Go ahead," Whitney urged. "See how lovely you look—"

Elizabeth's timid gaze travelled up the clingy folds of the elegant silk gown, past her slim hips and dainty waist, then riveted in shock on her exposed decolletage. Her hands flew to cover the tops of her breasts swelling above the bodice of the gown. "I can't," she gasped, blushing.

Whitney rolled her eyes. "Yes, you can, Elizabeth. Why in France, this gown would be considered only a tiny bit daring."

A nervous giggle trilled from Elizabeth as she slowly lowered her hands. "Do you think Peter will like it?"

"Not," Whitney predicted happily, "when I tell him that I think your gowns are much too demure and that when we're in London I intend to make certain you buy more like this one to wear at the parties we shall be attending."

At eight o'clock Peter strode into the candlelit drawing room and joined the two young women who were waiting for him. After a brief nod in Whitney's direction, he looked around the room for Elizabeth, who was staring out the window with her back to him.

"What is this 'extraordinary thing' the two of you are planning to do?" he demanded.

Elizabeth slowly turned and an expression of comical incredulity froze Peter's features. With slackened jaw and glazed eyes, he gaped at her.

Elizabeth, who had evidently hoped he would take one look at her and fall to his knee to propose matrimony, waited in expectant silence. When he neither spoke nor moved, her dainty chin lifted with stubborn determination and for the first time in her twenty-one years, Elizabeth consciously began to use the feminine wiles with which she was born. "Whitney is taking me for an extended trip to London tomorrow," she explained, while strolling back and forth, parading her blond loveliness before a staggered Peter. "Whitney thinks I shall be all the rage in London once I have new clothes and a new hair style. She is going to teach me how to flirt with gentlemen too," ad-libbed Elizabeth with wide-eyed innocence. "Of course," she finished with a spurt of inspiration, "I do hope I shan't have changed so much by the time we return that you won't recognize me . . ."

Whitney's lips trembled with admiring laughter which she quickly suppressed as Peter's outraged glower swung toward her. "What the devil do you think you're doing?" he snapped furiously.

Somehow Whitney managed to look almost as innocent as Elizabeth. "I'm only trying to take Elizabeth under my wing."

"Elizabeth would be safer under an axe!" he exploded. "I won't permit—"

"Now Peter," Whitney soothed, struggling desperately to keep her face straight. "Be reasonable. All I intend to do is take Elizabeth to London and introduce her to some of the gentlemen I met at a ball there this week. They are a most charming, eligible group, and all of them have impeccable backgrounds and unexceptionable reputations. They may be a *little* fast, but I'm quite certain Elizabeth won't fall violently in love with more than one or two of them. It's time for her to marry, you know. She's a year older than I."

"I know how old Elizabeth is!" Peter raked his hand through his hair in frustration.

"Then you should also know that you have no say in what she does. You aren't her papa, nor her husband, nor even her fiancé, so do stop arguing and admit defeat. I'll just go and see about dinner," she finished, hastily turning away to hide her brimming laughter.

Whitney was absolutely certain that Peter would propose when he took Elizabeth home. She was wrong; they were standing hand-in-hand when she returned to the drawing room ten minutes later.

"It grieves me to upset your plans," Peter mocked, "but Elizabeth will not be accompanying you to London. She has agreed to become my wife. Well," he demanded irritably, "what have you to say to *that?*"

"Say?" Whitney repeated, lowering her eyes to hide her delighted smile. "Why . . . how very provoking of you,

Peter. I had so wanted to . . . give Elizabeth a glorious taste of London."

Peter, who was innately good-tempered, glanced with smiling tolerance at his future wife and said in a friendlier voice, "Since you're so bent on being with Elizabeth in London, you can shop for her trousseau with her. If her papa accepts me tonight, I expect she'll want to leave tomorrow, and she has already informed me that she wants you to be a bridesmaid."

Chapter Twenty-three

UPON ARRIVING AT THE ARCHIBALDS' TOWNHOUSE, WHITNEY was greeted by a flustered Emily, her brown hair covered with a kerchief, her cheeks smudged with dirt. "You look like a chimney sweep," Whitney laughed.

"You look like a godsend!" Emily countered, embracing her. "Can a knight be seated beside an honorable at dinner?" she burst out desperately.

Whitney blinked in surprised confusion.

"It's this wretched party," Emily explained in the salon after Whitney had taken off her pelisse and Clarissa had been shown to her room. "Michael's mama said that I must begin to entertain as suits Michael's station in life. Have you any idea how much fuss the *ton* can make over the simple act of sitting down to dinner? Here, just look at what I've been going through." She went over to a desk and plucked up a seating diagram for the dining tables that evening. It was obvious she had repeatedly scratched out names to rearrange them. "Can you, or can you not, seat an honorable beside a knight? Michael's mama lent me a dozen books on etiquette, but they're so filled with contradictions and exceptions to rules that I know less now than I did before I read them."

Whitney scanned the seating diagram and then promptly slid into the sabre-legged chair at the desk. Dipping the quill into the inkpot, she deftly rearranged the guests, then sat back and flashed a sunny smile at her stunned friend. "Thanks to Aunt Anne's training, I can do that when there are nobles from five different countries present," she said.

Emily sank down on the sofa, her eyes still clouded with worry. "This is our first formal party and Michael's mama is going to be here watching every move I make. She's a stickler for formalities. She was less than pleased when her son married A Nobody, and I want more than anything to show her I can have the most perfect, grandest party she's ever attended!"

Whitney, who had been racking her brain for some excuse to see Clayton other than the obvious one, slowly began to smile with delight. Turning back to the desk, she picked up the quill and wrote his name and title in the proper place on the seating diagram. *"This* should make you the hostess of the year," she announced proudly, handing the diagram to Emily. "And it will also make your mother-in-law positively envious!"

"The Duke of Claymore," Emily gasped. "But he'd think me the most presumptuous person in the world. Besides, he'd not come—none of our guests is his social equal, despite their titles."

"He'll come," Whitney assured her. "Give me a spare invitation and a sheet of paper." After a moment's thought, Whitney wrote to Clayton and explained that she had come to London to visit Emily, and that she hoped very much that he would join her at the party. She enclosed the invitation and gave it to one of the Archibalds' footmen with instructions to take it to his grace's secretary, Mr. Hudgins, in Upper Brook Street and to tell Mr. Hudgins that the note was from *Miss Stone*—which was how Clayton had told her to reach him if she wanted him to come back early.

The footman returned a short time later with the information that the duke had gone to his brother's country home, and would be back in London early the next day—Saturday.

Emily looked simultaneously relieved and crestfallen. "He'll be too weary to come to the party tomorrow night," she sighed.

"He'll be here," Whitney said with smiling certainty.

After dinner, Emily tried to open the subject of Paul, and then the Duke of Claymore, but Whitney said very gently, and very firmly, that she didn't want to discuss either of them just yet. To take the sting out of her refusal to confide in her best friend, Whitney then regaled her with an hilarious account of how she'd coerced poor Peter into offering for Elizabeth. "Elizabeth and Peter, along with their parents, and Margaret and Mrs. Merryton, all left the village this morning when I did," she finished gaily. "They have come here to shop for Elizabeth's trousseau."

"If anyone had told me a few years ago that you would someday be Elizabeth's bridesmaid, I'd have accused them of being deranged!" Emily said with a laugh.

"I think Elizabeth means to ask you to be her matron of honor," Whitney said. "The wedding is going to take place here in London, since most of Elizabeth and Peter's relatives live here."

Not until Saturday afternoon did Whitney allow herself to dwell on her forthcoming confrontation with Clayton tonight. She and Clarissa spent the morning doing errands for Emily, and on the way back, Whitney asked the Archibalds' driver to turn into the park and stop. She left Clarissa in the open carriage and wandered along the path between the neatly tended beds of chrysanthemums.

She had told Aunt Anne that Clayton didn't care for her, but she knew that wasn't entirely true. He had said he "wanted" her, which must mean he *desired* her. Whitney sat down on the park bench, a faint blush staining her cheeks as she thought of his lips moving warmly on hers and his hands caressing her body, molding her to his masculine frame.

She thought about the times they had been together, beginning with the first time she'd seen him in England. He'd been standing beside the stream with his shoulders propped against the sycamore, watching her sunning her bare legs. He had already been betrothed to her that day, and she had virtually ordered him off her property. She felt a surge of righteous indignation when she recalled the way he had used the crop on her tender backside, but it dwindled away when she thought about what she'd done to deserve it. A smile touched her lips as she recalled the night they had played chess at his house, and her flush deepened as she remembered the stormy passion of his kisses before he took her home.

Clayton desired her. And he was very proud of her—she had seen that at the Rutherfords' ball. He didn't love her, of course, but he did *care* for her. He cared enough about her to be hurt by the dreadful things she'd said to him that day beside the pavilion. Tenderness welled in her heart as she remembered how furiously he'd rejected her kiss until he finally lost control and his arms went around her, crushing her to him. And she remembered how desolate she'd felt when she believed they were saying goodbye forever.

Sternly, Whitney reminded herself of the arrogant, tyrannical, and high-handed way he had negotiated their betrothal, and then she shrugged the thought aside. He was all those things and more, yet she cared for him too, and there was no point in denying it merely so that she could keep the fires of her resentment and rebellion alive.

She cared for him, and if she hadn't been so obsessed with marrying Paul, she would have realized it much sooner. Her mind shied away from delving too deeply into the exact nature of her feelings for Clayton; it seemed obscene to even consider the possibility that she loved him, when three days ago, she'd thought she loved Paul. Besides, after believing she was in love with Paul for all these years, only to discover that she'd merely been blindly infatuated, she had little faith left in her ability to judge her own emotions. But she did care for Clayton, there was no use denying it. She had always responded wantonly to his caresses and, although he often made her furious, he made her laugh too.

They were going to be married. Clayton had decided that last spring, and his indomitable will was going to prevail as surely as the sun was going to set.

It was inevitable; she was ready to accept that now. That

handsome, powerful, sophisticated nobleman was going to be her husband. He was also going to be furious tonight when she told him the villagers all believed she was betrothed to Paul.

Sighing, Whitney scuffed at a pebble with the toe of her slipper. Instinctively, she knew that she could assuage Clayton's anger simply by telling him that she was willing to marry him whenever he wished. Now, she had to decide what tone she would use when she told him. She could salvage some of her pride by being coolly unenthusiastic and saying something like, "Since I have no real choice except to marry you, we may as well wed whenever you wish." If she told him in that way, Clayton would undoubtedly look at her with that sarcastically amused expression which never failed to irk her and reply with something equally unenthusiastic, such as, "As you wish, Ma'am."

Whitney frowned unhappily. Although that would save a bit of her pride, it was an awful way for two people to begin a marriage—each pretending complete indifference. In all truth, she didn't *feel* indifferent to him. These past days she had missed him more than she would have believed possible; she had missed his quiet strength, his lazy smile; she had missed the laughter they often shared; she had even missed arguing with him!

Since she felt this way, it seemed not only silly, but wrong, to pretend she hated the idea of marrying him. Mentally, Whitney rehearsed a different way of telling him that she was ready to marry him. Tonight, after she told him that everyone at home believed she was betrothed to Paul, she could smile softly into those fathomless gray eyes of his and say, "I suppose the best way to put a stop to the gossip would be for us to announce *our* engagement." Her smile would tell him that she was surrendering, unconditionally giving over in the battle of wills that had waged between them all these weeks. True, her pride would suffer a bit, but Clayton was going to be her husband, and he truly deserved to know that she was willingly accepting him.

If she told him her decision in this manner, instead of

replying with mocking sarcasm, Clayton would probably take her in his arms and kiss her in that bold, sensuous way of his. Just thinking about it made Whitney feel giddy.

The devil with her pride! Whitney decided. She would take the latter course. As she walked back toward the carriage, anticipation and happiness began to pulse through her veins.

When she returned to Emily's house, Whitney was informed that Emily was in the salon with guests. Rather than intrude, Whitney went up to the luxurious guest room she was temporarily occupying.

Emily came in just as she was removing her bonnet. "Elizabeth, Peter, Margaret, and their mamas just left. Elizabeth asked me to be in her wedding." Apprehensively, Emily added, "I—I invited them to our party tonight. I couldn't possibly avoid it, with my whole household in an uproar, obviously preparing for a party."

Whitney pulled off her gloves, a puzzled smile on her lips as she studied Emily's worried expression. "Don't fret about it, we'll just make a few changes to the seating for dinner. It's as simple as that."

"No, it isn't," Emily said bleakly. "You see, while they were shopping, they encountered your friend, M. DuVille. He asked Margaret about you, and Elizabeth told him that you were staying here with me, and naturally *he* came here with them . . ."

Whitney felt a cloud of doom descending over her even before Emily said, "I had to invite him too. I knew it might make things awkward for you with the duke coming at your invitation, but I was absolutely certain M. DuVille would decline on such short notice."

Whitney sank down on the bed. "But Nicki didn't decline, did he?"

Emily shook her head. "I could cheerfully have strangled Margaret. He was obviously interested only in you, but she was hanging on his arm like a . . . a leech, imploring him to come. I wish her parents would marry her off to someone before she disgraces herself and them. She is the most clinging, indiscriminate, vicious female alive, and Elizabeth is so sweet, she lets Margaret trample all over her."

Unwilling to let anyone or anything dampen her joyous anticipation of the night to come, Whitney gave Emily a reassuring smile. "Don't worry about Margaret or Nicki. Everything's going to be fine."

Chapter Twenty-four

CLAYTON TOSSED THE REPORTS HIS BROTHER HAD ASKED HIM TO read onto the opposite seat of his coach and leaned his head back, impatient with himself for returning to the village a day ahead of schedule.

The horses slowed as they neared the cobbled street of the village, and he leaned sideways, glancing out the window. Heavy clouds roiled overhead, nearly obliterating the struggling sunlight of the early Saturday afternoon. The road through the village was temporarily rendered impassable by an overturned wagon and several abandoned vehicles whose owners were trying to right the wagon and catch the fleeing sheep. "McRea!" he called irritably, "when we get close to that snarl, stop and lend a hand. Otherwise we'll be here all day."

"Aye, your grace," McRea called from his perch atop the coach.

Clayton glanced at his watch and his mouth twisted with wry derision. He was behaving like a besotted idiot, racing back here a day early. Driven by a ridiculous eagerness to see Whitney, he had left his brother's house at six o'clock this morning and headed straight here, instead of spending the day in London as he'd originally planned. For seven hours, he'd been travelling as if his life depended upon reaching her, stopping only to change horses. He should never have given her this week by herself, he told himself for the hundredth time. Instead of offering her solitude, he should have offered her firm but gentle moral support. By now she had probably worked herself into a fresh fit of rebellion because he had forced her to turn down Sevarin. What a stubborn little fool she was to persist in believing she loved that weakling. A beautiful, spirited, magnificent little fool. If she cared a snap for Sevarin, she could never respond to his own caresses the way she did.

Clayton's loins tightened as he recalled the way she had kissed him and pressed herself against him after the Rutherfords' ball when he took her back to the Archibalds'. The champagne had loosened her maidenly inhibitions, but the sweet desire she felt for him had been there for many weeks. She wanted him, and if she weren't so damned stubborn, and so young, she would have known it long ago. She wanted him all right—and he wanted her more than he had ever wanted anything in his life. He wanted to fill her days with joy and her nights with pleasure, until she loved him as much as he loved her.

Loved her? Clayton scowled darkly at the thought, and then with a long, derisive sigh, he admitted the truth to himself. He was in love with Whitney. At four and thirty years of age, after more women and more affairs than he wanted to count, he had fallen victim to an outrageously impertinent, gorgeous girl-woman who blithely incurred his displeasure, mocked his title, and flatly refused to yield to his authority. Her smile warmed his heart and her touch heated his blood; she could enchant, amuse and infuriate him as no other woman had ever been able to do. He couldn't imagine his future without her at his side.

Having admitted all that to himself, Clayton was even more eager to reach her, to feast his eyes on her again and hold her in his arms, to hear her musical voice and to know the exquisite sensation of her slender, voluptuous body curved against his.

McRea pulled the coach to a stop in front of the apothecary's shop and climbed down to help capture the last of the loose sheep and put them in the righted wagon. Unable to endure the confinement of the coach any longer, Clayton climbed down and joined the knot of spectators who were watching the men scrambling after the loose sheep. A smile touched his lips as the baker made a frantic lunge for one of the woolly beasts, missed his target, and plowed into another villager who had just captured one.

"Quite a comic spectacle, isn't it?" Mr. Oldenberry said, coming out of his shop to stand beside Clayton and the other onlookers. "You've missed the real excitement though," he added with a sly poke in the ribs. "Whole town is buzzing with the news. Betrothals," he added.

"Really," Clayton said indifferently, his attention on the wagon which was finally being pulled from the street.

"Yes, indeed," Mr. Oldenberry said. "You won't be able to felicitate the brides-to-be, though; they're both in London." He lowered his voice to a stage whisper. "Personally, I thought the Stone girl would choose you, but she's wanted Mr. Sevarin forever and now she got him. They're betrothed. No sooner did I hear that than Miss Ashton announced her betrothal to Mr. Redfern. Amazing how nothing seems to happen and then—"

Clayton's head jerked toward the speaker, and Mr. Oldenberry's voice froze at the murderous look in those gray eyes. In a low, deadly voice, Clayton said, "What did you say?"

"I—I said Miss Stone and Miss Ashton both got themselves betrothed while you were gone."

"You're lying or you're mistaken."

Mr. Oldenberry stepped back from the furious blast of those gray eyes and hastily shook his head. "No—no, I'm not. Ask anyone in the village, and they'll tell you it's true. Miss Stone and Miss Ashton both left here yesterday morning within an hour of each other. On their way to shop for wedding finery in London—Mrs. Ashton told me so herself," Mr. Oldenberry reassured a little desperately. "Miss Stone is staying with Lady Archibald and Miss Ashton with her grandparents," he added to prove how fully informed he was.

Without a word, Clayton turned on his heel and headed toward the coach.

Mr. Oldenberry turned to his fellow villagers who had

gathered to watch the sheep being captured and remained to eavesdrop on his conversation with Mr. Westland. "Did you see the look he gave me when I told him Miss Ashton was in London buying her wedding finery?" he asked them, his eyes glazed with awe. "And all this time *I* thought he fancied the Stone girl."

"The Stone estate," Clayton snapped at McRea and leapt into the coach.

As they pulled up before Whitney's house, a footman ran out. "Where is Miss Stone?" Clayton said, his icy voice checking the servant's hand as he reached out to lower the steps.

"In London, sir," the footman replied, stepping back.

Before the horses came to a full stop in front of his temporary residence, Clayton flung open the coach door, and vaulted out. "Have fresh horses put to," he snapped at his astonished coachman. "And be ready to leave for London in ten minutes." Rage boiled inside of Clayton like fiery acid, destroying his tender feelings for her. To think that while he was racing back to her like a besotted fool, *she* was in London buying her trousseau, which—he reminded himself with a fresh surge of blazing wrath—*he* was paying for!

"Damn her conniving little heart!" He ground the words out savagely as he swiftly changed his clothing. As soon as he could get a special license, he was going to drag her to the altar, by the hair if necessary.

No, by God, he wouldn't get a special license! Why the hell should he wait for that? He'd haul her to Scotland tonight and marry her there. When they came back, she could endure the scandal of an elopement as her punishment for deceiving him.

Bitterly, he cursed himself for having denied himself the pleasure of her body because he was waiting and hoping she would admit she wanted to marry him. The hell with what she wanted! From now on things were going to be the way *he* wanted them. Henceforth, Whitney could either bend to his will or he'd break her to it—and he didn't give a damn which way she chose to have it.

Precisely ten minutes later, after changing his clothes, he bounded out of the house and hurled himself back into the coach. Clayton endured the long trip back to the city in alternate states of deadly calm and barely leashed fury. It was after midnight when the horses drew to a stop in front of the brightly lit Archibald house where a party was obviously in progress.

"Wait here. I'll be right out," he snapped at the coachman, and as Clayton stalked swiftly up the steps to the front door, the rage boiling inside of him turned to cold, hard resolve. He had been cuckolded by a spiteful, willful brat! Brat? She was worse, much worse than that. She was a scheming, lying *bitch!* he thought murderously as he strode past the astonished butler toward the music and laughter.

The chilly night air cooled Whitney's heated face as she turned a dazzling, artificial smile on the gentlemen who had followed her out onto Emily's terrace where she had fled to escape the overcrowded ballroom. Despite her bright smile, her green eyes were somber as they scanned the milling crowd indoors, searching hopelessly for Clayton, even though she knew it was too late now for him to arrive. Perhaps he hadn't gotten her invitation; perhaps he had gone directly to her home without stopping in London. Whitney shivered, wishing she hadn't written to Aunt Anne and suggested that she make her postponed visit to her relatives, since Whitney had everything under control in London. She should have waited until Clayton had acknowledged receiving her note.

No, she decided miserably, Clayton's secretary had been very positive about his employer's travel plans. There was no point in deceiving herself; Clayton had cavalierly ignored her invitation. Her indignation gave way to deep hurt.

She had worn her hair loose about her shoulders because Clayton had said he liked it best that way. She had even dressed especially to please him in an alluring ivory satin gown heavily embellished with pearls. She had done everything to please him, and he hadn't even bothered to come or to decline her invitation.

Perilously close to tears, Whitney tried to convince herself that this aching disappointment she felt was merely because she had finally gathered the courage to tell Clayton that she would willingly marry him whenever he wished, but her lonely dejection sprang from something much deeper: she had missed him. She had been longing to see his smile, to be able to tell him she was surrendering in this battle of wills that had raged between them, and then to have him take her in his arms and kiss her. She had hoped tonight would be a beginning for them. Whitney blinked back her tears and determined to enjoy what was left of her ravaged evening.

Clayton nodded curtly to those few guests with whom he was acquainted, while he waited like a panther, watching for a glimpse of his prey. He saw DuVille going toward the terrace doors, carrying two glasses of champagne. Clayton's eyes tracked him across the room, his jaw clenching into a tight line of rage when he saw Whitney standing outside on the terrace, surrounded by at least half a dozen men.

With deceptive casualness, Clayton strolled toward them. His eyes turned icy with contempt when he realized that the men were pretending to play musical instruments while his "betrothed" was giving a charming little imitation of leading them with her invisible baton. The role, Clayton thought scathingly, was eminently suited to her—leading men on. He was about to let himself out the doors beside the ones through which DuVille had just gone, when a detaining hand was laid on his arm.

"What a pleasant surprise to find you here," Margaret Merryton said.

All Clayton's attention was riveted on Whitney. He started to pull his arm away, but Margaret's fingers tightened. "Disgraceful, isn't she?" she remarked, following the direction of his gaze.

Thirty-four years of strict adherence to certain rules of etiquette could not be completely disregarded, and Clayton turned, albeit angrily, to acknowledge the woman who was addressing him—except he was so furious that it took several moments for him even to identify her. Too angry to attempt to hide his insulting lack of recognition, Clayton stared blankly into her worshipful hazel eyes while their expression changed from adoration to insulted hatred. Laughter burst from the terrace and Clayton's head jerked in the direction of the sound.

Margaret's hand tightened convulsively on his arm as she looked toward Whitney Stone, and wounded pride hoarsened her voice. "If you're so eager to have her, go and get her. You needn't worry about DuVille or Paul Sevarin. Neither of them will ever actually marry her."

"Why is that?" Clayton demanded, pulling his arm away.

"Because Paul has just discovered what M. DuVille has known for years—neither of them was *her first!*" She saw Clayton's face blanche and the muscle leaping in his clenched jaw. Turning on her heel, she hissed brokenly over her shoulder, "In case you're interested, a stableboy was the first! *That's* why she was sent to France."

Something shattered inside of Clayton, splintering his emotions from all rational control. At another time, he would have shrugged off Margaret's words, for he was well enough acquainted with female jealousy to recognize it when he saw it. But this wasn't another time. This was the day he had realized that Whitney had been playing him for a fool, that she was a treacherous liar.

He paused, waiting while DuVille departed, then he reached down, grasped the handle of the door and jerked it open. He stepped onto the terrace directly behind Whitney just as one of her drunken admirers dropped to one knee.

"Miss Stone," the young man joked, his words slightly slurred. "It occurs to me that two talented 'musicians' such as you and I ought . . . ought to form a permanent duet! May I have the honor of your arm . . . no, your *hand* in . . ." Suddenly he stopped and swallowed audibly, his alarmed gaze fixed on something behind Whitney.

Dissolving with laughter at the young man's comic antics, Whitney glanced over her shoulder, then half turned toward Clayton. Happiness soared through her and she smiled joyously at him, but Clayton's attention was frozen on poor Carlisle, who was still kneeling on one leg.

"Get up!" Clayton snarled. With withering sarcasm he added, "If you intend to request Miss Stone's hand in marriage, you will have to wait until she grows another. At present, she has only two, and she has already pledged them both." With that he caught Whitney's wrist in a vice-like grip and turned on his heel, dragging her with him.

Whitney ran, trying to keep up with him as he strode around the wide balcony and down the front steps to his coach waiting below a street lamp.

"Stop this, you're hurting me!" she panted, stumbling on the hem of her gown and falling halfway to her knees. Clayton jerked her up with such cruel force that a pain shot from her wrist to her shoulder blade, then he snapped a command at his driver, grabbed her by the waist and flung her into the coach.

"How dare you!" Whitney hissed, angry and embarrassed at being so ignominiously hauled from Emily's house, and then manhandled to boot. "Who do you think you are?" The horses bolted from the curb and the coach lurched violently, sending Whitney reeling against the back of her seat.

"Who do I think I am?" Clayton jeered. "Why, I am your owner. By your own words, your father sold you, and I bought you."

Whitney stared at him, her mind in a complete turmoil. She couldn't imagine why Clayton was so angry over Carlisle's mock proposal when he'd interrupted her cousin, Cuthbert, in the midst of a serious one, and had been laughingly good-natured about it. She had believed that tonight would be a time for sweet reconciliation between them, and it was harshly disconcerting to now find herself the target of Clayton's fury instead of his ardor.

Even so, she was absurdly happy that he hadn't ignored her invitation, and she couldn't really blame him for losing his temper when he discovered yet another gentleman offering marriage to her. Very gently, she said, "Mr. Carlisle was quite foxed, you see, and his proposal was only a joke. He—"

"Shut up!" Clayton snapped. His head twisted toward her, and for the first time, in the flickering light of the coach lamp, Whitney actually saw the savage, scorching fury that was emanating from the man beside her. His handsome jaw was taut with rage, his mouth was drawn into a ruthless, forbidding line, and his expression was filled with cold loathing. His contemptuous eyes raked over her . . . and then he turned his head away, as if he couldn't stomach the sight of her.

Never in her life had Whitney witnessed such controlled, menacing fury, nor had anyone ever looked at her with such scathing contempt, not even her father. She had hoped so much to see laughter, or warmth, or affection in those penetrating, soul-searching gray eyes of his tonight; she had never imagined he could look at her with this alarming, malicious hatred. Her shock faded to hurt, and very slowly, the first glimmerings of fear were born in her heart. Silently, she stared out the window until the lights of the city began to glimmer less frequently and the long stretches of lonely darkness lengthened. "Where are you taking me?" she asked unsteadily. He was coldly silent. "Clayton?" she almost begged. "Where are we going?"

Clayton turned and stared down at her beautiful, frightened face. He wanted to put his hands around her slender white throat and strangle her for defiling her body with other men, for betraying his own love and trust, and for finally calling him "Clayton" *now*, when he knew her for what she was—a lying, deceiving little bitch who had freely shared her lush, ripe body with any rutting pig who asked her to. He tore his mind from thoughts of her coupling with other men and, without answering her question, pointedly looked away.

Whitney tried to combat her mounting alarm by concentrating on where they were and in which direction they were travelling. North! she realized as they turned off the main road. They were heading north. Now she *was* frantic. Drawing a quick breath, she swallowed what was left of her pride and said, "I was going to tell you that I'm willing to marry you. It isn't necessary to take me to Scotland to marry me. I'll—"

"Not necessary to marry you?" Clayton interrupted with a short, bitter laugh. "So I have heard. However, I have no desire to elope, nor have I any intention of pushing my horses much further. They've already chased across half of England today in pursuit of you."

Abruptly, the coach turned west onto a smooth, but less

travelled road, at the same moment the full import of his words slammed into her. If he'd been on the road all day "in pursuit" of her, then he must have returned to the village today and heard the gossip about her betrothal to Paul. Pleadingly, Whitney laid her hand on his arm. "I can explain about Paul. You see—"

His fingers clamped down on her slim hand, wringing a gasp of pain from her. "I'm delighted that you're so eager to touch me," he drawled sarcastically, "because in a short while, you are going to have an opportunity to do exactly that." Distastefully he removed her hand from his arm and dropped it into her lap. "However, since this is not the place for you to demonstrate your affection, you will have to control your passions until then."

"Control my—?" Whitney gasped, and then hopefully she blurted, "Are you foxed?"

His lips twisted with cynical amusement. "I am not drunk, so you needn't worry that I will be unable to *perform* . . ." He emphasized the last word, making it sound ominous. Then almost pleasantly he added, "You should sleep now. You've a long and exhausting night ahead of you."

Frightened by his taunting and hurt by the disgusted revulsion in his eyes whenever he looked at her, Whitney tore her gaze from his. She had no idea what he was talking about. *She* was on the verge of hysterical terror, and *he* was sitting here telling her to control her passions, assuring her that he would be able to "perform." In the darkness of the coach, the vulgar crudity of his remark finally penetrated the turbulent agitation of her mind, and her eyes grew huge with fear. *Now* she understood his plans!

Whitney searched the starlit night for sign of a village, a house, anywhere she could seek refuge. There were a few lights up ahead on her side of the road—a posting house or an inn, she thought. She didn't know what kind of injury she would sustain by jumping from the coach and she didn't care, so long as she would be able to get up and run . . . run to the lights beside the road.

Biting her trembling lower lip, Whitney inched her hand cautiously along her skirts toward the handle that would open the door. She stole a final, parting look at the granite profile of the man beside her and felt as if something were dying within her.

Squeezing her eyes closed, she tried to clear them of the burning tears that would blind her when she hurtled from the coach. She edged her fingertips along the padded leather of the door until they closed around the hard, cold metal of the handle. A few more seconds until they were even with the open gates of the inn yard, and the horses slowed against the strain of the incline. Whitney's fingers tightened . . . She screamed as Clayton's hand clamped around her arm, jerking her away from the door.

"Don't be so impatient, my sweet. A common roadside inn is hardly the proper setting for our first coupling. Or do you prefer inns for your little trysts?" With a sharp twist of his arm, he flung her onto the seat across from him. "Do you?" he repeated savagely.

With pounding heart, Whitney watched the distance widen between the coach and the inn, and with it went her hope of escape. She couldn't possibly take him by surprise again, nor could she overpower him.

"Personally," Clayton continued almost sociably, "I have always preferred the comforts of my 'dingy' home to the questionable cleanliness and worn bed linen one usually finds in these places."

His cool mockery finally snapped her fragile self-control. "You—you are a bastard!" she burst out.

"If you say so," he agreed indifferently. "And if I am, that makes me eminently well suited to spend the night in bed with a bitch!"

Whitney squeezed her eyes closed and leaned her head back against the seat, trying desperately to bring her emotions under control. Clayton was infuriated about Paul, and somehow she had to explain. Swallowing convulsively, she whispered into the darkness, "Mrs. Sevarin is to blame for the gossip you heard. Despite what you think, as soon as Paul came home, I told him that I couldn't marry him. I couldn't stop the gossip at home, so I went to London—"

"The gossip followed you there, my sweet," he informed

her in a silky tone. "Now stop boring me with your explanations."

"But—"

"Shut up," Clayton warned with deadly calm, "or I will change my mind about waiting until we have a comfortable bed, and I'll take you right here."

Tendrils of fresh terror wrapped themselves around Whitney's heart.

They had been travelling for nearly two hours when the coach slowed and passed through gates of some sort. The dazed exhaustion which had blessedly numbed her mind vanished, and Whitney stiffened, staring out the window at the lights of a large house looming in the far distance.

By the time they pulled up before the house, her heart was hammering so wildly she could scarcely breathe. Clayton climbed down, then reached in and dragged her from the coach.

"I am not going into that house," she cried, writhing and twisting in his grasp.

"It's a little late for you to start trying to protect your virtue," he jeered, swinging her up into his arms. His hands bit into her thigh and waist as he carried her into the dimly lit house and up the endless, curving staircase.

A red-haired maid rushed out onto the balcony and Whitney opened her mouth to cry out, then choked on the cry as Clayton's fingers dug agonizingly into her flesh.

"Go to bed!" he snapped at the woman who watched them pass with wide, disbelieving eyes.

"Please, please stop this!" Whitney begged frantically as he kicked open the door to a bedroom and strode inside. Her mind dimly registered the splendid furnishings and a fire burning in the grate of an enormous fireplace across the room, but the object that claimed all her wild-eyed attention was the large four-poster bed on a dais to which Clayton was carrying her.

He dumped her unceremoniously in the center of the bed, then turned on his heel and headed across the room toward the door. For one relieved moment, Whitney thought he intended to leave. Instead he reached out and rammed the bolt into place with the finality of a death blow.

In a frozen paralysis, she watched him stride past the bed toward the fireplace across the room. He flung himself into one of the sofas at right angles to the fireplace, and minutes passed while he sat there, looking at her as if she were some strange, captive animal, a curiosity, deformed and loathsome to his sight.

The silence was finally shattered by his order rapped out in a cold, unfamiliar voice. "Come here, Whitney."

Whitney's whole body jerked. She shook her head and inched backward along the bed toward the pillows, her gaze flying to the windows, then the other doors. Could she possibly reach one of them before he could stop her?

"You can try," Clayton commented. "But I promise you'll never make it."

Swallowing a panicked sob, Whitney sat straighter, struggling against the hysteria welling up in her throat. "About Paul—"

"Say his name one more time," Clayton lashed out furiously, "and I'll kill you, so help me God!" And then he became frighteningly polite. "You may have Sevarin if he still wants you. But we can discuss all that later. Now, my love, are you going to walk over here to me unaided, or must I come and assist you?"

He lifted a dark brow at her, permitting her a moment to think it over. "Well?" he threatened, half rising from his chair.

Refusing to beg, or to give him the added satisfaction of subduing her, Whitney rose from the bed. She tried to hold her head high, to look scornful and proud, but her knees felt like water. Two paces away from him, her shaking legs refused to move again. She stood there, staring at him with tear-brightened eyes.

He surged to his feet. "Turn around!" he snapped. Before Whitney could utter a protest, he caught her by the shoulders and whipped her around. With one vicious jerk, he ripped her dress down the back and the sound of tearing fabric screamed in Whitney's ears, while satin-covered buttons scattered across the carpet to shine in the firelight. He turned her back toward him and smiled malevolently. "I own the dress too," he reminded her. He settled back in his chair, stretched his long legs out, and for several moments watched Whitney's clumsy attempts to keep the slippery satin bodice clutched to her breasts. "Drop it!" he ordered.

The satin bodice slid from her fingers and he watched impassively as yards of fine ivory satin swooshed down her hips and slender legs, landing in a heap at her feet.

"The rest?" he said blandly.

Choking on her humiliation, Whitney hesitated, then stepped woodenly out of the stiff petticoats, standing before him clad only in her thin chemise. He was waiting for her to remove the chemise, Whitney knew—because he intended total nakedness to be her final humiliation. He meant to punish her for the gossip about Paul by terrifying her like this. Well, she was terrified and degraded enough already, punished for whatever she'd done or thought of doing. In mute rebellion, she started to back away.

Clayton was on his feet before she could take the second step. His hand shot out and twisted tightly in the thin fabric at the neckline of her chemise, drawing it taut over her thrusting breasts. Her chest rising and falling in rapid, harsh breaths, she stared down at the strong, well-manicured hand at her breasts, the same hand that had once caressed her with gentle passion. Abruptly the hand tightened and with one sharp jerk he split the thin garment in two, flinging it away from her body. "Get into the bed," he ordered coldly.

Desperate to hide her nakedness, Whitney fled to the big four-poster and quickly pulled the sheets up to her chin, as if they could protect her from him. In a blur of unreality, she saw Clayton strip off his jacket. He unbuttoned his shirt and pulled it off, and she stared blindly at the rippling muscles of his powerful shoulders and arms. When his hands went to the waistband of his pants, Whitney twisted her head to the wall and squeezed her eyes closed. His footsteps bore down on the bed, and she opened her eyes to see him towering menacingly above her.

"Don't cover yourself from me!" He caught the sheets and tore them from her clenched fists. "I want to see what I paid so handsomely for." Pain slashed across his features as his gaze swept over her naked body, then his jaw hardened.

In a shivering trance of fear, Whitney stared at his hard, ruthless face while her tortured mind superimposed other, gentle memories of him. She saw him bending over her the day she fell from her horse, his face white with alarm. She saw him gazing tenderly into her eyes the day she had kissed him near the stream—*"My God you are sweet"* he had whispered. She thought of the night he had taught her to gamble with cards and chips. She remembered the way he had stood beside her only a few nights ago at the Rutherfords' and proudly introduced her as his fiancée.

Aunt Anne had been right; Clayton did love her. Love and possessiveness were driving him to do this terrible thing to her—*she* had driven him to it, by denying her feelings for him for so long, by her blind determination to marry Paul. He was deliberately compromising her so that she would have no choice except to marry him and not Paul. He loved her, and in return she had caused this proud man to become an object of public ridicule.

The bed shifted beneath his weight as he stretched out beside her, and Whitney's fear gave way to a deep, shattering remorse. Her eyes aching with unshed tears, she turned her face to his and hesitantly laid her trembling fingers against his rigid jaw. "I—I'm sorry," she whispered chokily. "I'm so sorry."

His eyes narrowed, then he leaned toward her, his weight supported on an elbow, his free hand gliding over her bare arm to boldly cup her breast. "Show me," he invited, teasing her nipple with his thumb. "Show me how sorry you are."

Overriding the shrieking protest of her conscience, Whitney complied, letting his fingers send shooting sensations from her breast to the pit of her stomach. She didn't struggle. She was prepared to show him she was sorry—she was prepared to let him do this to her.

His mouth came down on hers, parting her lips in a deep, languorous kiss, and Whitney tried to kiss him back with all the love and contrition in her aching heart. "You're very lovely, my sweet," he murmured as his hands began boldly to explore her body. "But then I suppose you've heard that before." His mouth burned a hot trail down her throat to the pink tips of her full breasts, his tongue teasing, flicking and then circling. Suddenly his lips closed tightly around her nipple, drawing hard, and Whitney gasped with startled pleasure. Instantly his hand moved down her thighs, then up between them to cover the soft mound of hair and she gave a leap of instinctive shock. He ignored her, his questing fingers parting her and then intimately exploring her, sending melting, tingling sensations racing along her raw nerve endings.

Nuzzling her neck, he continued the arousing movement of his hand against her most sensitive place, his skillful fingers moving with unerring certainty to linger and teasingly caress the precise places where his touch could send shock waves of desire shooting through her.

Whitney yielded helplessly to the hot, searing need he was expertly building within her, while a nameless panic slowly began to grip her. Something was different, wrong, in the way he was kissing her, touching her! For a man driven by possessive, unrequited love, his kisses lacked his usual smoldering ardor, his caresses were without tender urgency . . .

His fingers moved within her and she moaned in her throat.

"So you like that, do you?" he taunted in a low whisper, then he stopped. "I don't want you to enjoy this too much, my love," he explained abruptly and shifted his weight on top of her, wedging his knee between her legs. He grasped her hips, lifting them, at the same moment the cynical inflection in his voice pierced the thick, sensual haze engulfing her. Her eyes flew open. She saw his harsh, bitter expression just as Clayton drew back and then rammed himself full-length into her tight, virginal passage. Searing pain ripped through her and she screamed, burying her face in her hands, her back arching. Above her a savage curse exploded from Clayton's chest. He withdrew, and she stiffened hysterically, trying to brace herself for the next agonizing pain that would come when he entered her again . . .

But the pain never came; he remained withdrawn, motionless.

Whitney's hands fell limply from her face. Through a blurring haze of tears, she saw him above her. Clayton's head was thrown back, his eyes clenched shut, his features a mask of tortured anguish. As she stared at his ravaged face, her body jerked with suppressed sobs until the burden of holding them back was more than she could bear. She wanted to be held, to be comforted, and irrationally, she sought this comfort from her own tormentor. Shuddering on a lonely, convulsive cry, Whitney reached her arms up around Clayton's powerful shoulders and drew him down against her.

With aching gentleness, Clayton gathered her into his arms, and shifted to lie beside her. Without a word, she turned her face into his bare chest and wept, cried her heart out in harsh, racking sobs that shook her slender body with such violence that Clayton thought they would surely tear her apart. He lay there, holding her defiled, naked body cradled against him, stroking the rumpled silk of her hair, while he punished himself with the sound of her muffled weeping, lashed himself with the tears that poured from her eyes and drenched his chest.

"I—I told Paul I—I wouldn't marry him," Whitney cried brokenly. "The gossip w-wasn't my fault."

"It wasn't that, little one," Clayton whispered, his voice raw with emotion. "I'd never have done this to you for that."

"Then why did you?" she choked.

Clayton expelled a ragged breath. "I thought you'd lain with him. And with others."

Abruptly Whitney's crying subsided. Clutching the sheet to her naked breasts, she reared up on an elbow and stared at him with scornful green eyes. "Oh you did, did you!" she hissed, and tore herself from his embrace, rolling over onto her other side to face the wall. The bewildered terror that had seized her in the coach evaporated, along with her belief that he loved her. In a blinding flash of sick humiliation, she understood that he had done this to degrade her; his monstrous pride had demanded this unspeakable revenge for some imagined crime. Bile rose in her throat as she realized that she had submitted to him without struggling. He hadn't deceived her, she had deceived herself. He hadn't stolen her virtue, she had given it to him! *She had given it to him.* Drowning in shame and self-loathing, she struggled to pull the heavy bedcovers up to cover herself.

Clayton saw her and reached across to draw them tenderly over her lovely, naked body. Realizing too late that he had just added insult to her injury, he put his hand on her shoulder, gently trying to turn her toward him. "If you'll let me," he implored, "I'd like to explain—"

Furiously, she shrugged his hand off. "I'd like to see you try! But do it by letter, because if you ever come near me or my family again, I'll kill you, I swear I will!" The substance of this brave threat was diminished by the muffled sobs that followed it and seemed to go on forever until she sank into an exhausted slumber.

His grace, Clayton Robert Westmoreland, Duke of Claymore, descendent of five hundred years of nobility, possessor of estates and wealth so vast as to defy comprehension, lay beside the only woman he had ever loved, helpless either to comfort her or regain her.

He stared at the ceiling, seeing her as she had been only hours before, conducting a group of merry, would-be musicians.

How could he have done this to her, when all he had ever wanted to do was pamper and cherish and protect her? Instead he had coldly and deliberately taken her innocence. And in doing so, he had lost more than she had, for he had managed to lose the only thing he had ever really wanted to possess—this one headstrong, beautiful girl lying beside him. Loathing him.

He remembered all the coarse, vulgar things he'd said to her in the coach and in this room. Each degrading word he had spoken, each touch that had hurt her, paraded across his mind bringing a sharp agonizing pain, so he punished himself by going over and over every vicious thing he had said and done to her.

Near dawn, she turned onto her back. Clayton leaned over

and tenderly brushed a wayward lock of mahogany hair from her smooth cheek, then he lay back to watch her sleep. Because he knew that this would be the last time Whitney would ever lie beside him.

She awoke the next morning, vaguely aware of a tenderness between her legs and at her waist and thighs. Her lashes fluttered open and she rolled onto her back. Her mind felt sluggish and fuzzy as she glanced with half-closed, sleepy eyes at her surroundings.

She was in a gigantic bed situated on a dais. The immense bedroom was ten times the size of her large bedroom at home, and splendidly furnished. She blinked dazedly at the thick moss-green carpet stretching luxuriously across the vast floor. The entire wall to her left was a sweeping expanse of mullioned glass, and the one across from her had a marble fireplace so large that she could easily have stood up in the opening. The two remaining walls were covered with wide, richly carved rosewood panels and hung with magnificent tapestries. Wearily, Whitney closed her eyes and started to drift back into the peace of slumber. Odd that she would be sleeping in a room that seemed so masculine.

Her eyes snapped open and she sat bolt upright in bed. *His* bed! *His* room! Someone opened the door and she cringed backward, clutching the silk sheets to her bare breasts. The diminutive red-haired maid Whitney had seen on the balcony the night before came in carrying Whitney's mended ivory gown and chemise, which she carefully hung over a door that led into a dressing room. As she turned to go, she saw Whitney huddled watchfully in the bed and picked up an elegant lace dressing gown that was draped over a chair. "Good morning, Miss," she said as she approached the bed, and Whitney bitterly noted that the servant showed no surprise at finding a naked woman in her master's bed— obviously, it was nothing out of the ordinary.

"My name is Mary," the maid said in a soft Irish brogue as she extended her arm over which was draped the lace dressing gown. "May I help you up?"

Shamed to the depths of her soul, Whitney took her

outstretched hand and climbed unsteadily down from the bed. "Merciful God!" Mary gasped, her eyes riveted on the blood-stained silk sheets. "What did he do to you?"

Whitney smothered a trill of hysterical laughter at the idiocy of the question. "He ruined me!" she choked.

Mesmerized, Mary stared at the blood stains. "He'll pay an awful price for this in the judgment. The Lord'll not forgive this easily—the master being what he is, and knowing better, and you a virgin!" She dragged her eyes from the sheets and led Whitney to a sunken marble bath which adjoined the bedchambers.

"I hope God doesn't forgive him!" Whitney hissed brokenly, stepping into the warm bathwater. "I hope he burns in hell! I wish I had a knife so that I could cut his heart out!" Mary started to soap her back, but Whitney took the cloth from her and began to scrub every part of her body that Clayton had touched. Suddenly her hand froze. What insanity possessed her to climb obediently into this tub when she should be dressed already and planning a way to escape? She clutched at the maid's wrist, her green eyes wild with pleading. "I have to leave before he comes back, Mary. Please help me find some way out of here. You can't believe how badly he hurt me, the things—awful things—he said to me. If I don't get away, he'll—he'll make me do that again."

With confused, sorrowful blue eyes, the maid looked down at Whitney and gently shook her head. "His grace has no wish to enter this room or keep you here. He told me himself that only I am to look after you. The coach is already waiting for you around in front, and when you're dressed, I'm to take you down myself."

Two stories above the main entrance to his house, Clayton stood at the window, waiting for a last glimpse of her. Waiting to make his final farewell. The trees bent and sighed in the wind, bowing deeply to her as she stepped out into a day as bleak and dreary as his soul. Her gown flew about her as she descended the long sweep of steps to the waiting coach, and the wind caught her hair, tumbling it wildly about her.

On the bottom step, Whitney paused and for one agonizing, soul-wrenching moment, Clayton thought that she was going to turn and look up at him. Helplessly he stretched his hand out, longing to slide his knuckles over her soft, silken cheek. But all he touched was a cold pane of glass. As if she sensed somehow that he was watching her, Whitney lifted her head in that regal way of hers, gave it a defiant toss, and without looking back, she stepped into the coach.

The brandy glass Clayton was holding shattered in his clenched hand, and he looked down at the bright red drops oozing from his fingers.

"I imagine you'll be getting poison of the blood now," Mary, standing in the doorway, predicted with a certain amount of satisfaction.

"Unfortunately, I doubt it," Clayton replied flatly.

Whitney huddled in a corner of the coach, her thoughts marching dizzily in a tight circle of shame, misery, and anger. She thought of the vulgar things he had said to her, the businesslike way his hands had moved over her flesh, expertly evoking an unwilling response from her traitorous body.

Bitter bile rose up in her throat, choking her. She wished she were dead—no, she wished *he* were dead! Last night was only the beginning of the humiliating nightmare she would have to endure. Michael Archibald would undoubtedly insist that Emily send her home, for he would never permit a woman of questionable virtue to associate with his wife. Even if Whitney could convince him that she had been *forced* to spend the night with Clayton, she would still be just as soiled, just as unfit to be received in polite society.

Fighting down a surge of nausea, Whitney leaned her head back. Somehow, she had to think of a feasible excuse to give the Archibalds to explain why she had been gone all night. Otherwise, she'd be banished from her best friend's company, banished from the company of decent people. She would spend her life in lonely shame with only her father for company.

After nearly an hour, Whitney finally settled on an excuse she could give Michael and Emily; it sounded a little lame, but it might suffice if they didn't question her. Now she felt less afraid, but infinitely more alone, more vulnerable. There

353

was no one to whom she could turn for comfort or understanding.

She could write to Aunt Anne who was staying with a cousin in Lincolnshire, and ask her to come to London. But what could Aunt Anne do except demand that Clayton marry her immediately? What a punishment that would be for him, Whitney thought sarcastically. He'd get precisely what he'd always wanted, and she would be condemned to marriage with a man she would hate for as long as she lived. If Whitney refused to marry Clayton, Aunt Anne would naturally turn to Uncle Edward for advice. When Uncle Edward learned what Clayton had done, he would probably demand that Clayton give him satisfaction, meaning a duel, which must at all cost be avoided. In the first place, duelling was illegal now; in the second, Whitney was terrifyingly certain that that *bastard* would kill her uncle.

The only other alternative was for Uncle Edward to demand justice through the courts, but a trial and the public scandal attached to it would ruin Whitney for as long as she lived.

And so, here she was, forced to bear her hurt and shame alone, with no way of avenging herself on that devil! But she would think of something, she told herself bracingly. The next time he came near her, she would be ready. The next time he came near her? Whitney's hands grew clammy, and perspiration broke out on her forehead. She would die if he **ev**er came near her again. She would kill herself before she ever let him touch her! If he tried to speak to her, if he touched her, she would start screaming and never be able to stop!

Every servant in the Archibald household seemed to be hovering in the hallways, watching her with secret condemnation when Whitney entered the house. She marched bravely past the butler, three footmen, and a half dozen housemaids with her chin up and her head high. But when she closed the bedroom door behind her, she collapsed against it, her body shaking and her chin quivering. Clarissa descended on her a moment later, bristled up like a maddened porcupine, slamming drawers, muttering under her breath about "shameless hussies" and "slurs on the family name."

Whitney hid her mortification behind a stony expression and jerked off the hated ivory satin gown, self-consciously snatching on a dressing robe when Clarissa's eyes raked suspiciously over her naked body.

"Your poor sweet mother must be spinning in her grave," Clarissa announced, plunking her hands on her ample hips.

"Don't say such ghoulish things," Whitney said wretchedly. "My mother is resting in peace because she knows I've done nothing to be ashamed of."

"Well, it's just too bad the servants in this house don't know that," replied Clarissa, puffing up with ire. "As hoity-toity as royalty they are here. And every one of them is whispering about *you!*"

Whitney's interview with Emily late that afternoon was even more humiliating. Emily simply sat there, listening attentively to Whitney's lame tale of how the duke had escorted her to another party across town and when the hour had grown too late to return, her unnamed hostess had insisted that Whitney spend the night. At the end of the explanation, Emily nodded her complete, unqualified understanding, but her pretty, honest face reflected a stunned shock that was worse than any accusation she could have made.

Emily went directly to her husband's study and repeated the story to him. "So you see," she said in a determinedly confident voice while anxiously scanning Michael's face, "it was all perfectly innocent and not in the least scandalous. You do believe her explanation, don't you, Michael?" she pleaded.

Michael leaned back in his chair and regarded his young wife levelly. "No," he said quietly, "I don't." He reached out and drew Emily down onto his lap. For a long moment he studied her distraught features, then he said gently, "But I do believe in you. If you tell me she's innocent, I will believe that."

"I love you, Michael," Emily said simply, her body sagging

with relief. "Whitney would never do anything indecent, I know it!"

Whitney had dreaded the evening meal, but Emily and her husband seemed perfectly relaxed and natural. In fact, Michael even urged her to remain with them until after Elizabeth's wedding, which was slightly more than a month away. He seemed so sincere, and Emily so eager for her to stay, that Whitney gratefully and happily accepted their invitation. The last thing in the world she wanted to do was to go home to her father and face the rumors of her betrothal to Paul.

But that night, as she lay in bed, loneliness and despair washed over her in a tidal wave. She wished her aunt were here to tell her what to do, but she knew in her heart there was nothing Anne or anyone else could do to help her. She was going to have to bear this alone.

From this day forward, she would always be alone. She could never have a husband or children because no decent man would want her. She was soiled, dirtied, used by another. She had always wanted to have children, but now she couldn't. A painful lump of desolation swelled in her throat.

She didn't want a husband though, she told herself bitterly. She could never care for another man or bear to be touched by his hands. In her whole life, there had been only two men she had wanted to marry: Paul, who was shallow and weak, and Clayton who was—an animal. Paul had only disappointed her, but Clayton had destroyed her. He had insinuated his way into her heart, and then he had used her and thrown her away, sent her home without even an apology!

Tears trickled down Whitney's cheeks and she furiously brushed them away. Clayton Westmoreland had made her cry for the last time! When next they met, she would be hardened and calm. She was through thinking about him; she would never think about last night again.

Despite her resolve, the following days were the most harrowing of Whitney's life. Every time the butler appeared to announce a caller, Whitney's heart leapt with terror that the "caller" was the Duke of Claymore. She longed to tell Emily that she would not be at home to him when he called, but how could she, when he was an acquaintance of Michael's, and she was a guest in Michael's home? Besides, Emily would want to know why, and that would reopen the topic of Clayton, a topic which Emily had already tried to reopen several times. Which left Whitney with no choice but to cringe and try to steady her nerves every time a visitor arrived at the Archibald residence.

She rarely accompanied Emily out of the house because she was obsessed with the morbid certainty that she could come face to face with Clayton if she did. With each passing day her tension steadily mounted until she felt as if she would go mad with the helpless waiting, the fear and dread.

But she kept the promises she had made to herself almost a week ago. She meticulously refused to think of that hideous, fateful night. And she did not cry.

Chapter Twenty-five

TWO SLEEK, WELL-SPRUNG TRAVELLING CHAISES WAITED IN front of Claymore, the vast three-story stone structure that was Clayton's principal residence. The grandeur of the house and grounds was the result of loving restoration and extensive additions which had been carried out by Clayton, his father, his grandfather, and all of the Dukes of Claymore who had preceded them.

To visitors and guests, Claymore was a place in which to wander admiringly, from domed-glass rooms where one could see the sky, to rooms of breathtaking splendor where vaulted ceilings rose three stories in height, supported by graceful Gothic pillars. Looking up, one could behold the master genius of Rubens, who had lavishly embellished the ceilings with rich, exuberant scenes.

To Clayton, however, his house was a place of haunting memories where he could not sleep, and when he did, could not escape the recurring nightmare of what had happened there seven endless agonizing nights ago. It was a place from which he had to escape.

Seated at his desk in the spacious oak-panelled library, he listened impatiently to the solicitor who was repeating the instructions Clayton had just given him.

"Do I understand you correctly, your grace? You wish to withdraw your offer of marriage to Miss Stone? But make no attempt to recover any of the monies you expended to secure the agreement?"

"That is precisely what I just said," Clayton replied shortly. "I am leaving for Grand Oak today, and will return in a fortnight. Have the papers here for my signature the day after my return." With that he stood up, abruptly concluding the distasteful interview.

The dowager Duchess of Claymore glanced up eagerly as the butler appeared in the doorway. "His grace's coach is just pulling up the drive," the old family retainer announced, his dignified countenance lit with unabashed pleasure.

Smiling, the duchess walked over to the windows of the lovely manor which her husband had years ago set aside as her dower house. In comparison to the vastness of Claymore, Grand Oak was small, but she entertained frequently and lavishly in the spacious house which stood before five guest pavilions and was surrounded by glorious gardens and arbors.

She watched the two sleek travelling chaises draw up smartly before the front steps, then turned aside to check her appearance in the mirror. At five and fifty, Alicia, Dowager Duchess of Claymore, was still slim and gracefully erect. Her dark hair was threaded with silver strands, but they only added dignity to her abiding beauty. A worried shadow darkened her gray eyes as she patted her elegantly coiffed hair into place and thought about Clayton's strangely uninformative note which had arrived only three days ago, announcing his intention to pay her a two-week visit. Clayton's visits were infrequent and usually disappointingly brief; it seemed odd somehow that he had decided to come for such an extended time and on such short notice.

A controlled commotion in the entrance hall heralded Clayton's arrival, and with her face wreathed in a delighted smile, Lady Westmoreland turned to greet her eldest son.

Clayton strode swiftly across the pale blue carpet and, ignoring her outstretched hands, he caught her in a brief embrace and pressed an affectionate kiss on her smooth forehead. "You are more beautiful than ever," he said.

His mother leaned back, anxiously studying the deeply

etched lines of strain and fatigue at his eyes and mouth. "Have you been ill, darling? You look terrible."

"Thank you, Mother," he said drily. "I am delighted to see you, too."

"Well, of course, I'm delighted to see you," she protested with a sighing laugh. "But I would like to see you looking better, which is what I meant." Dismissing the subject with a cheerful wave of her hand, she drew him down to sit beside her on the sofa, but her eyes still worriedly scanned his drawn face. "Stephen is in transports over being able to spend an entire fortnight here with you," she said. "He has planned parties and is even now en route here with a large group of people. I doubt you'll have a moment's peace and quiet, so if that's why you've come, I'm afraid you're in for a rude surprise."

"It doesn't matter," Clayton replied grimly. Getting up, he walked over to the side table and poured himself a liberal glass of whiskey.

"Where is that scoundrel who forced me to be a penniless younger son?" Stephen Westmoreland called from the hallway. He strode into the salon, winked at his mother, and warmly clasped Clayton's hand. Jokingly referring to the jumble of voices out in the hall he said, "I grew tired, brother dear, of having to make excuses for your absence to the London beauties, so I brought a few of them with me, as you will soon see."

"Fine." Clayton shrugged unenthusiastically.

Stephen's blue eyes narrowed into a slight frown, a pensive expression which heightened the similarity of features between the two brothers. Like Clayton, Stephen was dark-haired and tall. Although he lacked the aura of power and authority that seemed to surround his brother, Stephen was friendlier and easier to know, and as the *ton* often remarked, he possessed the legendary Westmoreland charm in good measure. He was, despite his earlier remark, very wealthy in his own right and perfectly content to have the ducal title—and the hundreds of responsibilities that went with it—rest on his brother's capable shoulders.

Subjecting Clayton to a brief scrutiny, he said, "You look like hell, Clay." Then with an apologetic grin at his mother, he added, "I beg your pardon, Mama."

"Well, he does," the duchess agreed. "I told him the same thing."

"*You* told him he looks like hell?" Stephen teased her, pressing a belated kiss of greeting on his mother's beringed fingers.

"It must be a family characteristic," Clayton observed sardonically, "to ignore the common civilities and make unsolicited observations instead. Hello, Stephen."

Shortly thereafter, Clayton pleaded fatigue from his four-hour trip and excused himself. As soon as he left the room, Lady Westmoreland turned determinedly to her youngest son. "Stephen, see if you can discover what's troubling him."

Stephen firmly shook his head in the negative. "Clay won't tolerate anyone prying into his affairs, you know that as well as I, sweetheart. Besides, he is probably only tired, nothing more."

Despite his words, Stephen watched Clayton closely in the two weeks that followed. During the day, the members of the house party rode and hunted and jaunted off to a nearby village to explore and shop. But the only activity Clayton seemed to enjoy was riding—except that now he ruthlessly forced his mount over impossible obstacles and rode with a reckless, bruising violence that struck genuine alarm in Stephen's chest.

The evenings were filled with sumptuous feasts and brilliant conversation; games of whist and billiards; as well as the predictable flirtations one could always look forward to wherever seven lovely, well-born young women and seven eligible gentlemen were thrown into each other's constant company for nearly two weeks.

Clayton fulfilled his role as host to the group with his usual careless elegance, and Stephen sat through meal after meal watching in amusement as the women flirted shamelessly with him, doing everything within the limits of propriety (and frequently beyond) to hold his attention. Occasionally, a lazy grin would flash across Clayton's features as he listened to whatever woman was speaking to him, but the shuttered look never left his eyes.

Twelve of the fourteen days had passed and the guests were due to leave the following morning. They were gathered that evening in the drawing room and Stephen's watchful gaze slid with increasing, concerned frequency to his brother.

"I think your brother is bored with us," Janet Cambridge told Stephen, nodding playfully toward Clayton who was standing alone, his shoulder propped against the window frame, staring out into the darkness.

Clayton heard her, as she intended that he should, but he did not bother to gallantly reassure her that he wasn't bored, nor did he turn to pay her the flattering attention that Janet was seeking with her remark. Raising his glass, he took a long swallow of his drink, watching the low-hanging mist swirling and advancing in the night. He yearned to have it close over him and blot out his thoughts, his memory, as it did everything else in its path.

He saw Janet Cambridge's reflection in the window glass and heard her low, throaty laugh behind him. Until a few months ago, he had enjoyed her sensuous beauty and seductive voice. But now she lacked something. Her eyes weren't the green of India jade; she didn't look at him with that teasing, appraising, impudent sidewise glance; she didn't tremble in his arms with shy, awakening emotions that she couldn't identify. She was too available, too eager to please him, but then other women always were. They didn't spar with him or stubbornly defy him. They weren't fresh and alive and witty and wonderful. They weren't . . .

Whitney.

He took another long swallow of his drink to dull the ache that came with just her name. He wondered what she was doing. Was she planning to marry Sevarin? Or was she with DuVille instead? DuVille was in London; he would be able to comfort her and tease her, to help her forget. DuVille would suit her better, Clayton decided with a wrenching pain. Sevarin was dull and weak, but DuVille was sophisticated and urbane. Clayton hoped with all his heart that she would choose the Frenchman. Well, with half his heart; the other half twisted in agony at the image of Whitney as another man's wife.

He tortured himself by thinking of the way she had said, *"I was going to tell you that I would marry you."* And bastard that he was, he had mocked her! Viciously, deliberately, coldly stolen her innocence! And when he had finished, she had put her arms around him and cried. Oh Christ! he had all but *raped* her and she had cried in his arms.

Clayton dragged his thoughts from that night. He preferred the more refined torture of thinking about the joy of her: the jaunty way she had looked at him at the starting line of their race, just before the pistol fired. *"If you would care to follow me, I shall be happy to show you the way."*

He could still visualize her exactly as she was that night in the garden at the Armands' masquerade, her beautiful face aglow with irreverent merriment because he had told her he was a duke. *"You are no duke,"* she had laughed. *"You have no quizzing glass, you don't wheeze and snort, and I doubt you have even a mild case of gout. I'm afraid you'll have to aspire to some other title, my lord."*

He thought of the way she had melted against him and kissed him with sweet passion that day beside the pavilion. God, what a warm, fiery, loving creature she could be—when she wasn't being stubborn and rebellious . . . and wonderful.

Clayton closed his eyes, cursing himself for letting Whitney leave Claymore at all. He should have demanded that she marry him as soon as he could summon a cleric to the house. And when she put up a fight, he could have bluntly pointed out that since he had already taken her virginity, she had no choice in the matter. Then, in the months that followed, he could have found some way to make up for what happened.

Clayton slammed his glass down and strode past the guests and out of the room. There was nothing he could ever do to atone for the profane act he had committed against her. Nothing!

The guests departed early the following morning and the brothers celebrated their last evening together by getting purposely, thoroughly, blindly drunk. They reminisced about their boyhood misdemeanors and when they ran out of those, they began telling each other bawdy stories, laughing uproariously at the tavern jokes, and drinking all the while.

Clayton reached for the decanter of brandy and spilled the last drop of it into his empty glass. "Migawd!" Stephen rasped admiringly, watching him. "You drinked . . . drunked . . . finished the the whole damned bottle." He grabbed another crystal decanter and pushed it across the table toward Clayton. "Here, see what you can do to the whiskey."

Clayton shrugged indifferently and pulled the top from the decanter.

Through slightly bleary eyes, Stephen watched him fill the glass to the brim. "What the hell are you trying to do, drown yerself?"

"I am trying," Clayton informed him in a proud, drunken tone, "to beat you to the finish line of oblivion."

"Probably you will, too." Stephen nodded jerkily. "But I was always the better man. It was unkind in you to be born, Big Brudder."

"Right. Never should've done it. Wisht I hadn't, but she's . . . she's paid me back for it tenfold."

Although the words were slurred, they were filled with such bleak pain and despair that Stephen snapped his head up and stared, as alert as his sodden wits would permit. "Who paid you back for being born?"

"She did."

Stephen shook his head, desperately trying to clear the alcohol euphoria from his hazy senses and concentrate. "Which . . . she?"

"The one with the green eyes," Clayton whispered in an agonized voice. "She's making me pay."

"Whad you do to make her want to pay you back?"

"Offered for her," Clayton announced thickly. "Gave her stupid father £100,000. Whitney wouldn't have me though." He grimaced, taking a long swallow of whiskey. "Betrothed herself to somebody else. Errybody's talking about it. No," he corrected himself, "she din't get betrothed. But I thought she had and I . . . and I . . ."

"And you . . . ?" Stephen rasped softly.

Clayton's features twisted into a mask of anguish. He lifted his palm to Stephen as if asking him to understand, then let it fall onto the table. "I didn't believe she was still a virgin," he grated. "Didn't know . . . till I took her . . . and . . ."

The tense silence that followed was suddenly shattered by a terrible sound that ripped from Clayton's chest. "Oh, God, I *hurt* her," he groaned agonizingly. "I hurt her so damned much!" He covered his face with his hands, his voice a hoarse, ravaged whisper. "I hurt her and she . . . she put her arms around me because . . . because she wanted me to hold her. Stephen," he choked brokenly, "she wanted me to hold her while she cried!"

He crossed his arms on the table and buried his face in them, finally sinking into the oblivion he'd been seeking all night. His raw voice was so low Stephen could hardly hear it. "I can still hear her crying," he whispered.

In dumbfounded amazement, Stephen stared at Clayton's bent head, trying to piece together the disjointed story. Apparently his self-confident, invulnerable older brother had lost his heart to some girl with green eyes named Whitney.

There had been a wild rumor sweeping London this past week that Clayton was betrothed—or on the verge of it—to some female, but that was nothing out of the ordinary and Stephen had shrugged it off as being the usual idle speculation. But it must have been true, and this Whitney must have been the girl.

Stupefied, Stephen continued to gaze at his sleeping brother. It was unbelievable that Clayton, who had always treated women with a combination of amused tolerance and relaxed indulgence, could have been driven to rape. And why? Because the girl refused to marry him? Because he was jealous? Impossible! And yet the evidence was across from him; Clayton was tearing himself apart with remorse.

Stephen sighed. Clayton had always been surrounded by dazzling women; Whitney must have been very special to have meant so much to him, for it was perfectly obvious that he loved her desperately—and still did.

In fact, Stephen thought tiredly, if the girl had turned to Clayton for comfort after he had just forcibly deprived her of her virginity, she must have loved Clayton a little too. More than a little.

The following morning, the brothers shook hands on the front steps, neither able to look at the bright, sunlit day without flinching in pain. The duchess waved a cheerful goodbye to Clayton, then rounded on Stephen. "He looks awful!"

"He *feels* awful," Stephen assured her, gingerly rubbing his temples.

"Stephen," she said firmly, "there is something I wish to discuss with you." She swept into the salon, closed the door behind them, and sat down in the nearest chair. Then she took an extraordinarily long time arranging her skirts to her satisfaction. In a halting but determined voice, she said, "Last night I couldn't sleep, so I came downstairs, thinking I'd spend a little more time with the two of you. When I reached the library, I realized that both of you were shockingly in your cups, and I was about to say how stunned I was to discover that I had raised two drunken louts, when I . . . when I . . ."

Stephen's lips twitched with laughter at the "drunken louts" but otherwise he kept his face straight. "When you overheard what Clay was telling me?" he assisted her.

Miserably, she nodded. "How could he have done such a thing?"

"I'm not certain why he did it," Stephen began carefully. "Obviously he cared for the girl, and he's a man—"

"Don't treat me like an imbecile, Stephen," her ladyship interrupted hotly. "I am a grown woman. I've been married and I've borne two sons. I am perfectly aware that Clayton is a man and that, as such, he has certain . . . ah . . ."

"Certain urges?" Stephen provided when she began fanning her flushed face, looking agonizingly ill at ease. She nodded but Stephen said, "What I was trying to say is that Clay is a man who has always been sought after by women, yet he never cared for any of them enough to offer marriage.

Apparently, he finally found the woman he wanted. If he gave her father £100,000, I assume the girl is undowered and her family is poor, but even so, she refused him."

"She must have been seven kinds of fool to refuse your brother," Lady Westmoreland exclaimed. "She would have to be stupid not to want him."

Stephen grinned at her loyalty, but he shook his head. "It's unlikely the girl is stupid or foolish. Clay has never been interested in vapid, empty-headed misses."

"I suppose you're right," Lady Westmoreland sighed, coming to her feet. She stopped at the door and gave Stephen a sad look over her shoulder. "I think," she said quietly, "that he must have adored her."

"He did."

Clayton read the legal document dissolving the betrothal agreement, then signed it and quickly shoved it across the desk to the solicitor. He could barely stand the sight of it. "There's something more," he said when the solicitor began to rise. "See that this note and a bank draft for £10,000 are delivered along with the document to Miss Stone at her home."

Clayton pulled open one of the heavy, carved drawers of his desk and extracted a blank sheet of white parchment with his seal embossed in silver at the top.

He stared at the blank sheet, the moment freezing in time.

He couldn't believe it had truly come to this. How could it be ending like this, with this wrenching stab of pain and loss, when he'd been so confident only a few weeks ago that it would end with Whitney standing beside him as his bride, lying beside him as his wife?

He forced himself to pick up the quill and write the words, "Please accept my sincere wishes for your happiness and convey them to Paul. The enclosed bank draft is intended as a gift." Clayton hesitated, knowing that Whitney would fly into a rage over the money, but he couldn't bear to think of her having to pinch pennies for a new gown, which she would have to do as Sevarin's wife. If by some miracle she didn't marry Sevarin, then the money would be hers. At least her stupid father couldn't once more spend everything she had.

"Enclose the draft and this note in the same envelope as that." He jerked his head toward the hateful document dissolving their betrothal. Rising, he concluded the painful interview with a silent nod of dismissal.

When the solicitor left, Clayton sank back down in his chair, fighting against the impulse to have the man stopped at the gates and brought back, to snatch the envelope from him and tear it to pieces. Instead he leaned his head against the padded leather back of his chair and closed his eyes. "Oh little one," he breathed aloud, "why do I have to send you that damned envelope?"

He thought of the words he had really wanted to write to her: "Please come back to me. Just let me hold you and I swear I will make you forget. I'll fill your days with laughter and your nights with love. I'll give you a son. And if you still can't love me, then all I ask is that you give me a daughter. A daughter with your eyes, your smile, your—"

Swearing savagely, he lurched forward and grabbed the stack of correspondence that had accumulated in his absence.

With single-minded determination, Clayton threw himself into the task of forgetting her. He immersed himself in work, spending hours each day poring over reports on his present business investments and planning future ones. He drove his secretary, Mr. Hudgins, so hard that an assistant had to be hired for the man. He met with his business managers, his estate managers, his stewards, and his tenants. He worked until it was time to go out at night to attend a ball, the opera, the theatre.

Each evening he deliberately escorted a different woman, hoping each time that *this* woman would spark something within him—something that had died four weeks ago. But if she was blond, Clayton discovered that he had an aversion to pale hair. If she was brunette, her hair lacked the lustre of Whitney's. If she was vivacious, she grated on his nerves. If she was sultry, he found her distasteful. If she was quiet, he had a wild urge to shake her and say, "Dammit, *say* something!"

But slowly, very slowly, he found his balance again. He began to feel that if he continued to block a pair of laughing green eyes from his memory, he might actually forget her someday.

As the weeks passed, he smiled more easily, and, occasionally, he was even able to laugh.

Chapter Twenty-six

WHITNEY'S DAYS IN LONDON HAD ESTABLISHED A PATTERN. SHE went shopping with Elizabeth and Emily, or for an occasional drive through the park. Nicki called regularly at the house. Rarely did she let him escort her anywhere, but at least he came, and he made her smile. And he never asked her for more than she was able to give.

Elizabeth was a daily visitor. She was so caught up in her wedding plans, so eager to discuss her gown, the flowers, the banquet menu, and everything else that concerned the wedding which was only four days away, that Whitney could hardly remain in the same room with her exuberant joy, and even while she was frantically thinking up excuses to leave, Whitney hated herself for not being better able to take pleasure in Elizabeth's happiness.

She no longer lived in frantic expectation of seeing Clayton, but neither was she able to relax. She existed in a tense limbo, suspended between a past she refused to think about and a future she could not bear to contemplate.

Today was much like the others, except that when Elizabeth launched into an enumeration of all Peter's wonderful qualities, Whitney leapt to her feet, excused herself, snatched her cape from her room and practically ran out of the house. Ignoring the stricture which required that she take someone with her, she fled to the small park a few blocks away, then slowed her steps and wandered aimlessly down the deserted paths.

Aunt Anne and Whitney's father were coming up to London for Elizabeth's wedding—Elizabeth had surprised everyone by deciding she wished to be married in all the splendor London could provide. As much as she longed to see her beloved aunt, Whitney dreaded the confrontation. In four days Aunt Anne would arrive, expecting to find Clayton and Whitney acting like an unofficially engaged couple. Instead, Whitney was going to tell her that she was never going to marry the Duke of Claymore. And Aunt Anne would insist on knowing why.

Why? Whitney thought wildly, rehearsing the scene with her aunt. "Because he dragged me away from Emily's party, he took me to his house and he tore my clothes off, and he made me get into his bed."

Aunt Anne would be stunned and outraged, but she would want to know what had happened before that. She would want to know *why*. Whitney sank down onto a park bench, her shoulders drooping with confused despair. Why had Clayton believed she had given herself to Paul? And why hadn't he at least come to find out how she was faring? Or to tell her what he was going to do?

Not once in the last four weeks had Whitney allowed herself to think about that night, but now that she had started, she couldn't stop. She tried to remember Clayton as the man who had coldly and viciously ripped her clothes off. Instead she remembered him in that awful, pain-blurred moment when he had discovered her virginity. She saw his tensed shoulders above her, his head thrown back, his face a tortured mask of anguish and regret.

She wanted to remember the names he had called her and the insulting, degrading things he had said to her. Instead she remembered that he had held her in his arms while she cried, stroking her hair and whispering to her in a voice raw with emotion. "Don't cry, darling. Please don't cry anymore."

An awful, stabbing ache grew and grew in Whitney's throat, but now the pain she felt was for Clayton, not herself. When she realized it, she jumped furiously to her feet. She must be mad, utterly mad! She was actually feeling sorry for the man who had violated her! She never wanted to lay eyes on him again. Ever!

She walked quickly back down the path, the gusty wind blowing her cape around her like a tourniquet. As suddenly as it had come up, the wind died and a squirrel scampered toward her, then stopped, watching her half in fear, half in expectation. Whitney stopped too, waiting for him to move, but he sat up and chattered reproachfully at her.

She saw the acorn lying beside her foot and bent down to pick it up, offering it to him. The furry little animal blinked nervously, but came no closer, so Whitney tossed it to him. "Better take it," she told him softly, "it's going to be winter soon." The squirrel flicked its eyes to the precious acorn now lying only inches from him. For a moment he hesitated, then he turned, fleeing from it as quickly as his legs would carry him.

Not once in the weeks since that fateful night had Whitney broken her brave promise not to cry. She had succeeded, but she had also stored up a terrible burden of emotion. A little squirrel who preferred to starve rather than take something she had touched, was the last straw. "I hope you starve!" she choked as tears welled in her eyes and spilled down her cheeks. She pivoted on her heel and stalked down the path, past the park gates.

Tears streamed down her face and the wind burned her eyes, but she cried anyway. She cried until there were no more tears of bitterness or hurt left to shed—and strangely her spirits began to lift. In fact, by the time she reached the Archibald house, Whitney felt better than she had since "it" had happened.

Lord Archibald was away that evening so Whitney and Emily shared a cozy dinner in Whitney's room, and Whitney discovered she could actually enjoy herself again.

"You look remarkably restored tonight," Emily teased her, as she poured tea.

"I feel remarkably restored," Whitney said, smiling.

"Good," Emily replied. "Because there's something I want to ask you."

"Ask away," Whitney said, sipping her tea.

"My mother wrote me that you're betrothed to Paul Sevarin. Are you?"

"No—to Clayton Westmoreland," Whitney replied in quick defense.

A priceless antique tea cup slid through Emily's fingers and crashed to the floor. Her eyes widened, then grew wider still while a slow smile dawned across her pretty features. "You aren't . . . jesting?" she whispered.

Whitney shook her head.

"You're certain?"

"Very certain."

"I don't think I believe you," Emily said.

She looked so skeptical that Whitney's lips trembled with laughter. "Would you care to bet your new sable cape that I'm *not* betrothed to him?"

"Do you want it badly enough to lie?"

"Definitely. But I'm not lying."

"But how—when—did it happen?"

Whitney opened her mouth to explain, then changed her mind. She desperately needed to talk to someone about it, but she was afraid to begin. Today, for the first time in weeks, she had begun to feel alive again; she didn't want to risk her fragile, newfound tranquillity. "No, Emily," she said. "I don't think it's a good idea to talk about it." She got up nervously and Emily rose too, advancing on her with a determined, joyous smile.

"Well, you're going to!" Emily laughed softly. "You are going to tell me every single, tiny detail of this unbelievable romance if I have to wring it out of you with my own two hands. Now begin at the beginning."

Whitney started to refuse, but Emily looked so happy and so determined, that it was useless. Besides, she suddenly *wanted* to talk about it. She sat back down and Emily settled beside her. "I suppose it actually began several years ago, before my come-out," Whitney started. "Clayton said he saw me in a millinery shop with my aunt. The proprietress was trying to convince me to purchase a hideous bonnet covered with artificial fruit . . ."

At the end of the story Emily stared at her with a combination of mirth and wonder. "Oh lord," she whispered. "It's too delicious for words—and so romantic. Imagine, after spending all that money, he came to England only to discover that you were infatuated with Paul." She gulped down a giggle. "Michael was so worried that his grace would break your heart, but I wasn't. I saw the way he looked at you when he came to take you to the Rutherfords' ball, and I knew."

"You knew what?" Whitney asked.

"Why, that he is in love with you, silly!" Emily broke off in bewilderment. "But he hasn't been here in weeks, and I know he's in London because he's been seen at the opera and the theatre." She watched the familiar haunted expression return to Whitney's face. "Whitney?" she breathed. "What's wrong? You've looked like this ever since the night you didn't come home. What happened that night to make you so unhappy?"

"I don't want to discuss it," Whitney said hoarsely.

Emily took Whitney's cold hands in hers. "You *have* to talk about it, it's been tearing you apart. I'm not trying to pry; I already know you didn't tell the truth. You see, I was standing at the window the morning you returned, and I saw the gold crest on the coach that brought you back. It was the duke's coach, wasn't it?"

"You know it was," Whitney said, her head bent with shame.

"And I also know you left here with him—you said you did, and Carlisle said you did too. Although," she added with a bemused smile in her voice, "Carlisle was shockingly in his cups that night, and he kept insisting that the Duke of Claymore had descended from nowhere and forcibly dragged you off into the night. Of course, I didn't believe for a minute—oh dear lord!" she burst out. "*Is* that what happened? *Is* it?" she pleaded.

Whitney nodded.

"Where did he take you?" Emily demanded, her voice tight with apprehension. "Did he take you to another party?"

"No."

"I will never forgive myself for laughing at Carlisle," she

said, her hand tightening convulsively on Whitney's. "Whitney," she whispered painfully, "where did he take you? What did he do to you?"

A pair of vulnerable green eyes lifted to Emily's, and in them Emily saw the answer. "That monster!" she hissed, leaping to her feet. "That blackguard, that devil! He ought to be hung! He—" Emily stopped, obviously deciding that Whitney needed encouragement, not more fuel for her hurt and anger. "We have to look on the bright side of this."

"What 'bright side'?" Whitney said tiredly.

"It may not seem like it, but there is one. Just listen." Dropping to her knees, Emily took both Whitney's hands in her reassuring grasp. "I don't know much about the law, but I do know that your father can't force you to marry that . . . that monster! And after what he's done, Claymore must know you will never willingly marry him. Therefore, he has no choice but to release you from the betrothal agreement and forget about the money he gave your father."

Whitney's head jerked up. For long moments, she stared blankly at the wall across from her. Of course Clayton meant to release her. That must be why he hadn't come to see her. He was going to withdraw his offer. A strange, sick feeling swept over her at the thought. "No," she said firmly. "He won't withdraw his offer. I know he won't. Oh Emily," she cried, "do you truly think he'll just walk away and let me go?"

"Of course!" Emily promptly reassured. "What else can he possibly—" Emily's eyes widened on Whitney's unhappy face. "Whitney?" she gasped, slowly coming to her feet and staring down at her unhappy friend. "You cannot possibly mean— My God! You don't *want* him to let you go," she cried.

Whitney's gaze flew upward. "It's only that I never considered that he might release me."

"You don't want him to!" Emily persisted in rising tones. "It's written all over your face."

Whitney stood up too, nervously rubbing her palms against the folds of her dress. She willed herself to say she hoped above everything that Clayton Westmoreland would release her, but the words lodged in her throat. "I don't know what I want," she admitted miserably.

Emily dismissed that with a wave of her hand, her anxious eyes riveted on Whitney. "Has he sent word to you, or approached you in any way since that night?"

"No! And he had better not!"

"And you have no intention of trying to see him?"

"Certainly not," Whitney declared heatedly.

"He can't possibly approach you. First he would need some sign from you that you would at least listen to an apology. And you won't—can't—give him that sign, can you?"

"I would die first!" Whitney announced proudly, and she meant it.

"But if he cares for you at all, he will be filled with remorse for what he did. He'll think that you must loathe him."

Whitney walked over to the bed and leaned her forehead against the poster which supported the canopy. "He won't let me go, Emily," she said with more hope than regret in her voice. "I think he cares . . . cared . . . for me very much."

"Well!" Emily exploded. "He certainly has a peculiar way of showing his regard."

"So do I," Whitney whispered. "I constantly defied him. I would have shamed him in front of his friends by eloping with Paul. I never stopped lying to him." She closed her eyes and turned her head away. "If you don't mind," she said in a suffocated voice, "I'd like to go to bed now."

Emily went to bed too, but after lying awake for hours, she finally gave up trying to sleep. Propping up the pillows, she sat back, watching Michael as he slept peacefully beside her. "Could I still love you if you'd done that to me?" she whispered to his sleeping form. "Yes," she answered, tenderly smoothing the hair at his temple. "I could forgive you almost anything." But if Michael had done that, he would have an opportunity to make amends. They were married, and no matter how battered or angry she felt in spirit, they would still be forced to be in each other's company, in order to keep up appearances. Before long, matters would inevitably come to a head, and then the breach could be healed. But Whitney wasn't married to Claymore. They were both avoiding each other, and they would continue to do so. Whitney's pride and hurt would prevent her from making the first move, and the duke would continue to believe that she hated him and wanted nothing to do with him. Unless something brought them face to face—and soon—this breach could never be healed.

Torn between interfering in a highly explosive situation, or politely staying out of it, Emily pulled up her knees and perched her chin on them. After several minutes' contemplation, she slowly shoved the bedcovers aside. Trembling with guilt and uncertainty, she crept out of bed. Downstairs she groped in the darkness for a tinder and lit a candle, then she tiptoed into the yellow salon and put the candle on the desk while she searched through the drawers for one of the unused wedding invitations she'd helped Elizabeth address.

She slid into the chair and nibbled on the end of a quill, trying to think of what she could say. It was imperative that the duke not mistakenly believe she was acting on Whitney's instructions, for there was every likelihood that when Whitney first saw him she would turn on him in hurt outrage. The important thing was bringing them face to face and leaving the rest to fate.

Hastily, before she lost her courage and changed her mind, Emily wrote on the bottom of the invitation, "Someone we both care very much for will be in attendance on the bride this day." She signed it simply, "Emily Archibald."

A footman wearing vaguely familiar livery was shown into Clayton's library on Upper Brook Street. "I have an invitation which my mistress instructed be given directly to you, your grace," he explained.

Clayton was deeply engrossed in his morning correspondence. "Are you to await a response?" he asked absently.

"No, my lord."

"Then leave it there." Clayton nodded at a small table near the door.

He was getting dressed to go out for the evening when he recollected the envelope left lying in his library that morning. "Send someone for it, Armstrong," he murmured to his valet without looking away from the mirror which reflected the success of the intricate folds he was putting into his snowy neckcloth.

Clayton shrugged into the jacket Armstrong held for him, then he took the envelope a footman had just brought up. Opening it, he extracted what appeared to be yet another invitation for his secretary to attend to.

The name "Ashton" leapt out at him and his heart instantly contracted with painful memories. "Tell my secretary to decline, but to send an appropriate gift in my name," he said quietly, handing the invitation back to the footman.

As he passed it across, however, a tiny handwritten message along the bottom caught his eye. Clayton read it, then read it again, his pulse beginning to hammer. What in God's name was Emily trying to tell him? That Whitney wished to see him? Or that Emily wanted him to see her? Impatiently waving his valet and the footman away, he carried the invitation into his bedchamber and reread Emily's words three more times, growing more agitated with each reading. Futilely he tried to find something in the brief note to indicate that Whitney had forgiven him. But there was nothing.

That evening, Clayton sat through the play at the Crown Theatre paying no more attention to the raven-haired beauty beside him than he did to the performances on the stage. His emotions veered back and forth between hope and despair. There was nothing about Emily's note to give him any encouragement except that she had sent it to him. Emily Archibald and Whitney had been fast friends since childhood. If Whitney hated him, Emily would have discovered that by now, and she would never have sent him the invitation. On the other hand, if Whitney had forgiven him, she would have sent it to him herself.

Suppose Whitney didn't *want* to see him. Suppose she took one look at him in the church and fainted? A sad smile touched Clayton's eyes. Whitney might hurl her bouquet in his face, but she wouldn't faint. Not his brave, courageous girl.

Chapter Twenty-seven

At the back of the crowded church, Elizabeth Ashton stood with her father, watching her third bridal attendant drift slowly down the carpeted aisle, then she turned to Whitney who would be next. "You're going to steal the day from me," she smiled, surveying the yellow and white roses entwined in Whitney's lustrous hair and the flowing yellow velvet bridesmaid gown she wore. "You look like a jonquil in springtime."

Whitney laughed. "*You* look like an angel, and don't you dare try to begin another flattery contest with me. Besides, as a bride, you're supposed to be nervous. Isn't she, Emily?" Whitney whispered, looking over her shoulder at her friend, who would follow her down the aisle.

"I believe so," Emily said absently. This morning she had confessed to Michael that Whitney and the duke had had a dreadful rift (which was certainly the truth) and that she had invited the duke to the wedding in hopes of bringing them back together. Michael's reaction had been alarmingly unencouraging. He told her that she should not have interfered, that she might be doing both parties an injustice, and that, in the end, they might both despise her for her well-intentioned interference.

Now, Elizabeth was also involved in Emily's scheme. When the guest list was originally prepared, "Mr. Clayton Westland" had been on it, but at Whitney's panicked insistence, Elizabeth had removed his name. Three days ago, Emily told Elizabeth that a secret romance had been blossoming between Whitney and Mr. Westland, but that the couple had quarreled (which was also the truth). Elizabeth had delightedly agreed that sending him a secret invitation was a splendid way to effect a reconciliation. She still did not realize, of course, that Mr. Westland was actually the duke of Claymore, for despite her weeks spent in London, she moved in very different circles from the duke.

Today, Emily cursed her plan as the worst idea she'd ever had.

"You're next, Miss," Emily's maid told Whitney as she bent down and straightened Whitney's train.

The other bridesmaids had cringed in nervous terror from making the long, solitary walk down the aisle, but the prospect didn't bother Whitney in the least. She'd done it a dozen times in Paris for Thérèse DuVille and other friends, but today she felt especially joyous, for she had played a very large part in bringing this wedding about. With a breezy smile Whitney accepted her bouquet of yellow and white roses from the maid. "Elizabeth," she whispered affectionately, "when next we speak, you'll be married." And she stepped out into the aisle.

Clayton's gaze riveted on her the instant she stepped into view, and the sight of her had the devastating impact of a boulder crashing into his chest. Never had she looked so radiantly beautiful or so serene. She was a shaft of glowing moonlight moving down the center of the candlelit aisle.

He was standing only inches from her as she swept gracefully past him, and he felt as if he were stretched on the rack. Every muscle in his body tightened, straining to endure the torture of her nearness. But it was a torture he welcomed, an agony he didn't want to be spared.

Whitney took her appointed place at the front. She stood quietly through the ceremony but when Elizabeth began softly repeating her vows, the words held a poignancy for Whitney that she'd never felt before, and sentimental tears suddenly stung the backs of her eyes. Without turning her head more than an inch or two, Whitney could view half the audience in the church, and as her gaze touched the crowded rows, she noticed that most of the women were dabbing at their eyes. Aune Anne smiled a silent greeting. Whitney acknowledged it with an imperceptible tip of her head, feeling a surge of comfort at the sight of her aunt's reassuring face.

As the threat of tears passed, and the lump of emotion in her throat began to dissolve, Whitney let her eyes drift back over the rows of guests, past her father, past Margaret Merryton's parents . . . past Lady Eubank who was wearing one of her outrageous turbans . . . past a very tall, dark-haired man who . . . Whitney's heart gave a leap, missed a beat, then began to thump madly as a pair of penetrating gray eyes looked straight into hers. Paralyzed, she saw the bitter regret carved into his handsome features and the aching gentleness in his compelling eyes. And then she tore her gaze from his.

Dragging air into her constricted lungs, she stared blindly ahead. He was here! He had finally come to see her, she thought wildly. He couldn't be here to attend the wedding because he hadn't been invited to it. He was here! Here, looking at her in a way that he had never, *ever* looked at her before—it was as if he were offering himself to her! Standing very straight and very tall, he was humbly *offering* himself to her. She knew it, she could feel it.

Whitney wanted to scream, to drop to her knees and weep, to hurt him as he'd hurt her. Fury, humiliation, and wild uncertainty all collided into one another. This was her opportunity to repay him, she thought hysterically, to show him with a single contemptuous glance that she despised him. She might never have another chance. He hadn't tried to see her before this, and he would leave after the wedding; he couldn't attend the banquet without an invitation. Emily said he couldn't possibly approach her without some sign from her, and he was asking her for that sign now.

Oh God! He was silently asking for her forgiveness, standing there and offering himself to her. If her answer was no, he would walk out of this church when the wedding was over. And out of her life.

Whitney closed her eyes in an agony of indecision, not caring that Clayton would see her doing it and know the struggle raging within her. He had abused her body and ravaged her soul and he knew it! Her pride demanded that she look up at him and show him that she felt only contempt for him. But her heart screamed not to let him walk out of this church.

"Don't cry, darling," he whispered in her memory. *"Please don't cry anymore."*

Whitney couldn't breathe; she couldn't move. "Help me!" she prayed to someone. "Please, please, help me!" And then she realized that the "someone" she was praying to was Clayton. And she loved him.

The moment Whitney stirred, Clayton knew that she was going to face him, that his answer would be there. His knuckles whitened as he gripped the bench in front of him, bracing himself. Her eyes lifted to his and the gentle yielding in their melting green depths nearly sent him to his knees. He wanted to drown himself in her eyes, to pull her into his shaking arms, to carry her from the church and beg her to say aloud the same three words she had just spoken in silence.

Everyone rushed down the aisle behind the bridal procession, pushing and jostling gaily for position on the broad crowded steps outside. Clayton was the last to leave. He strolled slowly along beneath the high vaulted ceiling, his footsteps echoing hollowly in his ears. Outside the massive doors of the church, he stopped, watching Whitney smiling and nodding, her hair shining in the late afternoon sunlight. He hesitated, knowing that if he went to her now, they'd not be able to exchange more than a few words, yet he couldn't bring himself to wait until the banquet. Meeting as few eyes as possible to avoid being waylaid by any of his former "neighbors," he stepped into the crowd, wending his way toward Whitney until he was standing only an inch behind her.

Whitney instantly sensed his presence as if it were a tangible force, something powerful and magnetic. She even recognized the elusive, tangy scent of his cologne. But she scarcely recognized his voice; it was raw with emotion, a hoarse, aching whisper. "Miss Stone—I adore you."

The shattering tenderness of the words sent a jolting tremor up Whitney's spine, a reaction which was not lost on Clayton. He saw her stiffen, and for one chilling second he thought he'd only imagined what had passed between them in the church, but then she took an imperceptible step backward. Very lightly, he felt her lean against him. His breath froze at the exquisite sensation of her body pressing against him. He dropped his hand to her waist, gently sliding it around in front of her, drawing her nearer and tighter to him. And she made no resistance at all . . . but stood quietly in his embrace. Clayton's mind flew to the cleric in the church. If he led Whitney inside now, would she stand beside him like some gorgeous greenhouse flower and repeat the same words Elizabeth had just said? Would he need a special license?

With a sublime effort, he thrust the idea of marrying her now, today, out of his mind. Whitney would be a breathtaking bride and he'd not attempt to cheat her of her day of glory—he'd already cheated her of so much!

Emily turned to Whitney without seeming to notice that Clayton was standing shockingly close behind her friend, with his arm around her waist. "They're signalling us to go now," she said.

Whitney nodded but Clayton sensed her reluctance to leave him and he had to fight down the impulse to tighten his hand. Finally she stepped away, and without a backward glance, she melted swiftly into a flurry of bridesmaids.

Emily hesitated before climbing into the carriage behind Whitney. Turning, she looked for the duke and found his inscrutable gray eyes levelled on her. She smiled with shy uncertainty. He returned her hesitant greeting with a deep, formal bow, then he grinned at her, a broad, devastating grin filled with boyish gratitude.

"He was there!" Whitney blurted, twisting around in the carriage, her gaze fastened on the waning vision of Clayton who was still standing on the church steps, watching the Archibalds' carriage pull into traffic. "Did you see him?"

Laughter trembled on Emily's lips. "Indeed I did. He was standing right behind you with his arm around your waist."

"Please don't hate him for what he did," Whitney whispered. "I couldn't bear it if you hated him. Emily, I love him so much."

"I know you do," Emily said gently.

Clayton watched her carriage until it had disappeared from view, his heart filled to bursting. He knew why Whitney had never turned to face him. It was for the same reason he'd not told her that he loved her just now. Neither of them wanted to begin again, surrounded by a group of strangers.

Although some of the guests weren't strangers at all, Clayton finally noted, glancing around him. There were several people here whom he knew from London. Simultaneously, it dawned on him that the murmurings of the crowd were rising to a fever-pitch. He walked down the steps, past women who were beginning to curtsy to him and men who were respectfully murmuring, "Your grace . . ."

Clayton stopped in his tracks, staring at his coach which was pulled up smartly at the curb. The coach! In his agitated preoccupation with seeing Whitney again, he'd forgotten to tell McRea to use the plain black one which he'd purchased to use as Whitney's "neighbor."

Clayton turned to face his gaping former neighbors who had known him as "Mr. Westland." He looked at them ruefully, with a faint smile of wry apology for his deception. Then he climbed into a magnificent midnight-blue coach with his ducal seal emblazoned in shining silver on the door panel.

Whitney had arranged to spend the time between the wedding and the banquet with her aunt at the Archibalds' so that she could tell her aunt of the permanent estrangement between Clayton and herself. She had dreaded this meeting for weeks, but now she could scarcely wait to see her aunt.

"You are positively glowing!" Aunt Anne smiled, coming into the salon and hugging Whitney tightly. She stripped off her gloves and pulled Whitney down on the settee beside her. "Really, darling," she said with laughing severity, "I began to wonder if the two of you were going to be able to tear your eyes from one another in that church."

Whitney beamed. "I could never hide anything from you, could I?"

"Darling, you didn't manage to hide it from *anyone*. Half the people there were craning their necks to watch the two of you outside, after the wedding." Whitney looked so horrified that her aunt burst out laughing. "And you may as well know that there were at least two dozen people from London at the wedding who recognized him. The crowd started buzzing with his name the moment he walked into church. By the time I left, everybody knew who he was, including all your neighbors from home. I'm afraid 'Mr. Westland' has been unmasked."

Whitney heard that with an inward burst of pride. She wanted *everybody* to know who he was, and she wanted all of them to know she was betrothed to him. She wanted to shout it to the world!

They chatted gaily for an hour and a half before Whitney remembered to inquire about Uncle Edward.

"He's in Spain," her aunt said with a tolerant smile. "His two letters were almost as uninformative as yours are, but I gathered that there was some calamity brewing there, and he was dispatched with haste and secrecy to try to smooth matters before they got out of hand. He promised to be here in six weeks. Apparently none of my letters ever reached him."

After a moment, she said, "Would you mind very much if I didn't attend the banquet tonight? I only came to the wedding because you never mentioned Claymore in your letters, and I wanted to see for myself how the two of you were getting on. Since it's obvious that you're both in perfect accord, I would like to start back to Lincolnshire at once. My cousin is a sweet, helpless creature, and she's become quite dependent on me for company. As soon as you and his grace decide to put London out of its suspense and announce your betrothal, I'll return and we can start preparing for your wedding."

The day fled so quickly that Whitney could hardly believe it when it was time to hug her aunt goodbye. "By the way," Aunt Anne said, lingering at the front door. "Your father brought two more trunks of your clothes. I sent them upstairs and Clarissa is unpacking them. Oh—and your father said there's some mail for you, too."

Whitney flew upstairs and slid into the chair at the dressing table. While Clarissa fussed with the roses in her hair, Whitney joyously imagined her reunion with Clayton tomorrow. He would come to see her early, of course, and they . . . She noticed the thick packet propped against her mirror. She picked it up and opened it, dreamily extracting some official-looking documents. At first glance they were filled with so many "parties of the first part" and "parties of the second part," and "whereas's" and "wherefore's," that Whitney thought the packet must have been intended for Lord Archibald and put in her room by mistake. She flipped to the last page and a signature leapt out at her: Clayton Robert Westmoreland, Ninth Duke of Claymore. Dismissing Clarissa, she slowly began to read the documents.

They set out in cold legal terms that she was no longer betrothed to the Duke of Claymore, that his offer of marriage was herewith withdrawn, and that whatever "monies, jewels, considerations, tokens, etc.," the Stone family had received from the duke were to be retained by them and considered as gifts.

Whitney's hand shook violently as she unfolded a note in Clayton's bold handwriting enclosed with the documents: "Please accept my sincere wishes for your happiness and convey them to Paul. The enclosed bank draft is intended as a present." A bank draft for £10,000 slid from Whitney's numb fingers onto the floor while nausea surged in her throat. Clayton had used her to satisfy his vengeance and lust. Now he was paying her off with a generous check as if she were a common trollop or one of his mistresses, and suggesting that she give her soiled body to Paul in marriage. "Oh my God!" Whitney whispered. "Oh my God!"

Emily tapped on her door and asked if she were ready to leave.

"I'll be down in a few minutes," Whitney called hoarsely. "Emily," she added, dragging her voice through the constricted pain in her chest. "Do . . . do you know how the duke came to be at the wedding? I mean, did Elizabeth decide to invite him, after all?"

Emily sounded both guilty and gay. "Yes. And aren't you glad now that she did?"

The room reeled and tilted. Whitney started to lurch from her chair, thinking that she was going to be ill, but her legs refused to move. Gulping long uneven breaths of air, she stayed where she was. The tumultuous upheaval settled slowly, leaving a dull, throbbing ache that was intensified with every moment.

Clayton hadn't come to the wedding to see her, he'd been invited! Whitney realized with a blinding streak of suffocating humiliation. Since his note and documents were dated weeks ago, he would naturally think she'd known about them today, when she saw him. Wild, hysterical laughter welled up within her. He had simply been attending the wedding—and how gratified he must have been when she had smiled adoringly at him!

She hadn't merely *smiled* at him, Whitney remembered with a fresh streak of mortified fury—she had *leaned* against him! She had let him put his arm around her and hold her! And that vile, conceited, arrogant lecher probably thought she was inviting him to use her body again! He was probably planning to take her home with him after the banquet and, considering the way she had acted, he would be confident she was willing to go.

The banquet. Whitney put her face in her hands and moaned aloud. Clayton was going to be at the banquet. She would have to face him there.

When she joined Emily and her husband downstairs, Whitney was a little pale and there was a suspicious sheen in her eyes, but her head was high and her delicate chin was stubbornly set. Outwardly she was composed and very calm —but it was the deadly calm that precedes a hurricane while it gathers force, preparing to strike.

The first thing she did when she arrived at the huge home of Elizabeth's paternal grandparents, was to smile her very best smile at the two handsomest groomsmen. Clayton had accused her once of trying to collect as many fawning admirers as she could squeeze around her skirts, and for a beginning, that was exactly what she intended to do.

As she stood between both groomsmen in the receiving line, she spoke to each guest as they made their way past—but if the guest happened to be a bachelor, Whitney was her most dazzlingly vivacious self. Within fifteen minutes, she had caused a tie-up in the proceedings, and she was surrounded by six gentlemen all of whom were vying for her attention. Only once did her composure slip a notch, and that was when Paul bent over her hand. Her bright smile faded uncertainly as she gazed into his handsome face, but he looked so sheepish and so contrite, that she immediately decided to add him to her entourage. Tightening her fingers a little on his, she drew Paul into the circle of men surrounding her.

Now she was fortified, surrounded. Insulated from Clayton. For the moment, this was all she needed.

Clayton arrived just as the receiving line disbanded. He paused in the doorway, his tall, commanding frame clad in an elegantly tailored black suit and waistcoat. Whitney watched his glance slide over the guests, then instantly halt when it reached her. A rosy peach tint suffused her high cheekbones as she shifted her gaze from Clayton to the men around her. "We are quite ignoring the bride," she teased with a gorgeous smile, and without a backward glance she led her entourage toward Elizabeth.

Clayton was positive she had seen him, and his eyes darkened with surprise and puzzlement as he watched her walk away. After a moment, he realized that Whitney had an obligation to attend the bride, and he felt slightly better, but as he watched her laughing gaily with the men who trailed after her, no dammit, *flirting* with them, his patience began to fray.

A footman appeared beside him bearing a tray, and Clayton took a glass of champagne, his hungry gaze following Whitney. She knew he was here, and she was obviously waiting for the appropriate moment to come to him. He ached to touch her, longed to hear the soft music of her voice, had been driven half out of his mind these past two hours just thinking of being near her again.

Dinner was announced, but Clayton hung back, hoping that Whitney might come to him before she went in to the banquet. "Ah—Claymore! Good to see you again," a jovial masculine voice said at his elbow.

Clayton glanced briefly at the short, elderly man beside him, recognizing him as Lord Anthony, an old friend of his father's.

"How's your lovely mother?" Lord Anthony asked, sipping from his champagne.

Clayton watched Whitney walk into the banquet room; she was *not* going to come to him. "She's well," he answered absently. "And yours?"

"I imagine she's about the same," Lord Anthony replied. "She's been dead for thirty years."

"Good," Clayton said. "Glad to hear it." He put his glass down and strolled off to take his assigned place at one of the banquet tables.

In the true spirit of a matchmaker, Elizabeth had contrived to place Clayton at the table facing the bridal party's, directly across from Whitney. Clayton ate little of his meal, and what he did eat, he couldn't taste. He was too preoccupied with an elusive and beautiful young woman who owned his heart, but who seemed either afraid, or unwilling, to meet his gaze. He watched her chatting playfully with the groomsmen on either side of her, winding them around her slender fingers, and jealousy pulsed through his veins.

To add to his mounting frustration, he was seated between two matrons who had discovered his title and immediately singled him out as a prospective husband for their unmarried daughters. "My Marie plays the pianoforte like an angel," one mother said. "You must come to one of our musicales, your grace."

"My Charlotte sings like a bird!" the other mother instantly countered.

"I'm tone deaf," Clayton drawled without taking his eyes from Whitney.

After what seemed like an eternity, the guests adjourned to the ballroom. Peter guided Elizabeth to the center of the floor and they danced together, their fine young bodies moving in perfect harmony with each other, then the newly married couple was joined by the bridal party, who also danced together. When the required first dance was finished, Clayton waited for Whitney to come to him. Instead she drifted into the arms of another groomsman, and then another, smiling into their eyes in a way that made Clayton want to wring her neck!

She was dancing the fourth dance with Paul Sevarin, when it finally dawned on Clayton that Whitney was waiting for *him* to come to *her*, and he was dumbstruck at his own stupidity. She had taken the first step toward a reconciliation at the church, and naturally she expected *him* to take the next one.

The instant the dance ended, Clayton strode directly to her. "Good to see you again, Sevarin," he lied politely as he firmly placed Whitney's hand on his arm. "I believe the next dance is mine," he added, covering her long fingers with his and drawing Whitney onto the dance floor.

Although she didn't object, Clayton was a little taken aback by the courteous, but impersonal smile she gave him as she turned into his arms for the waltz.

She was slimmer than before, and Clayton drew her protectively closer to him. It was *his* fault that she had lost weight. "Are you enjoying yourself?" he asked, his voice unfamiliar to her with its tone of tenderness and guilt.

Whitney nodded brightly. She nodded because she couldn't trust her voice. From the moment he had walked into this house, her senses had been screamingly aware of his presence. She felt as if she were dying inside, slowly and painfully suffocating. He had stolen her virginity and then coldly withdrawn his offer of marriage, suggested calmly that she marry Paul and then tossed his money in her face to appease her. And even so, it was all she could do not to humble herself at his feet, to plead with him to tell her *why,* to beg him to want her again. Only one thing kept her silent and upright: pride—outraged, stubborn, courageous, abused pride. Her face ached with the effort it took to smile, but she had been smiling all night, and she was going to keep right on doing it until Clayton walked out of this room. And then she was going to die.

For the first time since he had met her, Clayton didn't know what to say to her. He felt as if he were in a dream, and he was afraid to speak lest he say the wrong thing and break the spell. He thought of apologizing for ravaging her, but in view of the crime he had committed against her an apology was ludicrously inadequate. What he really wanted to say was, "Marry me tomorrow," but having already deprived her of her wedding night, Clayton was resolutely determined that she would have a spectacular wedding, complete with all the splendor and trappings, all the glittering pomp and circumstance, that she was entitled to enjoy as the bride of a duke.

Since he couldn't beg her forgiveness, or ask her to marry him at once, he decided to say the only other thing that mattered to him. Gazing down at her bent head, he said the words he had never spoken to another woman. Very quietly and very tenderly, he said, "I love you."

He felt the emotional impact his words had on her because she went rigid in his arms, but when she lifted her beautiful face the laughter in her expression almost made him stumble.

"I am not in the least surprised to hear it," she teased breezily. "I seem to be all the rage this season—particularly with tall men." She tipped her head to the side, considering the possible reasons for such a thing. "I believe it is probably because I am rather tall for a woman. It must be quite awkward for tall men to be forever bent over, trying to speak to tiny women. Or," she added jokingly, "it could be because I have very good teeth. I take excellent care of them and—"

"Don't!" Clayton commanded, trying to stop her banter.

"I shall never brush them again," Whitney agreed with sham solemnity.

Clayton gazed down at her entrancing cream and roses face and wondered how in the hell he had started to speak of love and ended up in an inane discussion of personal hygiene. If his emotions weren't in such a turmoil, if he weren't trying so desperately to make things right between them, he would have noticed that her overbright eyes were sparkling with suppressed tears, not laughter, and that the muscles in her slim throat were constricting spasmodically. But he *was* in a turmoil, and he *didn't* notice. "Elizabeth is a beautiful bride," he said, trying to guide their discussion around to marriage.

Whitney laughed. *"All* brides are beautiful. It was decreed centuries ago—by a duke, no doubt—that all brides *must* be beautiful. And blush."

"Will you blush?" he asked tenderly.

"Certainly not," she said, managing to smile despite the catch in her voice. "I have nothing left to blush about. Not that I mind, you see, because I've always harbored a secret contempt for females who blush and swoon at the slightest provocation."

Clayton's frustrated confusion reduced his voice to a tense whisper. "What's wrong? You weren't like this when you were in my arms outside the church—"

Whitney's jade green eyes widened in apparent bewilderment. "Was that *you?*"

Ignoring the wild curiosity they were generating among the wedding guests, Clayton jerked her hard against his chest. "Who in the living hell did you think it was?"

Whitney felt as if her heart was breaking. "Actually, I couldn't be absolutely certain *who* it was. It might have been . . ." She inclined her head toward the two groomsmen who'd been dancing attendance on her all night. "John Clifford or Lord Gilmore. They say they 'adore' me. Or it might have been Paul. He 'adores' me. Or it could have been Nicki, he—"

In one swift motion, Clayton whirled her off the dance floor and thrust her away. He stared down at her with cold savage contempt, his voice dangerously low, hissing with fury. "I thought you were a woman with a heart, but you're nothing but a common flirt!"

Whitney lifted her chin in scornful amusement. "I'd hardly say I was *common;* after all, I've fleeced you out of £110,000, and even so, all I have to do is smile, and you still come straight to heel, just as you did today. We are neither of us common, my lord," she taunted. "I am an *accomplished* flirt and *you* are a sublime fool."

For a split second, Whitney thought he was going to strike her. Instead he turned on his heel and strode swiftly away. She watched him stalk past the staring guests, past the servants stationed at the doors and knew that he had just left her life forever. Forcing back her damned up tears, she searched the crowd for Emily. "Emily," she mumbled brokenly, keeping her face down, "please explain to Elizabeth that I—I felt quite violently ill. I'll—I'll send your driver back with your carriage as soon as he leaves me at your house."

"I'll come with you," Emily said quickly.

"No, I prefer to be alone. I have to be alone."

Later that night Emily and Michael both paused outside Whitney's door, listening to the wrenching sound of grief being poured into a pillow. "Let her be," Michael advised compassionately. "She'll cry it all out of her system."

However, when Whitney failed to appear for breakfast the next morning, Emily went up to her room and found her sitting in bed, her knees drawn up to her chest as if she were trying to curl into a cocoon. She looked pale and fragile but when she saw Emily, she managed a wan smile. "How do you feel?" Emily asked softly.

"I—I'm much better today."

"Whitney, what happened last—"

"Don't!" Whitney implored tightly. "Please don't." When Emily nodded, the tension in Whitney's face gave way to gratitude and she relaxed against the pillows. "I've decided to begin enjoying the remainder of my time in London. Would you object if I had callers in occasionally?"

"Of course not. In fact, Lord Gilmore and the other groomsmen are downstairs right now, hoping to see you." Despite Emily's determined cheerfulness, her voice wavered and she sat down beside Whitney, putting her arm around her. "Michael and I both want you to stay with us as long as you can. He understands that you're more like my sister than my friend."

Whitney gave her a hard hug and tried to laugh. "Sisters argue abominably. Friends are better."

Chapter Twenty-eight

THAT DAY BEGAN A MONTH OF FRENETIC SOCIAL ACTIVITY FOR Whitney. With courage and determination, she purposely kept herself too busy to think. Each night she fell into bed exhausted, and slept until it was time to dress for the next day's engagements. Nicki was her favorite and most frequent escort, but two of the groomsmen and the other eligible gentlemen she'd met at Emily's party and Elizabeth's wedding were frequently at her side, as well. With Emily normally acting as chaperone, she was escorted to rout parties, to musicales, the opera, the theatre, and balls. And she met more eligible men at those places, who then appeared with gratifying predictability at the Archibald townhouse to invite her to more parties and more balls.

If Paris had welcomed her, London embraced her with outstretched arms, for her charm and her wit were even more rare here. Whispers began and heads turned when she walked into a room. Her humor was softer now, and shy men who would have been terrified to approach her before, flocked around her.

She was courted and sought after. And she was unhappy beyond words.

She was never alone. And she was never at peace.

Occasionally at one of these functions, Whitney would hear Clayton's name mentioned, and she would die a little inside.

But no one who saw her dazzling smile brighten even more would have guessed she cared.

Only once during that first month did Whitney even come close to encountering Clayton. The young viscount who was her escort for that particular evening handed her into his closed carriage and announced with obvious pride that to-night he was going to escort her to "the ball of the year," then he had turned to his coachman and instructed, "Number 10 Upper Brook Street."

The address struck Whitney like a pitcher of ice water in her face. Number 10 Upper Brook Street was Clayton's London address, the address he'd given her long ago, in case she wanted to reach him. "I detest large parties," she desperately informed him. "They give me the vapors!"

"But Claymore gives the best parties in London!" he objected with equal vehemence. "And last week, you said you adored large parties."

"That was last week. This week the noise makes me quite ill!"

The viscount undoubtedly found her recently acquired allergy to noise rather extraordinary, but Miss Stone was beautiful and entertaining. And very popular. He took her to the opera instead.

That marked the end of Whitney's good fortune: she saw Clayton the following night. She was at the theatre with Nicki, seated in a private box with an excellent view of the stage and the five tiers of seats above it. Just before the play began, her curl caught in her amethyst brooch, and Nicki leaned across to help untangle it. As he did so, Whitney's gaze wandered aimlessly across the crowd—then riveted in stricken paralysis on Clayton and Vanessa Standfield, who were just entering a box nearby which was already occupied by the Rutherfords. Clayton's hand was resting familiarly on Vanessa Standfield's waist as the two couples exchanged gay greetings. Unable to tear her eyes away, Whitney watched them take their seats. She saw Vanessa speak to Clayton, who leaned closer, the better to hear her, and whatever she said to him made him throw back his head and burst out laughing.

Her body trembling violently, Whitney watched as the

Rutherfords turned to Clayton and Vanessa, obviously curious about the reason for his hilarity. Clayton spoke, and he must have repeated what Vanessa said, because Vanessa blushed gorgeously, and the Rutherfords also joined in the laughter.

In the rows of seats below and the tiers above, heads were twisting and turning, and Whitney heard the murmurings about "Claymore" and "his grace" and "the duke." Clayton's presence in the theatre (and Vanessa's with him) was being duly noted by all.

"Chérie, are you ill?" Nicki asked, frowning at Whitney's paleness.

Thinking that she was going to be sick, Whitney started to rise. As she did so, Clayton glanced up and saw her. His eyes turned as flinty as steel, and his expression changed from icy distaste to bored contempt. And then he simply looked away.

Whitney told herself that she had to stay in that box until the play was over, that she wouldn't, *wouldn't* let Clayton see that she was affected by his presence. She left ten minutes after the curtain went up. She left because tears had started to stream down her cheeks, and because she was so jealous, so unbearably, agonizingly, helplessly jealous that she couldn't bear to remain.

Two nights later, Nicki escorted her to their second party of the evening. Arriving extremely late, Whitney handed her fur cape to the butler, then took Nicki's arm as he led her through the throngs of departing guests who were all waiting for their conveyances to be brought round. Near the rear of the group, Whitney saw Clayton helping Vanessa with her wrap, grinning down at her in that bold, intimate way of his, and her fingers tightened convulsively on Nicki's arm.

"Where are you leading me next, my lord?" Vanessa asked Clayton as Whitney tried helplessly to move past them.

"Astray," Clayton told her with a blunt chuckle. He glanced up and saw Whitney standing directly in front of him, but this time Clayton didn't bother to communicate his loathing. He merely looked through her as if she didn't exist for him, and then he turned his attention back to Vanessa.

On a cold, blustery December afternoon two weeks later,

Nicki proposed. Without flowery, fervent professions of his affection, Nicki gathered a pale Whitney into his arms and said simply, "Marry me, love."

His quiet offering of himself nearly destroyed Whitney's fragile grip on her emotions. "I—I can't, Nicki," she whispered, trying to smile at him despite the tears gathering in her eyes. "I wish with all my heart that I loved you, but it would be wrong for me to marry you, feeling the way I do."

"I know exactly how you feel, cherie," he said gently, tipping her chin up. "But I'm willing to gamble that if you marry me and come back to France, I can make you forget him."

Whitney reached up and laid her hand against his jaw. Nicki had been someone she could count on and trust. If she refused him now, he would leave, but she couldn't bring herself to give him false hope. "My dear, good friend," she whispered brokenly. "I will love you forever, but always as my friend." Tears glittered on her long lashes, and Whitney's voice shook. "I cannot tell you how . . . how honored I am that you would have me for your wife . . . or how much you have meant to me these past years. Oh Nicki, thank you. Thank you—for being all the things you are." Pulling out of his arms, she turned and fled.

She ran blindly up the stairs, holding back her tears until she heard the front door close behind him. And then they came, streaming down her cheeks as she covered her face with her hands and rushed past Emily and Michael's open door, down the hall to the bedroom which had become her private hell, to weep out the misery which seemed to have no end.

Emily turned on Michael, her eyes wide with alarm. "Dear God!" she cried. "What could have happened now? If Clayton Westmoreland has done anything else to her, I'll strangle him with my bare hands."

Michael drew Emily back into their bedroom and firmly closed the door. "Emily," he said cautiously, "Claymore married Vanessa Standfield at her home four days ago. Everyone who is in a position to know has been talking about it."

"I refuse to believe it!" Emily burst out. "Ever since I came to London years ago, I've heard endless gossip about him, and it's scarcely ever been true."

"Perhaps. But this time *I* believe it. And whether it's true or not, what difference does it make? Whitney has forgotten him completely these last weeks."

"Oh, Michael!" Emily said miserably. "How can you be so utterly blind?" Without waiting for her stunned husband to reply, she pulled the door open and walked determinedly down the hall to the blue guest bedroom. She tapped once on Whitney's door and when there was no answer, boldly opened it and stepped into the room. Whitney was lying in a crumpled heap on the bed, her eyes tightly closed, her face streaked with tears.

"Why are you crying?" Emily asked in a kind but firm tone.

Whitney's eyes flew open and she sat up in embarrassed surprise, groping for her handkerchief. "It seems to be the thing I do best lately," she said ruefully, dabbing at her eyes.

"This is the silliest thing I've ever heard. I've known you since we were babies, and I can't ever remember you shedding so much as one tear until a few weeks ago. Now, Miss Stone," she demanded, *"why* are you crying?"

"Nicki proposed," Whitney sighed, too exhausted to try to evade the question.

"Which made you so happy that you burst into tears?"

Whitney smiled but there was a catch in her voice. "I seem to have a difficult time coping with marriage proposals. You would think, with as must practice as I had in France, that I—"

"What happened to the last one?" Emily interrupted flatly.

Whitney looked at her in silence for a long moment, then she shrugged and looked away. "Clayton didn't want to marry me, after all."

"Oh rubbish! How can you expect me to believe such flummery? I've seen the way that man looks at you."

Whitney dragged herself off the bed and went over to the little French desk from which she extracted the packet Clayton had sent her. Without a word, she handed it to Emily.

Emily sank into a chair as she began to read. Her face registered no particular reaction when she read the legal documents, but she frowned at the bank draft, and rolled her eyes in absolute disgust when she read Clayton's note. "Really!" she exclaimed in wry exasperation. "Sending you this note was too foolish for words. If he wasn't drunk as a wheelbarrow when he wrote it I can't think what was wrong with his brain. But what has all this—" she gestured to the pile of papers—"to do with the way you behaved at Elizabeth's banquet? I saw the way you avoided and ignored him."

"I should have avoided him at the church!" Whitney said feelingly. "And I would have, except that I thought we were still betrothed. I—I didn't know about these papers until we came back here after the wedding. They were with the things my father sent from home."

"Surely you aren't upset because the duke withdrew his offer? It would seem to me he acted correctly, knowing that he had wronged you—and believing that you could never forgive him. I'm certain he was only trying to excuse you from an obligation he believed would be repugnant to you."

Whitney gaped at her. "How can you be so gullible? Emily, he dragged me to his bed and stole my honor, then he gave me a bank draft to pay me off, broke our betrothal, and sent me a note suggesting I marry Paul!"

"I suppose," Emily sighed, "that were I as emotionally involved as you are, I might feel the same way. But please, just for the sake of argument, forget about the bank draft. That was too foolish for words—and very generous of him, too." Whitney opened her mouth to object angrily, but Emily shook her head and firmly interrupted her. "Whitney, I saw him at the church, *after* he sent you these papers. He loved you—a fool could have seen that. He stood in that church worshiping you!"

Whitney leapt to her feet. "He stood in that church because Elizabeth invited him to her wedding. And if I'd known it at the time, I wouldn't have made such a horrid fool of myself and—"

"Elizabeth didn't invite him," Emily said guiltily. "*I* did. I sent him a note on the bottom of one of Elizabeth's invitations telling him that you were going to be there. And he came because he wanted to see you. He scarcely knew Elizabeth and Peter, and I doubt he attends weddings of distant acquaintances he doesn't care in the least about."

Whitney looked as if she were either going to faint or scream. "You told him?! But why—why would you do that to me? He surely thought I had put you up to it."

Emily shook her head. "He couldn't have thought anything of the sort. I simply told him that you were going to be there. And he came because you were. Whitney, listen to me. He came *after* he signed those documents; *after* he wrote that note, which, by the way, seems to me to have been only foolish and not vile; and *after* he sent you the bank draft."

A torrent of conflicting emotions battered Whitney as Emily went determinedly on. "He probably knew that Paul's circumstances are very strained. Everyone in the village knew it but you."

"He knew," Whitney admitted. "He was in my father's study the night *I* found out about Paul's problems."

"And he also knew you wanted to marry Paul?"

Whitney nodded.

"Whitney, for the love of heaven, can't you see what he was trying to do? He thought you hated him and he knew you wanted to marry Paul, so he sent you this . . . this *fortune* to help make your life easier. He gave you money to help make your life better with the man you preferred to him. Dear God! He must have loved you even more than *I* thought, to do a thing like this."

Whitney snorted derisively and looked away, but Emily marched to the bed where she sat, and plunked her fists on her slim hips. "Whitney, I think you are a fool! You love that man—you told me so yourself, so don't deny it. And he loved you. He offered for you, he assisted your father when he didn't have to, then he stood by while you flirted with Paul and did a hundred other things that had to provoke him beyond words. What did you say to him at the banquet?" she demanded.

Whitney's eyes flew to Emily's face, then slid away. In a

small voice she answered, "I mocked him when he said he loved me."

"You mocked him?" Emily gasped. "Why in heaven's name would you do such a thing after standing in his arms on the church steps?"

"Please!" Whitney cried in agitation, leaping to her feet. "I told you why. Because I had just gotten the documents and his note and his wretched bank draft. Because I thought he had merely been attending Elizabeth's wedding and I had practically thrown myself at his feet!"

"And now I suppose you think he'll come crawling to you?"

Whitney shook her head and stared at the floor. "No. When he sees me he acts as if I don't exist."

"What else would you expect him to do? He loved you enough to want to marry you and he gave your father a fortune. He loved you so much he committed a terrible act out of jealousy, so much that he gave you up, hoping to make you happy, so much that he came to Elizabeth's wedding to be near you. But believe me, he will not come near you again!"

A kaleidoscope of disbelief, misery, loneliness, and despair hurtled through Whitney's mind—but the fragile hope Emily had given her burst like white sunshine in the midst of it all. She bent her head and her hair tumbled forward over her shoulders, concealing her face. In a pained, choked voice, she said, "However will I get him back without crawling to *him?*"

A smile of joyous relief flashed across Emily's features. "Actually, I'm afraid that's the only way. You trampled his pride every time you had the opportunity. Your pride is going to have to suffer now."

"I'll—I'll think about it," Whitney whispered.

"You do that," Emily applauded, cautiously laying down her trump card. "And while you're thinking about it, consider how you're going to feel when he marries Vanessa Standfield. The gossips say he already has—but they are never entirely accurate. Probably, he is *about* to marry her."

Whitney leapt to her feet. "What can I do? I can't think where to begin."

Emily hid her smile as she walked to the door. "You will have to go to him and explain why you behaved in such a freakish way at the banquet."

"No," Whitney said, frantically shaking her head. "I'll send him a note and ask him to come here."

"You can. But he won't do it. Which will only make it doubly embarrassing when you have to go to him anyway. Provided, of course, that in the meantime he doesn't marry Miss Standfield."

Whitney flew to the desk and snatched up her notepaper, but after Emily left she paused to think. There *had* to be some way to make Clayton come to her, some ruse she could use. It was too humiliating to crawl to him, particularly when he was on the verge of marrying Vanessa Standfield. After several thoughtful minutes, her eyes widened with inspiration and her cheeks pinkened with embarrassment. There *was* a way—it was a horrid deception, but she was in no position to quibble over niceties now. Clayton had taken her to his bed and if—*if* he believed he had gotten her with child, then he couldn't possibly refuse to come to see her. And what's more, he certainly couldn't marry Miss Vanessa Standfield! Not only that, he would also have to marry Whitney immediately! But if he loved her as much as Emily thought he did, then surely after they were married, he would forgive her for deceiving him.

Whitney wrote the date on the note, then paused. What sort of salutation was appropriate to use when addressing a man who never wanted to hear from her again, but who was to be informed he was the father of her forthcoming baby? "Dear Sir?" Hardly! "Your grace?" Ridiculous. "Clayton?" Not under these circumstances. Whitney decided to omit the salutation completely. She thought for another minute and then wrote: "To my very great mortification, I find I am with child. Therefore, I ask that you call upon me here at once." She signed it "Whitney," then reread it.

Her faced burned with shame. It was degrading and, because it wasn't true, it was contemptible as well. It was also nearly impossible for Clayton to have fathered a child in the incomplete act, but Whitney was blissfully unaware of that.

She called Emily and, blushing to the roots of her hair, she showed the note to her. "I—I'm not certain I could send it, even if it were true," Whitney said with a shudder, shoving the hateful thing in a box of unused stationery to prevent its discovery by a servant.

"Whitney," Emily said firmly, "send a note saying that you wish to speak to him and would prefer to do it in the privacy of his home, rather than in the busy confines of this one. Tell him that you will come there tomorrow. It's as simple as that."

"It isn't 'as simple as that,'" Whitney argued, staring apprehensively at the blank piece of notepaper. "Even if Clayton agrees to see me, there's every chance he'll let me apologize and then send me away. You can't imagine how awesome he is when he's angry."

"Then don't even try to see him. He'll marry Vanessa Standfield, and if Michael and I are invited to the wedding, I'll tell you all about it."

With that motivation, Whitney's quill fairly flew across the paper, and the note was dispatched to Number 10 Upper Brook Street with a footman who was instructed to learn from one Mr. Hudgins, the Duke of Claymore's secretary, where the duke was and then to deliver the note to that place.

The footman returned within the hour. The duke, he said, had been away from home visiting Lord and Lady Standfield, however his grace was returning to his estate at Claymore late this evening. Mr. Hudgins, who was leaving to join him there, had taken the note and promised to give it to the duke as soon as he saw him tonight.

In the note Whitney had told Clayton that if she didn't hear from him by noon the next day, she would assume that he was willing to see her at five o'clock in the afternoon. Now there was nothing for her to do but wait out the torturous hours until noon tomorrow.

Chapter Twenty-nine

AT PRECISELY ELEVEN O'CLOCK THE FOLLOWING MORNING, FOUR elegant travelling chaises swept through the gates of Claymore. The first was occupied by the Dowager Duchess of Claymore and her son Stephen. The second by Stephen's valet and the duchess's personal maids. The remaining two were filled to capacity with trunks of clothing and accessories which the dowager duchess deemed absolutely essential for any extended visit—particularly when one expected to meet one's new daughter-in-law, i.e., the future mother of one's grandchildren.

"It's always been so lovely here," her grace sighed, letting her gaze roam appreciatively over the vast estate's manicured lawns and formal parks which paraded majestically on both sides of the curving, paved road. Pulling her gaze from the familiar scenery, she gave her son a penetrating look. "You're quite certain that your brother is bringing me a daughter-in-law to meet tonight?"

Stephen grinned at her. "I can only tell you what I know, darling. Clay's note said simply that Vanessa and he had remained an extra night with her parents but that they would both join us here at four-thirty this afternoon."

"He only referred to her as 'Vanessa'?" her ladyship said. "Are you certain he meant Vanessa Standfield?"

Stephen sent her a wry look. "If the rumor mill is to be believed, her name is now Westmoreland."

"I saw her years ago. She was a beautiful child."

"She's a beautiful woman," Stephen said with a roguish grin. "Very blond, very blue eyes, very everything."

"Good. Then I will have beautiful grandchildren," the duchess predicted happily, her thoughts ever reverting to that. Glancing sideways, she discovered her son frowning out the coach window. "Stephen, is there something about her you don't like?"

Stephen shrugged. "Only that her eyes aren't green and her name doesn't happen to be Whitney."

"Who? Oh, Stephen, that's ridiculous. What can you be thinking of? Why the girl, whoever she was, made him positively miserable. He's obviously forgotten all about her, and that's for the best."

"She's not that easy to forget," Stephen said with a grim smile.

"What do you mean?" she demanded suspiciously. "Stephen, have you met that girl?"

"No, but I saw her at a ball at the Kingsleys' a few weeks ago. She was surrounded by London's 'most eligibles,' excluding Clay, of course. When I heard her name was Whitney and saw those eyes of hers, I knew who she was."

The duchess started to demand a description of the young woman who had brought such torment to her eldest son, then dismissed the idea with a shrug. "That's all over now. Clayton is bringing home his wife."

"I can't think he'd so easily forget someone who meant so much to him. And I can't believe Clay is bringing home a wife. More likely a fiancée."

"I almost hope you're right. There'll be the very devil to pay if Clayton married Miss Standfield so abruptly. The gossip will be terrible."

Stephen gave her a mocking, sideways glance. "Clay

wouldn't care two hoots about the gossip, as you well know."

"Time to get up," Emily announced gaily, throwing back the curtains. "It's past noon and there's been no word from his grace telling you to stay away."

"I didn't go to sleep until dawn," Whitney mumbled, then she sat bolt upright in bed, catapulting from deep sleep to total awareness in the space of an instant. "I can't do it!" she cried.

"Of course you can. Just swing your feet over the side of the bed. It works every time," Emily teased.

Whitney pushed the covers aside and slid from the bed, her mind groping frantically for ways to extricate herself from the arranged meeting with Clayton. "Why don't we spend the day shopping and see that new play at the Royal?" she suggested desperately.

"Why don't we wait until tomorrow and begin shopping for your trousseau instead?"

"We are both candidates for Bedlam!" Whitney cried. "This entire scheme is insane. He won't listen to me, and even if he does, it won't change anything. I've seen the way he looks at me now—he despises me."

Emily shoved her in the direction of the bath. "That's encouraging. At least he feels *something* for you." She came back, just as Whitney finished dressing.

"How do I look?" Whitney asked uncertainly, turning in a slow circle for Emily's inspection. Her gown of rich aquamarine velvet had long sleeves and a low square-cut bodice. Her heavy mahogany hair had been brushed until it shone, then pulled back off her forehead, and fastened at the crown with an aquamarine and diamond clip, letting the rest fall in natural waves that curled at the ends halfway down her back. The lush gown was enticing and yet demure; the hair style framed her slightly flushed face, setting off her heavily fringed green eyes and finely sculpted features, giving her a softly vulnerable appearance.

Solemnly Emily said, "You look like a beautiful temple goddess about to be sacrificed to the bloodthirsty gods."

"You mean I look frightened?"

"Panic-stricken." Emily crossed to Whitney and took her cold, clammy hands in her own. "You've never looked better, but that's not going to be enough. I've met the man you're going to see, and he'll not be swayed by a poor-spirited, terrified young woman with whom he is still furious. He loved you for your spirit and courage. If you go to him all meekness and timidity, you'll be so different from the girl he loved, that you'll fail. He'll let you explain and apologize, then he'll thank you, and say goodbye. Do *anything:* argue with him, make him angrier if you must, but don't go there looking frightened. Be the girl he loved—smile at him, flirt with him, argue or fight with him—but don't, please don't be meek and supplicating."

"Now I know how poor Elizabeth must have felt when I made her defy Peter." Whitney half sighed, half laughed. But her chin came up and she was once again regal and proud.

Emily walked her out to Michael's coach and Whitney gave her a fierce hug. "Whatever happens, you've been wonderful."

The coach pulled away with a much calmer Whitney and left behind a wildly nervous Emily.

After an hour of her journey, Whitney's fragile serenity began to slip, and she tried to calm herself by imagining their meeting. Would Clayton open the door himself, or would he have the butler show her into a private room? Would he make her wait? Would he stalk in and loom over her, his handsome face cold and hard while he waited for her to finish so that he could thrust her out the door? What would he be wearing? Something casual, Whitney thought with a sinking heart, as she glanced down at her gorgeous finery—which he had paid for.

With firm determination, she pulled her mind away from this nonsensical preoccupation with the possible dissimilarities in their attire and concentrated on their meeting again. Would he be angry—or would he be merely cool? Oh God! she thought miserably, let him be angry or even furious; let him storm at me or say terrible things to me; but please,

please don't let him be coldly polite, because that will mean he doesn't care anymore.

A terrible premonition of failure quivered through her. If Clayton still cared about her, he would never have waited impassively for her to come to him today; he would have at least sent her a terse note acknowledging that he would be there at five.

The coach made a sharp eastward turn and approached a pair of gigantic iron gates barring their way. He'd had the gates closed against her! Whitney thought frantically. A gatekeeper dressed in burgundy cloth trimmed in gold braid stepped out of the gatekeeper's house and spoke to the Archibalds' coachman.

An audible sigh of relief escaped Whitney as they were permitted to pass, and the coach lurched forward onto the smooth, private road. They swayed gently along the curving drive bordered with wide sweeping lawns and huge formal parks dotted with leafless trees. The gently rolling landscape seemed to stretch as far as the eye could see.

They clattered over a wide bridge whose arches spanned a deep flowing stream, and at long last a magnificent house with immense expanses of mullioned windows and graceful balconies came into view. It loomed against a backdrop of clipped lawns, rising to a height of three stories in the center. Gigantic wings swept forward on both sides of the main structure, creating a terraced courtyard that was the size of a London park.

So bleak had been her mood the last time she had seen this house, Whitney could scarcely remember it. She laid her head back and closed her eyes in sublime misery: Had she called the house "dingy," or was that *his* word? Her own large house would fit into one of the wings with room enough left over for four more like it. She felt as if she were coming to see a stranger; whoever owned this palatial estate was not the carelessly unaffected man who'd raced against her on Dangerous Crossing or taught her to gamble with cards and chips.

Darkness had settled on the November afternoon, and the windows of the great house were aglow with lights when the coach pulled to a stop and the coachman climbed down and lowered the steps for Whitney to alight.

Comfortably ensconced in the white and gold salon at the front of the house, Stephen glanced away from his mother's anxious face and considered with distracted admiration the eighteenth-century furnishings covered in white silks and brocades. A magnificent Axminister carpet stretched across the seventy-foot length of the room, and the walls were papered in white watered silk, with paintings by Rubens, Reynolds, and Cheeraerts hanging in ornate gold gilt frames.

His gaze shifted restlessly to the clock, and he rose to pace impatiently. As he passed the wide bow windows, he saw the coach pulled up in the front drive and, with a quick grin over his shoulder at his mother, he strode from the room.

The butler was just opening the front door as Stephen stepped into the foyer with a welcoming smile on his face, expecting to see his brother with Vanessa Standfield. He halted in surprise, staring instead at a vaguely familiar, beautiful girl wrapped in a blue-green velvet cape lined with white ermine. When she reached up and pushed the hood back onto her shoulders, Stephen's pulse gave a wild leap of recognition. "My name is Miss Stone," she told the butler in a soft, musical voice. "I believe his grace is expecting me."

In that brief flash of time, Stephen thought of his brother's anguished drunken ramblings, debated whether it was likely Clay was bringing home a wife or only a fiancée, considered the wisdom of involving himself in his brother's personal life, and on a wild impulse, made his decision.

Stepping quickly forward to intervene before the butler could say that his master wasn't at home, Stephen put on his most engaging smile and said, "My brother is expected at any minute, Miss Stone. Would you like to come in and wait?"

Two very conflicting reactions flickered across the beautiful young woman's face: disappointment and relief. She shook her head. "No. Thank you. I sent word yesterday that I would like a few moments of his time, and asked that he let me know if today wouldn't be convenient. Perhaps some other day . . ." she murmured, half turning to leave.

Stephen reached out and firmly grasped her elbow. The reaction earned him a surprised look from the young woman, which deepened to astonishment as Stephen gently—but forcibly—drew her back into the entrance foyer. "Clay was delayed and didn't return yesterday," Stephen explained with a disarming smile. "So he doesn't know you intended to call on him today." Before she could utter a protest, he reached up and politely lifted the aquamarine velvet cape off her shoulders, then he handed it to the butler.

Whitney's gaze was riveted on the immense marble staircase which swept in a wide graceful half circle, terminating in an arc along the broad balcony above. She remembered how Clayton had carried her up that staircase, and she recalled vividly how brutal his rage could be. Abruptly, she turned toward the door. "Thank you for inviting me to stay, Lord Westmoreland."

"Stephen," he corrected.

"Thank you, Stephen," she said, taken aback when he insisted she use his given name. "But I've decided not to wait. If I could have my cape, please?" She looked at the butler, who looked at Stephen, who firmly shook his head, whereupon the butler crossed his arms over his chest and simply pretended not to have heard her request.

"I would like you to stay," Stephen said, his voice firm, but his smile cordial.

Bewildered laughter crept into Whitney's voice as she accepted Stephen's outstretched arm. "I don't think I've ever been made to feel quite so *welcome,* my lord."

"Westmorelands are famous for their hospitality," Stephen lied with a roguish grin as he drew her inexorably toward the salon where his mother was waiting.

At the sight of the duchess seated on one of the settees, Whitney drew back in startled embarrassment.

"My mother and I will *both* be pleased to have you wait for Clay with us," Stephen urged gently. "I know he will be delighted to see you, Miss Stone, and that he would never forgive me for letting you go before he returned."

Whitney halted and stared at him. "Lord Westmoreland," she began with a hint of a smile touching her soft lips.

"Stephen," he corrected.

"Stephen—I think you ought to know that there's every chance your brother won't be in the least 'delighted' to see me."

"I'll risk it," Stephen said with a grin.

Whitney was overawed by the white-and-gold room, but she carefully refrained from gazing at the intricately carved plasterwork on the ceilings and the masterpieces displayed in ornate gold frames along the walls while Stephen led her to his mother.

"Mother, may I present Miss Stone," Stephen said. "Since Clay did not return last night, he is unaware of *Whitney's* intention to call, but I have persuaded her to stay and wait with us until he arrives."

As Whitney curtsied to the duchess, she heard the emphasis Stephen placed on her first name—which she hadn't told him—and she saw the duchess's blank, answering look.

"Are you a friend of my son's, Miss Stone?" the duchess politely inquired as Whitney took the indicated seat across from her.

"*Occasionally* we have been friends, your grace," Whitney replied honestly.

The duchess blinked at the unusual response, studied the jade-green eyes regarding her solemnly from beneath a heavy fringe of dark lashes, then suddenly half rose from her chair, caught herself, and sat back down. Her gaze flew to Stephen, who nodded imperceptibly at her.

Cheerfully ignoring his mother's apprehensive glances, he relaxed back in his chair and listened while she and Whitney discussed a variety of topics, from Paris fashions to London weather.

After nearly an hour the front door was swung wide and voices drifted in from the entryway. The words were inaudible, but there was no mistaking the soft murmur and throaty laughter of a woman as she answered Clayton. Stephen saw Whitney's stricken expression as she realized that Clayton was accompanied by a female. Rising quickly, he flashed a sympathetic, encouraging look at her and then carefully placed himself so that he was standing in front of her, blocking her from Clayton's view to give her time to compose herself.

"I'm sorry we're late. We were delayed," Clayton said to his mother as he leaned down and pressed a light kiss on her forehead. Teasingly he added, "I trust you had no trouble finding your rooms without me?" Turning aside, he drew Vanessa foward. "Mother, may I present Vanessa . . ."

Stephen expelled his breath in a rush of relief when Clayton finished. "Standfield."

Vanessa sank into a deep curtsy before the duchess and when the two ladies had exchanged the proper civilities, Clayton waved a casual arm in Stephen's direction and laughingly added, "Vanessa, you already know Stephen." With that he turned back to his mother and bent low, speaking quietly to her.

"A pleasure seeing you again, Miss Standfield," Stephen said with amused formality.

"For heaven's sake, Stephen," Vanessa laughed. "You and I have been on a first-name basis forever."

Ignoring that, Stephen reached behind him, touched Whitney's arm, and she rose with quaking reluctance to her feet. "Miss Standfield," Stephen raised his voice slightly, "may I present Miss Whitney Stone . . ."

Clayton jerked erect and swung around.

"And this stony-faced gentleman," Stephen continued lightly to Whitney, "is my brother. As you know."

Whitney actually flinched at the cold, ruthless fury in Clayton's eyes as they raked over her. "How is your aunt?" he inquired icily.

Whitney swallowed and replied in a barely audible whisper, "My aunt is very well, thank you. And you?"

Clayton nodded curtly. "As you can see, I have survived our last encounter without scars."

Vanessa, who apparently recognized Whitney as her rival for Clayton from the Rutherfords' ball, gave Whitney a faint inclination of her elegantly coiffed head and said with a frosty smile, "Esterbrook was introduced to you at Lord and Lady Rutherford's affair, Miss Stone." She paused as if trying to recall the occasion more clearly. "Yes, I remember that he spoke of you at some length to many of us."

Realizing that Vanessa was waiting for an answer, Whitney said cautiously, "That was very kind of him."

"As I recall, what he said was not in the least *kind*, Miss Stone."

Whitney stiffened at Vanessa's unexpected and unprovoked attack, and Stephen waded into the deafening silence. "We can all discuss our mutual acquaintances at dinner," he announced cheerfully, "providing that I can convince my beautiful guest to dine with us."

Whitney shook her head in a desperate, emphatic no. "I really can't stay. I—I'm sorry."

"Ah, but I insist." He grinned. Arching a brow at his white-faced brother, he said, "We *both* insist, don't we?"

To Stephen's infinite disgust, Clayton didn't bother to second the invitation. Instead he merely glanced over his shoulder and nodded curtly to the servant hovering in the doorway, indicating that another place should be set at the table. Without another word, he turned on his heel and strode to the sideboard where he snatched a bottle of whiskey and a glass.

Stephen seated himself beside Whitney, then looked around to where Clayton stood, his tall frame rigid with anger, his back to them as he poured himself a drink. "Me too, big brother," he called good-naturedly.

Clayton threw Stephen a look of unwavering distaste and said in a voice of tightly controlled fury, "I am certain, Stephen, that included among your other brilliant talents is the ability to pour your own drink."

"Correct," Stephen said serenely, getting up from the settee where he was seated beside Whitney. "Ladies?" he offered. "A glass of wine?"

Vanessa and Whitney both accepted, and the duchess stifled the urge to request a full bottle.

Stephen strolled over to the sideboard, poured himself some whiskey, and began filling three crystal glasses with wine, blithely ignoring the simmering rage emanating from his brother. Under his breath, Clayton snapped, "Is there the slightest chance that you don't know who she is—to me?"

"Not the slightest." Stephen grinned imperturbably, picking up three of the four glasses. As he turned toward the ladies he said in a carrying voice, "Will you bring Whitney's glass, Clay? I can't manage all four."

Carrying her wineglass, Clayton bore purposefully down on Whitney, and she unconsciously pressed further back into the seat cushions, searching his forbidding countenance for some sign that he still cared for her. But there was none.

In a state of acute misery, she absently sipped her wine surreptitiously studying Clayton, who was seated across from her beside Vanessa, with his gleaming booted foot resting casually atop the opposite knee, his long legs encased in superbly tailored gray trousers. Seeing him here, relaxed and at home in the splendor of this white-and-gold room, he was every inch the aloof, elegant nobleman, the master of all he surveyed. Never had he looked more handsome—or more unattainable. And to make everything worse, Vanessa Standfield, who was draped in flowing blue silk, was more haughtily, breathtakingly beautiful than Whitney had realized that night at the Rutherfords' ball.

In the hour before dinner was announced, Stephen carried the greatest share of the conversational burden, with Vanessa contributing two more pointed insults aimed at Whitney. Clayton spoke in clipped, abrupt phrases only when absolutely necessary, and Whitney replied to Stephen's light banter with weak monosyllables. The duchess had three more glasses of wine and said nothing at all to anyone.

Curled into a tight ball of suspended anguish, Whitney silently counted the minutes until dinner could be finished and the ordeal over, so that she could creep away. She now knew she should never have come. It was too late.

Mercifully, dinner was announced shortly thereafter. Clayton rose, and without so much as a glance in Whitney's direction, he offered his arm to his mother and, with Vanessa on the other, escorted both women from the room.

Whitney stood and took Stephen's arm, her gaze clinging hopelessly to Clayton's back. She started to follow in his wake, but Stephen stopped her. "Damn Vanessa!" he laughed softly. "I could strangle her. It's time for us to change our strategy—although everything has been going well so far."

"Strategy?" Whitney gasped. "Going *well?*"

"Perfectly. You've been sitting here looking beautiful and vulnerable, and Clayton can't tear his eyes off you when he thinks you aren't looking. But it's time for you to do something to get him off alone with you."

Whitney's heart soared precariously. "He can't tear his eyes ? Oh, Stephen, are you certain? I don't think he even knows I'm here."

"He knows you're here," Stephen said, laughing. "Not that he doesn't wish to God you weren't! In fact, I can't recall ever seeing him this furious. Now it will be up to you to push his anger beyond the limits of his control."

"What?" Whitney whispered. "Dear God, why?"

They had reached the entrance of the dining room, but Stephen turned and paused before a portrait on the wall opposite the double doors; their backs were in full view of the diners who were already seated at the table. He gestured at the painting as if pointing out its merits to Whitney. "You have to make him furious enough to leave the table and take you with him. If you don't, as soon as dinner is over, he'll find some excuse to draw Vanessa and my mother off somewhere else, and simply leave you with me."

The prospect of actively trying to engage Clayton in verbal combat filled Whitney with an odd mixture of fear and anticipation. She reminded herself of what Emily had said about not being meek, and told herself bracingly that if demure Elizabeth Ashton could do it, so could she. "Stephen," she said suddenly, "why are you doing this?"

"There's no time to go into that now," Stephen replied, guiding her toward the dining room. "But remember this—no matter how angry he is, my brother is in love with you. And if you can get him alone, I think you'll be able to prove it to him."

"But your mother will think I'm the gauchest female alive if I deliberately provoke him."

Stephen grinned boyishly at her. "My mother will think you are brave and wonderful. Just as I do. Now courage, young lady! I'm expecting to see more of the gay, spirited female I watched at the Kingsleys' the other night."

There was just time for Whitney to flash an astonished, grateful look at him as he led her to her place at the table. As Stephen seated her, Clayton remarked with withering sarcasm, "It's kind of you finally to join us."

"It was kind of you to *ask* me, your grace," Whitney returned pointedly.

Clayton ignored her and nodded to the servants to begin serving. He was seated at the head of the table, with his mother on his right, and Vanessa on his left. Whitney was next to the duchess, and Stephen took a place opposite Whitney, beside Vanessa.

As the servant poured champagne into Whitney's glass, Clayton drawled caustically, "Leave the bottle next to Miss Stone. She is overly fond of champagne, as I recall."

Whitney's spirits gave a leap of joy—Clayton was no longer able to ignore her! Surely he must still care for her to be angry enough to say such a thing. She smiled enchantingly at him over her glass and sipped the bubbly wine. "Not *overly* fond of champagne. Although at times it does help to reinforce one's courage."

"Really? I wouldn't know."

"Ah yes, you prefer whiskey to reinforce yours," she quipped as he lifted his glass to his mouth. His eyes narrowed ominously and Whitney quickly looked away. *Please love me,* she implored him silently. *Don't make me go through this for nothing.*

"Do you play the pianoforte, Whitney?" the duchess asked, nervously stepping in to cover the charged silence.

"Only if I wish to give offense," Whitney replied with a shy smile.

"Do you sing then?" her grace persisted in sheer desperation.

"Yes," Whitney laughed, "but without the slightest attention to tune, I'm afraid."

"Really, Miss Stone," Vanessa drawled, "it's extraordinary

to meet a gently reared Englishwoman who has not been taught either to sing or to play. Exactly what *are* your accomplishments?"

"Whitney is a proficient flirt," Clayton interjected scathingly, answering Vanessa's question himself. "She is conversant in several languages and could undoubtedly do a creditable job of cursing fluently in all of them. She plays a fair game of chess, a poor game of solitaire, and is a capable horsewoman when deprived of her crop. She claims to excel with a slingshot—a talent for which I can't vouch firsthand, and she is a convincing actress—a talent for which I can. Have I treated you fairly, Whitney?" he snapped.

"Not entirely, your grace," Whitney said softly, stinging from the cruel whips of his words even though she was smiling. "Surely my chess game is better than 'fair.' And if you doubt my skill with the slingshot, I shall be pleased to demonstrate it to you—providing that you volunteer to be my target, as I have just been yours."

Stephen gave a sharp crack of laughter and his mother croaked, "Have you attended many social functions since you've come back from France?"

Whitney felt Clayton's scorching gaze on her and could not quite meet it. "Many parties and balls. Although no one has given a masquerade, and I particularly enjoy them. I believe my lord duke enjoys them equally—"

"Do you also enjoy weddings?" Vanessa asked her smoothly. "If so, we shall be certain to invite you to ours."

The silence of an ancient tomb settled over the table. Whitney tried valiantly to continue eating but could not swallow past the lump of desolation swelling in her throat. She looked miserably at Stephen, who shrugged imperturbably, and arched a brow in Clayton's direction. She knew that Stephen meant for her to continue, but she couldn't now. It was over. As transparent as it would be to everyone when she pleaded sudden illness, Whitney couldn't bear to stay at that table. She was too bruised and battered to care that everyone would know that the announcement of Clayton and Vanessa's betrothal was the reason she was leaving.

She took her napkin off her lap and put it on the table

beside her plate. As she reached down to slide her heavy chair back, a feminine hand suddenly came to rest over hers. The duchess gave her fingers a brief, encouraging squeeze, then held them tightly in a gesture that clearly said, "Stay and finish what you have begun."

Whitney smiled uncertainly, hesitated, then replaced her napkin. She glanced at Clayton, who was moodily contemplating the wine in his glass, then at Vanessa. Whitney couldn't bear to think of Clayton married to such a haughty beauty—not when she herself loved him so much, and had come this far, in this embarrassing fashion, to tell him so. She thought of Clayton holding Vanessa in his arms and kissing her in that intimate way of his, and that made Whitney angry and jealous enough to stay.

Vanessa put her hand on Clayton's arm. "I hope you aren't angry with me for blurting out our secret in front of a stranger."

"I'm certain he isn't in the least angry, Miss Standfield," Whitney said quietly, but her eyes were on Clayton. "We all do foolish things when we're in love. Don't we, your grace?"

"Do we?" Clayton countered repressively. "I hadn't noticed."

"Then you either have a very short memory," Whitney challenged softly, "or a very convenient one. Or perhaps you've never been in love, after all."

Clayton's wineglass slammed on the table. "Precisely what is that supposed to mean?" he demanded.

Whitney withered before the blast of those gray eyes. "Nothing," she lied softly.

The clink of silver began again. She watched Clayton's hand flexing on his goblet of wine, clenching it and loosening, then clenching again, and she knew he was wishing that her neck, not his goblet, were in his grip. After several minutes, his mother nervously cleared her throat, and cautiously said to Whitney, "Tell me, my dear, were things very different here in England when you returned?"

Whitney started to reply impersonally, but then she realized that the duchess had just unknowingly given her exactly the opening she needed. Since Clayton wasn't willing to let her explain in private, perhaps she could at least make him partially understand, here, at the table. "Very different!" she said with feeling. "You see, shortly after I returned to England, I discovered that while I was still in France my father had arranged for my marriage to a man I had scarcely met, and did not even recognize when I saw him again here."

"How distressing," replied the duchess with a dawning look of understanding.

"Indeed it was—particularly because I have a freakish streak in my nature which positively rebels against being coldly ordered about by anyone. And the man I was to marry, although he was kind and understanding in many ways, was quite horridly arbitrary and imperious about the betrothal. He acted as if I had no choice in the matter whatever."

"These arranged marriages can be difficult to adjust to at first," the duchess agreed. "What did you do then?"

"She betrothed herself to another man who was thoroughly spineless and an idiot!" Clayton announced coldly.

"But *not* dictatorial and tyrannical," Whitney shot back. "And I did *not* betroth myself to Paul at all!"

Angry silence reigned until Stephen laughingly said, "My God, don't keep us in suspense. Then what happened?"

Clayton answered for her in a contemptuous drawl. "Since there were another thousand eligible men in London, Miss Stone set about seeing how many of those she could betroth herself to as well."

Whitney couldn't endure it when he used that tone of voice. She bit her lip and meekly shook her head. "No, I was only ever betrothed to one man, but he's so angry with me, he won't give me a chance to explain. He's already withdrawn his offer."

"The beast!" Stephen said cheerfully, helping himself to a second portion of duck à l'orange. "He sounds like an evil tempered sort. You're probably much better off without him."

"I—I have a rather formidable temper myself," Whitney admitted.

"In that case, *he's* better off without *you*," Clayton snapped, then his gaze swung on Stephen with deadly menace. "Stephen, I find this conversation not only excessively boring, but in excruciatingly bad taste. Am I making myself clear?"

Stephen met his brother's look with sham bewilderment and nodded, but even he didn't dare to reopen the subject.

Servants moved about the room, and all five people at the dining table studiously concentrated on the sumptuous fare on their plates, but only Stephen ate with any enjoyment. Whitney told herself she would try once more, just once more, to make Clayton leave the room with her. Although how she was going to cope with him if she succeeded, was beyond her imagination.

"Stephen asked you a question, Clayton," Vanessa whispered.

"What?" Clayton demanded, staring at Stephen with blazing animosity.

"I asked how your horses did at the last race."

"They did well," was the curt answer.

"How well?" Stephen persisted. Although he addressed the table at large, the smile that tugged at the corner of his mouth was aimed at Whitney as he explained. "We had a bet that three of Clayton's and two of mine would come in the money. I know mine placed, and only two of his did, which means he lost the bet, and he owes me £300." Stephen's conspiratorial grin widened meaningfully at Whitney. "He doesn't care about the money, but he hates to admit he lost. He's never learned to accept defeat."

Clayton laid down his knife and fork, preparing to give Stephen the brutal setdown he'd earned hours before, but Whitney, taking Stephen's cue, immediately drew off Clayton's fire. "How strange you should say that," she said to Stephen, looking genuinely amazed. "I have found that your brother accepts defeat without even putting up the slightest struggle. Why, faced with the tiniest discouragement, he simply gives up and—"

Clayton's open hand slammed down on the table with a crash that made the dishes dance. He surged to his feet, a muscle leaping furiously along the taut line of his jaw. "Miss Stone and I have something to say to each other which is best said in private." He gritted out the words, flinging his napkin down on the table. Swiftly, he strode around the table and jerked Whitney's chair back. "Get up!" he snapped in a low, terrible voice when Whitney remained frozen in her seat. His hand clamped down painfully on her forearm and Whitney rose unsteadily.

The duchess looked at her in helpless dismay, but Stephen lifted his glass to Whitney in a silent toast and grinned.

Forcibly pulling her beside him, Clayton strode purposefully from the room and down the carpeted marble hallway. As they passed the front door, he snapped at the butler, "Have Miss Stone's carriage waiting in front in three minutes!" He turned down a side hall and nodded curtly to a servant who opened the doors of a luxurious study for them.

Clayton hauled her halfway across the room, which was lined with books recessed behind richly carved arches of polished oak, then flung her arm away and stalked to the fireplace. Turning, he regarded her with a look of undiluted loathing, while he visibly strove to bring his rampaging temper under control. Suddenly his voice slashed through the silence. "You have exactly two minutes to explain the purpose of this unexpected and unwelcome visit of yours. At the end of that time, I will escort you to your carriage and make your excuses for your absence to my mother and brother."

Whitney drew a tortured breath, knowing that if he saw her fear now he would use it against her. "The purpose of my visit?" she said in a small, distracted voice, her mind frantically counting off the passing seconds. "I—I would have thought by now it was obvious."

"It is *not* obvious!"

"I've come to—to explain why I said what I did to you at the banquet. You see," she said, stammering in her haste to finish in the minutes he'd allotted her, "earlier at the church, I thought we—you and I—still had an agreement, and—"

Clayton's eyes raked contemptuously over her. "We have no agreement," he said scathingly. "It's over. Done with. It should never have begun! The betrothal was an insane idea, and I curse the day I thought of it."

Sick with failure and defeat, Whitney dug her nails into the flesh of her palms and shook her head in denial. "It never had a chance to begin because I wouldn't let it."

"Your two minutes are almost up."

"Clayton, please listen to me!" she cried desperately. "You—you told me a long time ago that you wanted me to come to you willingly, that you didn't want a cold, unwilling wife."

"And?" he demanded furiously.

Whitney's voice shook. "And, I am here. Willingly."

Clayton stiffened, his whole body tensing into a rigid line as her meaning pierced the armor of his wrath. He stared at her for a moment, his jaw tight and hard, then he leaned back against the mantel and closed his eyes.

He was fighting her, Whitney knew. Trying to shut her out. In a paralysis of fear, she waited, watching him. It seemed an eternity before he reluctantly straightened. His eyes flicked open, meeting hers, and Whitney's heart gave a wild leap. She had won! She could see it in the slight softening of his rugged features. Oh God, she had won!

He looked first at the long stretch of carpet separating them, and then at her. When he spoke, the harsh edge of his voice was tempered, but his words were low and meaningful. "I'll not make this any easier for you," he told her evenly.

The distance between them stretched like a mile, and Whitney knew that he meant she would have to make the trip across the room to him if she wanted him, that he would not so much as meet her halfway . . . because, even now, he didn't entirely trust her.

His eyes never left hers as Whitney started walking toward him on legs that felt like water. A mere step away from him, she had to pause to still the slamming of her heart and quaking of her knees. She took the final step on legs that felt as if they were about to buckle beneath her, and stopped so close to him that her breasts were only inches from his gray jacket.

With her head bowed, she waited, but the seconds ticked by, and Clayton made no move to touch her. Finally she lifted her head and raised green eyes shining with surrender to his.

"Would you please," she whispered achingly, "hold me now?"

Clayton started to reach for her and stopped . . . and then he caught her arms and jerked her to him, crushing her against his chest as his mouth came down hungrily on hers. With a smothered moan of joy, Whitney returned his kiss, glorying in the feel of his lips locked fiercely to hers.

Twining her arms around his neck, she pressed against him, fitting her melting body to the hardening contours of his. A shudder shook him as she leaned into him, and his hands tightened possessively on her back and hips, molding her closer to him, sliding up her spine, then lower, gathering her willing body into his. "God, how I've missed you!" he whispered hoarsely against her lips, and he deepened the kiss. At the first tentative touch of his tongue, Whitney's lips parted without further urging, and Clayton groaned, clasping her tighter as his tongue plunged into her sweet softness, searching with an almost desperate urgency, taking what she was offering.

The exquisite feeling of her in his arms, the taste of her lips clinging to his, the fullness of her breasts against his palms, was unbearable joy to Clayton. He couldn't go on, and he was afraid to stop . . . afraid that if he broke the contact, she would vanish, and the aching desire racking him would become an aching emptiness instead.

When he finally tore his mouth from hers, he kept his arms around her, resting his chin atop her shining head, waiting for his breathing to even out. And Whitney stayed there—as if being in his arms were the only place in the world she wished to be.

Drawing back slightly, Clayton looked down into the limpid pools of her eyes and quietly asked, "Are you willing to marry me?"

Whitney nodded. She nodded, because she could not speak.

"Why?" he persisted evenly. *"Why* do you want to marry me?"

From the moment he had made her cross the room to him,

rather than meeting her halfway, Whitney had known Clayton was going to require an unconditional surrender from her; she knew what he was demanding of her now. Through joy and tears and relief constricting her breath, she found her voice and softly said, "Because I love you."

His arms closed around her with stunning force. "God help you if you don't mean it!" he warned fiercely, "because I'll never let you go again."

Shamelessly yearning to be kissed, Whitney whispered, "I shall be very happy to prove I *do* mean it." She saw his eyes darken with passion as he bent his head to her, and she leaned up on her toes to prove it. She kissed him with all the aching longing that being this close to him evoked; she kissed him in all the ways he had ever kissed her, feeling faint with joy when he began to kiss her back, his mouth moving with fierce tenderness, then opening with fiery demand over hers, until their breaths were mingled gasps, and they were straining to one another.

It was Clayton who broke the kiss and forced his hands to stop their exploration, the pleasure-torture of caressing the cherished curves and hollows of the slender, voluptuous body that had haunted his dreams. But he kept her in his arms, tangling his hand in her heavy hair, loving the familiar texture of it. "Why did you make me wait so long?" he breathed.

Leaning back, Whitney tipped her head in the direction of the dining room where Vanessa was. "Why couldn't you have waited a little longer?"

"Little one," he chuckled tenderly, "you are the only female alive who would bring up Vanessa at a time like this."

Whitney's expression suddenly turned solemn, and Clayton didn't see the smile that glowed in her eyes as she said, "I have a confession—and it may make a difference in which of us you decide upon."

Clayton stiffened. "And that is?"

"I told your mother the truth about my talent at the pianoforte."

With a laughing sigh of relief, Clayton drew her close. "Can you sing any better?" he teased.

"No. I'm afraid not."

Although his tone was light, Whitney heard the huskiness of desire that deepened his voice as he said, "In that case, I suppose you will have to learn some other ways to please me."

Beneath the thin fabric of his shirt, his chest was warm and hard against her cheek. Whitney smiled as she slid her hand upward and spread her fingers over his pounding heart. "The last time we discussed my shortcomings in that area, you said you didn't have the time to instruct a tiresomely naive schoolgirl. But I think—if you have the time—you will find that I'm an excellent student."

He was silent a long moment, then he said, "Perhaps I should begin by teaching you a more suitable response than your last when I tell you that I love you?"

Whitney nodded happily, but her voice suddenly filled with tears. "If you'd care to try again, I'll show you that I've already learned that lesson."

Tipping her chin up, Clayton looked deeply into her eyes and quietly said, "I love you, little one."

"I love you, too," Whitney whispered, shyly laying her trembling hand against his smoothly shaven cheek and jaw. "I love you very much."

He grinned. "Now that, my sweet, is a vast improvement."

She tried to smile back at him, but Clayton saw the tears glistening in her eyes. Cradling her face between both his hands, he gazed at her misty green eyes. "Why tears, darling?"

"Because," Whitney whispered brokenly, "until this moment, I was certain you would never say that to me again."

With a groaning laugh, Clayton hugged her tightly to him. "Oh, little one, I have loved you since the night we played chess at my house and, after announcing that you would never call any man your 'lord,' you called *me* a conniving, black-hearted scoundrel when I took the game from you." He had loved her from the moment she had laughingly told him a story about a girl who used to pepper her music teacher's snuff box.

Stephen tapped lightly on the door, then stepped into the study and closed the door behind him. He grinned wickedly at his brother, who tightened his arms possessively around Whitney. "Excuse me, brother dear, but your absence is making things increasingly uncomfortable in the other room."

Clayton heard this with a frown of distaste. "Is dinner over?"

"Long since," Stephen confirmed. "And Vanessa is displaying a marked antagonism toward my charming efforts to enlighten her on the proper care and feeding of racehorses."

"Stephen, your brother is in something of a dilemma." Whitney smiled, turning sideways in Clayton's arms. "Let me think—how did he phrase it? Oh yes. He has only two hands and he has offered them both."

Stephen arched a thoughtful brow. "I have two hands, and they are neither of them promised, Miss Stone," he offered gamely.

"Stephen," Clayton said sternly, but with a slow grin, "do not strain the bonds of brotherly affection beyond what you already have this evening. I'll attend to freeing one of my 'hands' when I take Vanessa home tonight."

"I should be leaving too," Whitney sighed, reluctantly pulling out of Clayton's arms and smoothing her gown. "It will be very late by the time I get back to Emily's."

"You, my love, are not setting foot out of this house. I'll send a servant to the Archibalds' for your things when I leave with Vanessa, and he can inform them that you will return in a week. Not one day before."

Whitney knew perfectly well that Clayton was issuing this edict because of her unexplained change in attitude between the time she left him at the church and saw him again at the wedding banquet. Since she wanted with all her heart to stay with him, Whitney acceded to his flat command with a demure smile.

With one hip perched atop his desk, Clayton watched while Whitney sat behind it and wrote a note to Emily. She assured her that the duchess was in residence and asked that Clarissa and her clothes be dispatched post haste to Claymore. Winsomely, Whitney added a postscript. "This time, *I'll* send the invitations. This one is yours—will you please be my matron of honor? I love you. Whitney."

Clayton took the note from her and, serenely ignoring his brother's presence, pulled her to her feet and kissed her with tender thoroughness. "I'll be back in two hours, perhaps a little more. Will you wait up for me?"

Whitney nodded, but as Clayton started from the room, she turned away from him, tracing her finger across his gleaming mahogany desktop. "Clayton," she said softly, her voice threaded with tears, "when Vanessa asked about my 'accomplishments' tonight, I forgot to mention that I do have one. And it's—it's so splendid that it compensates for my lack of all the others."

Stephen and Clayton grinned at each other, neither of them hearing the emotion that clogged her voice. "What 'splendid accomplishment' is that, little one?" Clayton asked.

Her shoulders hunched forward and began to shake. "I made you love me," she whispered brokenly. "Somehow, some way, I actually made you love me."

The laughter faded from Clayton's face, replaced by an expression so intense, so profoundly proud, that Stephen quietly left the two of them alone.

Clayton emerged from his study a few minutes later on his way to face Vanessa in the salon and take her home. He flashed a quick, grateful grin at Stephen, inclined his head toward the study doors and said in a low, laughter-tinged voice, "Stephen, do not let her out of your sight!"

While Clayton was leaving with Vanessa, Whitney sat across from Stephen in the study, trying to vanquish her sudden embarrassment over the earlier part of the evening. Finally she clasped her hands in her lap and regarded him directly. "Whatever made you want me to stay for dinner, when it was so obvious that Clayton didn't want me here at all? What made you help me, when I could have been just any female who—"

"I knew you weren't 'just *any* female,'" Stephen corrected.

"Your name was Whitney and you had green eyes. And one drunken night many weeks ago, my fair brother could talk of little else."

Two hours later, Clayton strode into the salon and Stephen drily remarked, "I suppose Lord Standfield was not in the best humor when you left?"

"He was reasonable," Clayton said briefly. He sat down beside Whitney and, defying all the proprieties with his usual careless elegance, he put his arm around her shoulders, drawing her close. With a meaningful look at his smiling mother and brother, he ungraciously hinted, "I imagine you're both exhausted from your trip this morning and would like to retire?"

"I happen to be exhausted from a good deal more than my trip," the duchess said laughingly, and obligingly she bade them both good night. Stephen, however, did nothing of the sort. Leaning back in his chair, he crossed his arms over his chest and said, "I'm not in the least tired, big brother. Besides, I want to hear about the wedding plans." Ignoring Clayton's dagger look, he glanced expectantly from him to Whitney. "Well, when's it to be?"

Clayton sighed, resigning himself to Stephen's continued presence, and smiled at Whitney. "How long will it take you to get ready, love?"

Gazing up into his compelling gray eyes, Whitney thought she would much rather have his arms around her and feel his lips moving over hers than discuss the wedding plans right now, but, like Clayton, she had no choice except to answer Stephen's question. "I suppose it will be a large wedding?" she mused, considering Clayton's title, and the vast number of friends and acquaintances she knew he had.

"Very large," Clayton confirmed.

"Then it will take a great deal of time to plan. There are so many arrangements to make, the gowns to be chosen, endless fittings—and the dressmakers take forever. The invitations must be prepared, sent out, and acknowledged—" She paused. "About how many guests will there be?"

"Five or six hundred, I imagine," Clayton said.

"Closer to a thousand, unless you want to offend half the

ton and alienate our relatives," Stephen corrected, grinning at Whitney's expression of stunned horror. Taking pity on her, he added, "Westmoreland dukes are always married in a church, and the wedding celebration is always here at Claymore. It's an ancient tradition, and everyone will know it, so you needn't worry about anyone thinking it queer that it's at Clay's home instead of yours."

"Always married in a church, and the celebration *here?"* Whitney repeated, with an accusing look at her grinning fiancé. "When I think of how you threatened to abduct me and take me to Scotland!"

"The custom, Madam," Clayton chuckled, tracing the elegant curve of her cheek and jaw with his forefinger, then tilting her chin up, "began because the first Duke of Claymore abducted *his* lady from her parents' castle, which was several days journey from Claymore. On the way here was a monastery, and since my ancestor had technically compromised her honor, one of the monks was more than willing to marry them, despite the lady's temporary reluctance. The *celebration,"* he emphasized, "took place here because the young woman's outraged relatives were in no mood to celebrate in their home an occasion which, at the time, they viewed as more a reason to fight than to feast." His grin widened devilishly. "So you see, had I carried you off to Scotland, married you there, then brought you back here, I'd have been honoring the tradition almost to the original letter."

Having been silenced on that subject, Whitney returned to the length of time required to prepare for the wedding. "Thérèse DuVille's wedding was not even half so large, and it took a year to accomplish . . ."

"No," Clayton said irrevocably. "Absolutely not."

"Six months?" Whitney offered to compromise.

"Six *weeks,"* Clayton announced flatly.

His imperious tone didn't daunt Whitney in the least. "If it's to be such a large wedding, it could scarcely be planned even in six months."

Clayton winked conspiratorially at Stephen. "Very well," he sighed, "I'll give you eight."

"Eight months," Whitney agreed with a sad little sigh. "It will barely be time enough, yet it seems like forever."

"Eight *weeks,*" her fiancé corrected with finality. "Not one day more. My mother will help you and so will Hudgins. I'll put an entire staff of assistants at your disposal. Eight weeks will give you plenty of time."

Whitney shot him a dubious look, but since she didn't want to wait eight months either, she happily agreed.

Clayton was sitting with his arm around Whitney's shoulders, chatting amiably with Stephen, when the weight against his side suddenly grew heavier and she didn't respond to his teasing remark. He glanced down and saw her long lashes lying softly against her cheeks. "She's asleep," he said quietly. Gently, he moved her aside, then scooped her up into his arms. "It's been a more than exhausting day for you, sweetheart," he murmured as she stirred and snuggled into his chest. To Stephen he said, "Wait for me here. I have some things I want to say to you when I come down."

A few minutes later, after summoning a maid and seeing Whitney sleepily installed in one of the guest rooms, Clayton strode back into the salon and firmly closed the doors behind him. When he turned around, Stephen thrust a glass of brandy into his hand and raised his own in a silent toast. "I have two questions to ask you," Clayton said calmly when they were both seated.

Grinning, Stephen stretched his long legs out in front of him and crossed them at the ankles. "I rather thought you might, your grace."

"How did you know who Whitney was? To me?"

"You told me. During a very drunken night at Grand Oak, you told me all about her, including her green eyes—which, God knows, she has."

Leaning forward, Clayton rested his forearms on his knees, staring into his brandy glass as he rolled it between his palms. "How much did I tell you that night?"

Stephen considered lying because it was kinder, but he abandoned the idea when Clayton's disconcertingly perceptive gaze lifted to his. "Everything," Stephen admitted with a sigh. "Everything, including the harm you did her. So, when she appeared here tonight, thinking you'd received her note—which I understand Hudgins has—I took one look at her and decided that since her loss had done such damage to you, I would restore her to you."

Clayton nodded his acceptance of Stephen's explanation. "I have one further question," he said gravely.

"You said you had two questions, and you've already reached your limit," Stephen warned lightly.

Ignoring that, Clayton said in a low, solemn voice, "I would like to know what I have within my power to give you, to express my gratitude."

"Your money, or your life?" Stephen ventured with a lopsided grin at his bandit's demand.

"They're yours for the asking," Clayton said quietly.

Later that night, he lay on his bed, his hands linked behind his head, staring at the ceiling. He could hardly believe that Whitney was here, that after fighting against him so fiercely, for so long, she had come tonight and fought to recover what they had begun together.

He thought of the way she had faced him in the study, daring him to deny that he still wanted her. And then he smiled in the darkness, remembering the way she had crossed the long room to him, her head held high, her eyes shining with love and surrender. That memory, that one memory of her coming to him, casting aside her pride because she loved him, would endure in his heart for as long as he lived. Nothing would ever mean more to him.

Tomorrow he would insist on a complete explanation for what had happened to change her attitude so drastically between the wedding and the banquet. No, he corrected himself with a wry grin, he would *ask* her for an explanation —that tempestuous beauty sleeping across the hall would be far more likely to respond to a question than a demand.

Chapter Thirty

WHITNEY AWOKE FROM A DEEP SLEEP, GROGGY WITH UNFINISHED dreams, and rolled over, unwilling to relinquish them. She opened her eyes, simultaneously recognizing her approximate location and Mary, the redheaded maid who had helped her the last time she was here. "The master has been prowling about below for over an hour, watching the stairs," Mary's Irish voice gaily announced from the foot of the bed. "He said to tell you that the day is unseasonably warm, and he asked that you dress for riding."

"That man thinks he's the King of England!" Clarissa grumbled, bustling into the room with her mob cap askew. "He decides he wants to marry my little girl, and we're shipped home from France. He wants to go to a ball, and we're bounced off to London. This morning, he wants to ride, and he has me hauled out of bed at dawn and carted here with the rest of your luggage. Dawn!" she exclaimed sourly, pulling back Whitney's covers, "when decent folks aren't even about on the roads!"

Whitney laughed, scrambling out of bed. "Oh Clarissa, I love you!" She bathed quickly and put on the amber riding habit that Clarissa had brought with her trunks that morning. Eager to see Clayton, to reassure herself that he didn't regret letting her win last night, she pulled her long hair back and caught it at the nape with a bow, then she dashed out of the room.

She crossed the wide balcony and stopped. Clayton was waiting for her at the foot of the stairs, the winter sun glinting down on his dark hair through the domed glass ceiling three stories above. Dressed in a soft chamois peasant shirt with a deep vee at the throat and snug-fitting, coffee-brown riding breeches, he looked so masculine, so like a tall, broad-shouldered god, that Whitney's pulse raced giddily.

Clayton watched her coming toward him down the broad curving staircase. Warily he scanned her lovely face for signs that she regretted her capitulation last night, or resented him for making it so difficult for her.

And then she stood on the last step, gentled still, smiling shyly into his searching gaze. "It's most embarrassing," she said softly, "to know that everyone is going to say that the groom is much more beautiful than the bride."

Clayton couldn't help himself. He caught her into his arms, crushing her to him, burying his face in the fresh fragrance of her hair. "My God!" he whispered hoarsely. "How will I ever wait eight weeks to make you mine?"

He felt her whole body go momentarily rigid in his embrace. *That* hadn't been what he meant at all, but he realized that Whitney had just recoiled in fear from the thought of his making love to her. He grinned against her hair; he had eight weeks to hold and caress her. Eight weeks until his desire could run its natural course to fulfillment and, in that time, she would come to want him too, and to realize that he would never hurt her. And on her wedding night, even if the act itself frightened her, she would trust him enough to let him make love to her. *Then* he would show her how it was supposed to be, how it was meant to be. He would make her wild with wanting, until she was clinging to him, writhing beneath him in a sweet yearning to be taken.

"Would you like to see the estate?" he asked her as soon as they finished breakfast.

"Very much," Whitney said happily.

It was one of those bright blue winter days when the sun warmed whatever it touched. Together they strolled through vast formal gardens with sleeping flower beds arranged in lavish geometric patterns, their borders precise and manicured.

The gardeners and groundskeepers who were gathering fallen twigs and heaping them onto a small fire took no apparent notice of the couple strolling through the gardens. But when the young lady said something that made the duke roar with laughter and snatch her into his arms in a quick bear hug, several of them glanced up to stare in astonishment, and then exchanged knowing grins before quietly continuing with their tasks.

At Clayton's side, Whitney wandered through the dappled sunlight of the arbor, her mind picturing the splendor of spring, when the trees would burst into bloom, strewing flowers along the wide winding paths, blanketing the white ornamental iron benches in blossoms of pink and rose and white.

They turned and walked along the perfectly tended banks of an immense lake with a graceful pillared pavilion overlooking it from a wide knoll on the opposite bank. Clayton took her hand and they walked around the lake toward the pavilion. It was, Whitney thought in a daze of happiness, sheer bliss to have her hand firmly clasped in Clayton's strong, warm one; to be with him in quiet, joyous peace, without the barriers she had always kept between them. She gazed at the bright blue sky where fluffy white clouds slowly drifted past, and decided it was a halcyon day—the happiest day of her life.

The view of the lake and surrounding grounds from the higher pavilion was glorious. Whitney leaned her shoulders against one of the white pillars, breathing in the splendor of it. She knew perfectly well that Clayton had guided her here because, inside, the pavilion would offer some scant privacy, but she stood there anyway, delightfully prolonging the moment when they would step inside and he would take her in his arms . . .

Unexpectedly he stepped in front of her, blocking her view as he braced a hand on either side of her shoulders. Laughter lurked in his gaze as his mouth slowly descended to hers. "Have it your own way," he said huskily, his tone amused. "I'm not shy, so it matters not in the least to me if I kiss you out here or in there."

When at last he lifted his mouth from hers, Whitney was shaky with awakened desire. "Clayton," she whispered. "I—"

He interrupted her in a deep, quiet voice. "I love to hear you say my name. It makes me want to take you in my arms, to have your sweet tongue in my mouth, to caress your breasts and feel your nipples rise up proudly against my hand."

Whitney drew an unsteady breath and dropped her eyes, but not before Clayton glimpsed the fires kindling in their jade depths and the warm peach tint creeping up her soft cheeks. He smiled to himself. She might be afraid of his making love to her now, but she was still a warm, passionate creature, and she would soon dismiss her fears. He glanced over her shoulder into the pavilion. He wanted to hold her and leisurely kiss that stirringly provocative mouth, but not here, where he knew they could be seen. Idly, he let his gaze wander over the landscape, a little irritated by the lack of privacy available to him, then he saw the wooded ridge off in the distance to the west. That ridge would offer both privacy and a view.

"The home woods?" Whitney asked, following his gaze.

Clayton grinned at her. "Part of them. The view is supposed to be the best for miles. We'll ride up there in a bit." But not entirely for the view, he added silently. Turning, he leaned against the pavilion wall, pleasuring himself with the view of her vivid profile. With her glossy tresses caught at the nape in a wide velvet bow, she reminded Clayton of a little girl who ought to be wearing white stockings and a ruffled dress, sitting on a swing, while the boys argued over the honor of pushing her. But here the image ended, for there was nothing childish about the lush, tantalizing curves displayed to such advantage by her amber riding habit.

Reluctantly, Clayton turned his attention toward a less

pleasant direction. "There are some things between us that need to be settled, and I would sooner do that now, so that the past can be buried and forgotten."

Whitney turned her head away, and he added quietly, "I think you already know what I want to ask—"

Whitney knew he wanted an explanation for her actions the day of Elizabeth's wedding, and she nodded, drawing a long breath. "You see, when I saw you at the church, I thought we were still betrothed, and I had no idea that you'd received an invitation to the wedding. I thought you'd come there to try to see me . . ." She told him the whole story, simply, without trying to hide the hurt and anger she'd felt toward him.

Clayton listened without interrupting. When she was finished, he asked, "What made you decide to come here last night, after hating me as you have for all these weeks?"

"Emily made me realize that I was misjudging you."

"What," Clayton said on a note of alarm, "does Emily Archibald know about us?"

In a small voice, Whitney admitted, "Everything." She saw him flinch and hesitantly said, "Now may I ask *you* something?"

"Anything," Clayton said gravely.

"Anything," Whitney teased, "within your power, and within reason?"

"Anything!" he declared firmly, but with a grin.

"Why did you do that awful thing to me? What made you think I had—had given myself to Paul?"

With self-disgust filling his voice, Clayton answered her question.

"But how could you have believed Margaret, knowing how much she hates me?" Whitney gave him a hurt, accusing look, realized that she was only adding more pain to his memory of that night, and quickly pressed a kiss on his mouth. "It doesn't matter."

"It matters," Clayton said harshly. "But some day, I'll make it up to you." A smile softened his voice. "Let's see if you can handle my favorite mare—we'll race up to that ridge."

The view from the top of the ridge was spectacular. While

Clayton tied their horses, Whitney stood, gazing out across the wooded valleys, trying to imagine how they would look in the lush greens of summer or the vibrant red-gold of autumn.

"There is more to be enjoyed here than the view, my lady," a husky, laughing voice announced from behind her. "Come here, and I'll show you."

Whitney turned around and discovered Clayton sitting with one knee drawn up, his shoulders propped against a tree trunk behind him. She saw the warm sensuality in his gray eyes, and she felt a small tremor of dread. She wanted very much to be in his arms, to be kissed and held, but she suspected Clayton had more than that in mind. Because he had already lain with her, he might feel that marriage was no longer a necessary prerequisite for the two of them. Whitney not only felt that marriage was still a prerequisite to the sexual act, she wished she could avoid the sexual intimacy forever. She couldn't, of course, but she had eight weeks before she would be obliged, as his wife, to endure that painful, embarrassing act, and she wanted this eight-week reprieve. Reluctant to tell Clayton that unless it was absolutely necessary, she turned back to the valleys below and tried to divert him from thoughts of lovemaking. "The view is breathtaking," she rhapsodized. "Could we ride down there?"

"We could," he said agreeably, then he added, "another day."

"Why don't we do it now?" Whitney suggested with pleading determination.

"Because I want to kiss you," he replied simply.

Whitney spun around in relieved disbelief. "You only want to kiss me? I mean you won't try to—to—"

"Oh darling, come here," Clayton laughed softly, noting her flaring color. "That's all I want to do." *That's all I'm going to do,* he amended silently.

With a sigh of joyous relief, Whitney went to him. She started to sit down beside him, but Clayton caught her arms and drew her down onto his lap. "The view will be better if you're up higher," he teased.

Sliding his arms around her, he moved her tighter against

437

him. Without urging she turned her face up for his kiss. Clayton brushed his lips against her temple; he kissed her smooth forehead and her cheek. He closed her eyes with his lips, avoiding her mouth lest he frighten her with his ardor, but he drew back in surprise at her muffled laugh.

"Unless your aim improves, my lord duke," she warned, her eyes aglow with laughter, "I shall be forced to buy you a quizzing glass after all."

"You will, will you?" Clayton growled huskily as his mouth crushed down on hers. He felt her hands glide up his chest and go around his neck, and his heart began to hammer. As her lips parted beneath his, desire began to heat his blood, and when her tongue crept timidly into his mouth, a jolt slammed through Clayton's entire nervous system, exploding his control. He kissed her deeply, his mouth moving with half-fierce, half-gentle urgency, and she moaned, kissing him back with desire and passion exquisite on her lips. He tormented her with his tongue, retreating, then thrusting deep until she instinctively responded in the way he wanted.

His hand moved of its own accord, opening her jacket to cup her breasts, his thumb circling her hardened nipples. Under her silken shirt, her thrusting breasts came to life in his hand, thrilling and warning him at the same time. Her soft moan of pleasure raced through him, throbbing in his ears. He forced his hand away, only to have it slide downward, lightly grazing her flat stomach, then her shapely thigh, instinctively seeking the place where, without the barrier of her skirts, he could part her silken thighs and gently, tenderly, tease his beautiful trembling girl until she was melting with desire for him, wanting him as badly as he wanted her. His mouth began to plunder hers more urgently, more hungrily now, and he started to reach for the hem of her skirt.

With the last vestige of control he possessed, Clayton tore his mouth away from hers, and firmly pulled her arms down from around his neck. His breathing was hard and fast, his blood was roaring in his ears, and a fire was raging wildly through his veins. He moved Whitney up against his chest, off his lap, to avoid shocking or frightening her with the rigid evidence of his desire, and he looked down at her, still desperate to join his body with hers. He wanted to pour his life into her, to be able to look at her across a room and know that his seed was deep inside of her, to see her slender body swell with his child . . .

Clayton drew a long breath and slowly expelled it. Whitney was watching him, her beautiful upturned face mirroring puzzlement and concern. He grinned at her, feeling slightly betrayed by his own body's uncontrollable reaction to her. "Little one," he explained ruefully, "unless it is your wish to see me driven to madness, I'm afraid we can't do very much of this."

Whitney's eyes widened with bewilderment, then grew huge with understanding. She lurched into an erect sitting position, starting to pull away from him, but Clayton drew her back against his chest. "No," he said quietly, "stay in my arms a while longer. I just want to hold you." And she did.

"Is this ridge the boundary of your property?" Whitney asked later, as they walked toward their tethered horses.

Clayton looked a little stung. "No, the boundaries are farther away."

"How much land do you have?" Whitney asked, wondering at his odd, faintly wounded expression.

"About one hundred twelve thousand acres."

She gasped.

Her obvious shock reminded Clayton of something else, and he stopped abruptly, regarding her with laughter glinting in his eyes. "While I think of it, I've been meaning to ask you if you find my house 'dingy'?"

Whitney gave him a plucky smile. "I said 'dismal.' 'Dingy' was *your* word. And it is splendid—just like you."

To a man who had waited for months just to hear her call him by his given name, being told in the same morning that he was "beautiful" and "splendid" was unequivocally reason for another long, stirring kiss.

Standing at the wide bow windows overlooking the side-lawns, the duchess and Stephen watched Whitney and Clayton walking hand in hand toward the house. "They are splendid together, aren't they," her grace happily observed.

"Yes, sweetheart," Stephen chuckled knowingly. "And

you will have half a dozen splendid grandchildren. And in none too long a time, I'll wager," he added with a bald grin.

"Stephen, that is too bad of you!"

"Can't imagine why. I think it's rather wonderful."

His mother shot him an exasperated look that dwindled into laughter when she met his contagious grin. "What I meant, you wretched boy, is that she is a marvellous girl, and she makes your brother happier than I have ever seen him."

"She does indeed." Stephen looked out the window and saw Whitney, who had been walking beside Clayton, suddenly draw back laughing. She spoke rapidly to him, then turned and fled. In two long strides, Clayton caught her at the waist, flung her over his shoulder as if she were a sack of flour, and continued striding toward the house. Whitney struggled and pushed against him until he finally put her down, whereupon she walked sedately beside him with her hands clasped demurely behind her back.

"I believe that settled that!" the duchess laughed.

"Don't count on it," Stephen chuckled. Even as he spoke, Whitney began moving ahead of Clayton, a good four or five paces this time, then she turned, taking little backward skipping steps. She shook her head, laughing at whatever Clayton told her, then she pivoted on her heel and fled out of their line of vision. Instead of chasing her this time, Clayton leaned a shoulder against a tree, crossed his arms over his chest, and called something after her. Whitney was back in a flash, flinging her arms around him.

"Now *that* settled it!" Stephen laughed. "Remind me to ask Whitney if she has a sister," he added thoughtfully.

"Really, Stephen," her grace expostulated. "With half the mamas in London trying to put their daughters in your way these past five years, I can't imagine why you haven't already chosen a wife and—" she paused as if struck with an idea. "I believe Whitney did say she has a second cousin."

A lazy smile, very much like his brother's and just as fatal to a lady's heart, flashed across Stephen's features. "If she's

440

like Whitney, I'll marry her out of hand and give you enough grandchildren to make you blush."

"You can't possibly be serious!" the duchess gasped at lunch, when Clayton announced his intention to be wed in eight weeks.

"I am perfectly serious." Rising from his chair, he pressed a kiss on Whitney's forehead and lightly mocked, "I'll leave the little details of the affair to the two of you." He strode toward the door, turned back toward his mother and Whitney who were staring at each other, overwhelmed, and took pity on them. "Just draw up a list of things to be attended to, and give it to Hudgins. He'll be able to prevail upon the various establishments to act with haste."

"Exactly who *is* Hudgins?" Whitney asked. "I've never seen him."

"He's Clayton's secretary. And he's a wizard," the duchess sighed. "He'll employ the magic of Clayton's name, and everything will be ready in eight weeks, but I had so hoped to have more time for parties and—"

Her sentence was interrupted by Clayton, who poked his head back into the room and, grinning like a devil, said, "Well, is the list ready yet?"

Chapter Thirty-one

In response to Whitney's note, Lady Anne Gilbert arrived the following morning, ready to help with the wedding preparations, and an almost instant friendship sprang up between her and the duchess.

For Whitney, the next four days drifted by in a haze of comfort and togetherness, of smiles exchanged across the table, and stolen moments of joy in each other's arms.

True to Clayton's mother's prediction, all the various shops agreed to meet their eight-week deadline, despite the fact that the fashionable modistes were already overburdened with orders for the next season. Frequently, it was the proprietors themselves who arrived, carrying large sketches and boxes of swatches, all of them eager to claim that they had been of assistance to the future Duchess of Claymore in her wedding preparations.

On the fifth day, however, Whitney received a rather perfunctory summons from a footman who informed her that "His grace wishes to see you in his study—at once." Trying to smother the apprehensive feeling in her breast, Whitney hurried down the hall, nodded toward a distinguished-looking man she passed who was carrying a large, flat, oblong case under his arm, and entered Clayton's study. Closing the doors behind her, she bobbed a funny little servant's curtsy and said teasingly, "You rang for me, your grace?"

Clayton was standing in front of his desk, and he gazed at her silently across the room, his expression very somber.

"Is—is something wrong?" Whitney breathed after a moment.

Although he spoke gently, there was a strange new gravity to his tone. "No. Come here, please."

"Clayton, what is it?" Whitney said, hurrying toward him. "What has—"

He caught her to him in a crushing embrace. "Nothing is wrong," he said in an odd, rough voice. "I missed you." With one arm still around her waist, he turned aside and picked up a small velvet box from the desk behind him. "I thought about an emerald," he said in that same gentle, grave voice, "but it would be outshone by your eyes. So I decided on this instead." He unsnapped the lid of the box with his free hand, and a magnificent diamond shot prisms of color across the intricate plasterwork scrolls at the ceiling.

Whitney stared at it in awed wonder. "I've never seen anything so . . . ." She stopped as tears of poignant happiness welled in her eyes.

Taking her hand, Clayton slid the exquisite gem onto her long finger. Whitney looked down at her own hand which now bore the first tangible proof that she was actually Clayton's. She belonged to him now, and all the world would see the ring and know it.

No longer was she Whitney Allison Stone, her father's daughter, Lord and Lady Gilbert's niece. She was now the promised bride of the Duke of Claymore. In the space of one moment, she had lost her identity and been given a new one. She wanted to tell him that his ring was beautiful, that she worshiped him, but she only managed to whisper, "I love you" before the tears came, and she turned her face into his chest. "I'm not sad," she tried to explain as the reassuring strength of his arms encircled her, "I'm happy."

"I know, little one," he whispered, holding her until the same emotion that had unexpectedly rocked him when he'd chosen the ring a few minutes ago, had passed through her.

Finally Whitney drew back, smiling a little sheepishly, and held her hand out in front of her to admire the glittering splendor of the single stone. "It's the most magnificent thing I've ever seen," she said, "except for you."

A surge of hot desire swept through Clayton at the sound of her words, and he bent his head to capture her mouth with his, then he checked the motion—there was a limit to how much stimulation his body could tolerate these days. Instead, he said in a tone of mock severity, "Madam, I hope you'll not make a habit of crying whenever I give you a jewel, else we'll have to send for buckets when you see the ones that belong to you from my grandmothers."

"Didn't this ring belong to one of your grandmothers?"

"No. Westmoreland duchesses are never betrothed with a ring that has belonged to another—it's tradition. Your wedding band will be an heirloom, though."

"Are there any other Westmoreland traditions?" Whitney asked, her smile filled with love.

Clayton's restraint broke; he gathered her into his arms, his mouth descending with hunger and need on hers. "We could start one," he whispered meaningfully. "Tell me you want me," he said thickly, his mouth fiercely tender as it ravaged hers.

"I love you," she answered instead, but Clayton felt her intoxicating body straining automatically to be closer to his. A deep, knowing laugh sounded in his chest as he drew back. "I know you love me, little one," he said, tipping her chin up. "But you *want* me, too."

Whitney conveniently remembered, then, that her aunt and the seamstresses were waiting for her in the other room. Only half reluctantly, she stepped away. "Will that be all, your grace?" she smiled, bobbing another servant's curtsy.

Clayton's tone was politely impersonal. "For now, thank you," he said, but when she turned, he gave her an affectionate smack that landed squarely on her derriere.

Whitney halted. Over her shoulder she regarded him with an expression of exaggerated severity, and warned, "If I were you, I'd not forget what happened when you did that to me after the Rutherfords' party."

"At the Archibalds' house?" he clarified. "When I brought you home?"

Her lips twitched with laughter, but she managed a slow, haughty nod. "Precisely."

"Am I to understand," Clayton mocked, trying unsuccessfully to keep his face straight, "that you're threatening to knock these paintings off the wall?"

Puzzled, Whitney glanced at the portraits in heavy carved frames hanging along the wall, and then at Clayton's laughing face. "I thought I slapped you."

"You missed."

"I did?"

"I'm afraid so," he confirmed gravely.

Whitney muffled a giggle. "How provoking."

"Undoubtedly," he agreed.

Bemused, Whitney turned and started to walk away. His second smack landed with a little more force upon her derriere than the first, and although she managed to look quite disapproving, she couldn't stifle her laughter.

That night after dinner, the family all retired to the drawing room. The duchess and Aunt Anne were deeply engrossed in gossip, while Stephen was regaling Whitney with hilarious versions of Clayton's most infamous boyhood transgressions, to which Clayton was listening with alternating expressions of extreme discomfort and bored disgust.

"Then there was the time when Clay was twelve and he didn't come down to breakfast. When he wasn't in his room either, Father and the servants began combing the grounds. Late in the afternoon, Clay's shirt was found on the bank of the stream where the water is fast and deep. His boat was still there, because Father had forbidden him to take it out for one month . . ."

Breathless with laughter from the last story, Whitney turned to her betrothed and gasped, "Why—why weren't you allowed to take your boat out?"

Clayton glowered his displeasure at Stephen, then gazed down into Whitney's vivid, laughing face and grinned in spite of himself. "As I recall, I had not come down properly attired for dinner the night before."

"Not properly attired?" Stephen hooted. "You appeared a half hour late, in riding boots and hacking clothes, positively reeking of horse sweat and leather, with gunpowder on your face from sneaking out and practicing with Father's old dueling pistols."

Clayton hurled a look of excruciating disgust at Stephen, and Whitney dissolved with laughter. "Go on, Stephen," she gasped merrily. "Tell me the rest about finding Clayton's shirt by the stream."

"Well, everyone thought Clay had drowned and they came rushing to the scene, with Mother in tears and Father as white as a sheet, when, around the bend came Clay on the most rickety, makeshift raft you have ever seen. Everyone held their breath, expecting the raft to swamp when he tried to bank it, but Clay guided it right in. With his fishing pole in one hand and a stringer of prime fish in the other, he got off and looked around at us as if he thought we were all odd for standing there, gaping at him. Then he strolled up to Father and Mother, still carrying that huge stringer of fish.

"Mother promptly burst into tears and Father finally recovered his voice. He was in the middle of delivering a thundering tirade about Clay's irresponsible behavior, his recklessness, and even his lack of a shirt, when your future husband said very patiently that he did not think it was seemly for Father to be dressing him down in front of the servants."

"Oh, you *didn't!*" Whitney whispered hoarsely, slumping lower in her seat. "Then what happened?"

Clayton chuckled. "Father obliged me by sending the servants away," he said, "and *then* he boxed my ears."

Into this utterly congenial atmosphere of charming conviviality intruded the black-coated figure of the butler who intoned magisterially, "Lord Edward Gilbert has arrived." This announcement was immediately followed by the appearance of Lord Edward Gilbert himself, who strode into the drawing room, glanced around, and beamed his general approbation on all the occupants.

"Good heavens! It's Edward!" gasped Lady Anne, coming to her feet and staring at her beloved husband. Afraid that her letters had finally caught up with him and that he had hastened here to rescue Whitney from an unwanted match with the duke, she thought madly for some concise explanation to give him for the momentous events which had led to this gathering at Claymore.

Whitney also lurched to her feet, her thoughts identical to her aunt's. "Uncle Edward!" she burst out.

"Glad that everyone recognizes me," Lord Edward Gilbert drily remarked, looking from Anne to Whitney in obvious expectation of some more sentimental greeting than he had thus far received.

Unnoticed, Clayton rose and strolled over to the fireplace, where he leaned an elbow upon the mantel, and with visible amusement watched the unfolding scene.

Edward waited for someone to introduce him to the duchess and Stephen, but when neither his wife nor his niece seemed capable of speech, he shrugged and strode directly over to the duke. "Well Claymore," he said, warmly returning Clayton's handclasp, "I see the betrothal has come off without a hitch."

"Without a hitch?!" Lady Gilbert whispered in a strangled voice.

"Without a hitch?" Whitney echoed as she slowly crumpled to the sofa.

"*Almost* without a hitch," Clayton corrected mildly, ignoring the gaping stares of the other occupants of the room.

"Good, good. Knew it would," said Lord Gilbert. Clayton introduced him to his mother and Stephen, and when the civilities had been exchanged, Edward finally turned again to his rigid wife. "Anne?" said he as he advanced upon her and she retreated, step for step. "After months apart, Madam, it strikes me that your greeting thus far has been less than enthusiastic."

"Edward," Lady Gilbert breathed, "you clothhead!"

"Can't say that's much of an improvement over, 'Good heavens, it's Edward,'" he pointed out with asperity.

"You knew about this betrothal from the very beginning," she accused, transferring her dark frown from Edward to a grinning Clayton, who immediately smoothed his face into more suitably grave lines. "I have been subjected to enough suspense to drive anyone to raving lunacy, and the two of you have been in communication all along, haven't you?! I can't think which of you I should more like to murder."

"Do you want your hartshorn, my dear?"

"No, I do not want my hartshorn," his lady replied, "I want an explanation!"

"An explanation for what?" Edward asked, bewildered.

"For why you have not answered my letters, for why you did not tell me you were aware of this betrothal, for why you didn't advise me what to do . . ."

"I only got *one* of your letters," he defended a trifle brusquely, "and all you said was that Claymore was in residence near Stone's place. And I can't imagine why you needed me to tell you what to do, when it was perfectly obvious that all you *had* to do was chaperone two people whom anyone could see were ideally suited to each other. And I did not tell you I was aware of the betrothal because I was *not* aware of it until Claymore's letter was brought to me in Spain a month and a half ago."

Lady Gilbert was not to be so easily pacified. With a brief glance of apology to Clayton, she burst out, "They most certainly were not *'ideally suited!'*"

"Of course they were!" Edward defended stoutly. "What possible objection could you have to a match with Claymore?" Suddenly, a look of amused understanding crossed his face. "So you were worried about his reputation, were you? Lord, Madam," he chuckled tolerantly, momentarily oblivious to the presence of the Westmoreland family in the room, "haven't you ever heard the saying that 'reformed rakes often make the best husbands'?"

"Why, thank you, Lord Gilbert," Clayton said wryly.

Lord Gilbert cast a puzzled look at Stephen who was suddenly seized with a fit of strangled laughter, then continued speaking to his wife. "I thought they would make an excellent match the night I saw them together at the masquerade, and I knew something was in the wind when I was informed the Westmoreland solicitors were making inquiries about Whitney in Paris. Then I thought Martin had spoiled everything by sending for her, but when I got your letter and you said Claymore was in residence not three miles away from Stone's doorstep, I knew exactly what was happening."

"Oh no you didn't!" Lady Anne exclaimed heatedly. *"I'll* tell you what happened. From the moment Whitney clapped eyes on his grace in England, she was at daggers-drawn with him. And . . ."

Lord Gilbert turned his head and peered sternly at Whitney over the top of his spectacles. "Oh, so *Whitney* was the problem, was she?" He transferred his gaze to Clayton and said, "Whitney needs a husband who'll keep a firm hand on the reins. That's why I was in favor of your suit from the very beginning."

"Why, thank you, Uncle Edward," Whitney said ungratefully.

"It's the truth and you know it, m'dear." To Lady Anne, he added, "She's much like you in that respect."

"How very kind of you to say so, Edward," Anne said tartly.

Edward glanced from his wife's indignant face to Whitney's rebellious one, and then toward Clayton, who was regarding him with a dark brow arched in sardonic amusement. He looked at Stephen Westmoreland, whose shoulders were rocking with silent laughter, and then at the duchess who was much too polite to show any emotion at all. "Well," said he to the duchess with a sigh, "I can see that I've now offended everyone. Amazing, is it not, that I am purported to be a competent diplomat?"

The duchess broke into a smile. *"I* am not in the least offended, Lord Gilbert. I have a decided partiality for rakes. After all, I was married to one, and I have raised"—she looked meaningfully at Stephen—"two."

Chapter Thirty-two

THE ANNOUNCEMENT IN THE PAPERS OF THE BETROTHAL OF THE Duke of Claymore to Miss Whitney Allison Stone struck London with the force of a hurricane, and Whitney was caught in its backlash.

Invitations to every conceivable social function arrived daily at the Archibalds' house in staggering numbers. Between the parties in their honor, which Whitney and Clayton had to attend, and the extensive wedding preparations which required every available minute of her time, Whitney was feverishly busy and almost limp with exhaustion. Added to that was the anxiety which increased as her wedding day—ergo, her wedding *night*—approached.

Often she lay awake in Emily's guest room, telling herself sternly that if other women could endure the sexual act, she could too. Besides, she repeatedly reminded herself, the act itself, and the awful pain that accompanied it, didn't last all that long. And she adored Clayton, so if he wished to do that to her, then she would bear the pain to make him happy, and hope that it happened with minimal frequency. Yet she hated knowing not only the day, but practically the *hour,* when he was going to do it to her again.

In one of her more philosophical moments, she decided that the reason virginity was so prized for a bride was because early man must have realized that a bride who knew what was

450

in store for her on her wedding night, would not be smiling quite so radiantly when she walked down that aisle!

Unfortunately, by the time the wedding was a week away, her philosophical attitude had deserted her entirely, and her dread was steadily mounting. To make matters worse, as their wedding day approached, Clayton's attentions became decidedly more ardent—and therefore, more frightening.

Even her ivory wedding gown, which was hanging in her dressing room, sent a trill of fear up her spine when she looked at it, because it reminded her of the ivory satin gown that Clayton had torn from her body. Not that she was idiotic enough to think that the gentle, understanding man she worshiped was going to tear her clothes from her on their wedding night—but neither did she think Clayton was likely to allow her to keep them on for very long either.

Surreptitiously, she began watching Emily when Michael asked her if she were ready to retire. Emily didn't seem to dread going to their bedroom. Neither, Whitney recalled, had Aunt Anne tried to evade retiring with Uncle Edward. Why then, was Whitney the only woman who winced at the thought of the pain which came with the marital act? The more Whitney considered it, the more horrifyingly convinced she became that there was a physical defect within her which made the act hurt her, and only her, so dreadfully.

To add to her misery, as her wedding day bore down on her, her agitated mind began tormenting her with constant visions of that terrible night when Clayton had cruelly and deliberately shamed her with his hands and mouth and body. The humiliation of that night came back to haunt her, magnifying her remembered physical pain until she was a mass of fear and trepidation.

Five days before the wedding, she was simply too worn down to attend the ball being given by one of Clayton's friends. The next day she sent Clayton a note, asking him to excuse her from an afternoon party at the Rutherfords'.

Clayton, who had removed to his townhouse in Upper Brook Street to be near Whitney during the weeks preceding the wedding, read her brief note declining the Rutherfords' party with a faint frown of bewilderment. After a moment's thought, he ordered his carriage brought round and went directly to the Archibald townhouse where he was informed that Miss Stone was in the Blue Salon, and that Lord and Lady Archibald were out for the day.

Whitney picked up a fresh piece of stationery, dipped her quill into the ink pot, and continued with the exhausting task of writing notes of appreciation for the awesome number of wedding gifts which had been arriving in droves for weeks. In the doorway of the salon, Clayton stopped and gazed at her. She was seated at a desk, her dark chestnut hair twisted into thick curls bound with narrow green ribbons. Her head was bent slightly as she wrote, her flawless profile turned to him. With the sun streaming in the window beside her, Clayton thought she looked so fragile and lovely that she seemed ethereal. "Problems?" he said after a long moment, closing the doors behind him. He crossed to her, took her by the hand and pulled her gently, but firmly, out of her chair and over toward the sofa. "Young lady, is it your intention to treat me as a bystander in all of this, and only remember my existence when you walk down the aisle?"

Whitney sank down beside him. "I'm sorry about the Rutherfords' affair," she said with a tired smile that made Clayton instantly regret his mild reprimand. "It's just that I'm so busy with everything, that even I feel like a bystander at times." Turning her face into the comforting curve of his shoulder and neck, she said, "I missed you terribly last night—did you have a pleasant time at the ball?"

Clayton tilted her chin up. "Not without you," he murmured as his mouth covered hers. "Now, show me how much you missed me . . ."

Within moments, Whitney's tension and exhaustion had melted away in the heat of Clayton's passionate kiss. In a kind of sensual haze, she was dimly aware that he was inexorably drawing her down to lie beside him on the silk sofa, but with his lips moving persuasively against hers, and his tongue teasing and exploring, the shift in her position scarcely seemed to matter.

Her senses swam dizzily, assaulted by his deep kisses and

the gentle, arousing things he whispered against her parted lips as he kissed her. "I can't get enough of you," he murmured, leaning over her. "I'll never get enough of you." His hand roamed possessively over the sensitive skin above her bodice, his fingers nimbly unfastening the row of tiny buttons at the front of her lime-wool dress. Before Whitney could react, her chemise was down and his mouth was moving leisurely toward her naked, exposed breasts. "The servants!" she gasped.

"They're scared to death of me," Clayton said. "They wouldn't come in here to warn us of a fire."

His tongue touched a rosy nipple, and Whitney struggled in genuine, frantic earnest. "Don't! Please!" she said hoarsely, lurching into a sitting position and clutching her open bodice, clumsily refastening it.

Clayton started to reach for her, but she leapt off the sofa. Amazed, he sat up and stared at her. She looked slightly flushed, very beautiful—and frightened half to death! "Whitney?" he said cautiously.

She jumped, took three steps backward, then sank onto the sofa across from him, her expression tortured and embarrassed. As Clayton watched, she started to speak, changed her mind, then ran her hand over her forehead. Finally, she raised pleading green eyes to his and drew a long, unsteady breath. "There's something I've wanted to ask you—a favor. But it's dreadful and embarrassing. It's about our wedding. Night."

Frowning with worry over the tension and anxiety he saw on her face, Clayton leaned forward and rested his forearms on his knees. "What favor do you want to ask of me?" he said quietly.

"Promise me you won't be angry when you hear it?"

"You have my word," Clayton assured her calmly.

"Well, you see," she began hesitantly, "I—I would like to be able to really look forward to our wedding. But I can't, because I keep thinking about what is going to happen—you know—later that night. Other brides don't understand, not exactly, but I do now and I—" She was as pink as roses when she trailed off into pathetic silence.

"What is it that you wanted to ask of me?" Clayton said, but he already knew—God help him, he already knew.

"I was wondering if you might agree to wait," she explained miserably. "I mean, agree not to do that to me on our wedding night." Unable to meet his steady gaze any longer, Whitney looked away in sheer embarrassment. Uninformed she might be about some things, but she knew full well that wives made no such bargains with husbands, and that marriages were consummated on the wedding night. Why, in days gone by, a marriage was consummated with observers in the room, in the old—and thank heavens, *antiquated*—custom of "bedding" the newly wedded couple. A wife's duty, her vows, required that she submit to her husband in all things, and that included satisfying his passion.

"Are you absolutely certain this is the way you want it?" Clayton asked after a long silence.

"Positive," Whitney whispered, her eyes downcast.

"What if I refuse to agree?"

Staring at her hands, Whitney swallowed. "Then I'll submit to you."

"Submit to me?" Clayton repeated, stunned and a little irritated by her choice of words. He could hardly believe that after eight weeks, Whitney still thought of the final culmination of their desires as some form of punishment to which she must "submit." She always came eagerly into his arms, returning his kisses with a fervor and hunger that almost matched his. And whenever he held her, she instinctively fitted her voluptuous body to the contours of his. What in the living hell did she imagine he was going to do on their wedding night—turn into a crazed animal and tear her clothes off again? "Is it me you're afraid of, little one?" he asked quietly.

Her gaze flew to his and her response was emphatic. "No! I couldn't bear it if you thought that. I know you aren't going to—to treat me the way you did before. It's just that I feel embarrassed, because I know exactly what you are going to do to me. And there's something else too—something terrible that I should have told you weeks ago. Clayton, I think I am malformed in some way. You see, it—what you did to me that night—hurt dreadfully. And I don't think other females feel such pain or . . ."

"Don't!" Clayton interrupted harshly, unable to bear hearing how badly he had hurt her. With an inward sigh, he accepted this as the penalty he was going to have to pay for his callous cruelty that night. And in view of what he had actually done to her, it seemed a small price, at that. "I will give you my word to wait, on two conditions," he told her quietly. "The first is that, after our wedding night, the option of choosing the time is mine."

She nodded so eagerly and looked so relieved that Clayton almost smiled.

"The second condition is that you promise that during the next few days you will seriously consider what I am about to say."

Again she nodded.

"Whitney, what occurred between us before was nothing more than an act of outrage on my part; it was not 'making love,' it was an act of selfish revenge."

She was listening, and Clayton realized she was trying to understand, but to her at this point, an act was an act, and if it was painful and humiliating before, it would be again. "Come here," he said gently. "I can explain better with a small demonstration."

Apprehension flitted across her face, but she obediently crossed to sit beside him. Clayton tipped her chin up and kissed her deeply and tenderly. Her response was longer than usual in coming, but when it did, it was exquisitely warm and filled with love. "Do you remember the first time I ever kissed you, on the balcony at Lady Eubank's house?" he asked, drawing back and searching her eyes. "I was punishing you for trying to use me to make Sevarin jealous—remember?"

She nodded. "I slapped you," she recalled with a smile.

"Do you feel like slapping me now? Do you feel in any way the same about this kiss as you did that first one?"

"No."

"Then believe me when I tell you that what will happen

between us the next time I take you to my bed will be as different from before, as this kiss is from that first one."

"Thank you," she said with a beaming smile of relief.

She didn't believe him for a minute, Clayton knew. But she was overjoyed with her "wedding night reprieve."

Chapter Thirty-three

AT THE FIRST LIGHT OF DAWN, WHITNEY CLIMBED FROM BENEATH the cool sheets, groped for her dressing robe in the dark, then settled into a chair at the windows to watch the sun rise over London on her wedding day. She bent her head and tried to pray. But all her prayers began with "Thank you" instead of "Please."

She heard the house slowly stirring to life, the sound of servants moving about the halls, of footsteps passing her door. The wedding was not to begin until three o'clock, and that seemed like an eternity from now.

For hours, time scarcely seemed to move, and then, just after noon, time leapt forward, picking up extraordinary speed. People scurried in and out of her bedroom, while Aunt Anne sat perched upon the bed, watching Clarissa brush Whitney's thick mahogany tresses until they shone. Emily came into the room wearing a dressing robe, ready to slip into her gown, and Elizabeth was right on her heels. "Hello," Whitney said in a quiet, joyous voice.

"Nervous or just not talkative?" Emily teased gaily.

"Neither. Just happy."

"Aren't you the tiniest bit nervous?" Elizabeth persevered hopefully, darting a conspiratorial wink at Emily and Whitney's aunt. "I hope his grace hasn't changed his mind."

"He hasn't," Whitney assured her with perfect serenity.

"Well!" Clayton's mother laughed, coming into the room, "I can see things are not much different here than they are in Upper Brook Street this afternoon. Stephen is driving Clayton to the brink of madness."

"Is Clayton nervous?" Whitney asked incredulously.

"Beyond belief!" her grace said, smiling and sitting down beside Anne Gilbert on the bed.

"Why?" Whitney asked in alarm.

"Why? There are at least a dozen reasons why, and all of them are either directly or indirectly related to Stephen. At ten o'clock this morning, Stephen arrived at the house and told Clayton that as he passed here, two travelling chaises were being loaded and that he was quite, quite certain he saw *you* getting into one of them. Clayton was already bounding down the stairs to come after you before Stephen shouted that he was joking."

Whitney smothered a laugh and the duchess said, *"You* may find that amusing, my dear, but Clayton did not. After that, Stephen convincingly reported that he had discovered a nonexistent plot among the groomsmen to kidnap Clayton and delay his arrival at the wedding. Which is why all twelve of the groomsmen are now cooling their heels under Clayton's watchful eye at his house. And that is only the beginning."

"Poor Clayton."

"Poor *Stephen,*" the duchess corrected drily. "I came here because I couldn't bear to watch my elder son murder my younger, which is what Clayton was threatening—rather seriously, I might add—to do if Stephen came within arm's reach of him again."

Time flew on rapid, beating wings, and suddenly Whitney was fully dressed, walking into the bedroom for her aunt and her future mother-in-law's inspection.

"Oh my dear child," the duchess gasped, her eyes shining with wonder. "I have never seen anything like you in all my life!" Stepping back, she surveyed Whitney's ivory, pearl-encrusted gown which had been designed as a glorious representation of a medieval bride. Its low, square-cut bodice hugged Whitney's full bosom, then tapered to a narrow waistline, where a gold chain with clusters of diamonds and pearls set in each shining link rode low on her hips. The undersleeves were tightly fitted satin tubes terminating in deep points at the tops of her hands, but the satin over-sleeves, stiffly encrusted with pearls, ended in wide bells at her elbows. A flowing satin cape trailed behind her, bordered in pearls, and attached at her shoulders with jeweled links that matched those at her waist. She wore no veil. Instead, her long hair was pulled back off her forehead and held at the crown with a diamond and pearl clip. It cascaded over her shoulders in curving waves, ending in soft thick curls, midway down her back. Clayton had once said he liked it best this way.

"You look exactly like a medieval princess would have *wished* to look," Clayton's mother breathed reverently, but Anne Gilbert only stared in silent joy at the serenely beautiful young woman who was about to become a duchess, while in Anne's mind she saw Whitney as she had been not so long ago, wearing groom's britches and balancing barefoot on the back of a cantering horse. When she finally spoke, tears of happiness and pride thickened her voice. "We should leave early for the church. Your father said there were crowds of spectators already gathering when he passed there hours ago, and he said that traffic was dreadfully bogged down."

That turned out to be an understatement. Four blocks from the massive church, the coach bearing Whitney, her father, and her aunt, was at a complete stop, hopelessly caught in the tangle of conveyances and would-be spectators blocking the streets. It was as if all London had turned out to witness the wedding.

In a large anteroom of the church, twelve groomsmen looked up hopefully as Stephen came in from a side door. He walked over to Clayton who was leaning against a table, his rigid features reflecting the gathering storm brewing within him as it seemed more and more likely that Whitney had jilted him at the altar. Stephen, however, was imperturbably cheerful as he reported, "There is the most unbelievable snarl out there. The streets are swarming with pedestrians, and the horses and carriages can't move."

Clayton straightened abruptly and jerked his head toward the door. "Find McRea, he's in this church somewhere, and tell him I want the coach waiting in front. If she isn't here in five minutes, I'm going after her."

"Clay, unless your cattle have sprouted wings, it wouldn't do any good. Would you mind stepping over to this door and seeing for yourself why Whitney is late?"

With long, angry strides, Clayton followed him to the door which looked out from the side of the church onto a square. The street was teaming with humanity and hopelessly entangled conveyances. "What in the living hell is going on?" he snapped.

"A duke is getting married." Stephen grinned. "And to a beautiful girl who has neither aristocratic lineage nor even immense wealth. Apparently yours is the fairy-tale wedding of the century, and the cits mean to be here to see it."

"Who in God's name invited them?" Clayton demanded, his mind on where Whitney might have gone to elude him.

"Since we don't own the church, they undoubtedly think they have the right to be here. Although," Stephen added wryly, "there's no more room left out there. Even the balconies are filled to capacity."

"Your grace," a serene masculine voice interrupted. Fourteen concerned male faces turned toward the archbishop who was arrayed in all his ecclesiastical finery. "The bride is here," he said quietly.

Twenty thousand white candles illuminated the aisles and the altar of the church. The organ pipes gave forth an expectant note, and then music rose majestically, filling the echoing church from its marble floor to the high-vaulted ceilings.

One by one, Whitney watched her twelve bridesmaids drift down the aisle. Therèse DuVille Ronsard accepted her bouquet from the maid and straightened her train, then she turned to Whitney with a soft smile. "Nicki gave me a message, which I am to give to you at this moment. He said to tell you, 'Bon voyage—again.'"

The poignant message from Nicki almost shattered Whitney's composure. Tears momentarily blurred her vision and she purposefully focused her eyes on Emily, who was just stepping out into the aisle in a trail of apple-green silk and satin. Alone now with her father with whom she had only exchanged polite, impersonal comments since his arrival for the wedding two days ago, Whitney turned to him. He looked austere and gruff. "Are you nervous, Papa?" she asked softly, watching him.

"Nothing to be nervous about," he said in an oddly hoarse voice. "I'm walking down the aisle with the most beautiful female in England on my arm." He looked at her, and Whitney saw that his eyes were moist as he added, "Don't suppose you'll believe this, because you and I have always been at sixes and sevens, but I never would have promised you to the duke if I didn't think he was man enough to handle—no, *the man* for you," he corrected clumsily. "I thought to myself that first day, when he came to the house, that the two of you were cut from the same cloth, and I agreed to his suit right then. We never even discussed money until *after* I had agreed to the betrothal."

Whitney's eyes were misty as she leaned up and kissed his furrowed brow. "Thank you for telling me that, Papa. I love you, too."

The organ music suddenly stopped, followed by a long moment of suspenseful silence, then it gave forth two expectant blasts, and Whitney laid her trembling hand upon her father's arm.

With the music soaring through the eaves and four thousand people staring in awed, hushed silence as she took each step, Whitney started down the long aisle.

Clayton had carried a picture in his mind of how she would look at this moment—a picture of a beautiful bride in a veil and flowing white gown. But the vision he saw coming toward him through the candlelight snatched his breath away. Pride burst within him, exploding through his entire body until he ached with it. No bride had ever, *ever* looked the way she did. Whitney was coming to him without shyness, without even a veil to cover herself from him. As he watched, she raised her eyes to his—then kept them there—deliberately letting every man, woman, and child in that church see that she was proud to be going to him.

Her luxuriant hair spilled over her shoulders, the gold chain that rode her slender hips swayed gracefully with each step, and behind her trailed a magnificent cape glowing with pearls. She was a queen in all her breathtaking glory, serene but not haughty, provocatively beautiful, yet aloof, untouchable. "Oh my God, little one," Clayton whispered in his heart.

The crowd watched in breathless anticipation as the duke stepped forward, his tall frame resplendent in rich royal purple velvet. They saw him take her hand and smile into her eyes—and they knew he said something to her. But only Whitney heard his softly spoken, "Hello, my love." The sight of the handsome duke gazing down upon his beautiful bride with such gentle pride brought handkerchiefs to eyes before the couple ever began to say their vows.

Clayton led her to the altar, to her place beside him, the place that would be hers for all eternity.

Whitney stood with her hand in his strong, reassuring grasp. When the archbishop asked her to repeat her vows, she turned to Clayton and lifted her eyes to meet his warm, reassuring gaze. She made her voice sound firm and sure, but when she was promising to obey him, Clayton's expression changed. He lifted one brow in a look of such humorous skepticism that Whitney almost missed a word as she choked back a stunned giggle.

At last they were pronounced man and wife; the organ music rose and swelled; and Clayton claimed his right to kiss his bride. It was such a chaste peck, so unlike any kiss he had ever given her before, that Whitney's eyes registered visible surprise. "I will have to practice," Clayton whispered teasingly as they turned, "until I get the hang of it."

His gloriously beautiful bride nodded with sham solemnity and whispered demurely, "I shall be happy to help you with your lessons, my lord."

Which is why, as it was later reported, the Duke of

Claymore's shoulders were shaking with laughter as he left the altar with his duchess on his arm.

Whitney sat beside Clayton in his coach as they swept over the smooth roads toward Claymore. The Gilberts' conveyance was still hopelessly snarled in traffic at the church, so Whitney's aunt and uncle were grateful, but reluctant, passengers in the vehicle with the bride and groom which, as the four of them were all acutely aware, left no privacy for the newlyweds.

Listening to Clayton conversing with them, she looked at the heavy gold band he had slid onto her hand. It felt strange there, covering her long slender finger almost to the first knuckle—a bold proclamation to the world that she belonged to her husband.

Her husband? Whitney stole a glance at Clayton through her lashes. *My husband,* she repeated to herself, and a thrill shot through her. Dear Lord . . . he was her husband; six feet three inches of bold masculinity, elegant and sophisticated—but forceful too; a gathered power, carefully restrained. She even bore his name now. She belonged to him. It was a scary thought—and a little wonderful, too, she decided.

The bridal entourage moved decorously through the main gates at Claymore then swept along the winding private drive where festive torches were already ablaze on both sides of the road to light the way for the guests who would soon be arriving. When they pulled up before the main house, Clayton helped Whitney to alight, and she was amazed to see that all the staff—from butler, steward, housekeeper, footmen, and maids; to gardeners, keepers, foresters, and stableboys— were lined up on the front steps in immaculate livery and uniforms, according to their individual rank.

Clayton led her, not to the front door as she expected, but rather to the foot of the steps to stand before them. Whitney smiled a little uncertainly at the hundred and fifty faces, then glanced at Clayton.

"Brace yourself," he whispered, grinning. A second later the air was split with the thunder of cheers and applause.

He waited for the clamor to die down. "This is another tradition," he explained to Whitney as he remained there, regarding the servants gravely, but with a smile in his eyes. "Behold your new mistress, my wife." Clayton spoke the ancient words of the first Duke of Claymore, who had returned with his abducted bride, in a deep resonant voice that carried to all. "And know that when she bids you, I have bidden you; what service you render her, you are rendering me; what loyalty you give or withhold from her, you give or withhold from me." Wide smiles wreathed the faces of the staff, and as Clayton turned to lead Whitney away, a cheer twice as uproarious as the last went up.

In the white-and-gold salon, Clayton poured champagne for Whitney, Lord and Lady Gilbert, and himself. Stephen and his mother joined them and Clayton automatically filled two more glasses. All one hundred and twenty-six rooms of the main house and the seventy rooms of the combined guest houses were occupied with wedding guests, many of whom had arrived the day before. Already there was the incessant sound of carriages pulling up in the drive, which meant the house guests were returning from the church.

"Would you like to rest, love?" Clayton asked as he handed Whitney her glass. Whitney glanced at the clock. It was seven and the festivities were to begin at eight. In the meantime, Clarissa would need to press her gown, which meant she had no time to finish her champagne. Reluctantly, she nodded and put down her glass.

Clayton saw her wistful glance at her wineglass and, giving her a mocking grin, he picked up both their glasses and led her up the broad curving staircase toward their chambers. At the suite which adjoined his, and which she would occupy from this day forward, he stopped, opened the door for her, and handed her a glass of champagne. "Shall I have a full bottle sent up, my lady?" he teased, and before Whitney could make a suitably audacious reply, his mouth came down, lightly playing over hers in a sweet, fleeting kiss.

A crimson carpet stretched from the drive up the terraced steps leading to the great house which was ablaze with lights.

The guests arrived in a steady, endless stream, making their way up the grand staircase, which was flanked by thirty footmen standing stiffly at attention in burgundy-and-gold Westmoreland livery.

Beneath a six-tiered chandelier in the ballroom, Whitney stood beside Clayton while the butler intoned, "Lord and Lady . . . Sir . . . Mr. and Mrs . . ." as each individual passed beneath the marble portals into the flower-decked room. "Lady Amelia Eubank," she heard the butler say. Automatically, Whitney tensed as the gruff old dowager bore down on them wearing an outrageous green turban and purple satin gown.

"I trust, Madam," Clayton mocked, grinning at the old harridan, "that I did not fail to provide you with adequate 'competition' for Sevarin?"

Lady Eubank gave a sharp crack of laughter, then leaned closer to Clayton. "I've been wanting to ask you, Claymore, precisely *why* you happened to select the Hodges place for your 'rest?'"

"Precisely," Clayton said as he tipped his head toward Whitney, "for the reason you think I did."

"I knew it!" said she with a triumphant chuckle. "It took me weeks to be certain, though. You arrogant young pup!" she added almost affectionately as she put monocle to eye and turned, looking for one of her unfortunate neighbors from the village to pounce upon.

Dinner was a magnificent affair which began with a round of champagne toasts, the first of which was offered by Stephen. "To the Duchess of Claymore," he said.

Looking over at Clayton's mother, Whitney smiled gaily and lifted her glass, prepared to toast her. "I believe Stephen means you, love," Clayton whispered with a chuckle.

"Me? Oh yes, of course," Whitney said, quickly lowering her hand as she tried to cover her mistake. But it was too late, for the guests had seen her and were already roaring with laughter.

After toasts had been offered for the bride and groom's health, their happiness, and long life, the guests began calling for a toast from the groom. Clayton rose from his chair and

Whitney felt a burst of pride as he stood there, surrounded by that aura of quiet command that was so much a part of him.

He spoke and his deep voice carried to the farthest corners of the silent room. "Several months ago in Paris," he said, gazing for a tender moment at Whitney, "a lovely young woman accused me of 'pretending' to be a duke. She said that I was such a poor 'impostor' that I really ought to choose some other title to which to aspire—some title that would suit me better. I decided there was only one other title I wanted: that of her husband." He shook his head ruefully, while laughter kindled in his gray eyes. "Believe me, my first title was far more easily acquired than the second." When the deluge of laughter subsided, Clayton added solemnly, "and of far, far less value."

When the musicians struck up the first waltz, Clayton led her onto the dance floor. Taking her in his arms, he whirled her around and around for all to behold, but when the guests joined them on the floor, he relaxed and danced more quietly with her.

His senses were alive to the elusive perfumed scent of her, to the light touch of her fingertips. He thought of tomorrow night, or the night after, when he would truly make her his, and his blood stirred so hotly that he had to force the thought aside. He tried to concentrate on something else, and in the space of ten seconds, was mentally undressing and kissing her, caressing her with his hands and mouth until she was wild for him.

Her father claimed her for the next dance, and Clayton danced with his mother, and so it went for hours. It was long after midnight when Whitney and he left the dance floor to stroll together, arm in arm, laughing and talking with their guests.

Whitney was obviously enjoying herself and Clayton was certainly in no hurry to take her away from her party. After all, he had nothing to look forward to tonight except sleeping alone in his bed. As the clock neared the hour of one, however, Clayton began to have the uneasy feeling that the guests were *expecting* them to retire—a suspicion which was confirmed when Lord Marcus Rutherford remarked to him in a low, laughter-tinged voice, "My God, man, if you're wondering when you can leave without causing talk, it was about two hours ago."

Clayton went to Whitney. "I'm sorry to put an end to your evening, little one, but if we don't leave soon, people will begin to talk. Let's say good night to your aunt and uncle," he urged, but he wasn't particularly eager to leave either, and it irked him to be evicted from his own damned party in his own damned house by his own damned guests . . . which, he instantly realized, was an entirely hilarious way for a bridegroom to be thinking on his wedding night, particularly when that bridegroom was himself. Grinning, he shook his head at the irony of it.

Unfortunately, Clayton was still grinning when Whitney bade her uncle good night, and that gentleman, mistaking Clayton's grin as a leer, felt it incumbent upon himself to give the bridegroom a dark, reproving frown. Clayton stiffened under the silent reprimand and, feeling unfairly villified, said flatly, "We shall see you at breakfast," when he had intended but a moment before to bid Lord Gilbert a friendly good night.

In silence, Clayton led Whitney down the long hall from the west wing. Tension twisted within her as they crossed the balcony, and at the staircase, her steps began to lag. Clayton, however, was grappling with a new problem and did not notice: Should he take Whitney to his chambers, or should he take her to hers? There were servants swarming all over the damned place and he didn't want their lack of marital intimacy on their wedding night to be common knowledge among the staff.

He had just decided to take her to her chambers when two footmen came up the stairs and, feeling guilty as a thief in his own house, Clayton quickly changed direction, stepped back, and opened the door to his rooms instead of hers. He had started into his suite before he realized that Whitney had stopped in the doorway and was staring in stricken paralysis at the familiar room where he had savagely torn her clothes off.

"Come, sweet," he said, casting a quick look down the hall and forcibly drawing her within. "There is nothing to fear in here, no madman to ravish you."

With a toss of her head, she seemed to shake off the memories that were haunting her, and she stepped inside. Sighing with relief, Clayton closed the door behind them and guided Whitney over to the long green sofa at right angles to the fireplace, across from the chair he had sat in that fateful night. He started to sit down beside her on the sofa, took one look at her enticing profile, and thought it would be wiser if he sat in the chair across from her instead.

Whitney couldn't possibly sleep in her rooms tonight and he in his, he decided, because the servants would think it odd if both beds were slept in. She would have to sleep in his bed and he would sleep on the sofa.

He looked at her. Her dark head was turned toward the blazing fire on the hearth, away from the large bed on the dais. It dawned on him then that she must be wondering why, if he meant to keep his promise, he hadn't taken her to her chambers instead of his. "You will have to sleep in here, little one—otherwise the servants will gossip. I'll sleep on the sofa."

She looked up at him and smiled, as if her thoughts had been far away.

After an awkward moment, he suggested, "Would you like to talk?"

"Yes," she agreed readily.

"What would you like to talk about?"

"Oh—anything."

Clayton racked his brain for something interesting to discuss, but his mind and his body were both riveted on her exciting presence in his bedroom. "The weather was extremely fine today," he announced finally. He could have sworn that laughter flickered across her features, or was it only a trick of the firelight? "It didn't rain," he added, beginning to feel utterly ridiculous.

"It wouldn't have mattered if it did rain. It still would have been a beautiful, wonderful day."

God! he wished she wouldn't look at him with those

glowing green eyes and smile at him in that entrancing way. Not tonight. There was a discreet knocking upon his door, and also hers. "Who in the hell would—?"

"I imagine it's Clarissa," Whitney said, already rising and looking about her for the connecting door which would lead into her bedchambers. Clayton went to the door that led into the hall, pulled it open and stared irritably at his valet, who said blandly, "Good evening, your grace," and automatically came in. Damn! He'd forgotten about his valet and Whitney's maid. For his part, Clayton thought it would be less trying on his aroused senses if they both slept in their clothes. Mentally cursing all servants in general, Clayton showed Whitney to the connecting door, then turned on his heel and strode into the study adjoining his bedchambers, already having forgotten his valet's presence somewhere in his suite.

Staring at the shelves of books lining the study walls, he tried to decide what to read. What to read, for God's sake! On his wedding night! After eight weeks of the barely restrained passion they had shared, why was she still so frightened? And what insanity had possessed him to make her that promise?

As he reached for a book, Armstrong padded silently into the study behind him. "May I assist you, your grace?" Jerking his hand self-consciously away from the bookshelf, Clayton rounded on his hapless valet. "I'll ring if I need you!" he said curtly, trying to keep his annoyance hidden. The servants would say he was as nervous as a boy on his wedding night, if he snapped and growled. "That will be all, Armstrong. Good night," he added, then he personally escorted the surprised valet to the door of the suite, thrust him out into the hallway, and locked the door behind him.

Clayton strode back to his study, stripped off his jacket and neckcloth, and unbuttoned the top two buttons of his shirt. Pulling the stopper out of the decanter on his desk, he poured a liberal amount of brandy in a glass, then he took a book off one of the shelves, sat down, and stretched out his long legs. Intending to relax, he sipped his brandy and read the same paragraph four times before he finally gave up and slammed the book shut.

He was genuinely annoyed with himself, and a little surprised, at being so unnerved by what was, after all, only one more night of celibacy. After eight weeks of celibacy, why did this one extra night matter so much? It mattered, he realized ruefully, because he couldn't shake the conviction that a wedding night automatically, irrevocably, meant lovemaking—because that was the way it was supposed to be. Considering that in his entire adult life, he'd never paid much heed to the way things were "supposed to be," Clayton couldn't imagine why he should be doing so tonight. Unless it was because his wife's (he liked the sound of that—his *wife's*) intoxicating body was his now, by marital right. And it was also tantalizingly near his own starved body.

He allowed Whitney twice the amount of time she could possibly need before he finally got up and reentered his bedroom. She wasn't there. The connecting door was ajar, and he went through her dressing room into her bedroom. She wasn't there either. His heart began to hammer even though he told himself she could not have, would not have, actually fled from him. Surely she had more faith in his word than that!

With quickened pace, Clayton retraced his footsteps, drawing to a relieved halt in the doorway of his bedroom. Whitney was at the opposite end of it, standing near the dais, staring at the huge four-poster bed upon it. In the glow of candlelight, he could see the memories, the fear in her expression. He moved into the room and his shadow lengthened down the long wall.

Whitney looked up at him, and Clayton saw her quickly hide her fear behind an enchanting smile. "Who are you—really?" she asked in the same conspiratorial tone she'd used at the Armands' masquerade so long ago.

"A duke," he offered, smiling as he remembered the way they had bantered that night. "Also your husband. Who are you?"

"A duchess!" she exclaimed with a mixture of joy and disbelief.

"Also my wife?"

She nodded, slowly her smile widening delightfully. In his

mind, Clayton saw the provocative goddess she had been that night with yellow and purple flowers entwined in her hair. At the same time, he beheld her standing there near his bed, and suddenly it didn't matter that he couldn't make love to her tonight. All that mattered was that he had finally made her his! He had done it—she really was his wife! He felt exhilarated and triumphant. "My *'obedient'* wife?" he teased, emphasizing the word obedient.

Whitney nodded again and he could almost see the laughter in her eyes.

"Then come here, my obedient wife," he commanded huskily.

A shadow of apprehension crossed her vivid features, but she turned fully toward him and began walking to him with that natural, fluid motion of hers. That was when Clayton realized what she was wearing, and he almost groaned aloud. Her dressing robe was made entirely of fragile white lace, revealing glimpses of skin along her arms, her breasts, and even her long legs; and there was enough soft flesh swelling above her bodice to send him into fresh agonies of desire and regret.

She stopped a few steps away from him, gazing at him in fear and confusion, as if she wanted to come the rest of the way but couldn't make herself. "About . . . about your promise," she said in a hesitant voice. "Remember?"

Did he remember his promise! "I remember it, little one," Clayton said quietly. He went to her and gently enfolded her in his arms, trying to ignore the incredible feel of her almost naked breasts softly crushed against his thin shirt. He wanted to kiss her but she was trembling so violently that he was afraid to, so he just held her with her face cradled against his chest and slowly stroked her long, lustrous hair.

"When I was a little girl," she whispered unsteadily against his heart, "lying in bed at night, I used to imagine that there were things—in the closets."

She fell silent and Clayton urged her, "There were toy soldiers in my closets. What were in yours?"

"Monsters!" she whispered. "Huge, ugly ones with claws for feet and enormous, bulging eyes." She drew a shaky breath and said, "There are monsters in this room too—hideous memories lurking in the shadows and corners."

Clayton flinched with pained remorse. "I know there are. But you've nothing to be afraid of; I'll not ask anything of you tonight. I gave you my word."

She leaned back a little and looked up at him, her face so lovely and vulnerable that Clayton wondered for the thousandth time how he ever, *ever* could have hurt her that night. She tried to say something and couldn't; instead she rested her cheek against his chest, sliding her arms around his waist.

After a moment, she began again, "I used to lie in bed at night, afraid of what was in the closet. And then, when I couldn't endure it any longer, I would run across the room and snatch the door open and make myself look inside."

Clayton smiled inwardly. It was like her to grow weary of cowering under the blankets and confront the darkness—monsters or no monsters. When she spoke again, her voice was so low that he had to strain to hear it.

"The closet was always empty. No monsters . . . nothing to fear." She drew a shuddering breath. "Clayton, I don't want to spend our wedding night lying alone in your bed, afraid of what is in the shadows."

Clayton's hand froze in mid-air, then he made himself continue the soothing motion, giving her time to reconsider. "You're certain?" he asked quietly.

Whitney nodded and whispered, "Yes."

Leaning down, he swung her up into his arms and carried her to the big four-poster where he had taught her how degrading the act could be, promising himself, every step of the way, that this time would be so perfect for her that the other time would be banished from her memory. He slipped his hand from beneath her knees, and the gliding feel of her legs sliding down his thighs made his hands tremble as he untied the ribbons at her breasts and tenderly shoved the lacy gown aside.

Her ivory shoulders and full, rosy-tipped breasts gleamed in the light from the fire across the room. "My God, you are beautiful," he breathed, and felt her body quiver sharply when his hands slid down her arms, sending the fragile lace gown spilling onto the floor. He took her dewy lips in a long, sweet kiss, then swept the satin coverlet back and lifted her gently, laying her on the cool sheets.

She closed her eyes and turned her head away, and Clayton saw the flush that swept up her long shapely legs, her slender curves, staining the glowing ivory skin right up to her hairline. Out of consideration for her obvious embarrassment, he reluctantly extinguished the candles burning on the bedside table. Afraid to leave her alone with the memories she was ready to confront, he undressed there beside the bed, then stretched out alongside her and carefully pulled her into his arms. Whitney stiffened. He ran his hand soothingly over her naked back, and she stiffened even more. Clayton stopped caressing her and lay back against the pillows with her head on his chest.

In the next few moments her breathing went from slow and shallow, to rapid and shallow, and he was not even touching her. Christ, how he hated himself for what he had done to her that night! She was so tense, so taut in every fiber of her body that, unless he could help her relax, he would hurt her no matter how gentle he was.

So that she wouldn't be overly conscious of their nakedness, Clayton reached down and drew the sheet over them. "I want to talk awhile first," he explained. Relief flooded her features and he chuckled because she looked as if she'd just been granted a last-minute reprieve from the guillotine. "If you possibly can, I would like you to try to put out of your mind what happened before. I'd also like you to forget whatever you may have heard about what happens between a husband and wife in bed, and simply listen to me."

"Yes," she whispered.

"Expressions such as 'submitting to him' or 'taking her' should never have been applied to lovemaking, yet I know this is the way you must think of it. The first implies a duty, performed reluctantly. The second is rape. I am not going to 'take' you, and you are not going to 'submit' to me. Nor are you going to feel any pain." With a tender smile at her upturned face, he said, "I promise you that you are *not* malformed. You are perfectly and exquisitely made."

He ran a forefinger over her lovely cheek. "What is about to take place between us is a sharing, born of my desire to be as close to you as I can be, to actually become a part of you. Little one, when I am inside of you I am not *taking*, I am *giving*. I am giving my body to you as I gave you my love before, and my ring today. When I am inside of you, I will put the seed of my own life into you and leave it there for you to keep and shelter within you—a symbol of my love and need for you, like your betrothal ring."

In the flickering orange glow from the fireplace across the room, Clayton saw her hesitate, and then imperceptibly tilt her face up, offering her lips for his kiss. Very slowly and gently, Clayton leaned over and began to kiss his wife. He kissed her long and lingeringly, with all the aching tenderness in his heart and she, after a few moments of tense passivity, laid her slender fingers against his cheek and began to kiss him back with all the shy, trembling love Clayton knew she felt.

Her soft lips parted with only the slightest urging from his probing tongue, and her arms went around his neck as she drew his tongue into her mouth, then gave him hers. He teased her, tormented her, offered himself to her by thrusting deep with his tongue, then slowly retreating and thrusting again and again, until Whitney was clinging to him, her mouth moving back and forth over his in passionate surrender to the wildly erotic kiss.

He stroked her hair and slid his hand down over her throat to her breasts, circling the pink crests with his thumb until they stood up proudly. Whitney shivered with delight and started to fit herself to his hardened length—then jerked away as if she had been scorched. Clayton immediately knew what had terrified her and although she resisted, he moved his arm to hold her hips against his. "No," he said gently as she tried to pull her lower body away from his rigid manhood. "Nothing is going to hurt you."

Her long lashes swept up and she gave him such a doubtful, accusing look, that he nearly smiled. "Put your hand on my chest," he instructed gently. "Only on my chest,"·he assured her when she lifted her hand to obey and then hesitated. The instant she moved her fingers over his warm skin, his muscles leapt reflexively. "See how my body responds to your touch?" he told her quietly. "The part of me that you are afraid of is only responding to your nearness, reaching for you." He gathered her closer against his thighs and hips, but she remained stiff and tensed. "You aren't still afraid that I am going to hurt you, after I've promised I won't?"

Whitney swallowed convulsively and shook her head against the pillow. If Clayton said this wasn't going to be painful, she would believe him. Tentatively she moved her fingers over the furring of dark hair on his chest and felt the slight increase in the steady thudding of his heart, the rippling of his powerful chest muscles when she slid her hand a little lower.

Clayton felt it as a flame racing uncontrollably through his veins. "Oh darling," he half laughed, half groaned, "please feel pride in what you can do to me. It humbles me to know you can make my body respond to your slightest touch, even if I will against it. It humbles me more to tell you so. But I tell you anyway, because if you can take pride in having such power over me, I can find a reason for joy in it, as well. But if it frightens you or makes you ashamed, then our love must be a timid thing, a thing of shame."

Whitney drew a long, unsteady breath and, reaching her arms around his neck, she pressed herself to the full length of his hard, unyielding contours and began to kiss him. Trembling in his embrace, she kissed his forehead and his eyes and his mouth. She slid her tongue over his lips, feeling the warm smoothness of them, and Clayton groaned, his mouth opening passionately over hers. And when he shifted her onto her back and leaned over her, kissing her and caressing her with his gentle, skillful hands, Whitney didn't know if what she was feeling was pride, but whatever it was, it was drugging and delirious and wonderful.

"I want you," he whispered against her parted lips. "I want you so badly that I ache for you." He took his mouth from hers and his hand trembled as he lifted it to cup her face. "I'll never hurt you, little one," he promised, his voice hoarse with tenderness and love.

Whitney's answer made his throat ache. "I know you won't," she whispered. "But it wouldn't matter if you hurt me every night—as long as you always say those things—about wanting to be a part of me."

Clayton couldn't help himself; he covered her mouth with his and devoured her with tender violence. He fondled her breasts and teased her nipples with his fingers, and she moaned softly when his mouth began retracing the path his hands had taken.

Every slight movement of her awakening body twisting beneath his gentle assault—every sound she made raced through his bloodstream like an aphrodisiac. He could not believe the passion she contained, nor the violence of his body's craving for her; he was ravenous for her.

Her hands were tangling in his hair, running over his shoulders and back, her nails digging into his flesh. But when he moved his hand down to the soft triangle between her legs, Whitney gave a leap of fear at his intimate touch and clamped her thighs together.

"Don't, darling," he murmured hotly, capturing her mouth in a deep, consuming kiss as he gently, inexorably, parted her thighs, his fingers teasing and toying with her, exploring and delightfully tormenting her until she was soft and damp and more than ready for him.

When he shifted up and over her, however, Whitney was jolted from the sensual whirlpool that had been sweeping her toward sweet oblivion. In fright that would not be banished she felt Clayton part her legs, felt her hips being lifted to receive him, and she swallowed back a cry of sheer panic at the probing hardness of him coming into intimate contact with her. Despite his promise, her body automatically braced itself for pain . . . but there was only the proud heat of him sliding slowly into her. Instinctively, she relaxed and opened for him, then gasped with exquisite pleasure as he plunged full length into her welcoming softness.

She wrapped her arms around him, lost in incoherent yearnings to have him stay inside of her like this forever, to draw him somehow deeper. She thought this was how it ended, and she could have wept with longing to have it continue. And then Clayton began to move within her, and Whitney ceased to think at all. Something small unfolded in the pit of her stomach, then spread like a mellow glow, slowly building and gathering force, until it began to race in a trembling fury along her every nerve. Twisting her head fitfully on the pillows she began arching to meet his deep plunging thrusts. "Please," she begged him in a whisper, but she did not know what she was asking for.

Clayton did. And he wanted it so badly for her that his own rampaging desire was secondary. "Soon, darling," he promised and began to steadily quicken the rhythm of his driving strokes.

The volcano that had been threatening to erupt inside of Whitney exploded with a force that tore a low scream from her throat. Instantly Clayton throttled the scream with his mouth. When her tremors had subsided he took her sweet lips in a long kiss, and with one deep thrust, he poured his shuddering warmth at the mouth of her womb.

Afraid that his weight would crush her, Clayton gathered her to him and rolled onto his side, taking her with him. Lying there, with Whitney cradled in his arms, his body still intimately joined to hers, he experienced a joyous contentment, a languorous peace, unlike anything he had ever known.

He half expected Whitney to fall asleep in his arms, but after several minutes, she tilted her head back and raised shining green eyes to his. Clayton brushed a wayward curl off her cheek. "Are you happy, love?"

She smiled at him; the sated, happy smile of a woman who loves . . . and who knows that she is beloved. "Yes," she whispered.

He kissed her forehead and she snuggled closer against him, while he tenderly caressed the lovely contours of her back and hip, waiting for her to fall asleep. Instead, she lapsed into silence, tracing small circles on his chest, but she did not seem any more inclined toward sleep than he. "What are you thinking about?" he asked her finally.

Whitney's gaze flew to his, then she buried her face against his chest. "Nothing," she murmured unconvincingly.

Tilting her chin up, Clayton forced her to look at him. He had no idea what she could be thinking, but after having just removed the last barrier between them, he didn't want any new ones erected, ever. "What?" he persisted with gentle firmness.

She bit her lip in a combination of shyness and laughter. "I was thinking that if it had been like this—that other time—instead of fleeing from here, I would have stayed and demanded that you do the proper thing and marry me at once!"

She looked so beautiful that Clayton was torn between laughing and kissing her. So he did both. It was heaven to hold her in his arms like this, to be able to talk to her in the darkness and have her bare arms around him. Clayton felt more in the mood for celebrating than sleeping. When he looked down at her a while later and found her still awake, gazing into the firelight, he said, "Do you want to sleep?"

"I don't think I could. I'm wide awake."

"Good, so am I." He grinned. "Will you light all three of those candles on the table beside you?"

"Your smallest wish is my command," his "obedient" wife told him as she leaned up on an elbow and kissed him full on the mouth, but before she turned over to light the candles, she carefully drew the sheet up.

Clayton's lips twitched with laughter as she modestly clutched it to the luscious breasts he had just fondled and kissed. He propped their pillows up so that they could sit back against them, then he relaxed back and pleasured himself with the sight of her. When she turned from lighting the candles and saw him gazing at her, she self-consciously ran her fingers through her tumbled tresses and gave the luxuriant mass a hard shake that sent it spilling down her back. "Madam," Clayton reassured her with a roguish grin, "you are beautiful *en dishabille*—if that sheet you are trying to wear qualifies you for being in that fashionable state of partial dress."

"I don't think it does," Whitney mused thoughtfully. "In France and even here, it is all the rage for ladies to receive gentlemen *en dishabille*, but I'm certain they must be wearin more than this." Then Whitney realized with a rosy blush that Clayton undoubtedly knew a good deal more about that particular "rage" than she did, and the thought made her feel a little forlorn.

Everyone knew that Clayton had had mistresses before, and married men frequently kept mistresses discreetly tucked away, too. It crushed her to think of him doing the things he had just done with her, with another woman, too. Emboldened by her distress and ashamed of her shocking effrontery, Whitney said hesitantly, "Clayton, I think I would have a very difficult time pretending not to notice . . . no, passively accepting . . . accepting . . ."

"Accepting what?" Clayton whispered, his lips against her temple.

"A mistress!" Whitney blurted.

Clayton's head jerked up. For a moment he stared blankly at her, then he wrapped his arms around her and burst out laughing. But because he knew she was genuinely distressed, he made his face more appropriately solemn—as befitted the lifetime renunciation he was about to make. Then, gazing into her glorious eyes, he said in quiet earnest, "I will not take a mistress."

"Thank you," Whitney whispered. "I'm afraid I would feel very strongly about it."

"I'm sure you would," he said, striving to keep his face straight.

A few minutes later, Clayton remembered the velvet box tucked away in the table beside the bed. Reluctantly easing his arm from beneath her shoulders, he explained, "I have a gift for you."

Whitney remembered that she had one for him, too, and was out of the bed in a flurry of long, shapely limbs and creamy curves. "I asked Clarissa to put yours in my room," she explained as she started away from the bed. Clayton was devouring the sight of her exquisite naked form when she noticed his look, then hurtled herself toward the discarded lace robe.

He presented her with a necklace of square-cut emeralds, each surrounded with a row of glittering diamonds, and a matching bracelet and ear drops. "Fit for a duchess," he whispered as he kissed her.

Whitney laughed as she handed him his gift. "Fit for a duke," she said, sitting beside him with her legs curled beneath her, watching him open it. Clayton snapped the lid up, then threw back his head and shouted with laughter at the sight of the gorgeously made, solid-gold quizzing glass she had given him. In exactly the same tone she had used at the Armands' masquerade, she said, "A quizzing glass is an indispensable affectation of royalty." Then she reached behind her and produced another gift in a small velvet box. As she handed it to him, the laughter vanished from her face, and her whole expression changed.

Clayton looked at her for a long moment before opening the box, wondering why she suddenly seemed almost shy. Puzzled, he opened the lid and beheld a magnificent ruby set in a heavy gold ring. He took the ring from its bed of black velvet and it glittered in the dim light. Holding it closer to the candles to admire it, he was about to ask her sentimentally if she would like to put the ring on his finger, as he had placed her wedding band on hers, when he caught sight of a small inscription on the inside of the band. In handsome scroll were two words, the first of which was underlined. *"My* lord."

He groaned and pulled her almost roughly down onto his chest. "God, how I love you!" he whispered hoarsely as his mouth captured hers.

When the kiss ended, Whitney remained in his arms, and her long fingers lightly stroked the hair at his temple. Between the touch of her hand and the feel of her breasts against his naked chest as she half lay atop him, Clayton was acutely aware that his body was stirring to life with alarming intensity. His senses were alive to every inch of her form languorously stretched across him, but he didn't want to risk frightening her with too much lovemaking their first night. He stirred and Whitney raised herself up on her forearms, bracing them against his chest, affording him a view of her swelling breasts that made desire pour like boiling lava through his veins.

"Am I too heavy?" she asked him softly.

"No, but I think you ought to get some sleep, my love," he suggested with a tinge of regret.

"I'm not in the least sleepy," his wife said.

She looked like an innocent goddess draped across him, her softly tousled hair spilling over his shoulders. "You're certain you don't want to sleep?" Clayton asked absently, brushing his knuckles over her smooth cheek, marvelling at her vivid beauty. "Then what would you like to do?"

In answer, Whitney looked at him and blushed, then she quickly hid her overheated face against his shoulder.

A chuckle rumbled deep in his chest as he shifted her fully atop his aroused length and wrapped his arms around her. "I suppose we could do that," he laughed huskily.

Chapter Thirty-four

A WEEK LATER THEY LEFT FOR FRANCE ON THEIR WEDDING TRIP. They stayed one month. When they returned to London the couple did not, as everyone expected they would, repair to the duke's handsome mansion in Upper Brook Street. Instead they seemed to prefer the seclusion and serenity of Claymore. They did, however, appear regularly at social functions in town, sometimes arriving back at Claymore just as dawn broke.

In a society where it was considered unfashionable for a husband and wife to be too much in each other's company when they were out together, the Duke and Duchess of Claymore created a fashion of their own. For the duke and his duchess were rarely far from each other's side, and one could scarcely fail to notice how desirable they made being together appear. They were a striking couple, of course, the duke splendidly tall and elegantly masculine, grinning that lazy, approving grin at his beautiful young wife who seemed to be able to make him laugh with a joy that no one had ever before observed. But it was more than what one saw, it was a feeling that one had when watching them—as if the couple were joined together by more than just affection or even wedlock. It was, the *ton* remarked with collective sighs of surprise and occasional envy, a most unusual marriage by modern standards. A few members of the haughty elite quite forgot to be brittly sophisticated and even went so far as to muse aloud that it was quite, quite obvious that the duke and duchess were in love with each other.

Clayton harbored not the slightest doubt of the correct term for what he felt. He loved Whitney with a passion and devotion that were rooted deeply in his soul. He could not see, or hear, or touch her enough to satisfy his craving for her. At night he would feel that hot need rising within him that seemed to increase, instead of diminish each time he exploded inside of her; and she would press herself against him as if she, too, could not be near enough to him, for long enough. In bed she was a passionate, irresistible mistress intent on pleasing him. Clayton taught her in the first weeks of their marriage that there was no place for embarrassment or shyness between them, and Whitney responded by abandoning herself to his caresses. He allowed her to hold nothing back from him and, after a few feeble attempts to hide her passionate responses to his lovemaking, she surrendered herself willingly to the wild and stormy tides that he caused to rise and crash until she cried out. And then he held her in his arms, tracing the curves of her body, whispering until they both slept, happy, peaceful, and sated.

Whitney's days were filled with contentment. Whenever possible she would curl up in a corner of Clayton's spacious study during the day, reviewing the household accounts, planning menus or simply reading, stealing surreptitious, admiring glances at him as he leaned back in his chair, going over the correspondence and reports on his business ventures. Occasionally, Clayton would look up as if to reassure himself that she was there, and grin at her, or give her a quick wink before turning his attention back to the business at hand. In the beginning, Whitney had never dreamed that he might like having her here. This was his private world where he talked about staggering amounts of money with his business agents and gambled in investments that she soon realized were amazingly perceptive and prudent. He liked this work, though—he didn't have to do it. He told her that one night. And Stephen told her once that in the last five years Clayton had nearly doubled the vast Westmoreland wealth. He even handled Stephen's investments for him and—surprise of surprises—now her father's as well.

She loved listening to him meeting with his solicitors and business acquaintances. She adored the thread of quiet authority in his voice as he spoke with them. He was so quick, and sure, and decisive. He was also devastatingly handsome, she thought with a burst of pride whenever she looked at him. She felt cherished and protected when he was near—safe and loved.

When she went shopping in town or to a play with Emily, she missed the sound of his voice, his warm glances and engaging smile.

Her nights were a celebration of their love. Sometimes he lingered over her as tenderly as he had on their wedding night. Other times he teased her, deliberately tantalizing her, making her tell him exactly what she wanted; then there were times when he took her swiftly, almost roughly. And Whitney could never decide which way she loved the most.

At first she had been a little frightened of the stormy, tumultuous passion she could arouse in him with a kiss, a touch, an intimate caress. But it took very little time before she was shamelessly glorying in his bold, virile masculinity. She was his—body, heart, and soul. She was at peace with her world.

She was also pregnant five months later.

Now when Clayton slept cradling her in his arms, Whitney lay awake feeling both excited and vaguely distressed. Her monthly flux was three weeks overdue, yet for several reasons, she postponed telling Clayton. Thérèse DuVille had confided to Whitney at the wedding that she was going to enjoy the rest from her husband's amorous attentions that being *enceinte* would provide. Thérèse might be looking forward to it, but Whitney definitely was not. On the other hand, she didn't want to risk harming the baby if such might be the result of their continued lovemaking. To complicate things, Clayton had never voiced any desire for children, although it seemed to Whitney that all men must want children—particularly men with titles to be passed on to their heirs. When she missed her second monthly flux and began to experience occasional queasiness and the yearning to nap in the middle of the day, she was positive, but still she held her silence.

One day shortly thereafter, as Whitney went upstairs to change for their daily break-neck gallop across the open countryside, Clayton stopped her on the steps. "Khan is favoring his right leg a little," he said with a peculiar gravity, mingled with profound gentleness in his voice. "Suppose we go for a walk instead, little one."

Whitney hadn't noticed Khan favoring his leg at all, and there were dozens of other splendid mounts at the stables, but she didn't question his decision. She was a little relieved because they always rode at such a hell-for-leather pace that she shuddered to think of what might happen if she fell, and she hadn't been able to think of a way to suggest they slow down without telling Clayton why.

That night, Clayton's lovemaking took on a new pattern that repeated itself consistently thereafter. He would arouse her until she was delirious with wanting his possession, and then enter her with painstaking gentleness, penetrating deeply, but slowly, withdrawing lingeringly. It prolonged the inevitable moment of joyous release unbearably . . . and very pleasurably. It also provided Whitney with the rationalization that such a gentle invasion of her body could not possibly be harming their baby.

The next week she took herself firmly in hand and told herself she was being ridiculous. In the first place, she was bursting with her news. In the second, if she delayed much longer, her own body would provide him with the announcement of his impending fatherhood. Accordingly, Whitney went to London and purchased six tiny items of infant apparel at a particular shop. Immediately upon her return, she set to work in earnest with the embroidery thread in the privacy of her rooms.

She summoned Mary and Clarissa for an opinion of her needlework and said with a sigh as she produced her handiwork, "Amazing, is it not, that I could master Greek and not this?" Mary and Clarissa, who were both secure in their positions in the household, took one look at her embroidery, then looked at each other and collapsed on the bed amidst shrieks of laughter.

By dinner the next evening, Whitney was finally satisfied with a "W" she had embroidered in blue on the collar of an unbelievably tiny baby gown. "This will have to do," she sighed to Clarissa.

"When are you going to tell his grace that my baby is going to have a baby?" Clarissa asked with fond tears sparkling at the multiple creases at the corners of her eyes.

"That isn't *quite* what I planned to say to him," Whitney giggled, giving Clarissa a pat on her wrinkled cheek. "Actually, I'm not going to tell him at all—I'm going to let this tell him," she said, indicating the little infant gown. "And I think tonight after dinner will be a perfect time." With a gay, conspiratorial smile, Whitney tucked the little gown into the drawer of her desk beside her stationery and trooped downstairs for dinner.

She waited until Clayton had finished his port after the meal and they were sitting in the white-and-gold salon. Feigning absorption in her book, Whitney sighed. "I can't think why I have been feeling so tired lately." She did not look up and so missed the look of gentle pride and laughter that Clayton beamed on her.

"Can't you, sweet?" he asked cautiously. He thought she knew she was with child but he wasn't certain, and if there was a chance she feared childbearing, he wanted to spare her the worry as long as possible.

"No," Whitney said in a musing tone. "But I wanted to answer my aunt's letter tonight and I have just realized that I left it in the drawer of my writing desk upstairs. Would you mind terribly getting it for me? Those stairs seem like a mountain to climb lately."

Clayton got up, pressed a light kiss on her forehead, affectionately rumpled her heavy hair, and strode briskly up the curving marble staircase.

He went into her room and grinned to himself as he looked about him. A faint scent of Whitney's perfume lingered there. Her combs and brushes were on her dressing table. Her presence filled the airy room and made it seem pretty and fresh and vibrant. Like she was.

Wondering again if she knew she was with child, and wondering why in the world, if she did know, she wasn't telling him, he pulled open the drawer of her rosewood writing desk. Clayton took some stationery off the top of the thick stack for Whitney to use, then rummaged through the drawer, looking for her aunt's letter. Unable to find it, he pushed aside what he thought was a white handkerchief and flipped through the stack of unused stationery. Near the very bottom he finally discovered a folded letter. Uncertain if it was the one Whitney wanted, he unfolded it and scanned the words Whitney had written many months ago at Emily's house, in a foolish—and discarded—attempt to force Clayton to come back to her:

"To my very great mortification, I find I am with child. Please call at once here to discuss what can be done. Whitney."

To her very great mortification? Clayton repeated to himself with a bewildered frown. What an odd way for her to feel about the living culmination of the exquisite joy they had found in one another. And what a peculiar way for her to choose to give him the news. "Please call at once."

In the space of the next three seconds, three realizations stunned him: The note was dated two months before they were married—in fact, it was written on the day before he had brought Vanessa here and found Whitney waiting for him . . . there was no name on it to indicate who the note had been intended for . . . and the note was in Whitney's elegant, scholarly hand and signed by her. God *help* him . . . She had written it to some man she believed had made her pregnant.

Clayton's mind registered disbelief, it started to shout denials . . . even while something inside of him slowly cracked and began to crumble. He felt as if he were shattering and all of his pieces flying apart. Whitney had been playacting the night she came here to him. After all those months of treasuring the memory of the way she had surrendered her pride and crossed the study to come to him, it had been a lie, a contemptible, filthy lie! That tender scene in which she had whispered, "I love you" had been an act! She had played it because she believed she was pregnant, and whoever this note was intended for either refused his responsibility or couldn't accept it. Perhaps the son of a bitch was already married.

Whitney had come to Claymore that night to get herself a father for someone else's brat—Christ! They had probably concocted the scheme of her coming here together. Except in the end, she hadn't really needed a father for her bastard. She must have miscarried, Clayton thought with feverishly clear hindsight. No wonder she had looked so tired and wan in the weeks preceding the wedding.

And what a goddamned act on their wedding night! By then she had to have known she wasn't pregnant, but she must have been so horrified by her near calamity that she was willing to go ahead and marry him anyway. Perhaps it made it more convenient for her lover and her if Whitney were married. No one would think a thing about her becoming pregnant now. And then Clayton recalled all the times in the last months when she had gone to London on "shopping trips" and to "visit friends." Bile surged up in his throat. This child she was carrying now was as likely someone else's as his.

That bitch! That lying, deceitful little . . . No, he couldn't call her that again, even in his twisted torment. He had loved her too much, until a minute ago, to curse her. But he had loved a sham, a consummate actress, a hollow shell of a woman. A body. Nothing more. And the body wasn't even his alone.

What an instinct for survival she had, you had to give her that! She had faced him in that study with Vanessa in the same house, borne his fury and pressed her body against his, kissing him as if her whole heart were in it. Because she was pregnant! Clayton wanted to believe the baby might have been his. He even tried to convince himself of that for a moment. But he knew better—the night he had ravaged her, there had been no more than a moment's penetration. The act had never been consummated. The chance of the child's having been his was too minuscule even to consider.

Their lives were a charade. Each word she spoke, every

look on her face, the way she was in bed—all of it was a performance she put on every day. It was all an obscene, disgusting act!

His hand tightened on the piece of blue stationery, slowly crumpling it into a tight, hard ball. The pain inside of him began to dull as a cold, black rage swept over him. He dropped the crumpled note blindly into the desk drawer and slammed it shut, but it wouldn't close. A tiny white garment with a small "W" embroidered in blue threads on the collar had jammed between the drawer and the desk, half in and half out of it.

Clayton stared at it, then gave it a vicious jerk. *This* was what he had been meant to find, he realized with fury. How very touching of her to tell him this way! What a flair for tender drama she had! Distastefully, he dropped the tiny garment on the floor and deliberately ground it beneath his heel as he turned to walk away.

"I see you found it," Whitney whispered from the doorway, her gaze frozen in misery on the little gown crushed beneath his foot.

"When?" he said icily.

"In—in about seven months, I think."

Clayton stared at her, violence emanating from every pore. With deliberate cruelty he carefully enunciated each vicious word. *"I don't want it."*

Clarissa and Mary, who had been hovering on the balcony to have a look at their employer's beaming countenance when he heard the news, recoiled in amazement as he passed them on the way down the stairs, moving with an unleashed savagery that threatened to strike down anything in his path. The front door crashed into its frame behind him, and Clarissa slowly turned and walked into Whitney's room, then froze in horror at the sight that greeted her:

Whitney was kneeling on the floor near her desk, her shoulders jerking spasmodically with her silent weeping. Her head was thrown back and tears were streaming from her tightly closed eyes.

And in her hands was a tiny white gown with a little "W" he had lovingly embroidered in blue.

"Here, don't cry so, darlin'," Clarissa said in a suffocated whisper as she bent down to help her up. "You'll harm the babe."

Whitney thought she would never be able to stop. She cried until her sobs were dry and choked. She cried until there were no more tears left to weep and she felt dry and barren. *"I don't want it!"* The four words coiled around her heart, squeezing and twisting until she couldn't breathe.

When dawn came to lighten the sky, Whitney turned onto her side, staring out into the early gray light. She was alone in her bed, alone all night for the first time in their marriage. Clayton didn't want her baby. Their baby. Did he mean to disown it? Oh God, no! He couldn't—he wouldn't—*why* would he? Squeezing her eyes closed, she turned her head into the pillow. He was going to make her give up the baby. That's what he meant to do. He was going to get a wet nurse as soon as it was born and send the child away to have it raised on one of his other estates, out of their way. Was his need for her so selfish then, so consuming that there was no room for their child?

A few hours ago, she might not have known how she felt about her pregnancy, but she did now. Clayton's rejection of her baby had brought on a tidal wave of protectiveness in her so fierce that it shook her to the roots of her being. She would never let him send their baby away. Never!

Whitney awoke very late. Her head was aching and she felt horribly sick and dizzy, but she made herself go down to breakfast. Clayton's place across from her was still set. "His grace said he had no appetite for breakfast, my lady," the servant informed her. Whitney ate a Spartan meal for the sake of the baby then went outdoors for a long walk.

She didn't know where Clayton was; he hadn't come into his room until just before dawn.

She walked through the formal rose gardens, vibrant with separate beds of red, white, pink and yellow roses, and then across the lush manicured banks of the immense lake where swans floated aimlessly upon the tranquil surface. Her steps carried her to the white pavilion on the far bank overlooking the lake, and she went inside and sat down on the brightly colored pillows strewn across the benches.

She sat there for two hours while her thoughts tumbled over each other, trying to reconcile the fact that she was the same person she had been only yesterday, that this was the same lifetime she had inhabited.

She went back to the house and slowly walked up the staircase, only to find Clayton's valet and three servants busily moving his clothing out of his room. "What are they doing?" Whitney breathlessly begged Mary. "Mary, tell me why they are moving my husband's things." She felt as if she were teetering on the brink of insanity.

"His grace is moving into the east wing," Mary explained, forcing herself to sound both brisk and unconcerned. "We'll move your things into his room, and your room will make a nice nursery when the time comes."

"Oh," Whitney whispered faintly, knowing she could never bear to be in that suite without Clayton. "Would you show me where his new rooms are? I—I have to ask him about tonight. We were to go out." Mary led her to an elegant suite at the far end of the east wing and kindly left her alone there.

Whitney walked slowly into the room. Clayton had been there today, but he was gone now. His shirt was thrown over a chair and a pair of gloves lay on the bed where he had tossed them. She wandered into the dressing room and ran her fingers over the onyx backs of his brushes and had to swallow back a fresh onrush of tears. She opened a wardrobe and tortured herself by touching his shirts and jackets. You could tell what broad shoulders were needed to fill those jackets. Such broad shoulders, she thought. She had always loved his broad shoulders. And his eyes.

Whitney was walking toward the door when he came in. Without a word he strode right past her, went into his dressing room, and began shrugging out of his jacket.

She followed him, unable to keep the tears from her voice as she said, "Why are you doing this, Clayton?"

He jerked his shirt off but did not deign to answer her.

"Be-because of our baby?" she persisted in a whisper.

His eyes raked over her. "Because of *a* baby," he corrected her.

"You—you don't like children?"

"Not another man's children," he informed her icily. Flinging his shirt onto a chair, he turned, caught her elbow in a bruising grip and began forcibly escorting her from the room.

"But you must want children of your own," Whitney said brokenly as she was unceremoniously thrust into the hallway in full sight of a passing servant.

"Of my own," Clayton emphasized in a menacing voice. He loomed over her with one hand on the door as if he were about to shut it in her face.

"Are we going to the Wilsons' tonight? I—I accepted their invitation weeks ago."

"I am going out. You can do as you damn well please."

"But," Whitney pleaded, "are you going to the Wilsons'? If you are . . ."

"No!" he snapped. Then in a terrible voice, he added, "And if I ever find you in this room, or even in this wing of the house again, I will personally remove you. And I promise you, Whitney, you won't like the way I do it." The door slammed in her face.

Clayton stood rigidly still in the room on the other side of the closed door, his hands clenching and unclenching as he tried to bring this new onslaught of fury under control. By dawn this morning he had managed to drink himself into near oblivion in his study. But not before he had carefully, coldly considered all the ways he could avenge himself for his misplaced love and trust. He would take a mistress, flagrantly flaunt her until Whitney learned of her existence. Society would overlook a married man with a mistress; it always had. But Whitney would be caught in a vice. She'd not be able to go out alone very often without causing talk. And if she appeared with another man she would be publicly scorned and ostracized.

But even that wasn't enough. If she was going to bear a

child, and he was going to have to give it his name, then by God he wasn't going to have to look at it and wonder whose it was! He'd send the brat away from his sight. But not right away. First he would let her keep the child for a year or two until she was deeply attached to it; then he would wrench the babe away from her. The child—that would be his ultimate weapon. He didn't care whether it was the result of her dirty little liaison with her lover or whether it was the living proof of his own desires.

Whitney stood there staring at the oak panel. Her throat ached and her eyes burned, but she would not cry! The more she had tried to plead with him, the more pleasure he'd taken in verbally abusing her. Stiffly, she walked down the long hall to the sanity . . . no, not the sanity, this was all insane . . . to the safety of her rooms.

Mary and Clarissa were both working in the master suite, moving Whitney's clothes into the next room, and everything was in disorder. "If you don't mind," Whitney said, drawing a shaking breath, "I—I would like to be alone for a while. You can finish this later." They both looked so sad and so sympathetic that Whitney couldn't bear it.

When they left she looked all around her, trying to assimilate what was happening to her. Clayton was actually casting her aside because their lovemaking had resulted in her pregnancy.

For the first time since last night, Whitney felt a surge of genuine anger. Since when was pregnancy entirely the woman's fault? And just exactly what had he supposed was going to happen if they made love together? Naive she might have been, but even *she* had known that this is how babies were made. She had half a mind to go storming back to his rooms and inform him of that!

The more she thought of it, the angrier she became. Putting up her chin, Whitney marched over to the bellpull and summoned Clarissa. "Please have my blue silk pressed," she said. "And have the carriage brought round after dinner. I am going out."

Four hours later, Whitney swept into the dining room. Her

hair was twisted into elaborate coils entwined with a rope of sapphires and diamonds, with soft tendrils falling at her ears. If they were going to live like strangers, then they could live like friendly strangers. But if Clayton thought for one moment that after she bore his child he was going to be permitted to come to her bed again and take up where they had left off before yesterday—well, he didn't know her quite so well as he thought!

Except that when he automatically came to his feet when she walked into the room, Whitney took one look at him and felt a pang of longing and need so strong that she felt faint. He was so splendid, so unbearably handsome that if he had just smiled at her a little she would have flung herself against him and begged him . . . but begged him for what? For forgiveness for loving him? Or for carrying his child?

Several times during their silent meal, Whitney was aware of his gaze resting momentarily on her breasts which swelled beautifully above the sapphire bodice of her gown. And each time Clayton looked away again, she had the feeling that he was more furious than the time before. She almost wondered if it were possible that he was the least bit jealous. After all, this was the first time that they had ever gone to separate affairs in the evening. The next time his gaze slid to her breasts, she asked innocently, "Do you like my new dress?"

"If you mean to display your charms to the world, it suits you admirably," he said cynically.

"Are you settled into your new rooms?" she asked.

Clayton shoved his plate aside as if her conversation had ruined his appetite and rose from the table. "I find them vastly preferable to the ones I occupied before," he said icily. Without another word, he turned on his heel and strode from the room. A few minutes later the front door closed behind him, and Whitney heard the sound of his coach pulling away. She felt deflated, ill and miserable. But she went to the Wilsons' party and purposely stayed until well past midnight in the vague hope that Clayton might not like her being out late without him, and would accompany her the next time.

She was weary to the bone but she woke up abruptly as her

carriage pulled up in the Claymore drive, just as Clayton was alighting from his. They walked up the stairs together and Whitney could see the taut anger in the set of his jaw. "Continue to stay out this late and you will have all London gossiping about you within a week," he said tensely.

Whitney stopped with one hand on the door to her room. "I will not be able to go out in society once my condition becomes apparent," she informed him, and then out of sheer obstinacy, she gave her head a toss and added, "Besides, I was having a wonderful time!" She was not absolutely sure, but she thought he swore under his breath.

The next morning she went down to the stables and was bluntly refused a mount. She was hurt, confused, and angry. She was also embarrassed, as were the grooms who had to tell her that those were his grace's orders. Whitney was too distressed to reconsider her actions. Without a word, and looking very much like the young duchess she was, she swung on her heel and marched toward the house, through the front door, and down the hall to Clayton's study, which she entered without bothering to knock first.

He was in conclave with a large group of men seated in a semicircle around his desk. They all leapt to their feet, with the exception of Clayton, who rose with noticeable reluctance.

Smiling angelically at the circle of surprised men, Whitney said, "I beg your pardon, gentlemen, I didn't realize my husband had visitors." Then to Clayton who was standing rigidly behind his desk: "There has been a misunderstanding at the stables. No one there seems to realize that Khan belongs to *me*. Shall I tell them or would you prefer to explain?"

"Do not," her husband said in a terrible voice, "even consider getting on him."

"I am sorry to have interrupted your meeting," Whitney said, hot with embarrassment that he had spoken to her in front of strangers in that degrading tone. She stormed up to her room. This was madness, cruel, perverse insanity. Now

Clayton intended to keep her from doing anything to occupy her time. He wanted to deprive her of her smallest joys in life. She jerked off her riding hat. She hated wearing those silly hats when half the fun of riding was feeling the wind in your hair. She took two steps toward her dressing room, intending to change her clothes, and changed her mind instead.

She stormed back to the stables, gave the first groom who stepped in front of her such a haughty look of disdain that he stepped aside, and then she strode into Khan's stall. She curried him herself. She bridled him herself and then she marched over to the rack where her saddle was kept and dragged it down. She gained courage with each second. After all, not one of them would dare to lay a hand on her to prevent her from doing what she had set out to do. It took three tries to swing the heavy sidesaddle up and over Khan's back, but she finally made it. She tightened his girth strap as best she could and prayed that it would be tight enough to hold, then she led him out of his stall.

Whitney rode for three hours. She was tired after the first hour, but she hated to go back. From the minute she rode off on Khan, she had known that Clayton would be informed of her action, and she dreaded having to face him.

She had expected a confrontation later; she had *not* expected to find Clayton waiting for her at the stables. He was standing there with one shoulder propped casually against the whitewashed fence, his features composed as he conversed with the head groom. Inwardly, Whitney quailed at the sight of him. She knew that relaxed, almost indolent stance of his was only a surface calm, beneath which was a murderous fury which he would unleash on her.

As she trotted briskly past him, Clayton reached out in a deceptively casual move and caught Khan's bridle, jerking the horse around to a teeth-jarring stop. His eyes held a terrifying menace and his voice was so icy, so soft, that Whitney's heart pounded in fear. "Get down!"

Whitney had scarcely conceived the notion of whirling Khan and racing for parts unknown, when in that same awful voice he said, "Don't try it, I'm warning you."

To her consternation and fury, Whitney felt her cheeks grow hot and her hands shake. She swallowed and reached her arms toward him in an unconsciously childlike gesture. "Then will you help me down?"

Clayton lifted her roughly from the sidesaddle. "How *dare* you disobey me," he hissed, his fingers closing cruelly on her upper arm as he marched her away from the curious grooms and stablekeeps.

Whitney waited until they were out of earshot of the stable and approaching the rear door of the house before she pulled her arm away and turned on him. "Disobey you?!" she repeated, stamping her foot. "Do you mean to actually remind me of my vows? Why of all the— Would you like me to remind you of yours, my lord?"

"I will give you a warning. Just one," Clayton enunciated viciously. "Call it advice, if you prefer."

"If I wanted advice," Whitney retorted, her eyes sparkling with jade fire, "you would be the last person on earth I would ask!" She opened her mouth to say more, then changed her mind at the boiling wrath her outburst brought to his features.

"Defy me one more time—just once more, and I will have you locked in your rooms until your brat is born."

"I'm sure you would like nothing more!" Whitney said, hating him for calling her baby a brat. "You are the meanest, cruelest . . . you're a fraud and a liar! How dare you have told me you love me and then treat me so! And another thing, my lord duke," she added in choking fury, "which I'm sure will come as a *tremendous* surprise to you: It so happens that making love makes babies!"

Clayton was so stunned by her ridiculous "revelation" that he never saw the blow coming. She caught him full on the side of the face with the flat of her hand, then reared back, looking like a tempestuous goddess in all her fine fury.

"Go ahead and hit me back," she raged. "You want to hurt me. What's wrong—have you lost your desire to torture me?" she taunted, ignoring the drumming pulse at his temple. "Well good, because I'm just angry enough to do it again!" She swung wide, then gasped with pain as her wrist was caught in a vise-like grip a split second before her hand would have crashed into his face.

Jerking her wrist up behind her back, Clayton brought her slamming against his chest. "You are a beautiful, conniving, deceitful little bitch," he said furiously. "But just once in our misbegotten lives together, tell me one small truth. Just one honest admission. I swear that whether the answer is 'I don't know' or 'yes' I won't care either way."

"You *swear* to me?" Whitney hurled back at him. "As you swore at our wedding? As you swore in this house never to hurt me? Your word isn't worth the—"

"Is the child mine?" Clayton snapped, viciously tightening his cruel grip.

Her eyes widened until they were huge green orbs; her soft lips parted in shocked disbelief that was so convincing Clayton wondered for a split-second if somehow he was wrong about everything. Tears of outrage sprang into her eyes. "Is it *yours? Yours?*" Her voice rose and then, unexpectedly, she collapsed against him, her shoulders quaking violently.

Clayton released his grip on her wrist. He wanted to thrust her slender, shaking form away from him. And he wanted just as much to gather her into his arms and bury his face in her hair. But more than anything, he longed to take her into the house and ease the pain in his heart with her body. She was clinging with both hands to his lapels, her shoulders shaking, her face buried in his chest, saying over and over again, "Is it *yours?*"

Clayton put his hands on her arms, not gently but not roughly either, and moved her away from him. She was sobbing, he thought with an unwanted pang of guilt. He dropped his hands, and Whitney slowly raised her head. She wasn't weeping—she was laughing! She was laughing hysterically. She was still laughing when she hit him full across the side of the face with a crashing blow that snapped his head around, and then she ran inside.

Slowly, thoughtfully, Clayton followed her into the house. He went into his study, closed the doors behind him, and poured himself a liberal drink. He now knew two things for certain: Whitney had a powerful right arm. And the baby was his.

Whatever else she had lied about—the reason for her coming to him here, the reason she had married him—whatever else, her look of contemptuous scorn when he asked if the child was his—that look had been real. She had not lain with her lover on her trips to London. No human being alive who was guilty could have fabricated that look of stunned horror or shocked outrage. She had not betrayed him since they were married. Whatever else she had done, she had not done that. The child was his. Clayton knew it as surely as he knew she had come to him here seven months ago because she thought she needed a father for someone else's child. His wrath went from a roiling boil to a steady simmer.

Unfortunately, Whitney's did the opposite. Of all the vile, vulgar, contemptible . . . He was insane! Insane! And she would be too, if she stayed with him. For, even when he had called her terrible things a few minutes ago and hurt her arm with his punishing grip, she had felt joy in being pressed tightly to his heart again. Even then, she had wanted his arms to go around her. If she stayed, she would go mad.

Whitney tried to ignore the stab of anguish that came with knowing she had to leave him, while she tried to think of a place she could go. Her father wasn't strong-willed enough to shelter her from her husband if Clayton chose to demand her return to Claymore. Aunt Anne and Uncle Edward would help her. She would write to them and ask if she could come to France for a visit. When she was there, she would explain. She didn't know if Clayton's awesome power could touch her in France, or if he would retaliate by using his influence in England to damage her uncle's diplomatic career.

All she could do was explain to her Uncle Edward and let him decide.

Whitney sank down into the chair at her writing desk, pulled open the drawer and, as she reached for a sheet of blue stationery, she saw the crumpled ball of blue paper on top of the neat stack. Without much curiosity she turned it in her fingers, saw that it had writing on it, and smoothed it out to see if it was something she had kept because she might need it.

"To my very great mortification . . ." Blankly she remembered having secreted the unsent note among her unused stationery when she had been at Emily's because she didn't want a servant to find it. But now it was crumpled up and on top of the stack. *Someone* had found it, but only Mary and Clarissa served her at Claymore, and they would never search through her desk.

It was humiliating to think of someone reading that note, and she tried to imagine who could have been in her desk. Two days ago, when she had joyously tucked the little infant gown in the drawer for Clayton to find, the drawer had been neat and no one, other than Clayton, had been . . . Oh, my God!

Whitney half rose from her chair—she had sent Clayton to her desk and asked him to find her aunt's letter. "And you found this," she breathed aloud, as if he were in the room. "Dear God, you found this." Her hands were shaking and her mind was reeling as she tried to concentrate on what Clayton might have made of what he had read. She forced herself to look at the note as if she had found it, instead of written it. The date. They had promised to celebrate, each year, the date she had come to Claymore, and the note was dated just one day before that. Reading this, Clayton would wonder if—no, *believe*—she had come to him that night because she thought she was pregnant! That would hurt him deeply, because he had told her once that nothing she could ever do would mean more to him than the way she had come to him that night because she loved him and wanted him to know it.

Very well, then the next thing she would wonder about, if she had found the note, was whom it was meant for. Getting up with the note still in her hand, Whitney began to pace agitatedly back and forth. Based on Clayton's reaction, he must have thought the note had been meant for someone else. All right—but he knew he had taken her virginity that terrible night and she could have been carrying his child as a result of that. How dare he be so angry merely because she might have turned to someone else for help or advice! Well, why shouldn't she have done so—after all, when that note was written they weren't even on civil terms with each other. Why, she could have been writing to her father or her aunt or anyone! But judging from the violence of Clayton's reaction, he obviously thought not.

He was torturing her this way because he was hurt. And because he was angry that she might have turned to another . . . another *man* . . . for help. He was hurt. And jealous.

"You fool!" Whitney hissed into the empty room. She was so relieved and so happy that she could have flung her arms out and twirled around. It wasn't because Clayton didn't want their baby! Yet weak with relief though she was, she could also cheerfully have killed him!

He had done it again! Just what he had done the awful night he had dragged her here. He had accused her of something in his mind, tried and convicted and sentenced her, without ever telling her what crime she was accused of committing. Without ever giving her an opportunity to explain! And now—and now—he actually believed he could just set her aside, move to another wing of the house and pretend that their marriage was as dead as if it had never existed.

Whitney was shaking with relief and quaking with determination. This was the last, the *last* time his temper was going to explode against her before she was given some explanation for the reason first!

And if Clayton thought for one moment that he could love her as deeply as Whitney knew he did, yet turn his back on her and coldly walk away, well, he was now going to learn differently. How could he be so wise, so intelligent, and actually think he could set her aside in anger, no matter what she did—or what he thought she did?

Somehow, some way, she was going to make him explain why he was acting this way. Whitney didn't care how it came about or how he did it. He could hurl the accusations in her face, for all she cared. In fact, she thought with a sad smile, that was undoubtedly how it would happen, because she was not going to plead with him to explain; she had tried that already and it did no good. Which left her with no choice but to force his hand, to make him angry enough or jealous enough to lose control completely and confront her with what he thought she'd done.

And when he did, she would coldly explain about the note. She would make him grovel at her feet and beg for her forgiveness. A brilliant smile dawned across her features. Oh rubbish! She would never be able to do that. She would explain as quickly as she could and then fling herself against his hard chest and feel faint with joy and longing when his strong arms went around her.

But for now, she had to make herself be anything but meek or sad. She would be charming and gay until Clayton missed what they had together so badly that he couldn't stand it. She would goad and needle him gently at first, and only if that didn't work would she force his hand by making him truly angry.

The Clifftons were having a huge affair tonight. Whitney couldn't be sure whether Clayton still meant to go. But she did.

She dressed with great care in an emerald-green gown she had ordered in Paris on their wedding trip. It was the most revealing gown she had ever worn and she smiled to herself as she put on the emerald and diamond necklace and matching bracelet and ear drops. "How do I look?" Whitney asked Clarissa, twirling around.

"Bare as the day you were born," Clarissa decreed with a censorious stare at Whitney's bodice.

"It's a little less than I normally wear," Whitney agreed with a faint twinkle in her eyes, "but I don't *quite* think my husband will want me going anywhere without him in this gown, do you?"

In a rustle of emerald silk, Whitney swept into the drawing room. Clayton was pouring himself a drink at the sideboard, his tall, athletic frame resplendent in midnight-blue jacket and trousers. In contrast to the deep blue superfine, his shirt and neckcloth were dazzling white. He looked unbearably handsome. He also looked utterly furious as his insolent gaze swung over the shimmering green gown and froze on the daring display of tantalizing flesh swelling above her bodice.

"Where," he asked in a low, ominous voice, "do you think you are going?"

"Think I am going?" Whitney repeated, managing to look extremely innocent, despite the seductive allure of her gown. "We promised to go to the Clifftons' tonight. I would love a glass of wine, if you wouldn't mind," she added with a languorous smile.

Clayton jerked a bottle of wine from the rack built into the cabinet. "That's too damned bad, because *we* aren't going to the Clifftons'."

"Oh?" Whitney said as she crossed to him to take her glass. "That's a shame, for you will miss a splendid party. I have always thought the Clifftons' parties are the most delightful of any in . . ."

Clayton turned slowly and perched a hip on the cabinet beside him, one leg swinging idly, his weight braced against the other foot. "I am not going to the Clifftons'," he told her icily. "And you are not going out tonight at all. Is that clear enough, Whitney?"

"The *words* are quite clear," Whitney told him. She turned, carrying her glass, and swept regally off to the dining room, trailing emerald silk in her wake. She was crushed. Clayton wasn't going to take her to the Clifftons', and he wouldn't let her go alone.

In the candlelit dining room their meal progressed in stiff silence. Whitney watched him surreptitiously throughout the meal. It was nearly over when her gaze fell on his hand. It was devoid of the ruby ring she'd given him on their wedding night. Her heart constricted as she stared at the light mark across his finger; from the moment she had placed the ring on his hand on their wedding night, he had never taken it off.

She looked up and found him observing her pained reaction with a smile of cynical amusement. And as hurt as she was, Whitney was even angrier. She was going to that party, she decided with a determined lift of her chin. If she had to walk, she was going without him.

Before dessert was brought in, Whitney stood up and said, "I am going to my room. Good night." She was going to her room because she didn't want to alert him to the fact that she was also going to the party, and risk having Clayton forbid their drivers to take her anywhere.

It was well past one o'clock in the morning, but in the exclusive gentlemen's gaming club to which Clayton belonged, time was never of much importance. He was relaxing in his chair, not paying much attention to the discussions going on around him, or, for that matter, to the cards he held.

No matter how much he drank tonight, or how hard he tried, he couldn't concentrate on the game or the hearty masculine conversation of his friends and acquaintances. He had married a witch who had gotten under his skin like a thorn. It hurt unbearably to have her there and it hurt to pull her out. His mind kept riveting itself on the way Whitney had looked tonight in that goddamned green gown with her charms displayed in such gorgeous wantonness. His hands had actually ached for the feel of that petal-soft skin against his palms, and his lust had been almost past bearing. Lust, not love. He wouldn't call it love anymore. All he felt for Whitney was an occasional pang of desire. More than an occasional pang.

How dare she even consider going out in that dress alone! And what in hell did she mean by acting as if he'd forbidden her to ride in order to torture her? He had given that order at the stable days ago when he had suspected her pregnancy and thought she was unaware of it. Not that he gave a damn what the conniving little liar thought. He didn't have to offer explanations for his actions; she would have to do as she was bidden. And that, he thought as he threw chips onto the pile in the center of the table, was irrevocably that!

"Good to see you, Claymore," William Baskerville said with amiable cordiality as he took a vacant chair at the table of six across from Clayton. "Surprised to see you, in fact."

"Why is that?" Clayton said indifferently.

"Just saw your wife at the Clifftons' crush. Thought you must be there, too," Baskerville explained, absorbed in stacking his chips into piles, preparatory to joining the heavy play in progress. "She looked lovely—told her so, too." This innocent discourse earned Baskerville a look of such stunned disbelief from the duke that Baskerville hastened to heap on polite reassurances. "Your wife *always* looks lovely. I *always* tell her that." In dismayed bewilderment, Baskerville watched the duke slowly come erect and rigid in his chair, his expression glacial. Searching his mind frantically for how he could possibly have given offense, Baskerville unfortunately arrived at the incorrect conclusion that his compliments must sound watery to the lady's husband who was, according to gossip, inordinately fond of his young bride. With a helpless glance at the other men seated around the table, Baskerville said desperately, "*Everyone* thought the duchess looked ravishing—she was wearing a green gown that matched her eyes. I told her it did, too. Had to wait in line just to tell her, in fact. Surrounded by all the young bucks and old fossils like me, she was. Quite a gathering of admirers."

Very quietly, very deliberately, Clayton turned his cards over on the table and slid his chair back. He stood up, nodded curtly to the other men seated at the table, and without a word to any of his friends, turned on his heel and strode purposefully from the room.

All cardplay suspended as the five remaining men at the table watched the duke making his way to the door leading out onto the street. Of the five, four were married. Baskerville, a confirmed bachelor of five and forty years, was not. Of the five faces at the table, four of them were either grinning or valiantly trying to hide a grin. Only Baskerville's expression was alarmed.

"Blast it!" he whispered, looking around at the others. "Claymore gave me the *devil* of a look when I said I'd just seen his duchess at the Clifftons'," He paused, seized by a terrible thought. "I say—have the Westmorelands been married long enough to quarrel, would you think?"

Marcus Rutherford's lips twitched with laughter. "I would say, Baskerville, that as of about three minutes ago, the Westmorelands have now been married long enough to quarrel."

Distress furrowed Baskerville's kindly brow. "Good God! I'd never have mentioned seeing her if I thought it would cause a quarrel. She's a lovely young thing. Feel wretched about causing trouble for her. I'm sure she'd never have gone to the deuced party if she realized Claymore wouldn't approve."

"You think not?" Lord Rutherford said after sharing a derisive grin with the other married men.

Baskerville was positive. "Well, of course not! If Claymore told her not to go, she wouldn't have gone. She's his wife, after all. Vows, you know—obedience and all that!"

Guffaws greeted this announcement, bursting out around the table like cracks from a cannon. "I once told my wife that she didn't need the fur she was pining for—she had a dozen already," Rutherford told him as the gambling was temporarily forgotten. "I put my foot squarely down and told her she could *not* have it!"

"Surely she didn't buy it anyway?" Baskerville asked in a horrified tone.

"Certainly not," Rutherford chuckled. "She bought eleven new gowns instead, to match the furs she already had. She said that if she had to appear in outer rags, at least no one would have cause to criticize her gowns. She spent three times the cost of the new fur."

"My God! Did you beat her?"

"Beat her?" Rutherford repeated in amusement. "No— beating's not at all 'the thing,' you know. I rather dislike the idea of it myself. I bought her the new fur instead."

"But—but why?" Baskerville sputtered in shock.

"Why, my good man? I'll tell you why. Because I'd no wish to own all of Bond Street before she got over her being miffed. Gowns are devilish costly things, but jewels—jewels she hadn't even thought of yet! I saved myself a fortune by getting her the fur."

Dawn was already streaking the sky as Whitney trailed quietly up the broad marble staircase to her room. She had missed Clayton terribly tonight; missed the feel of his hand lightly riding her waist, of his bold gaze capturing hers, and of the joy of knowing he was near. How could he have become so essential to her life in so short a time? She felt desolate without him, and it was an awful temptation to bring the note to his room and explain. But what would happen the next time if she couldn't find a clue like the note, to explain his fury? Then he would punish her again with his wrath, and she would be helpless to defend herself—and it was agony to have someone you loved furious with you, without knowing why. She did not in the least regret her open defiance of Clayton's command tonight, because she was hoping that when he discovered her disobedience, it would bring about the confrontation she wanted and needed.

In fact, she wondered if she ought to mention—quite casually—that she had had a lovely time at the Clifftons', when she saw Clayton at breakfast in the morning. Yes, Whitney decided, as she groped in the darkness of her room for the lamp, it would be an excellent idea.

On second thought, it was not a good idea at all, she realized with a lurch of fear as the room flared to light and from the corner of her eye, she glimpsed a gleaming, booted foot resting casually atop the other knee, a pair of dark blue gloves being idly slapped against a blue-clad thigh. From somewhere in the depths of her momentary panic, inspiration seized her, and Whitney pretended not to have seen him. She reached up behind her and began to unfasten her dress on the way into her dressing room. If she could just make him wait until she could change into one of her most seductive negligees, she might have a slight advantage—then desire might overcome anger, and—

"Keep it on!" his voice slashed out, "until I leave."

Whitney swung around, startled by his scathing tone.

Clayton came to his feet, advancing on her with the predatory grace of a stalking panther. Reflexively, Whitney started to back away, then checked herself and held her ground. He loomed over her, his gaze a frigid blast. In a silky, menacing voice, he said, "Do you remember what I told you would happen if you dared to disobey me again, Whitney?"

He had threatened to lock her in her rooms until her baby was born. Whitney was angry and frightened—and so much in love with him that even her voice throbbed with it. "Yes, I remember," she said in an aching whisper. "I remember all sorts of other things, too. I remember the words you have whispered to me when you are so deep inside of me that you have touched my heart. I remember . . ."

"Shut up!" he snapped furiously. "Or so help me God, I'll . . ."

"I remember exactly the way your hands feel against my skin when you touch me and . . ."

He caught her shoulders in a bruising grip and shook her so hard that Whitney's head snapped back. "Damn you! I said stop!"

"I can't." Whitney shuddered from the pain his hands were inflicting. "I can't stop, because I love you. I love your eyes, and your smile, and your . . ."

With a vicious jerk, Clayton yanked her into his arms, his mouth capturing hers in a savage, punishing kiss that was meant to silence and hurt and retaliate. He was bruising her lips, and she was crushed so tightly against him that she couldn't breathe. But Whitney didn't care; she could feel the hardness of his need swelling rigidly against her, and when his mouth began to slant fiercely over hers with wild hunger and desperate urgency, she wrapped her arms around his neck and clung to him.

As abruptly as he had caught her to him, Clayton pushed her away. His breathing was harsh and ragged, his expression so incensed, so bleakly embittered that Whitney almost lost her resolve and brought up the note herself. Instead she raised her chin to its bravest angle and said in quiet defiance, "I will willingly commit myself to being locked in this room for as long as you wish—provided you are willing to stay locked in here with me. Otherwise, nothing—and no one—will keep me in here. If I have to set fire to the house to get out, then I will."

It took a moment for Clayton to react. She looked so unbearably beautiful, so young and vulnerable, facing him in this outrageous mutiny, that if he didn't hate her and hate himself, he would have grinned. He had to remind himself that she was a calculating schemer; even so, his earlier wrath was momentarily defused by her impertinent suggestion that he lock himself into her room with her. Lock himself in with her? Christ! He could barely stand to live in the same house with her, despising her with an uncontrollable virulence half the time, and wanting her until he ached with it the rest.

"If you ever again leave the grounds of this estate without my permission," he said in a low, savage voice, "you will yearn for the 'tenderness' I showed you the first time I brought you here."

Clayton had taught her to be proud of the power she held over his body, and that one brutal kiss had shown Whitney how badly he still wanted her. The knowledge gave her the courage to look at him and say with a faint blush, "I already do yearn for it, my lord." Then, reverting to her former air of proud rebellion, she added as she turned and walked into her dressing room, "However, I shall obey you to the extent of at least *asking* for your permission *before* I leave the grounds."

Whitney heard the outer door close and leaned weakly against the wall of her dressing room, more shaken by the confrontation than she had let him see. Her idle threat about setting fire to the house had not been what had stopped him from having her confined to her room. She knew, and he knew, that he could very easily have her kept there with a loyal servant acting as guard in her room to prevent her from doing anything harmful. But she had thrown him off balance by boldly inviting him to stay here with her.

She was playing with fire, Whitney knew. She couldn't risk angering him to the point where he might have her removed entirely from his presence. She had to be with him so that she could force him into accusing her of this nonsense he believed. She had to be near him so that she could continue to stoke the fire of his desire; one of them, either fury or desire, was going to drive him from his stony silence.

In the east wing, Clayton lay awake in his bed, coldly contemplating his past and his future. By now he had managed to find an explanation for every heretofore unexplainable word or action on Whitney's part. At long last, the reason for her behavior at Elizabeth's wedding banquet was crystal clear. She had meant every cold, vile word she had said to him as they danced. *After* the banquet, in the ensuing weeks, Whitney had discovered her pregnancy, or thought she was pregnant, and when the father couldn't or wouldn't offer her his name, she had concocted the scheme of coming here and renewing their dead betrothal. And he, like a goddamned fool, had, with great joy, allowed himself to be cuckolded.

He didn't know how long he could stand this living arrangement. His heart and his mind understood the harsh reality that there could never be anything between Whitney and him again, but his body tormented him with the same insatiable desire for her he'd always felt.

If they weren't living under the same roof, perhaps he could find some relief from his agony. He could remove to his townhouse in Upper Brook Street and resume a semblance of his former life, or he could go to France or Spain for a few months. That would be ideal, but Whitney was, after all, carrying his child and, in the event of some complication with her pregnancy, he shouldn't be so far away.

No, the townhouse would be better. His need for diversion and his physical needs could both be satisfied in London. All he had to do was take Whitney to a few social affairs during the next month or two, then, once her pregnancy was apparent, she would not be able to go out into society anyway, so no one would find it odd that she was no longer seen on his arm. When they saw him with other women, the old biddies would cluck their tongues and whisper to one another that "the little nobody" he had married hadn't been able to hold him very long, and that they had known all along that this was how it was going to end. The thought gave Clayton a certain perverse pleasure.

He hoped to God that Whitney was carrying a boy, for this was going to be his only opportunity to get an heir. Otherwise he would have to leave it up to Stephen to sire the heir. Thank God he *could* count on Stephen for that; the lands and title had always been held by a Westmoreland, and his father had been the only boy of five children.

The following morning, Whitney composed a carefully worded note to Clayton to the effect that Lord Archibald's parents were celebrating their anniversary and that Whitney had promised Emily and Michael to attend the gala affair this evening, and that she would appreciate it very much if Clayton would escort her. She sent the note into the east wing with Clarissa, then paced back and forth, waiting for Clayton's response.

With trembling fingers she unfolded her note across the bottom of which was a curt reply in Clayton's bold handwriting. "Advise my valet whether the dress is formal or informal." She could have laughed with joy.

That night she spent more time than ever in her life on her appearance. Clarissa swept her hair up into intricate coils entwined with a finely wrought gold chain which had belonged to Whitney's grandmother. Nestled in the hollow between her breasts was a simple topaz pendant surrounded by a ring of diamonds, which had belonged to Whitney's great-grandmother. She was not wearing any of the Westmoreland jewelry. She was not, in fact, wearing her splendid betrothal ring. For a few minutes Whitney actually considered removing her wide gold wedding band, but that she could not do—not even to make her point.

Clayton was standing at the far end of the white and gold salon, staring moodily out the windows with a glass of whiskey in his hand, looking utterly magnificent in his black evening clothes. With a gleam of mischief dancing in her eyes, Whitney floated into the salon in a swirl of glittering gold-spangled chiffon. She did not remove the golden stole that was lying softly across her breasts, draped in a gentle half circle down her back, nor did she intend to do so until they arrived at Michael's parents' home.

The hour and a half ride was made in frosty silence, but Whitney contented herself by relishing what Clayton's reaction was going to be when he saw the tantalizing display of swelling breasts exposed by the gown's provocatively plunging bodice. If Clayton hadn't liked the emerald gown in his current mood, he was definitely not going to approve of this one.

"We don't clash," Whitney remarked when they arrived at their destination and Clayton was helping her down from the closed carriage.

"Meaning what?" he said coldly.

"Meaning the colors we are wearing," she innocently explained. In a deceptively casual gesture, Whitney pulled off the gold stole and let it flutter from her fingers as she stepped forward beside him toward the house.

"I can't imagine what damned difference—" Clayton came to a complete halt, his eyes like shards of ice as they froze on the swelling expanse of glowing skin exposed above the glittering bodice. In a low, incensed voice he said, "Are you trying to see exactly how far I can be provoked?"

"No, my lord," Whitney replied demurely, aware of the curious looks from other arriving guests. "How could I possibly provoke you more than I already have simply by offering you a child."

"If you will take some advice," he snapped, making a visible effort to control his fury, "you will remember your condition and behave accordingly tonight."

Whitney gave him a vivacious smile, aware that his blazing eyes were riveted on her swelling breasts. "Of course," she said lightly, "I meant to do exactly that, but my knitting wouldn't fit inside my reticule." In humorous proof, she held up her little beaded bag, then gasped aloud in surprised pain as Clayton's hand locked onto her forearm, his fingers biting cruelly into her flesh.

"Do not fail to enjoy the party this evening to its fullest, because it is the last you will be attending. You will remain at Claymore until the child is born, and I am moving into the townhouse."

All the optimistic hope and determination went out of her, leaving Whitney numb and desolate. She tried to pull her arm free, but his painful grip was relentless. "Then please don't shame us both tonight by leaving the marks of your contempt on my arm."

His grip loosened so abruptly that it seemed as if he had been unaware of even touching her. "Pain," he snapped at her as they passed by the butler, "like love, is a thing to be shared."

From the first minute she entered the drawing room, Whitney was vaguely aware that something was amiss, but she could not quite put her finger on what it was. It was just that everyone seemed so . . . normal. No, too painstakingly normal—as if they were making a concerted effort to *seem* normal. Nearly an hour later, Whitney glanced up and saw Lord Esterbrook; she smiled at him and he nodded and bowed, but when he would have started toward her, Whitney made a great show of being deeply involved in her conversation with the group surrounding her. She had never believed that Lord Esterbrook had said "unkind" things about her to Vanessa at the Rutherfords' party, but he had an extremely perverse sense of humor and could deliver a cut with a razor's edge, so she always made a practice of keeping him at a distance.

Emily, who arrived shortly thereafter, immediately provided the answer to the strange atmosphere pervading the evening. "Oh good Lord in heaven," she said, hauling Whitney off to one side and whispering while she cast furtive looks around her. "My father-in-law is the veriest loose screw about some things. I could not believe my ears when he told me five minutes ago what great pains he'd taken to lure her here as a surprise for my mother-in-law."

"What are you talking about?" Whitney whispered back as premonitions of disaster began to pound in her brain.

"Marie St. Allermain. She's here! Michael's father went through friends of friends to entice her to come and sing here tonight. She's a guest at the palace where she is to perform tomorrow night, and . . ."

Whitney didn't hear the rest. Her legs and arms had begun to tremble from the moment Emily had mentioned the name of Clayton's beautiful and most famous former mistress. Marie St. Allermain was in London, in the very house with Clayton. And not more than an hour ago, he'd announced his intention of moving into the London house. Whitney didn't remember what she said to Emily or how she managed to return to the circle of acquaintances she'd left. She waited in sick dread for the moment when Marie St. Allermain would walk into the room.

The huge drawing room was packed beyond capacity. From the corner of her eye, Whitney watched Clayton enter the room at the same time the accompanist seated himself at the big grand piano, and the musicians picked up their instruments. There was a crackling tension in the room, although whether it was due to the appearance of a woman whose voice and beauty were legendary, and who was in demand in all the capitals of Europe, or whether it was because everyone was secretly waiting to see Clayton and her come face to face, Whitney didn't know.

Clayton, who had paused to talk to someone, finally made his way to Whitney's side. It was as if the crowd parted to clear a path so that they could both stroll to the very front row of guests clustered around the piano.

Whitney stood with her hand linked through Clayton's arm. She knew he didn't want it there, but she was feeling ill and desperately needed something to hold onto. "No voice in the world like St. Allermain's, if you ask me," the elderly man beside Clayton said. Beneath her fingertips, Whitney felt the muscles in Clayton's forearm tense into rigidity and then slowly relax. He hadn't known! she realized. Oh God! Why did he have to look so devastatingly handsome tonight, so completely desirable? And why, she thought, with tears burning behind her eyes as the blond singer entered the room, did Marie St. Allermain have to be so lushly, provocatively, enchantingly beautiful? Whitney could not tear her unwilling gaze from the woman. She had the body of a slender Venus and the magnetism of a woman who is confident of her extraordinary beauty without being at all obsessed with it.

And when she began to sing, Whitney felt the room swim dizzily. She had the sort of lilting voice that could fall gently upon the ears, or deepen until it was rich and sensual. There was a glint of laughter in her eyes while she sang, as if she found the silent adoration being lavished upon her by the hundreds of people who were listening and watching her, secretly very silly.

In comparison to her, Whitney felt girlish and plain and unsophisticated. And deathly ill. For she now knew *exactly* what being Clayton's mistress really meant. That woman with the laughing blue eyes had known Clayton's drugging kisses, had lain naked in his arms and shared the exquisite ecstasy of his body driving deeply into hers. Whitney knew she must be as pale as death; her ears were ringing and her hands felt like ice. She was going to faint if she stayed in here; if she left, she would create a scene that would feed the malicious gossips for years. She tried to tell herself that, after all, Clayton had broken off his affair with Marie to pursue *her*. But that was before; now he detested and despised her. And very soon, even if he came back to Claymore, her body would be ungainly and swollen with child.

Whitney wished, very sincerely, that she were dead. She was so anguished that she had no idea precisely when Clayton's hand had come to rest upon her cold, clammy one which was linked through the crook of his arm, or for how long he had been lightly, reassuringly squeezing her fingers. But when she realized it, she shamelessly took what little support he was offering her and curled her fingers tightly around his. At least now she felt as if she could breathe. But only momentarily. For when Marie St. Allermain was accepting the thunderous applause with a faintly amused inclination of her head, her blue eyes met Clayton's, and a current leapt between the two of them that Whitney felt with a painful jolt.

Soon after, the ballroom was opened for dancing. For the next half hour, Clayton did not leave her side, but neither did he speak to her or so much as glance at her. He was there though, and Whitney clung to that fact as if it were the beginning of the reconciliation she had been waiting for. Her hopes were dashed to pieces the moment Clayton led her onto the dance floor and took her in his arms. "Where in the living hell is **yo**ur betrothal ring?" he snapped angrily as he whirled her effortlessly in perfect time to the waltz.

"The token of your love?" Whitney asked him, her chin

proudly high, her pale face fragile and beautiful. "That betrothal ring?"

"You know damned well which ring."

"Since it was a token of the love I no longer have from you, I felt it was hypocrisy to wear it." She waited breathlessly for Clayton to say his love for her wasn't dead.

"Do as you damn well please," he said with cynical indifference. "You always have."

When the dance ended they remained together, each of them putting on a convincing performance of participating in the light-hearted conversation directed at them by the dozen guests surrounding them. A short time later, however, an imperceptible tension seemed to take root and spread through the group, and their laughter suddenly became too hardy and forced as they flicked nervous glances over Whitney's right shoulder. In her heightened state of nervous awareness, Whitney noticed the change in the atmosphere and turned to see what was causing it. One glance, and she jerked her head around, but it was too late to do more than brace herself. Lord Esterbrook, with Marie St. Allermain on his arm, was approaching them from behind.

"Claymore!" Esterbrook's mocking voice cut through the little group's forced joviality like a hot knife through butter. "I'm sure that no introductions are necessary between the two of you."

Every pair of eyes swivelled to them as Clayton turned automatically at the sound of his name and found himself confronted by a grinning Esterbrook and his former mistress. Whitney, who had no choice but to turn around also, heard the frantic buzzing and gasps, the muted laughter, and felt the weight of avidly curious gazes focusing on them. There was no doubt that everyone present in the huge ballroom was now fully cognizant of the import of the meeting taking place . . . everyone, that is, except Clayton and Marie St. Allermain, who seemed to find the situation rather amusing.

With a lazy grin, Clayton lifted Marie's hand to his lips for a brief kiss. "I see, Madam, that you still have only to walk into a room to bring the entire male population to your feet."

An answering sparkle twinkled in Marie's smoky blue eyes as she inclined her head in a gracious acceptance of his gallant compliment. "Not quite the *entire* population," she said meaningfully. "But then I would be astonished to find you in such an excessively silly position, your grace."

Whitney listened to this light repartée in a state of angry, humiliated pain, wondering if Clayton were going to introduce his wife to his mistress, being absolutely certain that he could not, in the interest of politeness do so, nor avoid doing so without being *im*polite. In that moment, Whitney hated Clayton. She despised Esterbrook. She loathed every prying eye in that room. They were all her enemies, brittle, sophisticated, gossiping strangers who resented her intrusion into their select society and who were relishing the mortifying position in which she was now placed. They were Esterbrooks, one and all. Including her polished, urbane husband. She wished she had married Paul and lived quietly in the security of a place where she could belong. And that was before Whitney realized that Esterbrook, with a look of sham innocence, was now introducing Clayton's mistress to *her*.

Fortified by her anger, Whitney met Marie St. Allermain's silently assessing gaze with quiet composure. Graciously, in flawless French, Whitney said, "Thank you for sharing the gift of your beautiful voice with me, Mademoiselle. It was a joy to be able to hear you."

With equal graciousness, Marie replied, "Most accounts of feminine beauty and charm are gross exaggerations. However, I can see that accounts of yours were not." A slow, sensual smile curved her lips. Glancing provocatively at Clayton, she added with devastating candor, "And, I must say it is excessively disappointing to find it so." With that, she nodded regally at both of them, took Esterbrook's arm, and swept away to content herself with the fawning admiration of the other three hundred male occupants of the room.

For a while, Whitney basked in the warmth of Clayton's unspoken approval; she knew he was proud of the way she had handled the confrontation. She also knew when, an hour later, Clayton and Marie each left the room via separate doors out onto the terrace. She had seen the subtle look Marie passed to him across the ballroom and witnessed the imperceptible inclination of Clayton's dark head in reply.

Smiling in the summer moonlight, Marie extended both her hands to be clasped in his strong, warm ones. "It is wonderful to see you, Clayton. Esterbrook must bear you great malice to have deliberately manipulated our brief encounter in there."

Clayton grinned down at her. "Esterbrook is a stupid son of a bitch, as you have already surmised on your own, Marie." He watched the way the moonlight turned her hair to shining silver, while he relished her lush beauty and the keen intelligence in her violet-blue eyes. She took no missish offense at his blunt summation of Esterbrook; she was as astute a judge of character as was he, and they both knew it.

"Marriage does not agree with you, my lord?" She said it as a question, but it was more a quiet observation.

Clayton stiffened slightly. He reminded himself that nothing would rock the foundations of London society so violently as his taking Marie St. Allermain as his mistress again. They were both so well known that the gossip created by a renewed liaison between the two of them would be endless, and the humiliation Whitney would suffer as a result of it would be immeasurable. And Marie was a passionate bed partner who suited him perfectly. And even while he told himself all this, he could almost feel Whitney's cold, trembling hand on his arm, the way her fingers had clutched his for support while Marie was singing.

Damn her! How dare she take off her betrothal ring! She was a schemer, a liar, and a fraud. But she was also his wife. And right now, she was young and afraid and pregnant with his child. To Clayton's intense disgust, he realized that he could not bring himself to make the overture which he knew would be welcome to Marie. He would take another woman as his mistress, someone who would create less notoriety.

"Marriage does not seem to agree with your wife either," Marie was observing quietly. "She is very beautiful—and very unhappy."

"Marriage agrees with both of us," Clayton said grimly.

A slow, provocative smile trembled on her lips. "If you say so, Clayton."

"I say so," he said irritably. If Marie had noticed that Whitney was unhappy and distressed, others in the ballroom may have noticed that as well. He didn't want Whitney shamed in front of their friends. It was one thing for him to hate her and humiliate her in private, another entirely for society to be taking notice of it. And he was thoroughly incensed to discover that he even gave a damn.

"In that case," Marie mused, displaying the perspicacity that Clayton had always enjoyed in her, "it might be wise if you now went back into the ballroom. Because I am of the opinion that Esterbrook's intent in bringing us together in front of your wife, was to make himself available to console her later." She saw Clayton's shoulders stiffen and the dangerous glitter in his eyes. A winsome smile touched her lips. "I've never seen you look like this before. You are terrifying—and devastatingly attractive—when you're angry. And jealous."

"Leave it at angry," Clayton replied in a clipped voice which he softened as he bid his former mistress farewell.

When he strode back into the ballroom, he looked first for Esterbrook, then for Whitney. Esterbrook was there, Whitney was not. With a feeling of relief, Clayton noted that no one seemed to have observed his absence with Marie, and judging by the boisterous level of conversation in the room, whatever gossip had begun at their public meeting had died a polite death. Clayton was glad of that because these people were Whitney's friends as well as his, and she would need to know that she didn't have to cringe from seeing them the next time.

Except that Whitney wouldn't know that. Because the duchess, as the butler solemnly explained, had already left. Damned little fool! Clayton thought savagely. What was she thinking of, walking out on him like this? Now there would be hell to pay! He couldn't go back in there without her, or everyone would immediately realize that she had left in distress or anger, and that *would* cause gossip. Personally, he couldn't have cared less about the talk, but Whitney would be the one who had to face it, and who had left because she couldn't. And he couldn't leave either, dammit—because she had taken the carriage.

Emily and Michael Archibald solved that problem within seconds by walking into the entryway and asking to have their carriage brought round so that they could leave. Without question or comment, they provided him with a ride to his London townhouse, where Clayton spent a very angry, uncomfortable night. He kept seeing Whitney in that glittering golden gown that displayed her ripe breasts to such glorious advantage. She'd worn it deliberately to provoke him and, by God, she'd succeeded! Hadn't he had to stand beside her all night, watching men's gazes lingering lustfully on the tantalizing display of her creamy flesh?

If she hadn't worn that damned gown and taken off her betrothal ring, if her hair weren't so thick and lustrous with that shining gold chain entwined in it, if she hadn't looked so heart-breakingly beautiful and desirable, he'd never have accepted Marie's silent invitation to join her on the terrace in the first place.

Chapter Thirty-five

CLAYTON DID NOT RETURN TO CLAYMORE THE NEXT DAY OR THE day after, or the day after that. Nor did he spend the three days entwined in naked splendor with Marie St. Allermain as Whitney's feverish, tortured imaginings told her. He spent the three days in London, in alternating states of righteous fury and quiet thoughtfulness. He spent the nights at his club with his friends.

Very late on the third night, as he sat staring out the window of his bedroom overlooking a fog-shrouded courtyard, Clayton arrived at a few conclusions. In the first place, he did not see why the hell he should have to go to the inconvenience of choosing a mistress and setting her up in a discreet home of her own, which he would have to do now that he was married. He was married to a slut, but she had a ripe, tantalizing body that intoxicated his mind and fitted his own body to perfection. So why should he take a mistress when he had Whitney? And he was not going to continue living like a damned monk, nor was he going to remain living like a guest in the east wing of his own house, either.

He was going home and he was moving back into his own bedroom. And when his body had need of her, Whitney would service him. She would be a servant, nothing more, a well-dressed servant whose duties were to act as his hostess on the occasions when he required one, and as his unpaid whore when he needed one. It was almost what she was anyway, he thought with a fresh surge of boiling wrath. Except that her price had been very high—a fortune in money, and his name, to boot! But he owned her. Permanently.

With those tender thoughts and several more of a similar nature, Clayton ordered his town carriage around on the morning of the fourth day and impatiently endured the hour and a half drive through an English countryside decked out in all its lush, summer glory. He scarcely noticed the passing landscape as he contemplated the scene that was going to take place as soon as he arrived at Claymore. First he was going to explain to Whitney her future status and duties in the crudest possible terms. Then he intended to tell her what he thought of her treachery and deceit, her outrageous temper, and her rebellion against his authority. And when he was done with that, he was going to cram that note down her lovely throat—figuratively speaking.

The carriage had scarcely pulled to a stop in the drive in front of the house before Clayton was striding swiftly up the steps, through the front doors and up the staircase to Whitney's rooms. He flung the door to her bedchambers open with a force that sent it crashing against the wall and brought Mary flying around in surprised alarm. Without a word to the staring servant, he strode quickly through the adjoining dressing room into his old chambers. But Whitney wasn't there. Because the duchess, as Mary tearfully explained, had left. Yesterday.

"Left for where?" Clayton snapped impatiently.

"S-she wouldn't say, your grace. She said she left a note for you in her desk." His formerly loyal housekeeper began to sniffle, but Clayton ignored her as he strode stiffly to Whitney's desk. It was empty, save for a single crumpled ball of blue writing paper in the top drawer. Clayton hated even to touch it, but he smoothed it out and made himself look at it in case she had written something else. She hadn't. It was just her way of telling him she had discovered the reason for his anger. He crammed the despised note into his pocket and turned in the doorway.

"I'm moving back into my own rooms," he said in a soft snarl to Mary. "Get her things out of there."

"And where shall I put them next?" Mary asked in a mutinous tone.

"Back in here, dammit!" Clayton was aware that the Irish housekeeper found something to smile about in his reply, but he was too furious at being cheated of his true prey to bother chastising a servant for her impertinence. Besides, he was in the mood for murder, and little gratification would be had in murdering Mary.

He was halfway down the hall on the way to the east wing when it dawned on him what had seemed vaguely different about the note in his pocket. It was stained now as if droplets of water had splashed on it. Tears! he thought with a mixture of disgust and an uncomfortable feeling of guilt. A great many tears.

For the next four days, Clayton waited like a caged tiger for his errant wife to return. He was positive she would come back when she realized he was not going to pursue her in a frenzied state of alarm over the danger to her delicate condition. She would have to come back. After all, who would shelter her from her own husband, in violation of the law of England? Her father was much too sensible a man not to order Whitney back to her husband's side where she belonged, Clayton decided in an abrupt change of attitude toward Martin Stone.

When she wasn't back by the fifth day, Clayton knew a wrath that was beyond anything he had ever felt in his life. She couldn't be visiting anyone for this length of time. By God! She had actually left him! He could scarcely contain his fury; it was one thing for him to have considered leaving her or sending her away—he was the injured party, after all. Besides, he hadn't actually done it. But Whitney had! She had obviously gone home to her father, and that stupid bastard was letting her remain.

He ordered the travelling chaise made ready and the horses put to and snapped at McRea, "I want to be at Martin Stone's house in six hours. Not one minute more!" Based on McRea's knowing grin, Clayton almost wondered if his driver had been lying about not knowing where Whitney had gone. It was McRea's story that Whitney had had him take her to the first posting house on the way back to London, where she had, according to the proprietor of the posting house, rented a hack. What in the hell was she doing traipsing all over the countryside, alone and pregnant with his child? The little fool! Obstinate, infuriating little fool! Beautiful little fool.

Martin Stone came out to greet Clayton himself, smiling openly as Clayton alighted. "Welcome, welcome," he said expansively, looking expectantly toward the open door of the coach. "How is my daughter? Where is she?"

Clayton tasted bitter defeat. "Whitney is fine, Martin. She wanted me to come and tell you that we are expecting a child," Clayton said, improvising quickly. After all, Martin Stone was a decent sort, and Clayton didn't want to worry him by admitting that he had driven his daughter away with his surly temper.

"The Hodges place," Clayton snapped at McRae a half hour later, which was the earliest possible moment he could escape from Martin without either looking ridiculous or raising the man's suspicions. Whitney was not staying in seclusion at the Hodges place. And McRea was not smiling when Clayton acidly ordered the chaise back to Claymore.

According to the investigation Clayton instigated the following morning, Whitney was not staying with the Archibalds. She had in fact vanished somewhere between the posting house and no-one-knew-where.

Clayton was no longer angry, he was worried. And when it was reported that she had not crossed the Channel on a packet for France, his worry became alarm.

Alone in his elegant bedroom suite a week after he had returned to Claymore and found her missing, Clayton considered the possibility that Whitney had gone to the man who had been her lover before they were married. Perhaps the bastard had been unwilling or unable to offer her his name before, but now was willing to keep her neatly tucked away and available to him.

That was an agonizing thought and an infuriating one. But only for a minute, because in the purple light of deepening dusk, Clayton couldn't actually believe that Whitney would go to another man. It might have been the mellowing effect of the half bottle of brandy he had consumed during the last two hours, but it seemed to him . . . it seemed somehow that Whitney must have grown to love him. A little. He thought of the way she had preferred to sit curled up in a chair in his study during the day while he worked and she read, or wrote letters, or went over household accounts. She had liked being near him. And she had damn well liked being in bed with him. No woman alive would have melted in his arms, and tried in every way to give him as much pleasure as he was giving her, if she weren't at least infatuated.

He had loved her desperately on the day they were married; she hadn't loved him. Then. But surely in the months afterward, in the shared hours of quiet talk and laughter and unbridled passion, surely she must have come to love him.

Restlessly, Clayton got up and wandered from his empty, lonely room into hers. It wasn't pretty and alive without her. She was gone and with her, his reason for living each day. He had driven her away, finally broken her spirit and defeated her. And she had so much spirit! So damned much spirit. She had stood up to his rage that day she'd taken her horse out, and then defied him openly by going to the Clifftons' party in that glorious green dress that made her eyes turn the color of emeralds. And when he had been waiting here, in this very room in the dark, to confront her with it, she had stood up to him then too. No woman alive but Whitney would have dared to gaze boldly up into his eyes and flatly refuse to be confined to her rooms unless he stayed there with her! And why would she have wanted him to stay with her, if she didn't care for him?

Walking back into his room, Clayton leaned a shoulder against the broad expanse of mullioned glass that ran the length of it on one side. Staring out into the dark night, he thought about what she had said when he had grabbed her and shaken her, trying to silence her. *"I can't stop,"* she had whispered, flinching from his harsh grip. *"Because I love you. I love your smile and your eyes . . ."* Oh Christ! How *could* she have said that to him when he had been deliberately hurting her? *"I remember exactly how your hands feel against my skin when you touch me,"* she had said, *"and the things you have whispered to me when you are so deep inside of me that you have touched my heart."*

Clayton slowly walked into his dressing room and opened the leather case where his shirt studs were kept. He took out the ruby ring she had given him and turned it in his fingers so that he could catch the inscription inside. With a ragged sigh he read the two beloved words: *"My* Lord." He hesitated, torn between putting it on now or waiting until Whitney could place it on his hand as she had the night they were married. She had put the ring on his finger, then she had kissed his hand and held it softly to her cheek. He put the ring on himself—he didn't want to wait any longer.

He felt better now that her ring was on his hand where it belonged, and he sat down and stretched his long legs out in front of him, slowly sipping brandy while he stared in silence at the big four-poster bed they had shared. He knew he had to come to grips with her betrayal now, before he found her. Otherwise he would take one look at her, and his temper would erupt and destroy them both again.

Very well, Whitney had given herself to another man before their marriage. If he didn't let himself wonder who the man was, it was easier to bear. It was he himself who had deprived Whitney of her virginity, he who had probably driven her into the arms of that other man. So whose fault was it that she had given herself once to someone else in a moment of loneliness and despair? Once. He would allow her that much—one time. With a sigh, Clayton leaned his head back and closed his eyes. Or a hundred times—because no matter what she had done before, he could not face living without her now.

In a state of frenetic restlessness, Clayton rode for miles the next day. He rode Whitney's horse because Khan was some thing that belonged to her—as Whitney had haughtily reminded him. Ultimately he arrived at the same high ridge where he had brought her the day after she'd come to Claymore. Sitting down, he propped his shoulders against the same tree trunk where he had sat that day with Whitney cradled on his lap. He gazed idly out across the valley where brilliant sunlight danced and glanced off the wide stream that meandered through it.

With one knee drawn up, he idly tapped the side of his boot with his riding crop, remembering how Whitney had wanted to ride down into that valley because she was afraid he was going to try to make love to her. God, that was almost eight months ago. Eight months! Eight of the most glorious, wonderful, tormented, miserable months of his life.

He smiled a little sadly. Eight months. If Whitney had had her way the night she came to Claymore, they would just be getting married in the next week or two. She had insisted she would need eight months to make the wedding preparations and . . . eight months! Swearing savagely under his breath, Clayton surged to his feet, his mind in a turmoil. Whitney had wanted *eight months* to prepare for the wedding. Even *she* was not that naive! If she'd believed she was pregnant, if she'd come to him because she was, or thought she was, pregnant, she'd never have wanted to wait eight goddamn months.

Hating himself with a virulence that nearly strangled his breathing, Clayton pushed her fleet-legged gelding to the limits of Khan's endurance. Whitney wasn't naive enough to want to wait eight months to get married if she'd thought she was pregnant—but she must have been naive enough to think *he* could have gotten her with child the night he abducted her. And she was proud enough to consider using that as a ploy to bring *him* to *her* . . . and honorable enough to give up the idea and come to him at Claymore herself.

"Cool him down," he snapped at the groom as he flung Khan's reins at the surprised servant and began half running, half walking toward the house. "Tell McRea to have the bays put to and be out in front in five minutes," he called over his shoulder.

Two hours later, Emily Archibald received a smoothly worded invitation from Clayton, which she correctly construed as an "order" to accompany his servant down to the coach which would carry her to his house in Upper Brook Street. She obeyed the summons with a mixture of concern and trepidation.

The butler showed her into a spacious, panelled library at the side of the house where the Duke of Claymore was standing, staring out the windows with his back to her. To Emily's surprise, he didn't greet her with any of his usual open friendliness, nor did he turn around and face her as he said in a cool, remote voice, "Shall we indulge in polite trivialities for the next five minutes, or shall I come directly to the point?"

A shiver of fear danced up her spine as he slowly turned and studied her. Never before had Emily seen *this* Clayton Westmoreland. He was, as always, implacably calm, but now he positively emanated ruthless determination. She stood there, staring at him.

With a brief, almost curt inclination of his head toward the chair beside her, he told her to sit down. Emily sank into the chair, trying to equate this man with the one she had known.

"Since you seem to have no preference, I will come directly to the point. I presume you know why I have asked you here?"

"Whitney?" Emily guessed in a whisper. She gave her head a slight shake and cleared her parched throat.

"Where is she?" he demanded abruptly. And then with a touch of his former gentleness, he added, "I have not approached you before this because I did not want to put you in the position of betraying her confidence, and because I had every reason to believe I could find her through my own sources. Since that hasn't been the case, I am going to have to insist that you tell me."

"But I—I don't *know* where she is. I never thought to as

her where she was going. I never dreamt she would stay away so long."

A pair of cool gray eyes held hers captive, measuring her response, judging it for truth.

"Please believe me. Now that I've seen you I'd never be so unkind as to keep her from you, if I knew where to find her."

He drew a long breath and nodded slightly, his expression no longer coldly forbidding. "Thank you for that," he said simply, "I'll have my driver take you home."

Emily hesitated, still vaguely intimidated by his aura of command, and yet grateful that he had trusted her enough to accept what she said as truth. "Whitney said you found that awful note." With a whimsical smile she shook her head. "You know, she couldn't *quite* decide at the time whether to send it to you as 'dear sir' or . . ."

Naked pain flashed across his handsome features, and Emily trailed off into silence. "I beg your pardon—I shouldn't have mentioned it."

"Since we seem to have no secrets from one another," he said quietly, "do you mind telling me why Whitney wrote the note in the first place?"

"Well, it was her pride she was trying to save. She hoped, no, preferred, to bring you to her, if possible. And she thought that with a note like that—I suppose it was really terrible of her even to consider it, but . . ."

"The only 'terrible' thing Whitney has ever done in her life was marrying me," Clayton interrupted.

Tears sprang into Emily's hazel eyes as she arose to leave. "That's not true. Whitney adored . . . adores you, your grace."

"Thank you again," he said humbly.

For a long time after Emily left, Clayton stood there, feeling the minutes ticking by and knowing that, as each moment passed, Whitney's hurt and anger would be hardening into hatred.

The Dowager Duchess of Claymore dined quietly with her daughter-in-law that evening, mentally berating her eldest son for his tardiness in coming to fetch his wife, who was growing more lost and forlorn with each day. When Whitney had arrived eight days ago and asked if she could stay here until Clayton had time to think things through and come for her, Alicia Westmoreland had considered urging her to return at once to her rightful place beside her husband, insisting upon it, in fact. And yet, there was something about Whitney's hurt, determined look that had reminded the dowager duchess of herself, many years before—of Clayton's father striding across her parents' drawing room, where he had found his wife after an absence of four days: "Get into that carriage immediately," he had ordered her. And then, "Please, Alicia." Having thus made her point, Alicia Westmoreland had dutifully and obediently done as she was bidden.

But Whitney had been here for eight days, and Clayton had not made the slightest effort to come for her. Lady Westmoreland wanted grandchildren, and she could not see how she was likely to have any if these two willful, stubborn young people were living miles apart. Really, the entire thing was preposterous! Never had two people loved each other more than they did.

It was over dessert that evening that a thought occurred to the dowager duchess that brought her half out of her chair. Accordingly, she sent word to Stephen in London that very night to present himself to her at the first possible hour the next morning.

"The thing is," she told a frowning, but faintly amused Stephen the next day in a very private meeting with him, "I'm not certain it has occurred to Clayton to come for Whitney here. Assuming he *wants* to come for her."

Stephen, who had been completely unaware of the estrangement, flashed a wicked grin at his mother. "Darling, this reminds me of some of the tales I've heard about you and Father."

The dowager duchess bent a quelling look upon her completely impervious son and continued, "I want you to find

Clayton. I rather imagine he'll be staying at his London house. But find him tonight if you can. Then drop a 'hint' that she is with me—as if you automatically assumed he would know that. Do *not* let him think he is being urged to come for her. Under those circumstances, I'm certain Whitney would reject any half-hearted effort of his at reconciliation."

"Why don't I just take Whitney back to London with me now and have it whispered about that I'm madly in love with her? *That'll* draw Clay's fire," Stephen grinned.

"Stephen, don't be flippant; this is serious. Here is what I want you to say . . ."

At seven o'clock that evening, as Clayton lounged in a chair at his club, he was only faintly surprised to look up from his cards and find his brother sitting down across the table from him and stacking his chips as he prepared to join the play. Clayton eyed Stephen with wary friendliness. He didn't want him to ask about Whitney because he couldn't very well explain that he'd "misplaced" his wife, any more than he could ever bear to tell Stephen of the estrangement itself. So it was with a sense of relief that he heard Stephen open the conversation with, "Are you losing or winning tonight, your grace?"

"He's cleaning us all out," Marcus Rutherford answered good-naturedly. "Hasn't had a losing hand in the last hour."

"You look like hell, brother," Stephen remarked in a grinning undertone.

"Thank you," Clayton answered drily as he tossed his chips onto the mounting pile in the center of the table. He took that hand and the next two.

"Good to see you, Claymore," William Baskerville said, bending a cautious eye upon the duke who had left so abruptly the last time they'd been playing cards here. Baskerville was on the verge of politely asking after the young duchess, but the last time he'd mentioned seeing her at the Clifftons' party, he'd caused a quarrel, so he thought it best to avoid mentioning her. "Mind if I join you?" he asked the duke instead.

"He doesn't mind at all," Stephen said when Clayton appeared not to have heard Baskerville. "He's perfectly willing to take your money along with everyone else's."

Clayton gave his brother a mildly sardonic look. He couldn't stay home or the worry would drive him out of his mind. And yet the cheerful conversation of his brother and the others was already wearing on his ragged nerves, and he'd only been playing for an hour. He was on the verge of suggesting to Stephen that they both adjourn to his house and indulge in an orgy of drunkenness, which was more suitable to his frame of mind anyway, when Stephen remarked to him, "Didn't really expect to find you here. Thought you'd be attending the little affair Mother is having for our relatives tonight."

Managing an excellent imitation of a man who has just said something he shouldn't have, Stephen shook his head and added apologetically, "Sorry, Clay. I forgot that with Whitney staying with her and naturally planning to attend the party, you wouldn't . . ."

Baskerville, who overheard the gist of this, forgot his earlier resolution and said with his usual unaffected cordiality, "Lovely young woman—your lady duchess. Give her my best and . . ." Baskerville's jaw slackened as he watched in horrified surprise while Clayton Westmoreland came slowly erect and rigid in his chair. "I haven't *seen* her anywhere," Baskerville hastily assured him.

But the duke had already risen to his feet. He stood there, staring down at his brother with a mixture of incredulity, amazement, and something else poor Baskerville was too confused to identify. And then, without so much as picking up the huge stacks of chips that represented his winnings, or bidding a civil goodbye to anyone, the duke turned on his heel and headed for the door with long, purposeful strides.

"Oh I say!" Baskerville breathed to Stephen as they both watched Clayton's retreating form. "You've really put your foot in it! I could have told you—your brother don't like for his duchess to attend parties without him."

"No," Stephen agreed with a wide grin. "I don't think he does."

The drive to Grand Oak, which normally took four hours, was accomplished in three hours and a half from the front door of Clayton's club. Whitney had been staying with his mother! With his mother, for Christ's sake! The one person alive who should have had sense enough to order his wife home to him. His own mother had collaborated in putting him through this torment!

The coach pulled up in front of his mother's brilliantly lit house, and Clayton recalled that Stephen had said there was to be a party tonight. He didn't want to see his relatives, he wanted to see his wife. And he hadn't brought formal clothes, hadn't even considered stopping at his house for a change of attire, and wouldn't have if he'd thought of it. He was sorely tempted to confront his mother with her treachery before he went in search of Whitney. He was tempted, but he wasn't going to.

"Good evening, your grace," the family butler intoned.

"Dammit!" Clayton replied as he stalked past the affronted servant on his way to look into the crowded drawing room. It seemed that every relative he had was present in those rooms. But not Whitney. He saw his mother though, and when she started toward him, her face wreathed in a smile, Clayton took a moment to direct a look of such frigid displeasure at her that it stopped her dead. Then he swung around and headed for the main stairs. "Where is my wife?" he demanded of a maid in the upstairs hall.

Clayton hesitated outside the designated door, his hand on the brass handle, his heart slamming with a combination of relief and dread. He had no idea how Whitney would react to seeing him, no idea of what he could possibly say to her. But at that moment, all that mattered was being able to see her and feast his eyes on her.

Opening the door, Clayton stepped silently within, then closed it behind him. Whitney was in a big brass tub with her back to the room. Her maid was hovering behind her, holding soap and a washcloth. Mesmerized, Clayton simply stood there.

He wanted to go to her and pull her, naked and wet, into his arms, to absorb her into his body, to carry her to the bed and lose himself in her. And at the same time, he didn't feel worthy of even speaking to her, let alone touching her. He *wasn't* worthy. Twice in their lives now he had treated her with a brutal viciousness of which he'd never known he was capable. God! She was nurturing his child within her womb and never once had he even asked how she was feeling. How could one slender girl bear the weight of such cruelty without hating him as he deserved? Clayton drew a long, labored breath.

Clarissa glanced up, saw Clayton rolling up his shirtsleeves as he walked toward the tub, and gave him a ferocious scowl. She opened her mouth with the obvious intention of endowing him with a liberal piece of her mind, duke or no duke, but Clayton forestalled her with a curt nod of dismissal. Reluctantly she handed him the soap and cloth and silently left the room.

With aching gentleness, Clayton soaped Whitney's back, carefully keeping his touch light and his hands out of her view.

"That feels wonderful, Clarissa," Whitney murmured as she bent forward and lathered her legs. Normally, Clarissa left her to bathe alone, but lately she had become so worried and solicitous that Whitney didn't give much thought to this unusual, added attention.

Sleek and glistening with droplets of scented water streaming down her, Whitney arose from the bath and stepped out of the tub. She started to turn and reach behind her for the towel, but Clarissa, in an excess of compassionate helpfulness, was already gently drying her off.

Clayton toweled her neck, her soft shoulders and her trim back.

"Thank you, Clarissa, I'll finish. I'm going to have my dinner up here and then I'll dress to go downstairs for—" Turning, Whitney reached for the towel. The color drained from her face, and she swayed unsteadily as she beheld the handsome, grave man who said nothing to her, but continued to dry her body. In a state of numb paralysis, she stood stock still, incapable of movement or speech. When Clayton toweled her stomach and thighs, Whitney was dimly aware that his hands lingered imperceptibly longer there, but they were not caressing her. Desperately she tried to assimilate what was happening. Clayton was here—no longer angry with her—but not speaking to her. Not smiling at her. He wasn't even touching her as a husband, but almost like a . . . a servant! A servant! An aching lump began to swell in Whitney's throat as she realized what he was doing. He was acting as her maid as a way of humbling himself to her.

His strong hands were gentle as he forced her down onto the chair beside the tub and, without looking up at her, he knelt down on one knee and solemnly began to dry her calves. "Clayton," she whispered brokenly. "Oh, don't . . ."

Ignoring her tearful plea, he continued his humble services as he said in a ragged, pain-edged voice, "If I ever think you are even *considering* leaving me again, no matter how good your reasons, I'll have you locked in your rooms and the doors barricaded, so help me God." He lifted her foot and began to dry it.

Her voice shaking, Whitney asked, "Will you stay locked in there with me?"

He raised her dainty foot to his jaw and tenderly laid his cheek against it, then turned his head and kissed it. "Yes," he whispered.

Standing up, he walked over to the wardrobe, removed a blue silk dressing robe and brought it over, holding it while Whitney put her arms into the sleeves. Like a puppet, she stood there while he reached around her and brought the sash to the front, tying it at her waist. Without a word, he leaned down and scooped her into his arms, carrying her over to the chair where her dinner was waiting on a low table. He sat down, cradling her on his lap. Leaning forward, he removed the silver cover from her dinner tray. When Whitney realized that he intended to feed her, she couldn't bear any more.

"Don't!" she cried out softly, reaching her arms around his powerful shoulders and burying her face in his neck. "Please, please don't do this. Just talk to me. Please talk to me."

"I can't," he whispered against her shining hair. He drew a long, tortured breath. "I can't find the words."

The naked anguish in his voice brought tears to her eyes as she leaned back and looked adoringly at him. "I can," she whispered brokenly. "You taught them to me—I love you. *I love you.*"

Threading his fingers through her hair, he framed her face between his hands and gazed at her. "I love you," he whispered hoarsely. "God! How I love you."

In the flickering candlelight, the hands on the ormulu clock across the room from the bed had just moved to half past one. Clayton gazed down tenderly at the beauty who was nestled up against him, asleep in his arms, her tousled head resting trustingly against his naked chest. Brushing a wayward curl gently off her cheek, he drew her closer to him and touched his lips to her forehead. "I love you," he breathed softly. He knew Whitney was asleep and couldn't hear him, but he needed to say the words again.

He had said them to her in his heart tonight, each time his mouth touched the dewy softness of hers in hungry urgency or aching tenderness. "I love you." It was a song his heart sang when she writhed beneath him and arched sweetly up to meet his thrusts; a melody that rose to a soaring crescendo as he led her to the peak of ecstasy and then joined her there.

His wife snuggled closer against him and dreamily whispered, "I love you, too."

"Ssssh, darling. Sleep," Clayton murmured. He had lingered over her endlessly tonight, deliberately delaying the final, exquisite moment of release until they were both wild with wanting. After such prolonged lovemaking he wanted her to rest.

"What took you so long?" she whispered.

Leaning his head down to better see her face, Clayton grinned. "I can't believe you mean what I think you mean."

She looked puzzled at first, then she blushed and looked away.

Surprised and concerned by her reaction, Clayton tipped her chin up. "What *did* you mean?" he asked gently.

"It—it doesn't matter. Truly it doesn't."

Gazing down into her pain-shadowed green eyes, he said quietly, "I think that, whatever it is, it matters very much to you."

Whitney wished she hadn't spoken, wouldn't have, except that the hurt was spreading through her like a bruise that would not stop aching. Knowing that Clayton would now insist on an answer, she gave it in a barely audible whisper, "Marie."

"What about her?"

"Was she the reason it took you so long to come for me?"

Tightening his arms around her, as if he could absorb some of the pain he had caused her, Clayton smiled wryly. "Darling, the reason it took me so long was that forty investigators could not find a trace of you. And I—who undoubtedly should have known better—failed to consider my own mother as a possible partner in a conspiracy to keep my wife from me."

"But I thought this would be the *first* place you would think of looking for me, once you had time to think things over."

"Well it wasn't," Clayton said quietly. "But then, neither did I 'think things over' within five miles of Marie St. Allermain—which I gather is what you're trying to ask me."

"You didn't?"

"No, I didn't."

Her green eyes filled with tears as she gazed at him and smiled tremulously. "Thank you," she whispered simply.

"You're very welcome," Clayton said with a tender smile at her upturned face. He traced his finger along the elegant curve of her cheek. "Now sleep, my love. Otherwise, this bed is again going to be put to another use."

Obediently she closed her eyes and snuggled into his arms. Her fingertips slid up to lightly brush the hair at his temple; a few minutes later they slipped down his shoulder to his chest.

Clayton felt his body's instant response and tried to control the mounting passion which Whitney was inadvertently igniting with her sleepy caresses. When her hand drifted down the planes of his stomach, he caught it and held it firmly in his own to prevent its further descent. He thought he heard a smothered laugh as she turned in apparent sleep, and her lips touched his ear.

Leaning back, Clayton gazed suspiciously into her face. She was wide awake, her eyes aglow with love.

In one quick, smooth motion, he rolled her over onto her back and pressed her into the pillows, his body half covering hers. "You can't say I didn't warn you," he whispered in a husky voice.

"I won't."